Howard Spring was born in C[...] career as a newspaper errand bo[...] *Manchester Guardian* and developed [...] city which would become the setting for several of his novels. It was not long before Spring took over the job of literary critic on the *Evening Standard* from J B Priestley and on moving to Cornwall at the outset of World War II he became literary critic of *Country Life*. His most well-known novel, *Fame is the Spur*, the story of a Labour politician's rise to power, was filmed by the Boulting Brothers and he continued to write until his death in 1965.

ALL THE DAY LONG

A novel by

HOWARD SPRING

HOUSE OF STRATUS

This edition published in 2000 by House of Stratus, an imprint of Stratus Holdings plc, 24c Old Burlington Street, London, W1X 1RL, UK.

www.houseofstratus.com

Typeset, printed and bound by House of Stratus.

A catalogue record for this book is available from the British Library.

ISBN 1-84232-324-5

For
JANE KELLY
This belated fulfilment
of a promise

*O Lord, support us all the day long
of this troublous life, until the shades
lengthen and the evening comes, and
the busy world is hushed, the fever of
life is over, and our work done.*

From a prayer by
JOHN HENRY NEWMAN

CHAPTER ONE

E UPHEMIA EMMETT was buried at dawn on May the twenty-first, 1881. That was my birthday, and I was five years old. Three years before, Euphemia was given to me for a birthday present. She was now a poor old thing without glory. She had come to me beautifully dressed, cheeks aglow, with charming kid leather boots. Father said: "She is far too good for the child," and for a long time after that I was ashamed to show my face in her presence. Surely she would despise me. But one day she lost a boot, and Mrs Solway, who was our cook and all sorts of other things, made another. I laughed when I saw the new boot on Euphemia, for it was a poor thing. The contrast between the two boots made her look slightly ridiculous, and that was a comfort to me. Then her clothes began to get torn or to wear out and she had to do with makeshifts. And the colour faded from her cheeks, for she was often left lying about in the graveyard, with the hot Cornish sunshine pouring down. I stole into Father's study one day and daubed her cheeks with red ink, and that didn't improve her. Louisa said it made her look fast, but I didn't know what she meant. Louisa often said things I didn't understand. She was eighteen, a tremendous age for one of my sisters to be. Roger was ten and Bella eight. There had been other little Legassicks besides us four, but they hadn't lasted. They were under the grass in the churchyard which was my playground and where poor Euphemia Emmett was so often left to dry in the sun if I had dropped her into the sea, or just to wilt there for no especial reason.

The big cool sitting room of the vicarage had a french window, and you walked out of that into a bit of garden, more trees and shrubs than flowers. There were splendid eucalyptus, great smooth boles reaching up into a rustle of blue leaves, each a sickle. And there was mimosa

1

and camellia, and all sorts of loveliness that we took for granted. You went through a gap in the hedge straight into the churchyard. The small grey church had a Norman door. A wooden belfry stood apart. I spent hours there, wandering through the gloomy avenue of Irish yews, and watching the blackbirds and thrushes gorging themselves in autumn on the ripe berries that hung like dusky jewels on the hoary English yew whose dark branches spread nearly as wide as the church itself. I remember Roger saying to me once, as we stood looking at that sight: "I'll bet Shakespeare knew a tree like that. That's where he got the line 'Like a rich jewel in an Ethiop's ear'." I knew nothing about Shakespeare, but Roger was like that. He talked to me as if I would understand things. He never snubbed me as Louisa did.

Usually, I was alone, and I would walk through the graveyard and out of the gate on to the narrow path that had the graveyard wall on one side and the sea on the other. It was that great arm of the sea known as the Carrick Roads. To the east, the land was a mile and a half away. To the north, three miles off, you saw the water take a turn, to run up through the hills to Truro; and to the west there was a mile-long creek where the water petered out at low tide. The herons came there, and the wild swans, and the curlews cried heart-brokenly by day and night. We had a dinghy, but it wasn't good enough for Louisa, who hated getting wet or dirty, and Roger was away at school, and Bella was often taking lessons from Father. So Euphemia and I would embark and splash about, and I didn't think she was too good for me now. I would shout orders that the poor thing couldn't obey, and I would call her a stupid lubber and duck her into the water to brighten her ideas, and then, when we were ashore, put her on a tombstone to dry.

And sometimes as I sat there like that, with half an eye on Euphemia and half an eye on the dazzling water or on the hawks hovering above the land on the opposite side of the creek, the bell in the wooden tower of the belfry would begin to toll, and through the droning summer day I would hear Father's voice droning "I am the resurrection and the life," and there he would be, tall and dark and stern in his white surplice; and I would listen and love the words. He never mumbled. His voice was full and clear whether, as now, in the summer heat or whether, in the winter, caught and tossed about by the wind like the rooks around the elms. "Man that is born of woman

2

hath but a short time to live, and is full of misery. He cometh up, and is cut down, like a flower, he fleeth as it were a shadow, and never continueth in one stay."

Listening there, I was not full of misery. I loved the graveyard and all that went on in it: the women gossiping as they tended the graves; the sexton slashing with a sickle at the winter heliotrope that flourished there and scented all the days of early spring; the brides in white who came through the Norman doorway with their grinning grooms: oh, yes, I was as happy in the graveyard as one of the wagtails that sprinted through the grass and with a hop and a flirt of the tail expressed a joy ineffable.

It was in the graveyard that I learned to read. Sometimes Mrs Solway would command me to pick peas for dinner, and then she and I would go down to the churchyard with the basketful and shell them as we sat in the sun by her husband's grave. She was a merry one, and many a laugh we had there sitting among the graves; and often enough old Thomas May, the sexton, who also looked after Father's horse, would be digging a grave nearby, and he would pause with only his head out of the pit and his hands like roots covered with clay grasping the sides, and ask what the joke was. And it was always a joke about the people who were buried there, even about Mr Solway himself, who had been, his widow said with relish, the biggest ole poacher and smuggler thereabouts, "and look at all that there," she would say, pointing to the slab above him which we used as a table for our peas. "I wrote it myself," she would say with an author's pride, and old May would shake his head and say: "Ay, a good piece of writing that be. A proper ole disguise." And sometimes he would heave himself up out of his pit, and Mrs Solway would say: "Like one of the blest heaving himself out on Resurrection Morning you be, Thomas May"; and he would take bread and cheese or a pasty out of the bag he always had with him and munch away with his leathery jaws as he sat at our side. They would discuss the tombstones like old companions turning over a photograph album by the fireside, and tales of joys and griefs would flow about me.

I learned to read from the tombstones, and it was Mrs Solway who taught me. She taught me first the A.B.C., picking out the letters from the lovely cursive writing on the slate that never weathered or from the carving upon granite crusted over with green and yellow lichens; and when I could read all my letters from A to Z – for fortunately a Zachariah Ponsharden was among what she called those in glory – we went on to words, and she said I was a clever little maid, I learned them so fast. "Ay, she'm a chip of the old block," Thomas May would agree, thinking of my father's books. "Here she be, reading it off like a proper little squire. Got me fair beat, she have that. I can't read at all. And if I could, I wouldn't want to read about all them ole sinners," he would say with a comprehensive look round at the holes he had filled. "Testimonials, that's all they be, testimonials writ by a kind master for them as is moving on to a new job. Well," he would say, getting up and rubbing the grease of his pasty on to the seat of his corduroys, "I better get on. Another foot, I reckon, 'll help to keep ole Mary Trebetherick quiet. About time, too. If she clacks up aloft like she did 'ere below the Almighty won't be able to 'ear his angels singing."

I could read when I was four years old. The graveyard was my first library, and in it I read the history of the parish. It was there that I learned of the sad fate of poor

EUPHEMIA EMMETT

Who left what the will of God
and the malice of man had made for
her a vale of tears on
May ye 21st 1820
Aged 21

A maiden pure, she to the paths of virtue kept,
Nor e'er the bounds of modesty o'erstept,
But sland'rous tongues pour'd forth their venom rank,
And gladly to the friendly grave she sank.

It was then two years since I had been given my doll, who had long since ceased to be a daunting princess. She had never had a name, and now I began to call her Euphemia Emmett and to look upon her with deep pity, a victim of venom rank. I ceased to be unkind to her and to throw her into the sea, and I put her to bed each night with a pillow beneath what was left of her faded hair and with a warm coverlet upon her. But it was clear to me that my solicitude had been awakened too late and that Euphemia was on her happy way out from the malice of men in this vale of tears. I was nursing her at breakfast one morning when Father said: "Dolls are like cats. One year of their lives equals seven in the life of a man. Maria's doll is nearly old enough to be her mother."

"She is almost twenty-one," I said, proud of my prompt arithmetic. "I don't see how she can put up with this world much longer."

There was a week to go to my birthday, which was also the birth and death-day of Euphemia in the graveyard; and I watched my Euphemia anxiously, fearing symptoms of recovery. For I had determined to do her in; not murderously, but as people are done in by the inscrutable will of God when their time comes. My uncle Reginald, the brother of my dead mother, was staying at the vicarage at the time, and I shall tell you more about him later on. For the moment it is enough to say that no one had treated me as my uncle Reginald did. He used to take me for walks and row me in the dinghy and talk seriously to me about his travels, so that I felt myself to be a grown-up person and was ashamed of this old doll that had been my companion for three years. She died abruptly on the evening of May 20th. I had put her head upon the pillow and was spreading the counterpane over her, and I asked anxiously "How are you feeling tonight, Euphemia?" She did not answer, but a choking gasp escaped her, and I knew that her spirit was fled. I was glad that she was at last free from the malice of men, and as it was still light and there was an hour to go before my bedtime I took a trowel from the tool-shed and went to prepare her grave.

I decided to bury her under the English yew that stands by the south-east corner of the church. It was so old that crutches had been placed under the lower wide-spreading arms, and thus I was able to go easily into the gloomy cavern where I always took my young sorrows, which were few enough.

Thither I went with the trowel that evening, and from a couple of feet of space I cleared the thick carpet of tiny yew-leaves that made one feel as though walking on sponges deep down upon the bed of a dark green sea. I remember Roger sitting there with me on a broiling summer day and reciting "Full fathom five thy father lies." When I had cleared a space I dug out the soil, and it took me a long time, for the tree, having in long centuries past decided to grow there, had had many a northeaster to withstand and had anchored itself down with an infinity of grapnels. I dug through them, and they were red and sappy and filled the dark space with an exciting charnel smell. When the work was done, I filled the hole in with rotting leaves so that no passer-by might see what I had been up to.

I shared a bedroom with Bella, who happily slept like a drugged dormouse. I knew that it would need the last angelic trump to make her stir. There was no need to take Louisa into account, for she had her own bedroom. I should have to be up at dawn, and when I knelt down to say my prayers I asked God to wake me up at 5 a.m. I needn't have worried, for I hardly slept at all. Our bedroom window looked east. As soon as it was grey I was out of bed and popped Euphemia into the boot-box I had put ready for her. I knew from my studies in the graveyard that one should not be buried without poetry, so in pencil on the lid of the box I scribbled:

EUPHEMIA EMMETT

Departed this Vale of Tears
May ye 21st, 1881
Aged 21 years

Sad was her lot, but when the trumpet blows
God give her a place in one of the front rows.

It didn't sound very good, even to me, but I dared not delay and it had to do. I put on my warmest clothes, wrapped my long white nightgown round the boot-box, and stole cautiously through the dark sleeping house. Into the sitting room, out through the french window, into the dawn.

It was so beautiful that I almost forgot what I had come for. I had never been up so early before. The eastward land across the water was still dark, but the sky above it was pulsing and vibrating and shifting about in ever-changing grey-blue and red that slowly warmed up like a Halleluiah Chorus. And the sea between me and the glory getting born over there was a vast seething of vapour, a milky smoke, waiting to rise at a touch and let the sun when he came fall splashing and sparkling. And then another Halleluiah Chorus began, first with a few drowsy tuning-up twitters, then with one clear call from a thrush or blackbird, which was like a conductor's rapping on his stand, and then the full orchestra of the birds surged into a splendid *aubade*.

6

I don't suppose the moment seemed to me then to have these components. I am looking a long way back, writing here in the sitting room through whose door the small Maria Legassick crept that morning. But I can recall at least the swift uprising of the heart, the forgetfulness of the errand, the dying away of the birds' chorus as if they were abashed to silence when the sun rose over the hill and threw the dense shadow of the yew tree towards me. Then I went quietly forward along the path to the church, carrying Euphemia to her last resting-place. In the church porch I slipped my nightdress over my head for surplice, and as I had to be both parson and bearers I put Euphemia in her box under my arm and walked slowly towards the yew tree intoning: "Forasmuch as it hath pleased Almighty God of his great mercy to take unto himself the soul of our dear sister here departed, we therefore commit her body to the ground: earth to earth, ashes to ashes, dust to dust."

I had so often lain in the summer grass, listening to Father's voice, and I knew the words so well and loved the music of them so much, that I could have run through the whole service; but it was difficult to be everyone at once, and I knew I was wrong here, for this was the moment when Thomas May should have been standing at the graveside crumbling earth three times through his fingers. So I decided to fill in the few yards to the grave with a passage that always delighted me, and I intoned: "When thou with rebukes doth chasten man for sin, thou makest his beauty to consume away, like as it were a moth fretting a garment: every man therefore is but vanity."

I had been keeping my eyes upon the path, and now I lifted them as the darkness of the yew fell upon my face. I gave a little cry and the box dropped, spilling poor Euphemia upon the ground. Louisa, wrapped in a warm cloak, whose darkness melted into the darkness of the tree, was nothing but a white horrified face with dark eyes blazing. She took me by the arm and shook me till my teeth rattled. "You blasphemous little fool!" she hissed. "What are you up to? You little spy!"

She had been so unexpected, her face, as though without a body, floating in the air at the mouth of the tree's cavern, that she had been ghost and terror till she spoke. Then she was Louisa, who seemed never to like me, who always scolded me because I was bold and unsubmissive. My rebellion rose now, and I said: "I am burying Euphemia. What is there to spy on?"

She stepped out of the cavern and walked a few paces till she was standing with the morning sun flooding her beauty. Bella didn't mind her beauty, but I did. I was a plain child, and jealous. I said: "I am not a spy."

She looked shaken and confused. To my surprise she said: "I beg your pardon."

"I should think so," I said righteously.

"It was a foolish word to use."

The toe of her shoe was uneasily scuffling at a patch of moss.

"I came out to see the sunrise," she said. "I thought I heard a horse being ridden away. Did you hear anything?"

"Not a sound."

"I must have been mistaken."

"Father would be annoyed if he knew you were up and in the graveyard at this time of day," I said, happy for once to be the reprover.

"Say nothing," she said. "We must both say nothing."

It appealed to me, because it sounded like a conspiracy. "Very well," I said. "Now get back to bed, Louisa. I must bury Euphemia."

Oh, it was lovely to be able to order her about like that!

She looked for a moment as though she would flare at me again, but she didn't. She went slowly away, with now and then a doubting backward look. She had quite spoiled the funeral. I pushed Euphemia back unceremoniously into the boot-box, dug the leaves from the grave with my fingers, pushed her in, and stamped the ground hard upon her. I took off my surplice, wound it about my neck like a muffler, and jumped over the churchyard wall on the the road that edged the sea. A long way out a man was rowing our dinghy. I saw that it was Uncle Reginald, coming towards the shore. I waited for him. He was not the sort of man who poked his nose into other people's business. He would not ask what I was doing out of bed at that time of day. He merely said, as he stepped out of the boat and heaved it a yard on to the shore: "Tide's falling. It'll be all right there for a bit. I've been out trying for a fish or two for breakfast. Let's go and cook 'em."

2

When you look at a nurseryman's catalogue you see that all sorts of shrubs and plants are Pallacei. This is the abiding memorial to my mother's brother, Reginald Pallace. I might as well tell you at once that not much happened in our family unless there was a parson behind it. My mother was a parson's daughter, and my parson-father was a parson's son. And so it had been with Pallaces and Legassicks for a long time. Not one of them achieved any distinction in the church. We produced not so much as a dean, let alone a bishop: nothing but country parsons. Uncle Reginald said that all the Legassick and Pallace men were born with dog-collars attached and that they were content to be kennelled in rectories and vicarages. I said: "What about you, Uncle Reginald?" and he laughed. "I was an exception. I was never a good sheepdog. I'm a rogue."

His father had had a vicarage on the other side of this wide water across which I found him rowing on that May morning. He had once taken me to see it. He rowed until the pleasant little tower of our church was out of sight, for the Carrick Roads turn in among the hills. We landed on the eastern side and walked among the woods till we came to a small clearing in which a church stood with a few cottages about it and one pleasant house, which was the vicarage. The whole of this hamlet, drowned there in the woods whose trees were shaggy with moss, looked like nothing but an appendage of the nearby mansion, which indeed it was. Here my mother and Uncle Reginald had been born and had grown up and had roamed the vast gardens of the mansion as though they owned them. We roamed them that day, startling the deer, catching glimpses of the blue salt river through gaps in the scrub oak, pausing now and then while Uncle Reginald felt the trunk of a tree as if shaking hands with an old friend. As he was. "Doing well," I remember him saying with pleasure. "Twenty years ago I sent home the seed. That was my first journey."

As a boy, he had not long been content to roam the gardens without aim. You won't find many gardeners there now, but then there was a large staff, and he worked among them in all the hours he could steal from the schooling which Mr Pallace, his father, was taking in hand. When the old man thought the time had come for Reginald to go to a public school, the boy protested. He said he wanted to be a botanist – "And one of these days," he added prophetically, "to go about the world and find new things."

Uncle Reginald told me all this as we sat that day under one of his trees and munched the sandwiches we had brought with us. I felt very important to be receiving these confidences, for Bella was rather dull, and Louisa so much older that she had no use for me, and father rarely out of his study, and Roger at school. I don't remember all the details: only that Mr Pallace was obdurate, that the boy ran away, and that he was not heard of again till he was working at Kew. It was not till he was thirty, and my father had for some time been married to his sister, that he reappeared in Cornwall as head gardener to the Polperro family, who had the great estate of Tregannock.

The Polperros had become rich out of the tin and copper of Cornwall. The Mr Polperro of that time was one of a syndicate of Cornish gentry who financed Uncle Reginald's travels in search of shrubs and plants. He was with us now, back from the third of his great adventures in country having names that fascinated me — Sikkim, the Salween River, Yunnan and Tibet. Cornish gardens were full of the lovely things he had found. Outside the french window through which I had carried Euphemia Emmett that morning was a superb camellia that would never have been there if Uncle Reginald had not said No to his father and trudged with his coolies through the steamy thickets that hang on the mountain-sides above the Salween River.

3

He looked a huge man as stood there on the edge of the water, a few fish, which he held by a string threaded through their gills, dangling from his hand. He was broad, brown and clean-shaven, blue-eyed, wearing a grey tweed coat and knickerbockers, blue woollen stockings, brogues, and an old tweed hat. He took my hand and I toddled up the beach at his side. At the western end of the vicarage garden, its wall flush with the road, was a grey stone building. Our only horse, a fat old brown thing named Neb, which was short for Nebuchadnezzar, whose job was to pull the trap when father did his visiting, lived on the ground floor. An outside stairway led to a floor above. Thomas May had lived there for many years, but recently, to everyone's surprise, he had married. Mrs Solway thought it a great joke, and she was not alone. Her conversations with Thomas May seemed all to be conducted with a mere leathery head standing out from the earth; and, addressing this, she said: "No fool like an ole fool, Thomas May." "Well," he said, "that ole Nebuchadnezzar 'ave taken to snorin' in 'is sleep, an' if I got to put up with snores let 'em be from a woman alongside, not from an ole 'oss below. Besides which, Mrs

Solway, I got so tired of they ole funerals I thought I'd try a weddin' for a change."

"There's more than a wedding in married life, Thomas May."

"Ay, that there be. There's someone to rub me for my lumbago."

Uncle Reginald was now quartered in Thomas May's old room. I followed him up the ladder and looked round his small domain. It was the first time I had seen it, for I had not been allowed to go up there in Thomas May's time. It was a big oblong, with one window opening on to the road and one on to our garden. The walls were whitewashed and the floor was bare. The fireplace was in the wall at one end, with a wicker chair in front of it, and there were shelves at either side. There wasn't much on them: a few tin plates and mugs. At the other end of the room was Uncle Reginald's folding bed, with a sheet and blanket neatly arranged upon it. There were a few books on a small table by the chair. It gave me the impression of a barrack room for one well-trained soldier, and this was not what I had expected, for in Thomas May's time the room had a bad reputation. My father, who made a monthly inspection, always turned in an evil report. "Of all the magpies!" I heard him say. "Everything goes into that room, except fresh air, and nothing comes out. Thomas May, you must have those windows open now and then."

"What are windows for then, Vicar, if not to shut against the air?" the old man challenged him. "Cut me down like a flower, that's what air would do, and who'd dig your ole graves then?"

My father was not a very firm man, and, having made his monthly protest, he would let things go.

But the loft, as we called it, was changed now. Though Uncle Reginald was to stay with us only for a month, he had scrubbed and scoured and whitewashed with his own hands, and the air of that May morning was blowing in at one window and out at the other. It was still only six o'clock. I had intended to creep back to bed so that no one but Louisa would know I had been out, but that would now be difficult. Father was always up at six, getting on with his everlasting writing.

At that time, I knew nothing about the writing except that it hung over us all like a threat. If Bella and I laughed or scuffled with one another when we were getting up, Louisa would be certain to appear, looking thundery. "Whatever are you two thinking about! Don't you know that Father's writing?" And we would make our toilets fearfully, afraid lest the splashing of our ice-cold water should reach the study. Louisa always had warm water carried up by Mrs Solway; and Bella confided to me once that, having sneaked into Louisa's room, which we had been forbidden to enter, she had found on the dressing table a bottle of lavender water and a pot of some red concoction. We felt in the presence of profound feminine mysteries and were awestruck. Father's work didn't worry us much in the daylight hours. Louisa had ceased to be his pupil, but he had Bella on his hands, and my turn would come soon. Then there were his parish duties and one thing and another; but after our evening meal quiet was expected for, having kissed the three of us, he went again into his study. I have read all his books now and am able to wonder that so much time should go to producing so unrewarding a result. Poor Father – and that is odd, that I should write "Poor Father" of one whom I held in such awe – hadn't a touch of creation in all his make-up. The titles of his books give them away. *Jeremy Taylor: a Re-assessment. Bunyan Re-considered. Stubb's Early Plantagenets Re-examined.* And so forth, volume after volume. He could take anybody he liked, read all that other people had written, regurgitate it with hardly a thought or emotion of his own added, and call it a re-examination or reassessment or reconsideration, and somebody or other would print it and sell it or, I imagine, fail to sell it. Father had one copy of each, bound in handsome red morocco leather, on his study shelves, and I suppose the sight of them comforted him, gave him a sense of achievement, as similar books abundantly do for similar men even to this day.

As I was thinking what I should say to Father if I went back now to the house, Uncle Reginald, who had put a match to the fire and planted a kettle upon it, said: "I'll tell Aubrey that I fixed up with you to come fishing. He can hardly object to that."

He never called Father anything but Aubrey, even to us children. Bella and I thought it fun that the Reverend Aubrey Legassick, M.A., should be just Aubrey, but Louisa was displeased. She said nothing, but we could always read her symptoms.

When the kettle was boiling he made tea and fried the fish he had caught. He had gutted them and rinsed them in salt water on the beach. He buttered some bread and we sat down at his small table to what seemed to me the most delicious and romantic meal I had ever eaten, with the now powerful sun streaming through the eastern window and making the white room a joy of light.

I said: "Thank you, Uncle Reginald. That's the loveliest breakfast I've ever eaten."

He said: "Well, I've eaten worse." And he went on to tell me of forests of rhododendrons and camellias, and tearing torrents, and little bridges above them made of rope and bamboo that swayed as you crossed them, and of his foreign porters and collectors and encampments, and of his journeys home by sea in sailing ships. "You know that vicarage I took you to the other day," he said, "where your mother and I grew up? Well, those are the sort of things I used to dream about there when I was a boy. What do you dream about, young Maria?"

I said: "Of having hot water to wash in in the mornings, and lavender water on my dressing table."

He roared with laughter, and I suppose gave me up as a hopeless case. "Well," he said, "let's wash up."

It was hardly a job for one, let alone two, but we did it together, and that, of course, was what he wanted. When I was drying the plates, he asked suddenly: "What was Louisa doing so early in the graveyard?"

I did not want anybody to know what I had been doing there myself, and I was sure that Louisa would never tell. She was bossy with us, but she was reliable. What is more, though I was too young to guess what it had all been about, I had an idea that it was something secret, and a secret was not to be treated lightly. "Louisa?" I said. "Was she in the churchyard?"

He looked at the nightdress which I had used as a surplice and had thrown upon his bed. I feared he would ask something about that, but he gave me a long, considering stare and then shrugged his shoulders as if washing his hands of the Legassick girls. He said: "I shall be going to Tregannock today to see Mr Polperro. Would you like to come with me?"

I jumped at the chance.

4

Mr Polperro was a name of awe, and Tregannock was a name of enchantment. Mr Polperro was patron of the living my father held, and they were more than parson and patron. They were friends,

13

though their ways of life had little in common. They had been undergraduates together at Oxford, and in those days my father used to spend most of his university vacations at Tregannock. Mr Polperro succeeded to his inheritance when my father was a curate in the East End of London, and one of his first actions was to instal his friend in the living that then fell vacant through my grandfather's death. They were now beyond their middle years, my father a thin dark ascetic, Mr Polperro big and ruddy, with a voice like rich plum cake, but Louisa, who didn't like him, said no one could get a voice like that except by a lifetime's overindulgence in cigars and port wine.

Tregannock was a few miles from the church as the crow flies, and five or six by our narrow twisting roads, and along those roads on Sundays the Polperros were driven to morning service. Mr Polperro liked everybody to be in church when the family arrived, so that they could make an entrance, walk unembarrassed to their pew under the wall-tablets which left no doubt that Heaven was the better for the many Polperros who had now gone into residence there.

Father was very strict about me and Bella and Louisa, and Roger when he was at home, being in our places; but once, when I had had measles and was thought not well enough to go to church – a notion which I encouraged, though I felt remarkably well – I wrapped myself in a large cloak and hid behind a hedge and watched the arrival. Even for those days, the Polperro coach was an antique: a vast lumbering contraption on iron-shod wheels but, like the King's daughter, all glorious within. The cockaded coachman wore a white wig and yellow gloves, and standing behind was a footman in full livery: white silk stockings, buckled shoes and all the rest of it. Down he jumped and opened the door, standing bowed as Mr Polperro got out and offered an arm to Mrs Polperro, and then Mr James Polperro, the heir, got out and offered an arm to Miss Jane Polperro. The two pairs stepped delicately across the bars of granite awkwardly spaced so as to discourage cows from straying into the graveyard, and went down the sloping path bearing the good news that worship could begin. Then the stiff face of the footman relaxed into a grin; he winked at the coachman; and the tumbril moved away, to amble up and down slowly for an hour or so. It had been well worth watching, and I returned to bed uplifted by a sense of sin and happiness.

There were a few other great houses in the neighbourhood, though now some are desolate, some drag out a living death as National Trust museums, and Tregannock itself is a shell, a mere container for the ashes of its own fiery destruction. In those days they took it in turn to entertain one another's servants at winter dances; and every Christmas-time Mr and Mrs Polperro gave a ball for their more resplendent neighbours, and by a stretch of social magnanimity included the professions: the doctors, a few lawyers from Falmouth and Truro, the parsons and their wives. Bella and I were too young for such diversions, but the Christmas before this May day of which I am writing Louisa, being then eighteen, was deemed old enough to be invited. Where bits and pieces are concerned, I am a worse magpie than Thomas May. Soon enough someone will burn all my rubbish, and that will be the end of the lot of us. But now I can still look at the bit of pasteboard, with the date 1880, upon which a thin copperplate hand invited the Reverend Aubrey Legassick and Miss Legassick to attend the ball.

Louisa pretended that she wasn't a bit excited, but Bella and I were in a ferment until Father made up his mind. How on earth were they to get there? he wanted to know. With Louisa wearing a ball-dress they couldn't amble through the countryside in an open trap behind old Neb. Ten to one, it would be raining. And what was he to do at a dance? It wasn't in his line at all. And Louisa was too young. Besides, the affair was on a Saturday night which he liked to spend preparing for his Sunday's work. We could have killed him. And Louisa said nothing to persuade him one way or another.

It was Mrs Solway and Mr Polperro who settled the matter. Mr Polperro rode over on his lovely dapple-grey to say that the famous tumbril would come for Father and Louisa and bring them back after the ball. With what joy Bella and I listened to his fruity voice as we lingered, guilty but unashamed, outside the study door. "Damn it all, Legassick, you can't let the girl rot in a vicarage all her life." As for Mrs Solway, she produced the young wife of a farmer, who before her marriage had worked for a Truro dressmaker, and told Father point-blank that here was someone who could make a ball-dress as good as any you'd find upalong, by which we understood towns given over to the devil, like London. "Made the wedding-dress for Thomas May's bride, she did, and to make her look anything but the resurrection morning, let alone a bride, was something, if you ask me."

"On the resurrection morning, Mrs Solway, we shall be arrayed in righteousness, I hope," Father said severely, though not, I now imagine, seriously. "Well, bring this young woman along, though she will not need to work miracles to make Louisa fit for company."

These words having virtually decided the matter, Bella and I began to think of our own part in the adventure. We were at the breakfast table, and "Oh, Father," Bella cried, "shall we be allowed to stay up to see you and Louisa come home?" And I chipped in with a cry seconding this exciting notion.

Father said: "You will be allowed to stay up to see us go – certainly not to see us return. We shall not leave here till nine o'clock."

There could not have been more excitement if the young woman had been commanded to dress the Queen for her coronation. For a week and more there was an intensity of snipping and sewing and fitting in Louisa's bedroom, and Louisa herself became even more than usually aloof and reserved. We besought her to tell us what material had been chosen, what colour it was, but not a word could we get out of her; and when we asked Mrs Solway she leased us with: "Oh, you'll see all in God's good time. It's a sort of Dandy-grey-russet."

And then the night of the ball came, and we could bear it no longer. It had been a glorious day, sunny from morning to night, and already the camellia by the house was in flower and violets were blue under the wall and a few primroses bloomed along the hedge. Roger was home for the Christmas holiday, and in the afternoon he rowed me and Bella on the Carrick Roads which were as smooth as silk, and we worked hard on him and persuaded him to fall in with our scheme. He was to take Louisa for a walk at six o'clock. Mrs Solway had gone out after lunch to see her sister and would not be back till seven. The young dressmaker, we knew, would be coming at eight to help Louisa with her dressing. Father would be in his study, and we would have an hour for gloating in Louisa's room.

The plan worked well, and we entered the room hardly knowing what to expect. To begin with, the fire had been lit, and a fire in a bedroom was an unheard-of indulgence in those days. Already the curtains had been drawn, and in the dim but cheerful light of the dancing flames we started back appalled, for there was Louisa, tall, already dressed, staring at us, immobile and accusing. The illusion lasted for only a moment, then Bella stifled a laugh as she said: "It's the dummy." We had seen it carried into the house a week ago.

The recovery from fright made us bold, and I said: "Let's light the lamp."

The paraffin lamp was rarely used. A candlestick carried up from the hall table usually sufficed. But there the lamp was, hanging from a chain above the dressing table. I climbed on to a chair and lit it, and then we gave ourselves to an orgy of looking.

I can go up to that room now. It is my bedroom and it doesn't amount to much. It has electric light and an electric fire, and there is carpet fitted right in to the skirting boards. That night it was enchanting, and I use the word with care. It put a spell upon us. It was a peephole through which we looked not so much at what was under our eyes but at feminine mysteries which we knew nothing about, but apprehended. The warmth, the firelight, the glow of the lamp falling upon the floor bare save for a strip of matting, the little iron bedstead with its plain meek coverlet, the silence, a pair of golden shoes. We held our breath.

I looked at the bottle of lavender-water on the dressing table, and at the pot of opaque white porcelain that I knew to contain the somehow sinful red paste, at the beautiful brushes that had belonged to Mother. There was a low glass dish full of the dusky red camellias from the garden. Everywhere I sensed, but did not understand, that there had been arrangement, Louisa's arrangement, of the place, as though here she would be robed to enter a shrine. And then my thoughts went beyond the shrine to the occasion which it must serve, and I saw the Tregannock ballroom full of candlelight, swirling with dancers, and I heard the music, and pictured Louisa there wearing the dress that had been the matter of so much speculation.

Bella and I looked at it with awe, but dared not touch it. It was of thick silk, so deeply cream-coloured as almost to be gold. Lying on the bed were what seemed to us miraculous undergarments.

At last the spell broke. Bella said: "I wonder whether she'll put red on her cheeks?"

She took up the pot from the dressing table and unscrewed the lid. "Look," she whispered.

But this was going so deep into the mystery that I hardly dared. However, having walked to her side, I was overcome by boldness, and not only looked but tried to dip a finger on to the coloured paste. Bella snatched the pot away so hastily that my fingers brushed the surface, and I stood there looking at the tell-tale colour on their tips. "Oh, you little fool," Bella said. "She'll see those marks now and guess what we've been up to." She gave me so petulant a push, and so unexpectedly, that I almost fell backwards, and, to recover myself, snatched at the first thing to hand. That was the silken dress. The dummy toppled, recovered itself, and we stared aghast. My fingers had dragged themselves down the silk and left their red tracks from waist almost to hem.

We knew there was nothing we could do about it. That was the dreadful thing. I began to cry. Bella snatched my hand and said: "For goodness' sake keep quiet." She dragged me into the passage and along to our own room. We sat there in the dark, trembling, till we heard Roger and Louisa come in. That must have been half-an-hour later. Now, I thought, now? I was trembling from head to foot.

We heard Roger go whistling through the garden towards the loft where Thomas May was still living till he could find a cottage for himself and his bride. Roger spent a lot of time there when he was at home. Ten minutes later we heard Louisa come up and go into her room. Instantly, she was out again, running along the passage, calling "Father! Father!" Her voice was full of agony.

We waited, fright making us feel more dead than alive, till Father came up. We followed him and Louisa to her room. We had expected to see her pointing out the red tell-tale smears. What in fact confronted us was beyond belief. We had forgotten the paraffin lamp. As such lamps may easily do if not tended, this one had smoked, and it must have been smoking for three-quarters of an hour. The air was thick with carbon cobwebs dense and oily, falling like filthy rain. The dressing table, the bed and the underclothes upon it, the dress upon the dummy: all were thick with horrid evil-smelling smut. The ruin was irretrievable.

I have never loved Father, or admired him so much, as I did then. While Louisa and Bella were staring at the dress his eyes caught mine. The thick eyebrows went up in an unspoken question, and I nodded.

18

In that flash all was confessed, understood, and forgiven. He said: "Go outside, all of you, or you'll be like a lot of sweeps."

We went into the passage and watched as he threw back the curtains, opened the window, turned down the wick and finally blew out the lamp. "Louisa, my dear," he said, "come along to my study." Louisa followed him, looking stony. Before closing the door, he said to us: "When the dressmaker comes, please send her in to me."

A few moments later Mrs Solway returned, and – the one lucky thing that happened that night – she had brought the dressmaker with her, an hour earlier than had been expected. We sent her in to Father, and he said to us: "Tell Mrs Solway to give you your supper. Louisa and I will need nothing." Then he and Louisa and the dressmaker went up to his bedroom. I had a sense that he was taking charge, and this surprised me, for normally, so long as nothing disturbed his routine, Father rarely intervened in anything. Somehow comforted, I wandered into the dining room, feeling subdued, sinful, but forgiven.

Roger had not returned, and Mrs Solway said: "He can eat when he comes for it. Once he and that ole earthworm get together they'll talk till doomsday." She put the food before us, and stood looking at us, hands on hips. "Well," she said, "there's something up when you two are as dumb as dead ducks. What's happened?"

We couldn't tell her. Bella began to snivel, and I said grandly: "Please leave us, Mrs Solway. We have grief to bear."

"Aye, I'll bet you have," she said, "something you've brought on your own heads by the look of it. Well, in God's good time all will be revealed."

She left us, and we couldn't eat a mouthful. We could hear footsteps overhead, but what was going on in Father's bedroom we could not understand. Presently Roger came in. Our supper was cold meat and pickles. Without calling Mrs Solway, Bella pushed her plate towards him. He cleared it hungrily. I pushed him mine, and he ate that, too. Then he echoed Mrs Solway's words: "What's happened?"

We told him. Always, we told Roger everything. Like Louisa, he was beautiful; but, unlike her, he was radiant, he threw out warmth. Louisa was contained. You could feel the heat within her, as though held back for an explosion. Roger had his own concerns. You would come upon him often standing quite still – in the graveyard or on the road or in the house – smiling. And you knew that he was with his own things, whatever they might be; but he would put them aside, and then he was wholly your brother. Now he entered at once into our sad concern. I said: "And we feel so dreadful because Louisa can't go to the ball without a dress."

"Of course she can't," he said. "But the dress in her bedroom isn't the only one in the world."

Bella and I looked up at once full of hope. Roger was like that. He made you feel that things were possible. I was so warmed and reassured by his words that the thought of food no longer nauseated me. I wished I hadn't given him my supper.

"Have you ever seen Mother's old dresses?" he asked. "She used to go every year to Mr Polperro's ball. She looked lovely."

I could not remember my mother. I was a year old when she died. Roger was six then.

"They're still upstairs," he said, "in a wardrobe in Father's room. Now I'll bet you what is happening is this. That dressmaker is doing a quick job on one of them. And it'll have to be quick. Lucky she came an hour before she was expected."

The shame and guilt lifted from Bella's face. "Oh, Roger!" she said. "What a wonderful idea! I hope you're right."

For myself, I felt so certain that Roger had seen in his mind what was happening that if he had said "Of course I'm right!" I should not have been surprised. But yes, I would. Roger was not like that. "Well," he said, "it seems to me the sensible thing to do."

There was now so much guessing what Louisa would look like that we were almost glad that our sin had been clever enough to contrive this new situation. We pressed Roger to tell us what he knew about Mother's dresses, but he was hopeless. "Oh, you know – the usual gorgeous things women wear when they go out," was as far as he could get.

At half-past eight Father came unexpectedly into the room. Mrs Solway brought him a sandwich and he drank a glass of wine. We looked at him anxiously as at an ambassador who could bring fateful news, but we dared not question him. At last he said: "Well, what are you and Thomas May up to this time, Roger?"

We knew that he was teasing us, aware of our tension but determined not to resolve it.

"We've been talking about the dinghy, sir. He thinks he could drop a centre-board through it and put in a small mast. It would be good fun."

"Oh, there's all sorts of fun to be had in the world," Father said. "Think of the fun you can have with a paraffin lamp."

He looked severe, but I could see a smile hiding in the corners of his eyes, and, emboldened, I said: "It was clever of you, Father, to think of a way out of the difficulty."

"Well," he said, "a man with three daughters gets practice enough in that. Eh, Roger?"

"I don't know, sir," Roger said logically. "I've never had three daughters."

They continued to tease us until we heard a crunching on the gravel outside, and Father said: "Well, that sounds like the coach. You'd better get into the hall and see Cinderella come down. Could you put up with the couch in the sitting room tonight, Roger? I've told Louisa to use your room. Her own has suffered from a fall of carboniferous deposits."

Oh, it was good to hear him putting on this gay act, because it wasn't easy or natural for him. But it meant that I was forgiven, and I stood in the hall holding Bella's arm and trembling with happiness.

Mrs Solway had opened the front door, and I rejoiced to see that Mr Polperro had given us the whole works, as they say nowadays. The splendid day had been followed by a full-moon night, and the pale shine of it was on the coach with its lighted lamps, and on the bewigged coachman, and the footman standing there already holding open the coach door. We looked up, and there was Louisa coming down, the dressmaker carrying a candle on the step above her. Two candles were lit on the hall table; and it was because of this not extravagant golden glow, so different from our fierce illumination of today, that she seemed to be webbed with light. She was dressed in yellow silk that rustled and caught sparkles as she moved, so that I thought of moongleams on a sighing sea. My father was standing with us watching her come in his dead wife's dress, and God knows what thoughts were in his heart. She smiled at Roger and not at me or Bella, and then he took her arm and handed her into the coach. We stood there till the great contraption turned slowly on our gravel sweep, passed through the gates, and lumbered away up the hill.

21

"Now come on in," Mrs Solway said. "That's the end of the show, and we don't want you girls catching cold. There's just a bit of frost in the air."

5

Bella and I never said to Louisa "Tell us." She either told us or she didn't, and she told us nothing about the ball. Neither, of course, did Father. And so in a day or two the ball might never have been. The mess in Louisa's room was cleaned up; the holiday ended and Roger went back to school; the spring rushed upon us; Uncle Reginald came home, and Euphemia Emmett died. If I hadn't decided to give her a fairly Christian burial I should not have been there with Uncle Reginald eating breakfast in the loft, and I should not have been going to Tregannock. Thus all things work together for good, as Mrs Solway was always reminding me, forgetting the conclusion of that phrase.

In many country parishes the church is in one place and the village in another. So it was with us. There were three ways of getting to the village. You could row yourself up the creek in the dinghy, and that was just about a mile. The village clustered round the head of the creek. Or you could go along the narrow road that followed the run of the creek, but you couldn't do this if you were driving any sort of vehicle, for the walls of fields closed in near the vicarage so severely that no vehicle could get through. So the third way was by the wide road that made a half-circle sweep to the village, and that added miles. It was the way the Polperro coach came.

My favourite way of making the journey was in the dinghy, and that was the way we went on that May morning. As soon as we had washed up the breakfast things Uncle Reginald went over to the house and told Father we should be out all day; and in five minutes we were off. There was no time for delay: the tide had turned, and soon the upper half of the creek would be a mud-flat. But now it was all beauty, and how beautiful our creek was! On the side opposite the vicarage, pastureland rolled steeply down to the water, and where land and water met small oaks grew thickly, and you could see the high-tide mark drawn upon the leaves stretching away in front of you as clean as a ruled line.

Uncle Reginald was rowing, and I had nothing to do but look about at the swans nesting, as they always nested, on the other bank, at the herons that lifted as we approached and seemed to saunter lazily through the air, the most unhurrying of birds, so different from the kingfishers that you could see there too: they went by like tiny thunderbolts, an eye-blink of red and blue and green, and buried themselves in the banks. I loved them all for one reason or another, but, as for noise, I loved most the lost-soul crying of the curlews and the querulous voices of the owls, like discontented old gentlemen for ever quavering about one grievance or another. I fell asleep to their noises every night – the curlews and the owls.

We just made it. Another half-hour and we should have been stranded. Uncle Reginald tied the painter to a ringbolt in the little quay, and lifted me up. Then he climbed after me.

We had still about two miles to go, but before leaving the village we peeped into the smithy opposite the Polperro Arms, and already a few old men, their pipes smoking placidly, were sitting near the forge. It was a regular club and parliament combined. Some of them snoozed and gossiped there through all of every day, going home only for their meals. That morning Mr James Polperro was talking to them amid the clutter of old ploughs that needed mending, and wheels that needed new rims, and harrows and piles of horse-shoes and miscellaneous ironmongery. Mr Rowe, the blacksmith and a chorister of Father's church, was not a bit like Longfellow's heroic bore. He was a little man who looked as though the fires of his forge had dried the sap out of him long ago and were now curing the leather of his narrow face. He looked at us over his steel-rimmed spectacles and said: "Good morning, Miss Maria. Good morning, Mr Pallace. Three years since I saw you. You don't change much except to grow bigger."

"While you dwindles, George," said one of the ancients, taking out his pipe and spitting. "Next time Mr Pallace comes 'ome, you'll be making nothing but mouse-traps."

"Dang it," said Mr Rowe, "it'll 'ave to be a small un to catch 'ee."

Not very smart repartee, but that was how it went in the smithy, and in those days I thought it smart enough. I laughed heartily.

Mr Rowe's son, three times his size, was working the bellows, and soon the hammering on the anvil was done, and the horse-shoe hissed in the cold water, and Mr Rowe said: "Well, there 'e be, Mr James."

They walked outside to where a horse was tied to a ring in the smithy wall. Mr James Polperro stroked its lovely neck, and Mr Rowe took a foot between his knees and couched it in his leather apron. "Lost a shoe this morning," Mr James said as the smith hammered.

"Out riding early, weren't you?" asked Uncle Reginald.

"Oh, yes. I often am," Mr James said easily.

"Well I must be on my way. I'm due at Tregannock."

"Yes." Father's expecting you, I know."

We had a fair way yet to go, for Tregannock was, on the other side, as far from the village as the vicarage was on ours. Uncle Reginald's stride made me think of the heron's flight: apparently lazy and lounging, but going on and on, tireless. The sun was warm. The daffodils were long since over. Hawthorn scented the air, and every cottage garden was lively with colour. Now and then my uncle would stop to look closely at a rhododendron or azalea. I didn't know then – or knew only vaguely – that these and camellias were his great gift from the East to the West and that he was paid a beggar's pittance by the wealthy landowners whose estates he beautified. Not, I am sure, that he would have minded that. He didn't talk much, but I remember his saying: "I shall have to go up to London next week, and then, as soon as I can fix things up, I shall be off to Tibet." He said it as casually as one might say "I'm going in to Falmouth," and I had neither the knowledge nor the imagination to understand the immensity those few words conveyed. For in those days one didn't reach the seacoasts of the East in a comfortable liner and go thence to the foothills of the mountains in an aeroplane, as plant collectors can do today.

The gates of Tregannock opened upon a field big enough to house a village, with a road running through it. Beyond an iron fence, upon a slight rise of ground, the house stood with a lawn in front of it. Tregannock was no Blenheim or Montacute or Longleat, but it was an imposing house with a granite balustrade in front of it and a sweep of balustraded steps rising up to the entrance. Standing there at the head of the steps, you looked upon a great stretch of level agricultural land, but not far behind the house the land fell away in a vast escarpment, wooded, so that you looked out over that falling sea of oaks to a prospect of enchantment, blue and tender on a summer's day. The gardens were not gardens in the sense that the word conveys to most people: not a municipal park or the garden of a seedsman's catalogue. Like most great Cornish gardens, it was mainly woodland, but woodland composed of rare and splendid trees that had been brought to prosper in that favoured climate, undergrown with blazing bushes that had known the steamy silence of forests climbing the foothills of the lonely Himalayas. It is all desolate now; and I often think how, from down there below the escarpment of oaks, where the road runs to Truro, night travellers must have looked up in wonder to see the great house flaming to death upon the hill.

Mr Polperro, with two retrievers at his heels, met us as we passed through the gate in the iron fence. He pointed to me with his walking-stick, and said: "This is one of Legassick's girls, isn't it?"

My uncle said that it was, and Mr Polperro, who must have known who I was anyway, said: "I shall be keeping you all day. What is she going to do with herself?"

My uncle said casually: "She can roam about, if you don't mind."

"Of course I don't mind, but what is she going to eat?" Mr Polperro asked, and he looked so well-fed himself that the question seemed to rise from some great depth of his being. "Well, come with us," he said to me.

We followed the path round the lawn, up the steps, and into the house, whose door stood open. I had not been in the house before, and it seemed to me stupendous, with the wings of a great double staircase rising to the first floor. The noble sweep drew my eyes inevitably upward to where the wings met in a landing, and there, looking down over the banister, was a young woman. She called a question to Mr Polperro and he answered her. Then she walked away along a corridor. Mr Polperro said to my uncle: "Well, Pallace, if you're away as long next time as you were last, I suppose you'll come back to find me a grandfather. That was Lady Mary Lacey, who is to marry that boy of mine."

Then he remembered me again and called to a footman who was standing about doing nothing, but looking as resplendent as though he had heavenly functions. "Go to the kitchen," Mr Polperro said, "and have some sandwiches cut for this girl. Put them in a basket and bring them to her here." He turned to my uncle and said: "Now, we've got a lot to talk about, Pallace." They were going, when Mr Polperro said to the footman: "You'd better bring the girl a glass of milk and a piece of cake before you do anything else."

Then I was left alone in the great entrance hall, and I sat on a winged chair upholstered in *petit point* work and looked at the portraits on the walls and the enormous porcelain pots in which shrubs were flowering. My milk and cake arrived, and I was munching happily when the young woman who had spoken to Mr Polperro strolled down the stairs. I thought it must be very exciting to be on the point of marrying Mr Polperro's son, but the young woman didn't seem at all excited. She trailed slowly through the hall, gave me a long look but did not speak to me, and passed out through the door into the morning. I thought she was very handsome but that she would not be much fun. She might at least have given me a smile.

The footman came back and handed me a little basket containing sandwiches wrapped in a linen cloth. He spoke for the first time. "Chickenanam," he said. "Orl right?" The heavenly being was at once diminished in my sight. I knew that Mr Polperro never employed local men as footmen. They were all Cockneys, people said. But even Cockneys should be aware of aspirates. It was something Father was very strict about, though in the pulpit he always referred to the 'umble and meek. Louisa tackled him about it once, and he said: "You no more pronounce the H in humble, my dear, than you do in honour."

I said to the footman: "They will do very nicely. Please convey my thanks to the cook," and I walked out through the door, trying to look as haughty as Lady Mary Lacey. She was nowhere in sight, and that didn't worry me. I was used to wandering about alone, and the gardens of Tregannock were certainly something to wander in.

When the sun was at its height I found myself behind the house, on the edge of the woods, and I sat down on the grass to eat my chickenanam and looked out over the trees whose leaves had not lost their springtime gold. As far as I could see to right and left that gold clothed the falling ground like an immense carpet, the uniformity broken here and there by the springing green of a larch. Beyond this was tender distance, blue infinity.

I had been up very early that morning to bury Euphemia Emmett and accidentally to surprise Louisa hidden in the darkness of the graveyard yew. I was feeling tired and I moved off the path, a little way down into the wood, and piling the dry fronds of last year's bracken I made a nest and fell asleep in it. There were peacocks strutting about at Tregannock, and the screeching of one of these beautiful stupid creatures wakened me. I sat up dazed and wondering for a moment where I was, and the screeching went on. I was terrified when I realised that it was now coming from a human throat. I could not retreat or advance without seeming an eavesdropper. I squirmed over on to my stomach, peeped through the bracken, and saw Mr James Polperro and Lady Mary Lacey standing on the path where I had eaten my lunch. The screeching was coming from Lady Mary. Her face was no longer beautiful, but white and furious. Mr James looked sheepish and miserable. I heard nothing of what was said, for I was no sooner fully awake than they moved on together, Lady Mary still screeching.

I was amazed. Glad at having escaped unseen, I sat pondering what was to me an unbelievable happening. If Bella and I quarrelled and raised our voices, Father would punish us by instructing Mrs Solway to give us at lunch time nothing but a plate of raw maize. It didn't happen often, because we liked our food, and to be thus reminded that we were a pair of cockatoos, to be fed accordingly, was something we didn't relish. But we learned our lesson. One of the ways you could tell a lady, Father said, was by the way she spoke. In no circumstances did she shriek. Pondering the syllogism: No lady shrieks. Lady Mary Lacey shrieks. Therefore Lady Mary Lacey is no lady: I sauntered on. It must have been an hour later that, walking outside the wall that surrounded the rose-garden, I came to the little wrought-iron gate through which I could peep in. I didn't peep for long. What I saw caused me to hurry on. Lady Mary and Mr James Polperro were sitting on the granite edge of the lily pond. She was looking as happy as the day is long and as gentle as a lamb. She was dabbling her fingers in the water, and Mr Polperro was kissing the back of her neck.

They were married in the autumn of that year.

CHAPTER TWO

SURPRISING THOUGH it had been to find Louisa under the yew tree, and sadly as this had wrecked the ceremony with which I had wished to commit Euphemia Emmett to the ground, her presence there made me feel important in the days that followed.

Nobody knew what was the matter with Louisa. I didn't know myself, but at least I could guess that it had something to do with her presence in the graveyard. This gave me a great sense of power over Father and Bella. Not for anything would I have told either what I had seen, not only because I had promised Louisa to keep silent, but also because I liked the feeling that I was the only person who had so much as a hint about the cause of all the trouble. Though in fact I knew nothing that had any relevance to the true situation.

On the morning after Uncle Reginald and I had visited Tregannock, he joined us at breakfast instead of cooking his own in the loft. He was full of talk about his interview with Mr Polperro, who was the mouthpiece of the syndicate that employed him, and with whom he had now come to final arrangements about his visit to Tibet. It was at this point that I butted in. I said: "Mr Polperro told Uncle Reginald that he will probably be a grandfather before the journey is over."

Father was not surprised. "Yes, indeed he may," he said. "He told me last week about Mr James' engagement to Lady Mary Lacey. She's the youngest daughter of the Earl of Aberavon. I haven't met her yet."

I was annoyed that Father knew, but glad that he hadn't met her. "I have," I announced, making it matter-of-fact. "I saw her yesterday three times."

"Then perhaps you will give us your mature impression of the future lady of Tregannock," Father said with a smile.

"She's a horrid stuck-up creature, and she's no lady because she shrieks like a parrot."

Father reproved me. "Maria," he said to Uncle Reginald, "tends to err from over-emphasis. She is full of rash opinions which she expresses immoderately."

Uncle Reginald said: "I'm not much of a judge of English ladies. The ladies I meet have different codes of conduct. However, I thought Lady Mary good-looking and well-mannered. She and Mr James joined me and Mr Polperro at tea time."

I rushed in impetuously. "I don't call her good-mannered. The first time I met her, she passed me without a smile. The second, she was shrieking at Mr James and he was looking unhappy. The third time, he was kissing her. She's inconsistent."

Louisa, so much older than the rest of us, was always our deputy-mother rather than a sister. She looked at me now with the dislike I have seen in many mothers' faces when their young are not all they're expected to be. "Control your tongue," she said sharply, and her face reddened.

Bella was uninterested in any of it. She went on eating bread-and-butter with deep concentration. Only at Louisa's sharp remark did she look up and ask her languidly: "What are you blushing about?"

Louisa said: "Father, these two children are becoming impossible. We have no manners at all in this house when Roger is out of it."

Father reproved us. "I will not have you speaking to your elder sister in that way," he said. "It is most unseemly." He looked at Louisa to see whether this satisfied her. There were times when he seemed a little afraid of her.

"Well," he went on, "we shall soon have an opportunity to form our own opinions. While Lady Mary is at Tregannock, Louisa and I had better call and offer our felicitations. It will be expected of us."

Louisa said: "That would be premature, Father. The engagement has not been publicly announced."

"Well," Father said gently, "I don't think we need stand on ceremony to that extent, my dear. Polperro is more than the patron of this living. He is my friend. Could you find it convenient to come tomorrow?"

Then, right out of the blue, there burst such a scene as the vicarage had not witnessed in my time. The red drained from Louisa's cheeks. She was white as a surplice. She asked in sudden fury: "Why should we kow-tow to these people? If they want to get married, they can do it, can't they, without our crawling to tell them how honoured we feel to wish them luck? Let them take their chance like the rest of us. Did you go to Thomas May and his wife with felicitations?"

Then she seemed downright terrified, as though all this had been torn out of her, and she wished it hadn't. Even Bella stopped eating and looked at Father with a keen expectation of his reply. He asked merely: "Louisa, are you well?"

It could have been an anti-climax, but Louisa did not permit that. She said: "I am very far from well, and going to Tregannock will not make me better. I would prefer that you went alone, Father, if you must go at all."

At last there was a little acid in Father's voice. "I shall certainly go," he said. "And I shall not feel that I am kow-towing when I visit a dear friend. If your Mother had been alive she would have been delighted to go with me. I thought you would like learning to take her place."

Louisa said: "I shall never be able to do so, Father, and I'm tired of trying. I'm tired of doing nothing but wander in the few miles about this place. Even going to Truro or Falmouth is an event, and it shouldn't be. I'm tired of the people, and I was ashamed to go to the Tregannock ball wearing Mother's old dress."

"You were not ashamed at the time," Father said. "You looked well and you felt well. Whatever has come over you has nothing to do with that. You have merely raked it up. In any case, you wouldn't have worn it if these children had learned manners enough not to intrude into other people's rooms. You haven't brought them up well."

"It isn't my business to bring them up at all," Louisa said flatly.

"Then whose business is it? Are we to leave them to acquire their manners from Mrs Solway and Thomas May?"

"They could do worse," Louisa said. "In any case, I wash my hands of them. Will you please excuse me?"

She went out of the room and Bella and I soon followed her. Believe me, we had plenty to talk about. It was a lovely morning and we ran through the graveyard, jumped into the dinghy, and rowed ourselves to the other side of the creek. A small semi-circular quay was there — and is there still — faced with grey local stone and paved with grass and seapinks. No one ever seemed to use it. It was our favourite place for being alone. We lay on the grass with the morning sun streaming down on us and discussed the incredible conversation at the breakfast table. We felt in some odd way that, whatever it had been about, Louisa had won, that she was strong and Father weak. It was Louisa who had started it, and Louisa who had had the last word. What most deeply impressed us was that she had spoken rudely of the Polperros. It was not for the first time. Not long ago Father had recounted to us at tea time how he had been in the village that afternoon and Mr Polperro had ridden through on his horse. A village boy had failed to remove his cap, and Mr Polperro had turned his horse, overtaken the boy, lifted his cap from his head with the bone handle of his riding-crop, and tossed it over the hedge.

Louisa said: "He needs to be civilised."

"Oh, well," Father answered, "Mr Polperro did his best to teach him."

"I mean," Louisa said slowly, "that Mr Polperro needs to be civilised. Do you call it a civilised action to treat a child like that?"

Father said: "It will be a long time, my dear, before class distinctions are abolished, even if one should think the abolition desirable."

Louisa said coldly: "I'm not talking about class distinctions. I'm talking about civilised behaviour. Mr Polperro is arrogant, and Mr James is as weak as ditch-water."

"I don't advise you, my dear, to propagate your views."

"Moreover," Louisa persisted, "Mr Polperro drinks far too much."

"Louisa!"

"Yes, Father?"

She looked coldly at him, and whatever it was that he was going to say, he didn't say it.

We admired Louisa enormously in moments like that when she seemed full of cold ferocity, but too often the cold ferocity was used on us, and we couldn't love her.

At eleven o'clock Bella was due to take her lessons with Father. We rowed across the water and ran up to the house in time to see old Neb harnessed to the trap and Louisa and Uncle Reginald sitting in it. They drove off before we were near enough to have a word. Bella went in glumly to her books and I went down to have a talk with Thomas May who was just due to emerge from his latest grave and have a pasty.

2

Whoever St Tudno may have been, which is something no one has been able to discover, and I don't think we are any the worse for that, our church was dedicated to him, and Legassicks had followed one another as parish priests of St Tudno for generations. What I am trying to do is give some account of the end of them. We all go the same way home; and throughout my lifetime methods of accelerating our departure have been fruitfully invented, ever better and better, so that now I am the last of the Legassicks, and the chances are fifty-fifty that I shall join the rest before my tale is done.

When my own bit of the tale began I was too young to know the significance of the fragments that came under my observation. And so, in order to keep the narrative straight, I must tell of many things as I came to understand them later. To begin with, I must tell what was the matter with Louisa.

3

Those poor Brontë girls! Like us, they were brought up in a vicarage looking upon a graveyard. Like us, they were motherless and had one brother, though Roger did not drink like Branwell Brontë. We had our Mrs Solway as they had their Tabby, and, with their Cornish mother and Irish father, they were full of Celtic blood, like us. I wonder what would have happened if their father had had the vicarage of St Tudno instead of the rectory at Haworth? However, there were differences as well as similarities. They were wonderful women, and we were not. Except Louisa. Being, like Bella, a commonplace person, I didn't know then that Louisa was wonderful. I came to admire her, but I was always a little afraid of her, too, as (I had even in childhood sensed) Father was. He kept her very busy. She wrote a beautiful clear hand, but you needed to be a diviner, not a reader, to make out what Father wrote. She became his amanuensis, making fair copies of his scribbles for the printer, and when I asked her long afterwards about those days she laughed. "One thing I have to thank Father for," she said, "is that he opened my eyes. His books were such rubbish. The dreadful thing is that he never knew it. But who in his senses would want to go on writing again what other people had written better twenty times before?"

We were sitting then almost precisely in the place where I had made my bed of bracken so long before, and had slept and awakened to hear Lady Mary Lacey screeching like a peacock. Now we heard

James Polperro's voice "Are you coming in, my dear? It's time for lunch."

"No," Louisa said. "I don't want any lunch. Leave me in peace."

"Very well, my dear."

He hovered there for a moment, and she gave him an impatient look, and he walked away.

She went on as though we had not been interrupted: "It was all like that. Just as though Thomas May had had nothing to do but dig up old skeletons and bury them again with the full canonical droning."

I don't know whether she had ever loved Father. Certainly she had no pity for him, and she made no pretences. "It opened my eyes to a lot," she said. "I mean the way that a thing went on once it had been started. There were the Polperros, for example. To see them arriving in church used to make me want to laugh fit to burst. Everybody knew that Mr Polperro was a heavy drinker and tyrant, that his wife and daughter were nitwits, and that Mr James couldn't have held his own in the simplest argument with Thomas May or Mrs Solway. Not that either would have dared to argue with him. That was the point. There the Polperros had been, and there they were, and that was reason enough for supposing that they ever would be. I used to seethe, and I broke out to Father once or twice."

I remembered that.

"He never argued the matter with me. That used to infuriate me more than anything. He just used to look at me out of his handsome eyes as though pitying my youth which would come, all in due season, to recognise that the social set-up had been devised by God once and for all."

Then she fell in love with James Polperro.

4

My brother-in-law James was a handsome man, and I recall my earliest impressions of him as a handsome youth. He was twenty when Louisa was eighteen, and had just been sent down from Oxford. How he had ever got into Balliol, of which Jowett was then Master, is one of the mysteries that may be revealed when the seals are opened; how he was sent down is a simpler matter. He used to tell the story with a frequency that became rather tiresome. He saw little enough of Jowett. The last time he saw him this was their conversation.

Jowett said: "Your tutor tells me you are studying Greek, Mr Polperro?"

"Yes, sir."

"He is normally a truthful man, but I find it difficult to believe that he is not somehow misinformed. Can you produce for me any *evidence* that you are studying Greek?"

"No, sir."

"Could it roughly be said that this negative covers the whole range of your studies, with the possible exception of horsemanship?"

"I fear so, sir."

"I am no advocate of specialisation, Mr Polperro, but in this case I feel compelled to encourage your bent. Unfortunately, the University has no chair of equestrian art — or is it a science?"

"A little of both, sir."

"Ah. Thank you. Well, go hence and specialise, young man. I suggest Cornwall, which I am told breeds admirable centaurs. I shall always be pleased to hear of your progress. Shall we drink a glass of sherry wine?"

"I shall be delighted, sir."

"Well, your good health, and my apologies that the University's curriculum is so tragically restricted."

So the young man came down to Cornwall and noticed that the vicar's eldest daughter was a handsome girl.

The ball which Louisa attended in Mother's old dress was in December, and it was in the autumn before this that the affair began. We were a fairly self-supporting family. When Thomas May wasn't digging a grave or slashing with his sickle at the churchyard overgrowth, he was among the vegetables in Father's bit of glebe land; and Mrs Solway found time to look after the poultry and milk the cow. We girls helped by gathering the fruits of the hedges, and it was while she was picking blackberries for jam and jelly that Louisa met James Polperro.

"It was on this very spot," she said to me once, and I can imagine that encounter because the spot hasn't changed. The land rises up from the vicarage, and at the top of the rise it falls down to a view of Falmouth in one direction and a view of the Carrick Roads in the other. On such a day it is an enchanting place, with the heat of the year gone, a tender light on the gold of stubble, the sky blue, the water blue with a sail on it here and there, and in the hedges all the leaves are flushed with the colours of their coming death. The blackthorns that, only the other day, were frothed over with clouds of white, carry harvests of purple sloes bloomed with a patina that a touch destroys, and the blackberries shine with dew. Flocks of goldfinches flirt and frisk along the hedges, and, amid so much that is ending, the honeysuckle twigs are tufted with the buds of next year's leaves, which caused Thomas May to say to me once: "They learn me more about the resurrection morning, midear, than your father ever do." And if the resurrection morning is as good as a spring day in Cornwall I shan't grumble.

I can imagine, then, Louisa on an autumn day, furnished with a crooked stick for reaching down the high fruit, seeing the horseman ambling along the lane, which then was dusty white, and recognising Mr James. She was thrusting her stick high to reach an alluringly perfect cluster when he sidled the horse in to the hedge, took the blackberry branch in his hand, and bent it down to her. "Allow me to help," he said.

He held it there while she plucked off the berries and dropped them into her basket, and then he let it swish up again, and she, not prepared for that, was scratched along the cheek by a thorn. She fumbled for a handkerchief to wipe away the thread of blood, and hadn't one. He dismounted, took a handkerchief from his pocket and, holding up her chin with one hand, dabbled at her face with the other. The touch of his flesh on hers made her shiver, especially as, when the blood was stanched, he continued to hold her chin cupped in his hand. He looked at her, smiling, then stooped and kissed her.

She glared at him, outraged. The Polperros had a reputation for meanness among their tenants. Louisa said: "You are acting in character, Mr Polperro."

He was too dim-witted to see what she meant, and she said: "You quickly grasp at payment for a small service."

He said: "You look enchanting when you are blushing with anger. You make me want to do it again."

He was standing with one arm resting on his horse's neck, and he made as though to steal another kiss. She swiped at him with her stick. He stepped aside and the blow fell across the horse's head. It was a spirited creature that he had just bought. It reared up on to its hind legs and began flailing with its fore hoofs. James shouted: "Look out, for God's sake!" and threw her unceremoniously into the hedge bottom.

She saw the creature towering over her, and a hoof come down and squash her basket flat, staining the dust with purple. She saw James, quite unexcited, take the reins near the mouth, and stroke the sweating creature's neck, and murmur softly into its ear. He appeared to be more understanding with horses than with women and soon, without a word to her, he mounted lightly and rode away, the proud beast seeming almost humble.

Louisa picked herself up from the ditch and sorted herself out as best she could – her emotions as well as her clothes. I can understand how she was vivid with anger, and fear, and gratitude that she had escaped that smashing hoof, and with a tangle of feeling that surprised and shocked her.

Being Louisa, she said nothing to anybody about this. The next day she took a basket and wandered along the same road. She confessed to me, in the days when I had reached the dull status of being a receiver of confidences, that she didn't know whether she went in expectation or with the idea of speaking her mind should Mr James again appear. No one appeared save a small boy named Jose Green who ran up to her eagerly and gave her a letter. "Save me a walk that 'ave, Miss Legassick," he said. "I were on the way to the vicarage. Mr James said to give this to you if it could be done with no one about. And 'ere you be, praaper private."

She thanked the small Jose, and when he was gone looked at the boyish writing on the envelope, which was what she would have expected. She opened it, and read:

Dear Miss Legassick. – I was very sorry to ride away like that without giving you a hand up, but you know how it is with horses. That smack you gave Paddy put him in a real murdering mood, and it was lucky I was there, because I'm what Irish grooms call a whisperer. They mean a man who can make the maddest horse calm down by whispering sweet nothings in his ear. But I find that when I've done that, it's best to be up and away on him, so that he'll know I'm both friend and master. So that's how it was, and I was rather ashamed at leaving you in the ditch and hope you'll accept this apology, which I'm sending by a messenger because I know what parents are and possibly Mr Legassick might be inquisitive if a letter to you came through the post and you didn't want to say anything about it which could quite possibly have been the case in the circumstances, I think. As for the circumstances, I can only say you were very beautiful and I acted impulsively.

Yours sincerely,

James Polperro.

It was anti-climax, and to a girl of eighteen anti-climax can seem a tragic reversal. "You will hardly remember Mother," Louisa said. "Just imagine what her life was! Living in that vicarage across the water till she was ready to be married, and then coming to spend the rest of her life in the vicarage on this side of the water." Louisa laughed. "No wonder she took to reading Ouida!"

The Ouida novels were in Father's study. Louisa used to slave in there most afternoons making her clear copies while Father was out and about among his flock. She noticed the novels, and took one to her own room, and was fascinated. These high romantics, guardsmen who lived in boudoirs, ladies with fantastic names and habits, were heady stuff for a girl of her age who had been provided by Father with only such fiction as *Queechy*, *Little Women*, and Miss Montgomery's *Misunderstood*. He was a bit afraid of fiction, and would have been surprised had anyone rated *Tom Jones* above his own *Reconsideration of Grace Abounding*.

"The odd thing was," Louisa said to me, "that while I loved Ouida's guardsmen and could have gone on reading about them for ever, I was full of doubts about this sort of thing." It was a winter's day, and we were lounging in front of the fire in her boudoir at Tregannock. "No one had ever talked to me about the social set-up, and I had no idea that there were books about such matters or how I could get hold of them if there were. But I know that watching the Polperros arrive in their coach at church, and watching James' father ride about the village like a touchy Lord God Almighty, whose law had been laid down on Sinai and must henceforth be observed – well, it just used to make me sick. I couldn't forget how much Polperro money had come out of the mines that poor devils had to climb into and out of. Did you know that? They climbed up and down two thousand feet and more of

37

vertical ladders. Can you imagine it? Two thousand feet, after working for hours in hot exhausted air. Sometimes the ladders broke, and anyway the life of those miners was twenty years short of the average. I had a feeling that it was the Polperros of this world who ought to be touching their caps. That's how I was when James gave me his first kiss: stuffed up with romantic notions and at the same time full of vague resentments against him and people like him. Do you remember how you and Bella ruined my ball dress with rouge?"

The sense of sin I had felt that night rushed back upon me, and I hardly dared to look at Louisa, for now she seemed to me even more formidable than she had been then: taller, thinner, lit by a kind of frustrated ferocity. I admitted that I remembered the night.

"It shows you the mix-up I was in. There was an old man in Falmouth whom I always called on when I was there – Mrs Solway's grandfather. He was the one who used to talk to me about the mining days. He could remember *his* grandfather, who was killed when a rotten ladder broke. The odd thing was that he was as mild as a lamb, bore no resentment against anybody. It used to make me feel that it was time such people had someone to voice their resentments for them. Well, I was coming away from a visit to him one day when I saw a pot of rouge in a chemist's shop window. It seemed to me the essence of Ouida wickedness. I bought it, and I remember sneaking it into my bedroom, feeling like a woman far gone in exotic sin. Indeed I was in a mess! I used to sit there, with my face coloured, reading about my guardsmen, then wipe the stuff off and go to sleep and have nightmares about falling off a ladder and going down endlessly."

This, then, was the odd creature that James Polperro tried to play with, and half her mind was full of the intrepid horseman, the Ouida type, whispering the rearing brute to gentleness, and the other half was full of the insolence of the undeserving lords of creation. His letter left her more mixed up than ever; and the secrecy of its coming – through a small messenger bribed with a few coppers – was not without its appeal.

We didn't see much of the Polperros at the vicarage. They faithfully set their example to the people by attending morning service on Sundays, even in winter when our little church could be deathly cold; and beyond such heroism what more could be expected? But occasionally Mr Polperro would call in if he were riding that way, and he would take a cup of tea and be jovial to us children. A week after Louisa's encounter with James, both father and son turned up, tied their horses to the rail outside the vicarage, and came in to tea.

Even when he had become my brother-in-law, James never talked to me about the lovely autumn day, and the rearing horse, and the squashed blackberries, and the tumbled girl, though I must say it seemed a romantic confusion to me. Indeed, James rarely talked. If you asked him about a more complicated matter than how his horses were getting on, he would blush and stammer and leave you wondering why God had ever bothered to endow him with speech. I can only guess at what he was thinking in the few days after sending Jose Green along with his letter. The fact of having written it – perhaps the first letter he had written to a girl in his life – would fix in his mind the happening that called it forth, and when there was no answer he would think about it the more. It seems to me, even now, that a man who had kissed Louisa once would want to do it again, despite her resentment.

I remember that she and Father took tea in the drawing room with the Polperros, and Bella and I were sent off to the kitchen, which we preferred because we didn't have to be polite. Mrs Solway said: "It'll be about that ole church Mr Polperro 'ave come to see your father. Thomas May says he wants some sort of heating 'gainst the comin' winter. About time. An hour in there take a week off your life, I reckon. Still, that's a short cut to 'eaven, when you come to think of it, and I suppose that's what a church is for."

Whether that was what Mr Polperro had come for I don't know. Certainly, from our watch-out at the bedroom window we presently saw him and Father go into the church, but Mr James was not with them. We went downstairs, and he was not in the house. We went into the churchyard, and there we saw him and Louisa. On one side of the churchyard there is an avenue of Irish yews, a cold repellent place with a footpath grown dankly with undernourished moss. Walking on this footpath, apparently in deep and earnest conversation, were Louisa and Mr James. Bella took my arm and whisked me away. We ran down to the creek as though we had not seen them.

Louisa grew into a woman who did not mince her words. She said that day, as we were talking about the matter in front of her boudoir fire: "When he threw me into the ditch I found that I liked it. I went home in a perfect dither."

After the talk in the avenue of Irish yews they met almost every day. She would walk to an arranged spot, and he would ride there.

On the night of the ball he asked her to marry him. She said that she would, and they agreed that no one must be told about it for a time. James was sure that his father would not willingly consent. Polperros always married money. And so after the ball they continued to meet as secretly as before. Louisa said: "I wasn't thinking now about Polperros as oppressors of the poor, believe me, and my dreams were full of other things than poor wretches falling off rotten ladders. We became lovers in every sense of the word."

So things went on till the May morning when I buried Euphemia Emmett.

"He and I," Louisa said, "were both using little Jose Green as a messenger if we couldn't keep an appointment. We invented an idiotic cypher. The day before you found me under the yew tree Jose brought me a letter that wasn't in cypher. James had been very odd and restrained during the last few days, and as soon as I opened the letter and saw that it was rather a long screed I knew that the affair was over. The letter said that he would like to meet me in the churchyard at the absurd hour of five in the morning, because he must leave the house and return to it without being missed. 'But there is something I must say, and I sha'n't have a chance to say it at any other time, because we have visitors here and I sha'n't be able to get away.' "

What he had to say was that he was engaged to Lady Mary Lacey. "I loathe the girl," he said, as if that cleared him. Louisa said: "He had then been engaged to Mary Lacey for nearly a week, while we were still meeting, and, what is more, while he was still enjoying me."

She asked him what he had said to his father about her, and he confessed that he had said nothing. His father had virtually commanded the engagement. He had known Lord Aberavon for years, and the young people had met off and on all their lives. Lady Mary, with her mother, had now appeared so that a family contract might be signed and sealed, and James had gone down before the first gust of his father's anger when he showed reluctance. He said bitterly: "That's how things are done in our family." She looked at him with contempt. "All the same," she said to me, "James is the only man I have ever loved. Can you understand that?" Frankly, I couldn't. I said: "Yes."

So that was Louisa, who had burst out against Father and against the Polperros, and whom Bella and I saw sitting in the trap behind old Neb and driving off towards Falmouth with Uncle Reginald.

5

I suppose Father wasn't bad as a parson, and as a writer he was at any rate able to go on and on, which is all you need if you write the sort of books that he wrote. But he wasn't very good at seeing what was happening under his eyes. When Louisa so unaccountably went contrary to all her usual conduct, he didn't see that something serious must be the cause of it. He merely looked hurt and went off in what is called for some reason or another dudgeon. It was Uncle Reginald who looked at her gravely and said, when we girls had gone away: "Louisa, I'm going in to Falmouth to buy one or two things. What about coming along and having lunch there with me?"

She was only too glad to go. As she had said, going to Falmouth was an event: having lunch there made it a jubilation.

As they were jogging along through that lovely May morning he said: "Has something gone wrong between you and young Polperro?"

She jumped and looked at him aghast.

"I love being out in the dawn," he said. "I went yesterday in the dinghy to see the sun rise. It seems to be quite a popular pastime. Maria was out, and you, and James Polperro. I had my field glasses with me."

She was flabbergasted. "I even tried to look indignant," she said to me. But it was no use.

He said: "Did I ever tell you about Vincent Wheatstone?"

"No," she said. "No one tells us about anything. We just rot here."

"Well," he tried again, "did you ever hear about the Baroness Burdett-Coutts?"

"Yes, vaguely. Father has talked about her. She's a very rich woman who gives away a lot of money. Isn't that right?"

"Yes. Well, Wheatstone belongs to that breed. He's a very rich man who gives away a lot of money. I know him pretty well. When I was last in England he asked me to call on him. He has a great objection to missionaries, but at the same time he thinks a lot needs to be done in the sort of places that I go to. He asked me to make a report on any useful secular work that I thought he could support out there. Before coming down here this time I called on him again and left my report with him. Not much of a report, I'm afraid. Fact is, the last thing I want is to see my country civilised, as they call it. I mean all that Eastern country. I like it too well as it is. Still, you might get on with Wheatstone. That is, if you can put up with a hard life."

"I should prefer a hard life to a soft one," Louisa said. "But I don't see how I can be interested one way or another."

"Wheatstone is an absolute miser," Uncle Reginald went on. "He pours out money like water on his causes. But he sweats himself to the bone, and everybody about him. If he finds that the officials of any cause that he supports have wasted as much as sixpence, down comes the guillotine and they don't get another penny. But his wealth is fabulous."

Louisa said frankly: "He sounds half cracked."

"Anything but. I think you'll like him. I shall be going up to town next week. Shall I take you to see him? If I can persuade your father?"

"But Uncle Reginald, I'd *love* to go to London! I've never been there. But why should I see this horrible old man?"

Uncle Reginald laughed. "He's not horrible, and he's not old. He's somewhere in his middle thirties. He inherited this fortune ten years ago, and in the interests of economy he's been doing his own secretarial work all that time. Now, he tells me, he is *reluctantly compelled* to find some one to help."

Neb was winding his way slowly down the steep twists of the road to Penryn. Louisa looked about her: at the hawthorn banks rising on either hand, at the familiar hodden grey of the church at the bend, and, when they had turned left on to the Falmouth road, at the flood tide filling the Penryn river. It was all so accustomed, and at that moment all so beautiful, that her heart was torn. She said: "There are times when I hate my life here – all the routine of little things that don't seem to add up to any one thing that is worth while. And there are other times when I pity people who live lives of strife and endeavour. In those times I think that if there's any answer to anything it's a quiet answer, and that one may find it in a place like this."

On the road to Falmouth Neb hit up his pretence of a gallant trot, and Uncle Reginald fell silent. He could be a very quiet man at times

42

and it was good to be with him then, because his quietness was full like the quietness of a smooth tide. Surrounded by this quietness, Louisa simmered down. They had a meal in the town, and then they drove to Pendennis Head and sat looking at the sea — not our land-locked sea of St Tudno but the vast sweep across which the Spanish armada had moved to its proud doom, sailing east, and the little *Mayflower* had sailed west with the seeds of a civilisation between her meagre planks. It is a place, as I know, to ponder comings and goings, beginnings and ends, and there they sat through the whole of that afternoon with hardly a word between them. It was only when they were approaching our vicarage gates in the evening that Uncle Reginald said: "Well, I'll speak to your father about this London visit"; and Louisa answered: "Very well. Thank you, Uncle Reginald."

6

They went a few days after that. Bella and I, of course, knew nothing of what was behind it all, and I don't imagine that Father knew much either. Uncle Reginald would have persuaded him to allow Louisa to go with him for a week's holiday. Something like that. And then, when the week was over, we watched Father reading a letter that seemed to disturb him very much. Before putting it down he read it several times, as though searching for something he had missed. At last he took off his spectacles, folded them neatly into their case as was his habit, and said: "It seems that your sister will not be returning from London."

He would have left it at that, but we questioned him unmercifully.

"This letter," he said, "is from your Mother's brother." That was the way he always spoke of Uncle Reginald, as though he did not exist in his own right, but had to be accepted as someone whom circumstances had dragged within the family circle. I don't think he approved of Uncle Reginald, and that was why he welcomed his sleeping in the loft and more or less living apart from us, though with us.

"I should never have consented," he said, "to allowing Louisa to go with him. It was against my instinct, and now he has betrayed my trust."

43

At last he told us: Louisa was going to stay in London and work there. "What we shall all do without her," he said, "I cannot imagine. She was more than a Mother to you."

We pressed him to tell us what work she was to do in London, but he was maddeningly vague. "She should be doing no work at all," he said, "and I shall write and tell her so."

He did, and when, for the purpose of these memoirs, I asked Louisa about that, she said that she had answered firmly.

"What did you tell him?"

"I said I was glad to learn that he thought I should do no work at all, because therefore he could take comfort from knowing that I was doing far less than I had done at the vicarage. And that was true. At all events, I didn't have so many *sorts* of work to do with Vincent. I was a secretary. At home, I was secretary, housekeeper and everything else that came along."

I saw Vincent Wheatstone five years later, when I was ten, and so I can visualise the man Louisa met. Father had put me on to the train for Paddington and given the guard a shilling to keep an eye on me, though once we had left Truro I never saw the man again. As an extra precaution, Father tied a label round my neck, stating that I was Maria Legassick of St Tudno, near Falmouth, bound for Manchester Square, London. Thus, safe as a railway parcel can be, and furnished with a basket of food, I set out. Louisa met me at Paddington. She seemed to me enormously changed. She was twenty-four years old and had been married to Vincent Wheatstone for a year. None of us had gone to the wedding. Indeed, it was not until she had been married for a month that she wrote to tell Father that she was Mrs Wheatstone. I asked her why she had been so reserved with him, and she said: "For one thing, he always exploited me. He took it for granted that it was my duty to be his drudge and yours. And for another, I had been dying to tell him about James Polperro, but I didn't dare. I knew that he would be on the Polperro side and point out the unsuitability of my conduct. That started something in my mind that I've never been able to get rid of."

But all this was in the future, and now here she was amid the afternoon bustle of Paddington Station on a June day, untying the label from my neck and saying:, "Really, Maria, how absurd you look! Did you travel in the luggage van?"

She gave me a perfunctory kiss and handed my small suitcase to a porter, and we followed him to a four-wheeler cab. More than ever, she seemed like an aunt rather than a sister, especially as she had developed a business-like way of talking and acting, and was severely dressed.

Although Father was displeased about this marriage, or at any rate about being kept in the dark concerning it, I had heard him say to Mrs Solway, not without satisfaction, that Mr Wheatstone could buy up the Polperros. Therefore, I had expectations of grandeur. I remembered Tregannock and its splendid furniture, and the powdered footman who had brought me my chickenanam, and the great coach that carried the Polperros to church; and not unnaturally I had been picturing during my journey the high old time I was in for. To find Louisa in duller clothes than I had ever seen her wear, and to be bundled into an old cab that might have been plying in Truro or Falmouth, gave me a shock of disillusion. But the liveliness of the London scene took my mind off these things, especially as I was telling myself that when we reached Manchester Square a footman at least would open the door to us.

Nothing of the sort happened. I liked the look of the square. I liked the painted railings round the areas, the gay boxes of flowers on the window-sills, the striped blinds that kept off the glare of the sun, the carved box-trees in fascinating spirals that screwed their way up from painted tubs by the doors. But our cab stopped at a house that had none of these delights. It had a dull flat façade whose paintwork looked none too fresh.

"Well, here we are," Louisa said. "Vincent is out. You'll meet him later."

The cab drove away, and Louisa rang the bell. Now, I thought; and comported myself haughtily to meet the footman's gaze. The door was opened by a middle-aged woman in black. Our Mrs Solway was better-looking, and not in mourning like this one.

For me, there is a feeling about a house as soon as the front door shuts behind me: a gay feeling, a feeling of happiness or content, of safety or danger, a harassed feeling, a feckless feeling. The feeling of this house rushed upon me: dull, dull, dull. A house full of Ps and Qs that would have to be watched, of rules, regulations and observances. Louisa was going before me up the stairs. "I'd better show you at once where you're to sleep," she said. "Vincent would like you to be in bed not later than nine. Breakfast is at eight."

How different this is from the square outside with its brave flowers and bright paint and stripes of dashing colour! The wall-paper was a dark green, unillumined with pictures. I looked about me on the landing, then followed Louisa up another flight of stairs. "Here we are," she said. "I thought it best for you to share my room. You won't feel so lonely."

The room was at the back of the house. It was like everything else: immaculate, but immaculately dull. The same dark green wallpaper; a washstand, a dressing table, a wardrobe, one cane-bottomed chair, two iron bedsteads side by side, no pictures.

I knew nothing much about married life but in my childish conception a large brass-knobbed double bed was in the middle of it. Father still slept in the one he had shared with my mother, and visits to his parishioners had shown me the same respectable monument in their lives as in ours. I said to Louisa: "Don't you sleep with Mr Wheatstone?"

She was not annoyed by the question, as I now see she might well have been. She said simply: "No."

"Unpack your things," she said, "and then come down," and she left me.

Mrs Solway, impressed by my going to stay with someone who could buy up the Polperros, had packed my smartest clothes, and while I was arranging them in the drawers there was a knock on the door and a girl who seemed not much older than I came in, carrying a japanned jug of hot water. She grinned at me and said: "I'm a norphan. At least as far as my old man goes. My name's Meg. My mother's on the streets and Mr Wheatstone rescued me."

She put the jug into the wash-basin, laid a folded towel over the top, as though proud of having mastered a complicated rite, said: "Well, goodbye for now," and went out.

I felt immensely cheered: by her grin, by her friendly look, and by the hot water which, short though my time had been in the house, seemed to me improbable and out of keeping. I was washing myself when the door opened again and Meg's head looked in. "Don't say nothing about that water," she said. "I pinched it from the kitchen. Goodbye."

She seemed such a friendly girl that I hoped her mother was having a nice time on the streets. They had looked so gay and exciting as we drove from Paddington that I couldn't understand why anyone should need to be rescued from them. I learned later that the dark forbidding Mrs Martin, who had opened the door to us, and who, with Meg, made up the domestic staff, had been rescued from a factory which made matches, and that the only animal about the house, a depressed black and white mongrel with tattered ears, that did a belly-slink away from me whenever I tried to pat it, had been rescued from a dog's home.

Mr Wheatstone came in just before seven o'clock. I suppose he was about forty years old at that time, but he had a beard, and that made him look like Methuselah. When Father was reading the lessons in church I always pictured the people he was reading about, and Methuselah, who was begot by Enoch and in turn begat Lamech, swam on my vision as very much like what Mr Wheatstone now turned out to be. I suppose he was in his way a handsome man. To give you a more modern instance, he was remarkably like the Tennyson whose bearded image appeared as a frontispiece to his poems. Warm though the day was, he was wearing thick broadcloth of the darkest grey. When he spoke, a voice utterly without vibration or colour came sepulchrally out of his beard, as though Lazarus was trying out damp vocal chords on rising from the dead. "So this is the child," and he looked at me with dark lustreless eyes, trying to discern something that he could rescue me from.

I said: "Yes, sir. I am the child."

I could call him nothing but sir. Incredible that this handsome unlit great pillar of a man was my brother-in-law! Louisa was so much older than I, and he was so much older than Louisa. In theory, one should address one's brother-in-law by his Christian name or even by a nickname; but the idea of calling Mr Wheatstone Vincent, or possibly Pogs or Wiggo, was stark blasphemy. I never addressed him save as sir.

Louisa said: "Father put a label round her neck. She looked incredibly absurd."

"Many things look what they are not," Mr Wheatstone pronounced, "and many things do not look what they are. Your father acted wisely. There are unfortunately such things as kidnappers."

I had read stories about kidnappers and how they stole the children of earls and dukes and such like, and used them for begging from door to door till the tell-tale strawberry mark was discovered by some old nurse. I didn't think they would bother with the youngest daughter of the vicar of St Tudno, and I didn't see how, if they had wished to bother, my label would have saved me. Still, it seemed to please Mr Wheatstone to be able to think that Father's foreseeing conduct had averted a situation into which he might have had to step in order to rescue me. It meant that much less work for him.

And how he worked! He looked now at a large watch plainly cased in gun-metal, and said: "Well, supper is ready, I hope," and strode off towards the dining room so purposefully that I felt it would be woe betide someone if his hope were unfulfilled.

Father was an abstemious man. At the midday meal and at supper he would take half a glass of wine topped up with water. My romantic dream, indulged during the journey, of the man who could buy up the Polperros, had included a footman leaning across his shoulder to pour wine from a splendid carafe into a splendid crystal glass. Mr Wheatstone took up a brown earthenware jug and said to Louisa: "Will you take a little water?"

She said: "Yes, please," and he then turned to me and poured water into a smaller glass by my plate, as though it were a luxury to be carefully meted out. We ate beef and carrots and potatoes, and then rice pudding. When he had finished, Mr Wheatstone rose unceremoniously. There was no grace either before or after meat. "Well, now," he said to Louisa, "I haven't altogether decided what we ought to do about the East End Widows Aid Society. I didn't quite like all that I heard this afternoon when I met the Committee. They seemed to me a lot of good-natured noodles who're not fit to be entrusted with half-a-crown a week. However, we shall see. I've brought along some figures. We'll work on them together and then discuss the thing right through."

Louisa gave me a peck on the cheek and said: "Now, get up to bed and have a good sleep. Your journey must have tired you."

I went up through the dusky house. On each landing an oil lamp burned on a deal table. To my surprise, the girl Meg was in my bedroom, turning down the sheets. She gave me her grin. "Not usual, this," she said. "Just a bit of extra service to celebrate the arrival of youth and beauty. Goodbye."

I had brought Miss Montgomery's *Misunderstood* with me, and now I lit my candle and got into bed, and worked myself up into a state about poor Humphie who, while dying, stretched out his arms crying: "Has God sent you to fetch me home at last, Mother?" And little Miles crept in and looked at the radiant smile and said: "Humphie has gone to sleep."

Then I went to sleep, too, with tears dribbling on to my pillow, but whether they were for poor Humphie or myself or Louisa I hardly knew. I was sure that Mr Wheatstone, who abhorred waste, would not expect tears to be wasted on him.

7

Long after this, when our newspaper had a headline about the Wheatstone Trust, whose founder had then been dead for some time, we exchanged some words about him, and Louisa said: "I often wondered how he impressed small children. What did you make of him during your first visit?"

I said: "I felt as though the sun had gone out. There was nothing but one tiny star in the sky – that child called Meg."

And then I dared to put a question that had long interested me. "How on earth did you come to marry him?"

She looked for a moment as angry as the girl whose ball-dress I had smeared with rouge and whose secret I had surprised under the darkness of the yew. Then she calmed down and told me.

Her flying out at Father on the subject of the Polperros had shown Uncle Reginald the way her mind was moving, and he must have guessed that the work she would have to do with Mr Wheatstone would chime in with her mood. It would be in a way so anti-Polperro – giving instead of getting – that it might well be the thing for her. And so it proved for a time. She worked like a horse, and under Mr Wheatstone's guidance learned a lot about finance. For example, she learned with wonder that, despite the flow-away through a thousand taps, careful investment kept the reservoir full. She discovered, and so did Mr Wheatstone, that she had a head for such things, and more and more work piled upon her, though there was never any question of more and more pay. Impressed by this ascetic life, she was filled with a spirit of self-sacrifice, and even gloried in her own poverty. She dealt with his enormous mail, sorting the begging letters into sheep for Mr Wheatstone's consideration and goats for the waste-paper basket. She hardly ever went out, unless to accompany him when he met some committee, and she made no friends. I was appalled at the thought of the mere writing she did. There was no typewriter; the careful beautiful script that she had cultivated for Father's benefit must have flowed over miles of paper.

This went on for about eighteen months. "I don't think I realised it," she said, "but some touch of revolt must have begun to move in me. Learning it all had been exciting, but now I was almost an automaton, and I don't think I was finding my life very happy. But I wouldn't admit it. Then the thing was touched off by something that seemed quite trivial."

Her office was a cold room behind the one where I slept when I visited her. She was working there one November night after supper, an oil lamp hanging from the ceiling above her table, a dying fire in the grate. She became cold, and got up to replenish the fire, but the scuttle was empty. So that was that. A scuttle-full a day was the coal-ration. She rubbed her blue hands together and sat down to write again, but could hardly hold the pen. Mr Wheatstone knocked and came in. He himself looked cold and tired. He passed a hand wearily across his forehead and then glanced at what she was writing. "Your handwriting is not improving, Miss Legassick," he said, "and you know it was the beauty of your writing that first commended you to me. This is positively slipshod."

"I was so tired," Louisa said, "and for the moment so doubtful of what he and I were doing, that I let out at him, just as I sometimes did at Father. He'd never seen that side of me, and he looked as if I'd hit him with an axe."

She got out of her chair and said: "How on earth do you expect decent writing when my hands are blue with cold? And what else can they be on a night like this when there's not a lump of coal in the bucket? What am I working for – a miser?"

He said: "I had hoped that, like me, you were working for the alleviation of human suffering. My hands are no warmer than yours. Feel them."

He put them on her cheeks, and she shuddered. She remembered James Polperro's hands cupping her chin by the blackberry bushes. She started away from him and said: "Don't do that."

He said: "Do you dislike me so much? I thought you were happy here? You have a task worth doing."

"If it's worth doing, it's worth paying for," Louisa said. "You give me a miserable pittance."

He looked at her as if she were a child who didn't understand what she was saying. "I should loathe myself," he said, "if I went among the wretched from a place of luxury."

They faced one another, Louisa still blazing, Mr Wheatstone calm but sad. "There was a time," he said, "when luxury was all I asked of life, and I lived like a blind fool. One night I came out of a theatre, and – I don't know why – instead of calling a cab and going home as usual, I wandered into the back streets around Covent Garden. I was wearing a cloak with a red silk lining and a dress suit and an opera hat, and I carried a cane. It was bitterly cold. Lying across a doorway was a dirty sack, and I poked at it with the cane as I strolled by. Then I stopped and went back. Something about that sack communicated itself to me through the cane. I picked it up with my beautifully gloved hands. It contained a girl child. Her arms and head were stuck through holes in the sack. She had no other clothing. I took off a glove and felt her. She was as cold and stiff as ice. She was dead."

Louisa was not blazing any more. She stood with her back to the grey grate and stared at him. This was the first human thing that had ever been said to her by the man of facts and figures.

"I didn't know what to do," he said. "I stood there with the child's head on my shoulder and her shrivelled legs sticking out of the bottom of the sack. It seemed to me such a monstrous, impossible happening that I half expected crowds to gather round, stunned by horror. Then a woman came along. She looked at me and the child for a moment, then pushed a hand up the sack and felt the body. She said: 'She's a stiff. Poor little bugger. Ah, well, there's plenty of 'em end up that way.' I said: 'What am I to do with her?' and the woman said: 'Shove 'er back where you found 'er. Don't bother your head. Let the cops deal with it.' She hovered about for a time, and then she said: 'Seems to 'ave worried you. I s'pose you're not used to that sort of thing. Come on 'ome with me. I'll soon make you forget it.' I began to cry. It was such a beautiful night, though so cold. Stars were shining. I asked the prostitute to go away, and she went, and then I carried the sack about till I found a policeman. He seemed as surprised as the prostitute had been at my concern. 'Don't upset yourself, sir,' he said. We were near another dark doorway. 'Just put her down there, and that's where I'll report I found her. Just a routine matter. We often finds 'em.' So I put the child down, and the policeman said: 'That's better. You get along home. No need to let a thing like this upset your night's sleep.' I went home. My man had a blazing fire ready for me, and a decanter of whisky. But I felt as though I could never be warm again, and I did not have a night's sleep. I'm sorry I criticised your writing. Good night."

He hadn't said anything about a bigger coal ration for Louisa or about more pay. When his autobiography was published after his death, he described that night much as he had described it to Louisa, and wrote: "That was my moment on the road to Damascus. If ever after that I felt a rekindling of the desire for soft living I shut my eyes and willed myself back to the moment, feeling again that small body of ice, so light, but as heavy on my heart as a monstrous crime. Soon my old desires died and I opened my arms gladly to hardships. They were nothing compared with what I had carried that night, and I expected this to be so, too, with those who worked at my side."

"What worried him," Louisa said, "was that his riches overwhelmed him with a sense of sin. And yet, being a rationalist, he couldn't admit this. A sense of sin involved the acceptance of an absolute, and to a rationalist reason is all one needs. Today they get out of it by dropping sin and speaking of a sense of guilt, as though that altered it. Guilt before whom?"

She got up impatiently. "But what's the good of talking about such matters? He had a knack of making me feel a worm, inadequate to a high mission, but ready to struggle on. Sometimes I hated him. Sometimes I worshipped his superhuman will."

So things went on through that winter, and towards the end of it he came in one night terribly disturbed. After supper he asked her to come into his room. They sat before his grisly fire, and without preamble he said: "Miss Legassick, you must marry me."

Louisa was stupefied. She could not answer. He got up and walked in agitation about the room. "You will understand," he said, "that a man in my position has many enemies. There are those who hate me. Their selfish clinging to wealth makes them see me as a traitor to their own way of life. As indeed I glory to be. They would stoop to any lie to discredit me. I have refuted a good many. Now they are whispering about my private life, as they did about Gladstone's."

He couldn't bring himself to say it, so Louisa, regaining her wits, said it for him. "They think I am your mistress."

"I don't suppose for a moment that they think it. But they say it, in the hope that others will think it."

Louisa said: "It seems to me an odd reason for marriage. You could bring an action for slander, or, perhaps better still, I could find work elsewhere."

"I have thought of both courses, but I cannot consent to either. A case in the courts would create the scandalous sensation they long for; and that you should leave me is unthinkable. I have come to rely on you. Your going would be most damaging to my work."

"I have certainly worked for you as I imagine few women would," Louisa said, not without bitterness.

"You have loved doing it," he asserted. "You pretend at times to be rebellious, but you stay. That is what I hold on to. You stay. And no woman would endure what you endure unless she shared my own visions."

He looked rather mad, and she hated the idea of visions. "Whenever I have thought of marriage," she said, "I have realised that a readiness to share difficulties, and perhaps even extreme hardships, is part of the matter. But it's not the whole thing, or the main thing. If it were only that, it would be no more than the self-protective comradeship of a chain gang."

She got up and walked towards the door. He took her by the arm and detained her. He said out of a dry mouth, his toneless voice more strange than ever: "I know that that is not all. This scandalous talk has revealed me to myself, has surprised me with myself. I have . . ."

She looked at him desperately. She knew and feared what he was going to say; knew, too, that once it was said the pin would be out of the bomb. She shook him off roughly, and said: "Please let me be," and he stood aside. She went upstairs, not to her office where there was work to do, but to her bedroom, where she shivered, though there were blankets enough.

8

The matter was not mentioned again, and it lay there between them. The winter passed uneasily by, and there were moments when Louisa thought of looking for other work and even of returning to Cornwall. But to come back would be to admit defeat, and all of her defiant spirit rose against it. As for other work, gruelling as life was with Mr Wheatstone, she knew it now inside out, and it satisfied something in her that could not have been satisfied by humdrum clerking. If only there had shone from Mr Wheatstone one spark of that radiant bliss to which he sought to lead mankind, her life, she thought, would have been happy indeed. But the thing between them had not been banished, "and", she said to me, "I don't know how long we could have gone on like that if I hadn't met James."

It was an April Sunday morning, and with an uplift of the heart she stepped out into the warm sunshine that was blessing Manchester Square. She held up her face to the tender blue sky stretched over the budding trees. She saw the first swifts in the sky, swooping in vast delirious arcs, and a butterfly staggered drunkenly in the lower air as though intoxicated by the day's promise. "Oh, God!" she thought with yearning, as Cornwall rushed upon her heart, and she saw the grey church and the light on the sea and Roger's dinghy that now had a centreboard and a sail.

She strolled into Hyde Park that was full of fashion drawn forth by the magnet of the sun. She sat down and watched the women and realised how dowdy she had become, how different from the girl who had walked hieratically downstairs in her mother's refashioned but splendid gown and had been driven to the ball at Tregannock. But she didn't care: it was a day to make the heart sing, and her heart sang.

James Polperro strolled up to her and raised a silk hat. "My God, Louisa," he said, "you don't belong to be dressed like that!"

That Cornish turn of phrase made her laugh, though she felt she had little reason to laugh with James Polperro. He was half turned to her, half to the strolling women. He appraised their dresses. "What do you say – this one? Just a little bit overdone, don't you think? This? Well, it's not bad. But it's hardly you. Ah, now, this with the lilac sunshade? Better, much better. But damn it all, I prefer you in your rags to the best groomed filly in the paddock."

There was nothing wrong with his own grooming. Leaning on his cane, he was the well-dressed man of the moment. Louisa said rudely: "You must be hard-pressed for company if you want mine."

He said: "You don't know how much I want it. But whether you want the company of a fool like me is another matter."

"Yes," she said, "I suppose it is." She smiled at him. "Oddly enough, there's nothing I should like better."

Louisa said to me: "I don't know what made me say it."

"Well," I said lightly, "I suppose the sun came out, and the little flower opened."

"Put it like that," she agreed. "There hadn't been a lot of sunshine. Vincent had preached duty into me so hard that I could almost feel his boots grinding me into the faces of the poor. I thought I had earned a day that had no moral lessons."

She got up, and they stood looking at one another. Louisa felt her limbs trembling and her cheeks burning. She owed him so much enmity, yet she could remember nothing but the joys they had shared. She said: "I shouldn't be with you," and James answered: "You're the only woman who should."

"Well," she asked, "what are we going to do?"

They were walking in the direction of the Marble Arch, and he said: "We'll find a hansom cab and drive out to Richmond. What else should one do on a day like this? We'll have lunch at the Star and Garter."

"I'm expected in to lunch."

"Oh, then we'd better think of something else. What would you like to do?"

"I should very much like to make my employer understand that now and then I can take my lunch where and when I please. So we'll go to Richmond. I've never been there."

In the cab he put an arm through hers, and she looked at the cuff and the stylish gloves lying against the dingy black of her clothes. A masher taking out a shop-girl for a spree. That's what the cabby's saying to himself, she thought. Well, let him think what he likes. She squeezed James' arm in to her waist.

He said: "They say at home that you've got a wonderful job with that feller Wheatstone."

"You know him?"

"No. But everyone knows *about* him. A wonderful feller. I could never be a feller like that."

"No," she agreed, "you couldn't."

The brilliant day spun by, and she tried to think of a bitter winter night and of James Polperro picking up a dead child wearing a dirty sack. She couldn't, and she felt a traitor. But such a happy one.

"Are you happy?" she asked him.

"At the moment – yes," he said. "But there are plenty of moments when I'm not. However, a man gets what he asks for."

"Well, you asked me to come to Richmond, and you've got that. Let's enjoy it."

They enjoyed duckling and green peas and a wonderful soufflé and a bottle of hock and the sight of the river sliding by under the sunlight, gay with young people in boats. Some of them, young though they were, were older than Louisa, and it was strange that she should be thinking of them as carefree youngsters, but she was. She was cut in two, and half of her was as old as human sin and misery, and half of her was grasping at this frail moment as though it were a life-belt on which she could be drawn to a green bank where she could lie in endless sunshine. Moreover, she was beginning to be afraid. There had been moments of silence, when she had sensed words banking up in James' mind, and she had rushed in with inconsequential talk to forestall their utterance. But they could not be kept back for ever. After lunch they walked in Richmond Park and presently sat down on the clenched green fists of bracken, and James said, groaning: "Oh, I hate that woman!"

It had been wrenched out of him at last, and, with his head on her shoulder, he went on and on, and she knew no way to stop him short of getting up and walking away. And she did not want to do that. So she endured, while pitying, and almost holding in contempt, this man she loved, for what was he revealing but the consequence of his own flabby acquiescence to another's will?

She stopped his mouth with kisses, and they sat for a long time in sad silence, their arms around one another. At last she got up, and he, still sitting on the ground, said: "I could divorce her. I have cause. I'm not living with her now. She's at her father's house, and I'm staying in a hotel. I would have tried again to make it up, but this time I can't. Not after this."

Always someone else to blame, she thought sadly. Now it's me.

They drove back in another hansom, and it seemed to Louisa that they were driving through another day. She hated herself, and her hate hazed the sunshine and made the springtime grey.

At Hyde Park Corner he said: "When shall we meet again?"

"When it happens as it has happened today. Never by arrangement."

"But, Louisa – my darling–" He tried to detain her, but she ran across the road and walked slowly back to Manchester Square.

9

Nowadays, when men take new wives and women take new husbands as casually as they change from one brand of cigarette to another, it is difficult to realise the sense, almost of shock and outrage, with which the word divorce was once heard, especially by a girl brought up as Louisa had been. It was no surprise to her to know that James Polperro was unhappy. That he should speak of the possibility of divorcing his wife filled her with dismay, the more so because she was never free from a sense of sin at having so readily and happily fallen in with his wishes in those few months before Lady Mary Lacey was produced by his father as the woman he must marry. She was certain that what had happened then had been a main cause of making the marriage fail. That James preferred her to a wealthy titled girl gave her small consolation. Enormously as she had enjoyed this day out with him, despite its accompaniment of spineless whimpering, she was a fool to have gone, and she blushed as she thought of their kisses. Never again must such a thing happen. Like other people, he must make what he could of a situation which, after all, he had not wandered into as a child, but had accepted as a man. The word divorce finished her. She would have no part in encouraging that sort of idea in his mind.

These were the moralisings that filled her mind as they drove back from Richmond, and to moralise came naturally enough to a Legassick, though nowadays it is spoken of almost as though it were an indecent occupation.

Her joy throughout the day had been so intense that the reaction was severe. "I don't think I had ever felt so miserable in my life," she said to me, "not even when James married, as I did when I turned in to Manchester Square that night."

When she rang the bell, Mr Wheatstone himself came to the door. He looked at her as though surprised by an apparition. "You're back!" he exclaimed. "I thought you had decided to leave me."

"He looked like an undertaker welcoming home his favourite corpse, and I felt well cast for the part."

She said to him: "I don't feel very well. I'll go straight to bed."

In the morning she felt even less well. Shivers were lightly fingering all over her body, and when she got up she swayed, light-headed, and had to hold on to the bed-head. She got back between the sheets and gave herself up gladly to the luxury of illness. She was aware of nothing more till the evening of that day, when she awoke to a miracle. The room was dark with the curtains drawn, but the darkness was irradiated. A fire was burning in the grate! Unheard-of indulgence! What is more, the dark silhouette of Mr Wheatstone was outlined against the glow. He was making up the fire from a full scuttle!

She shut her eyes as he turned towards the bed, and felt his hand laid for a moment lightly on her forehead. Then he tip-toed out and the door closed with a gentle click. She dozed and waked, and dozed and waked, and always the fire was a glowing companion, and pictures drifted through her mind like things half-seen in moving fog, and one that obsessed her was of Mr Wheatstone when he was a rich young man wearing a cloak lined with scarlet which his man would take as he entered his house. Then he would go to a luxurious room and sit by the fire with the whisky-decanter at his side and a glass in his hand. He would clap his hands like a caliph and ask for dancing girls, and they would come in: little starved girls wearing sacks, and they would hop about, ungainly, and then drop down with a brittle icy clatter dead at his feet. And the warmth of the fire would cause the ice in which they were cased to melt and dribble in water all over the carpet.

She was next aware of a man shaking a thermometer and holding it up to the light and saying: "She ought to be in hospital, of course," and of Mr Wheatstone saying with authority: "She will stay where she is."

The doctor said: "The deuce of it is, I can't account for it. It's almost as though she's *willing* herself to be ill."

Mr Wheatstone said surprisingly: "Of course she is. Well, I am willing her to get better. We shall see who wins."

She wondered whether all this was hallucination, like the dead dancing girls, but the thought made its way into her mind that the doctor was right, that she was willing this illness; and once she had laid hold of that thought she was appalled at the foolishness of her conduct. She said feebly: "I shall get better, never fear," and then she went to sleep again. She woke up to find Mr Wheatstone sitting by her bed, holding her hand, and to feel – she swore to me that this was literally so – to feel his command to her to get better tingling into her.

When he saw that her eyes were open, he asked: "How do you feel?"

"A lot better."

He put a thermometer into her mouth, examined it, and said: "Your temperature has fallen since the doctor was here this morning."

He went out and was back presently with a cup of soup. "Now sit up and eat this," he commanded.

She did so, and enjoyed it, and he said: "There. You are round the corner. Now Mrs Martin will be able to look after you."

"Have *you* been looking after me?"

"I have been holding your hand. Holding you back from suicide, if you like."

He went off with the cup and did not return. She lay enjoying the coolness of her body, the unclouded command of her thoughts. She was still desperately weak, but she knew he was right. She was round the corner.

10

Though she had been in bed for only a few days, Louisa found that her limbs were like water when she tried to get about again. The lovely weather continued to shine on London, not yet poisoned by the fumes of petrol and diesel oil, and she went out into it each morning. Mr Wheatstone went with her. They walked slowly round Manchester Square. Halfway round she stopped for a moment and he said: "Perhaps you would like to take my arm?"

She did so; and thereafter he offered his arm each morning as they left the house. On the third morning she felt so much better that she did not need his arm, but she took it. Her spirit was rising with her rising health, and she was emboldened to say: "I feel like a prisoner being conducted by a warder for his daily exercise in the gaol yard."

She looked at him, and the first smile that she had ever seen on his face drew crow's-feet at the corners of his eyes. "Yes," he agreed, "I suppose it must seem like that to you. I'm often surprised that people put up with me, you especially."

It was a human word at last. She said: "Oh, you needn't worry about me. But you're terribly hard on yourself."

He seemed to consider this, and then said: "When you decide as I did to give up everything in order to help other people, it isn't easy. There's a long time when you are in danger of relapse. You mustn't leave a loophole for the soft things to creep back upon you. It's warfare, and Berthier was right when he said that in warfare nothing is done till everything is done. Giving is easy. Giving everything is another matter. And so I had to watch myself, and I became what you see. I'm afraid nothing will change me now."

The next morning there was a letter for her in what she saw to be James Polperro's hand. James knew that she was with Mr Wheatstone, and it was easy enough to discover where so well-known a man lived. Even to see the writing troubled her heart desperately with its old desires. She looked at Mr Wheatstone sitting opposite to her at the breakfast table, and she remembered his words of the day before. She said to herself: "If you have done with this thing, have done with it," and when the meal was over she took the letter to her office, set a match to it unread, and watched it blacken to ash in the fireplace.

She went downstairs, and Mr Wheatstone said: "Do you feel well enough to take your little walk alone this morning, or would you like me to come with you once more?"

"Please come with me," she said. He had done to her something irrevocable. As he had willed her out of her illness, so, she knew, it was his will rather than hers that had made her burn the letter. She took his arm feeling strangely dependent, almost as though hypnotised; and when, a month later, he again spoke of marriage, she said yes.

11

That is how things were when I made my first visit to London. Poor Father, who had been told nothing of the marriage till it was a week old, had said to me when seeing me off: "Remember, Maria, I shall expect an intelligent account of how Louisa is getting on." It seemed to me that my report would be dull and colourless indeed so far as Louisa was concerned, for I saw little of her and would have seen little of anything else but for Meg Newman, who was commissioned by Mr Wheatstone to take me for a walk each afternoon. I said point blank to Louisa at luncheon: "Why can't *you* take me for my walks?" and I was puzzled by the embarrassed silence. I did not know then that in the early days of their marriage, when Mr Wheatstone's hypnotic influence over her was strong, she had told him everything about her past life. "And I mean everything," she said to me, "including James and the horse and what happened afterwards."

I said that I couldn't believe it: it would be like confessing murder to a hanging judge.

"Oddly enough," she said, "the confession seemed to give him pleasure. It was a superb chance to be magnanimous. After that, he cherished me as something to be saved. He never despaired of publicans and sinners, and now I was one of them. But in his heart he was afraid of James, terrified that I might meet him again. That's why I never went out unless he was with me."

So Meg was entrusted with steering me through the pitfalls of London life. Mr Wheatstone laid down each morning the route of our hour's peregrination and emphasized that we were to walk it smartly with no dallying in front of shops and, above all, no conversation with strangers. We faithfully obeyed the law, but, as Meg said, her Ma wasn't a stranger, was she?

We were coming at a soldierly pace through Bond Street, and, as I had done on other days, I was thinking that this hour with Meg was the loveliest of the twenty-four, when a smart lady, loitering along the pavement ahead of us, turned back and we almost ran into her. In a flash, Meg had handed me the lead of the rescued dog that we took with us because Mr Wheatstone considered him a protector, and had rushed upon the lady and thrown her arms round her waist. "Oh, Ma!" she cried, "can't I come 'ome with you?"

The words told me that this was Mrs Newman, and I looked at her with interest. Here she was, on the streets where I perpetually pictured her, as stylish a woman as you could wish to see, with blue eyes and auburn hair, billowing light blue clothes, and a blue silken parasol sloped across her shoulders and held in a hand gloved with blue lace. I curtseyed and said: "Good afternoon, Mrs Newman."

She smiled at me, and her teeth were wonderful. I couldn't understand how Meg, who spoke so badly, could have so lovely a mother, or how, having one, she could endure being separated from her in order to spend her time washing dishes in Louisa's dark kitchen and being chivvied all over the place by Mrs Martin.

Having smiled at me, Mrs Newman addressed her daughter, and her voice disappointed me. It didn't chime in with the rest of her. "Now you get along 'ome, Meg," she said, "and be thankful to 'ave such a good 'ome to go to. You know very well you're not supposed to 'ave nothing more to do with me, and if Mr Wheatstone finds that you 'ave, and turns you out, where you goin' to be then, eh? So run along 'ome like a good child. I'm expectin' my friend."

A gentleman in a frock-coat and silk hat who was loitering at a shop window and occasionally looking over his shoulder in our direction seemed to me the sort of friend Meg's stylish mother would have, and I felt embarrassed at delaying their meeting. Our protective dog, too, was developing the look that was apt to dawn upon him in the presence of friends and foes alike: a look which suggested that at any moment someone would begin upon him a process of keen and lingering torture. His tail curled in between his legs; the whites of his eyes began to implore heaven; and his long, protesting howl rose upon Bond Street.

Meg gave one distasteful glance at the johnny, and said "Oh – 'im!" snatched the lead from my hand, and we hurried away. To my surprise, I saw Meg's mother turn to the gentleman and heard her say: "Oh, go to 'ell!" and she flounced away in the opposite direction from ours. I was horrified. It seemed to me a dreadful way to speak to a friend. Meg said venomously and ungrammatically: "I know 'im. 'E's the son of the chap where Mother used to work in the big draper's." And that was Meg's mother's complete biography so far as I was concerned.

The encounter had impressed me deeply, and I could hardly have prevented myself from blurting out something about it if the whole matter had not been wiped off my mind by a surprising happening. As we ran across Manchester Square a cab drew up before Mr Wheatstone's gate, and Uncle Reginald got out of it.

12

Mrs Martin came to the door, and I said in a burst of enthusiasm, as though this were something that should impress her deeply, that here was my Uncle Reginald back from Tibet. Mrs Martin said flatly: "Mr Wheatstone won't be back till seven o'clock, and Mrs Wheatstone says she's not to be disturbed." Uncle Reginald said: "Perhaps you'll permit me to write a note?"

We went in and I brought him notepaper, and he, having scribbled a note, said: "Please give this to either Mr or Mrs Wheatstone when you can. I've explained that I'm taking out my little niece here. We'll be back this evening."

There was something so large and dependable and solid about Uncle Reginald that even Mrs Martin could not see him as a kidnapper and said: "Very well, sir."

We were about to turn from the door when Louisa came down the stairs. My mind unaccountably rushed back to the winter moment when Bella and I stood in the hall at home and watched her coming downstairs, moving slowly through a shimmer of candleshine, her face lit with a dream. Child though I was, I was struck suddenly with a sense of disaster. The woman coming downstairs now in rusty black looked almost middle-aged, and her face had done with dreaming. My heart cried out that Louisa didn't belong to be like this.

She was halfway down when she saw Uncle Reginald, and she paused for a moment as though doubting her eyes; then, with a strange glad little cry, she ran and put her arms about him, and kissed him almost hungrily. She stood for a moment, her chin resting on his shoulder, her face turned towards me, and I saw what I had never before seen in my life. There were tears in Louisa's eyes.

Mrs Martin had returned to the kitchen. Uncle Reginald said after a moment: "I had no idea you were married. I wrote to Aubrey as soon as I got back to England, and this morning I received his answer. I was staggered when I heard that you were married to Wheatstone. I came round to offer my congratulations."

She said tonelessly, as though she had caught Mr Wheatstone's very voice: "You needn't."

He put her from him and said gravely: "I don't like you in those clothes. Have you any others? If so, go and put them on. Maria and I will wait for you."

I felt enormously excited by all this, and sat there on edge watching him pace the hall ponderously. He was dressed as he always was, London or no London, in tweeds and knickerbockers, woollen stockings and brogues. His stick tap-tapped on the cold uncarpeted tiles. Louisa had looked so white and lifeless that he made me think of a vast St Bernard dog come to the rescue. I wouldn't have been surprised to see a brandy-keg tied round his neck. The idea made me laugh, and he turned and frowned as though I had laughed in a mortuary.

Our Mrs Solway, who always looked as though dressed in the left-overs of a jumble-sale, for some reason or other took a journal dedicated to stylish attire. Bella and I gloated over it, and I thought myself a considerable expert in what well-dressed women should wear. When Louisa at last appeared at the top of the stairs I didn't think much of her and asked brashly: "Is that the best you can do?"

She said simply: "I'm afraid so," and Uncle Reginald said: "Well, at all events, you don't look like the epitaph on a miser's tomb."

"Was it as bad as that?" Louisa asked; and he assured her that it was. "You looked as if you'd just got back from Kensal Green and listened to the reading of a very disappointing will."

She asked: "Well, what are we going to do?" and he said: "I've no idea, but for God's sake let's get out of this and do *something*."

13

When I read memoirs of the last years of Victoria's reign, I am sure to come upon "the Marlborough House Set" that pranced round the Prince of Wales and the Princess Alexandra. It is odd that such people should have had something to do with the obscure lives of the Vicar of St Tudno's daughters. Ernest Kopf. He is always there in the memoirs, close friend of Edward as prince and king. For one thing, he was married to a beautiful wife, and for another he was an invaluable financial adviser. The memoirs never fail to hint at the hundreds of thousands by which his prescient investment tips enriched his royal friend. He advanced by the customary stages. Mr Kopf became Sir Ernest, and Sir Ernest became Lord Lavernock, and the Lavernocks nowadays, married into the fringes of the royal family itself, do not often, I imagine, remember the boy Kopf working in the office of an Amsterdam diamond merchant, going thence to South Africa in his teens, smelling gold and diamonds like a hound smelling the wind for fox, and in his middle twenties appearing in England and setting up that incredible establishment in Park Lane to which he took the daughter of Lord Bettiscombe.

It was soon after this, while he was still Mr Kopf, that Louisa, Uncle Reginald and I got into a cab outside Mr Wheatstone's house and Uncle Reginald said to the driver: "Just drive about a bit – anywhere." We were moving sedately through Hyde Park when he said: "I don't like the smell of that house, Louisa. I seem to have come just in time. You've got Mr Ernest Kopf to thank for that."

The day after he had arrived back in England, Mr Kopf had asked him to call at the house in Park Lane and had talked to him about Coverdale. It stands to reason that a Park Lane mansion must be companioned by a country house, and this house, to be called Coverdale, had begun to go up on the brow of a hill near Dorking. Figures like ten or a hundred didn't mean much to Mr Kopf, so he had bought two thousand acres of land. He and Uncle Reginald drove out to look at it, and Mr Kopf became an eighteenth-century grandee talking to a Repton or Capability Brown. They stood on the hillside amid mountains of lovely red brick and looked at the upward slope of the land behind them and the fall down to the valley. A wood here, a lake there, a bridge, a summer house, lawns, gardens, enclosed walks and open spaces. Mr Kopf smoked a cigar and dreamed aloud. Arbours, kitchen gardens, pergolas, a long grass walk leading to clipped yews encircling a quiet place where statues gleamed and a fountain played. Oh, and conservatories, of course. Orchids. "I know you're a gardener as well as an explorer, Mr Pallace. What d'you think of it?"

Uncle Reginald smiled and said: "I think the land has great capability," but Mr Kopf, who didn't miss much, didn't catch that allusion. "You'll do it?" he asked.

"Do what?"

"Why, take on the job. You don't want to spend your life trotting about the world. There comes a time for a man to settle down. Look at me."

He was only twenty-eight. Uncle Reginald looked at him and saw a swarthy, stocky man, clean-shaven, rather vulturine, with bright restless eyes. He looked as settled down as a hawk settled on a wrist, waiting for the hood to come off.

Uncle Reginald, said: "It's going to take a long time."

"I know it is. You won't lack labour, and when it's done you can choose your own staff. You'll have a house. I thought down there, where that thorn bush is."

It would certainly be a lovely place for a house.

"You make it, and then you stay and look after it. That's my idea."

"The making will need an army; and you'll want all of thirty men to keep it going."

"Labour's cheap enough."

Uncle Reginald thought of the almost princely estate surrounding his father's vicarage that he had known so well as a boy. In all their lives, some of the men there had not seen more than twelve shillings a week, and those who earned a pound thought themselves lucky. He said: "The labour won't be cheap if I'm in charge of it, and I won't be cheap either. Anyway, I'd like to walk round the place for a few days on my own and think it over. There may be all sorts of snags that you haven't thought of."

Mr Kopf said impatiently: "I'd like to settle the matter right away," and Uncle Reginald answered firmly: "I daresay you would. But what you'd like and what a tree would like when it's got a hundred years to grow in are two different things. There's more than money involved in making a garden, Mr Kopf. Don't try to rush it, and don't try to rush me."

"He looked a bit startled," Uncle Reginald said as we bowled along in the cab, "but I thought we'd better start off on the right foot. Anyway, I spent a day or two out there, and I saw him again yesterday and we've fixed it up. It'll be a grand thing to do and a lovely place to live in. Wonderful soil for rhododendrons and camellias and azaleas."

He gave the cabby a Kensington address, and we stopped in front of a small hotel. "I shall stay here," he said, "till I've tied up a few ends with the Kew people and the Royal Horticultural Society. Then I must inflict myself on poor Aubrey while I settle accounts with my Cornishmen. After that, I shall live in Dorking till my cottage has been built. You must come out often and see me there, Louisa. You look as though you're not getting all the air you need."

Louisa said: "I'm not getting all sorts of things that I need."

He took her arm as though she were an invalid and led her up the few steps and into a quiet chintzy little room that he said was reserved for himself. He rang for tea, and when it came he said: "Now. Tell me what you're in mourning for."

Louisa said: "*Pas devant les enfants*", and I assured her brightly that I knew what that meant. I had found the phrase in a book and asked Father about it.

Louisa said: "Oh, well. I think we can trust her. I've found her reliable before." She was thinking of the morning under the yew tree. I felt flattered and said: "I am no longer a child. I met Meg's mother on the streets this afternoon. Anything I hear will be locked forever in my heart."

Uncle began: "My nieces seem to be leading very odd lives –"When Louisa put down her cup with a sudden clatter and said: "Oh, let's get it over and done with! I've had no one to confide in, and then seeing you so suddenly . . ."

She stopped, looking lost, and there was a grave silence that seemed to last a long time. She said: "I can't go back there. I won't go back there." She took up her cup and it chattered against her teeth.

"How long have you been married?"

"Oh, I don't know. About a hundred and twenty-five years."

"You should consult your father before taking so grave a step."

"Thank you, Uncle Reginald," she said bitterly, "but I could quote Father's views on the indissolubility of marriage without consulting him."

"Then what do you intend to do?"

"You must not know what I intend to do. But if you could lend me fifty pounds it would help me."

"Have you no money of your own?"

"No."

"Surely Mr Wheatstone paid you a good salary?"

"He paid me a small salary till we were married. Then it stopped. From that moment, seeing that I shared everything with him, the vow of poverty, chastity and obedience was included."

She looked desperate.

Uncle Reginald said: "Well, I suppose we must thank Mr Kopf for all this. If he hadn't detained me I should have been in Cornwall. He has been pleased to pay me what he calls a retainer. A handsome one at that. Otherwise I couldn't have helped."

He counted out fifty golden sovereigns and dropped them into a little leather bag. He took her hand and said: "I am not doing this very happily, my dear. I know that you and Aubrey don't get on well together in important things, though on the trivial surface there seems nothing wrong. Still, I can't imagine anything more serious than for you to hurt him without even attempting an explanation. There is Mr Wheatstone, too. I know he is a man who drives other people as hard as he drives himself. I know he has made himself a miser for what he thinks to be God's sake. He may be mistaken, but you have chosen to be his wife."

She said: "But I am not his woman."

He urged her again. "Think whether there is not reason for your going back, if only to try to show him where you feel he is at fault."

Louisa said: "There are a thousand reasons for my going back, but there is one why I shall not. He's killing me by inches."

Uncle Reginald had been standing there, looking at her gravely, weighing the little bag of sovereigns in his hand. He gave it to her and said: "Very well. What now?"

"So far as you are concerned, only this. Maria and I are going back to Manchester Square. It would be a good idea if you saw us into a cab and gave the cabman the address."

He still persisted: "Are you sure of what you're doing?"

"I was never more sure in my life. Do one thing for me. When you are settled at Dorking put an advertisement into the *Daily Telegraph* personal column. 'Sally. Sevenoaks next Saturday. Bob.' I am Sally. You are Bob. Sevenoaks is Dorking. I'll meet you at the station there at 2.30 on the Saturday after the advertisement appears."

She gave a nervous laugh. "I never knew I had the makings of a conspirator in me."

Our uncle walked us to the cab rank at the end of the street. He saw us in and gave the cabby the address in Manchester Square. He waved us off, and Louisa sat back, her face a dreadful blank. We were passing a draper's shop in Kensington when she tapped the window and asked the cabby to stop. She got out and said so that he might hear: "There's some shopping I must do, Maria. You go straight home and tell Vincent I'll follow as soon as I can. I shouldn't be more than half-an-hour."

We saw her go into the shop, and then I went home alone, hugging my cue.

Louisa, I know now, bought a suitcase and some night things and brushes, and then found a small inexpensive hotel on the south side of the river, in Battersea. She lay low there till Uncle Reginald advertised in the *Daily Telegraph*. Then she met him and arranged her next steps.

14

Mr Wheatstone was at home when I returned and told my story. He frowned and said it was most improper of Louisa to have allowed me to travel alone in a cab. It was about six o'clock. She had not returned by seven, and he and I sat down to a solitary supper. I sat down, at any rate. He left his meal untouched and strode restlessly up and down, glancing at the clock again and again as though that would bring her back. "You are sure she said in half-an-hour?"

"Yes, sir." I nibbled away as apprehensively as a mouse eating in the presence of a prowling cat.

I went up to my bedroom to get on with *The Wide, Wide World*, but had hardly settled down when he flung open the door and said abruptly: "We had better go to Kensington. Perhaps she has returned to your uncle."

Oh, what a day! Meg's mother and Uncle Reginald and Louisa's plot, and now into a cab again with Mr Wheatstone at my side, brooding and muttering through the golden light of the evening. Uncle Reginald had gone out, no one knew where he was, or when he would be back.

Almost frantic with frustration, Mr Wheatstone demanded: "Where was this cab rank from which you travelled home?"

I led him to it, and the cabby chanced to be there. But Louisa had plotted well. What could he do but confirm my story? Yes, he remembered picking up the two ladies. Yes, he remembered dropping one at the shop. No, of course he couldn't say what happened to her after that. All right – all right. Keep yer 'air on, guv'nor. Got daughters of me own. Know what they are.

Mr Wheatstone chartered him to take us back. "She *must* be there by now," he said as we drew near to Manchester Square. But she wasn't, and he turned on me and commanded me sharply to go to bed. I did so, and slept like a top, worn out by the day's excitements.

In the morning Meg brought me hot water and exclaimed dramatically: "The missus didn't come home last night! There's a proper do going on downstairs. I must fly. The master's talking about getting in touch with the police. My Ma always said to me, never 'ave nothing to do with the police. Keep clear of 'em, right or wrong. Goodbye."

Mrs Martin, who always looked as if she had been sentenced to death, now looked as though she had given up hope of a last-minute reprieve. Mr Wheatstone sat in grim silence, the working of his jaw causing his beard to twitch up and down in a frightening fashion. He ate nothing and did not speak to me, but from across the table he looked at me ceaselessly as though trying to divine what I could tell him if I would. I was sure that he had never liked me, and had been unable to understand why Louisa had been so sentimental as to allow a small sister to divert her thoughts from duty. Not that poor Louisa had worked a whit the less for my being there.

At last I called up enough courage to ask: "Is there any news of Louisa, sir?"

He said briefly: "None whatever," and then Mrs Martin came in with the letters. I was always staggered by the size of Mr Wheatstone's morning mail, for at the vicarage we rarely saw more than two or three letters a week. Mr Wheatstone turned over the pile listlessly till he came to one that made him start. He tore it open anxiously, and as he threw down the envelope I saw that it was addressed in Louisa's hand. He ran his eye quickly over the few lines and then stood up holding the letter in his hand, as rigid as a bronze image of a mayor clutching the municipal charter. Then, to my consternation, his eyes closed, he swayed, and fell flat to the floor. I ran round the table and looked at the sheet of notepaper lying by his side.

> Dear Vincent – I have left you, and do not intend to return to you. A thousand words would not explain why I have done this, so I ask you merely to believe that nothing will make me change my mind. I remain to all intents and purposes what I was when first I met you,
>
> Louisa Legassick.

It was only years later that I was able to understand how this brief but devastating repudiation must have pierced even his harsh armour and brought him down. It took me no more than a few seconds to read the note; then I called Mrs Martin and as she knelt over him the door-bell rang. I went to the door myself, and there was Uncle Reginald. I took him into what would have been the drawing room in another house, but was Mr Wheatstone's study, and told him what had happened. He said: "I am leaving for Cornwall tomorrow and you had better be ready to come with me. Go up and pack your things now."

I was back in a quarter of an hour, and by that time Mr Wheatstone was recovered, though looking ghastly, and was sitting on a dining room chair. What had passed between him and Uncle Reginald I do not know, but my uncle said to me: "If you're ready, we'll go now to Kensington. You can stay there with me today and we'll be off in the morning."

He held out his hand to Mr Wheatstone, who took it as though wondering what it was. There was no goodbye either to my uncle or me. I stepped into the porch, and the house seemed to fall off my shoulders like a weight that I had unaccountably been carrying. I was surprised to see what a beautiful morning it was.

CHAPTER THREE

I THOUGHT Miss Braddon the most wonderful novelist who had ever lived, and was anxious to get back to *Lady Audley's Secret*. Bella, who was now eighteen, had given it to me for my birthday in May, and, this being the end of July, I had still not exhausted its glories and was racing through a third reading. But Father detained me. I was fifteen, and for a year now I had waited on him in the study each morning at nine. I suppose he would have sent us girls away to be educated if he could have afforded it; but Roger at Rugby, and now at Oxford, had eaten up all the spare cash. Bella had graduated to Louisa's old job of copying Father's manuscripts. She didn't resent this, for she hadn't Louisa's spirit. The mechanical going on and on of her pen suited her phlegmatic nature. There was nothing tart in Bella. She was like rich gurgling cream. She laughed at little things in a rich gurgling voice and liked her food and her bed. If she didn't want to do a thing, she didn't make a scene. She left it undone, slid round it like warm treacle. She had become a beauty in her dull way: big blue eyes, a magnolia skin, and masses of fair hair, thick and rich. But it was a static beauty that never flashed or sparkled. She was utterly predictable. She was now in the loft over the stable, working away on Father's latest. The loft had become a common room that she and I shared. Ever since Uncle Reginald had cleaned it up we had been casting eyes on it, and slowly we had appropriated it to our own purposes. It was just a whitewashed oblong with a window in each long side, one looking on to the road and the other across the garden towards the front door of the vicarage. We had put curtains to the windows, scrounged a few bits of carpet for the floor and a couple of wicker chairs to sit in. Thomas May knocked us up a table and put book shelves along one wall; and on winter nights a log fire made the place homely. The oil lamp that we had disastrously lit in Louisa's bedroom hung over the table and Bella's favourite picture was above the fireplace. It was a copy of Marcus Stone's usual confection: a couple of well-dressed young people on a balustraded walk overlooking a garden, clearly ill at ease with one another because of a recent quarrel. I thought it pretty good, and it reminded me of Mr James Polperro and Lady Mary Lacey on the terrace at Tregannock. Bella would bring a bag of buns with her, and a glass of milk. The buns were made by Mrs Solway, an especially sticky sort crusted with sugar. And there Bella would loll munching and sipping through a whole winter evening, not even bothering to take a book into her hand, much less read one. For me, I read and read. Anything and everything. I was at the age of voracious and indiscriminate absorption. *Paradise Lost*, Bunyan's *Holy War* or *Lady Audley's Secret*: it was all one to me. Bella would suck the last taste of sugar from her fingers and say with her slow smile: "Come on. Time for bed, printomaniac." Then we would go in, cross the dark garden, filled with the sound of the sea's sighing and the noise of night birds, and climb to our bedroom. My head was going on and on listening to

> *They, looking back, all th' eastern side beheld*
> *Of Paradise, so late their happy seat,*
> *Waved over by that flaming brand, the Gate*
> *With dreadful faces thronged and fiery arms.*
> *Some natural tears they dropped, but wiped them soon:*
> *The world was all before them where to choose*

or to: " 'Very well,' Sir Hector sneered, crushing out his cigar on the onyx mantelpiece . . ." and the faint fall and swell of Bella's breath would reach me from the next bed. Her head had only to touch a pillow to become unconscious. I would stretch my hand across to her bed and let it lie there for companionship. Sometimes hers would unconsciously take it and fondle it as the words went on. "All before them . . . all before them . . ."

2

That morning, when lessons were done, Father said: "I'm afraid you'll never write well, Maria, unless you study better models. I see you have several novels by Jane Austen in the loft."

I had had a very severe attack of Jane, and adored Darcy.

"When I was at Oxford," Father said, "my tutor warned me against her, and I pass the warning on. She had an abominable habit of ending sentences with prepositions."

I always listened patiently to Father's lectures about books, and then read what I liked. "For a good firm style," he said, "you should go to Fuller or Hooker."

"Yes, Father."

"There is some excellent writing in Fuller's *The Cause and Cure of a Guilty Conscience*. I am speaking, of course, only of his style. His thought is a little beyond you at the moment. Have you seen Thomas May this morning?"

"No, Father."

"I wondered whether he had any news of Mr Polperro. I'm afraid he's sinking."

I had a vision of Mr Polperro awash on a tide of port wine, going down slowly with cigar-smoke pouring out of his funnel.

I said piously: "It is appointed unto all men once to die, and after that the judgement."

He looked at me gravely, but had nothing better to say than: "Yes. I'm afraid that is so."

I said: "It gets us in the long run, great and small. Look at Mr Wheatstone."

Mr Wheatstone had been dead for a year, and as he had died suddenly and without a doctor there had been an inquest. It was found that he had died of malnutrition, and the coroner said things about his being a martyr who had given his life for the poor and needy. Father turned away from me impatiently, dismissing me and Mr Wheatstone with the words: "Well, I shall drive over to Tregannock this afternoon and see how things are."

Through the window I saw Roger sitting on a tombstone, reading. I hastened to join him.

3

Life was always different when Roger was at home. Unfortunately he was at home very little, for even during university vacations, he would go off with other men on what he called a reading course, or on a tramp through Germany or Spain or France. This time he had brought Hugo Oldham with him. They had been with us for a week and promised us another week. Then they were going to stay for a few days with Hugo's people in Manchester before clambering about the Lake District.

All through the last term we had been hearing about Hugo who was younger than Roger and had recently gone up to Christ Church where Roger was in his second year. I suppose the freshman found a sheltering wing and Roger found something that he liked, for his letters became all Hugo. Bella looked up from her buns in the loft one night to say: "I suppose he's attached himself to this Hugo for the sake of his money, as Father attached himself to Mr Polperro when they were at Oxford. Ah, well! The Legassicks, so far as I can make out, have never had a penny, and they must attach themselves or starve." She was smiling her slow enchanting smile, asking me not to take her seriously. "What a fool Louisa was," she went on. "Wouldn't you have tried to handle a millionaire more profitably?"

"I wouldn't have handled Mr Wheatstone with the kitchen tongs," I said. Even now, when it had all been over for five years, the house in Manchester Square could recreate itself dismally in my dreams.

"Anyway," Bella said, "I must get Mr Oldham to help me with the flowers for the altar. It could be a beginning."

She did that; and we all four crossed over often to the small landing-stage on the other side of the creek and swam there; and we sailed together – once, I remember, on a moonlit night so quiet that the gentle drawing of the wind in the sail was the only reminder that all the world was not asleep. As we came in, we could see the roof of the church silvered, and the cattle moving quietly about the fields, and when we pulled in the chain of the moorings over the fairlead the sound was harsh and unseemly. The silence closed in again, and the dip of the oars as the dinghy moved to the shore raised nothing but crystal whispers. We went up through the graveyard where Thomas May, who didn't get on well with his wife, was wandering as though happy in the companionship of old friends he had long since tucked into bed, and Hugo said: "Thank you, Legassick. That was memorable."

We liked the masculine way they called one another Oldham and Legassick; but we didn't like the exclusiveness of their masculinity. It had been a softening night, but we had felt no softness, only a hardness of male comradeship to which a courteous concession had for a moment admitted us.

4

I went out now from my talk with Father and joined Roger on his tombstone. I asked him what he was reading, and he said "John Donne's Holy Sonnets."

I said: "This graveyard never makes me feel holy – only happy. Should the two things be the same?"

"Theoretically, yes. It depends on what you mean by happiness."

I didn't pursue that, and said, scratching at the moss of an inscription: "I think Father's potty."

"It must be hard," he said with a smile, "to live up to your vision of the ideal man. What has poor Father been up to now?"

"He thinks Jane Austen writes badly."

"Did you enlighten him?"

"No. I'm a moral coward. I'm not Louisa."

"Ah, Louisa! We had a lovely day together in London just before term ended."

I looked at him in amazement. "Roger!" I said.

"Yes?"

"You really are the most amazing and aggravating person. You wrap up mighty secrets in your breast, and then bring them out as though they were of no concern."

"She writes to me now and then," he said casually, "but this was the first time I'd seen her since she went away. She was looking very well."

"Go on!" I said impatiently. "What is she doing? Where is she living?"

"She's working in a draper's shop in Oxford Street, and she's living there, too."

I looked at him flabbergasted. "Something will happen," I said at last.

"Something has happened. Surely for Louisa to be working in a draper's shop is something?"

"I mean something dramatic." I thought of my vivid rebellious sister. " 'Madam, I said fourteen and nine-three a yard. If you stand there humming and ha'ing all day I can say nothing else. It's abominable stuff anyway, just what a vulgarian like you would fancy. But for heaven's sake make up your mind, if you've got one.' Something like that," I said, "and up rushes a shop-walker and says:

'Have you taken leave of your senses, Mrs Wheatstone? Madam, this woman shall be dismissed at once.' "

I was enjoying the scene, as though it were a memory, not a fabrication, and Roger smiled. "You underestimate Louisa," he said. "For one thing, she isn't Mrs Wheatstone: she is Miss Legassick. For another, she didn't go into this blindly. She knew the life she would have to live, and she's living it quite happily. Oddly enough, she's an excellent shop-girl. Louisa would never waste her tantrums. She keeps them for important occasions."

His acceptance of the situation didn't soothe me. "What on earth would Father say?" I demanded. "He would think it most degrading."

Roger chaffed me. "What does it matter if a potty father thinks this or that? Anyway, we had a lovely day together. We pooled our resources, which came to eleven and sevenpence; and on that we had a good lunch and a matinee at a theatre."

It was long after this that Louisa told me of her association with James Polperro; but I had seen the break-up of that meeting under the yew tree and I had put one and two together. Now, at fifteen, I was aware of many things. The parish of St Tudno was not notably chaste, and not all the girls who lugged their babies about the village had passed through Father's vestry to sign the marriage register. I longed to say to Roger: "I wonder what Mr James Polperro would think of Louisa working in a shop?" but Louisa had put me on trust; and I said instead: "Father thinks Mr Polperro is dying."

Thomas May, who was passing by, said briefly: "He's dead," and Mrs Solway, arriving at that moment to call me and Roger in to lunch, chided him. "You take it calmly, Thomas May."

"Well," he said, "when you've put as many under as I 'ave, you think no more about it than if they were broken crockery that you throw into the dust-bin. I'll put Mr Polperro away as calm as I'll put you when God calls you 'ome."

"That'll do, Thomas May," she said rather shrilly. "Don't fix your glance on me. You've got the eye of an obelisk."

"Well," he said with professional pride, "I can generally tell who's coming my way, barring people like old Ferris who fell off the haystack last week an' broke his neck. Sudden death is another thing. But I can see the long shadow. However, midear, cheer up. You've got a year or two yet to repent of your manifold sins and iniquities."

Mrs Solway said: "It don't seem right when great folks like the Polperros die."

"So far as I'm concerned," said Thomas May, sitting on the gravestone from which Roger and I had risen and opening his lunch basket, "I don't mind taking on all comers. But I do wish they danged fools up to Tregannock would go in the earth like anyone else. I don't mind digging among the daisies, but levering up stones in the church is another matter. But there they like to be, and there they'll 'ave to be: under all they flamin' angels and long words in foreign tongues. I s'pose you learn that rigmarole in college, Mr Roger?"

"Yes," Roger said. "It's Latin. I imagine it's a reminder of the time when the Church was universal and Latin was its language."

"Well," said Thomas May, "anyone who thinks the church is universal now wants his head looking to. What with Methodies an' Baptists and Seventh Day Adventurers it's about as universal as I am, and I'm Cornish an' want nothing to do with up-along."

He was in a bad mood. He took out his pasty, smelled it, and tossed it into the grave he had been digging. "That danged woman will never learn," he said. "She's soled a boot an' thinks she's made a pasty. Mrs Solway, I'm coming up with you. You'd better put me up a bite of Christian vittles. With that stuff weighing down my stomach I'd have a poor chance of rising on the last day."

5

In the good old fashion of the squires, Mr Polperro made his last journey to church on a farm wagon drawn by powerful horses. Roger and Hugo Oldham were gone. Father was distressed. He told Roger that he thought it most disrespectful to the Family to go away at such a time; but Roger had his engagement with Hugo's people in Manchester, and said he was sure that no one in the Polperro family would notice whether he was present or absent. Father said: "It's not a question of what they notice. It's a question of paying one's respects."

Roger said: "But what is there to respect about the Polperros, sir?" and all that old scene that had broken out so long ago between Louisa and Father rose up in my mind. I imagine it rose up in Father's mind, too, and that he remembered how, because of it, he had lost a child.

So he didn't press the point with Roger, even though Hugo urged him: "You stay, Legassick. I'll explain to my people."

But Roger wouldn't stay, and he was right enough in saying that he wouldn't be missed; for "all the county", as they say, was there. The roadway outside the vicarage gates was jammed with coaches, and our humble church was jammed with the local mighty. Old Thomas May was ding-donging at the passing bell in the wooden belfry as they came shuffling in, and as they were singing *For all Thy Saints who from their labours rest* he slid to a place near the grave, ready for his traditional task of sprinkling earth upon the coffin.

Bella and I were sitting with Mrs Solway, who couldn't restrain her tears at the thought that great people like the Polperros should die; and to us the excitement of the occasion was that open grave within the church itself. It was something new and fascinating. We had always known that Polperros lay there under the pavement, an uncommonly saintly lot according to the inscriptions; but now we should ever picture there the Polperro we had known, bloated with superfluity, and I, at any rate, found it an unpleasant thought. The corpses from whose simple tales I had learned to read, lying out there below the daffodils in spring, with the sun shining on them and the sea-breeze playing above them, had never disturbed me; they were intended to be forgotten and they soon were forgotten; but here commemorative pomp was intended to make me remember, and I should remember, and I should wonder whether there had been so much to remember after all.

It was a hot day, and estate servants had sweated up the aisle with the coffin, and Tregannock household men-servants were there, too, with their secret London faces, as though they were holding something back. I recognised the one who had gone to the kitchen for my chickenanam sandwiches on the day when I had stumbled upon Louisa under the yew tree and had later seen Lady Mary Lacey in the Tregannock garden. There had been great changes since then. Old Mrs Polperro had died, and Mr James' sister had married someone in far-off Scotland, and now Mr James would be simply Mr Polperro and would have all the pomp and glory of it to himself. There he was, looking very lonely, I thought, for Lady Mary Polperro was not with him, nor was she at Tregannock waiting to comfort him when this was over. She rarely was at Tregannock. There was one thing about the

Polperros: they hadn't bothered with all the nonsense of the London "season", and going on afterwards to shoot grouse in Yorkshire or Scotland. They were local squires, and they had stayed with us. Old Rowe the blacksmith said: "Mr Polperro may kick you in the backside now and then, but he's always here to do it. That's something." But this didn't suit Lady Mary. She had to be in London when all the nobs and snobs were sweating away at whatever it was they did there, and she had to have her hunting. Mr James loved riding, but all the rigmarole of hunting meant nothing to him. Lady Mary had a small house of her own in Leicestershire, and there she stayed so long as there was a fox with four legs to run on and hounds to chase him. Sometimes Mr James was with her; more often he wasn't. On her rare visits to Tregannock she brought her lady's maid, and the lady's maid talked to the footmen, and the footmen talked among themselves in the Polperro Arms, and what they talked about there was talked about again in the veterans' parliament round old Rowe's smithy fire. And so the parishioners of St Tudno, watching the burly woodmen carry old Polperro's coffin up the aisle with Mr James walking lonely behind it, had plenty to think about and plenty to guess concerning what would happen at Tregannock now. Lady Mary was in fact at that moment on a steam yacht in the Mediterranean, one of a very high-toned party indeed assembled by Sir Ernest Kopf. A Most Distinguished Person was among the merry-makers, and it was obviously desirable that there should be one good-looking lady unembarrassed by the presence of a husband.

Bella and I agreed that Father was pretty good. He piled it on a bit, but not too thick, comparing the late Mr Polperro with Elijah, and Mr James with Elisha who was to receive the mantle of the prophet and carry on the good work. There were few present, I imagine, who could conceive, or who wanted, anything better than that: Polperro to Polperro to Polperro, world without end.

The many people made the church feel intolerably stuffy; and I wasn't sorry when the words of the committal came and Thomas May shuffled forward and with his leathery hands that made me think of a mole's paws scooped the earth down upon the coffin. He looked about him with satisfaction, like a sportsman who had scored another notch, and in his characteristic way wiped his hands up and down his thighs, though he was wearing his best suit. "A bit of good stuff I put on 'un," he confided to me later. "Dug it up in the graveyard with worms in it. There's no nature in what you dig up in that church, an' I thought the old man ought to 'ave the best."

Bella and I walked down through the churchyard and sat on the wall and looked at the bright summer sea, dancing in sun-splashes. We were too used to funerals to feel depressed or even especially solemn. We listened to the villagers who were strolling there, exchanging their bits of gossip before going their ways, and what she would do now was the general matter of speculation, she being James Polperro's wife. As it turned out, it was not a thing about which speculation was long continued, for Lady Mary signalised the opening of the next hunting season by getting her neck broken the first day she was out with hounds.

6

If Mr Polperro's death and burial was nothing else, it was at all events a welcome break in routine. It is extraordinary how circumscribed were the lives that Bella and I led. It was in 1891 that Mr Polperro died, and life at St Tudno, I was beginning to think, could not have changed much since the Middle Ages. The country was threaded with railways, but these made little difference to rural lives. They were highroads, and there had always been highroads of a sort, if not iron ones. Off the highroads, the country still slumbered, and it was not till motorcars came to infiltrate, as they say now, into every side lane that village life virtually ceased. Villages continued to exist, but they were no longer occupied by villagers. A man like Thomas May, who could dig a grave, or build a wall, or sink a well, or fell a tree, or groom a horse, would have been at home in the days of Piers Plowman; but there's no call for him in St Tudno as I have come to know it, where trees are pushed over by bulldozers and walls are built of concrete blocks, and there is no man left who has the feeling of stone in his hands.

When the excitement was over we settled down. Falmouth and Truro were capitals, and to reach them we used our old horse, and for nearer purposes we used our legs. To buy a penny stamp we had to wait for high tide and row a mile to the village at the head of the creek or walk it along the footpath. In the winter time, once dusk had fallen, the church and vicarage were cut off from everything by that mile of silent and unlighted land. We made up the fires and lit the candles and snuggled down close to the earth, beneath the trees, at the edge of the water. Sometimes it was placid moonlit water. Sometimes, especially when the wind was from the east or north-east, it was howling chaos that threw the sea's bitter salt in among the graves. We didn't mind any of it. It was in our bones. Indeed, those wilder nights had their fascination, and now and then, as Bella and I sat in the loft, my book would pall, and I would pull on an old coat and run down the granite steps and through the churchyard and stand there by the wall with the wind streaming my hair inland and the sting of salt in my eyes and its taste on my lips. Looking back, I would see a hanging thread of light where Father's curtains didn't quite meet and would picture his hand moving patiently over his fruitless unending pages. So might a monk have gone placidly on through the rages of a mediaeval storm, and I would feel a great love and pity for him. I would wonder whether his hand ever paused, whether his mind ever speculated on the fate of his eldest daughter; and that would take me to Louisa herself and to London and the draper's shop. Her rebellion was the only thing that had deeply disturbed Legassick routine in my time; and at last the violence of the night, confounding earth and heaven, shouting and shrieking and tearing the sea to tatters, would drive me in, wondering whether, if it ever came to the touch, I should myself have the strength to rebel. Bella would look up and say: "Well, wild-cat, hadn't we better go in to bed?" but one night she hadn't been able to wait for bed and was sleeping where she lay, lolled back in a long wicker chair. Her lips were parted and dewy, her face was rather flushed, and I noticed for the first time how drowsily heavy the lids of her eyes were. I kissed her awake, and she started up and said: "I was having lovely dreams." She stood and stretched and yawned. "Far too lovely to be disturbed," she said, "by the smell of an old pilchard barrel like you."

This was a late autumn night of the year when Mr Polperro died, a time of equinoctial wrath, and the next day when the postwoman came with our letters she talked of a tree torn out of the hedge and lying across the road half a mile away as though it were news of national catastrophe. But that was the St Tudno way and we were not disturbed. Thomas May with a saw and an axe would deal with that inside an hour. The postwoman, however, was not to be robbed of her moment. "You be lucky to get your letter at all, Miss Bella," she said.

"Terrible gurt tree! How I got through 'un I don't know. 'Ad to bend fair double, I 'ad."

The vicarage was the end of the heroine's beat and we sent her to the kitchen to take a cup of tea with Mrs Solway. Bella scanned her letter. She didn't know the handwriting and neither did I. I looked at the postmark. "It's from Oxford."

Since it was from Oxford and wasn't from Roger, I made a guess. "Perhaps it's from Mr Oldham."

"What on earth would he be writing to me for?" Bella demanded.

I reminded her. "You can find out by opening it."

However, she didn't. She put it into her pocket, and didn't open it till we were snug in the loft that night. A letter to either of us was so rare that I was burning with impatience; but I wasn't going to let Bella know that, and I settled down by the fire with Keats. I had asked Father for Shelley, but he said the man was a revolutionary who had let down his family and had led a most disorderly life, and he would prefer it if I didn't read his work – not for some time at any rate. Which made me determined to get hold of a life of Shelley by hook or crook at the earliest possible moment.

So there I sat turning over pages as though I were reading while Bella maddeningly delayed her opening of the letter. At last she opened it, read it, and handed it to me. I took it carelessly, turned over another page or two of Keats, and then, as I had hoped, had Bella hopping mad. "Go on," she said. "Aren't you going to read it?" In a moment or two I condescended to do so.

My dear Miss Legassick. – Your brother and I will be coming down soon, and he hopes to spend part of the vacation with us in Manchester. That's rather complimentary to my family, for it suggests that he didn't dislike his stay with us in the summer, though Manchester has nothing to offer of the beauties that abound at St Tudno. I remember, for example, that day when we all went sailing and came back by moonlight."

I broke off to say: "Well! Fancy his remembering that! He didn't speak a word to either of us. I felt nothing better than a worm shrivelled on a path in summer."

I don't think Bella heard me. She was sitting back, her hands behind her head, dreaming at the fire. I went on reading:

Still, a great town has its own attractions, and if you and your sister would care to join our party I can promise you won't have a dull time. My sister and her husband will be there with their children. We Oldhams are quite a clan. Of course, my mother would write to your father to make the invitation in form, but I don't want to ask her to do this unless I am sure that you would wish it. And your sister, too." (I smiled at the way this sister was scooped in as an afterthought.) "So will you let me know how you feel about it, and forgive me for suggesting it if you think it rather an impertinence, as I do myself. By the way, after being undecided for a long time, I've made up my mind to take Holy Orders.

Yours very truly,

Hugo Oldham.

I folded the letter and slipped it back into its envelope. "The last sentence is the significant one," I said, feeling very wise and percipient.

"I don't see why," said Bella, beginning to munch one of her everlasting sugar buns.

"He's telling you what you are going to let yourself in for if you marry him."

"Nonsense!" Bella answered. "Marry him indeed! You read too many novels, Maria. I'm told Manchester is a horrible place."

"I'm sure it is," I agreed. "All fog and rain and smoke. And when it snows, the snow comes down black instead of white. And the language of the natives is unintelligible. One employs a dragoman to do the translating."

"Hugo's accent is as good as yours or mine."

"Hugo?" I asked innocently.

"Mr Oldham's I mean."

"Oh, Mr Oldham! Yes. He's beginning to speak quite reasonably well. But I'm not sure that one would want to be away from Cornwall for a whole Christmas holiday in order to listen to an improvement in Mr Oldham's accent."

"Neither am I, for that matter. I think on the whole I shall write and tell him not to bother."

"Do you remember when Mr Polperro persuaded Father to have a bet on the Derby and he won five pounds seven shillings? He was terribly embarrassed, as though he'd committed a mortal sin, and put the lot into the poor box."

"I remember."

"Well, I'll bet you twenty to one in pennies that as soon as my presence is removed you'll sit down at that table and write to Mr Oldham saying 'Only too delighted, I'm sure,' or words to that effect. So here goes."

I took up my Keats and left her to it.

7

It was dark when Roger and Bella and I arrived at London Road Station in Manchester. If you live in a place like St Tudno there's not much sense in going away for a holiday, and I had never left home except for my memorable visit to the Wheatstones in London. And that had been in summer. Now it was winter, and even the excitement of the adventure, even the presence of Roger whom we loved and saw so little of, could not prevent me, and Bella too, I am sure, from feeling melancholy and oppressed as our journey drew to its end. When we clanged over the viaduct at Stockport and looked down from that height into the stygian pit wherein the town lay – thousands of buildings that seemed to have been taken into a giant's fist and squeezed into one corporate mass from which plumes of black smoke rose as plentifully as ears of corn from an autumn field, and upon which squares and oblongs of light suggested an oppressive immensity of unknown human living – our hearts were very low, and for the short remainder of the journey I could think of nothing but what I had read in Dickens about Coketown, and I looked forward with dread to the Bounderbys and Gradgrinds I was about to meet.

Roger, who had been reading a Greek text, put the book into his pocket and began lifting down our cases from the rack. "Cheer up," he said. "Any minute now and you'll know the worst." And then there we were, with the train slowing into the vast station, and crowds of people sliding past, and one of them resolving itself into Hugo Oldham who caught sight of us through the window and began running with the train as though it might take it into its steamy head to charge right through the walls of the terminus and leave him behind for ever.

Hugo said to us all, but looking at Bella, whose fur-gloved hand he had taken and was, perhaps absent-mindedly, holding: "Oh, you poor things! You must be starving!"

The idea of Bella starving in any circumstances amused me immensely; and Roger, kicking a large wicker hamper, said: "My dear fellow, when we started out, you could hardly press the lid down on the Cornish pasties, saffron cake, heavy cake, sugar buns, sandwiches and bars of chocolate. Now you see it is empty. No army starves with Bella for *vivandière*."

Hugo, himself of Bella's tubby build, beamed upon her through his spectacles as though Roger's words had conferred upon her a certificate of moral and spiritual excellence.

Through the clangour of the steamy station we followed the trolley rattling our belongings to the stone setts of the station approach. There Hugo led us to a brougham with a cockaded driver sitting up aloft. We stood alongside the vehicle as the baggage was disposed of, and Bella and I looked our first on Manchester. I retain little but a general sense of bustle, of many lights burning in buildings, of a damp smell, and of a sky without stars, an ambiguous roof the colour of a bruise.

Hugo had packed so many fur rugs into the brougham that he might have been a hunter returning from a successful trip. We fought our way in amongst them, and, with beautiful self-abnegation, Hugo sat next to me, our backs to the horse, and placed Roger and Bella together, facing us.

We rattled through the town, sensing the throb of an urgent pulse that was altogether foreign to our Cornish way of life. Hugo pointed out this and that, though all he pointed out was nothing but a succession of moving blurs, so that the Exchange might as well have been the Free Trade Hall and the Town Hall the Theatre Royal. I whispered to him presently: "She's asleep." The length of the journey, the warmth of the furs, and the proximity of Roger's shoulder, had been too much for Bella. She was snuggled down, a faint bubbling purr coming from her lips. "The poor thing!" Hugo said reverently, and thereafter was silent as in a shrine.

For myself, I was wide awake, aware of the town dropping behind us but extending itself in mile after mile of suburban building. It seemed that we would never shake it off, that, travel as far as we might, it would always follow us: ribbon, tape, thread. Its monotony at last drowsed me, too, and I nodded, then slept. I was awakened by a new sound and feel beneath the wheels, and sat up. Gravel. We had turned in to a drive. I was aware of the shapes of trees, vague beyond the windows that our breath had steamed, and then of a light burning in a porch, and then, as Hugo rubbed the window clear with the sleeve of his overcoat, of a reception committee drawn there by the sound of the wheels. Identifying them by age, I took them to be Mr and Mrs Oldham and Hugo's sister and her husband, whose name I didn't know. It was Cumberledge – Dr and Mrs Cumberledge.

When you drive up to the vicarage at St Tudno you come to a small portico – so small that a trap, much less a brougham, had better not try to pass under it, and you enter a stone-floored hall bursting with its message of plain living and high thinking. At Grosmont, which is what the Oldhams' house at Bowdon was called, you passed safely under a small but adequate *porte cochère* and stepped into a hall that shone and twinkled with welcome. I have said before that the feel of a house envelops me as soon as I am over the threshold; and I could not help contrasting this with Mr Wheatstone's heart-freezing house in Manchester Square. Though only four people met us, we felt as though all human kindness was about us like an atmosphere. Bella and I might have been the victims of a gang of kidnappers, returned after long search and the payment of ransom. Bella gave herself to it like a cat snuggling down on to a knee at a fireside, but I am a little more reserved and was able to notice the components of the occasion: the fire, the warmth of the carpet, the shine of an old Welsh dresser gay with blue and white china, the immense picture in an immense gilt frame that even my inexperience was able to identify as a Burne-Jones. Plenitude, not selection, was the note, but it was a happy plenitude, radiating a sense that its owner loved to share all that he had. Some of the rooms I go into today, composed of a Ming horse, a Piper drawing and a white wall, leave me feeling adrift in a thin fall of aesthetic sleet. In Mr Oldham's hall there was a vast blue bowl on the Welsh dresser, overflowing with a tumble of apples and tangerines topped with a bunch of purple grapes. It was cornucopian, and symptomatic.

Everybody seemed to be laughing and talking at once. I forget what any of them said, but I remember that, when the time came for Bella and me to be shown to our bedroom, it was Bella's suitcase that Hugo seized, and Roger carried mine. They were dumped in the room, and Hugo said: "Well, dinner in half-an-hour." The door clicked, and we were left alone. Upon the long clattering boredom of the journey and the excitement of arrival silence fell and we were able to draw breath.

A fire was burning and on a white rug in front of it was a chintz-covered easy chair. Bella sat down on it at once, kicked off her shoes, and wiggled her toes in the warmth, her head back, her arms dangling. Chintz curtains were drawn. Two candles were lit on the mantelpiece and two on the dressing table. I loved the silence. It was as deep as the night-time silence of St Tudno. I had not expected this in Manchester, but I had not known that Bowdon was so far out from the city or that Mr Oldham's house stood in a couple of acres of land where great trees flourished. I stood there listening to this silence and to the gentle rustle of the fire, and then an owl, almost under the window it seemed, set up its quaver and tremolo. It was the last touch to my content, because I knew that though I had not met any Gradgrinds or Bounderbys, though this was a welcoming and happy house, the owl had whipped my heart back to St Tudno and that that was the place for me. I looked at Bella, wondering if she were asleep. "Get up now," I said. "We'd better put on our party frocks."

She yawned and stretched. "Isn't it lovely!" she said. "A whole week without copying out Father's reassessment of Stillingfleet's *Defence of the Doctrine of the Trinity*."

8

When I woke in the morning the first thing that came into my head was this remark of Bella's about Father. It was the sort of remark that all of us children were inclined to make about him, but we all loved him — all except Louisa, and even she was to come to an understanding with him, though it was never a cordial one. Cordiality, in any case, was not something you could expect from Father. He was a recluse who used his cure of souls as a refuge wherein he could follow a scholar's inclinations – rather dreary ones, it seemed to me, but that was his affair, not mine. I think it was his very helplessness, almost childishness, that made us love him. He depended on us so absurdly. Sometimes even I, the youngest of the family, felt the need to cherish him. And I never forgot how, on the day when Bella and I ruined the dress that Louisa was to wear to the ball, he had tried hard to be gay and to cover our offence when Louisa was ready to murder the pair of us. As I grew up and developed a frantic taste for reading that Roger alone shared with me, I came to think Father's tastes and opinions absurdly old-fashioned and his judgment undependable; but there was no reason why that should upset me. Having given his opinion, he never prevented me from following my own.

Lying in bed that morning and thinking of these things, I knew that Father was on the point of being very lonely, and that for all of us, indeed, the old St Tudno family life was as good as ended. Bella would marry Hugo. That was as plain as a pikestaff. All through last evening Hugo's obsession was obvious, and so was the kindness to her of Mr and Mrs Oldham. They treated her almost as though she were already a beloved daughter; and when Bella, who seemed born with the right tactics for an occasion of this sort, begged Mrs Cumberledge to let her see the sleeping children – "Just a peep. I think children look so lovely and innocent when they're sleeping" – why, Bella had then made a good stride towards the Cumberledge approval. Obvious her tactics may have been, but successful, too; so much so that Roger passed me a knowing wink as the doctor and his wife led her out of the room. For me, I had never felt so much merely Bella's sister; though the whole family, I must admit, was kindness itself, and I rejoiced that Bella would have this background of human warmth and solidarity.

Well, there was that; and, though we should see Roger at St Tudno, I supposed, as much as we had ever done, that had never been much. Now that he had achieved a First in Greats at Oxford and would be moving off in January to take a job as assistant classics master at a school in the north of England, we should have to regard him as a person with a life of his own and not to be depended on to consider us.

And Louisa? Right out of the count.

So there it was. It looked as though I was the only one on whom Father could now count. The thought gave me pleasure. I had seen nothing of Manchester and its environs save what could be glimpsed through a steamy window, and I didn't care if I saw no more. Already I was longing to be back at St Tudno.

9

When awake, the Cumberledge children were far from being the angels that Bella had declared them to be when asleep. However, we didn't see much of them, and after three days their parents bore them away to Warwickshire where Dr Cumberledge had his practice. Our visit lasted a week: such a week as I had never known. My surprise at the country delights to be enjoyed near Manchester grew as we watched the deer ranging under the great trees of Dunham Massey; and tramped along the wintry road to Knutsford, which thrilled me because it was Mrs Gaskell's *Cranford* – "Rather shallow, my dear, but pleasant enough, I dare say," Father had pronounced; and watched Roger and Hugo skating on a mere, showing off in good style before us who had never seen a frozen pond in our lives. And at night there was dining in a Manchester restaurant, which seemed a most daring and cosmopolitan thing to be doing; and a play at the Theatre Royal, and a Hallé concert in the Free Trade Hall. Mr and Mrs Oldham kept tactfully out of the way, leaving us four to our own devices; and it was soon clear that Hugo and Bella wished that Roger and I would show an equal tact. However, we couldn't do that; we were expected to be sheepdogs to these two lambs; but on the way home in the brougham we could at least feign tiredness and put back our heads and close our eyes, so as to be unaware of Hugo's arm round Bella's waist.

I became very fond of Hugo. He was a dear man, simple and good. He gave me my first experience of what was to be my life's occupation: watching the joys and sorrows of other people. Or had Louisa done that, on the morning when I buried Euphemia beneath the yew? But then I was unconscious of what was happening. Now I was fully awake.

Before driving to his office on the last morning of our stay, Mr Oldham, who was a cotton merchant, presented Bella with a charming watch. I was not forgotten. He gave me a brooch containing a chip of diamond: a neat little noncommittal gift for a younger sister.

CHAPTER FOUR

FOR FIVE years after his father's death, Mr James Polperro was not often seen at St Tudno. The splendid coach no more arrived at the church on Sunday mornings, and all we had to remind us of Polperro might was the marble slab over the family pew. On it Father had recorded, in Latin which I am sure was grammatically faultless if imperfect as evidence, the grace and glory of the departed. You could go to Tregannock now and find no footmen to be commanded to produce chickenanam sandwiches. They had all been cleared out, and the village was not sorry to see the last of them. Except in the servants' quarters, the furniture ghosted in penitential sheets; and the only servants left were the butler, housekeeper and cook, with a few maids to minister to their indolence. The great house rode above the valley like a disused ship manned by nothing but a maintenance party. The gardens were splendidly kept up, and the full force of woodmen remained. The gamekeepers nurtured the pheasants, and in October Mr Polperro would come down with a few male friends and ritually slaughter them. Then the house would open half an eye; but this was nothing like the wide-eyed splendour of the old days, when wives came with the sportsmen and ladies' maids came with the wives, and a social occasion of the first magnitude broke upon us in a wave that even overflowed into church on Sunday mornings when the pheasants, like all other of God's creatures, were expected to take a day's rest from their normal occupation of being flying targets. Mr James Polperro and his friends, who never numbered more than three or four, didn't come to church; but they did now and then send a brace or two of pheasants to the vicarage to show that they had not wholly forgotten their Christian duties. The names of these sportsmen got about, and one autumn day, when I was twenty years old, the only child left to look after Father, I heard that one of them was Sir Ernest Kopf. I had been doing a round of visiting with Father, and we had looked into the smithy to have a word with the gaffers there when one of them imparted this news to us, not without pride. " 'E be that chap that go everywhere with the Prince of Wales," he said, as though, through this visit of Sir Ernest, the most regal splendour shone reflected upon St Tudno.

Father made no comment on this. The Prince's horse Minoru had won the Derby that year, and thereby the Prince had become doubly endeared in the hearts of the people; but Father was hardly the man from whose mind the triumph of a horse would wipe out the memory of some rather fishy doings on the part of the horse's owner. But as we drove home he said: "I wonder whether it is my duty to call on Mr Polperro? He doesn't encourage me to do so, but after all he is not only my patron but a parishioner like any other. This man Kopf of whom they were speaking is your Uncle Pallace's employer. That might give me a loophole." But he was not an enterprising man. He said nothing more about it, and did nothing more. A week later Tregannock was asleep again.

2

Roger said: "Let's have a sail."

"If you can put up with me," I said.

He smiled, and I always forgave Roger when he smiled. He gave plenty of room for the exercise of my forgiving virtue. "It's a pity the Legassicks were not all boys, and all tramps like you," I said. "Then you'd have been happier."

"Oh, I'm happy enough," he assured me carelessly; but I knew he was regretting his ruined holiday. Now that Hugo was married to Bella and drudging away as a curate in Hunslet, he couldn't be counted on as a tramping companion, and to tramp about with men was Roger's idea of heaven on earth. I had been far too young to get on with Louisa; and although I could put up with Bella and was amused by her, I was capable of being enraged by her laziness. Roger was the nearest of them all to my heart, but I was a girl, and you couldn't tramp about the world with a girl. He had arranged to go to Sicily with a fellow schoolmaster who had decided to put in a bit of preliminary scrambling in the Lakes. There he had succeeded in fracturing his thigh, and so we had Roger fretting at home like a chained hawk.

As I was rowing him out to the boat he said: "One of these days I'll get some fellows to sail round the world with me."

"The trouble with you," I told him, "is that you're more Pallace than Legassick. You're like Uncle Reginald, always dreaming about foreign places."

"Yes, but he didn't stop at dreaming. He's come to rest now, but not before doing something that means that his name will always be attached to scores of lovely things. That must be wonderful. Did you ever hear of Porson?"

"No," I said, splashing the buoy overboard as Roger ran up the sail.

"He was a professor of Greek who drank too much."

I took the tiller and we began to move out towards St Just. "Like Mr Polperro," I said.

Roger smiled. "One of these days you'll be hanged for high treason. Well, Porson stated a theory of a pause in iambic metre. It is known as Porson's Pause. I fear that my fame, if any, will be something like that. I might discover how the stress on certain syllables should be lengthened. It would be known for ever as Legassick's Lengthening. There's a cause to dedicate one's life to – what?"

"Well, anyway," I said, "let's not dedicate this evening to it. Stand by. I'm going about."

We stood up towards the mouth of the Truro river, with the sunset flooding across from our port side on to the rising land on the other shore: land that was alight with golden bracken and the sombre purple of heather.

"Talking of Uncle Reginald," I said, "old Spargo tells me that that man Kopf who employs him is shooting at Tregannock."

Roger was always capable of surprising me. He did so now. "I've met him," he said. "He's quite a good chap in his way."

"Well!" I said. "You and Louisa! Was there ever such a pair for keeping their mouths shut!"

"I was with Louisa at the time. You remember I dashed up to Town during the last half-term? Or didn't I tell you?"

"No, you didn't!" I said emphatically.

"Well, let's go ashore, and I'll tell you now."

We were in the mouth of the river, and Roger downed the sail and threw the anchor overboard. I rowed ashore. A trickle of water that filters down through a wood of scrub oak flows in there from the eastward side. At high tide, which it now was, the inlet floods. It is too mean a spot for geography: the maps give it no name. We called it Ted's Bight. On one side of it, just where it meets the deep water of the river, a little bluff stands up with a rocky wall behind it – a wall grown with thyme that scents the whole place. In the woods across the thread of water there is a heronry, and sitting on the turf with sea-pinks blooming about us we watched the big grey birds coming in and settling down. "This makes me feel young again," Roger said, filling his pipe. Ever since we were children it had been our secret place, our best-loved destination for a picnic. The burned stones that we had piled for fire-places were still there, cluttered with ashes. It had always been Roger and Bella and myself. Louisa had been like a harassed mother, glad to see the children out of the way for a few hours. "Now tell me about Louisa and Sir Ernest Kopf," I said.

Roger had written to Louisa. They met on a Sunday morning and took a train to Dorking where Uncle Reginald met them and drove them in a pony trap to his cottage on the Kopf estate.

"I never saw the place," Roger said, "when Uncle Reginald took it over, but I'm told it was nothing more than a valley and meadowland. It's amazing now. It happened to be the best time for rhododendrons and azaleas, and the valley was blazing with them. You'd think the things had been growing there for ever. I don't know anything about Sir Ernest Kopf's taste, but at all events he has the sense to employ people whose taste is perfect. The house is most dramatic on the brow of the hill, looking down on Uncle Reginald's woods and gardens and water. I asked Uncle what it had cost. He just laughed and said: 'Aubrey once told me that you were no good at mathematics, so I won't trouble you with astronomical figures, my boy.' Well, that's one way of telling me to mind my own business."

A woman from near by came in every day to give Uncle Reginald's cottage a brush up and to cook his midday meal. For the rest, he looked after himself. When they had eaten, they saw some more of the place. "But nothing like all, I should imagine. It's immense, and it all has a look of being as old as the hills."

They were about to drive back to Dorking when they met Sir Ernest strolling alone through the rhododendron valley. Uncle Reginald raised his old tweed hat and was passing on when Sir Ernest said: "Introduce your friends to me, Mr Pallace."

"My sister's children, sir, Louisa and Roger Legassick, from St Tudno."

"Ah," he said, "that's near James Polperro's place, isn't it? He's asked me to shoot there this autumn. I think I shall go. I've never been in Cornwall."

"He hadn't much to say," Roger told me, "but he seemed a friendly sort of man. I rather liked him."

"You might have told me this before," I said. I was feeling hurt by the sense of missing all sorts of things that I ought to know. I was twenty. I didn't any longer think of Louisa with awe.

As we rowed back to the boat Roger apologised. "Louisa asked me to say nothing."

"Well, now you've broken your word," I said. "I think the way Louisa's going on is nonsensical. I shall go and see her and tell her so. I shall write to Uncle Reginald and ask him to have me for a week's visit, and while I'm there I'll get him to invite Louisa. This Legassick feud has gone on long enough."

Roger looked at me in surprise. He was not used to resolution in Maria, the youngest of the brood.

"I mean it," I said. "I won't have you or Louisa treating me as a child any longer, or Father for that matter. It's disgraceful to have you two more or less conspiring in this fashion." I really was worked up.

Roger said: "Will Father let you go?"

"I'll see to that," I promised.

I went in November.

3

I hadn't travelled to Paddington since, when I was ten years old, Father labelled me as though I were a parcel. Now I was twenty, and if it interests you to know what I was like, I was very thin, very dark, with straight hair and eyes that were almost black. This was the Legassick look that Father had handed on to me and Louisa, though her eyes were not black but dark blue. The Pallace strain came out in Bella and Roger. Both were fair with curly locks, but Bella had lazed and eaten herself fat while Roger was as thin as Louisa and I. He used to say that I only needed a bull terrier and genius to be like Emily Brontë, and I once bought a bull terrier from Thomas May's nephew to see if that would somehow help on with the genius, but Father wouldn't have a dog about the house, so I gave the terrier away and remained uninspired. Knowing more about Emily now than I did then, I see that one thing I had in common with her was the quality best described by the word *farouche*. It was this that had stirred me to make my present journey and seek a show-down with Louisa. Who was she to be going on like this as though the rest of us didn't matter a tinker's curse?

I was rather annoyed when Uncle Reginald met me at Paddington. It seemed another hint that I wasn't capable of looking after myself. However, as we sat in the Great Western hotel taking tea I thanked him for coming, but I couldn't forbear to add: "It's ten years, Uncle, since we met – ten years since you waved goodbye to Louisa and I dropped her at the shop where she disappeared."

He smiled and said: "Yes. And the odd thing is that when I think of you I still see a child of ten."

"So I realise," I said tartly. "You might have assumed that by now I'd have the sense to find my own way across London and get into the train at Dorking."

"I wanted a moment to talk to you before you arrived," he said. "When you proposed yourself for a visit, I was delighted that you were coming to see my place, but you won't find me alone. Louisa has come to live with me. Indeed, we have quite a household now. She's brought a young women named Meg something or other. Meg is a good cook and housekeeper. And Louisa is writing her book."

"I know nothing about Louisa or her book," I said sharply. I was feeling annoyed because my scheme to contrive a meeting with Louisa, a meeting that would leave her gaping with surprise, had been forestalled.

"So Louisa has at last given up being a shop-girl," I said. "About time. It was an odious thing for her to do. She was right in not letting Father know."

Looking back now on my absurd outburst, I am surprised that he didn't bark at me. Instead, he said gently: "I hope, my dear, that you'll treat Louisa with the respect she deserves. She had a living to earn:

your father had not educated her to earn one: and she did the best she could. I don't think being a shop-girl is any more odious than being a gardener like me or a parson like Aubrey. Anyway, she ceased being a shop-girl long ago."

Well, here was something else Roger hadn't told me! He must have known this when he saw her during the last half-term.

"I don't know what the grades are in the hierarchy of a big trading establishment," my uncle said, "but she moved from one to another, and was at last doing responsible work, buying materials, and this meant travelling. She was in Paris a good deal. Of course, she had long since ceased to 'live in' as they call it. She had rooms in Kensington, and this girl Meg, who used to work, I believe, for Mr Wheatstone, looked after her. Meg had been a shop-girl, too. Louisa got her the job, but Meg hadn't the brains to be anything else. However, they're devoted to one another."

"Quite an odyssey!" I said flippantly.

"Yes," he quietly agreed. "It showed Louisa a lot of things she didn't like. And that's what she's writing her book about. It was quite a sacrifice in a way to give up her job. I'm sure she was earning more than Aubrey gets out of his living."

So there it was. "I hope, my dear, you'll treat Louisa with the respect she deserves." It wasn't to be, after all, the respectable daughter of the parson confronting the bad girl of the family and asking her to explain herself. It was to be little Maria looking up to the figure on Uncle Reginald's plinth: the successful woman, the traveller, the writer of a book. Suddenly I felt again like the child with a label round her neck waiting to be met by the wife of the man who could buy up Mr Polperro.

4

Meg was at Dorking station with the pony trap. In the ten years since I had seen her I had often thought of Meg, and I had come to have no doubt about the meaning of that encounter with her mother in Bond Street. I could even work up a shiver of horror as I persuaded myself that I had run dreadful risks in being on the loose in London with a street-walker's child. I had moments of deep religious brooding when I would fall on my knees and thank God that His hand had guided me safely through the sinful labyrinth of London; but at other times I would look back almost wistfully to those few days which my imagination could elaborate into a frisking on the fringes of an inferno.

And here was Meg whom I had often imagined going her mother's way, and who, I now thought in a flash, might very well have done so but for Louisa. It is unlikely that she would have remembered me, but I suppose Louisa had freshened her mind, for she came forward shyly and held out her hand and said: "I'm sure you don't remember me, Miss Maria." She pronounced the "i" as though it were the first person singular. In my family it was pronounced as a long "e".

I let it go. I said: "I shouldn't have recognised you, but really I do remember you. I often think about you."

She beamed with pleasure. I shook her hand and said: "No, indeed, I shouldn't have recognised you. You have become so handsome."

She blushed. She had a fair skin that blushed easily, and I thought that if Louisa were in any way responsible for so attractive a young creature she certainly deserved the respect that Uncle Reginald said was her due.

Uncle Reginald said: "Drive Miss Maria home, Meg. I have some shopping to do. I'll walk along later."

The night was coming on. The cottage, which was like a Swiss chalet, looked warm and welcoming, huddled beneath tall beech trees with one or two windows glowing. The long journey had tired me more than I had expected. Louisa was standing at the door on the look-out for us. She was thirty-three. When last I had seen her she was a haggard girl worn out by overwork and a frustrating marriage. What I saw now was a woman of great beauty, but rather daunting: commanding and imperious. Without a word, she put her arms round me, kissed me, and held me close. At last she said: "Come in. I'll take you up to your room. Or rather mine. We're sharing. Meg has put a warm brick in your bed."

"Bed?" I asked surprised. "At this time of day?"

"You must be worn out," she said. "I'll send up some supper at once. Then you can have a good sleep. Besides," she added, looking at me with a faint smile, "you may want to be up at four or five in the morning."

It reminded me of the day when, a silly child, I buried poor Euphemia, and Louisa was already a woman. Somehow, despite the smile, it re-established that moment and the emotions of the moment. I said: "Thank you, Louisa. I shall love that."

She pushed open the bedroom door. "Well, here you are," she said. "This is your bed."

Meg came in and dumped my suitcase. "Now get straight into bed," Louisa said. "Meg will bring you some soup as soon as she's stabled the pony."

They both went out, Louisa closing the door softly, as though upon an invalid. By the light of a candle I got into bed, feeling subdued. This was a different beginning from what I had rehearsed. "Now, Louisa, don't you think it's about time you gave your family some explanation of your extraordinary behaviour?"

Meg's brick had warmed the bed beautifully, and when she came with soup and toast and half a glass of wine I was already tottering into dreams. I roused myself and ate. Meg sat on the bed, watching me with admiration, as though eating were a rare accomplishment and my mastery of it astounding. When I had done, she said: "She's a caution, isn't she?" And this, too, was something that she seemed to find commendable. "Well, goodbye now," she said, and tiptoed out with the tray.

A little wind had risen; the branches of the beeches sighed and whispered; and I went to sleep feeling oddly comforted, though I had not imagined myself to be in need of comforting. Perhaps I was relieved at having already decided to throw up my part of missionary to the heathen.

I didn't hear Louisa come to bed, and when I awoke in the morning the sun was shining in on me. The window looked east. The view was of trees and trees and trees. Many of them were still clothed. The sun burnished the thin gold of their leaves. Looking upward to the brow of the hill, I could see the mansion, the lovely brick that Roger had mentioned warm in the morning light, livened by sun-flashed windows.

Meg came in with a tray: coffee, toast, butter and marmalade. "You're to have breakfast in bed, Miss Maria," she declared. "Miss Legassick says you're not to be pampered, but just for this once."

"She's not Miss Legassick. You know as well as I do that she's Mrs Wheatstone."

"Begging your pardon, Miss Maria, she's been Miss Legassick since even before that old corpse gave up pretending to be alive. She was always so known in the shop, and she's so known to Mr Pallace. That's good enough for me."

I could not remember having breakfast in bed before, except when some childish ailment had laid me up. I said contentedly: "I don't see why she should treat me as a child."

"Maybe you don't, but that's how she's treating you, and, if you'll take a tip from me who knows her inside out, you'll just let her do what she thinks fit."

She looked hard at me, as though challenging me to dispute her wisdom. I didn't take her up. "Well, goodbye," she said. "I'll be back later for the tray."

5

It was ten o'clock when I went down, and Louisa said: "Let's take a little walk. We can't go far. I must be back by eleven. I work from then till one." She said nothing about the nature of the work. I guessed it was the book. We followed a rugged path down the valley to where it flattened, and here formal gardens had been laid out. We came to a great lawn, walled in with yew looking as solid as dark masonry. A long narrow pond, stone-fringed, ran its length, widening in the middle into a large square of water. In the middle of the square was a stone triton, with water pouring from an uplifted conch. In each corner of the garden was a small pavilion built in Portland stone. At any time of day one might sit and enjoy what sun there was. The sun was unclouded that day. Though it was November, we were warm in the pavilion. Louisa said: "Sir Ernest and his wife are good-hearted people. They don't mind my lounging about in the gardens."

I didn't say that Sir Ernest had recently been at Tregannock and was there still for aught I knew. After a moment she said it for me. "He's been at Tregannock, shooting."

I showed no surprise that she knew this. Since I was not to convert the heathen, I could at least be as reserved as Louisa had been for ten years. Her remark, I thought, was a lead, and I didn't take it.

Presently she asked: "Why did you come?"

"Why didn't you? Had you forgotten you had a family?"

"Have you only just remembered that I'm a member of it?"

"No. I remember it every day when Father mentions you in his prayers."

" 'And bless and preserve my wandering daughter Louisa.' Something like that, I suppose. How long does it take? Say three seconds. And for all the other seconds of the twenty-four hours I'm not thought of."

"If you believe that, you've got a very wrong idea of Father."

She surprised me by saying: "Of course I don't believe it. I'm merely trying to justify myself. When I went away to work for Mr Wheatstone I was bitter about Father. You were a child. You wouldn't have an inkling of what it was about. It was more than you think. Perhaps some day I'll tell you. When you've acted impulsively like that, and in a little while begin to have doubt about what you've done, you fight against it and find all sorts of reasons to back your action. As Father would put it, you harden your heart. What I should have loathed beyond anything was a prodigal's welcome: fatted calves and fine raiment, all that sort of thing. I can't imagine anything more calculated to make a home-comer feel a perfect fool. I didn't miss home so much that I could have accepted *that* as the price of going back. If I could just have slipped in to find everything as it was before . . . But that's nonsense, of course. That can never be done."

I said not a word. This, miraculously coming now without a jog from me, was all I wanted to hear. I feared to stop the flow. Grey and yellow water wagtails were running in their urgent way up and down the stone edging of the pond, taking off now and then to alight in the shallow baths that the water-lily leaves provided. There with their wings they winnowed the water into sparkling showers. I feared that even so charming and innocent a diversion might draw her mind away from what she was saying.

"So it went on," she said. "It was touch-and-go for a long time whether I should return or not. Mind you, it wasn't only the sudden gulf between me and Father that drove me out. I should have gone sooner or later. I imagine you're happy enough at St Tudno."

"Yes."

"I never was. Father and Mrs Solway and Thomas May. For that matter, you and Bella. And an occasional condescending glance from a Polperro. I wanted a bit more out of life than that. I suppose I had the itch that made Uncle Reginald dream when he was young of the

Himalayas and strange flowers. Well, working for Mr Wheatstone didn't turn out to be exactly that."

I ventured a timid word at last. "I didn't like him."

She laughed without mirth. "What do you know about Saint Francis of Assisi?" she asked unexpectedly.

"He preached to the birds."

"So they say, though what good that did the birds I can't imagine. However, there was more to it than that. He was a rich young man who loved all the nonsense of chivalry. He was baptised John, but he was so gay and fond of fun and so prodigal with his money that he became known as Francesco – the little Frenchman. Illness turned his thoughts to religion and you know the rest – the happy saint who wouldn't have a penny for himself or the order he founded. Mr Wheatstone was a rich young man, too, but his thoughts never turned to religion, and he never loved people as Francis did. Believe me, Maria, I've had reason to think a lot about Mr Wheatstone, and I've come to a very odd conclusion about him. But I think it's the right one. He never forgave humanity for revealing its seamy side to him. He decided to devote his money and his life to the poor and outcast, but he never ceased to regret the impulse that made him do it. He hated people, rich and poor alike. The newspapers always spoke of 'Mr Wheatstone, the well-known philanthropist.' They seem to imagine that a philanthropist is a person who gives away money. A philanthropist is simply someone who loves his fellows. I haven't forgotten everything Father taught," she said with a little smile, "and so I can recall St Paul: 'Owe no man anything, save to love one another.' Francis was a philanthropist, though he never had a cent to give away."

"Perhaps," I ventured, "it is harder to serve those you hate than those you love. What you say may be to his credit."

"You may be right," she said, "if credit is what one is after. He would know none of his pensioners personally. There was as much love between him and them as there is between an old Crimean wreck and the War Office that pays him his weekly shilling or two."

I asked timidly: "Why did you marry him?"

"I could no more answer that than solve the riddle of the universe. I was young, ill and friendless. You can put on your wisest look, if you like, and say that's a poor answer, explaining nothing. All the same, it's the only answer I can give. It would surprise me very much to know that human beings can logically explain all they do. Anyway, it was another barrier between me and St Tudno. Mr Wheatstone wasn't interested in my family."

"It's rather surprising then that he allowed me to make my visit."

"You may never have realised it, my dear Maria, but it was your visit that smashed the whole thing up. You were St Tudno – the other half of me – perhaps not the more important half, but the half that belonged to the first things I had known. I was never without longings to go back, and when you appeared they became overpowering. But to leave Mr Wheatstone and go back would have been to admit that my whole adventure had ended in nothing but the ignominious fatted calf. I decided to continue the adventure – without you and without Mr Wheatstone too."

"So you became a shop-girl."

"Why not? I knew I shouldn't remain a shop-girl for long. But – a shop-girl. The very way you say it, so contemptuously, shows how impossible it would have been to make Father see sense. Still, I repeat it – why not? It was fun, much more fun than being Mrs Wheatstone, believe me. Now walk around. No one will interfere with you. I must get in to my work. I'm glad you came."

6

The wall of dense yew that enclosed us had two ways out: straight-cut slits that only one person could edge through at a time. Louisa went through one, and after sitting for a moment pondering the unexpected talk – almost the monologue – that I had listened to, I went out by the other. Now I was in an enclosure bordered not by yew but by grey stone. The walls were high, their tops decorated by leaden figures: nymphs and shepherds, birds and beasts. The stone was clothed with climbing roses, and beneath them in wide herbaceous borders a few late flowers lingered on. The rest of the space was turfed save for a large circular bed in the middle wherein bush roses grew. The November sun shone upon the quiet opulence of the enclosure, and I thought what fun, and what profound satisfaction of the spirit, Uncle Reginald must have had in calling into being this alternation of small wild glens and patches of sophisticated beauty.

One end of this enclosure was built up into a turfed platform, retained by the same grey stone that made the walls, and this ramp was thickly grown with aubretia and rock roses and snow-on-the-mountain that must have been a joy in spring. A semi-circular sweep of steps led from the lawn to the platform on which a summer-house was perched. I went up the steps, and only then saw that the summer-house was occupied. A lady was stretched at ease on a long cane seat, cushioned in red. I paused, and was about to retreat, when she saw me and said: "Good morning."

There was nothing for it then but to go on. She did not rise, but stretched out a hand which I took, and she said: "I am Lady Jane Kopf."

Not just Lady Kopf. The Jane reminded me that Sir Ernest had married an earl's daughter. I said: "I hope I'm not intruding, my lady. I'm Mr Pallace's niece."

She was a fair lovely creature who seemed to be in her middle thirties. She smiled and said: "Intruding! I should think not. My father has been visiting me, but he returned to London yesterday. My boy has gone back to school, and my husband is in Amsterdam. I'm longing for company."

"I should have thought, my lady, that it would not be too difficult to induce company to visit you in so charming a place."

"Oh, I loathe formal company, invited people," she said. "They come with their maids and their playing-cards and their senseless gossip. No. Two's company, especially when one of them is unexpected. Why don't you come and live here for ever, and surprise me like this at odd times and in unexpected places? Don't stand about. Bring a chair and sit by me."

Little cane chairs were ranged against the wall. I brought one and sat by her. Her pose amused me. "I have read," I said, "that when one of the earls of Shrewsbury laid out the gardens at Alton Towers he built a grotto and put a blind harpist to live in it. I could hardly do that. Still, you might build me a retreat somewhere, and I could make spectacular appearances, now as a naiad dripping from a stream, now as a dryad draped with amaranth and moly."

She clapped her hands. "Oh, good!" she said. "You have imagination. I hope my boy will have imagination. I want him to be a poet. When I was expecting him, it was lovely weather, and I used to lie naked by our little waterfall so that music should enter into his soul."

I said: "Poor Keats! He had to do with the sound of horses blowing into the mangers in his father's livery stable."

"Do you know the *Ode to a Nightingale?*" she asked.

"Yes."

"Recite it to me, please. You have a voice for poetry."

I began: "My heart aches, and a drowsy numbness pains my sense. . ." when a quiet cough at the foot of the steps made me stop. Lady Jane had composed herself, leaning on her cushions, her eyes closed. Now she opened them and saw the silk-stockinged footman who threw my thoughts back to chickenanam.

"Oh, Robertson," she said, "how tiresome of you to choose so inappropriate a time."

"I wished to inform your ladyship that Mr Polperro has arrived. He was expected."

"But he is so tiresome, so earthy," she said. "He likes horses."

"Yes, my lady."

"Well, I must come and welcome him, I fear. Sir Ernest will be back this afternoon, and he has a fondness for Polperro."

"As your ladyship pleases."

Robertson went, and I was glad that Lady Jane did not ask me to go on with the poem. I was not word-perfect. She stood up, tall and slender. "Well, I must be off. This Mr Polperro can be of little interest to you."

7

You must remember that at this time I knew nothing of what had happened between James and Louisa before she left St Tudno. Bella and I thought the outburst against Father concerning the Polperros was the cause of it; but, as so often happens, it was merely the occasion through which a deep cause became operative. We were not altogether unaware of this, but thought the cause was dissatisfaction with life in the vicarage, boredom with us children, weariness of her everlasting transcribing of Father's scrawls into fair copies. As the years went by, even these immature ideas faded from our minds. Louisa was simply our sister who had gone away. We did not associate her at all with St Tudno, and certainly not with some one person there, especially not with James Polperro.

And so the footman's message to Lady Jane did not seem to me to have any bearing on us. It was nothing more than an interesting fact that I was anxious to convey to Louisa. It didn't surprise me. Mr Polperro had been entertaining Sir Ernest. What more natural than that he should make a return visit?

I spent the morning wandering about the estate. Tall yew hedges enclosing private places seemed one of Uncle Reginald's favourite devices. I came upon one whose only entrance was blocked by a canvas screen labelled: "Private. Keep out." Nevertheless, I peeped round the screen, saw nobody, and entered. It was a rough little place where rock obtruded through turf that looked aboriginal and where a minute fall of water made a constant pleasing sound. So this was the waterfall where Lady Jane had given her son a pre-natal push towards Parnassus! I had wondered whether she was merely babbling pleasant nonsense, and had thought that, if footmen were liable to seek her out with messages, situations were likely to arise that they might find agreeable and she embarrassing. But the narrow slit of an entrance, the screen and the keep-out notice, suggested that her story was true. She amused me, but I thought that, with her husband returning and with Mr Polperro to be entertained, I was not likely to see much of her.

So I returned to the cottage at lunch time with James Polperro once again foremost in my mind. In the dining room I was surprised to find only two places set, and presently Uncle Reginald, looking oddly disturbed for so equable a man, came in and exclaimed: "Louisa is gone!"

"Gone? How do you mean, Uncle – gone?"

Meg came in with the roast beef, and looked as though she had been crying. "It's all my fault," she said, trying hard not to cry again. "I always did do anything she asked me, and now I've gone and done this which Mr Pallace is angry with me because I shouldn't."

"All right, Meg," my uncle soothed her. "You must always obey the boss, and Louisa's been the boss here."

She went out, and I asked: "What is Louisa up to now?"

"Goodness knows. All that Meg can tell me is that a letter came for Louisa just after you and she had gone out this morning. Louisa read it as soon as she got back, and for some reason or other scooted."

"Does Meg know who sent the letter?"

"How should she? She says Louisa wasn't flustered but 'determined like.' She told Meg to go and harness the pony, and when Meg came back she had packed a bag and said: 'Drive me into Dorking.' Meg heard her ask for a ticket to London, and that's all she knows. Louisa sent her packing before the train came in."

I forgot all my liking for Louisa that had followed our talk that morning. I said angrily: "Louisa really is the limit! She upsets everybody without a moment's thought."

"I don't know about that," he said. "It seems to me that there must have been a good deal to think about before she'd do a thing like this."

"A mere selfish impulse!" I insisted.

"No. You are twice wrong. Louisa is neither selfish nor impulsive. I wish I knew what it is all about. Still, she's not a child. I refuse to worry."

We finished the meal without speaking of Louisa again. Indeed, we spoke of nothing, and I could see that, despite his words, he was worrying plenty.

I helped Meg with the washing-up and then went to the bedroom that Louisa and I had shared. There was no sign of sudden disruption. The packing, it was clear, had been methodically done. If I were looking for a clue, it didn't seem as though I was going to find one here. A drapery of muslin reached from the dressing table to the floor. I was about to leave the room when I saw, peeping from beneath this drapery, the edge of a piece of paper. So you were flustered after all, I thought. You brushed the letter from the dressing table and your shoes scuffled it out of sight, and you were in such a hurry to be away that you did not notice it was gone.

Without compunction, I read the letter. It was addressed from a London hotel:

Dear Miss Legassick. – After all that was once between us, and after that wonderful day we spent together at Richmond while my wife was still alive, I find this a cold way to address you, but I don't know whether you would want it otherwise. After

Richmond, you disappeared, and I didn't expect or deserve ever to see you again. But a wonderful piece of luck has put me on your track. Sir Ernest Kopf came down to Tregannock to do a bit of shooting, and talking of his place near Dorking he mentioned Mr Pallace as the designer of his gardens. I said that I knew Mr Pallace well, as he used to come occasionally to see my father, and I said he was the brother-in-law of our vicar, Mr Legassick. He said 'Then that will be the vicar's daughter who's living with him – a Miss Louisa Legassick.' You could have knocked me down with a feather. I said nothing to him; but I promised myself that I would propose myself for a short visit to him. I have now done this, and should be arriving on the day this reaches you. Do you forgive me? Do you look forward to seeing me? I am addressing this to you in the name of Legassick, since from what Sir Ernest said I gather you use it. I dare not sign myself as I would wish, so say merely that I am 'yours sincerely'

James Polperro.

The dull, almost illiterate, letter seemed nevertheless to flame in my hand. "After all that was once between us." "After Richmond." "I dare not sign myself as I would wish."

I was not now the small and innocent child who had come, years ago, upon her eighteen-year-old sister flushed and perturbed under the yew tree at St Tudno. That day came flooding back. I remembered a horseman riding away and myself rowing Uncle Reginald up the creek, and the meeting with James Polperro in the smithy. He had been out early, he told Uncle Reginald, and his horse had cast a shoe. I sat at the bedroom window, forcing my memory back, and everything clicked into place. I began to see the whole picture. I had no doubt at all that it was James Polperro who had ridden away. I heard old Mr Polperro saying to Uncle Reginald that James was engaged to marry Lady Mary Lacey; and, looking now at the letter in my hand, reading again that phrase "All that was once between us", I guessed that whatever had been between them ended there that morning under the yew tree. What *had* been between them? My mind boggled. It would not accept the answer. That it had been something serious I knew from the quarrel that I had witnessed between James and Lady Mary. It was unlikely that in what should have been so happy a moment he would have said anything to provoke the shrieking I had heard unless his mind was torn by regret for having put an end to – well, whatever it was that he had put an end to.

But this was not all. *Had* it been put an end to? There was "that wonderful day we spent together at Richmond" while Lady Mary Polperro was still alive.

Louisa's career, which Bella and I had so innocently thought of as a mere defiance of Father, began to seem more colourful than I could have imagined. What surprised me most was a reluctant admiration.

Uncle Reginald had gone off to superintend the planting of a new orchard. What an eye-opening story I could tell him when he returned! But I would tell him nothing. Fifteen years had passed since I promised Louisa under the yew tree to say nothing of what I had seen that morning. Now, more than ever, I must keep my word.

8

In the hot summer weather Father used the pony and trap for getting about among his parishioners, for he disliked exertion in the heat; but in the winter he walked. You would see him, tall and thin, wearing a black wideawake hat, with a grey woollen muffler flung round his neck and a home-made walking-stick in his hand, trudging along our muddy roads, innocent then of macadam.

So he was going, a few days after Louisa had left Uncle's cottage. It had been a lowering day, never a sunshine peep, and darkness was coming on. Louisa, travelling in an ancient closed-in carriage that she had hired at Truro, saw him through the window as she drove past and told the cabman to stop. She lowered the window as he came up, and said: "Hallo, Father! Can I give you a lift?"

Heaven knows what thoughts occupied his odd mind during those solitary rambles, but he looked, Louisa said, as startled as a fish lifted suddenly from water on to the grass. He stared at her for a moment as though adjusting his mind to an inconceivable situation; then said: "Louisa! You startled me! You look so like my mother."

Louisa laughed, though she felt like crying, for he was so much older and frailer and lonelier than she had expected. "I feel so old," she said to him, "that it would not surprise me if I looked like your grandmother. But get in, Father."

He leaned on his stick, gazing at her. Then he kissed her through the lowered window, and she saw that there were tears in his eyes. "It is so surprising," he said. "I was thinking of Thomas à Kempis, and here are you!"

"Quite another kettle of fish, Father. But get in."

"No, my dear," he said, "you drive on, and I shall walk. It will give me a moment to readjust my thoughts."

So she drove on down the last familiar stretch, and saw the Carrick Roads quiet and sullen as lead in the fall of the evening, and the red posting-box stuck into the wall of a white-washed byre, and the cows, that looked like the cows she had always known, sloven-slopping up the hill from the pastures, their udders fit to burst. The old winter-bare sycamores on the grass verge outside the vicarage wall, the short drive down which she had gone fifteen years ago, wearing her mother's dress, to go to the Polperro dance.

"Well, God send all his angels to protect us!" said Mrs Solway. "If you're not back!"

"Yes. I passed Father on the road. He'll be here in a moment. Have tea ready for him."

"You should have given him a lift. Break my heart he do at times, wandering home like a lost child."

"Well, now, make the tea."

"Easier said than done, Miss Louisa. I can't tear myself away from looking at you, as if you was Lazarus risen from the dead. An' looking quite a lady."

"Well, I hope Lazarus looked quite a gentleman. Get the tea now."

9

My visit to Dorking had been for the purpose of seeing Louisa and taking home to Father some news of her. Now that she was gone there seemed nothing to stay for, and my conscience got busy. I don't know how far he "worked" it, or how far it naturally arose from the circumstances in which we all found ourselves, but Father had the consciences of us three girls well in hand. The duty of looking after him was as unquestioned as our belief in God; and that in itself shows how profound was the emotional disturbance that drove Louisa out. After that, there was Bella, who never, for all her sluggishness, neglected the things that Father expected her to do. Now there was

myself, and, the cause for my absence from home being removed, I
began to think of the daughterless vicarage and the quarto sheets of
writing flowing remorselessly from under Father's hand. Another
thing was that I did not want to meet James Polperro.

I said goodbye to my uncle and to Meg, proposing to give myself
one day in London in order to find some gifts for Father and Mrs
Solway and Thomas May. I didn't reach town till late evening, and
booked myself in at a small hotel in a street off Baker Street. There I
stayed, not venturing into the night-time November streets, which I
was convinced were full of evil. I was up early in the morning, and
decided to slip round before breakfast to look at the house in
Manchester Square where Louisa had lived with Mr Wheatstone. It
was but five minutes' walk away.

It was an oppressive and gloomy morning, full of cold mist and
with no promise of betterment. Here was the house – and yet it
wasn't. It was impossible to believe that this had ever been the
sepulchre that I remembered. Despite the dreariness of the day, the
house had a look of warmth that captivated me. The railings were
painted black, tipped with gold. The door was black, shining like
Chinese lacquer, and the brass upon it was polished up to the nines.
The steps were whitened. The windows could not twinkle in such a
morning, but they hadn't the forbidding scowl I had known, and the
white window boxes, though empty, looked as though they could
hardly wait for spring to awaken the daffodils whose bulbs I imagined
to be buried in their loam.

As I stood there gawping the door opened, and I had a glimpse of
gas-light falling upon a rich interior. I remembered my manners –
Don't stare, Maria – and was moving to one side when I was helped
by the voice of a footman. "Do you mind standing clear of the gate,
please. No, the other side, please. Mr Lester will go that way."

He came down the steps and opened the gate and indicated to me
where I was to stand. His words annoyed me. (It had never taken
much for a flunkey to annoy me. I'm glad the breed has all but
disappeared.) But I could never tick these people off without getting
heated and flustered, and that was something that Louisa, when Bella
and I were children, had always scolded us for. ("Don't raise your
voice, Maria, especially to servants.") But I did raise my voice, and I

was blushing all over as I said: "Mr Lester can go any way he likes. But I hope a public pavement belongs to me as much as to him."

I was staring so hard, and I hoped so fiercely, at the footman that I noticed no one else and was surprised when a voice said: "Of course it does. What's the matter now, Chillingworth?"

"Chillingworth!" I exclaimed, trying to put a fine inflection of scorn into my voice. "What a name for a footman!"

A laugh that sounded enchanting in that grim morning and at that unhappy moment caused me to turn my head from the hated Chillingworth, and then indeed I wished I had remembered and followed Louisa's advice. I felt horribly cheap, utterly confused, and my face burned.

The young man was, I supposed, only a year or two older than I. His Greek curled head was bare, and he was wearing running clothes: a light blue vest and shorts. His eyes shone with laughter, and I thought of someone about to take up a torch and run somewhere with it in the odd way Greeks were said to have.

I said humbly: "I'm sorry," and he, still smiling: "I should think so. You're as bad as he is. You look a proper spitfire. Chillingworth, this lady is right. Outside the gate, the pavement belongs to her Majesty's lieges, who have full right to pass to and fro on their lawful occasions without any old buck from you."

Chillingworth said: "I feared a collision, sir, as you ran out. You always run out impetuous."

"Well, you have prevented my running out this morning, and there has been this collision nevertheless. That will do."

Chillingworth shut the gate, shut the door, and Charles Lester and I stood face to face. "Good for you," he said. "Always stand up for your rights. Well, I'd better get moving. I don't want a chill, and these are no clothes to stand about in."

I thought: He'll go, and I'll return to that horrid little hotel, and then I'll catch the train to Truro and never see him again. I said: "Do you run every morning?"

He said: "Oh, yes. In Hyde Park. Hail, rain or snow."

"We rarely have snow in Cornwall. Indeed, I've never seen any. Not there, anyway. But there are people who have."

He was prancing up and down to keep warm, gripping a piece of wood in each hand. "I should hate that," he said. "I rather like snow."

"I don't mind it," I said. "It's so white."

"Yes, I suppose it is, when you come to think of it. Well –"

"But I shouldn't think it's too good to run in. What weather do you like best for running?"

"Look," he said, "you write me a nice long thesis on Cornish weather, and I'll do you one on running. How's that?"

But still I didn't want to see him go. I was wondering what else to say, and also I was feeling a perfect fool because of all I had said so far, when the front door opened and a voice shouted: "Get going, lad. D'you want to catch your death of cold?" and Charles Lester said, I feared gladly: "Right, sir," and shot off without another word.

The man at the door said: "Come up 'ere, lass," and I walked trembling up the steps. I saw that, fixed to the right of the door, was a small brass plate: Sir George Lester, M.P.

"Now, lass," he said. "Is there owt I can do for you?"

"I'm afraid not, sir," I said. "I was just passing by and stopped to have a look at the house because my sister used to live in it. But," I added to placate him, for he was a formidable man, "it looks much nicer now than it did then. My sister was married to Mr Wheatstone, the philanthropist, and," I said primly, "I fear he didn't care much for worldly estate."

"Ah could've told you that," he said. "When I bought the place it were a fair pig-sty. Charity begins at 'ome, I say, so Ah've done myself proud. Come an' 'ave a look at it."

This odd turn of events left me too confused to notice much. A general hint of richness expressed mainly in gold, blue and crimson was all I could take in. I paused to look at a portrait of an old gentleman with a thin aristocratic face and eyes like blue ice. "So that's where the eyes come from," I thought, with Charles Lester, not his father, in mind.

"D'you like that?" Sir George asked.

"He's got a wonderful face," I said.

"It's my old father – a proper old devil if ever there was one," he said, looking affectionately at the portrait.

"He looks an aristocrat."

"Meaning I don't, eh? Well, never be taken in by faces. I've known peers with pedigrees as long as your arm and the faces of pork butchers. And there's my old father and there's me. And come to that there's that boy of mine. A proper see-saw. This chap," he said, indicating the portrait, "kept a barber's shop in Bacup. He were a Wesleyan local preacher and didn't smoke or drink. What's more, 'e leathered 'ell out of me with a razor-strop when I began to do a bit o' both. I were twenty-one at the time an' could've bent 'im in two with one 'and. But I took it. That's the sort o' man 'e was, and of course I should've 'ated him. But Ah didn't, you know. I admired 'im, an' I saw to it," said Sir George with an inflation of the chest, "that 'e rose in the social scale as I did. Spinning — that's 'ow I made my brass, but we needn't go into that. When I got elected to Parliament I bought this 'ouse an' brought 'im down to live with me. He were ninety then, but I 'ad time to get that painted. It's by W. P. Frith — you know, the chap that paints railway stations an' things like that. 'Owever, 'e'd painted Charles Dickens, an' that was good enough for me. I 'ope you read Charles Dickens. You know, that portrait makes me think of Little Nell's grandfather in *The Old Curiosity Shop*. Which only goes to show because, believe me, even when 'e was ninety 'e gave me a clout one day across the head with 'is walking-stick that fair dazzled me."

He looked long and affectionately at the portrait and said: "Ay, the terror of Bacup 'e were. 'E'd lam 'ell out of sin and sinners alike."

Mr Lester was evidently so proud of his house and his father and his son and himself that he would be ready to go on talking at the slightest push, and I so much wanted him to do so that I said: "So you are from Lancashire, sir. I have friends there. My sister married the son of a Mr Oldham who lives out at Bowdon."

"Well, Ah'll be damned now," he said. "Fancy that. The world's a small place. Ah knew Bill Oldham well all through my working life, and Ah watched that boy of his grow up. Pity 'e became a parson. Ah'm a religious man, mind you, but I always regret it when a lad becomes a parson. My old man wanted me to be a Wesleyan parson, but I thought to hell with that for a lark when there's the Lancashire cotton trade to chew at."

I said: "I'm rather used to parsons, sir. My father's one. It's been the family trade for generations."

"Well, Ah'm not denying it's a respectable trade so far as it goes, and if that's the way a lad's fancy lies, good luck to 'im. So I sent Bill Oldham's lad a damn great silver rose bowl. Fancy that, now. At this very moment p'raps your sister is sitting down to breakfast with that bowl on the table. And another of your sisters lived in this house. Well – we're almost related!"

He beamed upon me with such evident good-will that I said hurriedly: "I'm afraid I've intruded, sir. I must be off," hoping for a disclaimer of this idea, which came so promptly that I began to fancy myself as a diplomat.

"Nay, lass," he said. "Wait till that lad of mine gets back, and 'ave a bit o' breakfast."

"That's very kind of you, sir."

"Not at all. Come on in 'ere."

We had been standing in the hall, and now moved into the drawing room. It had been Mr Wheatstone's office. I recalled its repellent dinginess and marvelled at the change. It seemed to me hopelessly over-furnished, gross with comfort; and, sitting by the warm hearth whence, I remembered, a sullen eye of fire was all that once looked out; and feeling under my feet the rich carpet where a cold linoleum had lain; considering the opulent couch standing precisely where Mr Wheatstone's paper-burdened table had been, I pondered the contrasting too much and too little. Sir George Lester stood with his back to the fire, and, as though guessing my thoughts, he said: "Ah suppose this is a bit different from what Mr Wheatstone had here? A queer bird that was from all one heard about him."

"Yes, sir," I said. "He was not a *usual* sort of man."

"Neither am I," he said quickly, as though fearing my words belittled him. "If you'd seen the sitting room behind that shop in Bacup! Couldn't swing a cat. Well, Ah made up my mind to get out of it, and Ah got out of it. Ah used to watch the bosses drivin' up in their carriages and pairs, and Ah said to myself: 'George, that's you one of these days,' and Ah *made* it so. It's one thing to give away the brass someone else 'as made, an' quite another to make it for yourself."

He looked around the room as though to draw strength from its opulence, and said: "There's reason in everything, lass. Remember that. Ah've got a charity list as long as my arm. So long as the rich do their duty to the poor and the Liberal Party remains in existence things won't go far wrong. And Salisbury won't be Prime Minister for ever."

He was taking me out of my very humble depths, and I was not sorry to hear a rush of feet going upstairs. "Well, that's Charles back," he said. "We sha'n't be long now. I named 'im Charles after Dickens." Remembering Coketown, Mr Merdle, and one or two other things, I thought this strange, but let it go; and soon, sitting in the dining room, I had something else to think about. Charles had come down from taking a shower. He was glowing. Almost literally, he shone; and if some small antagonism had been creeping into my mind, roused by Sir George's self-satisfaction, it evaporated as his enslavement to his son became evident.

Charles seemed not at all surprised by my presence. Nothing, I imagine, ever surprised him. Life had been a golden tree for him to shake, and down fell all he wanted. "Well, my boy," his father said, "this young woman is nearly one of our relatives. One of her sisters is Mrs Wheatstone, who used to live in this house, and another of 'em is married to young Hugo Oldham. You remember Hugo?"

"Yes, I do, sir. Didn't he become a parson?"

"Ay, 'e did that. 'E 'ad a mind of his own and made it up. Not like some I could name." He gave Charles an adoring glance, as though this inability to make up his mind, which rightly or wrongly he imputed to him, were a rare and precious gift that the gods bestowed on few.

"But, sir, I have made up my mind. You know that very well. I intend to make the name of Lester known the world over."

"There's nowt wrong with the name Lester. Ah've lifted it off the board over a barber's shop an' put it on t'plate outside yon door." It was evident that never in any circumstances was the barber's shop to be forgotten, nor the wonder-chick hatched there, to develop into this senatorial swan. He almost swelled before my eyes like those swans on our creek who, in their most prideful moments, could arrange themselves into shapes of classic arrogance.

Charles looked at him affectionately. Their mutual admiration made me feel uneasy. I couldn't imagine Father and Roger going on like this. I preferred their way of taking one another for granted, decent but by no means peerless.

"What this lad lacks," said Sir George, taking my plate over to the sideboard and lashing it up with kedgeree, "is ambition. Ah've brought 'im up soft. What d'you think, Miss . . . Well, dammit, Ah don't even know your name!"

"Legassick," I said, "Maria Legassick."

"Well, Miss Maria Legassick, what do *you* think – kick 'em out to sink or swim, or keep 'em wrapped up in life jackets?"

I was embarrassed, but I managed to say: "I haven't given it any thought, sir; but I should think there's something to be said for teaching them to swim and then kicking them out. However, it's none of my business."

I must have spoken the last words rather crossly, for all at once Charles Lester became serious. "Father," he said, "you mustn't embarrass Miss Legassick, and you mustn't give her the impression that I'm a loafer. I work very hard."

A shadow passed over the old man's face. "You'll never be a W. P. Frith," he said.

"No, sir. I've reconciled myself to that."

" 'E paints, tha knows," Sir George explained, "but 'e paints the daftest stuff. Frith charged me a thousand guineas for that picture of my father. I tried to beat him down to pounds, but he wouldn't have it. Now that's what I call a painter."

Charles looked at him, still fondly, but sadly. Sir George got up. "Well," he said, "excuse me. Ah'm seeing a man at the National Liberal Club."

Charles said: "I wonder whether Miss Legassick would care to see some of my pictures?"

"I'm in London only for a day," I explained, "and I have some shopping to do."

He looked disappointed, so I added: "Still, if I'm allowed to stay . . . I think I could do my few errands this afternoon."

We watched Sir George set off in a hansom cab, then turned back into the house. I followed Charles up the stairs to a room that I remembered well – the room that Louisa and I had shared ten years ago, the smallish room looking north upon uninspiring buildings. But now it could at least be warm. Charles put a match to a gas-fire, and did not at once begin, as I had expected, to show me pictures. There were plenty in the room, with their faces to the wall, and there was an easel, and a trestle table with pots full of brushes and the paraphernalia I expected in a studio, though I had not before been in one. There was a long wicker chair, and he pulled it round to face the fire and put me into it. He sat on the mat alongside. I could look down on his curly head. I felt a mad desire to stroke those curls. I didn't much want to see the pictures. I was no judge of pictures. A few not very good prints of too-well-known old masters, decorating the walls at home, were about all the pictures I had seen. But I wanted just to sit there, in that room where I had once been oppressed by desolation, and where now I did not dare to speak or to move because I was spell-bound. At that moment, Charles had nothing to do with Sir George Lester and his too banal story of the rise from rags to riches, nothing to do with the over-furnished house and the stifling opulence. I had happily been conditioned against feeling moved by such things; but I had not been conditioned against the emotions that now stirred me. I don't know what to say about it. I shall be laughed at. But if the old tag of the novelists was ever true, it was true of me: I was knocked out by love at first sight. That the father of the man who had done this to me was even now riding in a cab to the National Liberal Club seemed to me the most incongruous thing in the world. I waited for Charles to speak, and at last he said: "I am so unhappy."

We were strangers. There was nothing I could say to so flat and final a statement. After a moment, he said: "I'm so sick of being my father's son. I'd give anything to do something that would put me completely apart from him, so that when people said Lester they thought at once of me, not of him."

"Perhaps you will."

"Did you know," he said, "that the great Turner was born in a barber's shop?"

"No. I'm very ignorant about painting and painters. I'm afraid I sha'n't be able to say anything intelligent about the pictures you show me."

"Oh, I didn't really ask you here to see pictures. I just wanted someone to talk to. Well, Turner's father had a barber's shop in Maiden Lane. But it was Turner who got out of it, not the old man, and so he didn't have to endure the ghastly feeling of everlasting indebtedness. All that stuff my father was talking – should we kick 'em out or coddle 'em? – that was just meaningless. I've got no ambition, he says, but that's the last thing he wants me to have. I represent for him the success of his own ambitions, and that's how he likes it to be."

He got up from the floor and looked out at the grey London morning. "The dickens of it is," he said, "that I *do* admire him. It's all very well to laugh at the rags-to-riches story, as I expect you do. People talk as though making money is just a bad habit that northern men get into. All the same, there's not one in a hundred thousand who can do it. And I've got nothing to complain about. He sent me to a good school, though not one of the super-posh sort, thank God; and when I said I didn't want to go on to a university, he said very well, that was up to me. Because by then I was thinking of painting. We had an art master at school who thought I was pretty good, though that's not much to go on. Schools are full of kids who are pretty good and who haven't the foggiest notion what a hell it is to become *very* good. And if I can't become very good I don't want it."

"Why don't you have a real talk with your father about it?"

He came back from the window and plumped down again on the rug. "That's the one thing you can't do," he said. "I've tried it. He's kindness itself, but he just hasn't an inkling of what I'm after. He feels that a son of his should be *born* an R.A., and that an artist who isn't an R.A. is some sort of scrubby ruffian . . . Oh, I can't explain it. It's like trying to fight a well-intentioned cloud of fog."

I asked him if he had had any lessons since leaving school, and he said: "Yes. There's a man in Chelsea I go to. I keep it dark and pay him out of my own pocket. I'm never kept short of money."

"And what does the man in Chelsea think of you?"

"I haven't the faintest idea, except that he tears me to pieces. I don't think I'm much good, really."

"And what would your father like you to do? Doesn't he suggest anything?"

"He wants me to study for the bar – says it'll be a great help when I enter Parliament, which, of course, is what he really wants. You see, that way I'd go on sprouting from his own branch. I wouldn't be a sport. Meantime, I must keep fit. The daily run and all that, with Chillingworth to open the door and waft me forth."

"Do you know what I'd do?" I asked, and I imagine I sounded belligerent, thinking of determined characters like Uncle Reginald and Louisa.

"Oh," he said, smiling for the first time, "a person with a fierce little face like yours, a person who tells Chillingworth where he gets off, would suggest something desperate."

"If I *really* wanted to paint, I'd tell 'em all to go to the dickens. If necessary, I'd walk out and live on tuppence a week, and I'd paint."

"Ah," he said with a sigh, "it's easier to walk out of poverty, as Father did, than to walk out of riches."

"I'm not talking about what's easy," I said with fine moral fervour. "If you want to go on being a schoolboy who's pretty good, all right. But you told me yourself that you realised there was more to it than that."

I was overwhelmed with a feeling that he was as weak as he was beautiful. "You began this conversation," I said, "by saying that you were very unhappy. Well, I'm not surprised."

I didn't want to see his pictures. There was nothing I could say to him about pictures, anyway. I got up. "I must be off."

He was still smiling, and I wondered how much a pose, a self-defence, his sorrow had been. He said: "How wonderful to be so resolute."

I looked at him, and my own sorrow was without pretence, without limit. I held out my hand mutely. "I'll come down," he said.

Chillingworth opened the door and Charles waved from the steps. Manchester Square seemed as glum as it had been in Mr Wheatstone's day.

10

I reached home the next day in the evening, and I was somehow not surprised to find Louisa there. St Tudno is a changeless sort of place. Three wars have rolled over our heads since then. I have seen American troops quartered outside our vicarage gate, but the buildings they put up are gone and briars sprout from the foundations, and the red posting-box in the wall of the byre is still inscribed V.R., though five monarchs have reigned since the old lady went home. It seemed natural that anybody, even Louisa, should come back to St Tudno and take up where she had left off. That is what she was doing. When I had eaten, Father said: "Well, I must get up to my work. By the way, Louisa is back. You'll find her in the loft." She had been away for about fifteen years, but he said it as though she had just returned from taking tea in Falmouth. I found her in the loft, with a log fire burning, working away at the old job on Father's manuscript. I sat down gladly, my toes stretched to the flame. She put down her pen and sat on the floor near me. I handed her the letter I had found under her dressing table at Dorking. "I've read it," I said. "It's fifteen years since I buried Euphemia Emmett."

She saw the connection; and I saw, as if in comment on the passage of time, a streak of grey in her hair.

"Yes," she said. "It's been a long time."

This was an admission – the first admission into Louisa's intimacy that I had ever known. And she had not flown out at me for reading the letter. I was emboldened to ask: "What are you going to do about it?"

She said: "I shall marry him."

There was a time, I suppose, when the thought of a Legassick girl married into the splendour of Tregannock would have thrown me into wild romantic speculation; but now I thought less of the great house and the renowned gardens. I thought of James Polperro. I knew little of him, but I had guessed much, and I had been able to piece together more or less accurately the outlines of the story that began (so far as I was concerned) under the yew tree fifteen years ago, when Louisa was younger than I was now. I had fitted it all in, and even the reference to the day at Richmond when Lady Mary Polperro was still alive – even that had slipped, not inaccurately as I was to discover, into its right place. I said: "Do you think you should?"

"Yes," said Louisa, and then sat gazing at the sparks flying upwards as though considering her own brief answer. "I know," she said after a time, "that it won't be what it once could have been. I've had fifteen hard and lonely years. I'm not complaining about that. I'm thankful for them. But they might have been the end of me instead of the beginning, and that would have been James Polperro's fault. Perhaps it's an advantage to marry without illusion, and I certainly sha'n't start with the illusion that my husband is faultless. He's a very weak man."

She said after a pause: "But I should have liked to discover his weaknesses gradually. That's one of the advantages of marrying when you are what people call madly in love. Your emotion is a buffer that absorbs all sorts of shocks. When you find he isn't *this,* you reflect that at all events he is *that*; and so it goes on till two far from perfect people adjust themselves to one another and make something that takes a lot of breaking up. I imagine that this process of adjustment is the most worthwhile thing in a marriage, and I've been done out of all that."

I said: "It isn't according to Miss Braddon or Mrs Henry Wood to discuss a marriage so rationally."

Louisa smiled. "Miss Braddon," she said, "was at any rate rational enough to marry her publisher; and if you think there's much that's rational in the present situation you're mistaken. I made a hideous marriage when I was weak and ill. If I were a rational being, it would have warned me off marriage for life. However, one day out with James Polperro, when I met him by accident, shocked me into the discovery that, despite all he had done to me, I'd commit adultery with him for two pins."

I was disturbed by the word. It was not one we were accustomed to hear in the vicarage except when Father read the lessons, and he read it as smoothly as though it meant no more than a kiss in the lane. And even that was unthinkable unless the kisser were pledged to marry the kissed. "Which is all very well if you don't look behind the tombstones on a dark night," as I once, when I shouldn't, heard Thomas May say to Mrs Solway.

"What have you told Father?" I asked.

Louisa got up, and for the first time in her life, so far as I remember, put her arms round me and kissed me. "Nothing yet," she said. "But don't worry and don't moralise. We'll see how things go."

11

Uncle Reginald told me later that he met Lady Jane Kopf and James Polperro strolling together in the garden. She said: "Mr Pallace, I believe that you and Mr Polperro come from the same part of the country?"

"Yes, my lady."

"Then I'm sure he'll have a lot to talk to you about. My subjects seem to bore him. I loathe the thought of shooting partridges, grouse, pheasants or stags. I hate the idea of getting fun out of watching hounds chase hares or foxes. Horses are so large that they terrify me. Why don't people use zebras? They are much smaller and so charming. I must ask Sir Ernest about it. He has large interests in Africa. Do you think they could be trained to draw a small carriage?

There's a lovely line in Keats: *Not chariotted by Bacchus and his pards.* Pards are out of the question. But what do you think of zebras?"

"They're not in my line, my lady. I've seen more of llamas, and they only carry packs."

"You have had a wonderful life," she said. "We must have a long talk about it some day."

She was carrying a cane in one hand and in the other a volume of poetry bound in puce leather. She pointed with her cane at a rhododendron. "Where does that come from?"

"From the forests up over the Salween river. A marvellous country. I remember I was shot at there by bandits. Very old-fashioned. They used bows and arrows."

"There, you see," she said. "That's the sort of thing I mean. We must have some long talks."

Poor James Polperro had been forgotten. He had fallen behind her and was kicking at the peaty soil of the path. She walked on as though he had not been with her, and then he shook hands with Uncle Reginald. "I went down to your cottage soon after you'd left this morning, Mr Pallace. I was looking for your niece Louisa. A young woman there told me she's no longer with you."

Uncle Reginald said: "She's a very unpredictable girl, Mr Polperro. Years ago she cleared out of St Tudno all of a hop, and all of a hop she left Mr Wheatstone while she was still married to him. I wasn't a bit surprised when I came home the other day to find that she'd left me, too."

James said ungallantly: "I can't stand that posing chatterbox of a woman. I met her once or twice when she was a girl, and she was just the same then. Kopf is all right. But I wouldn't have put up with his wife even for his sake if I hadn't thought your niece would be here."

Uncle Reginald looked at him gravely. He was remembering the morning long ago when he was out in a dinghy on our creek, catching his breakfast. He was remembering how he saw James ride away and Louisa, perturbed, come out of the graveyard, and how from that moment, the thought of leaving St Tudno had overpowered her. He had helped her: he had introduced her to Mr Wheatstone, and the responsibility of having done that was heavy on him. It had led to a disaster. Well, in a way. He had seen too much to think of life as something predestined to run on smooth tramlines. What some might call a disaster he could think of as an experience, adding to the stature of the person it had befallen. If the person had any stature to be added to. Certainly Louisa had. She was not now the child who had brooded rather hopelessly at his side during that long and far-off day on Pendennis Head. "I thought," he said to me frankly, "that she had become a person rather outsize for a man like Polperro."

He said to James: "A long time ago, Mr Polperro, I was on my way to Tregannock to see your father, and I looked in at the smithy to have a chat. You were there having your horse shod, and you said you'd been out for a very early morning ride. D'you remember?"

"Yes. I vaguely do."

"Is it really so vague as all that? Hadn't that ride been rather memorable?"

My uncle said that James flushed and became at once the squire addressing the gardener. "I don't think," he said, "that we can continue this conversation if you are going to be impertinent."

"If you think frankness is impertinence," Uncle Reginald said, "I advise you to leave Louisa alone. You won't find her the girl you played with and deserted."

For a moment, the Polperro need to be deferred to made the air thunderous. "Old Polperro was genial enough," my uncle said to me, "so long as he was the Lord God Almighty. But only as long as that. Everything with him was grace and favour, not a right. But young James never measured up to his father – not even in that."

James said at last: "I'm sorry, Mr Pallace. If you know where Louisa is, I'd be glad if you'd tell me."

"I don't know," Uncle said, "but as a guess I'd say she's at St Tudno, waiting for you."

12

About a month after this I followed Father up to his study, when breakfast was over, to pick up my day's stint of manuscript. He said: "Sit down, my dear, for a moment. Have you heard this surprising news?"

"What news is that, Father?"

"Louisa tells me she is going to marry Mr Polperro."

"Yes, I knew that."

He sat looking at me across his wide desk like a headmaster who never ceases to wonder at the extraordinary things young people get up to.

"Most remarkable," he said. "Most remarkable. Does Bella know?"

"Yes. I wrote and told her."

"Does Roger know?"

"I believe Louisa wrote to him."

He took off his steel-rimmed spectacles and rubbed his eyes. He seemed an oddly isolated person, sitting there with everything just so on his desk, as I had always known it: Mother's photograph in a green plush frame; a plaster bust of Dean Farrar, whose *Life of St Paul* he was ever urging me to read; a few bits of pottery from Egypt, fruit of the only journey he had made out of England; the ivory paperknife; the ornate inkstand; the pen-wiper; the tattered Greek dictionary; the neat pile of quarto sheets on the left of the blotting-pad; the few sheets that he had written upon yesterday under a paper-weight on the right.

"What would you say, Maria?" he asked gravely. "Am I a parent to be shunned? Do you young people dislike me? Or is there something about me that creates a barrier between us? Do you not think it a little odd that so important a matter should be communicated to me now – when every other member of the family has known it for some time?"

I was deeply embarrassed. We all loved him – except, perhaps, Louisa; but he was not a reciprocating man. Even when we were children, he had rarely kissed us, never sported with us nonsensically. He was at first a figure of awe, withdrawn upon tasks that we believed to be profound, and then he became a figure of pathos, a scholar isolated among rustic boors, turning more and more from them inward upon matters which, frankly, we did not think to have much importance. Roger already was as good a scholar, and I remembered how, ever and again, he would light up his scholarship with a comment, a laugh, a joke, that flashed brightly out of his own contemporary mind. They are finding uranium now in the old disused Cornish tin mines. That was the difference between Roger and Father. Roger could find the uranium amid the antiquated workings that were, for Father, things in themselves.

How could the youngest Legassick girl – though now she was twenty! – say anything of this to Father?

I said merely: "I'm afraid we're an odd lot, sir. After all, Louisa is my sister, but she never wrote me a line during all the years she was away."

He surprised me by saying: "I don't know that I shall be able to conduct the marriage service. Louisa mentioned her marriage to me merely, so far as I can see, to lay down conditions. For one thing, she wants me not to read the banns. She says it would serve no purpose but to fill the church with staring villagers, and she doesn't want that."

I said: "She is a widow and Mr Polperro is a widower. I can understand that they would prefer to be married without fuss."

I suppose it was an unfortunate word. "The form of the solemnisation of matrimony," he said, "is not *fussy*. It is designed to safeguard the civil rights of those concerned, and also to satisfy the laws of God. It specifically says that the banns shall be published on three Sundays, and who am I to presume to disobey the directions laid down for the government of my actions?"

He picked up yesterday's writing and handed it to me. "Thank you, Maria," he said, "for giving me your attention." I don't think he meant it ironically. He hadn't an ironical mind. He took up a few new sheets, put them on to the writing-pad, and dipped his pen into the ink. This was dismissal, and I went across to the loft.

James and Louisa were married in London. They went down to the South of France and did not appear at Tregannock until May of the next year, which was 1898.

CHAPTER FIVE

I F YOU were walking from the vicarage to the village, the creek
was on your right hand all the way. When half the journey was
made, you were at the point where you had water at all times: but
beyond this were mud-flats when the tide was out. Just here the land
moved out into the water, forming a small promontory. Its extent was
no more than a third of an acre, but it enchanted me. The building
upon it fell halfway between being a cottage and a house, and this
building was not clearly visible because, just inside the rusty iron gate,
there were tall conifers. The house had a secret air. From its windows
you could look at low tide eastward to the mouth of the creek where
the swans would be floating on the sparkling water and the oak trees
grew along the northern bank, or westward to the flats where the
curlews were running and crying and sandpipers foraged in the mud,
and the northward land flattened into a beach with pasture behind it.
From my childhood days the place had fascinated me. It had seemed,
isolated there in our land which itself was isolated enough, a perfect
home for a witch, and thus awe was an ingredient of my fascination. I
knew it well, inside and out, because it was on Father's visiting list and
I sometimes made the calls with him. The old lady who lived alone
there was reputed to be a hundred years old, and had been so reputed
ever since I had known her, as though a century was enough to be
going on with and one could stop and have a good rest there before
going any farther. I liked it best if our calls on Mrs Mitchell were
made in the winter when, at tea time, the light would be fading and
we would pass through the darkness under the conifers to the dark
door and, on our knocking, Mrs Mitchell would come shuffling along
her passage, open the door an inch, and ask suspiciously "Who's
there?" before, on hearing Father's reassuring voice, she would further

open the door, leaving a gap just wide enough for us to squeeze through. Then, in her small drawing room, I could give myself up fully to the contemplation of her witch-like attributes: the thin claws, the cheeks chiselled, as it pleased me to think, with innumerable sorrows, as desolate land is chiselled by the flow of waters, her black cat opening upon us now and then green slits of eyes from its place on the rag mat by the fire, her parrot which never spoke but would now and then burst into shrill laughter, as though the contemplation of human beings stirred ironic thoughts. Mrs Mitchell was dressed always in black, with a white fichu at her neck, embellished with a gold brooch carved into the shape of a negro's head. The room was lit by what seemed to me a fantastic number of candles. They burned on the mantelpiece and on the table and on occasional tables, and as she had a weakness for lustre-ware the room was full of twinkles as the candle-light shone on cups and saucers, teapots and jugs, and porcelain plaques inscribed with warning texts: *Thou God seest Me. Prepare to meet Thy God. The Trumpet shall Sound.* I loved the way the candleshine caused these menacing texts to twinkle, almost as though they were smiling, almost as though saying: "Don't worry. It'll be all right on the night."

Mrs Mitchell had an old-fashioned fireplace with a hob on which a kettle was always simmering, so that in no time at all she would have made tea and produced a barrel of ginger biscuits. Father would talk to her of this and that, but she said little in answer. At the end of half an hour or so she would say: "Well, I suppose you're in a hurry, vicar. Don't let me detain you," and this remark always threw the parrot into a gale of mad laughter and caused the black cat to unveil an emerald sliver, as though to be sure we were taking the hint. We always did. What surprised people was that her only other visitor was Mr Polperro – not James but his father. My father once said to me on one of those nights when we were homeward bound from the cottage: "Mr Polperro tells me that Mrs Mitchell was very beautiful when she was a girl. She was a lady-in-waiting to Queen Victoria." And that is all I ever knew about my witch who lived at the cottage called Little in Sight. When the wind was howling and I was tucked into bed, I would think of her and of all that she must have had in sight as she looked backward through her years. I would wonder whether the wealth of candles was a protest against the Prince Consort who was so stingy with the candles at the palace.

2

Soon after Louisa had gone to live at Tregannock I was taking a walk along the creek. It was May of 1899. Flowing out of the hillside on my left, the spring that comes down there through an earthenware pipe was singing and sparkling. It was an exceptionally hot day and I stopped to drink, making a cup of my hands. I had heard footsteps coming along behind me, and now they halted and a voice said: "I say, is that all right? Is that water good to drink?"

I turned and faced a tall thin man, dressed from head to foot in white linen. He had a pointed golden beard and grey-blue eyes. I liked the look of him. "Try it," I said.

He did so, and smiled, the water dripping in sparkling drops from his fingers. "By God," he said, "that's good."

"It ought to be," I assured him. "It's the best water you'll find anywhere about here. And it's never been known to fail. Not even when a drought lasts all through the summer."

He drank again, and said: "By God! Yes, that's good. You know, in France one hardly dares to touch a drop of water, and in my cottage down the road there's a well. I loathe sweating at that. I'll bring a bucket up here every day and get a fill."

"You're living about here then?" I asked.

"Yes, in a place called Little in Sight. Whoever called it that must be as blind as a bat."

Mrs Mitchell had been dead for a year, and I had heard that her house was now occupied. Father had said only that morning that he must call on the new occupier. But he was never in a hurry about that sort of thing.

We walked together towards Little in Sight, and at the gate he said: "Would you like to peep in?"

"Well," I said, "I've known it all my life. My father's the vicar here. I'm Maria Legassick."

"I'm Gerald Pickering," he said, "an artist sick of Chelsea. We get our water through lead pipes. Odious stuff. By God! That stuff you've got is *alive*."

He didn't seem able to get over our water.

"But as I say," he added, "you just can't drink water in France. A bit hard on a teetotaller like me. I spent a fortune on bottled stuff."

We were on the path under the conifers, walking towards the door.

"Were you in France for long?" I asked.

"Three years. Oh God! The liberation after English painting. I knew Monet."

"I'm afraid I don't," I said. "Who is he?"

"Oh, God!" he said, flinging open his front door. "You don't know Monet?" He groaned.

I had no time to think of Monet, so surprised was I at the transformation of the witch's lair. Everything was white. "Wonderful," said Mr Pickering, "what a scraper and a whitewash brush will do. For the last fortnight I haven't looked at an easel. Scrape – whitewash. Scrape – whitewash. From morning to night. My God. Fatiguing."

A plummy gloom had been Mrs Mitchell's fancy. Now the place was suddenly radiant and twice as big. There was hardly a stick of furniture in it. "I'm more or less camping out," Mr Pickering explained. "I'll furnish gradually – as more and more people come to know Monet. To say nothing of Manet and Renoir."

He looked at me, as though hoping I might at least have heard of these two, but I shook my head.

"My God!" he said. "Well, well. Look in again sometime. Perhaps I'll have a bit of work to show you. Now I'm off to get a bucket of hippocrene."

He came with me to the gate and went one way, I another. I looked back, and he was watching me and waved the bucket in a friendly sort of way.

3

I was on my way to Tregannock. One didn't boggle at walking a few miles in those days. As I went, with the spring bursting about my head – birds, flowers, water, all seemed incandescent – I thought of Mr Gerald Pickering and regretted that I must have seemed an ignorant oaf to him. Still, some people knew one thing and some another. I doubted whether he knew what a supralapsarian was. Next time he popped out one of his French painters, I'd ask him.

At the head of the creek I turned right and crossed the bridge into the village. The tide was full, blue under the blue sky, warm-looking in the balmy Cornish air. Creamy fountains of pampas grass sprang up in the cottage gardens, and women were there hanging out the Monday wash; and as I went by and waved to them I was aware of something new in their attitude to me, something a shade more deferential, and unhappily therefore a shade more cold and reserved, than the old greeting I could count on when I was nothing but the parson's maiden. Now I was Mrs Polperro's sister.

Well, there it was. This was the great house that I had approached with awe, holding Uncle Reginald's hand, so long ago; and now I was approaching it alone, and a woodman who passed me as I walked the path leading through the fields to the house raised his hat formally. There was a time when a flick of the finger in the general direction of the right ear would have served his purpose.

I went round the house and followed the path to the small disused chapel which belonged to the day when the Polperros didn't lumber to St Tudno church in their great coach but kept their private date with the Lord. I went there now because, of all the places in our region, this was the one I most delighted in for an enlargement of vision. The gold of the oak-wood falling down the escarpment towards the Truro road was already turning green, and over it, against the blue sky, were two pairs of buzzards, now poised, now in swooping flight, majestic and unbound, so that one's spirit rejoiced with them, soared with them, and was expanded.

I turned at the sound of a footstep, and there was Meg Newman, rosy and blooming. "Good morning, Miss Maria. Mrs Polperro saw you going round, and hopes you'll be coming in and staying to lunch."

"Yes, Meg, say that I'd like to do that. How do you find life at Tregannock?"

"Oh, I've come to a good end," she said.

I laughed. "You've hardly come to an end yet, I hope. Did you expect to come to a bad one?"

"Well, that's what old Mother Martin always said. You remember old Mother Martin at Mr Wheatstone's?"

I did indeed.

"Gosh, what a pair! It's 'er Mr Wheatstone oughter've married, not Miss Louisa. They'd 'ave brought forth dragons," she said with such relish that the scaly rattling of this progeny on the cold linoleum of Manchester Square could almost be heard.

"Wheat is something now," Meg said, plunging deeper into fantasy. "And what's more, Miss Maria, it's something good. There wasn't no wheat about *him*. Grindstone, that's what I called him to myself – a proper old grindstone. And old Mother Martin was another. 'You keep out of Bond Street,' she used to say to me. 'You know what the johnnies goes lurking there for. You'll come to a bad end.' But now I've got the laugh of her, because I've come to a good end. All right. I'll tell Mrs Polperro you'll be in for lunch. Goodbye for now."

When I went in, Louisa was coming down the grand stairway that once I had seen Lady Mary Lacey descend. I said: "Who is Monet?"

I expected Louisa to be taken aback, but not she. Without so much as a smile at what seemed to me an odd question, she said: "Come up to my room."

It was a small, beautiful room on the first floor, and the window commanded the view I had been admiring. The floor was carpeted in warm gold and the walls were painted a pale matt green. The fireplace was of white marble, and over it was the only picture in the room. "That is a Monet," Louisa said.

A girl in filmy white clothes, with a pale blue parasol sloped back across her shoulder, was in a boat on a river. A young man in a straw hat was rowing her. The sun flooded down, on the young people, on the water, on the willows that grew along the bank. That was all.

I once, in a moment of earnest gush, said: "Father, what is the purpose of Art?"

He looked at me gravely, then at the dark brown atrocious reproduction of Holman Hunt's *Light of the World*, which was on his study wall. "The purpose of art, my dear," he said, "is the glorification of God."

In the light of this, my only art instruction till now, I looked at the picture. I told Louisa of my question to Father and of his reply. "Well, yes," she said. "I should say that defines this picture."

I was baffled, feeling, as I had so often felt in Louisa's presence, the young girl who had a lot to learn.

"Who are Manet and Renoir?" I asked.

She smiled. "What has raised such questions at St Tudno?"

I told her of my encounter with Gerald Pickering, and his name excited her. "Good heavens," she said. "You don't tell me he's living on our creek? He's good, you know. I must go and see what he's doing."

We sat on a sofa facing the window, with the warm May air fanning the muslin of the curtain. "You probably learned from Uncle Reginald," she said, "that I used to spend a lot of time in Paris when I was a buyer. Well, the chief of one of the firms I dealt with was tremendously excited about painting. He often took me out to lunch or dinner, and he always chose the places where students and painters went to eat. They all knew him, and I got thoroughly soaked in their chatter. Monet, Manet, Renoir, and a few others were their gods, and my friend took to showing me round the galleries and exhibitions and studios where their work could be seen. Well, that's enough of that. You see how it was. I became infected. As for your man Gerald Pickering, I heard his name mentioned once or twice as a disciple of these Frenchmen, and later on I went to one of his shows in London. I loved his stuff, but this way of painting hasn't excited anyone in England yet, and he didn't sell a thing. I'd have bought one myself, but I was too hard up. That Monet is James' wedding present to me. We found it in Paris during our honeymoon. He still wonders why on earth I wanted it."

4

A few days later, looking from our garden down into the graveyard, I saw Gerald Pickering reading the inscriptions on the stones. He was again wearing white linen and a floppy black felt hat. He had a portfolio under his arm. He saw me and waved his hand, then walked up to our wall.

I said: "What is a supralapsarian?"

He looked a little surprised and said: "A parson's daughter ought to know that."

"Do *you* know it?" I challenged him.

He sat on the wall and said lightly: "You can't catch me out on those old Calvinist bits of nonsense. My God, fancy sane men being willing to tear one another's ears off for things like that! Or were they sane?"

I said: "You are dodging my question."

"Oh, yes. And I intend to go on doing so. I dodged that sort of question years ago, once and for all. Come and have a drink."

I must have looked shocked. He said: "I mean the true, the blushful hippocrene."

"Ah, you know your Keats!" It was one of my touchstones.

"I do that. More Keats, less Calvin. That's my simple recipe for salvation."

We walked together along the creek path towards the spring. The swans were on the water, proudly parental, their biscuit-brown babies tagging behind.

"Better than Balham," he said briefly.

"Have you lived in Balham?"

"Well, if you can call it living. I was born there and I remained there dying till I was seventeen. Then I was born again. My mother kept a greengrocer's shop, and brought me up a good little Calvinist, so that I could tell you more than you can tell me about supralapsarians and infralapsarians."

He gave me a sly laughing glance.

"She died," he said, "when I was seventeen, and left me five hundred pounds. There's one good thing to be said about a greengrocer's shop. It's full of colour. I was for ever painting piles of oranges, apples, cabbages and parsnips. I could paint you a carrot now that would make a donkey follow me hee-hawing from here to Truro. Well, good health."

He cupped the water and drank. I did the same. "Good health," I said. We walked on towards Little in Sight.

"Fortunately," he said, "my mother owned the little shop. I was able to sell it, with what they call the goodwill, for another five hundred. Then I proceeded to be born again."

"Did you go to Paris?"

"Not right away. I wasted a lot of time in England first. But I did get to Paris at last when I was pretty well starving, and I had five glorious years of it. Then I came back to England, still starving. That's my autobiography. Have you time to come in? I've got some trade goods on view."

I thought the trade goods looked better on the walls than the late Mrs Mitchell's Calvinist texts, even though these had not seemed to take themselves too seriously. "Just wander round," Gerald Pickering said, and he went out to the garden at the back of the house, where it overlooked the creek water.

Left alone, I wandered from white room to white room, dazed by light and colour. Ignorant though I was, I could not but be aware of the affinity these pictures had with the Monet I had seen in Louisa's room. All were of outdoor scenes; all were painted in sunlight. They so lacked what I could only call the solemnity of the pictures I had known till then, they were so without any pretence of doing more than be beautiful, that I rejoiced as, when I was younger, I had rejoiced to come out of church, run down to the graveyard wall, and look at the light raining on the sea and on the trees across the creek.

I was standing spellbound in front of a small canvas showing a ride through an autumn wood. Few leaves were left on the trees, so that the light came bursting in to fall upon the golden floor that reached away and away as though one could dance along it for ever. I turned from it to see that Gerald Pickering had come back. He didn't ask me what I thought. He didn't so much as say "Well?"

But I said: "Oh, they make me feel so happy!"

"Good," he said with a smile. "Then they haven't done a bad job."

5

Gerald Pickering, his white suit and his black hat, became features of our landscape. He was an open-air painter and refused to add so much as a brush-stroke indoors. You would see him trudging about with his easel and stool and a box containing paints, palette and brushes, or sitting down at work, or rowing a dinghy he had hired across the roads to look for new points of view on the St Just side. Where the water shallows over rocks just off-shore you get the loveliest blues and violets and green and purples; and sometimes you would see him, with a grapnel down, just sitting in the boat, watching as patiently as a heron watching for fish on the fringes of the tide; and, like a heron, he would suddenly make a dart, slashing away furiously at the canvas propped before him. He loved to sit on the bit of grass behind his house when the tide was flowing, looking at the slow spread of the sea over the mud-flats, the wide sludge-grey pool taking on its garment of water, and the water absorbing the colour of the sky and the clouds. The yachts would come up with the tide, their sails white or rusty-red, and sometimes the yachtsmen had pulled in a fish or two – for we had little to do with Cowes and stylish sailing – and would be gutting them and throwing the offal overboard. Then there would be a whirling of white wings as a screaming quarrel of gulls fought upon the water and in the air; and slowly all this would die away and there would be nothing but the pool, deep and fulfilled, and the quiet of the trees, and the luminescence of the sky from which the sun had withdrawn, and the calm of yet another day folding its grey wings for sleep.

I often at such a moment took out our dinghy and rowed lazily up, letting the tide do the work for me; and I did so the more often now, in the hope of seeing him sitting there. One evening I was surprised to see that he had company, and more surprised to see, as I edged the boat nearer to his shore, that the two women were Louisa and Meg Newman. Gerald Pickering gestured me ashore and said, as he gave me a hand out of the boat: "You're just in time to join us at our meal."

Louisa, it seemed, had trudged over from Tregannock, Meg Newman carrying a basket full of sandwiches and cakes and fruit. She had spent an hour looking at Mr Pickering's pictures, and had bought one. It was of the pair of swans that haunted our creek, their whiteness luminous upon the blue-shadowed water beneath the oaks on the far bank. Then Louisa and Gerald settled down, sitting there on the grass, to a long talk of Paris and the studios. I sensed their contentment, and guessed that for each of them it had been a relief from *ennui*, especially so for Louisa. Mr Pickering, after all, had his painting to do. His discovery of Cornwall had released him into a fury of creation. This was to his painting what Keats' wonder-year had been to his poetry. But I knew too little, either of him or of painting, to be aware then that this was so.

Meg had gone into the house and came out now with the hamper. She spread a cloth upon the grass and the night was so warm and still that the edges needed no stones to keep them still. We sat down and ate, except Meg, who had notions about "keeping her place", although Louisa invited her to join us. Mr Pickering brought out a large jug of pale blue Venetian glass, filled from his bucket of hippocrene, incongruously accompanied by tin mugs. He said he had found the jug in a junk-shop and paid less for it than for the mugs. But we didn't talk much. The quiet of the evening, the deepening of the shadows, forbade it; and I shall never forget one moment of it: the tranced trees, the breathless tide at full, the swallows high up where perhaps they could still see the sunlight over the curve of the world, the earth-bound bats blundering in the shadows.

Meg, too, was standing in the shadows, and I was aware of what a sturdy, lovely Hebe-figure she had become. She stepped out and took up the big jug of water and poured almost ritually into our empty mugs. I saw how Gerald Pickering was aware of the lovely lines of that bending figure, and how an almost secret smile passed between him and her.

At last we three stood up and Gerald walked to a bush of white lilac and cut a spray and handed it to Louisa. He bowed and said: "For my first Cornish patron. I'll bring the picture to you in a few days. It's not quite dry." But when they went, it seemed to me that his eyes were following Meg, not Louisa.

6

I had not given Charles Lester my address, and I did not expect that I should see him or hear from him again. I often thought of him, though I did my best not to; and I did not mention him to Father or Louisa. To talk about him would have been to revive an image I wanted to suppress. Or so I imagined. In fact, nothing could have been worse than this suppression. I brooded sadly on that brief encounter, and my feeling became so intense that at one time I was ready to invent any excuse for going to London. This, too, was suppressed; and the suppressed image burst out in my dreams. I was very unhappy.

My condition was not helped by what was going on about me. Louisa came for me in her dogcart and took me off to lunch at Tregannock. Father was at work in his study and she didn't intrude upon him. Indeed, she seemed glad of the excuse for avoiding him. Their relationship was another cause of the gloom that enfolded me at that time. Their attitude to one another was so correct when they did meet that I was hit to the heart by the absence of spontaneity and true affection. This again I could not mention to anyone. Something was broken between them, and when that has happened no pacts and understandings and reconciliations ever work. It is just something that one must watch and endure and grieve for.

May was nearly ended; and we drove between hedgerows lit with bluebells and foxgloves and campion. Nothing could have been lovelier under the blue sky. Already some meadows were so ripe that the haymakers were at work. The clack of their machines had always seemed to me one of the sweetest of summer sounds; but that day my heart did not respond to it.

Louisa said: "I've asked Gerald Pickering to lunch. I'm not sure that he's getting enough to eat."

"Has James met him?"

"Not yet. I don't think they'd get on very well together. I'm afraid poor James would think a painter an odd creature. Anyway, they won't meet today. James is in Truro."

She said that James was attending a County Council committee. He wasn't a member of the County Council but had been co-opted on to several committees. "He's not very happy about it," she said, "but really he must try and fill the place his kind of people have always filled. It's some sort of justification for them."

In time, she said, James must become a member of the County Council. It would give him an insight into public affairs, and then there would be no reason why he shouldn't stand for Parliament.

"But he doesn't reason," she said. "He's a mass of inherited prejudices. We had quite a warm passage this morning about the war in South Africa."

I knew nothing about the war in South Africa except what I read in Father's conservative newspaper. It all seemed far away and, I was foolish enough to think, an irrelevance. All the same, I could not believe that anyone, except a few radical hot-heads, could object to a war that the government had decided on. I said so to Louisa.

She flicked the pony, and said: "That's what I mean by an inherited prejudice. Have you *thought* about the war? That's all I asked James to do – to *think* about it; and all he could say was: 'What is there to think about?' 'Everything on God's earth', I said; and James said: 'I've got plenty to do without wasting my time on thinking.' "

She laughed at this merrily enough; so that I decided, and rightly, that things were not much amiss between them. "But really, I am desperately anxious," she said, "that James shouldn't live the life of a turnip. He has qualities, if he'll only wake up."

As we drove along the path through the great field that lies in front of the house we saw Gerald Pickering at work, sitting on the canvas stool before his easel. Meg was standing looking over his shoulder. Louisa stopped the dogcart and called: "Meg, get up to the house. I'm sure Mr Pickering finds it most distracting to have you standing there staring."

Meg turned round, and to my surprise there was a rebellious look on her face. Or was I surprised after all? I had caught the glance between her and Gerald during the supper on his lawn. She seemed about to speak, checked herself, and went up to the house.

Gerald Pickering got up and walked towards us. "She doesn't worry me, Mrs Polperro," he said. "I'm one of those painters who aren't distracted by an audience, especially by one girl who is so impressed that she hardly dares to breathe. I think if I did nothing but draw a dog with two tails she'd think it marvellous."

A groom was passing by, and Louisa told him to drive the pony away. Then she walked over and looked at the picture. It was of a magnolia against grey stone; the magnolia called *soulangeana nigra*, whose flower petals have an indescribable colour in which a rich purple merges almost into black. Looking at the picture, without turning her head, Louisa said: "You mustn't let Meg pester you."

Gerald said: "What pesters me is a very mundane question: How am I to go on paying my rent?"

Louisa said quickly, with her eyes still on the picture: "You needn't let that worry you. I can afford a picture now and then."

He said rather sadly: "That is a lovely charitable gesture."

"No, indeed it isn't," Louisa said, turning to him at last. Her face was a little flushed. "I've been just as hard up as you are in my day. Many a time I've wanted to buy a picture and couldn't afford it. So you see I'm being merely self-indulgent."

"All the same," Gerald said, "I've made my own arrangements. I loathe the idea of pupils, but when I was working in Chelsea I had to have a few. Since I've been down here one of them has been nagging me. He wants to join me. His father doesn't think painting quite the thing, but the boy has worn him down at last. The old man has agreed to his spending the summer here. It's a boy named Charles Lester. He's not much good as a painter, and I don't think he ever will be. But he's got enough money to keep all the world's wolves from my little door."

7

If we hadn't someone to blame for our follies life would be unendurable. I blamed Father for my not showing him Charles' letter. I hated the thought of inquisition and disapproval. His attitude to Louisa's two marriages was not encouraging. Neither had taken place in St Tudno church, and a girl should be married from her home, especially when her father would have the grave pleasure of conducting the service. Louisa's excuse concerning her marriage to

James, that she didn't want a lot of gaping villagers present, outraged him. The villagers were his flock; and if he wasn't, like so many parsons today, full of up-to-date notions about their political rights and the social implications of Jesus, he was an excellent parish priest according to his lights. His lights gave him an affection for his people and forbade him to preach what he didn't believe – that you could give men anything more than your love, in the hope, which need not necessarily be fulfilled, that this would help them to endure.

This may seem odd to a lot of people today, but the longer I live the less odd it seems to me. Nowadays we are ready to give everything except the one thing that matters, which is our love.

However, a girl of twenty was hardly likely to see things in this way, even though Mr Wheatstone was there, a kind of private precursor of the state's grim benevolence, to fortify Father's view. Indeed, there was no question of reasoning at all. Here was a letter from Charles Lester and I intended to keep it to myself. That was the long and the short of it.

Charles wrote:

Dear Miss Legassick. – I expect you remember that during our amusing chance meeting in London I mentioned that I had been taking a few painting lessons with a man in Chelsea. He disappeared some time ago, saying only that he was going to do some walking and that, if he found a good place for painting, he might settle down there for a bit and get on with it. He wrote to me recently to tell me that he had found a Cornish village full of colour – the perfect place for a *pleine airist*. You didn't give me your address, and I should never have known that this was your village if Pickering hadn't said that he had met a Miss Legassick, whose father was the local parson, and I at once remembered your telling me that that's what your father was.

I don't know whether it will interest you at all, but I've decided to join Pickering and spend the rest of this summer down there. I've rather gone off the painting idea, but the prospect of a long stay out of London – and especially out of the parental orbit! – appeals to me. Of course, it wasn't easy persuading my father, but if I nag him long enough there's not much that he won't do for me; and I've at last made him see that a few months' steady application under the wing of an accomplished painter will make me blossom into a Frith or Marcus Stone. Happily, he's never seen a picture by Pickering or any other Impressionist, or he might have doubts. However, he imagines me coming back qualified to paint an endless succession of on-the-line Academy successes entitled The Fireman's Wedding, Can He Forgive Her? and so forth; while I see myself hiring a good boat and giving old Pickering the time of his life.

Well, there it is, and it will be nice to have someone down there whom I know. I'll be along any day.

Yours sincerely,

Charles Lester.

I still have this letter. If ever I read it now, I am appalled to remember that it didn't kill my love; that, on the contrary, sitting on a tombstone in the graveyard, or under a hedge on the way to Tregannock, or in the quiet of the loft, I read it again and again as something too private to be entrusted to other eyes, too sacred for Father's profane glance; and I would literally tremble at the thought that here, in my own beloved St Tudno, for months on end, I should have the company of the young god who had burst so unexpectedly into my life on a November morning in Manchester Square.

8

Few who had known Louisa in her early days could get into the habit of calling her Mrs Polperro, and certainly Thomas May couldn't. "That be Miss Louisa's maid from Tregannock, bain't it?" he asked, and I looked across the water to the small stone quay on the other side that we so often used for a diving-place at high tide. It was high tide now, and Meg was sitting there, wearing no shoes or stockings, her legs dangling down from the edge of the quay. With an easel rigged in his dinghy, Gerald Pickering was painting her. I said that yes, that was Louisa's maid. Thomas May, holding the sickle with which he had been slashing at the long grass between the graves, looked to me a likely subject for Gerald, and I said so.

"That I bain't. It's women them artists wants. I knows 'em. First they paint 'em without their shoes, and then they paint 'em without

141

their stockings, and then they paint 'em with nothing at all and call 'em nimps. Well, 'e'd better not start painting nimps in my graveyard. That'd be a fine sight to greet the rising saints if the Lord should take it into 'Is 'ead to sound the trump at that moment."

He took an impartial look at his own statement, and added: "Not that there'd be many saints from this parish. Not many sheep, but plenty of ole billy-goats, an' p'raps they wouldn't mind."

It was a good tide, and Meg had no difficulty in dropping from the quay into the dinghy. The session was over, and seeing them set out towards the head of the creek I followed. Gerald rowed her to the village and helped her ashore. She sat on the grass and put on her shoes and stockings and set off for Tregannock. Then I raced Gerald back to his own landing-place at Little in Sight. He didn't ask me to look at the picture. We sat on his sun-baked lawn, and I said: "Have you heard anything more from Charles Lester? – you know, the pupil you are expecting to stay with you."

We had passed into June. It was ten days since the letter had come from Charles, and I was pining for news of him.

"No," Gerald said. "Perhaps he'll come and perhaps he won't. I never found him very reliable."

That was all he had to say about Charles – just brushed him off as a person of small importance.

"Well," I said, "whether he comes or not we shall have a lively summer. For the first time in goodness knows how many years, the whole Legassick clan will be here."

Gerald said: "I never had a clan. I was an only child. I suppose it has advantages and disadvantages. What does your clan amount to?"

"Well, you know Louisa. Then there's Bella. She's married to a curate and lives in Hunslet. I've never been there, but I understand it's not a bit like St Tudno. Hugo – that's Bella's husband – will have to stay where he is, but Bella's coming down for the whole summer, bringing her two babies. There's John, who is four, and Connie, who is just a year old. Then there's my brother Roger. You'll love him. He's nearly thirty. He teaches classics at a school in the north of Yorkshire. Of course, he wouldn't be due for a holiday for some time, but a wretched epidemic has broken out at the school, so they're closing down till the autumn term begins."

"I shall be afraid of him," Gerald said. "I never went to anything but a board school, though of course I picked up French, and I know my own job. But on the whole educated people terrify me. I'm much happier with people like Meg Newman."

I said: "I had noticed that."

He gave me a sharp glance, but made no comment. "So that completes the clan," he said. "Not very extensive."

"Well, there's my uncle, Reginald Pallace. But he doesn't come into the assembly we expect this summer. He looks after Sir Ernest Kopf's place in Surrey."

"Oh, now that does interest me," he said. "Isn't Sir Ernest married to Lord Bettiscombe's daughter?"

"Yes. Do you know her?"

"Only as a patron. My patrons are not so many that I'm likely to overlook one. But Lady Jane is among the few people in England who share with your sister the honour of owning a Pickering picture. Of course, they both know France and what's being done there."

I told him of my own amusing encounter with Lady Jane Kopf. "Yes," he said, "I found her like that. She is an oddity – half a *poseuse* and half a truly original mind. When I've finished my work here, I hope to have the pleasure of showing her what I've done."

"Would you like to show *me* what you were doing this morning?" I boldly asked.

He said frankly: "No. Do excuse me. For one thing, it isn't finished. For another, it's a picture I'm painting for my own pleasure. Well, they all are, come to that. But this one is rather special."

9

Roger was at the vicarage when I got back. He had ridden all the way from Yorkshire on his bicycle, and had taken a week to do it, carrying his few things in a knapsack. He looked extraordinarily well and handsome. His few things included the proofs of *The Greek Ideal*, his first book. It was characteristic of him that he said nothing to any of us about the book until it had reached this advanced, this almost final stage. He looked Greek himself – at any rate, he had what most people think of as a Greek look, though they were a mixed lot, I imagine, like the rest of us. I can't believe that old Socrates ever looked a woman's dream. Roger didn't wear a hat. His close fair curls were bleached by the sun, and there was the beginning of an attractive severity in his dark blue eyes. They looked as though they would shrivel anything mean. When I rowed up, he was on the beach, wearing flannel bags and a dilapidated blue sweater. Our small sailing dinghy was pulled up there, and Roger was giving it a look-over. He said, as though we hadn't been parted for months: "This is going to be a bit small, don't you think, for the lot of us?"

I looked at the boat, little more than a toy, that the economical Legassicks had made do with ever since I could remember. I said "We shall be quite a mob. Still, we can count Louisa out. She was never much of a one for sailing."

"And fortunately Hugo won't be here. He's that fat nowadays he'd have the gunwales awash. Bella, too, is looking uncommonly matronly. I spent a night with them on the way down."

"How do the children look?"

"Coddled. We'll have to take them in hand. For one thing we must teach them to swim."

"My dear, Connie's only a year old. I expect Bella will loaf about on the shore with her, eating buns, and there'll just be you and I and John afloat."

He looked rather ruefully at our sailing dinghy. "All the same," he said, "even though this faithful little tub has stayed afloat under the weight of you and me and Hugo and Bella, I wish we had something a bit bigger. Now look at that. That's the sort of thing we ought to have."

I looked up, and there was a lively thirty-foot cutter coming smartly into the creek before an easterly breeze – the kind of boat we call a Falmouth quay punt. Her sails were being run down, and, as we watched, the anchor was thrown over. There were two men aboard, and they busied themselves tying the mainsail to the boom and stowing the foresail and jib under the deck of the forepeak. They got into the dinghy and the elder man began rowing towards us. I watched them, trembling. I said to Roger: "I know the younger of those men. His name is Charles Lester."

My voice shook, and Roger looked at me in surprise. I looked at him, too, and I was suddenly overcome by a premonition of disaster. I had always dearly loved my brother, and I knew that this boy, now coming swiftly towards me across the narrowing stretch of water, had none of the quality, the sure foundation, that endeared Roger to me.

Roger, I am certain, guessed at once what was disturbing me. He said: "What solitary lives we Legassicks lead. We never confide in one another. Except perhaps you and Bella. If you don't want to meet this man, go up to the house and leave it to me."

But, despite my agitation, how much I wanted to meet him! "I'll stay," I said. "I shall have to meet him sooner or later."

The dinghy grounded, and Charles stepped out – an astonishing figure. He was wearing grey trousers and a brass-buttoned reefer jacket, a white collar with dark blue tie, white shoes and a yachting cap with some indecipherable badge on it. Roger, hatless, bare-footed, looked at him with a cold all-seeing and judging eye.

Charles took my hand and said: "Well, I said I'd come, and here I am."

I introduced him to my brother.

The quay punt belonged to this old man who had rowed Charles ashore. Charles had been in Falmouth for a few days, seeking a boat that he could hire for the rest of the summer, and he had found this one. Charles knew nothing about sailing, or even about rowing a dinghy; but he had assured the owner that, once in our creek, he would find friends capable of taking charge. It was to satisfy himself about this that the old man had sailed him round from Falmouth. He looked with approval at Roger as he explained this. "She'll be all right with you, sir?" he asked. Although we didn't know him we had often seen this boat of his on the water and he seemed to know us. "I've watched you two grow up with that little ole boat of yours," he assured us.

I didn't know whether Roger would accept the responsibility, for this distressingly perfect yachtsman was not the sort of sailing companion he would want; but he gave me and Charles a long considering look and said: "I'll keep an eye on her. I suppose Mr Lester has insured her?"

"Oh, ay. I never bothers with them ole insurances. I reckon I can keep a boat afloat without paying them chaps upalong. But I thought in the circumstances . . ."

"All right," Roger said. "There's a mooring out there I can have the use of. I'll tie her up to that."

"You got a dinghy to go with her?"

Roger assured him that we had.

"All right then," the old man said, getting into his own dinghy. "I'll row myself back to Falmouth in this'n."

He got aboard, and we three were left alone on the beach.

Roger said to me: "It's nearly lunch time. Don't be late," and vaulted over the churchyard wall: always our short cut home.

I was disappointed by Charles' almost casual greeting of me; but there was no reason why I should be. There had been nothing whatever between us except a few moments' conversation that had arisen from a chance encounter. Yet, as I stood there on our rough little beach – all stones and seaweed – I felt an irrational bitter hurt. He would never have sought me out: his being here arose solely from the accident of Gerald Pickering's visit. Nevertheless, I was resentful and unhappy.

However, I couldn't stand there being nothing but a Dido registering grief upon a seashore; so I said: "I like your boat. She'll be all right where she is. I reckon she draws about six feet, but there's plenty of water there to deal with that, except perhaps at low springs."

He asked: "What do you mean by drawing six feet? And what are low springs?"

I felt too discouraged to go into the matter. I said: "Is your luggage aboard?"

"Yes, stacks of it."

"Well, I'll take you to Gerald's. He has a dinghy, and I expect he'll bring you back here to pick up your stuff."

I rowed him up the creek, hoping that none of the parishioners were watching from the shore. I felt vaguely ashamed of this tailor's model of a yachtsman. Of course, to hope we were unseen was nonsense. Nothing was unseen at St Tudno. "They be born with special swivel eyes in this parish for peeping round corners." Thomas May was right as usual. Old bedridden Mrs Hicks had an arrangement of mirrors that allowed her, lying on her back, to see the road and the water.

Charles said: "I hope Pickering won't harry me. I've practically decided against painting."

"I've read somewhere," I said, "that it's one thing to go in for art, but a far more serious thing when art goes in for you. You don't feel that that's happened?"

He laughed. "No. I've never believed myself to have been chosen by a relentless demon. This is just a way to shake off the parental incubus for a month or two. Once I get back, I'm afraid the game will be up and the heavy hand of the law will fall on my shoulder."

I landed him on Gerald's lawn and left him to find his way round to the door. He didn't even wave a hand as I rowed away.

10

After lunch Roger said: "I shall work in my black tent this afternoon." That's what he always called the darkness under the great yew where I had buried Euphemia Emmett. My black tent, or sometimes Kedar's tent.

It was a grilling afternoon, and presently I followed him down there with a book. Seeing my intent, Father, who was setting out in his pony-trap to make a round of the village, said: "Mind you don't disturb Roger."

I think if the Lord had commanded Father to offer up either his son or his three daughters, we three would have found ourselves upon the altar, and there would have been no ram in the thicket. Roger had taken the proofs of his book down to his black tent. Father knew it, and his old heart, I imagine, was swelling with pride. I said that I would not disturb Roger, and watched him drive away, loving him, but loving Roger more.

I took my book down to the yew tree and saw Roger within, wrestling with long snakes of paper. I sat outside in the sunshine which never incommoded me however hot it might be. My book was an excuse. I waited for Roger to speak. Out on the water the quay punt called *Norah* was sitting, her one tall mast reflected below her white hull in the hardly-rippled sea. The sight of her there disturbed me profoundly, as though she were a symbol whose significance was not yet revealed. The two swans that owned our creek came flying over her, their great wings thrashing out majestic music as they pursued intruders who had looked into their domain. The heron was pacing his accustomed beat. Nothing was lacking of the beauty that had been my balm. Far away up the roads, where they narrowed into the river, the land was hazed and trembling like a mirage in the heat, and thus uncertain, thus tremulous, my nerves were twitching.

Gerald Pickering, in his vast black hat and white linen suit, came rowing down towards *Norah*, with Charles in the stern. Charles looked like an admiral commanding the services of a galley-slave. It

147

was Gerald who climbed aboard, made the dinghy fast, carried three suitcases out from the forepeak, handed them down, and finally rowed back towards Little in Sight.

Roger said from under the yew: "Quite an addition to the population. Who's the man in white?"

I told him what I knew about Gerald. It was little enough. I said that Louisa called him an Impressionist.

"Well," he said, "Louisa knows about that sort of thing. What does she think of Mr Pickering's work?"

I said she had liked it well enough to buy a picture.

"In that case he must be good enough to talk about. Let's talk."

How good it was to hear those words again! From the time I was little more than a baby Roger would say now and then: "Let's talk." They were always lovely times when Roger talked about his school and about Oxford, and about his beloved Greeks.

He came out from his black tent, tied some tape round his proofs and called Thomas May to carry them up to the vicarage. "Let's walk as we talk," he said to me, and I said: "Talk to me about your book."

"No," he said. "I could as soon talk to you about my first love."

We didn't go up the creek. We followed the path in the opposite direction, skirting the Carrick Roads, with rising fields on our right and the quiet water on our left, opening out southward to the great sea. "Then," I said, "I must talk to you about *my* first love," and Roger answered simply: "I thought perhaps you'd want to."

But it was a long time before I could bring myself to do it. We went on till the shore was broken up by deep rocky fissures and crevasses into which, when the tide was making with the wind behind it, the water raged, smashing itself into foam that flew up and fell back and ran out sucking and gurgling, a mere dithering lacy pattern of ineffectual fury, only to be caught up again, and to come on again, compounded and mighty, hammering the earth till it shook and yielded its infinitesimal grains to the sea that will have it at last.

Often on darkening winter days I had stood there, my hair streaming landward, and gazed with awe into that furious cauldron; but that day the water was purring, stretching itself in a lazy carpet of changing and dissolving colour: lilac and green and blue threaded over with white. We sat down with the sun pouring upon us, the gorse golden about us, and that innocent-looking dangerous beauty below us; and I told Roger of how I had met Charles for an hour and had not seen him again till he was rowed ashore that day from the quay punt and of how the time in between had been filled with the image of him.

But I could not tell him what I now knew in my heart: that I had loved Charles because, physically, he was so much like Roger, and that, with Roger here at my side, the image of Charles was becoming counterfeit and dim. Gold and brass. Gold is ever bright, but brass must be rubbed up continuously, and it was nothing but my emotional preoccupation that had been rubbing up the image of Charles.

It was my own story that had opened my eyes to myself. When it was done, I watched the cormorants diving and the gulls wheeling and crying, all the familiar beauties of land and sea and sky, and they were bitter to me. I felt the biggest fool God had ever made. If the two had not come together, side by side like that: the one with all his bogus show, the other in his self-forgetful simplicity: I might not, even yet, have seen where folly had led me astray. Now the revelation was complete, and I almost hated the pampered, indolent simulacrum that Charles Lester was.

Almost. I had to be fair to him. He had never for a moment pretended to feel an interest in me, much less an affection for me. It was not my presence that had brought him to St Tudno. And another thing. I could not at a stroke uproot the imaginations that had crowded my heart since meeting him. He had come in like a wind-driven tide into this crevasse, and now the thought of him, though diminished, yet lay there – lazily but not without beauty – like the indolent water beneath my feet.

Thus, with one consideration and another lapping through me, I lay back on the turf till I felt Roger's hand placed sympathetically on mine. At that, I got up, almost frightened, and we walked silently back to the vicarage.

11

We were hardly used to bicycles in St Tudno, and so you may imagine the consternation which greeted the news that James Polperro had bought a motorcar. He was learning to drive it, but for the moment employed a chauffeur. It was the chauffeur who would go to Truro to meet Bella and her children. When Roger and I got back from our walk we found Father filled with dismay at Louisa's announcement that she would go with the chauffeur to meet her sister. We sat down at the tea table with them.

"My dear!" Father said. "You surely don't propose to imperil the lives of *four* members of the family!"

"It's your life and your old pony's that will be imperilled if we meet you on the road," she said.

Father said: "Nonsense. I shall drive into Truro myself and follow behind you in case you need my assistance. That thing of James' will never get up the hills, and if it tries to come down one, heaven help it! You can take it from me, Louisa, that I and my pony will still be on the roads when all this nonsense has fizzled out and this experiment has been given up as something contrary to nature."

Go to Truro he did, the next afternoon; and he arrived home with his pony an hour after Bella had unpacked and the children were in bed. Louisa had stayed. She said she would take supper with us. Father asked Mrs Solway to take a tray up to his room. He pretended that urgent work would not permit him to dally among us. As he went out of the room I ran after him and, in the hall, put my arm through his. At times like this he was capable of breaking my heart, because I knew what was in *his* heart. How long it had been since all four of us Legassick children had sat down to eat together! Not since Louisa began the disruption by going away on that far-off morning. He felt that in one way and another we had all removed ourselves from him, that that was how we would wish it to be, and that his presence would disturb a coming together that meant much to us. Also, I think, he feared that his gesture in driving the pony to Truro had made him look foolish, a man hopelessly out of touch with the sort of things we understood, the movements of the times that we accepted and responded to.

I said: "Father, stay and eat with us. It is so long since we have been all together under your roof."

He looked at me, rueful but unshaken. "My dear," he said, "it is this sorry Atlas who must still bear the roof on his shoulders. What would you all do if I didn't continue to work?"

It was nonsense, and he knew it. I was the only one he now had to keep, and I doubted whether his writing had ever contributed much to the keeping. I could only look at him sadly. He put my hand gently from his arm, kissed me on the forehead, and said: "Tell them not to make a noise. Bella's children are sleeping. I think the boy is a little like me. Good night, my dear."

When I got back to the dining room Roger said: "It's such a lovely night! Let's not feed in here. I'll fix the trestle table on the terrace."

The terrace was the rather insignificant sweep of gravel outside the window. I went with Roger and helped him to carry the supports and the table-top from the stable, and Mrs Solway whisked a cloth upon it. She looked approvingly at Bella. She said: "It's good to see someone back here who *eats*. A nibbler, that's all Mr Legassick is; and Miss Maria's little better."

Bella's fruity gurgle of a laugh was good to hear again. "It's all right, Mrs Solway," she assured her. "I'm in good practice. There's one thing Yorkshire people know about, and that's eating. They accepted me from the beginning as an expert."

It was a cold meal: chicken and salad and a cold apple pie and cheese. Roger said: "I think this reunion demands wine," and he went off and came back presently with tall glasses and a bottle of hock. Then he brought four silver candle-sticks, spaced them along the table and lighted the candles in them. We all sat on one side of the table, looking across it at the quiet water and the dying flame of the day, fading over the hill to a few embers that would soon be gone.

We had not much to say, but we had much to think about and to feel, come together again for a moment after our small but divisive vicissitudes. I remember a feeling almost of solemnity. There was not enough breath to flutter the candlelight and the water was without stir under the moon rising over St Just. Roger's black tent was a ragged globe of darkness. I thought of how I had buried Euphemia there, and found Louisa there, and talked with Roger there, and I loved the tree and loved this night and my heart was desperately squeezed in the ring marrying my joy and my sadness in this moment.

Norah was lying out there on the water, her tall mast almost still but not quite. The deep heart-beat of the sea moved the truck against the sky, this way, that way, by hardly more than a finger's length. Her deck was so dusky that we would scarcely have seen anyone aboard had it not been for Gerald Pickering's white suit. He must have been in the forepeak, and then suddenly he was there and the darker clothes of Charles Lester could now be made out, too. They leaned on the rail, evidently looking towards us, as well they might, for candles shining in the dark were hardly to be expected.

Bella said: "That boat's new to me. Who is it?"

No one answered her, because at that moment the notes of a guitar both broke and enhanced the stillness. At first it was a random plucking, and then the player – I could see it was Gerald – went into *Stille Nacht, Heilige Nacht*. If you had to play at all, I suppose that is what would suggest itself to you at the moment. It could have been intolerably sentimental, but it wasn't. It was deeply moving, and a strange thing happened. Roger reached out a hand and took mine, and on the other side he took Louisa's. With my free hand I reached for Bella's; and we four Legassicks sat there, linked like that, silent till the music ended. Then there was a whimper from a window above us, and Bella broke the moment. "That's Connie," she said and hurried into the house.

In the darkness outside the range of our candlelight, but drawn nearer and nearer to it, Thomas May was fluttering like a moth among what he called *his* graves. I was glad that our people took their graveyard so much for granted. If something was there for tears, they were soon over, and no sophisticated monument rose up to feign an unfelt grief. The very flowers planted there were of the sort that bloomed in cottage gardens, and, as these gardens seemed but to extend the houses of the living, so these accustomed flowers made death less abrupt, a gentle fading away of life. Dog daisies were favourite flowers to plant here, and on such a night as this they were moon daisies, tranquil, luminous. Watching Thomas May, himself a shadow, moving among the shades, I remembered an evening when I found him here and asked him what he was thinking about. He said, looking down on the earth into which his clay-clodded boots seemed planted like roots: "I was thinking this would be a good spot for the vicar when 'is time comes. 'Tis the loveliest view in the graveyard, clear across the water, an' catchin' any sun there is." I found myself neither shocked nor offended. "Yes," I agreed. "It's a lovely spot," and Thomas May said: "Ay. And well deserved."

His roaming brought him now within the shine of the candles, and Roger called to him. "Come and sit with us, Thomas May. Come and eat."

He sat between me and Roger and drank a glass of wine and finished what food was left. Roger twitted him gently. "You know,

Thomas May, in old times men had a skeleton at the feast, or sometimes a skull on the table to remind themselves that in the midst of life we are in death. You are doing us the same useful service."

The old man said: "There's no need for any such nonsense, Mr Roger. A thing don't mean much if you're always needing to be reminded of it by dramatics. I heard Miss Bella's baby cry, an' I said to myself: 'That's a soul comin' in, so it stands to reason that somewhere a soul's goin' out.' I'd rather be reminded of such matters by a babby than by a grinnin' skellington. I like to be in the nature of things."

It was a long speech for Thomas May; he took a chicken bone into his fingers and worried the meat from it.

Bella rejoined us. "It was only fidgets," she said. She stood like a sturdy pillar, looking out over the moon-washed water.

"Now Miss Bella," Thomas May announced, wiping his fingers on his knees, "Miss Bella be the one to take life an' death as they come. Like a cow in a field she be. I expect you've watched 'em of a summer's dawn, Mr Roger. When the sun begins to appear they get on their knees facin' towards it, as if they was sayin' their prayers; an' when that's done they just get on with the business of eatin'."

Bella's laughter bubbled out at this summary of her character. "Look," she said, "they're coming ashore."

The dinghy was pushing off from *Norah*.

Thomas May got up. "Well," he said. "No cross, no crown, they do say. I must get back to my lawful wedded cross." He took a last affectionate look around the graveyard. "I often wonder," he said, "what that lot's up to now. Well, there's not much choice. 'Arps or 'obs."

Louisa said, kissing Roger: "The car must be waiting. I said I should leave at ten, and it's gone that."

I said: "Go up and say good night to Father."

"He won't want to be disturbed," she said. "Roger darling, mind you come out soon. James expects you."

12

Bella, who was no more to be deprived of sleep than of food, wished us good night. Mrs Solway came out to clear away the supper things. Roger blew out the candles, and he and I went down through the churchyard to meet the dinghy. I introduced Roger to Gerald

Pickering. I could see at a glance that they liked one another, but Roger was on edge with Charles Lester who took charge of the conversation. "You said you'd introduce us to the art of sailing, Mr Legassick. What about a moonlight trip?"

Gerald apologised. "It's getting late," he said. "Why are you so set on it, Charles? Mr Legassick is probably tired."

"You may not have a night like this again," Charles insisted.

The tide had been falling for some time. We had had to go a fair way out over the beach to meet the dinghy. Roger looked at the sky and the sea and sniffed the air. I knew that he was longing to go. A quay punt would be fun after our toy. He glanced at *Norah*. The burgee, which had been without motion all through the evening, was beginning to stir faintly.

"Would you like to come, Mr Pickering?" he asked.

"I'd love to, if it's not a bore to you and Miss Legassick, and if you think it's practicable. I've been pointing out to Charles that you can't sail without wind."

"Oh, we'll find wind somewhere," Charles said obstinately.

Roger said: "I'll get you a sweater, Maria, and an extra one for myself." And to the others: "Will you be warm enough? It can be pretty fresh even on a summer night. The wind's beginning to stir, but it's not going to be much. However, if you'd like it, we can crawl about."

Roger was rather a long time coming back. "I looked in to see Father," he said. "He won't worry now about our being late."

"It's a good thing someone thinks of his feelings."

"Yes," he said, understanding. "I thought I'd better put that right."

It was nearly eleven before we were away. Even with three sails drawing, *Norah* was no racer at the best of times, and the wind continued to be only a whisper. Gerald seemed to be very happy. He said nothing, but you could feel his content as he leaned over the gunwale watching the water or gazed at the sky or the moon-silvered shore. Charles fussed up and down. "Is this the best she can do, Mr Legassick?" he asked.

"At the moment, yes," Roger said patiently. I could see that he, too, wanted to be left alone with the tiller under his arm, no kick or pull in it. We were nearing St Just. "Going about," he said to me quietly.

154

Even the quietness of the words seemed to annoy Charles. "I always thought yachting was someone shouting orders and other people jumping at ropes."

Roger said: "The Legassicks are an old-fashioned lot. They don't yacht; they sail. Anyhow, keep your head down, please, Mr Lester. This boom *will* go across in time, improbable as it seems."

It did, trundling slowly, and I sheeted in the jib and foresail single-handed.

And that was how it went on: *Norah* moving as sedately as a drayhorse dragging a heavy load. She strolled along till we could look into Falmouth with the moonlight glistening on its grey slate roofs, and then Roger said: "Well, not a very good night, I'm afraid. We'd better put back. I hope to be able to give you something more exciting before your holiday is over. Going about, Maria."

We were doddering homewards when Roger said: "Would you like to take the tiller, Mr Lester? You'll have to get the feel of it sooner or later." Charles took the tiller. "Just keep her steady as she goes," Roger said.

I looked at the two of them standing side by side in the moonlight, and their faces, stripped of the harsh reality of day, were even more startlingly alike than I had supposed. I wished I hadn't come. Charles' presence robbed me of the comfort I felt in Roger's, and Roger's diminished even such a flicker of emotion as I continued to feel in Charles'. I felt dead, hopeless. I was aware that *Norah* was not being kept "steady as she goes", but I was too bored and unhappy to do anything about it. Roger said: "Bring your tiller up a bit, Mr Lester. We should be moving a little more out to starboard."

Charles said: "I'm bringing her in towards the creek. Surely there's plenty of water in the sea."

"In parts," Roger agreed, and said no more about it. I could feel his contempt. *Norah* was strolling along so amiably that the grounding was almost imperceptible when it came a few minutes later. She just stopped, and, as she had been as good as stopped all through her small voyage, Charles took a moment or two to realise what had happened. "Have I done something wrong?" he asked.

"No," Roger said, "it's *Norah*. She has decided to rest on a bank. Fortunately she has chosen sand. It might have been rock."

"Well, we sha'n't be here long, I hope," Charles said.

"Hope has nothing to do with it," Roger assured him. "We are in the realm of certainties. The tide is dead low. It will begin to make in about an hour. In about an hour after that we shall be lifted off."

"We sit here for two solid hours in the dead of night?"

"Unless you have some other course to suggest?"

"Well, I'm damned! I think yachting's a fool's game."

"It *can* be," Roger agreed.

We ran down the sails, found a riding-light in the forepeak and hoisted it. Roger said: "Maria, I can row you ashore in the dinghy, if you like, and then come back to bring *Norah* in."

I said I would stay where I was. "Well, then, let's make ourselves as comfortable as we can under the deck. It's a pity Bella didn't come. She'd have brought plenty to eat and would have laughed."

I bitterly felt his reproof to my glum countenance. We all got under the deck, but you couldn't make yourself comfortable. We lit a hurricane lamp that hung there, and the smoky flame revealed the sort of litter to be expected in a tough little working boat: fishing-gear, coils of rope, a spare anchor, old sails, a bucket, oilskins, a pair of sea-boots, and, of all things for reading-matter, an ancient copy of *Ruff's Guide to the Turf*. Gerald Pickering's white linen looked odd. He left us there, took his guitar, and began to strum away in the open. We sat on the lockers. Charles, in his yachting suit, looked faintly ridiculous, and he was peevish, too. Roger, in his old blue sweater and corduroy trousers, looked at home. He was capable of finding consolation in reading-matter of any sort. He lit his pipe, opened the Guide to the Turf, and appeared instantly to be immersed in whatever it contained. From up above, Gerald's guitar plaintively informed us that there was no place like home.

Watching the pair of them, side by side on the locker opposite mine, I suddenly laughed. Once started, I couldn't stop myself. I laughed and laughed. I was thinking of the Legassicks: Father, asleep now, I hoped, in his lonely loveless room; Bella warm and sensuous, snuggled down with her infants, half an ear alert for whimpers; Louisa in her mansion with her lymphatic James and her motorcar; Roger and I in this stinking little forepeak, waiting for the tide to come and for God knows what besides. We all suddenly seemed to me so tragic a synopsis of human hopes and fears and endurances that when Roger slapped my face sharply, sensing my hysteria, my laughing turned to tears. I dried them and bent my back to pass out of that noisome little hole, and found Gerald leaning on the gunwale, staring at the moonlight on the meadows. You could see the cattle couched therein — the cattle that Thomas May said bowed to the east when the sun appeared. I said to Gerald: "Do you ever paint moonlight?"

"No," he said. "I accept my human limitations. I find it a good idea to put up with what I've got. To paint that," gesturing towards the ghostly land, "is something I haven't got.

13

The next day Roger apologised to me for having been rude to what he called my young man. How could I tell him that I didn't care if I never set eyes on Charles Lester again? Sitting out on the cliff, I had told him so much about my feeling for Charles that it would have been embarrassing to say: "Still, that's only how it *was*. Now, it isn't like that any more," and even more embarrassing to say why. So Roger remained in his illusion and set himself out to be friendly with Charles. *Norah* became the affair of those two. I hardly went aboard her, and Gerald Pickering was not much interested in her either. Roger spent hours aboard, teaching Charles the difference between a halyard and a sheet, how to tie knots and splice ropes, and especially how to listen to the orders of the man in command and so avoid such misadventures as running on to sand-banks. Charles lost his weary peevishness. He became enthusiastic, and one day surprised us all by ceasing to be a "yachtsman". He appeared in a sweater and corduroys, frank imitations of Roger's. When I saw him one day shinning up the mast to unravel the burgee which had managed to tie itself in knots, and on another day standing in the dinghy swabbing down *Norah's* sides, I knew what had happened. My hopes of spending a lot of time with Roger were ended. The schoolmaster had found a pupil and, being a good schoolmaster, had roused him to endeavour. Now Roger would be happy as he had always been with men. Once it was Hugo, and it had been other men before that and after that: walking through Europe, climbing, now sailing. I sat in the graveyard watching Charles swabbing the decks and saw Roger come up wearing a bathing-suit. I could hear his clear voice across the water. "Come on, Lester. Chuck that for a moment. Let's swim."

Charles, too, was in a bathing-suit. He climbed aboard. They stood side by side, their toes clinging to the gunwale, dived together. They struck off for the little quay on the other side, shouting, urging one another on, full of emulation, the midsummer sun shining on their golden heads. They climbed out and stretched themselves on the short hot grass. Beautifully Greek, I thought bitterly. I thought goodbye, Roger, and I hated Charles.

Little John, Bella's child, brown as an autumn hazel-nut, wearing nothing but a loin-cloth, shouted: "Boo, Auntie!" and leapt from behind a tombstone. He threw himself into my lap, his satin limbs warm under my hands. Young though he was, there was a down on them that the sunlight made to glisten. He said: "I saw'd Uncle Roger and the man. They swam away."

"Yes, I saw them, too."

"When shall I swim away?"

"Soon enough, I expect."

"Soon enough for what?" the small sophist persisted.

"Soon enough for everybody's comfort."

"What is everybody's comfort?"

Well, we could go on like this all day. "You'll swim nowhere unless you learn to swim. You wait here and I'll take you into the water."

I went into the house and put on a bathing-suit. When I returned John and Thomas May were sitting side by side on a grave. "How old are you, old man?" John asked. His fist was strangling a bunch of daisies.

"As old as Methuselum."

"How old is Chooslum?"

"I can give you the Written Word for that, midear. 'All the days of Methuselum were nine hundred sixty and nine years.' "

"Is that old?"

"Well, it's gettin' on."

"Thank you very much, old man," John said. "Now Auntie Maria is going to teach me to swim away." He held out his brown paw, which Thomas May took, saying: "I'll be about, midear, any time you want to discuss suchlike matters."

We didn't get far with the swimming lesson. The water was awash with entrancing weed and young prawns and shoals of mackerel bait. The swans swam by, hissing at us. So we merely dabbled and paddled for half an hour, and then John said: "I can't learn to swim away this morning. I must ask Uncle Roger to teach me. I like men to teach me things. Daddy teaches me better than Mummy Bella."

"Yes," I agreed. "Perhaps that would be better."

14

We were having breakfast the next morning when Louisa's chauffeur arrived with a message asking me and Roger and Bella to lunch at Tregannock. Roger said: "I don't think I'll go. I'm not smitten with James Polperro. Besides, there's a decent breeze today and I've promised Lester to take him out in *Norah*. He's to be in command today. I don't want to disappoint him, and I want to see how he's shaping."

Bella, who had heard of our midnight sojourn on the sand-bank, said: "You've taken quite a fancy to that Jonah. I expect Mr Pickering is glad to be rid of him. It leaves him free to give his attention to that girl Meg. If you go to lunch, Maria, you might find out how Louisa likes having her handmaid stolen."

"Of course I shall go," I said. "Aren't you coming?"

"No. Mrs Solway's got plenty to do without having my pair on her hands."

"Louisa will think we're all giving her the cold shoulder."

"Well," said Bella, who was not often catty, "she gave herself a lot of practice in the art, didn't she?"

I rushed to Louisa's defence. "I'm afraid you know little about Louisa. She was very unhappy and very lonely. When one of us did go to see her, she was delighted. Roger knows that. He saw her more than any of us."

Roger said: "Please don't think I'm avoiding Louisa. But I've given Lester my word that we'd go out on the first decent wind. I can't take that back."

So I went to Tregannock alone. I started as soon as breakfast was done, and so had plenty of time to go all the way on foot and to dawdle at that. As I was passing the spring by whose waters I had first met Gerald, Charles Lester came along and stopped to talk. He was looking very handsome, very excited. "Good morning, Miss Legassick," he said. "What a gorgeous day! This holiday is proving worth while after all."

"After all what?"

"Well, it *did* seem a bit of a frost at first. Gerald kept on nagging me about drawing and painting, and *Norah* seemed a dead loss. That night we sat on the sand-bank I all but decided to chuck the whole thing and get back home. Did you know I'm taking charge of her today?"

I said that I did; and he exclaimed, like an earnest schoolboy determined to please his headmaster: "I hope I don't make a fool of myself again. Do you think I shall be all right?"

I had no means of knowing how he would be, and said so.

"Is Mr Pickering very displeased with you?"

"As I said, he was at first. But not now. Between you and me, I shouldn't be surprised if he's glad to see the back of me. He seems to prefer the undivided company of that girl Meg. Well, I must hop. I mustn't keep the maestro waiting."

The maestro. Well, there it was. Dr Arnold and Tom Brown.

I thought of looking in at Little in Sight, but as I approached the cottage I saw Meg hurrying towards it from the opposite direction and went on to meet her. She had found what I had lost. How is it that you can always tell? She was lit up, while I felt like a lamp whose light had been blown out. Seeing her almost dancing towards me, I hoped that Gerald loved her and that he would be very successful and very rich. Of course, I told myself moralistically, the success and the riches are not important. But they do make such nice trimmings. I wanted to detain Meg, but more pressing things than I were in her mind. "Oh, good morning, Miss Maria!" she said, hardly pausing. "What a lovely day! Well, goodbye now."

I suppose it must be a lovely day, I thought. Charles says so, and Meg says so. I'm sure Roger thinks so, and to Bella every day is lovely. Let's hope Louisa and James are equally caught up in thanks to God for all his kindness.

I said to Louisa: "Is it such a lovely day as all that?"

She looked at me, a little astonished. We were walking on the broad stone terrace. "Well, now I come to look at it," she said, "it is pretty good. A perfect day for sailing. But I hadn't noticed. I've been working all the morning on the proofs of my book."

That did move me to laughter, and the day seemed brighter. "Oh, the Legassicks!" I cried. "Books, books, books! 'Too much damned ink in this house.' Who said that?"

"I don't know," Louisa said. "What's wrong with books?"

"Too many of 'em, and no one ever hears of them except the family. It only remains for Bella to produce a masterpiece called *Laugh and Grow Fat*."

"Why didn't Bella come today?"

"Just a Christian thought about not over-burdening Mrs Solway with the brats."

"Why didn't she bring a nursemaid?"

"My dear, she's married to a curate, not to the Lord of Tregannock."

"The curate's father is very rich, I understand."

"Yes, but the curate isn't, and he insists on living on his salary."

"He must be mad. Now that I'm married to the patron of a living, I know something about these things. Do you know how much Father brought us up on? – five pounds a week. I tell James he should be ashamed of himself. He spends more on bringing up a horse, and far more on his car and chauffeur."

"And how is James?"

She said seriously: "Good, my dear, as good as men are made. But weak and foolish. Still, for that you can blame Tregannock and all it stands for – not him. I'm doing the best I can with him. I'm afraid it won't be much."

I said: "To be a good man is much."

She said: "Thank you," and added sadly: "But the waste!"

The motorcar turned in at the gate from the road and we watched it come along the path through the field. James got out, and the car was driven away. James kissed me dutifully. He was beginning to be immense and red in the face like his father. "I've had a garage built far from the stables," he said. "Can't have that damned thing disturbing the horses."

Louisa took his arm. In his other hand was a dispatch case. I had the impression of a mother welcoming home from morning school a son with a satchel of unloved books. "How did you get on, darling?" she asked.

"Well, I *did* speak," he said, with an attractive shy pride.

161

"Good for you."

"Yes. I said just what you told me. It went down all right, I thought."

"Splendid. You'll soon have them hanging on your words."

"Well, I wouldn't go as far as that. Is lunch ready?"

At lunch I asked Louisa about the proofs she had been working on. "Is it the book you were writing when you were staying with Uncle Pallace?"

I felt at once that it was a bad topic. James said: "D'you know, Maria, I don't approve of this book. I don't approve much of any books, come to that. Not of my wife writing 'em, I mean. But when Louisa tells everybody that she's been a shop-girl – well, that seems to me a bit thick – eh?"

My foot was deep into trouble. I looked from one to another helplessly.

Louisa said soothingly: "Now, James, I've met your wishes by using a pen-name. I didn't want to do that. I don't care who knows what I've been. Being a shop-girl – among other things – has made me a more important person than the poor creatures I meet here who haven't done a hand's turn in their lives and think that somehow or other that dignifies them. I *don't* think so, and those of them I don't pity I despise."

"Well," James said, "you're certainly better value than any of that lot, which is why I hate the thought of their gossiping about you. And it'll soon be out, however many pen-names you use."

"It's out already, you can be sure of that. What the vicar's wicked daughter has sunk to has been common gossip for years. Haven't you noticed the gracious way they treat me? – like visitors being kind to the girls in a Moral Welfare home."

James turned for comfort to his cold salmon and Chablis. He was a little pacified, but not convinced.

"I promise you," Louisa said, "that I shall never write another book. I couldn't. I haven't the talent."

James growled: "Nonsense. Talent enough for anything."

"No. I can't invent or imagine. None of us Legassicks can. Not even Roger, the best of the lot of us. But I can say what I've seen and known. It's time other people knew it. It may do some good. Why," she added slyly, "even when I was a buyer, I earned hardly more than a parson."

"I don't want any pudding," James said abruptly, with an air of supreme renunciation. "I've got work to do."

He apologised to me, took up the dispatch case that had been resting against the leg of his chair, and left us.

Louisa said: "Poor dear. He's going to have a snooze."

"Don't press him too hard," I said.

She laughed. "Impossible, I assure you. It needs Archimedes' lever to shift him an inch."

We walked out to stroll round the lake deep in a hollow. The banks of this hollow were a glory of azaleas and rhododendrons – Uncle Reginald's imports – in their season; but now that was over. We sat down and watched the torpid carp and the lively orfe; and the water-lilies were wide open to the sunshine. I said: "I met Meg as I was coming along."

Louisa said: "Thank God, Meg is saving me from myself."

I knew what she meant. I had half-guessed it, but had put the idea resolutely out of my mind. It was unworthy of me, I told myself, a horrid little suspicion that I should jump on with all my weight. Now that she had said it, I was silent and appalled.

Louisa said: "I'm terribly given to falling in love, you know."

We sat there watching the lilies, and the fish lifting their snouts to gulp flies, and the steel-blue swallows scooping them up on the wing; and Louisa, whom I had seen so long ago come out from the cave of the yew tree, and who had commanded me to say nothing, knew that I had kept my word and would always keep it.

"I feel sometimes," she said, "that I must talk about it or die."

It was now that she told me what I have already set down: the story of her first meeting with James and the lengths to which that went.

"Apart from that," she said, "I have always remained what Father would call a good girl, but it hasn't been easy. I suppose," she said, "I'm a wanton without the courage of her convictions."

I asked her how she got on with James. She said: "I'm happy with him – at a price."

She meditated for so long that I thought that was the end of it. Then she said: "When I married him, I thought I had beaten the Polperros. But I'm not sure they haven't beaten me. All that I ever loved in James is still there, but I hoped to do more with him than they could ever have done. I'm not sure it isn't too late. When Gerald Pickering came here, the contrast was enormous."

She left it at that, and indeed there was no need for her to go on. She was too many women. The passion that had overwhelmed her in her teens, the grim resolution that had carried her through her years with Mr Wheatstone, the adaptability that had made her a success in business, the love of the arts that had been kindled in Paris; I marvelled as, for the first time, I seriously considered her and realised how swiftly I should have sunk where she had triumphantly kept afloat. I considered James and Gerald, and agreed that the contrast was enormous.

"I found," she said, "that I was making too many excuses for being at Little in Sight, and that I was annoyed with Meg for what I called wasting Mr Pickering's time. Not that she's doing anything of the sort. She's keeping him fed, and he finds her an excellent model. And so, for her sake and mine, she can now go there as often as she likes."

"Mr Wheatstone wouldn't have approved."

"Well, that's something," she said.

James appeared on the other side of the lake, corpulent and comfortable. We got up and went to meet him. "Where have you been all this time?" he asked rather petulantly. "I finished work half an hour ago."

Louisa took his arm. "You mean you woke up half an hour ago," she said. They exchanged a look of such perfect understanding that I did not fear for what she called her wantonness. There was only one man with whom she had ever gone all the way, or, I felt sure, ever would.

I said I'd better be getting back, and James said he'd have the car brought out.

"No. I'd rather walk."

"Walk!" he said. "You Legassicks! Walking, swimming, sailing. You'll wear yourselves out. You're all as thin as sticks."

"Except Bella," I reminded him.

"Yes," he agreed. "She's all right. Good breeding stock."

15

During that summer I saw little more of Roger. I knew what his ambition was: to be headmaster of Rugby, his own school. It says much for what we all felt about him that not one of us doubted for a moment that he would do this. As a preliminary step he had applied for the

headmastership of a small but excellent school near London. His name
had been on the short-list when his holiday began, and he was now called
to London to be interviewed by the governors. It meant a three days'
absence, and during that time Charles Lester was like a lost child. On the
middle day I saw him aboard *Norah* and rowed out. He was scrubbing and
polishing, and *Norah* certainly looked a different ship from the old
slattern he had brought from Falmouth. But it was not of the ship, it was
of Roger, that he wanted to talk. I sat on a coil of rope, leaning against
the bulkhead of the forepeak; and, watching this new Charles, hearing
him talk, the embers of my own feeling for him began to feel a little
returning warmth. The sensible clothes he had taken to wearing, his
preoccupation with some other thing and some other person than
himself, the falling away of his self-pity, all showed me a Charles I had not
known, a Charles that might have been. Roger's absence, too, delivered
me again to Charles. He had stripped to the waist, and as he stood there
with the sun pouring upon him and the gulls wheeling and screaming
over him my divided heart was full of joy and bitterness.

"I never dreamed," he said, "that sailing could be so marvellous.
Next summer Roger and I are going to make a voyage."

This was news to me. Roger had said nothing about it. "Oh," I said.
"It's all fixed up?"

"Yes. Not in this." He looked round *Norah* with affectionate
contempt. "She's been a good boat to learn in, but of course there's a
lot more to learn."

"When it comes to the sea, there always is."

"Don't I know it! However, we have a scheme for sailing down to the
Mediterranean. We'll want a properly decked boat, of course, with a
decent cabin, and we'll have to find a third man. I'm going to work hard
at navigation during the winter. We mustn't run on to sand-banks."

He looked at me with his frank, glorious smile, but he wasn't
seeing me. I wasn't there. He was seeing Roger and himself and a
third man running under all sail through the Straits and into
Mediterranean wonders.

"I'll need to know a lot," he said, his eyes on a splice he was making.
"The sea about here is all right for beginners."

"The sea," I said, "is the sea — anywhere. Don't treat it lightly. How
will your father like the idea of your spending the winter learning
navigation?"

"Oh, hasn't Roger told you about that?"

No, he hadn't, whatever that might be.

"I've decided on the law. Roger gave me a proper dressing-down. Gosh! I wouldn't like to be a kid in his form, unless I was a hard-working kid, or a master in his school if he gets this headmaster's job. Has he ever told you off?"

"No."

"Don't do anything to make him. That blue eye of his can be very cold. I was telling him about having Father where I wanted him, and he said, like a bark, 'Stop that!' Then he laid into me. Quite right, too, I deserved it."

He pulled on his splice, deemed it satisfactory, and put it down. "Well," he said, "the scheme is that I should read in someone's chambers and do my navigation in any spare time that comes along. That'll please my father and help me when I put up the idea of his buying me a good cruising ship. Of course, I haven't put it to Roger like that. He'd think it smelt of bribery."

"It's all right," I said, "so long as you're not taking up the law just for that purpose."

"Oh, no," he assured me earnestly. "That was an afterthought. I'm not a painter. Pickering says so frankly. Now the painting *was* a get-out if you like. Something to keep work at bay. You see, I haven't wasted my time down here. I've learned a lot of things beyond the elements of sailing a boat."

I was sure he had, but he had learned nothing about me, and didn't seem to want to. He was leaning over the gunwale, looking down into the shoals of bait swimming by, and the sun lighted up the taut skin drawn over his golden spine. I got up hastily. "I must be off," I said. "I've neglected Father shamefully this summer."

"There's one other thing," he said. "As soon as Roger gets back we're going to stay out all night in *Norah*. We're to sail to Fowey, sleep aboard, and sail back the next day."

I climbed into the dinghy. "Make it a happy day," I said, and rowed ashore.

I found Father walking about the graveyard, and this surprised me. It was his sacred working-time. Only an event of great significance could have brought him from his study at noon. He walked up to Thomas May, and as I approached I saw that his stern face was relaxed.

He had been telling Thomas May the news. He would have wanted to tell the first person he met. He told it to me. "Roger's got the job." He was clutching Roger's telegram.

I kissed him. "I never doubted it, Father. I'm so glad it makes you happy."

"I'm a natural doubter," he said. "I can't take things for granted. Except perhaps this thing. I prayed about it," he said simply; and, his smile beaming again, "I never pray for anything unless I'm certain God wants me to have it." And then, with for him a tremendous daring: "I think God wants me to share a bottle of hock with you and Bella at luncheon. Thomas May, come up to the house. You and Mrs Solway must join in our toast."

I had never known him so gay. He looked like Savonarola about to impart a good one he had just heard to some such cheerful fellow-sprite as Dante. I hoped – with what yearning I hoped! – that God indeed wanted him to have this thing. I see us still, the five of us, standing there in the cool room with our glasses raised. Father said: "To Roger. God bless him and keep him and prosper him."

We drank. Through the window I looked out on the burning day. I could see *Norah*, and Charles Lester dropping down into the dinghy to row away to his meal at Little in Sight.

16

Roger and Charles set out on their sail to Fowey early in the morning. Bella had been consulted about what food they would need for two days' travelling, and I had seen going aboard enough for Columbus starting on an unpredictable voyage. A fresh breeze was blowing as from the graveyard I watched the moorings dropped over the bows and *Norah*'s three sails filling taut with wind. It was hardly nine o'clock. Thomas May, shading his eyes with his hand from the morning dazzle on the water, said: "In my young days, I'd've done without they two fores'ls till I wanted 'em, an' maybe I'd've 'ad a bit of a reef in the mains'l."

I watched till they were nearly over to the St Just side, and there they tacked to take their fill of the sharp wind, which was blowing out of the north-west. They scudded along, lying over. That tack would take them right out into the open water of the English Channel.

I went in and ate my breakfast. I had arranged with Louisa to send the car to take me in to Falmouth. I wanted to look around and see if I could find a book that I might give to Roger, with my love and good wishes on his appointment. It was not till noon that the car came, and to my surprise James himself was driving it. He said he'd had a heavy morning's work on "papers" unspecified, and wanted a breath of air. He'd give me lunch in Falmouth.

He got his breath of air. The car, like many cars of the time, had no cover. My hat was held on by a scarf wrapped over it and knotted under my chin. As we climbed up from the vicarage on to high land the wind hit us sharply. It was an odd, exciting, and excited day. The sun shone with what would have been grilling heat but for the cut of the wind. There wasn't a cloud in the sky, but all the air was in agitation. The steady blow from the north-west had changed to a wind that didn't seem to know what it wanted to do. At the top James stopped the car, and we looked down on the Carrick Roads. You could see no strong tide running such as sends predictable and reliable waves rhythmically up a beach, but there was a fickle agitation everywhere, a white stippling all over the dark blue. It was an angry feminine sea full of rage without direction.

James merely said: "Pretty horrible – what?" and started the car again.

We didn't have lunch, and I didn't buy a book for Roger. James stopped the car by the Customs House, and so many people were moving down the side-road to the Customs House quay that we followed them. Standing there in the wind, with my clothes whipping now one way, now another, I listened to its strange, whining, petulant voice, rising at times to a short hysterical screech. And still not a cloud, still the bold midsummer sun pouring down, lighting up the white stippling that fretted and fumed everywhere, as though it were that furious complaining wind-voice made visible.

The harbour was full of little ships – working-boats and yachts and the insane non-rhythmical nature of the weather had them reeling north, south, east and west, sometimes seeming as though they wanted to leap out of the water, sometimes as though they were about to sink below it. My eyes were fixed on one of them when suddenly it was not there. I gasped and clutched at James' arm. I had seen boats capsize, even go down, but never before like that. Then, far from the first, another went. It was as though they had been gripped from below and ruthlessly jerked to the bottom. The little crowd of us stood there gaping as another went and another. I suppose it lasted for ten minutes, and seven boats went. The wind had risen to a high sustained keening, and then it tailed off into a moan, a whimper, as though a maniac's rage had been sated, leaving it exhausted and afraid.

We knew it was over, whatever it was. After that climax, the wind wept itself away. Whatever it and the sea had conspired to do was done.

James said: "I don't feel like eating. Let's go home."

We said nothing during the return journey. But each knew that the other knew, and I felt a kinship with James that I had not felt before. At the vicarage gate he helped me out and held me till my tottering legs could walk. "I'm sorry," he said. "I'll tell Louisa."

CHAPTER SIX

FATHER WAS buried in that sunny piece of the graveyard that Thomas May had selected for him, but Thomas May did not scatter the earth upon his coffin and the sun was not shining. Thomas May had always been outraged if anyone suggested doing something for him. The "whole man" was a Renaissance ideal – the man who was not a specialist, the man who was at home in war and peace, in art and science. But there are all sorts of "whole men", and Thomas May was the wholest man I have known. To see him lay the straw of thatch or the stone of a wall was to feel the very life of the material he worked in flowing through his hands. I once heard him say to a recalcitrant cow: "Stop your dang nonsense, midear. We belong together." And he belonged together with all natural things. He was never a lord of creation, and from him more than anyone I learned the little I know of the majesty of humility.

But one thing he couldn't do, and that was dig his own grave. That was done by young Barty Spargo, who had come back from the Boer War with one leg shorter than the other and who, when given the sexton's job, said that our sloping graveyard would suit him fine as long as he always walked with his short leg uphill.

It took a long time to persuade Father that he would never see Roger again, but no one ever did see him again, or Charles Lester either. No one ever saw anything but some fragments of their dinghy, washed high and dry on to the Gull Rock outside Portscatho, that lovely lonely breeding-place whence, as you approach, the wings rise and the hoarse voices desolately call.

I had never before in my life felt so lonely – lonely through to the heart and bone – as I did while that summer dragged to its end. Thomas May died. One August afternoon I saw him lying on the grass among the

170

graves. It was very hot, and I thought he was taking a rest in the great shadow which fell across him. And so I went my way on whatever my errand may have been, and was alarmed only when, on returning, I saw him there again in a stillness so absolute that it spoke its word at once to my heart. It happened that there was to be a burial in the graveyard that afternoon, and even as I stood there looking down at Thomas May I saw the white flutter of Father's surplice and heard his voice saying: "I am the resurrection and the life." There would be no Thomas May to crumble the earth upon the coffin, and Father, in the bemused and absent mind that had been his since Roger's death, would be so pulled up short and startled by the omission that I walked over to the open grave and, when the moment came, took up a handful of soil warm with summer and let it fall upon "this our brother". Father, I am sure, didn't notice that I was there or that Thomas May wasn't there. He carried the service through as automatically as he put on his boots in the morning, and when it was done he walked away without a word to a soul.

I told one of the men standing by the grave what had happened, and he, with a friend, carried the body away. I stood with the others among the heaps of soil that had been dug up and the bright summer flowers, and I felt as though the dust I had thrown into the grave had symbolically marked the end of a span of life that began when I buried Euphemia Emmett. I looked through the blazing heat at the invincible old tree: Euphemia's graveyard, Louisa's trysting-place, Roger's black tent, the dark shroud of Thomas May. Bella and her children were gone. My two loves were indissolubly one in death. Gerald Pickering and Meg had disappeared, so lost in happiness that they had left no word behind them. Louisa and James were in Paris. Life was shrunk to me and Father and Mrs Solway. Not far from where Thomas May had lain down to sleep, a pile of grass and withered flowers that he had fired was slowly smouldering. The blue smoke rose into the blue air, solemn, beautiful as all that day. I stood there long after everyone else was gone, and my life seemed to me to have as much meaning as that wavering and insubstantial column, or as the dead grass that fed it.

2

Father was the next to go. I never saw the death certificate. I suppose some doctor wrote upon it what was the cause of his death. But there was no cause at all except that he wanted to die and died. Just as you snip off the cotton when a sewing job is done, so suddenly and finally Father ceased to have anything more to do with life. He went through the motions of living, but for a long time before he was dead he ceased to be alive. He waited with a dreadful unnerving patience for news of Roger, going on with the book he was then writing, doing his visiting, eating his meals, occasionally finding fault with me when I misread his writing and put some absurdity into my fair copy. I remember he wrote: "All this is mere Arian heresy" and I rendered it "Asian hearsay", which made just as much sense to me. I bore his rebukes mildly, and had not the heart to point out that his handwriting, always difficult to decipher, had suddenly gone from bad to worse; and this, I knew, was because, alone in his study, his mind, as he wrote, was torn between the knowledge that Roger was dead and his refusal to believe that God, in this case, had not wanted what he had prayed for.

One morning I went down from the now so lonely loft to hand in what I had done and to pick up the next instalment. Instead of being at his table he was sitting in an armchair, doing nothing. His hands hung down; his face was desolate. It was clear that his moment of acceptance had come, and I stole out to leave him alone with it. After that he wrote nothing. The cessation of that out-pouring of multitudinous words affected the whole house. I hadn't realised, till it was ended, how it had shaped our lives, moulded our days: Louisa's, Bella's and my own. It had fixed our times of doing and not doing; it had modulated our voices, eaten up what otherwise we could have been doing and perhaps should have been doing. And now it was over.

This was soon after Christmas. He gave up visiting his flock, but he continued to conduct the church services. It moved me to see that even those who had not been regular in their devotions came now, as though they were aware that they would be hearing a voice that soon they would hear no more. I think – I hope – that in their way they loved him and were saying so as best they could. Even Louisa came, and James with her. There was no more a coachman and a footman. James drove the car. I was glad to see them there, even though Louisa's presence meant that she knew her father was dying.

It was on the first Sunday in March that he climbed the pulpit steps for the last time. His face and figure were shrunk, and he held to the ledge of the pulpit not giving the sense, which he had always done, that that was how he liked to stand, but that now he stood thus to hold himself from falling. It was one of those days when, down there, March can shout a Halleluiah Chorus. Uncle Reginald's camellias lit the garden. The mimosa floated round the trees in golden clouds, and the daffodils were gold on the ground. The sea was still, and as I went down through the churchyard the thrushes and blackbirds – greybirds old Thomas May had always called them – were singing their early heartening songs to hail the year's resurrection.

He had said nothing to me, but I knew that this was the last time I should see him there. Perhaps I loved him and understood him better than any of the others. I was the only one who had been with him all the time. I was recalling many things, and, looking at James and Louisa, I recalled the night when Bella and I had watched Father and Louisa coming down the stairs in candlelight, she wearing the hastily readied dress of Mother, and they had driven away, Louisa's heart fluttering with the thought of James, though we did not know that then. All the years between were in James' burly form and ruddy face, and in Louisa's thin stern countenance. She was no longer beautiful: she was what they call, doing their best for a woman, handsome.

And something happened which has haunted me with joy and sadness all through my life: Father spoke to me directly from the pulpit. He was reading from *Ecclesiastes:* "The grasshopper shall be a burden and the caper-berry shall fail: because man goeth to his long home, and the mourners go about the streets: or ever the silver cord be loosed, or the golden bowl be broken, or the pitcher be broken at the fountain, or the wheel broken at the cistern; and the dust return to the earth as it was, and the spirit return unto God who gave it . . . Of making many books there is no end; and much study is a weariness of the flesh."

It was in speaking that last phrase that he spoke to me: not in words, but he lifted his head and looked at me, and a pallid but beautiful smile dwelt transiently on his face. It was almost as though he was saying that he understood the burden he had laid on me and was asking my forgiveness. He did not then finish the chapter, but spoke only the next few words: "This is the end of the matter: all hath been heard."

Not that it has. It has been so often spoken, so rarely heard. Even all those long years ago I knew that – knew how few had found the way that gave my father peace.

As we left the church, through the little round-shouldered Norman portal, tears were streaming down Louisa's face. But what was the good of that? It puzzled me that I could love her and him; but I could. And I could love Charles and Roger. I wondered whether I loved too much, whether that was to be my life: always to love, but never to find a love that would take me and not let me go.

I waited for Father to come out of the vestry and offered him my arm, for the way to the vicarage, though short, was rather steep. He took my arm and said: "Thank you, my dear. What a beautiful day!" He had never taken an arm before.

He died, as he had lived, quietly and unobtrusively. A few days after preaching his last sermon he didn't get up, nor did he get up at all after that. He was never again fully conscious, and said no word to anyone. He was dead before the week was out, and he was buried on a boisterous wind-rushing day when all the daffodils were flattened and the sky was grey chaos. He was buried in the grave where Mother had long lain, the spot Thomas May had chosen. A stone records nothing but their names and their years, and beneath that is a line, "In memory of their only son, Roger, lost at sea."

3

Born though I had been into a parson's house, I didn't know what was to happen now. The house was a perquisite of the parson's job, and there was no parson. Had I a right to be there at all? At any rate I stayed, and Mrs Solway with me. There was no Thomas May to chop wood for us and do many other small things. I took to doing them myself, and on Sundays I gave lunch to a young curate who bicycled over from somewhere or another and took the morning service. He was a rosy hopeful boy, given to blushing, and I felt motherly towards him. I hadn't a penny. Mrs Solway received no wages, but she didn't seem to mind that. I was untrained for any sort of work, and sometimes wondered how much longer we would be able to pay the tradesmen's bills. This unhappy phase ended when James, who had now got rid of his chauffeur, drove over one morning, told me that he had opened an account for me in a Falmouth bank, and explained how a cheque-book was used. He was diffident and apologetic, a large good-natured oaf, whose very size was somehow reassuring; and I began to understand how Louisa would find comfort in him, as a masterful man would find it in a homely wife. He was obviously anxious to flee from the scene of his well-doing, and I did not seek to detain him. He said: "I'm sorting things out. Don't worry. If you like, we can shut this place up till we find a new parson. You could come and stay at Tregannock and bring Mrs Solway with you."

I didn't want that, and said so politely. "All right. As you wish," James said. "But I don't want to appoint a parson in a hurry. It's my job, you know."

I had forgotten that: it seemed odd that this large carnal brother-in-law of mine had the power to choose St Tudno's spiritual director. But there it was.

So I stayed on, and enjoyed the strange sensation of paying the butcher and the grocer by the simple means of signing my name on bits of paper. Mrs Solway baked our bread and I learned to do something about the kitchen garden. We had fruit and vegetables in abundance.

It was the antique Legassick dinghy that went on *Norah*'s last disastrous voyage. I missed her, but I managed to borrow a neighbour's boat and spent a lot of time rowing about the Carrick Roads and torturing myself with memories. Towards the end of the summer there was a day when my mood lifted. A letter came — a letter that sprawled a few lines across three pages of paper.

Dear Miss Maria. — We are happily married! What do you think we went to Parris! When we got back Gerald said we better get married because he'd been brout up a Calvinistick. So we live in Hamstead. It's a small house and Gerald has sold some pictures. So I came to a good end after all let old mother Martin say what she like. Being married is very happy, and hoping it will be your fate too,

Yours truly,

Meg Pickering.

I didn't see it being my fate, but I was happy for Meg's sake, and for Gerald's, too. I read and reread the letter. It was a warm voice speaking in my loneliness.

I wanted to share this good news with someone, so I rowed my borrowed dinghy to the head of the creek and walked on to

Tregannock. James was not at home. Louisa and I took tea together. "Well, thank goodness we've got his address at last," she said. "I haven't been worrying about Meg, but I have been worrying about those pictures. He would have come here to take them away some time, I suppose, but I've been bothering my head off about them. One of these days they'll mean a fortune."

"Who owns Little in Sight?" I asked.

"I do."

I looked at her, amazed, and that for two reasons. To buy a house – just like that - while I was badgering my brains about how I was to live! Money! And why *that* house?

"You don't seem to realise," Louisa said, "that that house is an art gallery. I told the owner that Mr Pickering had instructed me to look after the pictures till he returned to claim them, and that I didn't want the fag of shifting them to Tregannock. I found that Gerald owed a lot of rent, and I was afraid the man might claim the pictures. I thought the simplest thing was to pay the back rent and buy the house, pictures and all. I needn't have worried. He took one glance and said: 'You're welcome to that lot, Mrs Polperro.' So there it is. Gerald can have the pictures whenever he wants them. He can have the house, too. Now that they're married, I'll give it to him and Meg for a wedding present. A painter of that sort needs Cornwall."

Money! I listened to her, dazed.

There was another surprise to come. She said: "James has chosen the new vicar for St Tudno."

She waited, with a sense of drama, for me to ask who it was.

"Who is it?"

"Hugo. It'll be nice to have Bella back."

4

I rowed down the creek towards the lonely house thinking that yes, it would be nice to have Bella back, and Hugo, too, and the children. Nice for me. But was it going to be so nice for them? Would they want me to stay? If Hugo had only his parson's pay, could they afford to have me hanging on there, a ghost out of a page of the story that was now turned over so that a new chapter might begin? Even Meg, it seemed to me, would have more rights in the parish than I. Louisa had seen to that.

We had moved into May – almost to the end of it. The year was bursting with glory, but I rowed slowly, with a heavy heart. Little in Sight slid by on my left and I noticed smoke rising from the chimney. Louisa knew enough about pictures not to leave them at the mercy of mildew, the curse of the damp warmth that was our climate. Gerald was being thought of, and Gerald's pictures, and Hugo and Bella would be better off than they had been on a curate's pay in Hunslet. I had no doubt that Louisa had worked on James, and that the parson's stipend would be better than it had been in Father's time.

"Why, Miss Maria," Mrs Solway said, "you've got a face as long as a fiddle! Ah, well, I suppose you'll be happier when Miss Bella's back."

I was going to tell her; now that she knew, I didn't bother to ask how. Nothing was secret for long in St Tudno. A maid at Tregannock could have heard a word pass between James and Louisa, and before the day was out the whole parish would be chewing it over.

"It'll be like the lamb returning to the fold," Mrs Solway said with sentimental relish.

"Bella is no lamb," I said crossly. "She's got lambs of her own, as you well know."

"I don't envy Mr Oldham," she said, "him bein' a foreigner."

"I'm sick of hearing that word, Mrs Solway. Everybody's a foreigner to you, if he only comes from across the water at St Just."

"Well, so he be," she defended herself. "And what with Mr Oldham coming from upalong, he'll be lucky to have Miss Bella to guide his footsteps."

Miss Bella! Miss Bella! She seemed already to be in the house, taking charge, remoulding. It was odd that Bella, who, though my elder, had always somehow been an object of quiet amusement to me, should have the power to say to me: "Come" or "Go".

Frantic with self-pity, and knowing it and hating myself for it, I left the house and climbed up to the loft, to be alone. But I wasn't alone. The place was too thick with Legassick ghosts. Bella was there, fat and lazy, lolling in a fireside chair; and, because I had transcribed so much of Father's work at this rough old table that Thomas May had knocked together, Father was there, too; and in a corner was a pair of old sea-boots that had been Roger's. The light was fading, and for a dreadful moment I saw the ghost of Roger standing in the substantial boots. One half of me felt as though I were going mad; but the other half said

"Stop it! Stop it!" and took hold of the mad woman and banged her head upon the wall, just as Roger, on that night when Charles landed us on the sand-bank, had hit the hysteria out of me with a hard smack. I came to, and found myself fingering my skull, where a lump was swelling up. And that, thank God, was that. I was able to think; and I thought: "The sooner I leave St Tudno the better."

5

Hugo and Bella did not move in till the beginning of August, and on the first of September partridge-shooting began. Everything went better than I had expected. Hugo, who had refused money while his father was alive, couldn't help having it, now that he was dead, in the shape of a useful block of shares in the family business. And so there was such a clean-up of the vicarage as I had not known in my life. The walls were stripped and repapered. New carpets went down and new curtains went up. Old furniture was ditched or recovered, and the place was altogether so changed that, more than ever, I wanted to leave it. It was no longer the home I had grown into like a hermit-crab into its shell. It was Bella, eager and extrovert. She was heavy with another child, and lolled as she directed my efforts.

"What about Father's books?" she asked. "Hugo has such masses of his own and says there's not much room on the study shelves."

"Let him dump what he doesn't want in the loft," I suggested. "Then you could pick them over, and if there are any that you don't want either, perhaps you'd let me have them."

So it was done. Neither Hugo nor Bella wanted the books that Father had written himself – all those reassessments and reconsiderations on which we three girls had spent so many years of our lives. When a Falmouth bookseller came to take away the finally rejected junk, those were among the ones I couldn't let go. I put them with a few dozen others on the shelves in the loft. It had been a sad, revealing task. A man is on trial in the eyes of those who dispose of his books. There wasn't a novel among them, unless you can call *Pilgrim's Progress* a novel, and little poetry, save poetry with theological overtones like Milton's. He was represented only by *Paradise Lost*. That, to Father, was Milton – not my beloved *Comus*, not *Lycidas*.

I sat in the loft, looking at the new arrangement of my shelves, when Bella came heavily climbing the stairs. I found myself often in this place – the only place that the new broom hadn't swept over and transformed into something I couldn't come to terms with. I said to myself: "You're getting old, Maria my girl. You're getting as hidebound as Father." Bella was carefully balancing a tray containing a glass of milk and a few of Mrs Solway's sticky buns. She looked down complacently at her swollen stomach and said: "I've got to see that this is well-fed. I find myself eating like a horse nowadays. Well, somebody must keep the family on the march. Louisa seems to be nothing but a married old maid. What about you?"

Well, what about me? She knew nothing – nobody knew anything – about the wave that had swept over me, leaving me both enriched and miserably poor. Despite John and Connie and the one on the way, I couldn't help thinking of Bella as an inexperienced child. She lived with everything but her mind.

"Oh," I said carelessly, "I shall be all right."

She licked the sugar from her fingers in her old way and said: "Having you here is a godsend. You've been a dear with John and Connie. Goodness knows when I shall be able to look after them again."

She rose from the table and spread herself in the wicker easy-chair. Her mouth was pearly with milk. Her red tongue licked it up sensuously. "I've been talking it over with Hugo," she said. "He agrees with me that it would be an excellent thing for you if you stayed."

For *me*? Well, it could be salvation of a sort, but I knew that I didn't want to be saved. Dear, patient old Auntie Maria, taking the children for walks, darning the socks, at a pinch giving Mrs Solway a hand in the kitchen. Perhaps Hugo would permit me to arrange the flowers on the altar. I didn't like it, and it could go on and on. As James had once said, Bella was good breeding stock.

I said: "It's kind and generous of you and Hugo to think of my comfort. But I'm sure it would be a mistake. If I were married, I wouldn't want a sister sharing my home, and I can't believe that in your heart you do, either."

"But we do," she insisted. "We've looked at it from all angles."

I was sure they had, even from the rather risky ones. But, on balance, they had decided that the proposition was useful. I detested myself for my analysis, but didn't abate my opinion.

"Thank you, my dear," I said. "I don't know what I shall do, but I'll find something sooner or later. I shall be most grateful if you and Hugo will put up with me till the something comes along."

She looked crestfallen. "Well, if you must go . . ." she said.

"There's one thing I should be enormously grateful for – if you and Hugo would let me keep my books and odds and ends in this room, and let me use it if I want a holiday down here. I could sleep in it, just as Uncle Reginald used to do, and be out of the way of all of you."

She was not quite so gracious now. "Well," she said doubtfully, "I expect the children will want a place to knock about in, just as we used to do. I must have a word with Hugo about it."

And when she did in my presence, Hugo said: "Good lord, yes, of course. Maria was brought up here. If she wants a stake in the old place, let her have it."

He was a good fellow. Roger, I thought, would never have taken him for a friend if he hadn't been. He was getting stout. His eyes beamed through thick-lensed spectacles. He was aware of the local aversion to "foreigners". "Think what a thing it will be for me," he said, laughing, "to be able to say now and then 'My sister, Miss Legassick, is coming down to stay with us.'"

"I'm a Legassick," Bella reminded him.

"You don't look it," he said frankly. "I must keep in touch with the old firm."

6

In James' day, game was not preserved rigorously as in the days of his father. He said he hadn't time for that sort of thing. Louisa's tactful but insistent hand was guiding him into those paths of "public service" which she thought of as some small return for immense and hardly justifiable privilege. At last James was beginning to like it a little. He was even known to take a book into his hand now and then, to hold it as though it were not something that would bite. But that autumn Louisa said casually that he was having a few people down to shoot partridges. I had the feeling that she was awarding him a prize for good work. She didn't say who was invited, and I was not interested enough to ask.

On a golden September morning a week later I was wandering along the hedges, gathering blackberries and sloes, when a motorcar came along in a travelling cloud of dust. A motorcar was still so rare a sight that I scrambled down from the hedge to watch it go by. But it didn't go by: it stopped. I was amazed to see that it was driven by a woman. I had seen few enough motorcars, and, if there were women in them, they were timid-looking passengers with tied-on hats who seemed to have no other purpose than to admire the astounding prowess of some male at the wheel. This woman had a helmet of white felt hiding her hair and buttoned under her chin. A long white linen coat covered her clothes from neck to ankles. Have you noticed how anonymous a woman's face is with the hair covered! And yet those bright and rather mischievous eyes, that little pointed chin, seemed familiar to me, and she was looking at me as though she, too, were fumbling towards a recognition. At last she said: "Yes, of course you are. I was on the way to call upon you."

Suddenly I was back at Coverdale, Sir Ernest Kopf's place near Dorking. It was a long time ago, and since then Sir Ernest had become Viscount Lavernock. I remembered my encounter with his wife and her pretty, prattling nonsense. I laughed and said: "Well, you've changed your taste in transport."

She got out of the car and took matches and cigarettes from a patch-pocket on her overalls. She did not offer me a cigarette, judging rightly that a country parson's daughter would hardly yet have acquired advanced habits; and, indeed, I was a little shocked, but fascinated, too, as I watched the blue smoke shredding out into the blue air.

"What do you mean about transport?" she asked.

"My Uncle Pallace told me that you were once talking about Keats and that you rather inconsequentially got from his leopards on to zebras, and said you'd like some to draw a chariot."

"Did I say that? Well, well, I'd forgotten. But I did get the zebras. Four-in-hand. They were a *sensation* in Hyde Park." Her voice had a trick of underlining words as heavily as Queen Victoria's hand did. She looked at the motorcar and stroked the bonnet. "But one *must* move with the times," she said.

She looked at my baskets and said: "How divinely rustic you are to be gathering blackberries! And those purple things. What are they? Can one eat them?"

"They're sloes. One makes sloe-gin with them."

"So you *drink*," she said. "I'm sorry. I'm a total abstainer. However, with your bonnet and your baskets you look quite like dear Marie Antoinette at the Petit Trianon. What a pity they cut off her head! I didn't mind so much about her husband. Could you milk a cow?"

I said that I could. "You are altogether delightful," she assured me.

I said: "I take it you are staying at Tregannock?"

"Unhappily, yes," she said. "I always thought Mr Polperro dull, and now he has also a conscience – I believe it's called a *social* conscience. I shouldn't be surprised to find him asking that man Keir Hardie down to shoot. And your sister is so intense. I read her book. All true, I've no doubt, but I'm perfectly sure evolution will put that sort of thing right in due course without any help from us."

I said that possibly my sister was part of the evolutionary process. She said: "I doubt it. Still, she has some nice pictures by that man Gerald Pickering. She tells me he was painting down here this summer."

I said that I had seen a lot of him.

"Now that's *just* what I want to talk about. I'll drive you home, and you can put on something to keep the dust out of your hair, and then we'll go somewhere and talk. We'll talk about poetry and painting – much better than partridges and politics."

And that is what we did; or, rather, we mentioned things. Lady Lavernock was not a delver: she was a mentioner, flitting from Shelley to sparking plugs with no apparent sense of incongruity.

"These men named Wright," she said. "Have you read what they're doing in America? Such an *appropriate* name for them. A wright is someone who does things. Don't you agree that that's what a wright is? A wheelwright, a playwright, a cartwright. Do you see?"

I said that I saw, but that I didn't know who the Wrights were. "You're so *honest*," she said. "I *like* that about you. You don't pretend. It's so dreadful the way people *pretend* to know things when they don't. You would agree that that is dreadful? Well, these Wrights make aeroplanes. They have been in the air for almost a whole minute. Think what that means."

I thought I had better remain honest, so I asked: "What does it mean?"

"Why, it means," she said, "that this thing I'm driving now will soon be as dead as the dodo. We'll all be flying about like birds. Of course, men will want to keep it all to themselves. The bother I had with my husband when I said I'd drive my own car! But here I am, doing it; and so it will be with an aeroplane. You must come up with me. You'll *love* it!"

I said that what we were doing now was adventurous enough for me; and indeed it was. James was the only driver I had had so far, and he was cautious. With Lady Lavernock we seemed to be flying, though I doubt whether we were covering thirty miles an hour.

"What I *like*," she said, "is when a tyre bursts and I have to change a wheel. You see I carry a spare one. One gets such a sense of mastery when turning the nuts with a spanner, and arrives home positively *filthy*. It dismays Ernest – really *dismays* him. You don't mind if I call Lord Lavernock Ernest? I feel we're old friends because I know your uncle, Mr Pallace, so well."

Thinking of Uncle Reginald reminded me of the garden and the little enclosure with the waterfall where, she had told me, she lay naked to induce poesy in her unborn son. "How is your son, Lady Lavernock?" I asked.

"Oh, a stupendous great fellow," she said. "He's spending the holiday with my father. Thank goodness, he has a completely modern mind. I've seen him mending his own bicycle."

The waterfall seemed to have misfired.

We got as far as Helston that day and had lunch there. Lady Lavernock, wearing her helmet and white overalls during the meal, was an object of great curiosity in the Angel dining room, but she was unaware of it. I felt that if she had wished to walk across the floor on her hands she would have done it, without seeing in it anything to raise an eyebrow. She belonged to the privileged order, and did as she pleased. She said to the waiter in her clear penetrating voice: "I am a teetotaller. Bring me some water, please. But this lady *drinks*. You'd better ask what she'd like." She seemed disappointed when I asked for water, too.

After lunch, we stood on the pavement, looking at the car. A small crowd had collected before this novel object. Lady Lavernock said, when we were both seated: "Now this is where I must have some help. I can't start the thing. The starting-handle is too heavy for me."

Now I understood why she had left the engine running when she first met me and when she was waiting for me at the vicarage. She addressed the crowd: "Will someone help me, please? It's that thing sticking out from the front of the bonnet. You take hold of it and swing it *violently* from left to right. It won't bite you, but it may dislocate your wrist if you are not *careful*. So you must be *very* careful. It's something to do with what they call back-firing."

A volunteer with the physique of an ox took hold of the handle and gave what seemed a playful twiddle. But the car at once purred and trembled. "Masterly," she said. "Quite, quite masterly."

The giant grinned and touched his cap. "Child's play that be," he said.

"Thank you. Thank you *very* much," said Lady Lavernock, "You are a good child."

7

Lady Lavernock said: "Now that we know one another so well, you must call me Jane, and I shall call you Maria. I promise that I shall *never* pronounce it as though I were a *Cockney*."

We were on a small beach of the North coast. It was empty save for us, as Cornish beaches usually were in those days. The horrors of the summer invasion had not yet begun. Jane and I had bathed in the breakers that came rolling in monstrously, and now we were lying on the sand in a cove, with the mild September warmth falling upon us. The golden sand, the blue hazy sky, the thunder of the surf, and crying of the gulls: I reproached myself for finding all this so much more satisfying than holding a picture for Hugo to hang it, keeping an eye on John and Connie as they paddled on St Tudno's unadventurous little stony beach, waking Bella at tea time from the afternoon sleep that she found necessary now that a new baby was on the way. It seemed to me that I had been rather too much given to reproaching myself. Even now, lovely as this dalliance was, I could not free myself from the thought that it had gone on for a long time, and that there was so much I could have been doing at the vicarage.

It was a Saturday; and on Monday, Tuesday, Wednesday, Thursday and Friday, I told myself, ticking off the days like sins remembered, I had gallivanted about the country with Jane. "I shall call for you *every* morning," she had said, "and you shall show me Cornwall."

But it was she who had shown me Cornwall. When you have nothing but a pony and your own legs to rely on, you don't get far, and really I knew little of Cornwall beyond Truro one way and Falmouth the other, and such of the coast as we could reach in our little boat. Now the boat was wrecked and there was no pony. Hugo made his explorations of the scattered parish on a bicycle. And so these days with Jane Lavernock were an eye-opener to me rather than to her. We had been lucky. We had not had a single breakdown of the car, which was something in those days. There was ever the question of the starting-handle, and that was solved by leaving the car near a farmhouse likely to provide a brawny male, and then lugging our lunch-basket to a quiet place.

I sat up and looked at her lying there. She opened her eyes and smiled. "You know, Maria," she said, "it would be *charming* to do this all along the southern coast of France."

"How would you get the car across the Channel?" I asked innocently.

"Oh, there are boats that would do that sort of thing for me; though perhaps," she said with the airy *insouciance* of the rich, "it would be better to buy a car over there. Much less bother."

I reached behind me and pulled out the lunch-basket. She jumped up and said: "Now let me do that for once. Seeing that you are to be my companion, we must learn to look after *one another*."

The remark so startled me that I said nothing for a moment. We had almost finished the excellent food that Louisa's cook had put up for us before I could say: "What do you mean: that I am to be your companion?"

She was throwing food to the gulls, who were a battling whiteness on the sand and in the air. Amid their frantic greedy screaming she said: "Did you know that Gerald Pickering had been down to St Tudno this week?"

I hadn't known this. I suppose Louisa would have told me, but I had not seen her. Jane had come to the vicarage each morning and returned me there each evening.

"Yes," she said. "He came for a day only, to arrange about having his pictures packed and sent to London for a show. When your sister told me he was there, I couldn't resist going down to his cottage late one evening. I bought a picture. Well, that's how I met him. He told me about you and that boy named Lester."

My face must have been flaming. "What on earth could he have known about it?" I muttered. "Charles Lester didn't care a pin about me."

She took my hand and asked: "Did you know that Gerald Pickering was in love with this girl he has married?"

"It was as plain as a pikestaff."

"You were in love, and so it was plain to *you*. Gerald Pickering was in love, and so perhaps things were plainer to him than you imagined."

I cried in desperation: "I really don't know what all this . . ."

She broke off my sentence by getting up, stroking my head, and beginning to pack the things into the basket.

All the greedy gulls were gone save one who stood a little way off screaming at me through a thrust-out neck and gaping beak and regarding me with a cold venomous eye. It looked the incarnation of the wild, unpredictable, man-hating sea. I got up trembling and followed Jane and took the basket from her hand.

She asked: "How is Mr Oldham settling down in the vicarage?"

"Oh, well enough. But I think that he and my sister Bella will be glad when I can be a bit more useful to them. I'm beginning to be conscience-stricken."

"Is that a dreadful thing to be?"

"To me – yes."

"Don't deprive them of the opportunity to be conscience-stricken, too. Perhaps it will be good for their souls if they are conscience-stricken because they have been making a convenience of you. Not intentionally, I am sure.

"Am I interfering?" she went on as we were trudging back to where we had left the car. "*Do* tell me if I'm *interfering*. But I've heard so much from your sister Louisa about your virtues. You sounded like a dear patient little pit-pony, cheerfully – or so his driver likes to think – slogging away in the dark."

I said at last: "Louisa left us when she was young. I don't blame her. But perhaps in her eyes that magnified the virtue of my staying at home. However, I don't for a moment regret having done it. I loved my father, and anyway there was nothing else that I could do."

"I do so *horridly* feel that I'm *interfering*," she persisted. "But your father's death set you free. Should you begin it all over again? There's so much now in St Tudno that it would be better for you to forget."

"I'm not good at forgetting."

I might go; I had told Bella that I would go; but I would not forget.

We were both a bit puffed with our uphill climb, and we dumped the basket and sat down in the purple wilderness of heather at the cliff top. We looked out to sea. The water was blue and calm except where it fretted on our shore, as though the touch of our restless contagion could bedevil even the deep. Gazing into the autumn tenderness of mist that shrouded Wales, my eye saw the procession of things that could not be forgotten, from the morning when I left Bella snoring in bed and went out carrying poor Euphemia in her cardboard coffin up to the day when James and I watched the weather in its fantastic death-dance, and the day not so long afterwards when Father smiled at me from the pulpit as though asking my forgiveness for hurts I chose not to remember. As I sat there with the purple sea behind me and about me, and the sea of blue before me, it was as though a balance was struck, the accounts of my life to date made up, and a line ruled under the sum.

I said: "Jane, I don't want to forget anything that has ever happened to me. I can remember it with you as well as I can remember it at St Tudno. If you do indeed want me to be your companion, I should love it."

8

Ever since I was a child I have begun a diary on New Year's day. Few lasted so long as a month, and I thought that none had survived, but rummaging among old rubbish when waste-paper was being collected during the last war – or, perhaps more accurately the most recent war – I came upon a survivor belonging to my sixth year. It is a record for scantiness, for it contains only one entry. "January the First. My new year ressolusions to be good, beautifull and happy. I can be good if I do what Papa tells me, and being good will make me beautifull because all angels must have been good and they are all beautifull. And if I am good and beautifull I can't help being happy, so this ressolusion is not dificult."

Poor child . . .

Well, on January the First in 1904 I began a new diary or, rather, a journal; and this one went on. I have kept it intermittently ever since, and so now I shall not have to rely entirely on memory.

"Jan 1, 1904. – I have agreed to go and live with Lady Lavernock as an experiment. At least it will get me out of St Tudno – a good place to come back to, but altogether too narrow for continuous living. We never took holidays in Father's time, and never felt that we needed to; so that I know next to nothing of England, much less any other country. My brief visit to Louisa when she was Mrs Wheatstone, to Manchester with Bella, and to Surrey when Louisa was there with Uncle Reginald: that is the poor extent of my geographical knowledge.

"I decided to stay until Bella's baby was born, and that happened on December the first. There he is now, Richard Oldham, and Bella was for ever calling me to watch him feeding at her breast. It gives her great delight, as though she were herself vicariously feeding. 'Isn't he good at it?' she demands, as though her Richard were already showing himself a master of one of life's most important accomplishments. 'Oh, Maria', she would say, 'you are a cad to leave me now', but I went the more readily when Mrs Holmfirth arrived. She is a broad-bosomed Yorkshire widow whom Bella and Hugo knew at Hunslet, and who appears to be devoted to them. They will be able to afford more help than poor Father ever could, though how Mrs Solway will get on with this foreigner remains to be seen. However, the vicarage is filling up again. One more infant and there'll be as many as Father had to struggle with.

"Hugo was very nice about it all. He dotes on Bella as much as she does on her children, but he stoutly opposed her wish to keep me. On my last night there he came to me with two keys. 'This one is yours,' he said, and handed me a key of the loft. 'Do please always consider the loft to be your retreat. Not that we want to banish you,' he smiled. 'The run of the whole house is yours whenever you want it. But I still feel an intruder, you know. I remember how you used to love the loft when I came here so long ago with Roger.'

"The name reminded him of all that I had lost. He paused, and then kissed me affectionately. 'I think', he said, 'that you all loved Roger, as I did. But I know that he loved you most of all.'

"I was glad that he had said it; glad, too, that he had *finesse* enough not to dwell on it. He went on at once: 'I, too, have a key of the loft, you see. But regard me just as the caretaker. The place will need now and then to be dusted and aired. I'll put Mrs Holmfirth in charge.'

"I asked how she was hitting it off with Mrs Solway. He said: 'Happily, they are both passionately concerned about the stomach. I overheard a heated dispute about the merits of Yorkshire pudding and parkin on the one hand and of Cornish heavy-cake and pasty on the other. Each considers the other to have barbarous tastes.'

"The dear fellow, with his *good* face and his kind eyes beaming through thick spectacles, made me feel very happy.

"And here I am now, writing this at the end of my first day at Coverdale, which is the name of Lord Lavernock's place. It is enormous, like Tregannock, but it has a better gardener."

I well remember making this entry on the day of my arrival. I was too excited to go early to bed. Uncle Reginald had met me at Dorking station, driven me and my solitary trunk to Coverdale, and left me on the doorstep. Jane herself, in her impetuous way, came running to the door, delivered me from the servants, and took me up to the first floor. It was late in the afternoon and darkness was coming on, but this didn't matter as it did at the vicarage, or even at Tregannock. There was no fussing about with lamps and candles. Coverdale was the first house I had known to be lit by electricity, and Jane went before me like a magician, causing lights to spring up as she passed.

"Now this is your place," she said, opening a door at the end of a long corridor. She touched a switch, and my place sprang to view. "I don't want you to meet anyone today," she said. "Poor dear, you must be exhausted. I shall send up some tea at once, and later I shall send up some supper. Go to bed when you like. Your bedroom is through there."

She went at once, and I walked through there, which was another door, and through yet another door leading to a bathroom. It was all rather flabbergasting. Hugo was talking about putting a bathroom into the vicarage, but we had never known such a luxury. In the summer the beach was our bathroom, and once a week in the winter there was a great to-do carrying hot water upstairs to a tub in what we called the Black Hole — a windowless cubicle. As a kind of induction ceremony, I at once washed my hands and face and then went back through the bedroom to the sitting room, postponing a complete examination.

Someone had been in and drawn the curtains, which were of night-blue velvet. Everything was silence. In the bathroom the floor was of rubber. Here and in the bedroom the carpets were thick. I felt as though walking on moss. The fire purred, and an electric lamp was alight on a table. The small elegant room was easy to move in. There was little furniture: a sofa and an easy-chair upholstered in the same fabric as the curtains, a small writing desk, a few book-shelves in a recess on one side of the fire; a few charming pieces of pottery in a recess on the other. The walls and the paintwork were white.

I pulled back the curtains, almost wondering whether I had a right to be so self-assertive, seeing that someone had taken the trouble to draw them. To my delight, I found that I could look down the valley towards Uncle Reginald's cottage. There it was, sheltering among winter-bare trees, a light or two shining. It comforted me, and I needed comfort. I was twenty-seven years old – no child. But too much had happened to me too suddenly. Roger, Charles, Father. Those lamps had gone out, leaving the place dark and cold. Then Bella's arrival, filling the vicarage with home-making bustle, had not helped. For her, it was resurgence; for me exile. Watching the child at her breast had made me feel sterile and not-belonging. There had been nothing for it but to go. And so I went, but not bravely. Even now, with this enchanting perch beneath my feet, I felt a lost bird. I felt very young – a child almost, which was a strange feeling to have at my age; but it has recurred again and again. Even now, in old age, there are times when I cannot *believe* in my age and I feel quite lost amid people who seem grown-up and sure of themselves, though some of them are half-a-century younger than I.

So I was glad to see the lights burning in Uncle Reginald's cottage. There had been a little snow, but it was now clear and a young slip of a moon was lying on her back in the sky, not shedding enough light to dim the lustrous stars. The night was still and cold, lovely but loveless, as some women are. I tried to send a warm thought through the glittering cold down to Uncle Reginald, then pulled the curtains across the window and sat down by the fire.

There was nothing to complain about. I was being well looked after. A trim girl came in with a tray and put it down on my little table. Tea and toast and a pot of "Gentleman's Relish". I found that I was not expected even to make up my own fire. A footman came in and did it for me.

The tea-tray was gone and the footman was gone, and I lay back in my chair, tired, ready to fall asleep, when I noticed the picture hanging between the shelves of books and the charming figures on the other side. It gave me a start. I got up to look at it more closely, and then I could have wept. It was one of Gerald Pickering's. High summer. The blue water of our creek, the little quay from which we had so often dived, the oak trees, the swans. And on the water beneath which she had now for ever disappeared, *Norah* was waiting for whatever was to befall.

I could understand the good-hearted thought that had caused Lady Lavernock to hang it there. It would be something I knew, something to remind me of home. But all it did was make me wonder whether I should ever know home again, ever again know someone whom I could love.

9

In the autumn, when we were motoring about Cornwall, Jane Lavernock had spoken of her son. A strapping great fellow, she had called him, capable of mending his own bicycle. I had pictured a raw schoolboy with dirty hands and unformed manners: something quite different from the poet that Jane had once told me she hoped to breed. In the autumn he had gone for his first year to New College, Oxford, and when I came to Coverdale he was in London, staying with his grandfather, Lord Bettiscombe, whose heir he was. I had been with Lady Lavernock for about a week when she announced: "Arthur will be arriving today."

I asked her who Arthur was, and she said: "Why, my *son*. I'm sure I told you about him *ages* ago. I called him Arthur because when he was on the way I was simply *mad* about Tennyson's *Idylls*."

I suppose Tennyson's Arthur was a beautiful blond with a beard. At least, that's how I always pictured him when I, too, gloated over the *Idylls* in the loft at St Tudno. A corn-coloured beard and blue, gentle eyes that could flash with fire at the very thought of an unknightly deed. Well, Jane's Arthur was not a bit like that, and not a bit like the rough schoolboy I had foolishly imagined. At the sound of wheels on the drive that afternoon, Jane, who had been gossiping in my room, seized my arm, crying: "He's here!" and, in her impulsive way, ran me down the stairs and into the hall. She could never be the calm hostess.

191

She always, in this way, ran, skimming like a bird, to welcome those she loved or for some reason wanted to see; but if the visitor were not congenial she would say: "Oh, that's old Lady Biggleswade" – or what not. "I'll see her at dinner. Soon enough."

I lagged behind her on the stairs and watched the greeting. The first thing I noticed about him was his height. He was only nineteen then, but he was six foot tall, and was to be taller, though Lord Lavernock was short and inclined to be stout. But he wasn't a blond Arthur. He was as dark as his father, and had, too, his brown intelligent eyes. The resemblance ended there, for Lord Lavernock's eyes were, as a rule, shrewd and calculating, while Arthur's were kindly and humorous. In dress and looks he conveyed a sense of breeding, of elegance, that his father never had.

Lady Lavernock waved impatiently to me and I came forward. "This is my son," she said. "Arthur, this is Maria Legassick."

He shook hands and smiled at me and said: "Mother has written to me about you. Are you any relation of Roger Legassick?"

"He was my brother."

"Was?"

"Yes. He was drowned at sea last year. You can't have known him?"

"I'm sorry. No. I didn't know him, but I've been reading his book *The Greek Ideal*. My tutor advised it, and I've enjoyed it enormously. Even though it's not my subject. Not *really*. I'm *doing* classics, but that's only to please my mother. I'm a mechanic *really*. I like to know how things work."

He had his mother's way of underlining words.

"But you liked the book?" I insisted.

"Oh, yes. You can *feel* how the author loved writing it. That's the thing – don't you think so?"

Jane bore him away, and I went back to my room, badly shaken. I hadn't wanted to hear Roger spoken of again. Not yet, at all events. Perhaps in time it would be possible to hear his name without the feeling of being torn that overcame me now.

10

I saw little of Lord Lavernock. This splendid mansion seemed to be only an adjunct of his life, not the centre, as it was of Jane's. He had called upon architects and builders to make it, and on Uncle Reginald to create the gardens, and on artists and antique dealers to fill it with lovely things, and this, I suppose, satisfied the sense of power which had caused him, when he first stood on the hill, to decide that a great house should be built there. Occasionally he came down with a party of brilliant-looking people, and even then he must have Mr Robertson, his private secretary, with him; and every morning, before doing anything else, he would spend an hour in his office-wing, telephoning to people in London. But, for the most part, he lived at his house in Park Lane.

The weekend after Mr Arthur arrived, on the Sunday, a day of mild winter sunshine, I had been to say good-morning to Uncle Reginald, and was walking back to the house when I met him and Mr Arthur strolling in the grounds. When here at Coverdale, he liked to be an English country gentleman, and was wearing tweeds and brogues and a deer-stalker cap. He raised this cap and said: "Good morning. Who are you, please?"

Arthur said: "Haven't you met Miss Legassick, sir? She's mother's companion."

He said: "No. Legassick? Where have I heard that name before?"

"Down at Tregannock, I expect, sir. You were there in the autumn with Mr Polperro. He is married to Miss Legassick's sister."

Lord Lavernock smiled. "Ah, that's it. Yes. Polperro's wife is turning him into quite a politician."

As if reassured about my respectability, he now shook hands, but seemed at a loss for conversation. At last he said: "Well, I'm taking my son to see my black swans," and off they went.

I walked back to the house, pondering upon the brief meeting. Coverdale was, of course, a house large enough for a thin and insignificant person like me to remain hidden for a long time, but that Jane had not bothered even to let her husband know of my existence seemed to me odd indeed. I found her in the hall, arranging masses of flowers that Uncle Reginald had sent up from the greenhouses.

I said: "Jane, I've just met Lord Lavernock."

She stood there nursing an armful of exotic-looking stuff, her head on one side, considering a great Chinese vase, rampant with green dragons. "What's so remarkable about that?" she asked. She began to put in the flowers. "Ernest loves to see the place stuffed with flowers," she said, "but what a shame to ruin the shape of this lovely thing by filling it up with what it was never intended to hold. It was not intended to hold anything. It is a thing-in-itself. Hundreds of years ago some dear old Chinese was nodding his head over a wheel as his hands moulded this lovely shape. I wish I had known him. Ernest doesn't care at all about the people who make things. He's only interested in the things they make."

She took out all the flowers and started again. "Mind you," she said, "he *is* interested in the things. He's not a *barbarian*. I'd rather have his opinion about a pot or a picture than my own. But he doesn't care a hang about the potter or the painter."

"Perhaps," I said, "that is why you decided that he wouldn't care a hang about me. He's taking his son to see the black swans, who appear to be more important inhabitants of Coverdale than I am."

She laughed. "I wish," she said, "that I had your capacity for anger. You look as though you really *cared* for what he thinks."

"I care about your keeping me hidden like a guilty secret," I said.

She tumbled the flowers into a long basket and took my arm. Without a word, she led me to my room, and we sat down by the fire. "Let me tell you something, Maria," she said. "To begin with, would it surprise you to know that I was brought up in a country vicarage, like you?"

I said that it would indeed.

"Well, then. Listen."

Her father, Lord Bettiscombe, had not married till he was approaching middle age. Then, to the horror of his relatives, he fell in love with a beautiful penniless child, the daughter of a village doctor. He married her when she was eighteen, and she died in giving birth to Jane when she was twenty. "My father," Jane said, "had been a gay man-about-town. For a time after my mother's death he was desolate. He lived at his place in the country and saw no one – not even me. I imagine he hated me as the cause of his wife's death, and I can't blame him. I lived more or less with the servants till I was five years old. Then my father began to revive. He opened up his London house again and made a few steps into society. Before long he was in the full swing once more. However, he had to do something about me. He could have left me in the care of a governess, but he had the sense to realise that a child needed a home of some sort, and he found one for me."

The doctor who was Jane's maternal grandfather had a brother holding a living in a Kent village, and, being as hard up as most country parsons, he was willing enough to accept the handsome payment offered if he would take this young grand-niece into his crowded home.

Jane spoke of her years there as the happiest she had ever known. Mr and Mrs Drake loved her, and she them, and there was a houseful of children. She stayed there till she was seventeen; and then her father, whom she rarely saw, suddenly took her away and sent her off to a finishing school in France.

"Three years of that," she said, "and then a London season with my father's sister, Lady Wivelsfield, for chaperone. She was the oldest of my father's relations. It was like going out with Boadicea. Her chariot was furnished with scythes for mowing down undesirable young men."

"Were you sorry about that?" I asked. "Were there any young men you wanted to encourage?"

She thought it over. "No," she said at last. "Of course there were young men I liked well enough, but when you've grown up with a large, rather amusing but desperately poor family like the Drakes, all this other thing seems such nonsense. I used to go for long weekends to great houses all over the country. The people there can never have realised how fabulous they seemed to me. The men with their valets, the women with their ladies' maids, the shooting, the guzzling, the utter *dreariness* of the talk. I had my own maid, of course, and that was the funniest thing of all. To think that I couldn't slip a dress over my own head or put on my own shoes! Why, I'd been used to cleaning my own boots and even chopping wood and lighting fires. I remember once – I think it was at Trentham – I was in my bedroom, and, having nothing better to do, I was turning down my bed when old dragon Wivelsfield came into the room. She couldn't have been more shocked if I'd been cutting the butler's throat. 'Jane!' she said. '*Whatever* are you thinking about? Are you gone quite mad?' "

She paused, turning the moment over in her mind. "Well," she said, "you see how it was. I was all a mix-up of Bettiscombe's daughter and Mr Drake's grand-niece. And I preferred the Drake side of it. Oh, we had such *fun* at the vicarage and such good *talk*. And that's why, at last, I married Mr Kopf. I was fascinated by his talk. He had been as poor as a church mouse. He had travelled. He'd known all sorts of people, and he had that *flair* for lovely things that some Jews have. He had imagination. Well – look at this house and the gardens."

"Poor Jane," I twitted her. "It must have been terrible to marry a man like that – and a millionaire into the bargain."

"Well, you see," she smiled, "that's what comes of being so odd as to turn down your own sheets and blankets. I suppose the dragon reported to Father, and between them they decided that I'd better be married to the first bidder before I became *déclassée* – a byword and a scandal."

She was twenty and Mr Kopf thirty when they married. They were very happy. "I suppose," she said, without any self-consciousness, "that I was never in love with him. I don't think I've ever been in love with anybody, though I *imagined* I was with a groom, just before Father packed me off to school. Indeed, I think that's why I *was* packed off. But Ernest and I got along famously. We still do. I *admire* him enormously. But more and more we live separate lives. His work is making money, and I can't take the faintest interest in that. Indeed, he doesn't expect me to and would be horrified if I did. But his *recreation* is society, and that's something I have no use for – *no use at all*," she cried, almost passionately. "Too much Drake in me. I'm the reversal of the old fairy-tale. The swans hatched me, and I turned out to be a duckling, or a Drakeling."

"No one would guess it," I laughed. She was still, at forty, a beautiful woman.

"Guess it or not," she said, "that's how it is. What an inheritance for poor Arthur! – Bettiscombes and Drakes and a heavy dash of the Jew. Whatever will *become* of him?"

Thinking of the handsome elegant youth, I said: "If I were his mother I shouldn't spend many anxious hours over that problem."

"Now you see," she said, "why Ernest knew nothing about you. He doesn't *expect* me to tell him all I'm doing. I *love* having silly little secrets. It gives me the idea that there's some part of my life that belongs to no one but me. It's a small point anyway, and you mustn't let it fuss you. You'd have met him at dinner tonight, anyway."

I did, and I got on with him well enough – as well as one would expect to get on with a stranger next to whom one was placed at a public dinner. We had at least James and Tregannock for common ground, and I'm afraid we ploughed it rather more deeply than the soil warranted. However, it saw us through without disaster. I remember the scene rather than the conversation. When Lord Lavernock was away, Jane and I did not bother to use the dining room. There was a room next door to it called the Little Room, and there we could be cosy and, so to speak, unofficial. Neither of us was much of an eater. But when Lord Lavernock was at home, whether there were visitors or not, the full panoply was turned on. Jane had said to me simply: "Put on your best things for dinner tonight," and I did so, though my best things didn't amount to much. At a quarter to eight she came to my room to take me down, and to my surprise she was dressed to the nines and glittering with diamonds. Her dress was of Cambridge-blue chiffon, so that she seemed a moving cloud, lit with stars. She was very beautiful, but so unexpected that I waited for her to say something about her appearance. But I had the sense quickly to realise that there are people to whom the extreme of luxury is nothing unusual. She said simply: "We must get down. Ernest is annoyed by unpunctuality."

She led me to a small anteroom off the dining room. That is, it was small comparatively, but it was as big as the biggest of our rooms at the vicarage. I had not seen it before, and I thought it the loveliest room in the house. It was octagonal, the walls were dull gold and the ceiling a deep crimson lacquer. There were book-cases, also crimson-lacquered, containing books bound in leather of many colours. A few leather chairs, shining like well-cared-for saddles, and an octagonal table, were the only furniture. The room was dimly lighted, and warmed by an electric fire – the first I had ever seen.

I don't know whether dinner jackets had at that time intruded anywhere. They had not intruded here. Lord Lavernock and his son were wearing what we now call full-fig: breast-plated with starch, and elegant with tailed coats. A decanter and glasses were on the table.

Lord Lavernock glanced at a small sunburst clock on the wall, checking us in. He did not ask us what we would drink. In that house, before dinner, one drank sherry or nothing. Jane drank nothing. She said: "Miss Legassick *drinks*, Ernest," and he handed me a glass.

Precisely at the moment when the little clock gave a ting before striking the hour, the door leading to the dining room was opened, and the butler announced, as if the undertakers had arrived, that dinner was served.

We went in processionally, though there were only ten paces to walk, Lord Lavernock taking my arm and Arthur Jane's. I had not before been into the dining room at night or seen it prepared for a meal. Lord Lavernock's taste was for dim lighting, and here the lighting was completely concealed save for the strips above the pictures. I had examined them before: Gainsborough, Reynolds, Hoppner, Raeburn, Lawrence – they were all there, all the conventional and approved portrait-painters that rich men liked to have. A fire roared in the large grate; swags of curtain shut us in. Our footsteps made no sound.

There would be only the four of us, Jane had told me. The table would take twelve; and, a startling note in what was becoming for me a phantasmal evening, I saw that twelve places were laid. A river of flowers, breaking here and there around tall épergnes of fruit, flowed down the table. The footmen were in full-fig, silk stockings and all.

The meal proceeded, ritually; and part of the astonishing ritual was that one footman did not move. He was posted like a statue behind a chair when we came in, and there he stayed till the meal was over. Jane explained to me, later: "That is the chair the Prince used when he came down here four years ago." Presumably, the footman's task was to preserve the chair inviolate from any profane bottom.

At the end of each course the footman removed the cutlery which our ghostly fellow-diners would have used had they been flesh and blood; and empty plates containing nothing – unless it were unseen heavenly manna – were put down. Alice was never more puzzled in Wonderland than I was as I watched these gorgeous mutes bending deferentially over the shoulders of invisible guests, whipping away plates, wine-glasses, knives, forks, spoons. I hoped the spectres, at the end, felt as replete as I.

At last – and not too soon for me – Jane rose, tilted her head towards the door, and I followed her out. We left the gentlemen to their port.

11

After their port, the gentlemen did not join the ladies. I was not sorry. I had never before sat down to a dinner like that, and though Jane had

merely pecked at one or two dishes and declined the others, I thought
it would be fun, now that I was living an Arabian Night, to live it to
the full. I ate everything that was put before me, including a sorbet
that helped me over the last hurdles, and I drank. I don't remember
what I drank, but I know that, as well as the sherry, there was red wine
and white wine. The white-gloved hand of a footman above my glass
was a recurring theme in a symphony that became more and more
hazy and ethereal. And so I was glad that the gentlemen did not join
us. Anyway, we had not gone to the drawing room. Jane led me
straight to my own room, went through to my bedroom to see that
all was in order, and then said: "Get into bed, you little fool." I did so
gladly. She went away, and came back carrying a glass. "Drink this,"
she said. I smiled for a moment at the bubbles chasing one another
up the glass and exploding, and then downed it at a gulp. "In the
morning," Jane said, "you'll feel better than you deserve to." She
switched out the lights and left me. I slept, and when I awoke I did
feel well. Indeed, I had forgotten that I should be feeling anything
else. The girl who brought my morning tea asked: "Are you feeling
all right, madam?" I asked why I shouldn't, and she said: "My lady had
to consult Mr Summerskill last night. He's a great authority on –
diet."

I blushed, and imagined myself branded henceforth, a byword and
a reproach to all the staff. The news would reach Uncle Reginald, and
doubtless he would inform Louisa, who would tell Bella, and Bella
would pass it on to Hugo, who would have public prayers for my
redemption said in St Tudno church.

I drank my tea, had my bath, and felt more cheerful. It was a
morning of sparkling frost. The fire had been lit in my sitting room
and my breakfast was brought up. The stimulating smell of coffee
filled the room. Then I noticed that the tray had been laid for two.
Jane came in. "May I join you at breakfast?" she asked.

"Yes. If you haven't come to scold me."

"Why should I?"

"For my indiscretion."

"You weren't indiscreet. You were a plain fool. However, I didn't
want to talk about that. You have sense enough, I hope, to learn
lessons without my having to beat them into you."

I poured the coffee and handed her a cup. "Well," she asked. "What did you think of it all?"

"The dinner?"

"Well – if you care to call it such. The masquerade."

"Masquerade," I said, for Father was always urging me to look up the true meaning of words, "is founded on mask, a disguise, a pretence to be something or someone else."

"Thank you, teacher," she said. "You'd better write it on the blackboard, and then I sha'n't forget."

She nibbled a bit of toast, and said: "You know, Ernest isn't in the least degree an eccentric, and so you may wonder why he insists on this one eccentric thing. For he does. It *always* happens when he is here to dinner, however many people eat. Imagine what it's like when not even you and Arthur are present – just Ernest and I, and with me eating no more than a tom-tit. *Can* you imagine it?" I couldn't.

"Well," she said, "I don't want you to think he's quite a lunatic. There is an explanation. The King and Queen dined here once when they were Prince and Princess of Wales. When you've been brought up as Ernest was – much poorer than you ever were in your vicarage or I in mine – you can imagine what a thing that was for him. It wasn't all grace and favour, either. I've heard him say that his suggestions put at least half a million into the Prince's pocket."

I looked at her nibbling a bit of unbuttered toast, and I felt more dazed than I had been with wine last night. She talked about these people and these vast sums of money as casually as though she were discussing the price of bread.

"Well," she said, "the Waleses were one thing, the King was another. At last Ernest bagged him. He and Alexandra were to come down here to dinner, and to spend the night and do a day's shooting afterwards. Oh, the fuss about invitations! It was sheer hell. At the last permissible second there was a message from the Palace to say that the King had developed a sudden feverish cold and was forbidden by his doctors to travel. That was at five o'clock. Ernest was so shattered that he couldn't face the other guests. He went to bed, and I had to handle them alone. I fed them in the Little Room, and Ernest didn't get up till they'd all gone the next day. And that is why we have this rigmarole. Ernest must remind himself that he is fit to entertain a King, even though he's never done it, thanks to a microbe in the mucus membrane, or wherever these things get."

I said, truly, that it was the most fantastic thing I'd ever heard.

"Yes," Jane said. "But, of course, he's not often here, so I don't suffer much. Oddly enough, the servants love it. Old Summerskill would feel dreadfully put out if he didn't have his masquerade now and then."

I asked if we should have the masquerade again tonight.

"Oh, no," she said. "Ernest and Mr Robertson and Jacot are on the way to town by now."

"Jacot? I didn't meet Jacot."

"No. He's Ernest's chef. You and I and Arthur will put up with Mrs Comstock's cooking, and that suits me. But Jacot goes with Ernest, whether he's here or in town or on the yacht or down at Minstall."

"Minstall is new to me."

"It's Ernest's training place. Horses."

"Oh." It was all I could get out. I hardly dared open my mouth again lest my words draw back the curtain from some new incredible splendour. However, she didn't wait for me. "There's Voortrek, too," she said. "That's Ernest's place outside Cape Town. He has to be in South Africa a lot to see how his gold and diamonds are behaving."

I said feebly: "We shall be eating off gold plate next."

"Well, we do in town. That's the only point where the masquerade falls short. The gold plate was brought down for the King's dinner. But, as you perhaps noticed last night, for these *reminder* occasions, we content ourselves with Crown Derby."

I said: "With the three of them gone back to town, what do we do with ourselves today?"

"The four of them," she corrected me. "There's Massingham, Ernest's valet."

I said: "Poor Mr Arthur! Is he left to pull on his own trousers?"

"No. Finchley will look after him. He's the house valet here. He looks after any stray gentleman so unfortunate as to come down without his own valet."

She took another piece of unbuttered toast and I refilled her coffee-cup. "Ernest is very particular," she said, "about being properly dressed for all occasions. Not long ago, Arthur dashed down from Oxford, not knowing his father was here. He brought nothing but the clothes he was standing in and his night things. When we gathered for sherry, Ernest was in full fig. He was outraged. He said: 'Is your allowance so small, Arthur, that you cannot afford to keep a proper wardrobe here for use when you need it?' He rang for Summerskill and told him to bring Godfrey at once."

"Who is Godfrey?"

"Godfrey was the house valet before Finchley. Ernest handed him a week's wages and said: 'Please leave the house at your earliest convenience. You do not appear to understand your duties.' Godfrey dared to say: 'Mr Arthur has no evening clothes here, sir.' 'Then,' said Ernest, 'it was your duty to point out that fact and see that it was put right.' Then he rang again for Summerskill and said: 'Mr Arthur will take his sherry, and dine, in the Little Room.' "

She sipped her coffee, thinking back over the moment evidently without pleasure. "Half way through dinner," she said, "he asked me to excuse him and went up to his own rooms. He was soon back, wearing his shooting clothes. He said to Summerskill: 'Please ask Mr Arthur if he will be kind enough to join me at port.' Arthur appeared, and his father said: 'Come in, my boy. Sit down. I want you to feel at home.' I left them to it."

"I can think," I said, "of several easier ways of making a boy see a point."

"So can I. But Ernest is an autocrat. Did you notice that I was wearing diamonds last night?"

Did I not!

"If one had been missing I should have heard about it. He gave me every one, and every one is a symbol of the beneficence which his power permits him to shed upon me. Do you see the jewels I'm wearing now?"

I looked in vain for the jewels. I saw nothing but a thin gold chain round her neck and, attached to it, a not very becoming garnet. She fingered the garnet and said: "I'm fond of this. Mr Drake gave it to me when I left him to go to the finishing school."

She got up to go, and I was suddenly filled with an awareness of my great affection for her, and with contrition for my foolishness last night. "I'm so sorry, Jane," I said, "that I gave you so much trouble."

She stood in the doorway, fingering the garnet. "That's all right, Maria," she said. "We vicarage girls must hang together. Amuse yourself today. I'm taking Arthur out in the car. I must keep my hand in for our journey through France in the spring."

12

When they were gone I walked down to Uncle Reginald's cottage. He himself came to the door and said: "You're just in time. Come in."

He took me to what he called his den, a small room with a heavenly view. "What am I in time for?" I asked.

"To stop me working." He gave me a grin and pointed to a litter of papers on his table. "I'm told there are writers who loathe being interrupted. For me, I welcome intruders."

"You're not writing a *book*?" I cried.

He nodded.

"Oh, dear! Father, Louisa, Roger, and now you! Can nothing keep our tribe from the ink-trough?"

He said apologetically: "I didn't want to do it. A publisher badgered me, and after a masterly resistance I gave in."

He went out to his kitchen and came back with coffee. He lit his pipe and sprawled in a wicker chair. Nothing seemed to change him. His very clothes might have been those he was wearing when he rowed ashore at St Tudno on Euphemia's burial morning.

"What's it about?" I asked.

"Mainly about plants. I'm afraid that will be dreadfully scientific – masses of dull tables recording the marriages and inter-marriages of azaleas, rhododendrons and what not. And then there'll be the tale of my life in China and Tibet. It was rather exciting, you know, at times. The devil of it is that recording it brings it all back so vividly that it makes me feel like a tiger in the zoo."

"Aren't you happy here?"

He looked through the window at the winter-bare trees underplanted with evergreen. Here and there an early-flowering shrub was announcing the glory that would soon spread through all the woods.

"Isn't that a grand thing to have done?" I urged him.

"It makes the zoo habitable," he agreed. "But compared with the real thing – the mountains, the gorges, the torrents, the incredible plants growing in God's plenty, the solitude – oh dear, how shall I ever say it, make people see it? I wish I could *write* as well as remember."

"A lot of people do," I soothed him. "I'm sure you'll make a fine book of it."

"Don't think I'm ungrateful for what I've been allowed to do here. I shall dedicate the book to Lord Lavernock."

He fished for his wallet and produced a letter. "Talking of Lord Lavernock," he said, "I wonder what he would think of this?"

He handed me the letter. It was from Louisa.

Dear Uncle Reginald. – I hope you are keeping an eye on Maria. I'm not at all happy about her being in such a household as Lord Lavernock's, though it was not my business to do anything to stop her from going. Indeed, she *had* to go somewhere, since to stay at the vicarage after Hugo and Bella were installed would have been most unsuitable. But she's taken rather a jump – St Tudno vicarage to Coverdale might well test a person with some experience of society, and poor Maria has had no experience at all. From the little I saw of Lady Lavernock she was here with her husband in the autumn, I should say she is rather an unstable character, though her affection for Maria seemed genuine enough. We can only hope for the best.

I rudely poked my tongue out at the letter, and Uncle Reginald laughed. "I thought you'd like that bit," he said.

Louisa continued:

Well, the most surprising news I have to give you is that James is to try his hand as a parliamentary candidate. He has worked very hard on County Council business and has done a lot of public speaking during this winter. I have always gone with him and sat on the platform at his meetings, and have even done a bit of speaking myself. But the most valuable thing has been to watch him and to correct his deportment when necessary, and now and then to prime him with facts. He has come really to *enjoy* this sort of thing, which shows how people brought up as he was were *wasted*. They expected to be esteemed merely for being landowners, and all too often, alas, they were. But to get out, as James is now doing, and meet all sorts of people eager to criticize and question him – that's another matter and makes a man depend on what he *is*.

James is showing up reasonably well. I don't think a General Election can be long delayed, and it is as plain as a pikestaff that this scandalous Chinese slavery in the South African mines will throw the Conservatives out of office, and the sooner the better. Poor James wasn't even aware that a lot of his family's money came, not so long ago, from slavery in our own Cornish mines, but I have briefed him on that; and whenever he now speaks publicly on Chinese slavery, he begins, on my advice, by saying: 'I appear tonight as one who loathes slavery, whether English or Chinese. I know something about it. My ancestors grew fat on it. I am addressing you from the penitents' bench.' That takes the wind out of a good many sails, though it doesn't make James much loved by some of his old cronies. However, when the election comes, he will not fight here. He has been adopted as prospective Liberal candidate for a seat in Northamptonshire.

I imagine, and indeed hope, that this will end his not very warm friendship with Lord Lavernock, who no doubt imagines Chinese to be people created by God to serve his interests. It is wonderful how, during the war and in the years of depression following it, he has kept his head above water. I find it very, very difficult to imagine poor Maria in that *milieu*. However, give her my love, and accept it yourself, dear Uncle Reginald. James has been reading this over my shoulder. He says: 'Oh, come! Lavernock's not a bad feller. I doubt if he's seen a Chink in his life.' Which only shows how far his political thinking has still to go.

Louisa.

I handed him the letter. "Louisa is one of those people who think you shouldn't go into the water until you can swim," I said. "However, she took the plunge herself."

"Yes. I was partly responsible, do you remember? I knew Wheatstone slightly and took a risk."

"It worked out pretty oddly."

"I agree. Perhaps I wouldn't have done it if I'd known I was being a match-maker. The nuptials of shrubs are the only ones that should be entrusted to me."

"You've nothing to reproach yourself with," I assured him. "She'd have gone whether you helped her or not."

"Yes. She was all to pieces over James Polperro. How do you see him as a Liberal parliamentarian?"

I said: "It's working out exactly as I expected. He was her idol, and the idol was broken. When she at last picked up the pieces, she tried to fit them together again in a different shape. I'm afraid there'll always be strange-looking jagged angles."

He smiled at me through a cloud of tobacco-smoke. "Oh wise young judge!" he said.

"But don't you agree?"

"Yes. She's a remarkable woman. If women were allowed to sit in Parliament, she'd be the candidate herself. As it is, she does the best she can with James. If she had trained a crow to sing like a blackbird it wouldn't be more astonishing than to teach James to open his mouth in public. I shouldn't be surprised if he's elected. There is, you know, an awful lot of feeling about what they call Chinese slavery in South Africa. Well, we shall see. And how are you finding things?"

I told him that I was very happy with Jane, rather daunted by Lord Lavernock.

"Keep out of his way as much as you can," he advised me. "He's a brute force, and that's not his fault. He can no more help it than Niagara can help plunging over its cliff. I've watched a few financiers in my time, and most of them are ambitious bullfrogs who swell till they bust. Lavernock is not like that. There are few men like him in a century. Perhaps it would be a good idea if there were none at all. I don't know."

"How rich is he?" I foolishly asked, and Uncle Reginald said: "I don't suppose he knows within a million or two from day to day. But there are plenty of states whose Chancellors don't control as much money as he does."

"What is the *point* of being all that rich?"

He grinned at me. "When you're in an adventurous mood," he said, "you might ask Lord Lavernock. But I doubt whether he could give you an answer. Some men are made to hunt plants, some to paint pictures, some to make money. They don't know why. All they know is that they can't help it and they're miserable when they're not doing it."

I was in an argumentative mood. "But isn't it wrong to have so much money? Doesn't it hurt other people?"

"My dear Maria," he said, "you will never begin to understand people like Lord Lavernock if you imagine that such problems enter their minds. Right and wrong are difficult questions even for philosophers. Niagara doesn't ask them. It just goes pounding along."

CHAPTER SEVEN

O
N MAY the 21st, 1906, which was my thirtieth birthday, I paid my bill at the Green Bank Hotel in Falmouth, hired a boatman to row me across to Flushing, and took the road that would lead me over the hump of land on whose other side St Tudno vicarage nestled by the water's edge. I could be there in half-an-hour, but it was a day for loitering, and I was in a mood for loitering, and there was good reason why I should loiter. I left the suitcase containing my few clothes at the Green Bank. I could pick it up later if things turned out well.

It was odd to feel that I had no home. Uncle Reginald had died while I was abroad with Lady Lavernock. I had considered going to Tregannock, but Louisa would not be there. Now that James was a Member of Parliament, they had leased a London house in Brook Street, and there she stayed while the House was sitting, conscientiously entertaining the people who should be entertained and doing all the other things that might help to turn her plodding Dobbin into a racehorse. Anyhow, whether she would want to see me now was something I had no means of knowing. It had to be St Tudno.

At the top of the hill I paused. From here you could look back and see Falmouth, grey and homely, with a few sailing-ships on the water; or you could look forward and see the Carrick Roads and the land beyond carpeted with the gold of gorse. Already the grass in the fields about me was ripe enough for the mowers, and they were there, swinging their scythes, and the hedges were rich with bluebells and foxgloves and campion. The air was full of birdsong; and butterflies — red admirals and peacocks and the small pale blue ones whose name I did not know — dithered about as though drunk with the day's felicity.

I sat on the warm roadside grass and it seemed a day miraculously recreated out of my innocent childhood. How often, on such a day,

208

Roger would shout "It's May! It's May! Let's go for a walk!" and off we would go – he and Bella and I – like young animals released to gambol. In the dusty road, under the hedges frothing with hawthorn whose scent seemed to fill the space between earth and heaven, we were without goal or purpose – just being young on a morning in May.

And still it goes on, I thought. Look at these children now! They came belting along the road, shouting in glee – a tall thin boy, a chubby girl, a toddler with a bunch of hedgerow flowers held tightly in his fist, wilting already. Yes, I thought, that is Richard, and when last I saw him he was feeding from Bella's breast. Those others are John and Constance.

They looked at me and smiled as children will to a stranger, and I was a stranger to them. John is eleven, I said. When last I saw him he was eight. Three years to him is eternity, and I am standing on eternity's other side.

Richard's fat brown legs brought him to me and he shyly held out his bunch. "Fool's parsley," he announced with a scholar's pride.

"Oh, you know the names of flowers, do you?"

"Father teaches me. I know more than John."

"You don't," John challenged him.

"I do. I know fool's parsley and pennywort and viper's bugloss."

"That's a fat lot," John said. "Do you know stitchwort?"

"I know *everything*," Richard maintained stoutly.

"That's nonsense," Constance said. "Even Daddy doesn't know everything."

"I know more than Daddy," Richard affirmed, looking doubtful and blasphemous, his toe scraping the dust.

Daddy! The word struck me, a minute indication of change, of *rapprochement* between the generations. With us, it had been Papa, or, more often, Father.

A village girl, pushing a perambulator, came up and intervened with the authority of fourteen or fifteen years. "Don't worry the lady," she commanded.

John, obviously annoyed at being ordered about, joined Constance, and they ran on down the road. Richard said to me: "That's Millicent." He peeped in fondly beneath the green hood of the pram. He waved his flowers over Millicent's face, announcing pedagogically: "Fool's parsley."

I looked at Millicent, asleep, oblivious of all that she must learn of fool's parsley and much else. She was seraphically withdrawn, almost still in the womb. Her warm lips looked as though dewed with Bella's milk. I asked how old she was, and the girl said six months. Richard continued to wave his educational bunch over her face. It tickled her nose and she opened her eyes. She looked at me and smiled with the complacency of the utterly protected.

Richard said: "Goodbye. I must find stitchwort."

They disappeared presently round the bend of the road and I walked slowly on towards the vicarage, wondering how much I had to learn. I hadn't known of Millicent's existence, or even that she was on the way.

2

It was just three years ago that Jane and I crossed over to France. Lord Lavernock was in South Africa, and, so far as Jane knew, was likely to be there for some time. He was often away for as much as a year, she said. I remember asking innocently: "Who looks after his business when he is away?"

She glanced at me for a moment as though wondering whether I was trying to say something amusing, but seeing that I was serious, she laughed outright. "Really, Maria," she said, "Ernest is not a fishmonger's assistant. He doesn't *have* to be in an office at all, though I believe he's fairly faithful when he's in town. As for anyone looking after his business – well, I don't suppose there's anyone who *could* do that. I don't understand it all, but there *are* other ways of making money, you know, than going to an office at nine, coming home at five, and drawing your week's pay on Saturday morning."

We were sitting on the terrace, looking down the valley through which colour was flowing like a celestial river. The May sunshine was warm. I said: "If I ever marry, I shall marry someone who works at home – a painter or a writer – someone like that. Perhaps even a parson would do. Don't you find it dreadful when Lord Lavernock goes away for a whole year at a time?"

"Why should I?"

"Well, if you love a man . . ."

She looked at me rather wearily. She said: "I wish you wouldn't talk nonsense. And don't *pretend*. You must never *pretend* with me. Even a girl like you, whose whole life has been spent in a small village, must have noticed that people who love one another in the story-book fashion don't add up to one in a thousand. After a few years of marriage, feelings of that sort tend to diminish, not increase. I know very few women indeed who would want a husband about the house all day. Think, child, and tell me frankly – isn't it your own observation that that is so?"

It was so. I knew it was so. But I wouldn't admit a fact that I faced for the first time. I remained rebelliously mute.

"People talk about a marriage of convenience," she said, "as though that were some wicked contrivance of the rich. Almost every marriage is a marriage of convenience. It is completely convenient for men and women to live together, but that doesn't mean they want to live in one another's pockets. And," she added with a laugh, "it would be *most inconvenient* if children were born all over the place without the security of a home in their early years. Love builds the nest, but commonsense and tolerance hold it together, even though a window gets smashed now and then."

"Nests don't have windows."

"All right," she said, "quibble. But I see you agree with me."

I didn't say Yes or No. We sat uneasily, listening to a torrent of bird-song, watching a few fledglings trying their wings. She said: " 'The year's at the spring.' 'Sweet lovers love the spring.' All that sort of thing."

I said, surprised at my daring: "You are trying to defend your own position. You would like to be the one in a thousand."

She said: "Yes . . . Go away."

I went into the house.

3

We sailed from Folkstone to Boulogne. It was my first voyage in a steamboat and I wondered how I should stand it. I enjoyed every moment of it, though the sea was a bit fresh and choppy. But Jane was devastated. When we landed she decided to remain where she was. In the hotel she went to bed at once and stayed there till morning. According to our programme, we should by then have been in Paris, but Jane was not a slave of programmes. She awoke full of energy and decided that Paris could wait. "We have nothing to do there, anyway, but pick up the car I've ordered. We have years before us, so we'll go first of all to Montreuil. That naughty fellow Laurence Sterne was there. If you *do* ever marry a parson, mind you choose one like him. But, there. I don't suppose you've so much as heard of him."

However, I had. Alone in the vicarage, unpacking and arranging Hugo's books, I had come upon the *Sentimental Journey*. Hugo's books seemed altogether more broadminded than Father's. I had skipped through the book, and, though I often blushed, I did not desist. So I was able to assure Jane primly that I knew something of Sterne, but had not been aware that he was a clergyman. "Well, he was," she said, "though I don't imagine that the fact troubled him."

So we went to Montreuil and stayed at the Hôtel de France, with the broad *place* in front of it, and the bedrooms opening on to a balcony that overlooked the courtyard, so that one could gaze down as if into the pit of a theatre. I left Jane in her room and walked about the little town. Swallows were flying over the *place* whose trees were in new green, and under the trees the market women sat at their stalls. It was gay and animated. Even the oldest of the women – earthy creatures with calm but formidable faces, wearing black clothes and cloddish boots – could not make the day anything but young, anything but May. And to hear nothing but a foreign language being spoken touched it all with unreality. Father had taught me what French I knew, and I was amused to find that it was none. None, at any rate, that was of use here. They knitted and chattered, and what they said meant no more to me than did the chattering of the jackdaws who strutted upon the cobbles, taking the sunlight upon their neat grey necks.

I am abroad, I thought.

For the first time in my life I was abroad. From the cliffs of Boulogne, which were not many miles away, it would be possible to see England in clear weather; but how far away England was! Distance is not altogether geographical. How distant you can be from someone sitting on the other side of the room! Goodness knows, I was familiar enough with swallows and jackdaws. Why did these seem strange and unfamiliar? But they did. They had the lustre of things seen for the first time. I saw them under a foreign sky, with foreign words falling upon my ears, incomprehensible but enchanted.

I wandered, loitering before the shops and the lovely portal of the church, and from the ramparts I looked at the river flowing through the level fertile land. Down there the light was pearly. The fields and the trees seemed not sharply defined, as though the air between was screened by the invisible exhalation of the river and the marsh.

I walked back to the *place,* the reservoir into which all the streets of the little town flowed, and all the people, too, it seemed, on this market day. I paused to take in the scene once more, and suddenly a moment out of my past raced to meet me. I was walking along the creek path towards the cottage called Little in Sight, and before me, where the spring gushed out of the hedge, a man was standing, looking at the sparkling water. He was wearing a white linen suit and a black sombrero, and I stopped and we talked about the water and drank from our palms.

The rushing back of this moment hurt me to the heart, for it was the moment when Roger was at St Tudno and when Charles Lester was expected.

My feet dragged as I walked across the *place* towards the man in the white linen suit. Yes, it was Gerald Pickering.

He was leaning against a tree, slashing away with a stub of pencil at a sketch-book, so absorbed that for a moment he took no notice of me. At last he turned his head, and was as startled to see me as I had been to see him. "My God!" he said. "Miss Legassick! The Hippocrene nymph!"

He stuffed his sketch-book into the large pocket of his coat, and we shook hands. "Well," I said, "this is a surprise. I thought I was a stranger in a strange land. And here are you! Is Meg with you?"

He had seemed pleased to see me. His face, that had been gravely intent on his work, had lighted up. My question clouded it. "No," he said.

I waited, but nothing more came. It was so clear from his face that more was there to come, but was being clamped down, that I said: "I'm sorry."

There were mounds of snow-white cauliflowers, overflowing baskets of spring bloom, great wicker cages through whose osier bonds the cockerels lustily sent their flying challenges. But now he

213

was seeing and hearing none of it. Perhaps he was seeing Meg sitting on the quay wall, her bare white legs dangling, as he painted her from the dinghy. Whatever he was seeing, he was silent for a long time before saying: "Well, what are you doing here?"

I told him. "I expect," I added, "that Lady Lavernock is wondering what I'm up to. It's lunch time. I'm sure she'd be glad to see you. Would you care to join us?"

4

The house in Hampstead to which Gerald had taken Meg was rather beyond his means. He was happy about the pictures he had painted at St Tudno, and it is agreed now, I believe, that they were the best he ever did. The exhibition at which he showed them in London had been encouraging, and it was this that caused him to rent the small house. He left Little in Sight empty save for a couple of beds and a few pots and pans. It would be a good place to camp in when he wanted a change from London. He and Meg settled down with a view of the Heath. They would wander out in the mornings and watch the birds on the ponds and the grey squirrels flinging themselves about in the branches of the hawthorns. Meg loved them and would take a pocketful of crusts for them to eat. She would hold a crust between her teeth, and the squirrels would run up her dress and sit on her shoulders and paw her face as they snatched at the food. Their feet, cold and wet with dew, would make her squeal with delight.

"Well, you knew her," Gerald said. "She loved simple things of that sort. She brought home a sparrow with a broken leg, and made it well. It used to live in the kitchen. She had minnows there, too, in a big glass jar. She caught them in the ponds."

He didn't tell her of his troubles, and he had plenty. The half-success of the exhibition didn't develop. One or two of the art magazines had articles about him; he continued to sell a picture here and there. His second exhibition was not so successful as the first. The Manchester and Birmingham art galleries bought pictures, and that was about all.

"I began to be worried," he said, "and that was something new for me. Before I was married, I could live on a crust. I thought of looking out for the sort of place I'd been used to – just one room somewhere, with a gas-ring and a bed. But Meg was so happy at Hampstead. I couldn't face it."

He began to fall behind with the rent of the little house. "And that was another thing I couldn't tell her about. My mother had a horror of debt. Most poor people have, you know. She paid her bills weekly – that is, when she had bills at all. As a rule, she paid on the nail. Well, I was that sort of puritan as well as an artist. I began to feel like a criminal when the rent-collector appeared. Then I by-passed him and took a picture along to the landlord. I offered it in settlement. He said: 'Are you trying to be funny, Mr Pickering?' "

I can never forget how he looked when he told me that small story. He had offered the essence of his being. "It was one of the best things I ever painted. The chap said: 'I'm a business-man, Mr Pickering, not an old junk merchant.' "

I put my hand on his, to let him know that I understood. He turned towards me with a faint shy smile. We were sitting on the balcony, looking down into the courtyard of the Hôtel de France. A country cart had lumbered in behind a great horse wearing hairy fetlocks like dirty shredded doormats.

"You'd never believe," he said, "how difficult it is to raise a few pounds if people don't want what you have to sell."

"I *do* believe it," I said, thinking of the time when Father had died and I had nothing – not even something people didn't want to buy.

"I'm afraid your sister will never forgive me," he said. "Meg and I were deeply grateful to her for giving us Little in Sight. I sold it for a few hundred pounds. I said nothing to Meg, and we kept going for a bit that way."

He was still selling a picture now and then, charging thirty pounds each for them. "In my room at Chelsea, living alone, I could have managed . . . Did you ever meet Meg's mother?"

"I saw her – once. I've never spoken to her." I strove to force my thought back to the moment. A child visiting her sister who was Mrs Wheatstone. Being entrusted to Meg Newman. Walking about Bond Street and meeting the handsome lady. My mind had long since interpreted the details that had meant nothing to the child. I understood the significance of the masher hovering in the background.

"She was a prostitute," I said.

"Yes."

"I remember her as a fine-looking woman."

"She wasn't when we met her."

Now and then he took Meg up to town. "With a bit of money in hand I thought we could afford a splash now and then."

They had been having a splash. I suppose it cost about as much as one of Lord Lavernock's cigars. "But it was fun being with Meg in the small Soho restaurant," he said. "It was so wonderful to her. Everything was wonderful to Meg. Then we went to a music hall. I'm very fond of music halls. Meg laughed fit to burst." He was remembering everything about Meg, as in a dirty winter day one remembers April.

It was a steely winter night, hard and cold, and when they came out of the music hall the wind made them hurry. The old woman was sitting on a canvas stool in the doorway of a closed shop. She was huddled up in black clothes and she was knitting a magenta muffler. A tray of match-boxes lay in her lap. "I didn't want matches," Gerald said. "I don't smoke. But seeing her sitting there looking as though that wind would cut her open, I fumbled in my pocket for a few loose coppers and threw them on her tray. She looked up with a whine of thanks. 'Gawd bless you!' she said. Well, there was no blessing in that moment. The blessed thing would have been if I'd never seen her."

Her eyes and Meg's met. They recognised one another at once. The old woman got up, spilling the tray of matches, dropping the knitting to the pavement. She threw her arms round Meg and cried: "Oh, my dear daughter! My sorrows are ended!"

"I knew who it was," Gerald said. "Meg had told me about her. She told me about everything. I shuddered as I looked at her. She was a dreadful old woman, coarse and dirty. I knew in my bones that we had stumbled on something that was going to do us no good."

It must have been a bad moment for Meg. She was fastidious. She had been taken early away from her mother's influence. She had lived for years with Louisa. She did not kiss her mother. Indeed, she did not know *what* to do. She said with sad perplexity: "So you've come to this!" And to Gerald: "This is my mother."

Mrs Newman said: "Yes, dear. I've come to this at last with Gawd's help. I've come to honest work. I've repented of my sinful ways."

It was all a whine and a wary look-out for what advantage there might be in the encounter. "Who is the gentleman?" she asked.

Gerald said: "Who I am has nothing to do with you, Mrs Newman. Now we must be off." He fumbled again in his pocket and found half-a-crown. "Give yourself a warm meal," he said, "and get back to your home. This is no night to be out in."

"We can't all live on the fat of the land," she whined. "We can't all have roofs over our heads. It's easy for those that have homes to say 'Go home' to them that have none."

At that, Meg cried out in distress: "Oh Mother! You don't mean to say you have nowhere to go? – nowhere at all!"

Mrs Newman managed a tear, and wiped it away with the back of her hand. "My own daughter to doubt my word! My own daughter anxious to learn that I have a hole to crawl into, so that she may leave me to it!"

Gerald, full of foreboding, said: "That is what we are going to do, Mrs Newman." He took Meg's arm firmly. A Hampstead bus drew up at the kerb, and he pulled Meg on to it. All the way home they didn't speak. It wasn't the silence that comes from perfect understanding. There was something between them. Meg was unhappy. There was not a shred of self-righteousness or self-seeking in her. She could tell herself that her mother had come inevitably to the end of her chosen road; but that didn't cancel the bitter night, and the blue hands, and the hard frozen face. She felt that something should have been done that had been left undone. Gerald's half-crown didn't assuage her. It seemed to aggravate an iniquity.

He said: "I kissed her when we got home and asked her if she agreed that I had done the right thing. She said: 'Yes, darling. You always do the right thing. But somehow. . .'"

"Somehow what?" he asked.

"Oh, I don't know," she answered. "If she'd been a sparrow with a broken leg I'd have brought her home but because she's my mother . . ."

He put a match to the fire, made some tea, and then sat down with her on his lap. They drank from the same cup. It was the way they liked their evenings to end. As a rule, they had nothing to say to one another at this moment; and that was the happy thing about it: just to be there, at one, drinking from the same cup. Tonight it was different. "You see, my love," he said, "you're not dealing with a sparrow. You might find it was a vulture and that it had no intention of saying 'Thank you' and going back where it had come from. It might want to stay. I rather think that was the idea. Well, that would be a piece of generosity I can't afford. It's difficult enough as it is."

Meg's brow was furrowed. She didn't know what to say or do, but she knew that there was something she ought to do and was torn to pieces because she knew also that Gerald would not want her to do it. "If we just asked her here to a meal now and then . . ." she said.

Gerald hadn't told her that he had sold Little in Sight, that they were in a tight place for money. But it wasn't only that. If he had been without anxiety about money it would have been the same. He wouldn't have wanted Mrs Newman. But he didn't want to hurt Meg by repeating a refusal, so he said nothing, and she said nothing, and they went to bed with their fine evening out fallen to ashes and with their first difference still lying between them.

For a moment we watched the traffic below us in the courtyard of the Hôtel de France, and then Gerald said: "If she'd met her mother as she used to be, all dolled up and out on her own business, I'm sure she would have felt about it as I did, but she'd forgotten all that. As soon as I woke up in the morning I knew that she'd forgotten it."

Meg was awake before him, and began at once: "I know what we can do, darling. I don't blame you for not wanting my mother here, and I'd hate to do anything you didn't want. You know that, don't you, darling?"

He knew that, but he was disturbed to find the subject come up again so soon. He had hoped that by this morning she would see it as he did. He kept silent.

"Well," said Meg, "what about me going to town now and then to see her? She looked so cold."

So that's what she'd been thinking about all night, off and on: this new mother who looked so cold, sitting in an entry with the winter wind whistling round her. "I could take her somewhere for a cup of tea now and then," Meg said.

He said, with sad reluctance and foreboding, hating to deny her anything: "Well, if you'd like to do that . . . But are you sure you can find her again?"

"Oh, that'll be easy," Meg assured him, all joy now that she had his consent. "Those sort of people always stick to the same pitch."

She jumped gaily out of bed, happy Meg again, and prepared the breakfast. All through the morning he tried to work, but nothing much came of it. After their midday meal Meg dressed herself up and announced: "I think I'd better go today. Then I can go once a week after that."

"I shall come with you," Gerald said.

They went on a bus to town, and in Oxford Street Gerald left her. "Meet me on the corner of Bond Street," he said. "I'll be there sharp at half-past four. Don't be late."

"I won't," she promised. "Goodbye now."

He mooched about the art shops, was encouraged to find that he had sold a picture, and was consequently more cheerful when he met her. She was there promptly, and talked about her mother on the journey home; altogether they were happier than they had been last night. His forebodings dwindled and he was able to work.

So it went on for a month, with Meg going to town every Monday and coming back none the worse. He didn't bother to go with her except that first time. After all, she was London-bred, and able to take care of herself.

It was after Meg's fourth visit to town that she came back not so gay as usual. "How is your mother?" he asked, for the woman had ceased to be a hag in a nightmare. He could speak of her as though she didn't matter.

"She's not so good," Meg said. "I don't like it."

Instantly, he was alert, and she was aware of the swift change of mood. She said defensively: "She's coughing her head off. She could get pneumonia. I told her she ought to stay in for a few days and she just laughed. 'Some place for an invalid that is,' she said. And she told me about the room she lives in. Oh, it's dreadful, dreadful. There ought to be some place she can go to."

"There are hospitals."

"She wouldn't go. Poor people hate hospitals. Didn't you know that?"

"I hope you didn't offer her the hospitality of our roof."

"Well, I did tell her . . . just in case . . ."

"You mean you gave her this address?" His alarm and amazement were so sharp that she could not speak. She mutely nodded her head. After a moment she said quietly: "I thought it right. She's my mother. She's got no one else."

He was overwhelmed with love and pity for her. He kissed her and comforted her, all anger dead. They were very happy that night.

It was snowing heavily when Mrs Newman arrived two nights later. It was Gerald's habit to read to Meg in the evenings – simple childish tales that she loved: *Barriers Burned Away*, *The Wide, Wide World*, *Queechy*, and things of that sort. They were at it that night, the fire piled high, when the doorbell rang. Gerald stopped in the middle of a sentence, and they looked at one another. They knew. A caller was so rare, the hour and the weather were so unpropitious, that the question in their minds answered itself.

Gerald's old carpet slippers flapped on the oil-cloth of their narrow passageway. He turned up the gas and opened the door. A cab-horse stood with whitened back and bowed head outside the front garden gate, only a couple of yards away, the snow dithering about him. The cabman, carrying one of those brown tin trunks that domestic servants used to lug from place to place, was already on the doorstep. He thrust the trunk inside, and stood back for his passenger, a woman Gerald would not have recognised as the match-seller he had met a month ago. She said nothing, and Gerald was too taken aback to speak, either. She pushed past him, and it was she who shut the door. Meg had come out from the sitting room, and there they stood, the three of them, looking at one another in the gaslight. The tin trunk alone spoke. It said eloquently: "I've come to stay."

I said to Gerald, laying a hand on his: "I hope it didn't turn out too badly."

Not answering this, he said: "D'you know that Sherlock Holmes story – *The Man with the Twisted Lip*? He used to sit on a corner, a street-beggar like Mrs Newman, scarred and horrible. He was making a handsome living out of it, and he could remove his scars with a wipe of the sponge. As I looked at Meg's mother I thought of that. She'd so obviously disguised herself with dirt and rags and a put-on look of misery. Now she was washed and rouged and well enough dressed. There were a few rings on her fingers, and a hat full of flowers and fruit was on her head. She was wearing a feather boa. I could see that behind the make-up she was an old woman – too old for the trade she once followed. But she didn't look an ill woman."

Meg said: "Oh, Mother! You look so much better!"

Mrs Newman looked round the bleak passage with insolent dislike. She shot the bolt of the door and said: "For God's sake let's get alongside a fire. It's a perisher tonight."

They moved into the sitting room and she dumped herself into Gerald's chair. She took off her hat and dropped it on the floor. "Oh, yes," she said. "I'm all right. Nothing much the matter with me. A bit lonely. That's all."

Gerald said, with what he hoped was a pointed firmness: "Meg, make your mother a cup of tea. She can't go back on a night like this with nothing warm inside her."

Mrs Newman said: "Go back? Who says I'm going back? Didn't Meg invite me?"

"Oh, Mother!" Meg cried. "You know I didn't do anything of the sort. I thought you were ill, and I said that if . . ."

"Well, that's not what I thought," Mrs Newman rudely interrupted. "And another thing I didn't think," she said, looking contemptuously round the bleak room, "is that you'd thrown yourself away on this. I expected something better. Hampstead! Hampstead sounds classy, but this looks bloody awful. I feel proper let down."

Meg was near to weeping. Too late, she felt the impact of the fears that Gerald had earlier felt and too easily dismissed. She remembered his objections now, and looked at him in shame and contrition. "Oh, Gerry darling," she cried. "I didn't know!"

Mrs Newman said: "Oh, I'm something to apologise for, am I? Well, that's modern women, I suppose. That's gratitude. That's family affection."

She went out into the passage and came back with her brown tin box. She unlocked it and, rummaging among scented clothes, unearthed a bottle of gin. "Tea!" she said. "On a night like this! Tea! If you could oblige with a glass and a drop of hot water."

Gerald gave her what she asked for, and she sat back, sipping.

"I felt so damned inadequate," Gerald said. "What could I do? There she was. I couldn't take her by the neck and chuck her out into the snow."

So Mrs Newman sat there, getting warm with the fire and the gin, mellow, confidential. She refilled her glass, reached out and took from the table the book that Gerald had been reading to Meg. "*Queechy*", she said. "Well, well. *Queechy*. Read it when I was a kid." She began to laugh.

"She was wearing absurd high buttoned boots," Gerald said, "and she sat there with one leg thrown over the other, considering the toe of one of these boots as though it gave her great satisfaction." She said: "There's more in life than *Queechy*. Let me tell you that, my girl. Time you woke up. Look at this now."

She rummaged again in the brown tin trunk and pulled out a garment that filled the little room with scent. She held it up proudly against the gas-light: a nightdress so diaphanous as to be all but non-existent. "I had to bring it," she said. "Had to bring my dear old souvenir. *Souvenir des nuits inoubliables*. Know what that means? Neither do I. But I can guess. And that's what he called it – my old Frenchman. Bald as a coot on top, but with a chest like a bear's." She folded the garment and put it away. She began to snivel.

Gerald caught Meg's eye and made a gesture which said: "Take her to bed." He had made up his mind what to do. Meg said: "Let me show you your bed, Mother."

Mrs Newman was sagging by now, but Meg was sturdy. She got her up the stairs and put her into the only bed there was, which was hers and Gerald's.

Meg came down twenty minutes later and found Gerald dressed for going out, even to hat and overcoat. "Get your things on," he said.

"Where are we going to at this time of night?" It was just about ten o'clock.

"Get your things on. You'll see."

Before doing so, she clung to him, her head in his shoulder. "Oh, darling," she said. "I did this to you! I'm sorry."

"Don't worry," he assured her. "You won't see *her* again. Neither will I."

She looked at him, rather shaken by his note of resolution. "We're going away?"

"We're going away. It's as simple as that."

"What will Mother do in the morning?"

"Nothing could interest me less than what Mother will do or what the landlord will do, or what becomes of the few wretched relics we leave behind. We're on our way. For me, it's not the first time. When things become too much, hop it. It works."

"But Mother . . ." she persisted.

"Mother can go back to her Frenchman with the bear's chest, and for all I care with a monkey's tail."

They stole quietly out of the house. The snow was falling more heavily. They went to town on a bus, and Gerald said: "Now we'll finish the journey by cab. It'll surprise Joe to see I've got enough money for that."

"Who's Joe?"

"Joe Carpenter. Don't worry about Joe. If he's sober we'll be all right."

It was just after eleven by the time they reached Joe's, and Joe arrived at the same time as they did, for the pubs shut at eleven. Joe was concealed in an Inverness cape, and a St Bernard dog, wearing a small barrel where St Bernard dogs wear barrels, mooched along at his side as though he had just rescued him from a snow-drift. Joe looked at Gerald and said: "Hallo, Gerry. Come in," and Gerald said: "This is Meg, my wife." Joe said: "Hallo, Meg. Come in." Then the four of them – Joe and the dog, Gerald and Meg – climbed some snow-dumbed wooden outside stairs and hunched together on a small landing before a green door. Joe took off his Inverness cape and shook it and the dog shook himself, and looked a lot smaller, though immense. Joe opened the door and repeated: "Come in", and they all went in, and the dog at once sat down by the fire and began to steam. "Don't boil that damn' stuff," Joe said, and detached the barrel.

"I don't know whether you've ever heard of Joe or seen his work?" Gerald asked.

I said that I hadn't, and Gerald explained that Joe was a lithographic artist – "One of the best going," he said.

Joe lived up here in the loft, and in what had been the stable down below he did his tough heavy work with stones and rollers. "I've known him for years," Gerald said. "We always fly to one another in trouble – no questions asked. He's rather lazy because he's got just enough to live on – a curse for anybody. Give me plenty of money or none at all. And Joe drinks too much. He always keeps Tiny's barrel filled, so that he can have a drink if he's walking about between pub hours."

Well, there they were, with the snow falling outside, and the fire blazing, and Joe Carpenter frying steaks and onions. Meg, contemplating the satisfying but unfamiliar scene, the immense Joe, black-bearded, as outsize among men as Tiny was among dogs, must have found the swift transition from Hampstead rather difficult to take. Joe was wearing dangling circles of gold in his ears and a golden crucifix over his blue jersey. He looked as though he would be more at home in a pirate's cabin than an artist's studio. Tiny was slumped on the hearth-mat, and Joe straddled him as he flipped the steaks over with a fork. It was midnight.

When they had eaten Joe replenished the fire, filled his pipe, and asked: "So what?" They were spraddled about in long wicker chairs, and Joe had a glass of brandy and hot water in his hand. "Go to bed if you like," he said to Meg. There was only one bed in the room. Meg decided to stay up. Gerald explained what had brought them there and Joe raised his glass. "Well, here's death and damnation to all unwanted women," he said. "But what about your pictures, Gerry?"

"I left 'em. I can paint pictures any day," Gerald said.

Joe looked at him sadly, and merely asked: "This was in your Hampstead place, was it?"

"Yes."

"Well, let's all go to sleep. We'll talk about it in the morning."

Meg was asleep already. Worn out with the night's doings, she was snoring gently in her chair. Joe threw himself clothed upon his bed and Gerald put his head back. When he woke, Meg was still asleep, Joe and Tiny were gone.

During the next few days, Joe let slip here and there a detail of his adventure. Fitted together by Gerald, it went something like this.

Joe and Tiny set out at about seven o'clock. It was cold and dark, but the snow had ceased to fall. They gave themselves some breakfast at a coffee-stall and reached Hampstead by half-past eight. Joe called on a doctor-friend of his who had a practice there. He was an Irishman, young enough to have still the irresponsibility of a medical student, Irish enough to relish Joe's proposal. He was bolstering his yet precarious position with a certain amount of show which included a victoria and a cockaded coachman. He would not be going out on his rounds till ten o'clock, and Joe said that would give him all the time he needed. The victoria set off at nine. Joe had removed his earrings and crucifix and borrowed a rather tight fit in frock coats from his friend. A top-hat, too. He left Tiny behind. A professional looking black bag contained a stethoscope and a thermometer. He alighted from the victoria and rapped peremptorily with the knocker. It was some time before he heard feet shuffling downstairs. The door opened a crack. Joe raised his topper. "Mrs Newman?"

The astonished lady admitted it. "Dr Jenkinson-Jones," Joe said with a slight Welsh accent. "I'm surprised to see you up, ma'am. It's in bed you should be. Your daughter and her husband have just been to my surgery. They've had to go away to town now. Have you no maid?"

Astonished by this solicitude, impressed by the coachman, Mrs Newman shook her head mutely. Joe, ostentatiously carrying his black bag, edged gently into the passage. "Away to bed with you," he commanded. "I'll be up to give you a look over. And once you're in bed stay there. Your poor daughter's in a state about your health, I can tell you."

Mrs Newman must have thought things were turning out better than she had dared to expect. So she'd got 'em frightened, had she? She went with what she hoped was an invalid's gait back to bed, and soon Joe entered the bedroom, looking professional with the stethoscope round his neck. He took her pulse. He put the thermometer into her mouth. He made great play with the stethoscope and was amused by the *souvenir de nuits inoubliables*. But he managed to look grave, and stood with a hand on her forehead looking earnestly into her eyes. He even raised the lids. "Yes," he said consideringly, tapping his teeth with the thermometer-case. "Yes. As I feared. Now, ma'am. You'll stay just where you are. Your daughter'll call for the medicine as soon as she's back, and to be going on with I'll make you up a draught."

What Dr Maguire had mixed for him he didn't know, but she was soon asleep and he made a swift dash around the house. "And here they are," he said to Gerald, "all brought home in a cab: your easel and paints and brushes – the whole damn' outfit – and all your pictures. If you must flit, leave what else you like behind you. But your pictures, never on this earth. Come on, Tiny. We've earned one." And he left Gerald and Meg astonished and gloating.

They had stayed with Joe Carpenter for a week, and then, while they were walking along the Chelsea Embankment on a day that was surprising with a warmth of sunshine, they stood leaning on the river wall, looking at the gulls bobbing on the hurrying tide, and Gerald was aware that something was wrong with Meg. After a long silence she said: "I don't think we're being fair to Joe."

"Good heavens, Meg," Gerald said, "Joe loves company – especially mine."

"Are you sure," she asked, "that it's not especially mine?"

He was shocked. "Now don't fill your head with illusions," he said.

"It's not an illusion," she said, "that I had to slap Joe's face last night. I didn't like doing it, and I don't think he bears any ill-will. All the same, I've been thinking about Little in Sight. Shouldn't we go down there?" She took his arm, almost pleading. "It can be so lovely at this time of year," she said. "The camellias will be out."

He had to tell her what he had been concealing from her: that he had sold Little in Sight to pay the Hampstead rent. She looked desolate. "I'd been counting on it to get far away from my mother and Joe Carpenter."

Poor Gerald, even by the telling of this story, was so shaken that I said: "Forget it for the time being. Let's go for a walk."

I went back from the balcony into the hotel and peeped into Jane's room. She was lying on her bed, half-asleep. She complained that the crossing to Boulogne had shaken her up dreadfully and that she didn't yet feel alive. So I told her to stay in bed, that I was going out, and Gerald and I took the road into the level country and after a few miles came to an estaminet with a bit of garden. We sat there and I ordered grenadines, sweet sticky stuff that I loathed, but I remembered that Gerald was a teetotaller. He had told me so the first time we met by the spring on St Tudno creek. Thinking of that moment, I was aware how much I had instantly liked him, but there was a lot on my mind then, and more, disastrously more, was to follow. And by the time that was over he and Meg were gone. I hoped that he would leave Meg and her mother out of it for a while, so that we could be quiet here together in this bit of ragged unpretentious garden where the bees were bumbling and the swallows were overhead.

He said, as though he had not stopped talking: "It blew up into the first row Meg and I had ever had – this business of my selling Little in

Sight. I don't think I'd ever had a real row in my life before. I'm like that. I dodge things. Walking out at Hampstead, as I'd walked out of other places – it was just dodging, wasn't it? Joe is a different type – large, active, positive. His act of bringing back the pictures – I could no more do a thing like that than fly. It impressed Meg enormously. She's such a child. Even the dog and the brandy-barrel. She'd be out walking with Joe and he'd decide he wanted a drink. He carried a small silver cup in his pocket, wrapped in a silk handkerchief. He'd turn the spigot of the barrel and draw his drink. He's a bit of an exhibitionist. I'd noticed that he always waited till there was a lot of people about before doing this. It got a laugh, and I suppose Meg felt in the middle of the picture. Mind you, Miss Maria," he said, "I've always liked Joe. I like him still, and I take my hat off to his work."

"For the love of the Lord, Gerald," I said, "don't call me Miss Maria. And do come to the end of this story. Is Meg living with Joe Carpenter?"

"Yes."

"The bigger fool she," I said. "Now you've got it off your chest, try and forget it. Tell me what you're doing?"

"Doing?" he asked, rather surprised. "Why, painting. This is a cheap place to live, and I talk the language, and get along well enough."

5

Jane was herself the next day, and when we had breakfasted she said: "Now we'd better find out where Mr Pickering lives and see what he's been up to."

In so small a town there was no difficulty in finding Gerald's lodgings. He ate with the widow who owned the place and had one large whitewashed room to himself. His bed, washstand and chair didn't take up much space, and there was no other furniture. He was a quick and industrious painter, and the work he had done in Montreuil was hanging on the walls. In my eyes it was all lovely; but, though I could not any longer go into raptures about *The Last of the Garrison* and *When Did You Last See Your Father?*, I had no talent for judging pictures and could do no more than utter little exclamations of pleasure. Jane uttered nothing. Indeed, at one moment she said rather sharply: "Do be quiet, Maria," and after half-an-hour of looking she said to Gerald: "I'll have that one and that one."

Gerald said: "Trust you to pick the best, my lady."

"I should think so," she said simply. "What are you doing about selling?"

"I send a few to a man in Paris. He sells one now and then."

"Oh, Paris!" she said impatiently. "That's all very well. But you're an English painter and it's time a bit more was done about your English reputation. I must get Groggenheim over."

Gerald and I, poverty-stricken, were silent in the presence of Wealth talking. I didn't know who Groggenheim was, but Gerald looked both impressed and dubious. At last he said: "I never knew that one gave orders to Groggenheim. I thought one went to him on bended knees."

Jane said: "*I* don't."

She strolled about looking at the pictures again, and then she began to laugh. "The Memlinc will fetch him," she said.

She sat down on Gerald's neatly-made bed and began to enthuse about the Memlinc. "Oh, I love that man!" she said. "And Groggenheim has got hold of a beauty. You never *saw* such stained glass! The whole picture glows with it. And then for contrast there are the simple cows in the landscape you see through the windows, and, inside, a pale lovely little Virgin. I've been a good customer to Groggenheim, and that'd bring him anyway. But this Memlinc will clinch it. I've been bargaining with him for weeks, and he'll think I've made up my mind. Well, so I have, come to that." She was very gay at the thought of Mr Groggenheim coming to toe the line.

"All the same," Gerald said, "I don't see what it's got to do with me."

"Ah, well. Perhaps you don't know as much about selling pictures as you do about painting them. We shall see. Now, Maria and I will go and send a telegram."

Jane's telegrams were never businesslike and brief. I suppose today it would go something like this: "Groggenheim, Picdeals, London. Wish finalise Memlinc quickest." This was Jane's telegram: "Dear Mr Groggenheim. I've been thinking about the lovely Memlinc picture, and the more I think the more I am enraptured by it. Stop. I have almost (underline almost) decided to buy it even at your exorbitant (underline exorbitant) price. Stop. Do you think you could come here, if you wouldn't find the journey excessively tiresome, and persuade me to make up my mind? Stop. This is a delightful little place, though it's such a bore having to cross the Channel to get at it. (Stop.) Why do the artists all herd together at Dieppe and thereabouts? Query, stop. I expect you know that Laurence Sterne, who wrote the *Sentimental Journey* was here. Stop. I mean in Montreuil. Stop. But I shall be moving on, probably the day after tomorrow, so don't delay if you wish to pull off what with the best will in the world I cannot but think a positively monstrous (underline monstrous) deal. Stop. All my good wishes, and believe me, my dear Mr Groggenheim, ever yours sincerely Jane Lavernock. Stop. P.S. Stop. Have the goodness to excuse the brevity of this line. Stop."

Mr Groggenheim was with us the next day. I had expected someone with a disreputably slurkish Levantine air, and was surprised to meet a tall, dark, thin man, handsome, and dressed as if he were bound for the Royal Enclosure at Ascot. Gerald had turned up at the Hôtel de France after breakfast with a rucksack on his back. He was off for a day's tramp, he said, and it was not likely that he would return that night. He was clearly wishing not to come within talking range of Mr Groggenheim. Jane did Mr Groggenheim well at lunch, and after that we sat on the balcony. Mr Groggenheim smoked a cigar that smelled expensive and sipped brandy that the waiter had brought, addressing him, not unnaturally, I thought, as Milord. Jane talked to him about the Flemish Primitives. She was in love with them, with *all* of them, she said, and gave the impression that she was in that expensive market if anything came Mr Groggenheim's way. He was non-committal. Those things weren't to be had every day. But there was a Van der Goes that possibly he might persuade the owner to part with. I wondered when we were coming round to the Memlinc, but that magic name was not mentioned. We sat there till three o'clock, and then Jane got up. "I had the luck to run into an English artist living here," she said. "I'm rather inclined to buy a couple of his pictures. Would you give me your advice about them?"

"Who is he?"

"Gerald Pickering."

Mr Groggenheim considered this for a moment. Then he grunted: "Not bad."

We went to Gerald's room. Mr Groggenheim lit a new cigar and walked about for a long time. At last he committed himself. "He's come on. Those are the two you ought to buy – that one and that one."

Jane was delighted. "Those are the two I *have* bought. What should I offer him for them?"

"Since you're buying from the artist," he said with a grin, "fifty each would be more than reasonable. But you wouldn't get 'em at that price if you bought 'em from me."

"Sit down," Jane said, and patted Gerald's bed on which she was already sitting. Mr Groggenheim sat by her, a hand that held the cigar on his knee. He occasionally put the cigar to his lips, drew on it, and then expelled the smoke slowly and thoughtfully from half-parted lips. All the time his eyes were moving over the pictures.

Presently he said to Jane without looking at her: "So you decided to blackmail me?"

"Yes," she said gaily. "When I think of all the money you've had out of me, I don't see why I shouldn't get something back. I've bought a lot of pictures in my time, and that's something; but I'd like to feel that I'd helped to *make* an artist. There the stuff is," she said, waving a hand round the walls, "and you know as well as I do that it's important painting."

Mr Groggenheim looked sideways at her, smiling. It was the first smile I'd seen on his face. He had been all caution, walking like a cat amid broken glass. Now I saw that he admired Jane as a woman, and that she, though she didn't turn her head to meet his smile, knew this and was counting on it.

"This Pickering is lucky," he said, and got up. He walked over to a picture, took a small magnifying glass from his pocket, and scrutinised the paint. "What's your wonderful idea?" he asked.

"Don't be restless," Jane said, though nothing, I thought, could be more self-possessed and quiet than Mr Groggenheim. "Come and sit down."

"Tell me," he said, "how you propose to ruin me."

"You will arrange the usual campaign," Jane said. "First, you will get George Curtis to write one of his nice little books. You know what he is: he can turn out a thing like that in a fortnight. He can come over here to talk to Gerald about the personal side of the story, and so far as the painting goes he knows all the claptrap that impresses people. There'd better be at least half-a-dozen of the pictures reproduced in colour. Well, that's my contribution. Any loss on the book I'll make good. You could have a little pile of them on sale at the exhibition."

"What exhibition?"

"Don't be tiresome."

"Pickering has shown before, hasn't he?"

"Yes, but never at a gallery like yours, and I doubt whether he's ever made enough to pay the cost of showing."

"So you're asking the Groggenheim Gallery to boost a failure? It's never been done, dear lady."

"Then you'd better see that it isn't done this time."

"I should of course want to handle his complete output from now on."

"That would be to pay him a great compliment."

Mr Groggenheim took from one of the breast pockets of his waistcoat a slim note-book. The edges of the scarlet covers were bound in gold and the paper was a pleasing azure. He made a few notes with a gold-cased pencil. He got up and said: "In your telegram you said you wanted me to help you to make up your mind about the Memlinc. Have I succeeded?"

"Yes. I shall be away for a long time. Keep it till I return to London."

"Are you serious about the Van der Goes?"

"Yes. About all of them. I'm trying to persuade Lord Lavernock to get rid of his Gainsboroughs and Reynoldses. The place is crowded with the sort of stuff every rich man is told he ought to have. I'd like the dining room to be all Flemish Primitives."

"If his lordship decides to sell his English stuff, you'll come to me?"

"To whom else?"

"Thank you," he said. "Now, I must get back to Boulogne. I'm crossing on the night boat."

Jane went as far as the door with him, and returned excited to the room that was filled with the opulent incense of Mr Groggenheim's cigar. She fanned herself with her tiny handkerchief. "Open the window, Maria," she said. "My word! I never thought I'd crack that tough nut."

6

Gerald was rather shocked when he learned what had happened. Not shocked in a moral sense: he was as glad as any sane creature would be to find a prospect of success opening before him. But he was mentally and almost physically shocked at the thought of having to deal with the preliminaries. "George Curtis!" he groaned. "He'd write a eulogy of a pavement artist for a hundred pounds."

"George Curtis," Jane told him, "is not in my view a notably honest man. But he *is* the man people believe to know more about contemporary painters than anyone else. For our present purpose, that's all that matters. And so you will stay here and meet him and tell him anything he wants to know. When that's done with, you can join me and Maria. We'll be doddering about, and we'll keep in touch with you. I expect you'll find plenty of paintable stuff wherever we are. Then you'll have to go back to London when the exhibition opens. After that, you can please yourself whether you rejoin us. I expect you'll be too busy furnishing a London mansion."

When Gerald joined us, we were at a village called Douze Maisons, and that is what it was. The houses were sprinkled over a stony hillside that sloped down to a few stony fields where ancient olives grew, and through the fields there was a stony path that led to a beach of glittering white sand. The little place was drenched and bleached by the sun. The low whitewashed cottages were scattered about the hill like skulls, souvenirs of a battle that had happened long ago. The men fished and tilled the small tough fields and assembled at a pub called grandly *le Café de l'Agriculture et de la Pêcherie*. They played dominoes, and billiards with balls so long in use that they were octagonal. To be in the pub after the long day's heat was to feel as a loaf must feel just before the oven is opened. All the same, we went there most nights. Jane drank grenadine and I a little rough wine, and we listened to the chatter of the men and the clank of the balls. They sounded like toy engines going for ever over points. After a *bon soir, mesdames*, the men took no notice of us. Their own women didn't come to the pub, but everyone understood that the mad English were *capable de tout*. When we had had enough of that we would climb the path to our own cottage, the topmost of all, and watch the sea, and the western distance going violet-dusky, and when the flaming stars came out we would decide that perhaps it was cool enough to try and get some sleep. During our first week at Douze Maisons the nights had been moonlit, and then I hardly went to bed at all. It was new to me, enchanting; and Jane, who was used to that sort of thing, would laugh at me and leave me alone, sitting beglamoured on the bench outside the cottage, looking at the grey ghosts of the olive trees that sometimes netted a sigh of wind, and stirred, and uttered small sounds in their sleep, like memories of their hundreds of years. And the sea looked older than the Cornish sea, fuller of ancient wisdom, a palimpsest, written over by the keels of Greek and Phoenician ships. It looked as though it had known all there was to know.

Sometimes, in the moonlight, I would make up my journal, or write to Louisa in London or to Bella in Cornwall, hoping to stir their envy as I told them of my wonderful life. We had zig-zagged through France in a great confusion of geography and of social conditions. Now it would please Jane to be Milady, perched for a day or two in the gilded cage of a grand hotel; and then some roadside *auberge* would attract her, despite the farmyard midden that the French love; and yet again we would linger in a sedate little township as prim and proper as Truro, with the municipal band playing on the square in the evenings under the lime trees. But when Jane found Douze Maisons, which is not far from the Italian frontier, she decided that this was what she had been looking for and that there we should stay. We left the car on the rutted track which was all the road the place had, and she stood gazing about her with a look on her face which I knew announced a decision. "We shall stay here," she said, "indefinitely."

"But where?" I asked, for the *Café de l'Agriculture et de la Pêcherie* didn't look as though it knew what a tourist was.

"Why – there!" she said, pointing.

Attached to the cottage was a notice which said "*A vendre*."

"But it's for sale," I said. "It's not to let."

I hadn't, even yet, got used to the ways of the very rich, who happened also to be full of whims and fancies.

"I shall buy it," she said, and that is what she did.

There was an agent's name on the notice-board, and we drove on at once to the small town where he had his office, and in the heat of the day, when the poor man was clearly intending a *siesta*, Jane whirled him into negotiations. The house, he pointed out, had belonged to a widow who had died, and it was *admirablement meublée*, and not till after the sale of the furniture, which mightn't be held for another month, could a buyer take possession.

But how fortunate, Jane said, to have a house which was *admirablement meublée*, and therefore ready for immediate occupation!

She would buy the *ameublement* with the house, and so save him the boredom of conducting a sale. When he discovered that Jane was an authentic *vicomtesse anglaise*, who, for whatever mad English reason, wanted to live in Douze Maisons, he decided to forgo his siesta and to return at once with us to the village. Jane stocked the car with food, and soon the agent was opening the door, handing Jane the heavy iron key, and conducting us round. The place was small, but the widow had had a sense of decency. The furniture consisted of nothing but things of bare necessity, all as clean and well cared for as it was neat and solid. The agent assured us that our presence *tiendrai du prestige* for Douze Maisons; but we were glad to find the villagers rather dour and unforthcoming. There were no flags or red carpets. We were given simple civility, which suited us very well.

Looking from our bench to the sea, you would have the nearest cottage to ours a little lower down and to the left. Madame Maillard lived there, and was willing enough to increase her scanty income. As soon as we were up we would put on our bathing-suits and mackintoshes and run down to the beach which faced into the morning sunlight. We were both good swimmers, and these occasions were a delight. Tingling with salt, warmed by the sun, we would go back to our cottage, dress, and walk to Madame Maillard's where a bowl of *café au lait* and a hunk from a baton of bread would await us. At one o'clock, if we were at home, we would go to her for lunch. She was an admirable cook, a master with *bouillabaisse*, capable of transmuting even the scrawny chickens that scratched in her stony soil into memorable food. As for our own cottage, with no one in it but two naturally tidy women, it made no problem, and an hour's work in the morning permitted me to do all that needed to be done. The cottage, like all the others in Douze Maisons, was on one floor: a scullery, a kitchen-sitting room, and two bedrooms. Crouching, thick-walled, into the earth, it had a satisfying aboriginal feeling. Only the *Café de l'Agriculture et de la Pêcherie* had two storeys and justified its status as the chief building in the village by being as ugly as sin and built of repulsive imported brick.

We had been in the village for about a month, and one evening were sitting as usual on our bench in the last of the light, when we saw a young man come out of the *café* and start climbing the hill in our direction. He was playing a mouth-organ, and playing it well, too:

jigging dance tunes that made even me, no dancer, tingle in the toes. He came near enough for us to see that he was a handsome youth, florid, with dark curly hair, and dressed differently from the men of the village. They all wore black, Sundays and weekdays alike, their weekday clothes being merely the discards of old Sundays. Their boots were always huge. This boy was wearing espadrilles, pale blue trousers, and a black velvet coat. His shirt was white, and a bit of crimson silk was knotted carelessly round his neck. He shouted: "*Bon soir, mesdames*," and branched away towards Madame Maillard's cottage.

Jane said: "We seem to have a village Romeo," and the youth laughed. Clearly, he had understood the English words. He shouted back: "*Mais sans une Juliette*," and disappeared into Madame Maillard's. Thence the strains of the mouth-organ soon issued, and went on for a long time.

When we came out from the sea after our swim the next morning I was reluctant to go to Madame Maillard's for breakfast, though the lazy open air life we were leading made me as hungry as a horse. I didn't want to meet the young man, who was presumably still there. I had always disliked the raffish, knowing sort of person that he seemed to be. At the moment, this dislike was so acute that it was almost physically holding me back. But Jane was calling to me to come, so I gave a last tug at my tapes and went.

Madame Maillard was alone, and exceptionally silent. It was only when Jane spoke of our having seen the young man that she said: "Yes. It is my son Aristide."

"Aristide Maillard. Aristide Maillard," my mind said, as though registering a significant fact.

Jane said: "He appears to have some knowledge of English"; and Madame Maillard said reluctantly: "He knows a little about many things."

Jane's curiosity was wide awake, and she was a skilful unobtrusive cross-examiner. We discovered that Aristide was his mother's pride and despair. He was twenty years old, and since his father's death five years ago he had lived an unpredictable life. His mother had adored him for his beauty as a child, and his father had detested him for his wilfulness. The father's heavy punishments, the mother's unending defence of the boy, had utterly disrupted the family life. Aristide wouldn't do a hand's turn on the hard little fields. He wouldn't go out with the fishermen. He wanted to be an opera singer, and possibly, I thought, he might have been one had his life at the right moment been given the right twist. From my brief glimpse, he seemed to have at any rate the physical equipment of a self-assured vain Italian tenor.

We lingered long over our coffee that morning, for, once launched, Madame Maillard could not be restrained from expressing her love and sorrow. Aristide was fifteen when he first disappeared following one of the quarrels with his father. Monsieur Maillard, as usual on these occasions, took a leather belt to him. But by now Aristide himself was wearing a leather belt, and for the first time he retaliated. They slashed at one another through all the rooms of the house. It must have been a dreadful scene, and it ended with the old man lying battered and bleeding on the floor and the young man walking out.

A year passed before Aristide returned, and his father was then dead. The boy's disappearance had not brought peace to his parents. Madame Maillard complained that her husband had driven away all that made her hard life bearable; and her husband replied that no doubt Aristide reminded her of her lover: he certainly was no Maillard. In this bedevilled atmosphere they bickered out his few remaining months.

Aristide, who had hung round his mother in the kitchen from his earliest days, had learned to cook, and as a cook he had embarked on an English liner. He came home talking English, and told his mother that only a fool worked as a cook. He would go to sea again, but as a steward. A steward's life, he said, had far more opportunities. He didn't say what opportunities, but he had become more handsome than ever, and his mother could guess. Perhaps he tried to take opportunities too rashly, for his mother gathered that he had left the ship against his will in New York. He remained there for a time, unhappy, and later made his way to Rio. Thence he worked his passage on a sailing ship to Marseilles. This was something different from the smooth life on a liner, and he didn't want the sea any more. Marseilles suited him much better, but, confident as he was in his looks and his prowess, he was an amateur, a minnow among sharks, in that cosmopolitan sink. He returned to Douze Maisons subdued, and with an unexplained scar running from the shoulder to the elbow of his left arm.

This second adventure had lasted for two years, and his absences were not so long thereafter. But they were frequent. He would be away for a week, for a few weeks, even for a few months, without explanation. He was, Madame explained leniently, a bit of a one for the girls. And they were not good girls: they got him into trouble. If only he could find a good girl, he would be all right, for he was a good son, a *garçon de bon coeur*.

Jane asked how Aristide had lived in the time between first leaving home and finding work in the liner.

"There were no secrets between him and me," Madame Maillard said. "It is a hard life, you understand, and there was not much. But he knew where I hid it. *Ça ne fait rien.* He had only to ask and I would have given it to him. But he was in a hurry." *Il se trouvé pressé.*

We were walking slowly and thoughtfully back to our cottage when Jane said: "How she loathes that young rascal! And yet with her dying breath she'd deny it."

One of our English oddities was to sleep with our windows open and uncurtained. Jane and I shared a room. The only piece of furniture we had got rid of was the widow's immense brass-knobbed marital bed. We had had single ones sent over from the neighbouring town. That night Jane had got into her bed, and I was about to get into mine, when I went, as I often did, to stick my head through the window and take a good-night look at the stars. I could have screamed, but I repressed it for Jane's sake. After all, I was perhaps mistaken. But I could have sworn I saw a shadow slip round the angle of the house. Or was Aristide too heavily on my nerves?

I got into bed and slept well enough, but the next morning when we came out of the sea Jane said: "Don't take your bathing-suit off. Just put on your mackintosh and let's go."

As we were climbing up through the fields I asked: "Why all this?"

"That odious Maillard boy," she said. "He's playing the peeping Tom. I just caught a glimpse of him ducking down behind a rock."

I wondered what Jane would do about it. Despite her gaiety and light-heartedness and her, to me, very casual association with Lord Lavernock, she was a woman of great propriety. I once even jollied her about it, and she quickly put me in my place. At the *café* she had made friends with a young man named Anatole. She had only to call "Anatole!" and he was before her, at her service. Her motorcar was the link between them. Anatole dreamed of driving cars as some men dream of empire. He was a born mechanic, and Douze Maisons offered no opportunities. Jane first came on him rubbing the car down without having been asked to do so. He started away guiltily, but Jane smiled at him and asked if he liked cars. He replied extravagantly that he adored them, and as Jane did, too, they got on well. From books and from fiddling about in a little workshop when he had finished with his toil in the fields, Anatole knew it all theoretically. When Jane permitted him to sit at the controls, and start the engine and then put it into gear he trembled with delight. She took him for rides, and he learned to drive the thing. One Sunday we spent a whole day out, with Anatole at the wheel most of the time.

When we came out of the sea on the morning after Aristide had been peeping at us, I was aware of a wild commotion among the rocks. Then I saw Aristide running, and Anatole behind him slashing with a horse-whip. And not gently. I could hear the whip whistling and thudding. "Now," said Jane, who was not surprised, "you can take your things off and have a rub down."

The next morning Madame Maillard said that *cet pauvre Aristide* was *encore une fois disparu.* "Ah," she said in disgust, "*ces filles! Ces sales filles!*"

7

We didn't regard Douze Maisons as more than an occasional harbour. To stay there without change would have been intolerably boring. We motored all over the south of France and into Italy. Anatole, whose surname I discovered to be Marmont, sometimes went with us. He was a boy whose parents were both dead. He lived with an uncle, a widower, who scraped a livelihood from the sea and from a patch of land. He wasn't sorry to see Anatole go, for the boy was of small use to him. He spent too much time tinkering in the shed that he called his workshop. Jane couldn't resist fiddling about with other people's lives, if she thought those lives had a purpose that was being frustrated. Just as she had dragooned Mr Groggenheim into an attempt to "make" Gerald Pickering, so she now took Anatole's life in hand. Early every morning for a month she drove him to our small neighbouring town where a reasonably good motor mechanic had a workshop, and she paid what she called his apprenticeship fee. It was like teaching a duckling to swim. At the end of the month Anatole declared that he knew "everything" about internal combustion engines. It was perhaps not so, but he knew enough to be going on with, and he had the indispensable quality called *flair*, which, I suppose, is as vital to a mechanic as to anyone else.

Jane bought him overalls and a uniform and engaged him as a chauffeur, it being understood that she was to do most of the driving. There was a shed behind our cottage, and Anatole asked permission to occupy it. Jane dubiously consented. He made himself snug there. When we were invited to inspect the place we found it swept and garnished: a chair, a camp bed, hooks for his clothes. He said it was not *comme il faut* for Madame la Vicomtesse to be unprotected. *Comme il faut* became Anatole's watchword. It was not *comme il faut*, he assured us, to take our meals with a peasant like Madame Maillard. Why should he not carry the meals to us on a tray? It was but a step. Jane squashed that; but clearly Anatole was aiming at being more than a chauffeur. He was to be the Vicomtesse's major domo and factotum. He did not suppose we should want to spend our lives at Douze Maisons, and when we returned to England, he assured us, he would still be there to take care of us. "Every day," he told me, "I shall drive Madame la Vicomtesse, if necessary, to see the King at Ascot." He had a tumultuous notion of aristocratic life in England. As for Douze Maisons, he was doubtful whether we ought to be there at all. It was not *comme il faut*. There were bad types about. *Ce salaud de Maillard* would be back before long. I noticed that the whip with which he had thrashed Aristide was hanging on a hook in his shed.

8

Gerald Pickering didn't turn up till August when our stony village was grilled to the bone. He brought two copies of George Curtis' book, one inscribed to Jane and one to me. He thanked Jane courteously for making the book possible; but to me he said: "I loathe being written about by that paid prostitute. Anybody'd think I was the climax of all painting since Noah daubed his ark."

I suppose the words *paid prostitute* made me think of Meg's mother, and so of Meg. We had left Jane in the cottage and strolled down to the seashore. As we walked on the burning sand, I asked, wondering if I dared ask, but asking all the same: "Have you seen anything of Meg?"

He said: "Meg? Do you think I've come all the way to this Godforsaken blistering hole to talk about Meg? You're looking very beautiful. Let's talk about you."

I had dreamed often enough of a man saying that to me, and now it was said. I was terrified. I replied with the first foolish words that came into my head. "Gerald! You are married!"

I was too shaken to go on walking, and I sat down on a rock trembling. I said: "Please go away, Gerald."

"Very well." He walked away along the beach.

Beautiful! It was the last thing I had expected ever to be called. Certainly, this carefree sunny summer had made me better to look at than I was likely to be again: brown as a biscuit, lithe as a sapling, brimming with health and vigour. But I knew in my bones that Gerald no more loved me than I loved him. Looking at him pacing the sand, I could see in every movement of him the unhappiness of a deserted lover, nothing of a lover eager to persuade. I was sure that at this very moment it was Meg he was thinking of, not me. If I encouraged him I should be an escape from anguish and nothing more. All the same, it was a shattering moment, and not the less so because, though I loved him not at all, I liked him so much and felt his sorrow so deeply.

Presently, his pacing brought him back to the rock and he stood looking down at me – awkwardly, for he was no Lothario, only a temperate man carried away by a hard moment. I wonder what I should have done had he been a skilled amorist? But the decision was not called for. He said simply: "I am intolerably lonely. I find life too difficult. I thought Carpenter was my friend and that Meg loved me."

I got up and gave him what I hoped was a non-committal motherly kiss. "There, Gerald," I said. "You see what it is. Carpenter and Meg – not Maria at all."

"I've made a fool of myself," he said. "I beg your pardon."

"Oh, don't talk to me as if we were diplomats observing protocol. You are my dear friend, Gerald, but you know as well as I do that there's no more than that between us. But there is enough to make begging pardon rather foolish."

I took his arm and we walked back to the cottage together.

9

Jane wrote regularly to Lord Lavernock – at least once a week – and a letter occasionally reached her from him. In late September he wrote to say that he was leaving South Africa and that before returning to England he would spend some time cruising in the Mediterranean. He had invited a party to join his yacht at Southampton. They would sail to Nice and he would go aboard there. He would be glad if Jane would join him.

Jane decided to go. "Would you care to stay here?" she asked. "I really don't think you'd enjoy yourself on the yacht. There'll be all sorts of people you wouldn't like meeting. I sha'n't like meeting them myself, but it's just as well to remind some of those women now and then that I'm Ernest's wife, and I want to see Arthur. Besides," she said, "Gerald is being such a bore. Perhaps he'll be gone by the time I get back."

Gerald certainly was doing nothing to add to our gaiety. He had brought his painting things with him and went tramping off alone most days, but he would come back complaining that it was a Golgotha of a region, a place of skulls, and that he could find nothing in it that he wanted to do. "Give me a place with a bit of flesh on its bones."

I didn't look forward with any joy to being alone with him, and I should be alone, for Anatole was to go with Jane. "I expect," she said, "I shall want to go ashore now and then to find a moment's sanity, and Anatole can drive me about, or I'll drive him about. Besides, it will be a treat for him. He's never seen anything but this region."

That, more than ever, would shut me up with Gerald, for, with no car, I should be confined to Douze Maisons. This point troubled Anatole. It was not *comme il faut*, he pointed out, for Mademoiselle to be in the house alone with Monsieur Pickering when Madame la Vicomtesse was away. Gerald was amused by this, and it was good to find something that amused him. "*Il n'y a pas de quoi rire*," Anatole assured him. "It would be more *comme il faut* if monsieur slept in my little shed."

Gerald shared our liking for Anatole, and said: "Very well then. I promise to sleep in your little shed and on your return to hand over Mademoiselle Maria as good as new."

Gerald and I saw them off: Anatole looking as grave and responsible as a knight's esquire, Jane exceptionally gay. I think she was getting a little bored with all of us and with Douze Maisons as well. The car bumped along very slowly over the rutted track towards the tolerable road beyond and passed from our sight. Gerald gathered his painting things together and at once set out. "Perhaps I'll have better luck today," he said.

Those were the last words I heard him speak until his great cry of anguish awakened me. It must have been about one o'clock in the morning. I had retired to bed at ten, and heard Gerald return soon afterwards and go into the shed. It was an exceptionally brilliant moonlit night, so that as I sat up in bed I had a glimpse of him, his white linen suit shining. Then I lay back and slept.

10

Nobody in Douze Maisons had any use for Aristide Maillard. It was a small, tough, hard-working community, unlikely to take kindly to a loafing braggart. The thrashing that Anatole gave him was well received; and when he returned in the evening of the day that saw Jane's departure it was noted with satisfaction that weals still decorated his cheeks. He did not go to his mother's cottage but turned in at the *café*.

"He was in a very aggressive mood," said M. Thouillez, the proprietor. "He told us he had come back to take the hide off Anatole Marmont."

"Didn't he know that Anatole Marmont had left the village?"

"No, sir. No one liked Maillard. No one would speak to him. No one told him anything. He drank alone."

This was at the trial. It seems that Aristide sat there drinking himself into a boisterous mood. He played on his mouth-organ. He treated the audience to sentimental tenor songs. But the audience was unresponsive, and that nettled him. Someone at last, looking at the weals, said: "You shaved yourself badly this morning, Aristide." Aristide said: "Someone else is going to be shaved before the night is out."

"In short," Aristide's counsel asked, "you goaded this poor boy all through the evening?"

"No, sir. As I say, nobody liked him enough to talk to him much. That's all I remember being said to him, except when Louis Roussignon said that Anatole Marmont had left his uncle and was sleeping in the shed behind the house of the Vicomtesse."

"Maillard didn't know that Anatole Marmont at that moment was nowhere near the shed?"

"No, sir."

"But he was deliberately and falsely led to believe that that is where he was at that moment?"

"Yes, sir. I suppose Louis Roussignon thought . . ."

"Never mind what Roussignon thought. That is a matter on which he will himself inform us."

Roussignon said: "Yes, sir. I knew that the Englishman was there at the moment. I thought he was a man who would be able to take care of himself. I thought it would be a good joke to put Maillard in a bad situation."

"You thought! You thought! It seems to me that thinking is the last thing you were capable of. So it comes to this. Knowing that Maillard was in a dangerous mood because he had been thrashed, and believing that he intended that night to revenge himself, you deliberately incited him to go to the shed, even though you knew that an unsuspecting person who was not Anatole Marmont was sleeping there defenceless?"

"But I intended to be there myself, sir. If I *had* been it wouldn't have come to this. I followed him when he left the *café*. He didn't go to the shed. He went to his mother's house and let himself in. I waited for half an hour. Then I thought he wasn't going to the shed after all, so I went home."

"What was his condition?"

"He was staggering a little."

That was the situation when, sitting up in the moonlight, I saw Gerald go to the shed. Three hours later Maillard crept out of his mother's house.

He said: "It was dark in the shed. I didn't know it wasn't Marmont. I took him by the throat and started to shake him. He woke up and shook me off. He was very strong and wiry. The whip was hanging on the wall, and he seemed to know where it was because he jumped straight towards it and unhooked it. Then he started lashing at me. I still thought it was Marmont. We got into a grip, and I didn't know I'd stabbed him. I swear that, sir. I didn't know I'd stabbed him till I heard him cry out. Then I walked out into the moonlight and saw the knife and the blood, and I thought: 'My God! I've killed Marmont.' Then I went back to my mother's house and had a wash and hid the knife and went to sleep."

243

Prosecuting counsel asked: "You were very drunk?"

"Yes, sir. I didn't know what I was doing."

"But you were not so drunk that you didn't see at once that you had killed a man?"

No answer.

"You were not so drunk that you didn't think it would be a good idea to have a wash?"

No answer.

"You were not so drunk that you couldn't hide the knife?"

No answer.

"You were not so drunk that you couldn't wrench up a loose floorboard, put the knife there, and fasten the board back?"

No answer.

"You were not so drunk that you couldn't see it might produce a look of innocence if you were found asleep in the morning?"

No answer.

The case created a tremendous sensation in England. Jane had to give evidence about the feud between the two young men. She had to confess that she had bought the whip and asked Anatole to use it on Aristide. "Lady Lavernock incites lashing." I had to speak of the dreadful scream I heard, of my rushing to the shed, and my finding of Gerald's body. "M.P.'s sister-in-law in the witness-box." And there was poor Gerald himself. "The murdered artist was recently the subject of a monograph by Mr George Curtis, and the Groggenheim Gallery, oddly enough on the very day of his death, had announced an exhibition of his works."

Anatole wept in the witness-box. Maillard's counsel asked: "So it is enough for a woman to instruct you to assault a man, and you proceed to do it?"

"Maillard is a dirty-minded peeper."

"I don't want your opinion of Maillard. I want an answer to my question."

"I would do anything for Madame la Vicomtesse. She was very kind to me. She understood me."

So it went on; and into the papers there crept the subtle unexpressed suggestion that ours had been a very strange *ménage* indeed, with Lord Lavernock safely away in Africa and a handsome boy at my lady's command.

11

Lord Lavernock had come back with Jane and Anatole when the police said that their presence was necessary. He remained throughout the preliminary investigations and the final trial which took place in our neighbouring town. I somehow had not expected to find him admirable, but I did so. Hitherto, in my brief meetings with him, I had looked on him merely with the curiosity of the very poor for the doings of the outrageously rich. Of course, his riches were useful now. He came accompanied by his valet, and a lady's maid for Jane, and Anatole. He all but bought the only hotel in the town. We all had our own private rooms and unlimited service, but these things that he could buy were not the end of it. His presence was strengthening, and he washed away the feeling of smear and stigma that some of the newspaper comments induced. Poor Anatole was in a most depressed condition. He should never have thrashed Maillard, even at her ladyship's command. "Nonsense, boy," Lord Lavernock told him. "If I'd been about, I'd have laid it on thicker than you did."

In my room and Jane's flowers were renewed daily, and he came down to our private dining room each night as impeccably dressed in evening clothes as if he had been at home. He talked about everything except the horror that was hanging over us, and he was very efficient in dealing with journalists who wanted to see us. I played chess with him most evenings. He made the arrangements for Gerald's funeral, and forbade us to attend it. He went himself. When at last it was all over, he and Jane travelled back to England together, taking Anatole with them.

On the evening before they left he asked me after dinner to go to his room. All that he had been doing for us had been done so unobtrusively that it had seemed effortless. I noticed now as he sank into a chair that his face was drawn and pale. "I'm afraid, Miss Legassick," he said, "that my wife has landed you in some difficulty. I'm sorry."

I assured him that I didn't look upon it at all like that, and thanked him for the care he had taken of us.

"My wife tells me that you don't wish to return to England. I should have liked to see you safely home."

"I don't know how I should be received," I said. "I've had no letters from either of my sisters. I'd rather not go back just now."

"I know one of your sisters," he said. "She has been my hostess at Tregannock." He smiled. "I'm afraid," he said, "I sha'n't shoot partridges there again. Mr Polperro doesn't have time nowadays for such frivolities. Your sister is a very earnest woman, isn't she? I admire her enormously. Forgive me saying something personal about your brother-in-law, but he never struck me as having either the wish or the aptitude for public affairs. Now that he is in them, I can understand your sister's annoyance at finding his name so unnecessarily dragged into this affair. So she hasn't written?"

"No. Nor has my other sister. She's married to the vicar of our parish."

"I expect," he said, "she feels a bit like Caesar's wife. I don't know much about parish ladies, but this wretched business has been seething all over the English newspapers. So you see . . ."

"Her husband has written to me."

"Is he annoyed, too?"

"No."

Dear Hugo! It was a lovely letter. It was the sort of letter that would have come from Father or Roger. Thinking of them, I couldn't prevent a tear from falling.

Lord Lavernock said: "Do forgive me. You, after all, had the worst of it. My wife and this boy Anatole were away. It was you who . . ."

Yes, it was I who heard that awful scream, and ran out, and in a shaft of moonlight streaming through the door saw the tumbled bed and Gerald sagged across it, and the stain that looked black spreading upon his nightshirt. He reached for my hand and held it tight, but did not speak, only groaned horribly, and then his grasp loosened as a long shudder shook him. I didn't know what to do. Water, I thought. I should give him water. And my mind flew back to the lovely familiar path along the creek, and the sunny water bubbling out of the wayside rock, and the pair of us cupping our hands and drinking. And because of all this Louisa had not written and Bella had not written; only Hugo had written the sort of letter that would have been written by Father or Roger. And that is why I felt desolate and did not want to go home.

Lord Lavernock said: "Come and sit here by me, Miss Legassick." He patted the sofa he was sitting on. I sat by his side and he took my hand, and for a time we said nothing. But his silence, his contact, were comforting. I sighed, giving myself to his comfort. And a part of me was startled by this. I had heard so much about Lord Lavernock: of his autocracy and ruthlessness, even of his wickedness. But now I knew also that he was a good man. I was surprised by the discovery of how many things it could take to make a man, and I thought that perhaps any man beyond the commonplace was a battlefield of qualities, with no victory anywhere, no abiding city. And the longer I have lived the more this has seemed so to me; the more it has seemed so not only where men, but where man himself, is concerned.

At all events, I know that as I sat there I felt stronger and less lonely, *enabled*, as they say; and that is a great word. I remembered how Father had once been reading the Lessons and my young heart had leapt up at the words: "Thou worm! I will make thee an instrument having teeth."

I suppose we sat there for a quarter of an hour, and then Lord Lavernock said: "Thank you for all you have done for my wife. Now what are we to do about you?"

I had nothing to offer, and he asked with a smile: "Would it surprise you to know that I have a mother?"

Somehow it did. One might as well think of an avalanche or a tornado having a mother. It was to her I went as a companion: a little, simple, old Dutch lady living in splendour in a Renaissance villa near Florence. I learned to love her, and I stayed with her till her death. Then I went back to St Tudno.

CHAPTER EIGHT

WHEN I returned to St Tudno in May of 1906, and had watched Bella's children disappear round the bend of the road, I walked slowly on towards the vicarage. John, Constance, Richard, Millicent . . . The names were singing in my head. A family. A fairly large family. What use — what space even — would the vicarage have for me? And what right had I to expect it to have any? I felt as stable as a cork bobbing in on the tide. I wondered where I should be washed up, little knowing on to how unexpected a shore.

At a twist of the road, where it makes its last run down the hill to the vicarage, there is a gate leading into pasture, and I could not remember the time when I had not climbed upon it. Always, returning from my small expeditions, my fat little legs would take me up a rung or two and I would hang on gazing at the view that, coming back to it now, seemed as fair as any in the world. I didn't need to climb. I leaned on the gate and looked at the fields sloping down to the sea, and the land rising beyond the sea, and a few sails of yachts putting movement into the picture. I was so absorbed in reverie that I started when a young voice said: "Excuse me, but are we on the right road for the vicarage?"

I turned and saw a boy and girl, each carrying a small suitcase. Without waiting for me to answer, the boy said: "What a gorgeous view! Don't you think so, Augusta?"

"Yes," she said. "I wonder whether we could borrow a boat? Could we learn to manage one?"

"Oh, yes. You can learn to do anything if you give your mind to it," he assured her easily.

"Are you going to the vicarage?" I asked them.

248

"Yes. When we got to Penryn there was a chap with a pony cart who'd been told to look out for us and bring us along. However, we decided to walk it. We walk everywhere. He seemed disappointed, so I gave him a bob. Well, if this is the right road we'd better be moving."

"What is your name?" I asked him; and he said "Cumberledge. I'm Miles. That's Augusta."

I recalled my far-off visit to Manchester when Bella and Roger and I stayed with Hugo's father at Bowdon. Hugo's sister was there with her husband, a Doctor Cumberledge, who lived at Warwick. I had hardly thought of them from that moment to this.

Miles said: "Mr Oldham, the vicar here, is my uncle – my mother's brother."

Augusta said: "But our mother is dead."

There was a silence in the sunny day. The two young faces were grave. Augusta looked at Miles. I had the feeling that she adored him, as I had once adored Roger. She waited deferentially for him to speak.

"It's been a bit of an upset," he said rather gruffly. "It was only a month ago that Mother died. But as you see, we're not in mourning or any nonsense of that sort. Father doesn't believe in it."

"No, he doesn't," Augusta corroborated.

"Well," Miles went on, "we lived in Warwick then. But when Mother died Father didn't want to stay there, so he's bought a practice in Manchester. That's what all the upset's about. He's just moving in and didn't want us in the way. Not that we would have been. We could have helped. However, one knows what parents are."

"Yes," said Augusta. "One does."

"So now we're on the way to Uncle Hugo's till the dust settles," Miles concluded. "He invited us, and jolly decent it was of him. I expect I shall loathe Manchester. However, I sha'n't be there long. I'm off to school in the autumn."

Augusta said nothing to that, but I could see she didn't like the thought of his going to school. "I'm afraid that will leave you feeling lonely, Augusta," I said.

"Yes," she agreed; but Miles assured her: "You'll get over it. You can get over anything if you give your mind to it. Remember how we agreed to get over Mother's death? – and *did*."

Augusta remembered, and burst into tears.

I looked at the pair of them, valiant-seeming, but tormented by doubt, and my heart ached for them. I, too, was putting on a bold face, but had I been as young as Augusta I should have been sharing her tears, just as I shared her apprehensions. Does life teach us anything more, I wondered, than not to cry over all there is to cry about?

"Well," I said, "you'll have a lovely time here, I'm sure. Shall I help you to? I think I shall be able to get you a boat. I'll teach you to sail."

"Oh, I say!" Miles exclaimed. "That would be wonderful!"

"I'll walk along to the vicarage with you. Your uncle Hugo is married to my sister Bella."

"Oh, good! What a stroke of luck meeting you like this. Isn't it, Augusta?"

Augusta, choking back tears, agreed that it was. I hoped they were right. We finished the last lap of the road together.

2

There is a hedge or a wall, and in it there is a gate or a door. No matter how familiar the world is that presses up against the wall or the hedge, it is not till you have opened the gate or the door that you are home. That is the bridge over the frontier. The rest is foreign.

I was reluctant to open the gate, to step back into the core of my being. If that rejects me, I thought, I am done for. And there couldn't have been a worse moment for arriving. Bella and Hugo would be expecting these two children, and that would be enough of an upset seeing that there were already four. An unexpected adult could be a nuisance. It is dreadful to feel unwanted. All very well to say "This is my home." But it wasn't. It was Bella's home and Hugo's. I said to the children: "Well, there's the vicarage. Don't say anything about meeting me."

I watched them walk up the gravel path, the boy alert, looking here and there, weighing up the place and the moment; Augusta keeping close to him, as though no place or moment could now be tolerable except in so far as he shared it with her. Coming down the hill towards the gate I saw the rest of them: the pram with the sleeping Millicent pushed by the village girl, John and Constance on either side, Richard tagging behind, clutching his fistful of wilted flowers. I wondered if Mrs Solway would be ready to regale them with sticky buns, but I didn't know whether Mrs Solway was dead or alive.

I went into the churchyard through the lych-gate, which Father had explained to me meant the corpse-gate. On either side, under the canopy, an oblong granite block made a table on which the coffins were set down, and the floor was made of slabs of granite, too, running from side to side with deep spaces between so that cows would find it difficult to stray into the churchyard. When I was a girl I loved to stand outside the lych-gate and watch the coffins coming, pushed on a flat handcart by men in black clothes and followed by crying women. The men would lay the coffin on one of the granite slabs till Father came, surpliced and book in hand, and then they would take it up and follow him as he began: "I am the resurrection and the life."

I stood there once like that till the small procession had moved off; and then a cow strayed down the road and looked at the lych-gate, and I knew I should shoo it away lest the difficult stones prove not so difficult as all that. But I was full of curiosity and let the cow have a go, and she managed well enough and followed the mourners with gallons of milk bloating her udders. It would have been unseemly for any of the mourners to raise an halloo in that solemn moment, so the procession followed Father, and the cow followed the procession, and I followed the cow, and we all stood around the grave, and there was no sound in the June sunshine except Father's voice and the snivelling of some women and the wrench of grass as the cow browsed upon an overgrown grave. When it was all over, Thomas May went up to the cow and laid a hand gently on her flank. "Come on, Maudie," he said. "This be immortal grass nourished on the bones of the saints and you a mortal beast. 'Tis no place for 'e, midear." And so he guided her down to the lower gate that opened on to the path along the sea, and he let her through to find her way home.

Well, there it all was, miraculously unchanged, as, for the most part, it is to this day: Roger's black tent, and the bricked-in spring whence women drew water to fill the jam-pots that held the flowers on the graves, and the old crumbling sea-wall, and the wooden bell-tower that stood apart from the church. I wandered among the graves, and found the inscription concerning that Euphemia Emmett who had given my doll a name, and I was dreaming of all that had followed Euphemia's funeral when a hand was laid on my arm. I turned and Hugo looked at me, and his look was so loving and full of welcome that

I burst into tears. He was a stout, spectacled little man, embarrassed by my crying, and he made absurd, soothing, clucking noises, but they were not absurd to me. He said: "Young Miles told me about you. He shouldn't, he explained. You had told him not to. But he said you seemed unhappy, and so he thought he'd better disobey. Why on earth didn't you let us know you were coming?"

"I was afraid."

He looked at me sorrowfully, as though I had insulted him, and took my arm and led me up the hill towards the vicarage. But we didn't go into the house. We climbed the outside stairs to the loft, and when we were inside I saw the chair and the table, the books in their cases, the bed with sheets and blankets folded and ready upon it.

"I told you when you went away," he said, "that this would always be here for you."

"But what on earth will you do with all these children?"

"We'll tuck 'em in somewhere," he assured me. "Now have a rest. Have an hour's sleep, and then come down and join us."

3

I slept longer than I had intended and was awakened by the sound of the door opening. Miles put his head in. "I say, may I come in?"

"Yes," I said, swinging my legs down from the bed.

"May I call you Aunt Maria?"

"Yes, do."

"Well, Aunt Maria, would you care to come down now? The evening meal is just going on to the table. Augusta and I are being allowed to sit up and eat with Uncle Hugo and Aunt Bella. I'm three years older than my cousin John, so I suppose that's all right. He and the others have gone to bed already."

He was rather a tall boy for his age, with straight fair hair and blue eyes. I imagined that at this moment he was feeling disrupted, with not much to stand on except what he could call up out of his own spirit. It was a condition I knew well.

"How brave are you, Miles?"

"Oh, enormously," he said, and then considered this. He decided to modify it. "Well, you see, there's Augusta. Father said I was not to let her mope. So I try to keep her up to scratch. I've had her out swimming already."

"Pretty cold, wasn't it?"

"Yes, but we both happen to swim like fishes, and that soon warms you up. We're used to cold baths. Father believes in them. He was a great athlete, you know, in his young days. I'm surprised he let us come down here."

"Oh. Why is that? I should have thought he'd want you to spend all your holidays down here."

"No. He doesn't believe in the south. Says it's a soft place. We've always spent our holidays up on the Northumberland coast. That's where he taught us to swim. It's cold there if you like! This year he was going to take me alone to North Wales or the Lake District to start me on a bit of climbing. I was enormously looking forward to that, because Father's been a great climber in his time. And then Mother died . . . Well . . . there it is."

I wanted to kiss him, but I could see he was the sort of boy who wouldn't like that and wouldn't need it. His next words confirmed this. I had said: "Well, you must try and give Augusta a good holiday," and he said: "Oh, we shall be all right if Aunt Bella will leave us alone. She's been fussing all over us. We don't want that sort of thing."

I was glad that he was there to go down with me. I dreaded the meeting with Bella. It was a long time ago now, but I felt as though I were walking straight out of the witness-box, with all the slime of that dreadful case still dripping about me. Louisa had always been to me the elder sister, a person apart, unpredictable, admired, and a little feared. She was granite, but Bella was of the stuff they call in these days foam rubber. Things bounced off her: she would never allow herself to be hurt. She would certainly not allow me and my unfortunate experiences to hurt her. It could well be, I knew, that what had been to me a tragedy would be to her only a scandal. She was married, and very happily married, I knew, to the vicar of the parish. If she felt in the slightest degree that my presence was compromising – though, heaven knows, there had been no guilt on my part – she would find some way of making my stay at St Tudno impossible. I felt sure she would think it all very odd: gadding about France with a woman whose husband was in Africa, hob-nobbing with an artist, exposing oneself to a peeping Tom, sleeping alone in a house with a man in the garden shed outside the window, and then, to cap all, getting involved in a murderous *cause célèbre*.

She got up from the familiar dining table, with the oil-lamp burning above it, and waddled to meet me. It was the only word. She had always been on the fleshy side; now she was very fat, complacent and matronly. I was much taller than she, thin, still brown from the Italian sun. I might have been a child whom she was welcoming home from a short holiday. She put her arms around me and kissed me. She said: "Maria! How lovely to have you back!"

I embraced her. She felt as though she had no skeleton. She was swathed in web upon web of flimsy arty-coloured stuffs. It was like embracing an immense dandelion puff. She gave at all points.

Over her shoulder Hugo sent me his shy friendly smile, and Augusta seemed to shudder slightly, as though she, not I, were being enveloped.

She sat at one end of the table, Hugo at the other. Miles pulled out my chair, and then took his place alongside Augusta, facing me.

Hugo said: "Grant, O Lord, that these Thy mercies be used to Thy service. Amen."

That is where Father would have been sitting, I thought, and Louisa there where Bella is. Bella and I would have been sitting where those two children are, and here, where I am, would have been Roger when he was at home. Outside the window I could see the flowers of the camellia that Uncle Reginald had planted, and beyond that were the slope of the garden and the quiet evening sea. I saw all this, but all of it was unreal.

I am not at home, I thought. I have no home. The sooner I am gone the better.

A woman who was a stranger to me took away our plates. There was no sign of Mrs Holmfirth who had come south with Hugo or of Mrs Solway. I supposed Mrs Solway was dead, but, looking at Augusta, I decided that whether this person or that was dead was not a matter to be discussed. It was all small-talk, with a *pas devant les enfants* undertone.

"We're packing Miles into John's bed," Bella said, "and Augusta into Constance's. It's so lucky that you can have the loft. I shall help you to feel at home there by coming and having one of our long old-fashioned chats."

"Perhaps," Hugo said, "Maria would prefer on her first night to have a long old-fashioned sleep. She's looking rather tired."

"Oh, she'd never forgive me," Bella assured him, "if we didn't immediately resume our old customs."

And there we were resuming our old customs. During dinner someone had come and made up my bed, and a fire was burning, which was welcome, because May though it was, the evening was a little chilly. Bella lolled as of old in the wicker chair and I sat on the rug before the fire.

"Did Hugo tell you," she asked, "about the letter from Frank?"

"Frank?"

"Dr Cumberledge, the father of these poor children."

"Oh, I see. No, he didn't mention that."

"It came this morning." She handed me the letter.

Dear Hugo. – All my thanks to you and Bella for looking after the children while I'm settling in here. Miles didn't want to go, for he had the idea that I would need him. Augusta didn't care whether she went or stayed. Since Claire's death she's been utterly apathetic, appallingly obedient, hardly alive. Go easy with her. But I think she'll be all right so long as Miles is about. She is always happier with him than with anyone else. That is, since Claire died. As you know, they were all in all to one another. That, more than anything else, is why I've made this move. There was too much in Warwick to remind the child of her mother. She was always wanting to go on 'Mummy's walk' and do this, that and the other that she had done with Claire. You, of course, are not so much her uncle as 'Mummy's brother'. Try and edge her off gently if she keeps too much on that tack.

I think I shall find this a worthwhile practice. Didsbury is a pleasant enough suburb. You'd hardly think you were within five miles of the heart of Manchester. Our house is in a leafy little street, or rather half a street, for there are houses on only one side. Opposite is an open field. But I'm forgetting that you are a Manchester man and know more about Didsbury than I do. You'll know all about the flowering shrubs and trees and the fields towards the Mersey river. I hope the children will like it. It's flat country. They can get about on their bikes.

In the autumn Miles will be off to school, and that's when I shall be seriously up against the problem of Augusta. She'll hate his going and I'm afraid she'll be desperately lonely. I have my own problem, too, and I'm fishing round to see if I can solve hers and mine in one go. I've found an admirable woman here who will live in as what is comprehensively called cook-housekeeper, but I should like to find also an educated woman who could, not too obtrusively, be a companion for Augusta. You know that Claire, once the children had ceased to be mere infants demanding all her time, helped me no end. Only to have someone who can be relied on to take a telephone message accurately is a lot. So if this woman could do that sort of thing as well as prevent Augusta from moping, you see how I might get over a few obstacles that really are worrying me.

However, none of that is your business, and no doubt I shall sort out the tangle somehow. I'm writing because it soothes me to be sending a letter to the place where the children are. It's immensely good of you and Bella to have them, and I know them well enough to be sure that they won't be too much of a nuisance. Give them my love, which is yours and Bella's always.

Ever,

Frank.

It was dusky in the loft. I had been holding the letter down to the firelight. I sat back on my heels and looked at Bella. She was munching a chocolate and her eyes were on me with an extraordinary, an unmistakable, eagerness that I should understand.

I said: "It seems providential, doesn't it, Bella?"

She didn't answer, but relaxed in her chair, smiling.

I said: "I like this letter, and I think I shall like the man who wrote it. There's no reason why I shouldn't even like Manchester. Do you mind if I write personally to Dr Cumberledge, proposing myself for the situation?"

She looked a little flustered, and I don't know what she would have said, for at that moment Hugo knocked at the door and came in. He looked at his wife overflowing the chair and at me crouched on the floor. "We must have more chairs up here," he said. "This is Maria's room, and I expect she would like to see her guests seated."

It was a mild, good-humoured reproof, but as harsh a one, I suspected, as he could ever bring himself to administer.

"Maria won't be here for long," Bella said. "She tells me that she hopes to leave us soon."

She knew me well enough to be sure that I would not make a "thing" of it. Besides, in my very moment of despising her, I was aware that even if she had begged me to stay I should have gone. Dr Cumberledge's letter was indeed, as I had said, providential. The vicarage felt uxorious, oppressive. My travels with Jane, and my long stay with the sharp astringent Mrs Kopf, made Bella unthinkable. I should have felt like Carroll's dormouse living in a treacle-well.

Hugo lit his pipe and was silent for a time. I think he was absorbing the atmosphere of the moment and suddenly "got" it rightly. He said: "But this is very disappointing, my dear Maria. I was hoping that, even if you decided to go at last, you would give us a good long visit."

"May I stay," I asked, "as long as Miles and Augusta are here?"

"You know," he said uncomfortably, "that you may stay as long as you like."

I thanked him, and picked up the letter. He looked from it to Bella, and understood.

"I think," I said, "that I ought not to stay if Dr Cumberledge will have me. I intended to write to him myself, but will you do it, Hugo? That might be better. You can tell him that I have fluent French and Italian and that I am used to answering the telephone. If you wish to add anything on the other side, there's no reason why you shouldn't."

"My dear," Hugo said, "I assure you there's nothing."

I began to laugh, as I had laughed that night when Charles Lester ran *Norah* on to the sand-bank, and Roger brought me to my senses with a slap in the face. "You could tell him," I said, "that I'm the sort of woman who is rather an embarrassment in an English vicarage."

Hugo did not slap me. He looked unhappy and said: "I shall write, if you wish me to. Now, Bella, I think we should allow Maria to get some sleep."

Bella heaved herself out of the chair and kissed me. "Sleep well, darling," she said.

4

I did. When they were gone I made up the fire, put a guard in front of it, and got into bed. If Bella had expected me to be rebellious she was mistaken. She had handed me salvation on a plate. Looking at the shadows dancing on the white wall, I was tranquil and content. Obviously, I could not have stayed at the vicarage. Bella was right about that. I could have wished for a little more warmth, a little less of the impression she gave that I smelled of leprosy, a little less eagerness to see the back of me; but I was glad that Dr Cumberledge's letter had allowed the thing to arrange itself with a bit of face-saving, so that the dread word hypocrisy need not appear.

Thus I was able with a calm mind to allow St Tudno to embrace me. Always the place, if not the house, would be my home, and some day I should come back. Thinking this, I listened to the owls and to the squawk of a heron and to the sigh of a quiet tide; and was then, without knowing I had fallen happily asleep, awake to a room full of morning light and to that most wondrous noise of the curlew in springtime: that rapturous bubbling of joy which is the more moving because the curlew's only other note is of wild and unassuagable desolation. "Rachel crying for her children, and would not be comforted." Nothing between that and the Song of Songs that now drew me from bed to look out of the window.

It was going to be a good day. The weather-lore of this remote crumb of the world's coasts was in my blood. I knew that this opalescent mist moving on the water would draw slowly aside and let in the light to flash and sparkle. It was on such a morning that, when a child, I would shake Bella, lying at my side in the bed, and call upon her to come out and swim. But she never would. "I'll wait till the sea warms up," she'd say. "You go." And I'd go, while Bella pulled my share of the warm blankets about her.

I felt that I wanted to go now, but I had no bathing-suit. All my things were still in a bag at the Green Bank Hotel in Falmouth. I had slept naked, and was standing at the window now with a blanket round me, like an Indian squaw.

Young Miles came out of the front door of the vicarage. He stood still, bareheaded, taking in the morning. Caught unawares, he looked a child of sorrow and acquainted with grief. So small a man, with so many days, so many years, implacably before him.

I put on some clothes and went down. At the sound of my steps on the gravel he fitted a brave mask over the face I had seen unprotected. "Good morning, Aunt Maria," he said. "I loathed sharing a bed, so I got up early. I hope Augusta slept well."

I took him into the house, through to the kitchen. Bella's house-keeper was brewing herself a cup of tea. "Good morning, Miss Maria," she said. And, seeing that I didn't recognise her: "I'm Daisy Andrewartha. Just about your own age, I reckon. I expect I've changed a bit."

I remembered Daisy. She had been a child who used to come to Sunday school and then left the village to go into service upalong, as they say in Cornwall, meaning a foreign place that might be some inconceivable distance away — as much as ten miles.

She gave us some tea and biscuits. "Breakfast in an hour's time," she informed us.

I took Miles out into the garden. "Now," I said, "let's have a bit of a walk before breakfast. It doesn't look as though Aunt Bella has a boat, so I want to try and find one."

"Thank you," he said gravely. "That's what I'd love. And you *will* teach us to sail, as you promised yesterday?"

"I hope so. But for today we'll make do with rowing, if there's a boat to be had."

The mist was rising in gauzy scarves, and sun was beginning to warm the day, as we walked along the path that ran with the creek. I was glad he was seeing it like this. I felt joy in his quiet joy.

"It's not a bit like the Northumberland coast," he said.

"I've not been up there, but I suppose not."

"Up there it's rather — well, gruff. You know — Border ballad stuff."

"And how do you find it down here?"

"Well, rather King Arthur. Not fighting to steal someone else's cattle, but because of all sorts of ideals and things. Still, it seems they always had to fight. If not about one thing, then about another."

I looked at him appreciatively, surprised.

"Do you read much about those things?"

"Oh, I just read — anything that comes my way."

"Good," I said. "That's the way to read, especially when you're young."

"I'm not so young as all that. Would you call fourteen very young?"

"Well," I conceded, "I suppose it's getting on."

"What did you read when you were fourteen?"

"I was rather like you. I read anything I could lay hands on. But I liked lords with names such as Hector or Algernon and ladies called Ermyntrude and so forth."

"Sounds a bit frothy," he said. "Father can't stand froth."

We came to Little in Sight, and on the tiny pool that nibbles a way there into the edge of the creek a dinghy was bobbing. Barty Spargo, the lame young man who had succeeded Thomas May, was hauling on the line attached to a grapnel that held her. I knew little about him and had gone abroad with Jane soon after he took the job, but I spoke to him as the dinghy grounded, and he remembered me.

All along the edge of the creek, where the tide doesn't come except at high springs, you will find tables with their legs made of stout logs dug into the soil and with a transverse plank or two instead of a solid top. In the late autumn, dinghies are hoisted on to these and roped securely down, and there they spend the winter. By the springtime their seams are gaping and they need to be on the water for a day or two before they take up and become watertight.

Barty Spargo said he had put his boat out only the day before, and she was still wet. Miles took hold of the gunwale and helped him to heave her over and empty out the water. I had hardly known a boy who didn't love to play about with a boat, and I was glad to see that Miles was no exception.

I asked Barty if we might hire the boat while Miles and Augusta were at the vicarage, and he said: "You can 'av'n without hiring, Miss Maria. I don't use'n except to go out now and then an' catch an ole bass. Not that she's ready to go out yet. She needs a lick of paint."

"Oh, we'll do that, Mr Spargo," Miles promised eagerly, and I backed this proposal because something interesting for the children to do seemed to me what was needed. Nowadays, of course, it must have a wonderful name, as though it were something just thought of. They call it occupational therapy; but, bless my soul, we've been doing it, without calling it anything, since Adam.

So that was agreed, and they tipped the boat back on to her keel, and Miles helped to push her to the water's edge. "Now you see," Barty explained, "here's this ole hook called a grapnel. There's a ring at one end of it and prongs at the other. You being a town boy, I must make myself manifest."

I rejoiced to hear this small echo of Thomas May's idiom, and left the lesson to Barty. He explained how you gave the boat a hearty shove, and when she was far enough out to be still afloat at low tide you used the shore-line, fastened to the prongs, to jerk the grapnel in from where you had balanced it on the dinghy's bows. Then you made your shore-line fast and there you were, with the painter tied to the ring so that the boat couldn't float away, and the shore-line tied to the grapnel so that you could pull her ashore.

Miles listened with grave attention, and said: "Now let me do it." He hauled in the boat, balanced the hook, shoved her out, and jerked the hook overboard. The small job successfully done, he looked at her bobbing there on the water from which by now the sun had sucked away the mist, and he smiled very happily. "Thank you, Mr Spargo," he said. "I think you can safely entrust her to us."

"Ay," said Barty, " 'tis clear you're a proper li'l navigator. You'll be round the world and back before harvest home."

He limped away towards the vicarage, and I said: "Now pull her in again, Miles. I'll row you home."

I was glad to see that, without my having to tell him, he coiled the long shore-line neatly in the bows. Then he held the boat steady while I got in. He got in after me, and I said: "Now sit down. Unless you're in charge of a boat, always sit down till you're told to do something else."

"Sorry, Aunt. I should have seen that. I'm stupid."

"You're not a bit stupid, but it would be a pity if I threw you overboard when I push the boat out."

I pushed her out, shoving the oar down into the gravel. He watched every movement intently. I rowed across the creek to where the morning sun was falling strongly and the small scrub oaks that lined the shore still shone with the gold of immature leaves. Miles looked at them and noticed the straight line ruled along their lower branches. "That shows you where the high tides reach to," he said. I was glad I hadn't had to point it out to him. He was a boy who saw things quickly.

Five minutes' rowing had us back on the beach under the vicarage. The water was sloshing about our feet. The seams still had some taking-up to do. As I ran her ashore Miles sat still. "Now you can step ashore," I said.

He did so, and I laid the oars tidily down and unshipped the rowlocks. "Is that always done?" he asked.

"Yes."

Augusta was on the shore, astonished by the unexpected fashion of our arrival. "Now," I said, "show Augusta how the boat is pushed out and secured."

He went through the drill neatly. Hugo appeared, leaning over the graveyard wall. "Come on up to breakfast," he shouted. "Bella's ravenous."

5

After breakfast Bella said: "Would you like to take John and Constance out for the morning? I think they should get to know their cousins."

"Are they used to boats?"

"Not particularly. We haven't a boat, but they go out now and then in other people's."

"Are they good swimmers?"

"Well, John paddles like a puppy. Constance doesn't like the water."

"Don't you swim now?"

"Oh, no. It hardly seems becoming."

"Life has changed here a little," I said.

I thought of our own childhood when she and Roger and I always had some sort of a tub to play about in and swam like fishes.

I said: "I've managed to borrow a dinghy from Barty Spargo, and I should like to row Miles and Augusta round to Falmouth. My things are at the Green Bank, and I can pick them up. Four children who're not used to boats, two of them non-swimmers, are a bit more than I'd care to have in one rather leaky tub."

"I was counting on your giving us a hand."

"You can count on anything reasonable. I don't think this would be. Besides, if I'm to go and look after Miles and Augusta in Manchester, I'd like every chance to get to know them."

She switched from the children. "This Manchester thing seems an excellent solution of your problem."

"What problem?"

262

"Well, I suppose you'll have to earn a living somehow. I do hope Frank will think it a good idea. Hugo got a letter off first thing this morning."

"That was very good of him. I *do* want to go and see what living in Manchester is like. I got rather tired, at the end, of living with rich people. It tends to give one wrong ideas of what life's about."

She laughed. "You talk like Louisa. Living in Tregannock and always on about social injustice."

"Though," I added, "so far as earning a living goes, I don't need to do that. I can be as lazy as the next one if I choose. When old Mrs Kopf died, Lord Lavernock was quite fulsome about what his mother owed me for comforting her last years. He said he felt he should provide for me, and so he did. Mind you, I can't be riotous on it, but it's enough to keep me from starvation. About five pounds a week. A flea-bite to Lord Lavernock."

I went down to the beach and found Miles expounding to Augusta the mysteries of pushing out the boat. I said: "If you'd like a swim, go and get your bathing things." I was carrying my own.

Augusta said: "Mother was a beautiful swimmer."

"I'm sure she would want you to be an even better one," I said.

They were soon back with their bathing-suits on and dressing-gowns over their shoulders. "You two sit in the stern," I said.

"And once you're sitting, you stay sitting till you're told to move," Miles commanded. "Remember, Aunt Maria is the captain and gives the orders."

I rowed towards the little grass-grown half-circle of a quay on the other side of the creek. The sun was fully out in a cloudless sky. Through the clear water we could see the bright fish darting and the fretted edges of the seaweed lifting up, undulating to the water's complex compulsions.

"The boat's leaking," Augusta announced, looking down at her bare feet in an inch of water.

"It's what they call taking-up," Miles explained. "The boat has been out of the water for months and so the seams have parted. When the wood is swollen enough by damp it will be all right."

Augusta accepted this, as she did all he said. I looked at her and wondered about Dr Cumberledge. She was a beautiful child. Her mother was Hugo's sister, but there was nothing at all of the Oldham looks in her. In Miles I could already see something of the young Hugo as he was when he came to stay with Roger long ago: a youthful earnestness and gravity, a solidity rather than handsomeness. Augusta was something else. I had heard Hugo say that the Cumberledge family hailed from Northumberland, and there is a good deal of Norse blood up there. I couldn't recall Frank's looks. The memory of my long-ago only meeting with him was quite blotted out. Well, forget him, and look at Augusta. Light blue eyes, and corn-gold hair streaming over her shoulders from which the dressing-gown had slipped. Her arms and legs were lovely. Whether she had ever had puppy-fat I don't know. Now she was as slender and golden as a stalk of ripe corn. I could see the earliest budding of breasts beneath her bathing-suit. What a picture for Gerald, I thought: this fair child, and the blue sea, and this weightless floating of gulls upon the warm air! Her face and limbs were pale, but give her a few weeks of this sun! My goodness, I thought, we should have something!

It was a splendid tide, almost lipping the top of the quay wall. We climbed out and tied up the boat. The children couldn't wait. They were no sooner ashore than Augusta stuffed her hair into a rubber cap and they were gone like a pair of arrows shot into the water. They came up and paddled for a moment, and then they were off, swimming with a trudgeon stroke up the creek on the last dying push of the tide.

I went behind some bushes and threw off my clothes, thinking sad thoughts. That was how it had been: Roger and Bella and I; and over there Louisa had been transcribing yesterday's instalment of Father's work, and Father had been writing today's. And it had seemed that it would never end, that there was no such thing as tomorrow, only and for ever today, blue and burning. And, silently as a thief, Time had stolen a generation, and Aunt Maria found herself in danger of loving this child who had the golden looks of Roger and Charles Lester.

Less impetuous than the children, I sat on the warm granite stones that edged the quay and dabbled my toes in the water; and, because this moment of my return to St Tudno was reminding me of so much, I allowed it to remind me of Meg, sitting here, on this very edge of granite, dangling her bare legs as Gerald painted her from the dinghy. And, thinking of Gerald, I thought of his last anguished cry in the shed at Douze Maisons, the cry which, ever since it was uttered, recurred in my dreams; and then, as though to wash all that past away and submerge myself in the present moment, I slipped quietly over the edge and swam to meet the children who were now returning as unexhausted as a couple of young seals at play.

6

I had had a word with Mrs Trewince, the woman who had waited on us at dinner the night before and had asked her to make up a lunch-basket for me and the two children. She said she would speak to Mrs Oldham about it, and apparently Bella had no objection, for I found the basket in the kitchen. Daisy Andrewartha dug out an ancient tin kettle and a stone jar that would hold a gallon of water. "You'll want firewood, too, Miss Maria," she said, "if you're going on a picnic."

But that was against the rules, and I had learned the rules when young. The rules forbade the taking of even a newspaper to start the fire. Half the fun of a picnic was finding one's own fuel, including the handful of small dry twigs that made the kindling. I drew the line at leaving matches behind. Only once, so far as I could recall, had Father joined us on a picnic, and he had said no matches. He started the fire by concentrating the sun's light upon a handful of moss through a lens of his spectacles, and this success so excited him with pleasure that he dropped the spectacles and Roger stepped on them. Both lenses were smashed on a piece of rock. It spoiled the day for all of us.

So I put a box of matches into my pocket, and Miles carried the water-jar and Augusta the basket of food and we walked down again to the boat. "We'd better stow this heavy jar amidships," Miles said. "It might upset the balance of the boat." Stow. Amidships. Nice nautical words. He seemed to love using them. They both indeed seemed to be loving all they were doing that day, and I was determined to make it a crowded day. They had plenty to forget.

I rowed out of the creek into the Carrick Roads, a mile-and-a-half across. Plenty of water for fun on a day like this, and for trouble on other days that I had known. The tide was ebbing, so I had nothing to do but keep the dinghy on her course.

"Augusta," I said, "the tide is carrying us in towards Falmouth, and so rowing is not a hard job against the push of the water. Would you like to try?"

"Oh, Aunt Maria! May I? I've been longing to, but I didn't dare to ask."

"In a small dinghy like this," I said, "it's not a good idea to have two people scrambling about at the same time. So you come over to me."

When she was sitting in the bows I went and sat in the stern alongside Miles. I gave her no instructions. I let her do as she liked. There was a lot of frantic splashing and heaving, and once an oar went awash. I reached out and lifted it aboard and slipped it back into the rowlock. She looked annoyed with herself and blushed and bit her lip, which made her look more beautiful than ever.

"I'm not good at it," she said. "What am I doing wrong, Aunt Maria?"

I laughed. "You're fighting like the dickens against an enemy who isn't there. Some day you'll be rowing against the tide, and perhaps against a heavy wind at the same time. Then you'll need to put your back into it. But just now you have nothing to do but swing your oars astern, let them dip into the water, and then lean back a little as you pull them through it. Take it easy and find the rhythm."

She took it easy and she found the rhythm – well enough to be going on with. Then Miles took a turn, and it was lunch time, and we went ashore and lit a fire and boiled our kettle. As we sat there in the glowing light, watching a lovely four-masted barque coming slowly in to anchorage, I felt that I had never been happier in my life. And then Augusta, her bare toes wriggling in the sand, a chunk of Cornish pasty in one hand and a mug of tea in the other, looked at me with the first full-hearted smile I had seen on her face. She said: "And we didn't even know we *had* an Aunt Maria, did we, Miles? Aren't we in luck!" I could have wept for joy.

Miles said: "Well, I rather thought the idea might be trailing round with a lot of kid-cousins and a nursemaid. I must say this suits me better."

We could hear voices coming across the water from the barque as the great white towers began to crumble, and the anchor went down and the tall sticks stood up against the blue sky. I was moved by the sight, as I always was when one of the barques came home and our herring-gulls looked down on her as the lovely albatrosses had done and our breezes played about the rigging that had been strummed upon by winds howling off the antarctic ice as she made her bitter boisterous southing. "And some ships," I said to the children, "have lain where she is lying now, and you would have thought their sorrows were over, but even then the sea smashed them to pieces." I told them of the transport ship *Queen*, bringing home men, women and children from the Peninsular War. There they were, anchored, leaning over the rail, so near to home that they could count the very cows in the fields; nothing more to do than paddle ashore in a dinghy the next morning. "But on that January night in 1814," I said, "a great storm blew in from the south-east and the *Queen* dragged her anchor and went to pieces on these very rocks that lie about us. Two hundred men, women and children were drowned."

Dinghies were being rowed out to the great ship. The sun shone warmly down, and the treacherous sea was smiling. The children sat silent, pondering that old tragedy, and the sweet smell of wood smoke was in our nostrils. At last Miles said: "They shouldn't have gone to war."

But war had touched this place with many a wing. I pointed out the castles of Pendennis and St Mawes and explained their significance. I spoke of the Spanish armada surging through the water out there beyond the lighthouse, and of the small swift ship sailing in here with the first news of Trafalgar and Nelson's death.

"It's all the same to me," Miles said. "King Arthur, border raiders, Trafalgar and the rest of it. I shall never fight. It's all nonsense."

I didn't want the day to be spoiled by thoughts too sombre and heavy for their years. "Well," I said, "we must make some decisions about our own small peaceful craft. We promised Barty Spargo that we'd paint her. Let's have a look at her. What colour shall she be?"

We decided on a black bottom, dark blue sides, a black gunwale, and white inside. "Very well," I said. "Pack up the basket, and then we'll row into Falmouth and buy some paint and brushes."

"And some sort of scraper," said Augusta.

"And sandpaper," said Miles.

"And the dinghy will be only a beginning," said Augusta. "You promised that we shall sail. Shall we sail right out till we can see no land anywhere?"

"Yes. If we can borrow a sailing boat and if the weather is right, we shall do that."

Augusta laughed. "That's two ifs, Aunt Maria. You're being cautious."

"There are times," I assured her, "when one needs to be." Around the lighthouse and a little east was the Gull Rock. I didn't tell them what had happened there. I didn't tell them of *Norah's* dinghy, stove-in and thrown up high and dry on the ledges where the wild seabirds nested. I said: "Never trust the sea. Love it, if you must. But never trust it."

We paddled into Falmouth and went ashore. A lane – what they call an ope down there – gives off Church Street, and at the bottom of it, right on the edge of the water, is a building of grey Cornish stone that I had loved from my earliest years. And the children loved it now. Windows opened on the sea and let the light in to fall on the exciting miscellany: coils of rope of every thickness; chains whose massive links would hold the biggest ships, ships' bells, figureheads of piratical men and of women with eyes and breasts straining to strange horizons, and all painted in blue and white and red and green and black; lanterns and oars and anchors; lamps hanging in gimbals; boathooks, fenders, buoys and ladders; glass baubles that were floats for fishing nets, and nets themselves and fishing-line and hooks and bunting and signal flags; clocks to fit into bulkheads, mops, buckets and sextants; ships in bottles and ships in old engravings, opening fire gallantly against impossible odds; heaps of cannon-balls and guns of brass and iron, grappling-irons for boarding an enemy and cutlasses for slashing an enemy down – oh, there was no end to what that place contained of evocation, souvenir, and up-to-the-minute use whether in a dinghy or a four-masted barque. The floor was of trodden earth, saturated, by the feel of it, with the rise and ebb of tides beyond remembering, and this dumbed the sound of footsteps, so that the children walked there now, as my own infant feet had walked so often, noiseless, as befitted magic and invocation.

We needed a few pots of paint. I felt as though we were going to the Horse Guards Parade to buy a penny tin soldier.

The old man, who had seemed to me when young so withered, weather-beaten and beyond reckoning that he might well have trafficked with Phoenicians, bartering the dyed goods of Tyre and Sidon for Cornish tin, was still there; and with careful respect Miles opened the question of how much paint would be needed to makeover a dinghy. They went into matters of undercoating and final gloss, anti-fouling for the bottom, and so forth, and when all that was settled I bought a bailer to replace the old salmon-tin that Barty had aboard and a small ship in a bottle for Augusta. And after that it was still some time before the children wished to end their loitering. They moved about on silent feet, whispering, gazing wide-eyed; and when at last we went, and the hot blaze of afternoon struck us, it was as though we had come out of a cave full of sea-whispers. "You know," Miles said, "there's one thing about that old man. He ought to be carrying a trident."

We had tea in a shop overlooking the harbour, and then we went back to the dinghy and rowed to the Green Bank Hotel, where I picked up my bag. I rowed them out beyond the lighthouse to show them the full water of the Channel. We looked west. The sun was sloping down. "Soon it'll be waking people up in America," Miles said.

Augusta asked: "Will they be having the day we've just had? When it gets there, will it be full of all the things that have happened here? – me and Miles, and Aunt Maria and old Mr Neptune?"

I didn't know the answer, and on the tide that was making nicely I paddled lazily back to our familiar creek. "Now," said Augusta, "I must write a long letter to Daddy."

"What will you tell him about?"

"About you," she said.

7

A few days later Hugo received from Frank Cumberledge an answer to the letter proposing me as the kind of secretary-companion that the doctor had in mind. It was short, and said little more than that I sounded all right and that he would write to me. Two days after that Hugo came down to the beach, bringing me the letter. Miles, wearing nothing but khaki shorts, and Augusta wearing as little as Bella permitted, were at work on the overturned dinghy, one scraping down the old paint, the other sandpapering what had been scraped. On Hugo's arrival, Augusta paused, tossed her head to clear the hair from her eyes, and rubbed the back of her hand across her hot forehead. She said: "I wish she was carvel-built."

I was amused by the way the pair of them were picking up nautical words and throwing them about. "What is carvel-built?" Hugo asked.

"My goodness, Uncle," Miles exclaimed, "you living here with your church almost afloat and not knowing a thing like that! But you're joking."

"Indeed I'm not," Hugo assured him. "I don't get into a boat from one year's end to another, and I know nothing about them."

"Clinker-built," Augusta explained proudly, "means that the strakes overlap. In a carvel-built boat they lie edge to edge. That makes scraping-down easy. It's far more niggly with a thing like this."

"Mr Spargo is going to allow us to give her a name," Miles said. "She's to be *The Cowrie*. Augusta paints well, and she will paint a cowrieshell on the stern."

They got on with the job, and Hugo handed me the letter. "Looks as if it's from Frank," he said. "Well, Sunday tomorrow. I must go and prepare my groat's-worth of wit."

When he was gone, I left the children to their work and took the seat on the graveyard wall, with the sea spread glittering before me, that from childhood times I had used for private cogitation. I found myself agitated, reluctant to open the envelope. I dreaded to find that Dr Cumberledge could do without me, for in these few days it had become clear that I could not do without the children – except at the cost of a deeper wound than I felt I could bear. It was rather terrifying to find how much I was a child myself. Here, lonely in the place of my childhood, they had been my solace. It was as though we had entered into a compact on their terms, not mine. We were doing together, and on an equal footing, all the things that I had done when young, and that no one was left to do with me now. Sitting there with the letter in my hand, I should not have been surprised to hear Father's voice. "Well, young Maria, what makes you mope on a day like this?"

I opened the letter.

My dear Maria, as I suppose I must learn at once to call you. – My mind was twiddling about with a proposal that reached me from Hugo, but it was very far indeed from made up. Where Miles and Augusta are concerned, it isn't made up easily. Especially Augusta. Miles, as you may have learned, will soon be off to school, and that is causing me no anxiety. He's a fairly self-reliant person and he'll have new things to occupy his mind. Augusta will be alone, and a general medical practitioner doesn't have much time to spare for his family. So you see why Augusta is important.

I couldn't make up my mind about a woman whom I dimly remembered as a girl of long ago. Then Augusta wrote to me. What she said I needn't tell you, but her letter settled it. So far as I am concerned anyway. What your own feelings are I don't know. Perhaps when you told Hugo you would be willing to come here you were speaking impulsively. You may have had second thoughts. I hope not. I hope you will come. I am anxious to have the matter settled, so please write promptly to say Yes or No.

Yours sincerely,

Frank.

The happiness I felt must have shone in my face. I got up and stepped down into the graveyard and Barty Spargo, who was working there, said: "Good news, Miss Maria?"

I didn't answer that, but I asked: "Do you know anyone, Barty, who could hire me a small sailing-boat?"

"Ay," he said. "Up there where you picked up my dinghy the other day you'll find a little ole boat all ready to go to sea. Belong to Bill Hammill. You take 'er, Miss Maria. I'll explain to Bill."

I thanked him and ran down to the beach where Miles and Augusta were still scraping away. "You can take a rest from that this afternoon," I said. "We're going sailing."

8

It's no good pretending that Cornish weather in these days is any better than the weather in other places. It's milder, and that's all you can say for it. It is also wetter, and in the winter we expect snow and frost, which are things I never knew in my childhood. I've seen the lovely migrating redwings so overwhelmed by cold that they have died in hundreds. To enjoy the lesser amenities we have greater crowds. You are lucky indeed now to find in the summer a strip of beach belonging only to you and the sea and the sun.

However, in that summer when I first met Miles and Augusta it was heaven, especially after Frank's letter came and I knew we were not to part. We became so flagrantly a trio, living separate from the

271

others, that I suffered many a twinge of conscience. Bella's children were good and obedient and I could have got on well enough with them, but I wanted Miles and Augusta alone.

We did all that we had promised ourselves. The dinghy was painted and admired. I taught them some elementary sailing, and we went right out, as they had wished to do, beyond sight of land. We lived on the beaches, lighting fires, cooking meals, exploring caves, swimming, sun-bathing, gathering shells and gazing at the life of rock-pools. One morning I said: "We won't come home today! We'll stay out all night!"

I was in a foolish headstrong mood. Bella and Hugo had been reconciled rather than approving. But at this last proposal, made abruptly at the breakfast table, they thought the moment had come to draw the line.

Hugo said mildly: "Well, really, Maria . . ." and Bella said, almost with passion: "You must do nothing of the sort. Are we gypsies? I shall forbid Mrs Trewince to put up food for you. And where would you sleep?"

I said: "Roger's old tent is about somewhere. Augusta and I could sleep in that. And there's a sleeping-bag that Miles could use."

"Some intelligent expedition with *all* the children," Bella said pointedly, "would be more desirable. I don't think Frank would approve, and I don't want pneumonia cases on my hands."

"My dear Bella, the world has been roasting for the best part of a month. The earth is dry a yard deep."

"Besides," Bella insisted, "Miles and Augusta were entrusted to care. Your being here was accidental and unexpected."

Poor Hugo looked crestfallen at those last words. There was a touch of venom in them. "I think," he said, "Maria has given the children a very good time."

This mild support deepened Bella's opposition. "What on earth," she demanded, "would Augusta's mother have said to such a wild-cat scheme?"

Augusta winced. I had taken care, all through the time she was with me, never to mention her mother.

Hugo chipped in again. "I know more about Augusta's mother than you do, my dear. After all, she was my sister. We had a bit of orchard attached to our house at Bowdon, and when she was a girl she had a tent there. If the weather was exceptionally hot, she sometimes slept in it."

Bella said: "Sleeping in a tent in a private orchard with civilised people all round is one thing. Sleeping in a tent in the wilds is another."

"Come, Bella," I said, "Cornwall is not full of roving desperadoes. After all, when we were in France Lady Lavernock carried a tent in her motor-car, and, if she felt like it, we just pitched down for the night in a field."

"We know," she said darkly, "what came of all that. Well, I shall instruct Mrs Trewince."

She left us, and Hugo went up to his study. This was the first rough passage the children had known at the vicarage. Miles took it phlegmatically. Augusta looked shaken. "That cowrie shell on the boat needs touching up," Miles told her, and took her away.

I was seething, and worked it off in action. Very well, I thought. With Mrs Trewince or without her.

I found Roger's tent and sleeping-bag, took them to my loft and bound them into a rough bundle. In the loft were the knives, forks and spoons, and the tin mugs and the frying-pan and kettle that we took on our expeditions. I put them into a large basket. These and our bathing things were all we should need. For the rest, I said to myself, there are, after all, shops. I didn't need to go begging in the kitchen for a crust.

I went down to the beach and found the children disconsolate. Augusta was not painting. Miles was practising knot-making with a couple of rope's ends. He looked up and said: "It would have been such a lark, Aunt Maria."

I said: "It's *going* to be a lark. I have everything ready. Come up and help me bring it down to the boat."

Augusta's face brightened. "Oh, you darling!" she said. And then she looked worried again. "Would it be right?" she asked. "When Miles and I are safely back with Daddy, Aunt Bella might be angry with you."

I didn't tell her that I would be in Manchester, too, and I had asked Bella and Hugo not to do so. I said: "I think we'll chance it. There are times when you have to chance things."

We didn't go into the vicarage. We climbed the hill on to which one side of the loft looks out. Miles waited below while I went in and heaved the tent-bundle through the window. I came down carrying the basket. "Go in and get your bathing things," I told them when we were on the beach, and while they were doing that I rowed out with the stuff to Dick Hammill's sailing-boat. I shoved the things over the gunwale and rowed back for the children. It was eleven o'clock when we cast off and sailed towards Falmouth, towing the dinghy behind us.

There wasn't much wind and it was lunch time when we reached the town. But before we ate I went to the post-office and sent a telegram to Dr Cumberledge. "Do you approve my keeping the children out tonight, sleeping in tents. Reply G.P.O., Falmouth. Maria." The post-office clerk, reading this, grinned, and I felt a bit of a fool. But if Bella was going to make a "thing" of it I thought I'd better have the final authority behind me.

While we were eating our lunch I said: "There will be a full moon tonight, and a full moon means a high tide somewhere about six o'clock. We shall need it for where we're going."

"Where are we going?" Augusta wanted to know.

"It's a secret. But I can tell you this: it's a creek, smaller and shallower than our creek at St Tudno, and there's a sand-bar at the entrance that you can't get over without a good tide under you. We sha'n't be able to come out till the next high tide. That'll be about six o'clock tomorrow morning. So you'll have to be up early. We sha'n't want to keep Aunt Bella worrying longer than we can help. However, I think there'll be enough water up to seven o'clock or thereabouts."

Miles said: "I wish I knew all about the tides, like you."

"I was born with tides, and anyway," I assured him, "you can buy a tidetable for tuppence. Now, we shall need something to eat tonight and for breakfast in the morning. You and Augusta had better write out a list, and this afternoon we'll lay in our stores."

And so over the lunch table the two heads went together. Two loaves of bread. A quarter of a pound of tea. A pot of raspberry jam. A tin of pineapple chunks. ("We mustn't forget to buy a tin-opener.") A pound of bacon-rashers.

"What about eggs?"

"What about milk?"

"There's a farm nearby where we can get both," I assured them.

"Ginger-biscuits?" Augusta asked.

"Anything you like. Yes, go the whole hog and put down ginger-biscuits."

"What about a teapot?"

"Oh, we'll be real rough like me and Roger. We'll just tip the leaves into a kettle of boiling water."

"Who is Roger?"

"I'll tell you about him some day."

She handed me the completed list. "It doesn't seem much," I said, "for a great voyage like ours. We'd better add some apples and a box of chocolates."

Miles asked hopefully: "What about an axe for cutting down brushwood?"

"Very well," I conceded, and wrote: "Axe for cutting down brushwood."

"Will you read to us round the camp-fire?" Augusta wanted to know; and I said that I would.

"Read about Huckleberry Finn," she said; and I promised to see if Falmouth could provide the book.

So out we went with my big basket, and we found all we wanted, to say nothing of supernumeraries like nuts and bananas; and then we went to the post-office to see if a telegram had come from Dr Cumberledge.

It had.

"Expedition approved provided you guarantee no lions, tigers, hyenas and such like prowling beasts available to eat my children. Anyone else's, yes, gladly. But not mine. Cumberledge."

With this ship's clearance safely in my pocket, I said: "Well, let's go," and we went down and rowed the resplendent *Cowrie* out to Bill Hammill's rather disreputable-looking *Cormorant*.

We dallied hither and yon in the harbour till the tide turned, and then I put her about to sail up the Carrick Roads, with the afternoon drowsing over St Tudno on our left and St Just on our right. I was aware of a feeling of disappointment in both children. "Cheer up," I said. "You don't know the half of this water yet. You're not going to be let down."

When St Tudno was behind us they were happier. "It looks," I said, "as though you could go no further than you can see, and that's not far. But these Carrick Roads bend to the right and then to the left and flow between wonderful banks right up to Truro. Heavenly little openings go off here and there, and one of them is the Ruan River. That's where we're going. Now the sealed orders are open. You know the destination."

As I swung her into the river they exclaimed with delight. And there was reason for it. Scrub oak is the customary growth on our creeks, but nowhere is it lovelier than here, a dense green fleece upon the hills, flowing down on either hand to the edge of the river which is not, in fact, a river, but a mighty sea-filled gulch torn out of the earth by some old convulsion of nature. It is so deep that battleships can anchor there even at low tide, yet it keeps a smiling domestic flavour with heronries in the oaks and little bits of bays opening here and there: a few yards of shingle with a boat drawn up and a cottage behind: and sometimes, as now, with great caravans of cloud plodding across the blue desert of the sky and reflecting themselves in the blue water beneath our keel.

"Well," I asked, proud as a conjuror showing off a new trick, "will it do?"

I didn't want an answer: I wanted to enjoy it for myself. It was years now since I had seen it, and even when I was seeing it often it was new at every seeing. It would always mean my childhood, and Roger and Bella, and the secure base on which, it seemed then, life was founded. "You know," I said to the children, "that the Phoenicians used to trade for tin in Cornwall. There's a legend that sometimes on a winter's evening the ghost of one of their ships is on this water, and that, if you see it, you die before the winter's out."

Well, I thought, I don't need Phoenician ghosts. There are plenty of my own here. Even the old *Queen of the Fal*, high-built like a Mississippi river boat, coming towards us now bound for Falmouth, had a ghostly look: looming up out of a past so recent but containing so much that I would never know again.

I left the tiller to Miles. There was not much to do, with the tide bearing us steadily up-stream and just enough wind blowing the same way to keep the sail taut. I watched the herons standing reflective, with hunched shoulders, on the edges of the water, rising leisurely, drifting with lazy beats of great grey wings to settle farther on; and a pair of buzzards, high in the blue, swooping about in enjoyment of their wild fierce freedom. Oh, dear, I wondered, will Manchester ever become bearable after this?

A bend of the river brought the towers of a lordly house into view on the right bank. Beneath the high land on which it stood the water flowed away from the main body of the river. "This is it," I said to Miles. "Let me take her in."

We tacked to starboard. "The sand-bar is under us now," I said.

"Once the tide ebbs, it'll be like locking the front door. No one will be able to get at us."

We slid into shallower water. On our left a bluff rose, grown with shrubs and bracken, and gradually on our right the land flattened down to meadows. "Look out for the deer," I told them. "There's a herd wandering about up there on the high land to the left."

Augusta was sighing with content. "I do hope," she said, "the front door gets locked before anyone else sails in."

We were all right. No one else sailed in. We went about half a mile up the water, lowered *Cormorant's* sail, and dropped the hook. Miles claimed the privilege of rowing us ashore, and when we were landed on a yard or so of shaley beach which would soon be wider he and Augusta went back and loaded the stuff into the dinghy.

I sat on the shale with the declining sunlight falling round me, watching their joyful eager activity, and I knew that Manchester was going to be all right. I could get on with the man who sent me that telegram, and, as for the children, there were already meshes binding us together, meshes that would soon be strong enough, I hoped, to take life's tug and strain.

"The key is turning in the lock," I told them. "We've timed it well. You see, the shale has already dried out by a couple of inches since we arrived."

"I must learn to notice such things," Miles said.

The gear lay there in a heap, and they were all for laying into it at once, but I told them there was plenty of time. "What we'd better do now," I said, "is have our evening swim. For one thing, the work will warm us up after it, and for another this isn't a good bathing-place once the tide has gone out a bit."

"Yes," Augusta said. "Father says half the battle is doing things in the right order. He's a great believer in keeping life what he calls tidy."

So we swam in the deep evening hush. There was not much bird song, and the plop of a leaping fish was quite a noise. In the meadows beyond our bit of beach the cows were grazing and we could hear the wrench of the grass. The smell of the evening was all ripe meadow grass and warm bracken and the salt smell of the water, mingled with the oozy drench that from time beyond count it had carried down from Lamorran Woods, where the ferns are cool and green, rooted in the dissolution of centuries. I lay on my back, looking at the paling sky. Even St Tudno seemed, in that enchanted river, a noisy metropolis.

We dressed, and while the children put up the tent I wandered the river bank, gathering wood. There was plenty: dried and withered limbs that the winter had torn from trees, driftwood brought in on the tides, small twigs of blackthorn bearded with grey-green moss that would start the fire going at the touch of a match.

On the non-committed strip where shale and meadow met, a strip neutral between land and sea, the tent was up when I returned to drop my armful. "I think," Augusta said, "we should do without the eggs and milk that you said we could get from a farm. Let's not go to the farm. Let's not see anybody but us."

I understood and approved her feeling.

Miles was bringing in the largest stones he could find, and soon our fireplace was built and our fire roaring. Flat stones for "tables" were ranged round it, with knives and forks upon them, and then I busied myself with the frying-pan, while the kettle stood at the side, getting what heat was left over. When the bacon-fat was spluttering I cut hunks of bread and dropped them in. They came out golden-brown and crisp and lay upon the plates crowned with curls of bacon.

It was a long time since the children had eaten. I was glad to see them fall upon the food like wolves while I prepared a second helping. When they had done with that, I opened the tin of pineapple chunks. Augusta asked: "What do we do for dessert-plates?" and I said: "The Legassick children solved that problem long ago." A drop of water poured on each plate from the boiling kettle and a wipe with a piece of paper dealt with the matter. Then I put tea into the kettle, filled the cups, and we sat down to our dessert. Pineapple chunks, biscuits, chocolates. At last they had had enough. "Now wash up with the tea that's left in the kettle," I commanded. "We do things rough in camp."

Miles was swinging the short axe that we had bought in Falmouth. He seemed disappointed at not having found a use for it, almost as though he had pictured himself hewing down redwoods. "I think," he said, "I'll cross the river and see what I can find."

He rowed off alone over the quiet water, and I told Augusta that we should need a lot more firewood if we were to keep the fire going till the moon came up. We busied ourselves with that till Miles returned. The dinghy was looking more like a haystack than a boat, and going down to meet it, we found it piled with bracken. "Last year's," Miles assured us, "and as dry as tinder. I was hoping to hack you down some pine branches to sleep on, but I think this will have to do."

He backed into our minute tent and drew the bracken in after him armful by armful, till the place seemed filled halfway up to the top. "It'll squash down," he promised, "and you'll sleep soft."

I thanked him and said: "We've plenty of wood now for tonight and for tomorrow's breakfast fire. So let's sit down and rest for a while."

But there was still something he wanted to do. "A tip I got from a man who was in the Boer War," he said.

So off he went again, disappearing this time into the meadows behind us. He came back dragging the arm of a tree which a winter storm had torn down, and loaded upon it, as upon a truck, was a pile of dried cow-dung. He threw a handful upon our blaze as proudly as if he had been all the way to the African veldt to find it. "That's what the Boers and the Kaffirs use," he explained. "It makes a fire that will last. And this man who was one of Father's patients told me that the Boers use it, too, in their houses. He said that if you spread it wet over a floor it dries out into a hard surface that you can polish with beeswax."

Be that as it may: it deepened the glow of our fire and filled the air with a strangely wild evoking flavour.

The day was done, and in the deepening dark we sat there with the glow on our faces, and I asked Augusta whether she would now like me to read from *Huckleberry Finn*. "Mother used to read it to us," she said, "but now I somehow don't want to hear it. Let's just sit and be very quiet."

She hitched herself closer to my side, put an arm around my waist, and dropped her head upon my shoulder. She had never done this before. I didn't dare to shift a muscle: I was so moved, so happy.

So we sat there, and it seemed right to be very quiet, and the quiet was deepened, not disturbed, when the owls began to quaver, and a heron ripped his harsh call into the night, and, as if in answer, the curlew began their crying, which is the loveliest and saddest crying in the world. We sat there till the eastern sky was flooded with the moon's pale promise, and then the moon climbed clear of the trees, and the disc widened, dropping silent light upon the now narrow water, and upon the little mud-stranded *Cormorant*, and upon the shy deer which I could see on the other side, the heads of the delicate hinds and the horns of the stags moving slowly against the luminescence. I felt, as I always feel under a full moon, as though I were being looked down on by something that had died and, from beyond death, was forgiving life for its senseless bustle and trivial concerns. Why this should make me happy I don't know, but I was happy, with the child, unaware of all this, sleeping on my shoulder.

Miles moved off and got into his sleeping-bag and lay down on the shale. Augusta did not wake when I got to my feet. I carried her to the tent, laid her upon the thick mattress that the bracken made, and, dressed as we both were, stretched myself beside her. Roger's tent, I was thinking. She wakened enough to murmur "Good night. Thank you." I kissed her and said: "Good night, my darling," and I fell asleep with tears on my cheeks and my heart rejoicing.

9

We bathed in the morning light and ate our breakfast and were over the bar soon after that front door was unlocked. Augusta said: "That was the best thing to happen to me since Mother died, and you are the best woman since Mother."

I was happy to hear this because it was the first time she had spoken of her mother except out of a void – hopelessly, as though the void could never be filled. Of course, it always is – so far as the young are concerned at all events; but the time of waiting can be longer and more cruel than Augusta, I hoped, would find it. I must think of more new things, I told myself, to keep their minds off obsession with what they have lost and fear of what they are to find.

"You said the other day that you didn't even know that you *had* an Aunt Maria. Did you ever hear of Aunt Louisa?"

Miles didn't answer. I had put him in charge of our homeward voyage, and he was concentrating on his small job as earnestly as a man who has just gained his master's ticket and is taking a "leviathan" into an unfamiliar harbour. "Ease out the sail," he ordered. Augusta loosened the sheet. "That'll do. Cleat it down."

"No," Augusta said. "You see, I'm not sure that you're *really* an aunt at all. Mummy was Uncle Hugo's sister, and so we heard something about Aunt Bella because Uncle Hugo married her, but we never heard her sisters talked about. Are there any more after you and Aunt Louisa?"

"No. Just the three of us, and Louisa is the oldest. She's thirteen years older than I am, so I dare say she'll seem terrifically old to you. I haven't seen her for a long time."

"Are we to meet her?"

"Yes."

"Then perhaps," Augusta said reasonably, "you'd better tell us something about her."

As soon as I landed in England I wrote to Louisa at her house in Brook Street and said that I was going straight on to St Tudno. A letter from her had reached me soon after my arrival there, inviting me to call on her at Tregannock. "James," she said, "has been dreadfully overworking. He has quite knocked himself up. I have managed at last to persuade him to see a doctor, who prescribes a long rest. James wanted to put it off till the House rises, but the doctor wouldn't have it, and so I'm bringing him down to Tregannock as soon as we can get away . . ." and so forth.

Poor James! "Bringing him down!" It sounded as though he were still a reluctant parcel that Louisa carried about.

"Your Aunt Louisa," I explained to the children, "is married to a Member of Parliament. That means that they have to spend most of their time in London, but James — who may or may not be your *Uncle* James — also owns a large estate near St Tudno. His doctor in London has ordered him to take a rest, as he's been overworking; so I think we'll go over to Tregannock — that's the name of his house — and see him and Aunt Louisa."

"Tell us something about Tregannock," Augusta commanded; so I told them about old Mr Polperro, and the state coach that used to bring him to church, and the gardens and fish-ponds and footmen, the house-parties, the shooting, the balls.

She listened, wide-eyed. Already a woman, she said: "But, Aunt Maria, I couldn't possibly go to such a place in any of the clothes I have here!"

"How do I look?" I asked her.

She considered me, wearing the clothes I had slept in, bits of bracken still clinging to the skirt, and even to begin with they had been the disreputable rags I used for sailing.

"Dreadful," she said.

We both burst out laughing. "Dreadful or not," I said, "they're what I shall wear. You can please yourself. But you won't find footmen at Tregannock now, or much of the state that I've been telling you about. Things have changed a lot."

Miles, impatient with women's talk, said in a voice of quiet sorrow: "Might I ask you now to give me your attention, please? We're going about, to enter the creek. Will you do the sheets, please, Aunt Maria, and lower away the sail when I tell you? Augusta, be ready to get hold of the boathook to grab the buoy. Now – going about!"

10

We walked to Tregannock that afternoon, and as soon as we entered the gate I saw James. He was coming towards us on horseback, and he was huge, red and heavy. He got down and gave me a brotherly kiss, which was like a collision with an immense ripe melon. "Well, Maria," he said. "Long time since I've seen you. You don't get any fatter. Are you eating enough? Are these your children? No. Of course not. Sorry."

"So far as I can make out, James, they are your wife's sister's husband's sister's offspring by a medical practitioner named Cumberledge. You can just call them Miles and Augusta."

His red paw enveloped the children's hands. I could see from the way they were looking at him that, to them, he was very much what old Mr Polperro had been to me. He had become startlingly like his father.

"I was off for a ride," he explained unnecessarily.

"Does your doctor approve?" I asked. "I was sorry to hear from Louisa that you haven't been too well."

"Rubbish," he said. "Never been better in my life. It's something they've cooked up between 'em. The feller says I must get my weight down. Rubbish. The more there is of a man the more of a man there is. Obvious."

It was incontrovertible, and there certainly was an immensity of James.

"Well," he said, "I'll give up the ride. You go an' see Louisa. I'll show these shavers round."

He led the horse back towards the house, and we parted company at the path that led to the stables.

I entered the house alone. A butler whom I didn't know was mooching about in the hall. He and the cook and a few village girls now made the indoor staff. Outdoors, things had not been so drastically cut down. I found later that the old coach still existed, but it was not used, nor was any sort of carriage. So the coachman and all the hangers-on concerned with that sort of thing were gone. But James still kept riding-horses and employed two grooms; and as for the gardens there had been no cut at all. They were splendidly maintained. There was now no more shooting than a man might get out of a casual stroll round the estate; no preserving, no gamekeepers.

I explained to the butler who I was, and he took me up to Louisa's room. We looked at one another for a wordless moment, weighing one another up. I found that I was without the slight sense of being an insignificant youngster that had been till now my reaction to Louisa's presence. She got up from a desk where she had been writing and removed her spectacles. Standing behind the desk, tall and thin, with the fingertips of both hands resting upon her papers, she had the air of someone about to begin: "Mr Chairman, my lords, ladies and gentlemen." I guessed, correctly, that she was used to doing a lot of that sort of thing.

While these thoughts were passing through my mind, she was considering me. At last a small smile appeared on her austere face. She came round the desk and kissed me. "You look improved," she said. "How wise it was of you to get out of this place and see something of the world."

Never, since the night when I had ruined her ball-dress with rouge, had I been able to speak easily to her; but now inhibitions were gone. "Thank you, Louisa," I said. "But I should think the world I saw was hardly one you would approve."

"I hope you don't approve of it either," she said. "That's no reason why you shouldn't be improved by knowing the people who live in it. And I imagine that in all these years they were not the only people you saw."

"No. I saw a good deal of the dreariest poverty crawling under the surface of Italy."

"There's a good deal of poverty crawling under the surface of everything. I learned that much, at any rate, when I was with Vincent Wheatstone. However, let's leave that. I brought James down for a holiday, and I must try and take one myself."

We sat on a sofa, and through the window the dropping woods and the noble rise of the land beyond the valley spread before me, full of its old reassurance and peace. "Tell me about James," I said. "He met me on the way here. He looks fairly robust."

"There's nothing much wrong with him," she said, "except that he needs a good rest. I'm afraid I've been rather overworking him."

She said it calmly, as though he were a willing horse that she had driven too far.

"Doesn't he *like* his work in Parliament?"

"Well, yes and no. I have to keep him up to it, and he likes pleasing *me*."

She leaned back, with her fingers interlocked behind her head, looking out at the superb landscape bathed in late springtime sun. As if making a sudden decision, she said: "Shall I tell you the whole truth about me and James?"

"Please yourself. I'm quite good as a mother-confessor."

She pondered for a moment, then said: "There was a time, as you must know, when we were madly in love with one another. If he had married me then, I suppose I should have settled down and become the châtelaine of Tregannock in the old style. But he didn't. And I know in my heart that I've never forgiven him. Can you love without forgiveness?"

"You should know."

"Well, you can. *I* can, anyway. I love him for his kindness and simplicity and fidelity, but I can't forgive him for the weakness that left me in the lurch. No doubt that's self-esteem, something unpardonable, but it's there. I doubt whether there is such a thing as perfect love – I mean as the romantics see it. We have to make do with the best we can give and get. Now you know my best."

Through the window we could hear the young voices of the children and a great bellowing laugh from James. They were down there somewhere in the woods.

"It might have been different," Louisa said, "if I had been able to give him children. But I couldn't – not after I had been frozen by Vincent Wheatstone. Perhaps that's something else I can't forgive. I was left too long to learn all sorts of things that I'm glad I learned, but that, all the same, I would gladly have left unlearned. Does this all sound a muddle, a mix-up?"

"I think I understand."

"Well, that's how it was, and when I married it was far too late for any châtelaine business. I had seen too much that I wanted to do something about, and I dragged James along. Shall I bore you if I say a few political things?"

"Go on."

"Well, this Liberal government is going to last a long time, and it's what I call a townsman's government. It is opposed, and will become more so, to the landed-gentry party. In his heart, James belongs to that party, and that's the answer to your question whether he likes his work in Parliament. He likes it because I want him to like it. That far, and no farther."

"No wonder it takes it out of him."

"I suppose it isn't. But time works miracles, and I'm always there to read what he doesn't want to read and to digest it and show him the point of it. I even had to prevent his accepting a peerage."

This did startle me. I must have looked so surprised that she laughed outright.

"Oh, we shall have trouble with the House of Lords," she said. "With their precious veto they can always put a spoke in our wheel. From that point of view, the more Liberal peers the better. And so a shift to the Upper House was suggested to James. But I didn't see it. It meant moving out of the thick of the fight, and that's how he sees it now, too. Let's go and see these children. First of all, tell me exactly who they are."

I told her, and we got up. I noticed then what I hadn't seen before. There was quite a show of Gerald's pictures on the wall behind me. I looked at them and loved them. I had learned a lot about pictures from Jane Lavernock. "New, aren't they?"

"Fairly. I got them at the exhibition at Groggenheim's just at the time he was killed."

The time he was killed.

It all rushed back to me: the hot southern night with great lumps of blazing stars, the small black shed crouched beneath them, the cry, the silence in which my heart stood still for a moment and then raced and knocked.

I sat down.

"I'm sorry, Maria," Louisa said. "I had intended to say nothing about all that."

"Well, now that you've said it, tell me about the exhibition. Was it a success?"

"Oh, yes. The circumstances naturally crowded the gallery. There were thirty pictures, and nothing was priced under a hundred pounds. Every picture was sold. Very good for young Meg."

I looked at her enquiringly. "She did well," Louisa said with some bitterness. "After all, she was his wife, and he died intestate. So there you are. She was at the show."

"You saw her?"

"Yes. She came with a great bearded fellow leading a St Bernard dog. They were quite part of the exhibition."

"Have you kept in touch with her?"

"Not intentionally. But I go to most of the picture shows and occasionally I came across them there. However, they've left London now. I imagine they've exhausted what Gerald made for them, and I don't think the man earns much. So he's taken a teaching job in Manchester. They're married."

"I hope I don't meet them."

"Why should you?"

I told her about my arrangement with Dr Cumberledge, and then we went to look for the children.

They were by the lake across which, years ago, I had watched James talking to the girl who had come proudly down the great staircase and had given me a cold look as I sat waiting for the footman to bring me my chickenanam sandwiches.

There was a punt on the water, not one that you poled but one that you paddled. We watched James help the children in, and then he got in gingerly himself, as though doubtful about entrusting his weight to so frail a craft. It was all right, and he paddled away with the two-bladed implement – right, left, right, left – uttering as he did so eerie cries which puzzled me till I saw that Augusta's hair was stuck all over with feathers and that streaks of red earth made warpaint on Miles' face. They were Indians on Lake Erie. "Hence," said Louisa, making perhaps the first joke of her life, "the eerie cries."

It was a lovely picture. The lake filled a small valley whose rising sides had been planted by generations of Polperros, and on the water was a small island planted thick with azaleas. Yellow primulas with flower-stems a foot high fringed it, and in the middle was a little summer-house with a thatched roof.

Louisa and I stood still and watched the punt run aground and Miles leap out with a stag's agility. James followed him with more caution, and then both seized Augusta, hauled her, resisting, ashore, and began to drag her towards the summer-house.

Louisa shouted: "Hey! What's happening?"

Miles' clear voice came back: "We're going to sacrifice Augusta. She's a Pawnee. We're Winnebagos."

"Who says so?" Louisa shouted back.

"Uncle James."

"Does Augusta mind being sacrificed?"

"No. She's all for it."

"All right then. But don't take too long over the job. It's teatime."

We strolled back to the house to await them. Louisa was quiet and thoughtful. At last she said: "What a waste this place is! Think of the thousands of children whose holidays never take them out of a slum, and who would love to be doing what those children are doing now. Who *ought* to be doing it. And for three-quarters of the year it's doing nothing but house a handful of servants eating their heads off."

I didn't know it; but I was listening to prophetic and fateful words.

11

James wanted to drive us home in his car, but the children preferred to walk. Their energy was inexhaustible, and so in those days was mine. We walked.

"Well, did you have a good time?"

Miles had been commanded to wash his face before tea, but Augusta was still wearing her feathers. The great house had overawed them, but now, on the road again, they were full of spirit.

287

"Oh, yes," Augusta said. "Uncle James never ought to be an M.P. He ought to be always an uncle."

Miles said: "In the cave — that's the house in the lake — we didn't sacrifice Augusta. It was too near tea time. So we just swore a blood-bond between the two tribes. And" — rather inconsequently — "Uncle James is having the old coach out for tomorrow."

"What old coach?"

"The one you told us about," Augusta said. "The one they used to go to church in. It's still in the coach-house."

"It's a bit dirty," Miles filled in. "But the coat-of-arms is still on the doors. Uncle James says he'll have it all dusted out and borrow two of the farm-horses. He'll drive it himself, and we're going all over the shop in it."

"So you're going again tomorrow?"

Augusta looked at me contritely. "Sorry, Aunt Maria," she said. "We should have asked you first."

I was shocked with myself. The quick pang of jealousy had been apparent, even to a child.

"But of course you must go. May I come with you?"

"Oh, yes," she assured me earnestly. "We made sure of that with Uncle James, didn't we, Miles?"

"We did, and he said that you were a good sort, and that you could sit in the coach and be his mother, and I would be his father, and Augusta would be his sister, and he'd be the coachman, driving us all to church."

All this was done, and we had a great day. James had even found in a wardrobe the uniform that the coachman used to wear. I remember the coachman well. He had always seemed to me immense, but on James the uniform was a tight fit. Sitting up aloft, he cracked his whip over the two apathetic horses. They shambled to a reluctant start. Louisa was standing on the terrace, and waved us goodbye. James had asked her to come with us, and when she refused he pressed her hard. Because of the children, she did not allow her annoyance to appear, but I could see that she was very annoyed indeed. "Don't over-persuade me," she said. "I have said no and I mean no." After watching us go, she turned quickly and went back into the house.

As the old coach on its broad iron-tyred wheels lurched and swayed uncomfortably towards the road, I was thinking that even though James was the sort of fool I could love, he was undoubtedly a fool. He was without percipience. He wanted to give the children some fun, and he was giving them some fun. At the same time, he was giving himself fun, recalling the many times when this clumsy, gaudy, jolting box had carried him and his parents hither and thither. But he was incapable of seeing it as Louisa saw it. The coach had not been *for her* an accustomed vehicle. She had used it on one night only; and when James, to her great surprise, drove the thing to the front of the house, it was that night which detached itself from all other days and nights of her life and stood before her in stark and horrid isolation. I myself perhaps would not have found that night recalled had not the memory blazed so sharply in Louisa's mind that I almost caught the heat of it. But James would never be attuned to such intimations as that; and when he came into the house, explained what he had in mind for the day, and invited her to join us, he was surprised at her refusal, and a little hurt by the hint of asperity that came into her voice when his invitation was pressed.

So far as the children went, the day was a soaring success. Even though motorcars were beginning to appear in some numbers, our roads were still medieval, and eight enormous hoofs can make a lot of dust. James was no longer driving the family to church. He had recast the roles for all of us. Miles was a young gallant who had abducted Augusta and was flying with her to London, and I was her ever-faithful old nurse. There wasn't much flying about it as the horses ground their way over Carnon Downs and the coach at last squealed downhill into Truro with the brakes jammed on. We had lunch at the Red Lion, and that was the first time, I should imagine, that a coachman wearing full-fig had been permitted to sit down among the respectable eaters in the dining room. But the Polperros were well known at that venerable inn. The street down which we had driven to the doors bore their name, and Mr Polperro's prank would be talked about for a long time.

He and I were rather tired of the joke before we got back to Tregannock, but we kept it up for the sake of the children. Once we were there, James put us into his car and had us home in ten minutes. A telegram had arrived from Frank Cumberledge. "Come as soon as convenient – tomorrow if possible."

I decided that tomorrow it should be, and charged James with our farewells to Louisa.

CHAPTER NINE

T O THIS day I don't know what a hidalgo is, and I'm too lazy to look it up. But when I was a girl given to romantic reading a man had only to be described as "looking a perfect hidalgo", or some such nonsense, and my heart was his. Thin — dark — Spanish — aristocractic. Those were the adjectives that my infant mind provided to go along with the noun hidalgo. Odd that in books I should have so completely approved the hidalgo, seeing that, in fact, the men I have loved have been fair.

The train had not quite stopped in London Road Station, Manchester, before the children were on the platform. They were as though ejected from the compartment like a jack from his box when the lid is raised. By the time I had got myself out, their running legs had taken them to the barrier. Running. Running away from me as though I had never existed. Feeling diminished, a thing of no consequence, I followed slowly. I didn't matter. The *Cormorant* and the *Cowrie*, the camp on Ruan River, the Polperro lake and island and coach: none of it mattered. All that mattered was this hidalgo. With one child nestling, so to speak, under each wing, he was impeded from shaking hands. He looked at me, and then he looked down at the children, as though assessing a weight of obligation. The faintest smile came on to his dark grave face. "Thank you," he said. At last he got an arm free and held out to me a long, thin, hairy hand. The grasp was strong and warm. The small smile lingered. I rarely heard Frank Cumberledge laugh. That ironic shadow of a smile, just wrinkling the creases alongside his dark-brown but not quite black eyes, was all he needed to express his aloof amused contemplation of the world about him. I noticed that the children hadn't been kissed and didn't expect to be kissed. All the same, on that drear and depressing platform, amid the hurrying people, and the clanging trollies, and the hissing steam, and the northern voices, I was aware of accord so complete that it could do without formal expression.

A four-wheeler cab was waiting in the stony forecourt of the station – a cab almost as venerable as the Polperro coach. The pigeons were pecking about beneath the horse's feet and a gentle afternoon sunlight gave me a happier impression than that of my first visit to Manchester in the dark of a winter's evening so long ago.

"How long is it since we met?" Frank Cumberledge asked, his mind recalling the same occasion.

I couldn't remember: I had been little more than a child, hardly older than Miles was now.

"I think," I said, "we'll have to forget all that and start from scratch."

"As I did," Augusta said. "And now I feel as though I'd known Auntie Maria for donkey's years."

The long journey had tired her, and she had hardly spoken before her head was on her father's shoulder, his arm was around her, and she was asleep.

Her remark made me think of my own father and his old-fashioned way of speaking some words. Just as he *would* say umble, so he would *never* say ears, but always years. So I saw why donkey's years should mean a long time. Recalling Father recalled St Tudno; and, now that the excitement of the journey was ended, the doubts and fears that always afflict me in the presence of the unaccustomed came upon me heavily. On that night when I faced Manchester long ago, Roger and Bella and Hugo were with me. Now I was alone, charged with an unexplored responsibility, and I felt not only inadequate but depressed. The cab, on leaving the station forecourt, had turned sharply into London Road, and London Road is not something that soars the heart. For all the mild sunlight that fell upon it, perhaps because of it, the long grim street pushed my heart down unbearably, and when I thought how little time ago it was that the children and I had been behind the locked doors on the Ruan River, I wondered whether I could endure. Through the rumbling of horse-drawn lorries and the metallic clangour of the trams, the little houses, little shops, grimy and somehow seeming beyond hope, accompanied us as far as a railed patch of grass labelled Ardwick Green. It was green comparatively, and I suppose it had once been green in full and happy fact; but now it served, with me, no purpose save to remind me of all the green I had known: green sea, young green springing wheat, green boughs, green evening skies sparkled with stars.

We turned to the right, into a street of dwelling-houses. They were old and grey, clinging to the last vestiges of respectability. In many of the windows were cards: "Rooms to let." "Lodgings." The small front gardens were bleak and uncared for. Indeed, care could have done nothing for them. I was glad when we were through that little street and going left again along a broad high-road. Frank Cumberledge, who faced me, was regarding me with his faint smile. "Cheer up," he said. "The worst is now over. Manchester is about to lay its splendours before you."

Certainly, things improved once we had passed the open space called Platt Fields, though I could have done with a knoll, a hillock, to break its monotonous level. It looked as though even a molehill would be frowned upon with municipal displeasure and promptly smoothed out by a municipal roller. However, as we plugged along through Fallowfield and Withington, there were reputable houses and trees and shrubs, some of them bearing yet the lingerings of springtime bloom.

So we came to an inn called the White Lion, and there the road forked, and we drove down the fork which a signpost told us led to "Cheadle and the South".

"Lift up your heart," Frank said. "We're almost there."

The way now was pleasant and suburban. The houses were mostly new, their gardens as trim and polished as manicured finger-nails. There was a calceolaria-and-lobelia feeling about everything. We rolled past the entrance of the Didsbury railway station, and a greater sense of age was to be felt. For this road we were on was old. It was an immemorial road to London, and just here Didsbury had clustered about it when Didsbury was not a suburb but a village.

Houses were fewer now and in big gardens, with noble trees, especially beeches, their branches folded about them like wings in the deepening dusk. Dusk was earlier then: no one had thought of "summer time", and men adapted themselves to nature's rhythm. When trees had their own shadows stolen in to sleep beneath them you knew it was noon.

"Here's the Cock," Frank said. "If I were a boozing man I should find it irresistible."

A little clearing opened off the road, with a drinking-trough for beasts in the middle, and to one side the flat pleasant face of an inn. Above the entrance a great golden cock shone, the bird of dawning, proud and imperial.

"It's all going to be better than I hoped," I said.

"I'm not a complimentary man," Frank said, "but so are you, I think."

I suppose I achieved the blush that this called for. "However," Frank continued, "you must try to keep the shutters down a bit. You don't hide much, do you?"

"I'm sorry."

"There's no need to be sorry. I haven't much use for hard-baked people, but it's been rather alarming to read your hopes and fears making their commentary on our journey all the way from London Road station. Well, here we go. This is the scene of your martyrdom."

We turned into Kingsley Avenue. Then, the road had not been "made up", as they say, and I liked that. There was nothing made up about St Tudno. I suppose my eyes shone at the pleasant brick houses, not "semi-detached" but all in a row, with bow-windows on each floor, with small front gardens, and on the other side of the road there was a hedge, with open meadows beyond it. Above all, there was the smell. Even in the ancient cab, before we got out, there was the smell. It was the smell of evening. In Eden, Adam heard the voice of God walking in the garden in the cool of the day. I think it must have been this smell. I got out of the cab, and it came fully upon me. It is one thing by the sea, and another thing in the country, and another thing on the wild moors. But it is always the same thing. It is the smell of evening; and the cities cannot give it. It is the smell of the evening star, of hands folded in laps, of birds and children going to bed, of flowers closing, and grass ceasing even to sigh. It is the smell of the recurring death without which life cannot go on. It was here. The city had not advanced far enough to kill it, and I was glad.

I stood there with these emotions washing me, and Frank said: "You're at it again. Take this infant. She's still asleep."

He handed Augusta to me, and I carried her into the quiet house.

In his letter to Bella, Frank had written of his cook-housekeeper. She was Mrs Deal, a sad widow whose husband and only child had been killed in an accident. Hearing the cab arrive, she had turned up

the gas in the entrance passage and was waiting there to receive us.
"You'll be Miss Legassick?" she asked.

I shook her hand and said that I was. "Augusta's asleep. We'd better
put her to bed at once."

The cab had driven away, and Frank and Miles had come in. Miles
was wide awake, looking with interest upon his new home. "Don't put
me to bed at once, will you, Dad?" he said; and Frank said: "No, no.
You stay up and eat with me. Yes, Maria. Please pack Augusta off."

"If you don't mind, I'd like to pack myself off, too. It's been rather
an exhausting day. I don't want anything to eat."

"As you wish," he said. "Mrs Deal will show you your room. I'll
show Miles his."

In her bedroom on the first floor I unpacked Augusta's suitcase, put
her into her nightclothes, and tucked her into bed. She hardly stirred.

"You're up aloft, next door to me," Mrs Deal said.

She carried up my suitcase. There were two attic rooms. She
showed me mine and made to light the gas. I asked her to leave it,
thanked her, and she went. There was just enough light to see what I
was doing, and I wasn't much interested in the room, anyway. I can
sleep anywhere. I wanted to see what was beyond the window. It was
more than I had dared to hope. I should have liked a hill, but there was
no hill. However, in the dim I could make out trees, and fields
stretching beyond fields, as far as my sight could carry. A mist was
rising from them, and that suggested a river, which here, I guessed,
must be the Mersey; and against a red streak which was the last of the
day a church tower was blocked darkly. It would do, I told myself. I
could live here. I got into bed, felt the deep blessed silence, and was
almost at once asleep.

2

About a week after this, Miles and Augusta had gone off together,
taking a midday meal with them. Frank and I had eaten lunch, and he
lit his pipe and said: "Well, how's it going? Any regrets?"

"It's all right with me. What about you?"

He looked at me with his dark smile. "I'm wondering how you'd
react if I piled a bit more work on to you."

I said that I was doing precious little, and asked him what work he
had in mind.

"It's Augusta's education. She's never been to school, you know."

I said that I hadn't been myself, and had never felt the loss.

"I suppose your father taught you?"

"More or less. So far as reading goes, our old servant taught me in the graveyard. We spent a lot of time there. Tombs were my textbooks. Father taught me to write and tried to teach me arithmetic. But the chief part of my education was in reading books that Father thought unsuitable."

"I suppose," Frank said, "you could get away with that sort of thing in the Cornish backwoods. In big towns the education authorities are more alert."

I asked him what had been done about Augusta till now.

"Well, you know that you aren't compelled to send a child to school so long as you can show that it's in the hands of someone capable of educating it. Augusta's mother was. When I married her she was history mistress in a girls' high school. So we had no difficulty."

"There's no difficulty now. A child isn't compelled to go on to a high school, and she must have passed the elementary school age."

"Just about. But I don't want her to be suddenly loose-ended. It's all right at the moment. I'm thinking of when Miles goes off in the autumn."

"Well," I promised. "I'll take it on. I could teach her something about French and Italian, but I expect it'll make her loathe me."

"I doubt it. By the way, you've been here a week. This is pay-day."

He took from his pocket an old-fashioned purse, a little bag tied with a string of leather. He rolled a few sovereigns on to the table.

"We weren't very business-like," he said. "We didn't arrange anything about wages. What would you think was fair?"

He looked embarrassed, and I felt shocked and rather hurt. It was absurd: we were both blushing. "I didn't come here for pay, Frank," I said. "I have a roof and food to eat, and I happen to be very fond of Augusta."

He slid the coins about on the table and managed a smile. "So we mustn't allow lucre to stain a beautiful association?"

"Put it how you like, but please don't insist on paying me. I have an income from one of my wealthy admirers," I said, trying to laugh it off.

He took up the frivolous tone. "Very well. I won't intrude on his privileges."

He scooped the coins from the table into his palm, dropped them into the purse. He looked at me, delving for the right words of thanks. "Augusta'll be all right," he said at last, and could have found no words to please me better.

Through the window I watched him mount his bicycle and set off on his afternoon round. I climbed the stairs to my attic bedroom and set about arranging my books. I had written to Hugo and asked him to send on all the books I had left in the loft at St Tudno, and here they were, with the word *all* literally obeyed, for they included even the elaborately bound copies of Father's works. I looked on them with a sad affection: poor neglected things that had meant so much in the begetting – so much labour to him and to us girls. No one else would want them now, I was sure: not Louisa, not Bella. I was glad to have them. Nothing could more sharply spell my childhood. Somehow, not only Father but Mrs Solway and Thomas May, Roger and his dark tent, and much else that I didn't want to forget, was bound up there in all that dear futile work.

I had had a carpenter in to make shelves. They reached, breast-high, across the whole of one wall, and they were painted olive-green. I put in the odd salvage of my years: Keats and Tennyson, *Lady Audley's Secret* and *Under Two Flags*, a small volume that had been published in 1808 and contained, among other matter, Lady Pennington's *Unfortunate Mother's Advice to her Daughter* and Moore's *Fables for the Female Sex*. There was the *Decameron* in Italian and a mass of stuff that I had gathered in my journeys through France, and Roger's little book on the Greeks, and a bound volume of *Sunday at Home*. A tearful and sentimental collection, and I was glad to have it about me, even down to the small book that had been written to boost poor Gerald's painting before his painting so tragically ended for ever.

Now that the books were in, the room looked more furnished and homely. When you opened the door, there were the books on your right hand and on your left was the narrow bed, with just room for a small wardrobe between it and the wall. Happily, it had sliding doors. If they had opened outward they would have been jammed by the bed. There was no dressing table. The average sort of woman in those days didn't have a dressing table that looked like a chemist's shop-window, and for that matter a chemist's shop-window didn't look like an actress' dressing room. I had a brush and comb and a hand-mirror in a drawer of the writing table and a tooth-brush in the bathroom. As for my face, to this day I have used soap and cold water on it, and left the consequences, which, I admit, are not outstanding, to speak for themselves. Between the books and the bed a strip of pale green carpet ran to the window, and under the window was the writing table . The walls were painted in the same pale matt green as the carpet, and the curtain was of white net with pale green spots. It was a cool little room even on the hottest days, but it was cold in winter. There was no fireplace.

Father had given me a photograph of himself in a rose-pink velvet frame. I detested the frame, but kept it for love's sake. I put it on the top of the bookshelves, with Roger's photograph alongside it. They made a nice balance of Greek and Hebrew. Between them I put a cheap plaster bust of Dante that I had bought in Florence. I had had an intensive and disturbing Dante phase while living with Mrs Kopf.

Well, there it was, finished. That was my room so long as I lived in Manchester. If I wanted to lounge, I did it on the floor, with a few cushions under me and my back against the books. That was the best place for reading at night, for the gas-globe was in a bracket on the wall over the books.

I stood with my back to the door and looked at it with satisfaction. The telephone rang and I went down to answer it. It stood on a small table in the passage. On the table were sheets of paper held down by a brass elephant that had never been nearer Benares than Birmingham. There was a cheap clock. There was a pencil tied by a string to a ring in the back of the table. I felt proud of these my arrangements. Professionally secretarial. I looked at the clock, wrote "May 29, 3.42 p.m.", and took up the receiver. When I had put it down I wrote: "Could Dr Cumberledge call at the *earliest possible moment* at Mrs Maxwell-Moxon's, 36, Farthingale Avenue. Her daughter, aged 4, suffering from repeated convulsive crying-fits."

Frank came in an hour later and read the message. He shouted through to the kitchen: "Tea, Mrs Deal," and sat down, looking rather tired, in the drawing room.

"Aren't you going to Mrs Maxwell-Moxon's?" I asked. "She seemed to think you should get there at once. She sounded very anxious."

"I'll bear her in mind, Maria," he said. "If you care to ring her up and suggest interim treatment, you may."

"What shall I tell her?" I asked, eager to serve.

"That she should up-end her darling daughter, who is well known to me, and administer three smart smacks to the bottom. After an hour, if there has been no improvement, the treatment as before. Now, let's have some tea."

3

Augusta's bedroom and Miles' were all-purpose rooms like mine. There wasn't a lot of space to spare in the little house. When you came from the street into the passage there was a door on the left. In it we had our meals and, when meals were done with, we used it as the family common room. With the flaps let down, the table was shoved against a wall, and there was space enough for a couch to stand in front of the fireplace and for a couple of easy-chairs. If you by-passed the door of this room, another opened into Frank's consulting room, whose window overlooked the back garden. The only other room on this floor was the kitchen, where Mrs Deal made herself snug enough in the evenings. On the first floor were three bedrooms: Frank, Miles, Augusta: and a bathroom; and there was nothing else but the two attics.

Frank's consulting hours were immediately after breakfast and immediately before our evening meal. You will see that the snag was where to put those who came to consult him while they were waiting their turns. There was no option: they had to use our common room. And so for about two hours a day that was out of commission for the family. The consequence was that we tended to live very personal and individual lives, like monks in their cells. It was understood that admission to anyone else's bed-sitting room was by invitation only.

I had never lived in such close quarters before. The vicarage, old-fashioned and inconvenient in many ways, at all events absorbed us comfortably, and there was the spacious loft for a refuge. When I was with Lady Jane at Coverdale I had a comfortable flat to myself; and my years with Mrs Kopf had been spent in a Renaissance palace. I remember the old girl, small, dark, gnarled, with piercing little black eyes, standing one day on a red and white marble floor, looking about her at tapestries and pictures and splendid furniture, and suddenly giving a throaty chuckle. She said to me: "How's this for a return on fifty pounds of investment?"

I asked her what she meant, and she told me that when her son Ernest was a boy and they were living in Holland he had come to her one day and said he wanted to go to South Africa. "He was a good boy," she said. "He was already keeping me. Only just. We had food, and clothes on our backs. That was about all. We didn't argue about it. I had fifty pounds hidden under a floor-plank, and I gave him every penny. I had been a dressmaker, and I became a dressmaker again. He took the fifty pounds and made no promises. He just went, and for a few years I worked my fingers to the bone. One day he came back and bought me a little house and gave me a little income. It was five pounds a week. He was still a good boy. He hadn't waited till he was very rich. It was hard for him to do. And then he *was* very rich, and there it was: the house in London, and Coverdale, and his racehorses at Minstall, and Voortrek in Cape Town. And this for me . . ."

It must have been a long time ago, but she still couldn't get over it. "All nonsense," she said. "What am I? An old caretaker."

There was a Rembrandt on the wall: that incomparable light and shade, with an old woman's face materialising out of it. Mrs Kopf looked at her. "She didn't have a son like mine, I'll bet," she said. So much for Rembrandt.

There was Louisa with Tregannock and her house in Brook Street; there was Bella with room to turn round in, even though she seemed set on populating it thickly; and here was I in a slice of living-space so narrow that it meant sitting on the floor to read. I looked through my window at the trees and the fields and the summer day blue over them, and I didn't want to swap with anybody.

4

Frank asked me: "How are you getting on with Augusta?"

"I'm leaving her alone," I said. "It's obvious that for the moment she wants nobody but Miles."

While we were at St Tudno, there was a lot that I could give her. Now there wasn't much except my company, and she was getting along well enough without that. I didn't mind, but I hoped she would soon be able to get along without Miles' company, too. Do what we will, we are alone. The sooner we learn that, the better; and the more we are fit to be alone with ourselves, the more we are respectful to the individuality of others, and therefore the more we are fit to associate with our kind. This was a paradox she would have to learn for herself. I had no intention of trying to shove that or any other lesson down her throat. I didn't see education as a conveyor belt on to which you put every child you could lay hands on, so that someone could chip a bit off here and someone else dab a bit on there, ending up with a population of Model Ts. But that is the way it is more and more seen nowadays.

So there we were, leading by force of circumstances this cellular life. It was broken up when the summer ended and Miles went away to school. As we were at breakfast on the day before he went Frank asked: "What about tomorrow, Miles? Would you like me to take you? I could manage to sneak a day off."

Miles said: "No, thank you, Father. If you can give me a cab as far as Stockport station I shall be all right. The train goes straight through from there – no change."

Augusta said: "I've been looking forward to going with you and Daddy."

Miles asked reasonably: "But why? When we got to the other end you'd have to say 'So long, see you at half-term.' Why not say it here and have done with it?"

Augusta said: "It's Tom Elthorne. You don't want me because you want to be with him. He'll be travelling on the same train. You've arranged it."

"No need for any arrangement," Frank told her. "Seeing that Tom is due back at the same school on the same day, naturally he'll be travelling on the same train."

I looked at Augusta. She was not eating. She was miserable, and because all this had happened to me I knew there was nothing to be done for her. I could see the vicarage breakfast table, and Roger sitting there with Hugo or one of the other boys who had come to share his holiday, and I could feel again the loathing for them that I felt as I listened to their eager talk about a day whose arrangements had no place for me.

Tom Elthorne's father was a solicitor who lived a few doors away. Tom was more enthusiastic than knowledgeable about chemistry. In the back-yard he had a shed that he called his laboratory, and there, playing about with a test tube over a Bunsen burner, he had induced a respectable explosion that scorched his hand and pitted his cheek with splinters of glass. Frank was out, but I knew he would be back soon, and asked them to wait. I fell into conversation with them. Pale lank-haired spectacled Tom seemed to me a bit young to be playing with lethal chemicals, and I said so to Mr Elthorne, who laughed. "You have a go at trying to stop him," he said. "I can't. Not that I've tried very hard."

And Tom said: "*Experientia docet*, don't you think? I wanted to know what would happen." He grinned. "Well, now I do."

Frank dealt with the hand and flicked the bits of glass out of the boy's cheek. "Lucky you were wearing spectacles," he said.

"Yes," Tom agreed, with a self-confidence that belied his pale weary looks. "That's something else I've learned. There must be some contraption with a fine wire mesh that I can wear *over* my spectacles. In that way I'd make doubly sure. You see, theoretically there shouldn't have been an explosion. I want to find out why it happened."

Frank was taken with him. "You'd better build yourself an asbestos shed," he advised him with a laugh. But nothing seemed a laughing matter to young Tom Elthorne. "That's an idea, sir," he said solemnly. "Could you run to it, Father?"

Mr Elthorne did not commit himself. "I foresee a precarious future for this street," he said. "Don't try to make me an accessory before the fact."

Tom shrugged. "You lawyers!" he said. "All caution."

He was wearing a blazer which Frank recognised as that of the school Miles was to attend. So he called Miles down from his room and introduced the pair. They appeared to be not impressed with one another, but now, it seemed, they had at least come to this understanding about travelling together. And on the morrow they did travel together. Mr Elthorne and Frank had agreed to share the cost of the cab. After breakfast, when the cab drew up outside our house, Tom came along hauling his school trunk. Miles said goodbye to Augusta rather casually, and Tom, putting his head through the window, said seriously: "I say – your hair is like Lyle's golden syrup, and that's jolly good on steamed pudding," quite a flight of fancy for him, but one which Augusta appeared not to find to her liking.

Mr Elthorne, who had come to see them off, said: "Give this boy stinks and steamed pudding, and that were paradise enow. Isn't that so, Tom?"

Tom, the most poker-faced boy I had ever seen, said: "Yes, sir. Hadn't you better be getting along now? You don't want to be late for the office."

5

Off they went, and Frank hopped on to his bicycle and set out on his morning round. I was left alone with Augusta under the mild autumn sunlight. On a day like this, Manchester was better than I had expected – our part of it, at all events. The sky was blue and gentle and the air had an astringent touch. No more than a touch, but, as I looked at the trees in the field facing us and saw here and there a leaf detach itself and spin silently down, the touch had significance and spoke of asperity to come. It was a day to be on the road, and I stood for a time hoping that Augusta would suggest this, but presently she said: "I think I'd better start my letter to Miles," and went in.

I took up *The Manchester Guardian* from the table in the passage, went up to my room, and put some cushions on the floor. Manchester-born Hugo had said: "There are newspapers that one glances at. But one *reads* the *Guardian*. All right-minded Manchester men read it devoutly."

Trying to feel devout, I opened the paper. I read a headline: "Woman Suffragists Demonstrate. Siege of the House."

It didn't much interest me, and I was about to flick over the page when one word arrested my eye: the word Polperro. Then I read carefully. There had been, I gathered, a prolonged demonstration by what was called an "army" of women outside the House of Commons. It had gone on for hours. The women tried to force their way into the House and mounted police were called to repel them. Many were arrested, including Lady Lavernock, "wife of the international financier", and several were injured. "Mrs James Polperro, whose husband is a Liberal member of the House, fell under the hoofs of a policeman's horse. She was removed to hospital."

Nowadays, when people telephone to New York or Antofagasta almost casually, it is odd to think that, then, any sort of trunk call seemed an adventure. It did to me, at all events. However, I decided to see whether the miracle could be achieved, and timorously asked the telephone girl to put me through to James' house in Brook Street. I was staggered to find that this could be done and to hear what was indubitably James' port winey voice speaking to me, asking who was there?

"Oh, James, this is Maria. How is Louisa? I've been reading about her in *The Manchester Guardian*."

"She's here – upstairs in bed. I had her shifted from hospital and brought in my own doctor."

"Is she desperately ill?"

"She's not ill at all, in any life-and-death sense," James said, sounding almost cross. "It's her foot. Some damn' great brute of a horse stamped on it. She always was a fool where horses are concerned. You shouldn't lie under 'em. And I told her so."

I could imagine what Louisa said to that.

"Is her foot very bad?"

"Yes. Bones broken. Ligaments damaged. All sorts of damn' nonsense."

He sounded very cross indeed. I gathered that he had small sympathy with women who made a public spectacle of themselves and fell under horses.

"Give her my love."

"All right. But she don't deserve it. And how are you?"

"Bearing up."

"How are those two nice children?"

"Very well, thank you. Miles has gone off to school today."

"Poor little devil. Mind you bring 'em down to Tregannock again some day. That a promise?"

"Yes, if you'll have us."

"All right then. Look after yourself and keep out of politics."

I was putting down the receiver when Frank came in. I showed him the paragraph in the *Guardian* and recounted my conversation with James.

"What do you think?" I asked. "Does it sound serious to you?"

" My dear, a doctor doesn't diagnose without seeing his patient."

"Don't be stuffy. I'm not asking you to diagnose. You're a doctor, and you should have a rough idea of what happens when a damn' great horse, as James calls it, stamps on a woman's foot."

He considered it, and said: "Well, speaking unprofessionally, a foot's a complicated bit of machinery. It contains umpteen joints and umpteen bits of string holding 'em together and making 'em wiggle at the word of command. A damn' great horse's hoof coming down into that lot could mean that the foot will never be the same again. In fact, I guess – *guess*, mind you – that your sister will have a certain lameness for the rest of her life."

He was right about that. When next I met Louisa she was using a stick, and, what is more, using it with an air. She somehow succeeded in wearing her limp as a soldier wears a decoration gained in action.

6

A week or so later Augusta, rising from the breakfast table, said: "Excuse me. I must get on with my letter to Miles. I promised to post one every week."

She was hesitating by the door and Frank said: "Give him my love."

"Why, Daddy? Haven't you written to him yourself?"

"Not yet. I'm finding life rather demanding."

"What about you, Aunt Maria?"

I confessed that I hadn't written, and she went out, looking as though she despaired of us.

Frank gave me a rueful smile. "We're dirt, Maria. We're not living up to her standard."

She had hardly left the house since Miles went away. She was losing her beautiful Cornish colour.

"Can't you get her out a bit?" Frank asked.

"Oh, yes," I promised. "When the time comes."

I went up to put my room in order and to make my bed, and then I sat down to write to Louisa. I hadn't been much given to writing to her, but now, when a damn' great horse had stamped on her foot, I made an exception. I was in the midst of a kind sisterly letter when there was a knock, the door opened an inch or two, and Augusta asked: "May I come in?"

"Yes. Come in, darling."

She fidgeted near the door for a moment, then asked: "Do you know the poems of D. G. Rossetti?"

"Yes, pretty well. Sit down on the bed."

"I don't want to intrude."

"Nonsense. You know as well as I do that you're not intruding."

She sat on the extreme edge of the bed. "I haven't a copy of the poems," she said. "Mother had. She used to keep it on her dressing table."

I got up from the writing-desk and sat on my floor cushions. Very well, I thought. If you want to talk about your mother, that is what you'd better talk about.

"I haven't a dressing table, as you see," I said. "I keep a few things in a drawer. What was hers like?"

"It was of beautiful wood. She told me it was walnut. It had an enormous round mirror and she used to sit on a stool covered with pale blue silk and brush her hair with a silver brush. Sometimes she let me brush it. On each side there were four drawers with ivory handles. On the table there was a china tray. Mother said it was Meissen, whatever that means."

I told her what Meissen meant. "What was in the tray?"

"Oh, odds and ends. Pins and needles, and buttons that had come off and hadn't gone on again, and safety-pins and hair-pins. On one side of it was my photograph and on the other one of Miles when he was a baby. Usually, there were a few flowers in a glass vase."

Obviously, it was there in front of her again, and her mother sitting on the stool covered with pale blue silk. "There was even a small pot of rouge," she said. "Do you think rouge is wicked?"

I laughed. "In the wrong hands," I said, "it can have serious consequences. Would you care to hear a sad story about rouge?"

She slid off the bed, sat on the floor alongside me, and put her arm through mine. "Tell me. I love stories."

"It's a story about people you know – me and your Aunt Bella and Aunt Louisa and Uncle James Polperro. And about the old coach that Uncle James drove you in to Truro. There was a real coachman on it that night."

She listened, entranced; and when it was finished I brought her back to the point. "And Rossetti's poems were on the dressing table near the rouge-pot."

"Yes. The pages had gilt edges and the covers were made of soft purple leather. I used to read them when I was waiting for Mother to come and have her hair brushed. Inside, it said: 'From Hugo to Claire, with love.' "

305

She said after a moment: "It seems years since I read them, and I wanted to write a line out of them in my letter to Miles, and there's a word I can't remember. The ground-swirl of the something leaves of hope."

I quoted:

> *The ground-swirl of the perished leaves of hope,*
> *The wind of death's imperishable wing.*

"That's right!" she said, and squeezed my arm.

I said: "Rather a solemn line. I wonder whether Miles will be feeling up to solemnity? I expect he's a bit lonely, with everything new and strange."

"It's a tremendous long letter," she said. "I've been writing it all the week. I think a bit of solemnity will fit in, because there's all sorts of other things. Would you like to read it?"

"No, thank you, darling. You must write what you like. Only remember this. If you're carrying a heavy weight of bricks, it may not be a good idea to use a letter in order to land some of them on someone else. Someone else may have plenty of bricks to carry, too."

"Yes," she said simply.

I got up and took my Rossetti from the bookcase. I inscribed it: "From Aunt Maria to Augusta, with love," and gave it to her. "One of these days," I said, "I'll tell you something about the Rossettis. They were an interesting family."

"Tell me this afternoon," she said. "Let's have a good walk and a good talk."

"What about your father's telephone?"

"Oh," she said gaily, "he says that half the people who ring him up have nothing worse than a bellyache."

7

I didn't want to read the letter to Miles because I knew it would contain a good deal of what nowadays they call sob-stuff, for the emotions are looked on with distrust or even scorn. With clear heads and noble brows we bravely face a world that has none but a mechanical meaning.

However, it seemed to me then, and seems now, natural enough that Augusta should feel and express anguish. The young are extremists. When they are happy they cannot believe in sorrow; and when they are sad joy is not gone for a holiday: it is dead beyond resurrection.

So I didn't at the moment want to read what Augusta had to say; but a few weeks later when she asked me to read her weekly letter I did so because, being in a sort her governess, I wished to see how she wrote English. I remember some of her phrases. "The tree in the field opposite has taken off every stitch, and I like the look of its bare bones." "Father came in late and tired. I pitied him. How I should hate spending a life on the exploration of human ruins! Let the ivy grow over them and have done with it." I couldn't approve of all the sentiments, but decided that there need be no lessons in English composition.

Looking back on those days, I can't remember anything that could rightly be called lessons. She knew nothing of mathematics beyond adding, subtracting and dividing. Neither did I, and we left it like that. Her mother, who had been a history-mistress, had given her a start in that subject, and in geography. I confined myself to the only things I was good at – French and Italian. The quickest way to her mind was through people. I'm a reasonably ill-educated sort of woman, but I've done an immense amount of reading, and I was able to go on from the point most of her questions raised. For example: she had an anthology of poems containing Yeats' "When you are old and grey and full of sleep". She quoted it to me one day, and I pointed out how much it owed to Ronsard.

"Who is Ronsard?"

That was a typical starting-point, and we talked all the morning about Ronsard, du Bellay, and all that group. The Dante bust in my room was another start. "Who's that grim man, Aunt Maria?"

She took to using my room, sitting on the floor with her books while I was writing my journal and letters. Something she read would start her off and start me off, and so the morning would go by. It was not till she said to me: "I wish I knew French like you," that I pointed out to her what systematic study meant, but here I'm covering in a phrase a process that occupied years.

I loved the child, and it fascinated me to watch her stand, like Longfellow's maiden, "where the brook and river meet". It was a delicious moment. I never knew what I should find her reading. It might be Mrs Ewing or Mrs Molesworth; but also it might be Meredith or Thackeray. The temptation to over-persuade the stream this way or that was terrific; but I managed to hold my hand from building ducts and conduits. She was very untidy. She raided my bookshelves and left my books all over the house, but I did no more than lament one day: "Augusta, I wanted a quotation from Tennyson this morning. I wasted half an hour looking for the book. It was behind the breadbin in the kitchen."

She was instant penitence, and a wave of deserters flowed back to stand in the ranks on my shelves. She was more careful for at least a week.

8

"I suppose," she said to me just before Christmas, "that when Miles comes home he'll want to spend a lot of time with Steamed Pudding."

She had disliked Tom Elthorne's remark about her hair, mainly, I think, for she was not touchy, because she was in a high-charged emotional state when he made it. I was glad that she was able to turn it into this mild joke about himself.

"Well, if Miles wants to, that will be that. Now that he's thrown among a lot of boys, we can hardly expect him not to make a friend or two."

"Still," she said hopefully, "I shall see *something* of him, sha'n't I?"

"Oh, surely. They'll spare us a smile now and then."

As it turned out, we had more than a smile. That very night, after we had pushed back the table and were sitting round the fire, Mr Elthorne looked in. He sat and smoked a companionable pipe with Frank and obviously had something on his mind. In the course of an hour we gathered that this something was a favour he wished to ask. But Mr Elthorne was a tremendous beater about the bush, no man of Yea and Nay. He seemed to fear that every word he uttered might be used in evidence against him. When all came to all, we learned that his antique father – "Eighty-nine or ninety – or there-abouts – I wouldn't swear to a year, mind you" – had died, and that besides the funeral there were complicated family affairs to clear up – "not that I distrust

my sister, or her husband either, come to that. But he's pretty sharp –
I don't say a sharper, but sharp" – and consequently Mr Elthorne had
to be in Sunderland over Christmas. "Perhaps till the Friday after – or
it might be the Thursday – I wouldn't care to fix it to a day or so" –
and could we look after Tom.

"Of course, Elthorne," Frank said. "There's a camp bed. We can
shove him in with Miles. No trouble at all."

I didn't see much of any of them during that holiday. I remember
that it was for the most part sharp but sunny weather and that the
three of them would set out in mid-morning, taking food with
them, and not return till the mists were rising on our fields, and the
night's nip was beginning to be felt, and the sun was going down,
red as a Christmas apple, beyond Northenden church. After our
evening meal, Tom and Miles would go upstairs to their room, or to
the stinks shed behind the Elthorne house, and Augusta would sit for
a while with me and Frank, drowsing over a book, like a bee swaying
on the lip of a foxglove, aware of the honey, but too dithered by the
sunshine of a summer day to go in and get it. She would nod, yawn,
and at last go early to bed.

She was naturally a child of good manners. It was clear that she
would have loved to have Miles to herself now and then, but she
would not say so for fear of hurting Tom Elthorne's feelings. And so
one evening when they were discussing at dinner the programme for
the morrow, I said: "How long have you lived in Manchester, Tom?"

"I was born here," he said.

"Then you'll know a lot about the town?"

"Everything," he said confidently. "I used to go to the Grammar
School. Do you know the place?"

"No. I know nothing of the town at all. I was in Bowdon years ago
and now I'm in Didsbury. I don't suppose either is aboriginal
Manchester. I wondered if you'd show me round tomorrow. We could
have lunch somewhere."

"All right," he agreed with no notable enthusiasm. But I didn't
mind that, for Tom had an imperturbability that could have looked on
worlds in ruins and done no more than take a few careful notes.

"I'll show you the Grammar School," he said, "and I can tell you
now it's older than Eton. And I'll show you Chetham's Hospital next
door to it, which isn't a hospital at all but a place for poor scholars

who wear long blue coats, with leather belts, and long yellow stockings and buckled shoes. A few things like that."

I thanked him and said that would be fine.

"Mind you, it's all dreary and dirty. The Irk and the Irwell are mucky little rivers."

"I sha'n't mind."

"You can scrape enough chemicals off the face of the Town Hall to set up a laboratory."

"Good. I'm dying to see it all."

"The Ship Canal's unspeakably foul. I'm sorry there won't be time to see it. But I can promise you some pretty filthy things."

He peered at me through his spectacles as though hoping to see me wilt, but I smiled bravely.

"I should still be at the Grammar School," he said, "if I hadn't been born a delicate child. I have a constitutional addiction to colds, catarrhs, consumption and all that sort of thing."

I looked hard at him. Young as he was, I could never be sure whether he was pulling my leg. His unblinking mask gazed at me unrevealing.

"There was a severe attack of inflammation of the lungs and pleurisy. It may have developed into double pneumonia. I'm not sure. I was unconscious most of the time. However," he said with a sigh, as though life were an intolerable burden, "I survived."

"Perhaps you were born to do something great," Augusta said earnestly; and Miles, lightening the moment, suggested: "Like eating more steamed pudding than anyone else in the world."

Tom turned impassive lenses upon him. "It was no laughing matter, Cumberledge. Anyway, that was the end of the Grammar School for me. The doctor said I must live in country air. We moved out here from Lower Broughton. So I have reasonably clean air during the holidays, and I was sent off to this school in Derbyshire where the lab. is unspeakably inadequate. Well, let's get round to the shed."

And off they went to continue their task, which we had been told was the manufacture of fireworks.

Frank watched them go with his ironic smile. "I don't know," he said, "how much Elthorne expects under his father's will, but he'll be lucky if he doesn't have to spend some of it putting a new roof over his head."

An hour or so later Miles came back and said: "Will you please all go into the garden and watch the sky in the general direction of Northenden?"

We obliged, and shivered for twenty minutes. Then, not in the general direction of Northenden but almost overhead, something roared into the sky as though the moon at least were its destination, changed its mind, spluttered a couple of red and green sparks, and fell like Lucifer, never to rise again.

A few minutes later the boys came back. "That," Tom said, "might inaccurately be called a *ballon d'essai*. May I go to bed? I must think it out."

9

Augusta had been reading *Cranford*, and the next morning she and Miles set off to walk to Knutsford, where Mrs Gaskell had set the story. Tom Elthorne, taking seriously his job as cicerone, said: "That reminds me, Miss Legassick. I must show you Cross Street Chapel, where Mrs Gaskell's old man was parson. Don't expect much. It's a prim little shack built in brick – rather depressing, like Mr Gaskell himself. I can never make out why his wife stuck to him. Still, that was her affair. I'd better show you the place."

It seemed to me that he would make a poor tout or dragoman, but at least he was comprehensive. Nothing missed him. We had decided to walk the five miles to Manchester, and had hardly passed the Cock Inn when he pointed to some buildings standing in a fair-sized garden on the right. "That's Didsbury College," he said. "A Wesleyan place. They turn out parsons there. Rather grim, don't you think?"

I warned him: "You'd better be careful what you say, Tom. My father was a parson, though not a Wesleyan one, and my sister is married to a parson who is Miles' uncle. We're a rather parsonical family."

"Oh, don't think I've got anything against parsons *qua* parsons," he said. "I rather like what I've read about old Wesley himself. The way he used to go tooling round the country on his old nag was quite enterprising. But don't disturb my ruminations for a moment. I'm thinking up what you should see. Ah, yes! What about the Lit and Phil?"

"I'm afraid I don't know what that is."

"The Literary and Philosophical Society. Not much to look at," he said with grim relish. "Just the house where John Dalton used to live."

I confessed my ignorance of John Dalton. "Like everyone else, I know the name, but I'm not sure what he did."

"Well," he assured me easily, "he was pretty hot on the elasticity of vapours and the expansion of gases – that sort of thing. Then, of course, there's Joule. He worked under Dalton. There's a statue of him in the Town Hall. You might care to see it. But if you don't want to, say so."

I said we'd see how time panned out.

"Perhaps the Romans are more in your line," he suggested. "They had a camp here. Well, to me that doesn't matter tuppence. But if it interests you, there's a bit of brick or stone under a bridge in Salford that is undoubtedly Roman. The whole place round about there is quite unspeakably filthy. Perhaps you'd rather see the pub where Bonnie Prince Charlie stayed? There *are* people," he said with scorn, "who are interested in that sort of romantic nonsense. I think the fellow was a cheap little cad."

To save my reputation, I said No: we wouldn't bother with that. "It's in the oldest part of the town," he said. "The general region thereabouts is called The Shambles, and that about describes it."

We plodded on through Withington and Fallowfield, and thereafter the way was houses, houses, houses, as though, once Platt Fields were left behind, an invisible knife cut off town from almost-country with one sickening guillotine-smack.

We marched along this hideous way for what seemed a long time before Tom spoke again. Then he said: "Well, here we go – you and I in one direction, Miles and Augusta in another. We're back to back, with the distance between us increasing in a satisfying manner."

I was almost shocked by his perspicacity. I said weakly: "What do you mean, Tom?"

"I'm not complaining," he said. "I like Cumberledge, and to be with him I can put up with his sister. If you think they should have a chance to be without me now and then, well and good. But remember, I'm a wily young bird."

I suppose he was about fifteen – a year or so older than Miles. I was possessed by a sudden respect for him – almost a fear of him. I could find no answer to give him. After a moment, he said: "I've been brooding about that. Well, it's off my chest now. But always be candid with me. I like people to be candid with me."

We spent a satisfactory day together and were back in time to join Miles and Augusta at their evening meal. Tom really did have a knowledge of the town and he showed me many interesting things. But he showed me nothing half so interesting as that peep into his own mind. After this, I was never quite comfortable with him. He seemed a bit uncanny. What made it worse was that my little plot was wasted. Augusta said: "Don't take Tom away more than you can help, will you, Aunt Maria?"

"Why, darling? Did you miss him today?"

"Yes."

"Why?"

"Oh, dear," she said. "I hardly ever know the answer to why. But I did."

10

Behind Kingsley Avenue there was a lane, with the doors of the back-gardens opening into it. Inside our door was the bicycle-shed. Both Augusta and I rode bicycles, though we preferred walking to riding. But when we went into Manchester we used the bicycles, because walking that five miles was not something that either of us relished. And we were going into Manchester often as the spring days came on. My association with Jane Lavernock and Gerald Pickering had opened my eyes to pictures, and my stay in Italy had deepened my interest. Mrs Kopf's house was full of masterpieces of furniture and painting. Lord Lavernock used it as a depository for what he couldn't hang in his other houses. The Lavernock Collection now belongs to the nation and is displayed in what was Lord Lavernock's London home. It had been built up under Mr Groggenheim's supervision into one of the most famous private collections of our times. It is not surprising then that I had become picture-conscious and fairly knowledgeable, and while I lived in Florence I assembled a lot of folios of reproductions. These were in my nun's cell, as Frank Cumberledge called it. Inevitably Augusta came upon them.

It was a new world to the child and she was enchanted. For the moment, all her other studies went by the board, if our haphazard goings-on could in any way be called studies. I let her have her head, as usual, standing by to answer any questions she cared to ask. By suggesting the right books, I tried to lead her mind into some understanding of the trend of the thing, the development from the beginning up to our times. But that was secondary. As with reading, the main thing was to let her soak herself in the product. The rest could come later.

But though these reproductions were all very well in their way, they were not the real thing. That is why we were often now riding our bicycles into Manchester. I wanted to see for myself, and I wanted her to see, what there was at the town's art gallery in Mosley Street.

Painting, then, was our main concern throughout the rest of that summer and autumn. It was broken into by half-term visits to Miles' school and by the long summer holiday. We didn't go to Cornwall. Frank wanted the children to see the Lake District and it was not my business to oppose the scheme.

Augusta was rather disappointed. James had written inviting us all to Tregannock, and Augusta would have liked to go. "Of course," she said, "we needn't have played at Indians on the lake and that sort of thing."

She sounded as though she despised the little girl who had been tickled by such straws; and, indeed, looking at her as she sat on the cushions in my room, I rejoiced at the change in her. She had come my way just at the right moment. The chrysalis was cracking; the wings were about to appear.

"But I *was* looking forward," she said, "to having the *Cormorant* again and plenty of exploring and swimming. But there it is. I suppose you *can* swim in the Lakes. They'll be very cold, and that will please Daddy."

She looked as though it wouldn't please her; and watching her relaxed there, leaning against the books, with her white wheaten hair streaming down her shoulders, I couldn't see her as the sort of young woman we have lamentably come to see increasingly from that time to this: wearing uniform, dashing along foot-race tracks, smashing at hockey-balls, leaping in a scant swirl of lingerie about tennis-courts. Not, I think, that Frank would have liked any of this, either.

I didn't go with them. I saw them off, and then caught my own train to London.

11

Louisa met me, and couldn't have been more gracious if I had been Mrs Pankhurst coming up to town for a conference on window-smashing and letter-box burning. She had a porter ready to carry my suitcase to a taxi. She kissed me, and, somehow made more regal by her limp and her ebony stick, accompanied me along the platform. She was forty-four. We're getting on. We're all getting on, I thought. If Louisa had married James when first they were in love, she could have been a grandmother by now.

"How is James?" I asked, when I had helped her into the taxi.

"Shooting somewhere in Yorkshire," she said. "What is it they kill at this time of year? Grouse, isn't it?"

She knew as well as I did. "Yes," I said. "Grouse."

"James should be very happy," she said. "His rather gross sovereign is one of the party. Therefore, the Queen is not. The affair has been organised by Lord Lavernock, the imperial pimp."

"Louisa!"

She laughed. "Are you shocked?"

I didn't answer. "*I'm* not," she said. "It's a long time since I left St Tudno vicarage."

She looked bitter, and I guessed that this was because she suspected backsliding in James. It was years now since he had joined such a party as this.

"Do you see anything of Lady Lavernock?" I asked.

"As little as I can. She's not much seen except by mechanics on airfields. She flies in those crazy things they're making. She'll kill herself yet."

"How is James' health?"

"I don't think there's much wrong with it now. He is taking care not to strain it."

I looked sideways at her harsh but handsome profile. And suddenly a feeling I had never before had for Louisa flooded me. I had often completely failed to understand her. I had feared her. I had admired her. Now I was filled with compassion, and with sorrow that frustration had led her to say so many stern and perhaps not truthful things. I put my hand upon hers. She looked at it for a moment in surprise, as though, in a strange dream, a rose had pushed up suddenly through an iceberg and bloomed there. Her face twitched; then she was stern again, as though in the dream she had crushed the rose underfoot. She took my hand and laid it back on my knee. "Thank you, Maria," she said. "But please don't." And then, as if to squash me in her old fashion: "If you had accepted James' invitation to bring those children to Tregannock, he wouldn't have been with his present company."

12

I hadn't before been in this Brook Street house. I wandered about in it during the next few days. It was beautifully furnished. The Polperros had never been important, except within a mile or two of their house, but they had been rich for a long time. At a moment when land was already ceasing to be wealth and was becoming a financial worry, they had remained in clover. They were commercial people who had bought land, and though for some generations they had had nothing to do with the metals that had enriched them, the riches were still there, cosily nursed for them by lawyers and agents. It was the much older families, the men of the manor houses, who for centuries had had nothing but land, and to whom land was a trust, a religion and a way of life: it was these who were feeling the pinch and would soon feel the kicks from their largely urban parliamentary lords and masters. And so it had not been necessary to economise on the house in Brook Street. It was, of course, Louisa's idea, not James'. James himself was Louisa's idea. I had an uneasy feeling that for the first time Louisa was doubting herself, doubting whether she could, after all, make James into something that was (as it had always seemed to me) flatly contrary to his lazy, good-natured and unforceful being. James' absence made this feeling in my heart sharper day by day: this feeling of Louisa moving unhappily about her splendid stage-set, oppressed by a foreboding that her leading man, who had seemed so co-operative to begin with, was going to turn down the part after all.

Especial care had been paid to the dining room and drawing room. The dining room was an impressive solemnity of dark furniture and subdued lighting. Louisa's greatest political triumph so far was that Mr Asquith with his wife, and two other members of the Cabinet and their wives, had sat with her and James at this long elegant Sheraton table. Not that she set much store by Mrs Asquith. "That brittle chatterbox," she called her.

316

If the dining room was as splendidly sombre as one of Bossuet's *Oraisons Funèbres*, so that one could imagine the destinies of nations being gravely and nobly decided over the nuts and wine, the drawing room was all grace and gaiety. The pictures made my heart yearn with memory's ache, for they were all by Gerald Pickering: seas and skies; the cool flow of little, unknown rivers decked with all the flowers Ophelia could have needed for her watery bier; the white walls of a house that looked as though it must be full of ghosts, swooning beneath the moon.

These rooms were the show-pieces. The rest of the house was so-so. It was, indeed, what Louisa's austerity would have wanted a house to be. Not that there was anything to complain about. My bedroom could be lived in. It had an easy-chair and a writing table, and each evening after dinner I sat down and gave Augusta an account of my day. I told her of the galleries I had visited and the pictures and statues I had seen, and towards the end of my stay I was able to tell her that the purpose of this visit to Louisa had been achieved. Not that Augusta knew anything of my purpose; but it had seemed to me that a good long stay in London would do her no harm. I had sounded Frank, and now I was able to write: "Your Aunt Louisa would like you to come and stay with her and Uncle James here in Brook Street as soon as a visit can be conveniently arranged."

She replied:

How lovely it will be! Let's go early one morning and stand on Westminster Bridge and see the

> *Ships, towers, domes, theatres and temples lie*
> *Open unto the fields, and to the sky.*

You see, I've been reading Wordsworth. One can't not read him here. Oh, how lovely he is!

Tom Elthorne writes to Miles nearly every day, and he has written once to me. He explained how with a cake of sulphur he could make electric sparks fly from the tip of a cat's ear. He is such an odd creature. He seemed to think this very important, which I am sure is more than the cat did or than I do. He also

317

says that his father has come into some money and is going to have a proper laboratory built for him, in place of his shed.

Do you find London a dreary place? Apart from Wordsworth, I find the Lakes trying. They have three sorts of days – wet, wetter and wettest. Shall I tell you the best place I know? Your little room in Kingsley Avenue when we are there together.

All my love.

Augusta.

13

Sir Christopher Onslow-Purley called on Louisa every day. I looked forward to him if only for his resounding name. There was, too, his appearance. He was about six foot four in height, thin as a thread, clean-shaven, aristocratic. He carried his clothes so well that he might have been born in the Royal Enclosure at Ascot and there absorbed with his earliest breath an addiction to fashionable elegance. He had the air of being at any moment about to lead in the winner of the Gold Cup. A hansom cab brought him to Brook Street every morning.

His father had been a pawnbroker named Purley, living in the East End of London, who made a lot of money and sent young Christopher to a good school. He could pick up scholarships as easily as other boys could drop goals or knock up a century; and already his languid and aristocratic air made him an object of wonder. His height was so great and his manner so frosty that he was known at school as the North Pole.

His cautious and sceptical approach in all his relationships, his aptitude for languages and his distinguished bearing caused his tutor at Oxford to hint tentatively at the Foreign Office as a career. Christopher said: "Yes, sir. I decided on that some years ago."

The year after he came down he married a middle-class girl named Onslow, changed his name by deed poll to Onslow-Purley; and now, at this time when I met him, he was a childless widower, retired, who had been British Ambassador in three capitals. He was about seventy years old, had chambers in Albany, and spent most of his time in hansom cabs and the Athenaeum. He detested the country: nothing would induce him to leave London. Once when asked to join a shooting-party, he inquired: "What do you shoot?" "Oh, various sorts of birds," he was told. "Birds?" he said. "What are they?"

14

Neither Louisa nor I knew these things about Sir Christopher Onslow-Purley at that time. That he was a most distinguished old gentleman who had been an ambassador was as far as it went. Louisa had met him at a luncheon given by a marchioness who sympathised with the woman suffrage movement, though her sympathy was all she was prepared to give, and she wouldn't have given that if she had known it was a contribution to the domestic-servant problem that was to harass her daughters. What Sir Christopher was doing at the luncheon I don't know, but he was something of a snob and compensated perhaps for his humble beginnings by cherishing the denizens of Debrett. However that may be, he was Louisa's neighbour at table, and the conversation got on to her childhood. He learned that she was the daughter of a parson named Legassick. That name is common enough in Cornwall, but not well known outside the county; hence it "rang a bell", as they say, in Sir Christopher's mind. He recalled it from his Oxford days. He and Father had been under-graduates together, though never closely associated. However, there it was, that insignificant link, and it was enough to permit Sir Christopher to suggest, when the luncheon was over, that, as his hansom cab would be passing Brook Street, he might take Louisa to her door. She accepted his offer, and a week or two later returned the courtesy by inviting him to be one of a small dinner-party. Then, to her surprise, and at first to her annoyance, there began his daily calls. We sat one night and talked about Sir Christopher in the room she called her office, a room remarkably like one I remembered in Vincent Wheatstone's house, bleak and cluttered with papers.

"James was amused at first," she said, "and then became rather annoyed. He said he disliked the way I was getting myself talked about as a suffrage agitator, and now this, on top of all the rest, was a bit too much. I asked him what he meant by 'now this'. Well, he said, people were given to gossip and one couldn't be too careful. He was very lame and apologetic, but obstinate. I laughed, and that's always the wrong thing to do with James when he's in a fit of moral earnestness. But what on earth! Here's an old man who's obviously lonely, who likes talking to me, and whom I like to have about. His merest gossip is more full of information, to say nothing of wisdom, than all the considered speeches I hear from the politicians."

That was all very well, but there is no doubt that Sir Christopher innocently undid all that she had done with James. James had never taken kindly to the harness in which, with infinite patience, she had persuaded him to run, or rather to amble with a vast good-natured patience. I am no psychologist, but I can make a guess now and then; and my guess is that James remembered the day when he and Louisa had taken love where they could find it, and his betrayal of her with Lady Mary Lacey. He had not forgiven his own cowardice, and he was happy to compensate for it by doing what he could to please Louisa. That, I am sure, more than any response to her reasoned arguments, had brought them to where they now were. It must at best have been a delicate equilibrium, and Sir Christopher shook it fatally.

Sometimes when Sir Christopher called he would suggest a drive through the parks. On a summer day they had returned from one of these drives, and the courtly old skeleton, his tall grey hat in his hand, helped Louisa out of the hansom, held her hand till they reached her door, bowed over it and kissed it. Then he got into the cab and drove away to take his lunch in the Athenaeum.

James was walking home and saw the performance. He came in so hard on Louisa's footsteps that she was in no doubt that he had seen it. He said nothing and sat glumly through lunch. Louisa said: "What's the matter, James?"

He replied like a sullen boy: "Nothing. What makes you think something's the matter?"

"Well," she said, smiling, "you don't seem notable for lightness of heart today."

"I'm sorry," he answered stiffly, "that I can't supply the charm of continental chatter."

"I suppose you are referring to Sir Christopher. Well, he never *chats*. He's a good talker, and I like listening to him. And I can never condemn a thing because it's what you call continental."

"I don't like foreigners."

"On the whole, Sir Christopher doesn't, either. He's told me more than once how refreshing he finds it to be back in England for good. But when he talks about foreigners, he speaks with knowledge and doesn't damn whole nations whose countries he's never visited."

"He's picked up their manners with their lingo," James said. "I don't like him, and I don't like these daily visits."

"There's nothing much the matter with his manners. After all, I'm rather lame. Isn't it natural that he should hand me out of a cab?"

"Englishmen don't kiss ladies' hands."

"I'd rather he didn't kiss mine, but if he wants to, I'm sure I don't mind. He was in Vienna for years. It's mere formality there. It means nothing."

He was silent for so long that she said: "James, may I tell you exactly how I see this?"

"If you wish to – yes."

Louisa said: "In all my life I've had very few men friends. I've never had a woman friend. I don't like women, so that doesn't matter. But I do like men. When I was a working girl there was one in France who opened my eyes to all sorts of beautiful things that I'd been utterly blind to – pictures and music and the theatre. He was a Frenchman, and he was most respectable. You mustn't think that a friendship with a man is necessarily passionate. He never tried to seduce me, though he was a foreigner. If he had tried, he might have found it the easier because, not many years before, I *had* been seduced. You may remember it was by an Englishman, who deserted me – for all he knew, with a child. I've had a few other men friends, on the same terms as with the Frenchman, but one thing and another has caused them all to fizzle out. There was one friendship that I can tell you could easily have developed into something else, and that was with Gerald Pickering. However, I was determined that it shouldn't develop, and anyway Gerald's fancy was elsewhere – not very flatteringly for me.

"Well, I do want you to know that *I like men*. So far as passion goes, I think Vincent Wheatstone destroyed me for ever, and that's something I can never forgive him for. But I still like men. It's a long time since I've had a man friend. I do ask you not to interfere between me and Sir Christopher. He's old, and something of an oddity, but he gives me what I deeply want. Do you understand all this?"

The dear dense fool said what was perhaps the most impercipient thing of his life. "I think your remarks have been more than a little indelicate."

That James, of all people, should talk of delicacy! What did he think the word meant? Louisa left him there and went off to her own room.

It was not long after this that Lord Lavernock arranged his shooting party. He had hired a mansion and the servants who went with it and the moors that surrounded it as casually as I might have gone into a shop and bought a packet of hairpins. Why he remembered James and Louisa Polperro, with whom he had never been more than casually acquainted, I couldn't see; and some years afterwards when I had one of my infrequent meetings with Jane Lavernock I asked her about it.

"Oh," she said, "I remember quite well. Ernest was making up his list, and, of course, as Edward was to be present, it was as tricky as forming a Cabinet. One had to think not only of people who could shoot, but also of people who could afford to lose money at cards, or reputation in bed, and so forth. The obvious men and women leapt to mind – the dear old gang. I didn't mind. I'd made it clear I wasn't going to be there. There were a few places left, and I said for fun: 'What about the Polperros? You could tell me how they're getting on. I haven't had news of them for years.' "

For fun! It had been as casual as that!

Jane went on: "Ernest was shocked! So shocked that, though I hadn't been very serious, I thought he ought to be taken down a peg. I said: 'Who are you to look down your nose at the Polperros? Or, come to that, who's the King to do it?' I've always loathed Edward, so I suppose I put a bit of venom into it. I said: 'The Polperros at any rate are English, which is more than Edward is, or Alexandra, come to that, or you yourself.' I liked to goad Ernest now and then. He tended to get above himself. I said: 'I don't suppose the Polperros would regard your invitation as such an almighty honour. Ten to one, they'd turn it down.' He couldn't believe it. I think it was just to prove how wrong I was that he sent the invitation."

The invitation came soon after James had made his protest about Sir Christopher. Louisa laughed. "Really!" she said. "These people forget themselves. Whatever makes them think one would want to keep such company as that?"

James said: "We entertained Lord Lavernock at Tregannock. It's not unnatural that he should want to entertain us in return."

Louisa didn't even bother to answer that remark.

Throughout the whole of my visit I had the feeling that her life, as she had planned it when she married James, was in ruins, and that she knew it. His going off on that visit, which would take him among people whom he knew to be deeply antipathetic to her, was an act of self-assertion cloaked as the fulfilment of a social obligation. The tiff about Sir Christopher would have come to nothing in itself. It was merely a symptom of his growing feeling that Louisa was running his life for him. He had to protest about *something* or go under for ever. And he must have known that, politically, he hadn't a hope of being what she wanted him to be. Possibly he felt that Louisa knew this, and accepted it, and was content that he should be no more than the prop of her own designs, with this expensive house the base of her campaigns.

He didn't remain in Parliament for long after this. There was a prospective Labour candidate in the constituency which James represented, a young ambitious lawyer with a clever tongue, who in his speeches during the next winter exploited James' presence at the shooting-party. He made great and rather scandalous play with some of the people who had been there, the way in which they had made their money and now lived their lives; and after each point he would add: "Let your member from the backwoods answer that." Birds of a feather, he said, flocked together; and he asked his hearers to consider what plans for the good of the people had been discussed over the meagre meals that followed the counting of the bag each day.

All these questions were hurled at poor James when he spoke in the constituency, and questions, especially crude personal ones, were what he loathed and could never deal with. A *claque* pursued him from meeting to meeting and made his life hell. It was not without relief, I imagine, that he informed the Committee of his local Liberal Association that he would not seek re-election, and he left Parliament for ever when Asquith succeeded Campbell-Bannerman as Prime Minister in April of 1908.

15

However, while I was visiting Louisa in Brook Street this was some way ahead and James was enjoying himself, one hoped, with the shooting-party. Sir Christopher Onslow-Purley continued to call for Louisa, and I continued to ramble about the autumnal streets of London. I discovered new things every day that I should want to show Augusta, and every evening I wrote to her. I occasionally persuaded Louisa to go with me to a theatre, but, as a rule, she spent the evenings in her own room. Her correspondence was immense. Sometimes it seemed to me that there was small difference between her life now and that which she had lived with Vincent Wheatstone, except that she was living it in charming surroundings and had the boredom of her days (though I don't suppose it was boredom to her) broken up by Sir Christopher's visits. A letter from James came every morning. When she had read it she would hand it across the table to me. There was nothing that she needed to keep to herself. The letters were about happenings. Lovers' letters rarely are: they are about emotions. I know, because I have received them and written them, but only in imagination when Charles Lester was alive. And I am always prepared to accept as my guide what happens in imagination, which Wordsworth defined as "absolute power and clearest insight." James' letters were bored, and always ended mechanically "Love to you and Maria."

It was after we had both flicked our eyes across one of them, which was all they needed, that Louisa said: "I shall have to be looking round soon for someone to take the lease of this house off my hands."

"But why?" She looked so heavy in mood that I tried to lighten the moment. "It's such an attractive free lodging for me and Augusta when we visit town. We could never forgive you."

"The trouble is," she said, "that I shall be no more than a visitor myself before long. I shan't need a place like this."

I waited for the explanation that was bound to come. "There's a point beyond which you can't go," she said. "I've reached it with James."

I didn't need to be told that. The brief talk I had had with James when I rang him up on reading that Louisa had been taken to hospital had convinced me that he was tired of the life that he and Louisa were living. I said: "It was clumsy of me to come. I shouldn't have planted myself on you at such a moment."

"I wanted you," she assured me. "You were an odious little wretch when a child, but I could trust you." A faint smile passed over her face at the thought of days that now seemed almost pre-historic. "I wanted someone to talk to."

She talked. It was as saddening as listening to the talk of a disillusioned mother who had imagined her child to have qualities that she now saw had never existed. Her Derby winner was just managing to jog along between the shafts of a milk-cart, and would never do anything else. What was maddening Louisa was frustration. James had never, I imagine, been anything but her deputy sitting in Parliament. She would have liked to be sitting there herself, and, being prevented from doing it, had chosen James as her voice. It was perhaps harsh to say that she had chosen him as her ventriloquist's dummy, but, harsh or not, it was true. His failure left *her* without her platform, and I deeply sensed her inward rage.

The trouble had long been as clear as daylight, and now Louisa explained it to me. That was one of the things about her that made me want to throw a boot at her. She could never credit you with seeing what was there under your eyes. She was born to expound.

I let her go on, and she told me that she would always have plenty to do in London, but, if James gave up, nothing to justify entertaining in a house like that. She would take a flat. James, she presumed, would find something to do at Tregannock. So far as public work went, she doubted whether so much as a parish council sub-committee would see him again.

However, before James threw in his hand in the April of the next year Augusta and I managed two visits to London. We filled them with concerts and theatres and art galleries, saw all the things that tourists are told to see, had tea with James on the terrace of the House of Commons. That small social event ended with embarrassment for James. It was a mild spring afternoon, and Augusta was entranced. The gulls flying over the river; the tugs going by with tails of barges; Big Ben's four rich notes vibrating in the air; St Thomas' across the water and the sense of the town's immensity reaching behind it out to the Surrey hills, and reaching around us in all directions to a remote suburban dwindling into the countryside: all this seen and sensed for the first time by an imaginative child flushed her cheeks and brightened her eyes. Suddenly she got up and put her arms round James' neck and kissed him. "Oh, Uncle James," she said, "I didn't know your life was so wonderful."

A white-haired M.P., who had the unmistakable look of an experienced woman's man, laughed loudly. He called across: "How d'you do it, Polperro? I've taken 'em to Romano's and given 'em all that's going and they don't do that to me. How d'you do it on a cup of cold tea and two stale buns?"

It was the sort of moment poor James could never meet. He hurried us away, blushing like a girl. Since he had to leave Parliament, it was, I thought, a charming exit.

CHAPTER TEN

I SAW with satisfaction that Augusta was becoming less dependent on Miles. She enjoyed the half-term visits we made to the school, and especially the school play in which, as term followed term, Miles had an increasingly important part. He was mad on the theatre, and during his holidays could not be kept out of the repertory theatre that Miss Horniman had founded in the old Gaiety. But during term-time Augusta did not go on composing the non-stop letter that began at their first parting. A letter once a week had to do.

I remember a winter afternoon in 1909, when Augusta was sixteen. They had been for a walk together, and we were taking tea. Miles asked: "Coming tonight?"

There was no need to ask where. It could be nothing but the Repertory Theatre. When he didn't go there, he spent his evenings in his bedroom, writing. I suspected that he was writing plays.

Augusta said: "No. I've one or two things to do."

He looked up sharply in surprise. That was the first time, so far as I know, that she hadn't followed his lead. He said: "It's Synge's *Shadow of the Glen*. A marvellous thing. I've just read it."

She said: "I'd love to see it some time. But I can't go tonight."

This was one of the moments that gave me satisfaction. Their taste for plays was precocious. They were hardly out of what would be, for most children, the pantomime stage. But I knew that anything by Synge would interest Augusta, and therefore I was pleased to find that she was strong enough to leave it, even if it meant doing without Miles' company.

Frank was attending a doctors' meeting in Manchester that night, and he and Miles went off together. When they were gone I went up to my room and got down upon my cushions with a book, expecting that Augusta would join me soon. She didn't, so I went to her room, tapped at the door and peeped in. "Are you coming up tonight?" I asked.

She was sitting at her table in the fireless room with a shawl round her shoulders. Her smile was as lovely as ever, but she said firmly: "Not tonight. I've given myself rather a tough job, and I want to be alone at it."

I knew I ought to go. It was one of our unwritten rules. But I was fool enough to believe that there was nothing I couldn't help her to do. I dallied at the door.

"You don't know any Latin, do you, darling?" she asked.

"Not a word beyond the obvious quotations, which I mispronounce."

"Well, there you are. I've started on Latin."

"What on earth for?"

She got up and said: "Well, I'd better come to your room after all. I'll explain things."

Wearing her shawl, she came up to my cold attic and sat on the floor alongside me. "I want to pass the London Matriculation," she said.

I was tempted to ask again: "What on earth for?" but held my tongue.

"It's just a matter of discipline," she said. "If I pass the matric. I may go on and take my B.A. Wouldn't that be lovely – Augusta Cumberledge, B.A.? It would show that I'd stuck at something, instead of just enjoying myself with books indiscriminately."

I felt left behind and unhappy. She sensed this and put her arm through mine. "I have to pass in five subjects," she said. "English and French, and thanks to you there'll be no trouble about those. History – and thanks to Mummy and my own reading I don't imagine that need worry me. Mathematics I shudder to think of, but something will have to be done about it. Then there's Latin. I'm starting that on my own. I expect Miles can give me a tip or two, and perhaps Daddy. Doctors do have to know a bit of dog Latin, I think. But in the long run I shall probably have to ask Daddy to get me a tutor."

2

The next morning she and Miles were off again as soon as breakfast was over. I guessed that Miles wanted to talk to her about Synge, and that she wanted to talk to him about her programme of study. She was, of course, emulating him, as usual. It was clear that Miles had at last found something that was going to be with him all his life. Writing, painting, music, religion: I had seen people dabbling in them all; but it was rarely that the thing dabbled in the people and at last got its claws into them and would not let them go. It had happened to Miles, and so Augusta wanted a master-motive, too.

When they were away into the sharp bite of that lovely morning just after Christmas, leaving Frank and me at the breakfast table, he said: "Have another cup."

I had learned by now that "Have another cup" meant that he had something to say. I handed him my coffee-cup. He filled it and his own and lit his pipe. In the few years I had been with him he had built up a good practice. He worked hard, but he was lean and tough. His professional success made him happy. His hair was greying, and he looked very handsome.

"Have you noticed anything going on around here?" he asked.

"Yes. I've noticed that I'm mere lumber. The children don't need me any more."

I should have loved a disclaimer, but he was never a flatterer. "That's true enough," he said. "But do you need them?"

"Yes."

"Enough to make you willing to go on as you've been doing – an unpaid dogsbody at everyone's beck and call?"

"Is that how you've seen me?"

The faint ironical smile came to his face. "You're dying to hear me say that you've been indispensable, that you've held the home together. You want to be flattered, don't you?"

"I've never had so much flattery that it does me harm."

"Well, you'll get no flattery from me. I'll merely say that you've done a good job."

We looked at one another in silence for a moment, and then he said: "I'm not saying only that you've made the children love you, which is what they needed – especially Augusta. I'm saying that, even though they may not now need you as they did at the beginning, you may need them. So don't go – unless you want to."

I said frankly: "I should hate to go. I've had too much experience of moving on and leaving my heart behind me. I don't want to do it again."

"All right, then. Now tell me something about Augusta. She asked me to buy her the best Latin primer I knew of. 'Something that even a fool like me can understand,' she said. What's she up to?"

I told him.

"How's her French?"

"She reads it easily and, what's more to the point, with pleasure, and she speaks it well enough. The same goes for Italian."

"Good. But I wish she'd asked for music and dancing instead of Latin and mathematics."

"So do I. But I don't think we should thwart her."

"No. What about Miles?"

"He's all right. He has genius."

"What do you mean by that?"

"Well, briefly, that he can't help himself. Something's got hold of him and won't let him go."

He gave me the look of a handsome inquisitor. "That won't do. That won't do at all. Genius is like God. Genius may *be* God for all I know. A bit of God, anyway. And God helps those who help themselves."

This rather startled me, and I waited for him to go on.

"Nobody is a born actor or a born anything else. Born with possibilities – yes. But this thing you call genius needs a devil of a lot of encouragement and coaxing. It'll only work with you if you work with it. If you don't, it soon pushes off. If a man poses as an artist, I like to have a look in his pocket and see if it contains a sketchbook that he's always squiggling into."

I had a vision of Gerald as I came upon him in the *Grande Place* at Montreuil, leaning against a tree, sketching even in the midst of his life in ruins.

Frank said: "I've been impressed by Miles in the school plays, though that's not much to go on. A lot of boys like dressing-up and declaiming. They grow out of it. I'm more impressed by his passion for watching actors and reading plays. But his voice is hopeless."

I was surprised at this. I thought Miles' voice good. Inconsequently, as it seemed, Frank said: "Would you like me to take you out tonight? We've not been out to dinner since you came to Manchester."

That was true, and I was pleased to find that I could accept that offer unemotionally.

We had an early dinner in Manchester and then Frank called a cab. "I want you to come and hear a chap named Raybould," he said. "He does a good deal of public reading. He's reading the *Christmas Carol* tonight."

We listened to Mr Raybould reading in a Wesleyan chapel not far from our own suburb. He was a middle-aged man who had never learned the first thing about acting. He just sat there and read. When he was well under way Frank whispered: "Listen with your eyes shut." I shut my eyes, and the place was peopled. The people lived and moved, laughed and cried, roared and whispered in a silence that was absolute.

We walked home: there wasn't far to go. "I wanted you to hear," Frank said, "what the human voice can do. Raybould is a professional teacher of elocution. I shall see whether he'd care to take Miles on."

I saw now what he was getting at. Miles had a good voice, but it was always the same voice: it was Miles' voice. The school plays were ambitious. I had seen him as Lear, mad as a hatter, and as Prospero uttering ripe wisdom, and in voice there was little enough to choose between them. Before he went back to school at the end of that Christmas holiday Mr Raybould had begun at work on him, and Augusta was going out on three evenings a week to study Latin with a woman who, I should have thought, had enough of it in the daytime, for she taught Latin among other things in a girls' high school in the town. She was a frail, anaemic spinster living not far from us, and Frank had professionally attended her. She seemed to be fond of him. "The worst of it is," he said to me, "that I daren't tell her what she really needs. Holiday visits to the ruins of the Colosseum and such like places are all very well in their way. But a woman needs more than that."

"We'd better take care, then," I said, "that Augusta doesn't develop into something like poor Miss Vesey or me."

I'd never seen Frank blush, and he didn't exactly blush then. But he looked disconcerted. "I beg your pardon," he said.

3

In May of the next year, 1909, I was thirty-three. Augusta, at sixteen, was no longer mine. She could even infuriate me now and then by quoting Miss Vesey's opinion against something I had said. And she was beginning to have opinions of her own which she would express against both of us. I gathered that they did more than sit down and apply themselves to Latin. They seemed to discuss everything on earth, as Augusta and I had once done. Young Tom Elthorne, who was a little older than Miles, had already left school and was in his first year at Manchester University. This young man, his spectacles more thickly pebbled than ever, his fingers stained with ink and chemicals, his black lank hair looking as though he used it as a pen-wiper, was the cause of the first sharp words between us. Augusta was at Miss Vesey's. Her lesson ended at nine, and as it was a pleasant evening and I was tired of writing my journal and my letters, I decided to go out and take a mouthful of fresh air and walk towards Miss Vesey's to meet the child.

I turned left at the end of our street and went past the Cock Inn. Then there is a long wall over which that night the beech trees in their loveliest spring green were drooping their branches. It was dusk: a star or two had appeared, and bats were flittering over the road. Beyond this long wall were a few houses set well back with gardens in front of them. Miss Vesey lodged in one of them. The style of those houses always pleased me, and I crossed the road so as to look at them from the other side, which gave a bit of perspective.

Well, I stood there, waiting to see the front door open and Augusta come out. I had never gone to meet her before. I had brought with me the letters I had written, but suddenly I knew that it was not in order to post them that I had come. It was to meet Augusta, to take her arm, to walk home with her through the bat-light full of the smell of young leaves, and to feel again in its full surge that reaching out of her young heart, needing me. I told myself this, even while knowing that it was my heart that was reaching out, that my need must grow more and more, and hers less and less.

As I lingered there feeling guilty in the presence of these emotions, I stepped within the shadow of a large open gate that belonged to a garden on my side of the street. I didn't want her to see that I was waiting. It might embarrass her with a sense of being supervised. I would give her a start; then overtake her as though by chance.

At last the door opened and Augusta and Miss Vesey appeared in the tall oblong of light. They stood talking for a moment. Then Miss Vesey put her arm through Augusta's and they began to walk down towards the garden gate. It is a long narrow garden. They seemed to be walking and walking and walking, and I felt sick to the heart. I was thinking of Frank's words about the void of Miss Vesey's life. "A woman needs more than that." "My God!" I thought, "she's not going to have it at my expense!" And while thinking it I knew what nonsense it was, because there was nothing I could do.

Miss Vesey turned back towards the front door, and Augusta went towards our street. Now was the time to overtake her, but my heart was beating so erratically that I stood still for a time in the shadow. And at that moment Tom Elthorne appeared. Just where the row of houses ends there is a lane leading up from the banks of the Mersey. Tom might well have been taking a walk and have arrived by chance. I couldn't believe that it was so. I told myself that he knew when Augusta's lesson ended, and there he was – perhaps with her collusion. In any case, seeing her, he hurried and came up with her, and they walked on together. There was no question of joining them now. I let them go, walked on to the Didsbury post office, and dropped my letters in the box. I went home slowly, feeling as lonely as Crusoe, as feeble as if I were a hundred years old. When I reached our gate in Kingsley Avenue she and Tom were standing there talking. He waved a hand to me and moved off towards his own house.

My commonsense said to me: "Now leave it alone. Leave it alone." All the rest of me said to Augusta: "That boy gets scruffier and scruffier."

There must have been something odd and strained about my appearance and voice, for Augusta looked at me intently. "I expect it's just a phase," she said.

"It's a phase I don't like."

At that, her blue eyes opened wide in surprise. "Really, Aunt Maria!" she said.

She said the words with such adult emphasis that I felt humbled, put in my place. She was taller than I.

"How can it concern you?" she asked. "Tom is a very clever person. He's promised to help me with mathematics."

Frank came along on his bicycle. "What's this I hear?" he asked. "Who's going to help you with mathematics?"

"Tom Elthorne," she said.

He laughed as though it were a matter of no concern. "Rather him than me," he said. "Poor Tom!"

I felt a fool, and a sick fool at that. I went in, and straight to bed.

4

At breakfast the next morning Augusta said to her father: "What have you done to Miss Vesey, Daddy?" There was a dance of mischief in her eyes.

Frank put down *The Manchester Guardian* and looked with obvious admiration at his handsome child. I had never been much of a lady's maid to her. Now she was taking the job on for herself. Her hair was shining. She was dressing herself with care. I was morbid enough to imagine that Frank was comparing her with Miss Vesey and with other women who needed what they weren't getting.

"Miss Vesey?" he said. "I'm afraid I'm doing nothing. And what is more," he added with mock severity, "a doctor doesn't discuss his patients even with his favourite human being."

She got up with a lithe movement and put her arms round his neck. "Oh, Daddy," she said, "am I really that?"

He discouraged the emotional response. He kissed her briefly and said: "Yes – at the moment. But don't presume on it. I have some affection for Miles and a soft spot in my heart for your Aunt Maria."

"Well, of course," she conceded. "One takes that for granted."

"You are a stupid child," he said, trying unsuccessfully to quench the beam of affection in his eye. "As you grow up you will learn that nothing can be taken for granted." I am sure that his quick intuition, one of the qualities that made him a good doctor, had divined the tension between me and Augusta last night. "Why should your Aunt Maria take your affection for granted?"

She looked at me, but before she could speak he intervened. "Now what's all this about Miss Vesey?"

"I mustn't discuss her with her doctor," she said.

"Do you know that Pope means papa? Very well then. I am your Papa. I grant you my Papal dispensation. You may speak to me about Miss Vesey."

She tried to brush it off. "Oh, it's nothing. She fusses about me, that's all. She says it's a shame your children haven't a mother."

He tried to keep it light. "Perhaps she bestows a maternal kiss upon you now and then?"

"She tried to last night, but I managed to dodge it. And she wants me to go to tea with her next Saturday. Should I?"

"Do you want to?"

"Not particularly. I don't mind one way or the other."

"Then go by all means."

A letter had come for her from Miles. She went off to read it, as she liked to do, privately in her own room.

Frank took up the coffee-pot. "Have another cup, Maria?"

I sipped the coffee as he looked at me musingly for a moment. "What do you make of all that?" he asked.

I was still smarting from last night. "Should I discuss your patient and your favourite human being?"

He looked at me sternly, and that thin Spanish face could go very stern. "I know," he said, "that Augusta is finding interests outside what you can provide. What do you want – a homely parable about the young bird finding its wings and the old bird left behind feeling glad about a job well done but now ended? Or have you the sense to see that for yourself?"

I said: "It's happened a bit suddenly for me."

"It does," he said. "You came when she was a girl, and girl into young woman happens very quickly – far more quickly as a rule than boy into young man."

"Are you wise to let her go to that woman next Saturday?"

"No harm will come of it, seeing that she doesn't care whether she goes or not. If she had wanted to go, I think I could have found some means of stopping it without hurt feelings on either side. By the way, it's not very kind of you to call Miss Vesey *that woman*. It's easy to laugh at her, but I'd like to be excused from joining in the laughter."

Every word was right and reasonable, and that did not prevent me from feeling as miserable as sin.

"It's rather a long time," Frank said, "since you visited your sister in London. Wasn't it understood that she would like you and Augusta to go and stay with her?"

It was, but things had changed since then. The lease of the Brook Street house was sold and James was no longer a Member of Parliament. Louisa had written to me of her top-floor flat in Kensington Square. She and James lived now as Lord and Lady Lavernock had lived (and, I supposed, still did). Their meetings were all but accidental. Louisa occasionally went to Tregannock. James occasionally came up from Tregannock and stayed in the Kensington flat.

I explained all this to Frank, who said: "If your sister will be kind enough to put up with the pair of you, I don't think there could be a better time for the visit. If Tom Elthorne has a passion for teaching mathematics, he can come in and teach me."

I looked at him with admiration. He missed nothing.

5

I wrote to Louisa that day. "My dear Maria," she answered. "By all means come and do what you can to cheer me up." I opened my eyes. Had Louisa ever before in all her life confessed that she needed me or anyone else?

I am beginning to understand women who become nuns in an enclosed order. I could become one myself if there were a chance of my promotion to Mother Superior in fairly quick time. As it is, I endure. It is abominably unfair that women can't stand as parliamentary candidates. The only alternative is to push forward the career of some man, and the hope that I shall be able to do that is extinguished. Consequently my days seem to have precious little reason. I still work with the women's suffrage people. I go every day to headquarters like a paid clerk and take my orders. It amounts to little more than what I once did for Father – the dullest sort of secretarial work, and in company that I detest. I always did dislike women, and there are times now when I loathe them. Those I meet here, anyway. There are a few saints who are willing also to be martyrs, but most of them are bossy hunters after any limelight that's going.

James came up for last weekend. He is flourishing and perfectly happy. He laughed as he told me how a few local farmers had called on him and asked him to become chairman of a committee they had formed to keep an eye on something or other. 'But never again,' he said to me. 'Not even the smallest beginning. You start with the parish pump, and before you know where you are you're considering the international implications of the Nile dams.'

He seems quite unaware of what he has done to me, and the odd thing is that I don't resent this. I asked him if he intended his retirement to be permanent or did he think of starting again some day. He said: 'For God's sake forget your politics. Get it into your head that not one person in ten cares tuppence about politics, and all that's happened to me is that I've discovered I belong with the nine. I've come up to London to spend a weekend with a woman – not with a Liberal, a Tory, a Suffragette or a Latter Day Saint. One more word about politics and I'll go and stay at my club.'

This, quite suddenly, was the James I had once known, and I found that, though I should have liked him to be something else, I preferred even a blusterer to the half-thing that I had made. So we spent the weekend on his terms, and ate out and went to theatres, and I was sorry when he went away.

Since we last met I've been down a few times to Tregannock and have seen Bella once. We didn't get on terribly well, but perhaps that was my fault, for, as you know, I'm not much of a getter-on with people. I liked her husband, though St Tudno has made him slothful. If he'd stayed in industrial towns he might have been something by now. But that was my fault. I jockeyed James into making that appointment. The children seem an average vicarage brood.

This child Augusta that you are bringing I recall as a young beauty. I liked her and her brother, but I hope that if ever they get down to Tregannock again they will be beyond the stage of provoking James' more childish proclivities. But perhaps he won't have much time for them. He's rushing through the estate – sacking this man, engaging that – with all the enthusiasm of an heir who has just inherited. He said to me: 'How much better it

337

would have been if you had become a farmer's wife instead of trying to turn me into a politician's husband.'

Did you see the report in the newspapers of the unveiling of a statue of Vincent Wheatstone in Whitechapel? The committee asked me to unveil it and 'say a few words.' Oh what words I could have spoken! But I declined, and I haven't seen the thing.

I told you, didn't I, that Meg Newman had gone to live in Manchester? Have you ever come across her?

Give this child Augusta my love, and say I welcome her. And the same to you, dear Maria.

Louisa.

Frank was gone on his rounds; Augusta was working in her room. I popped my head into the kitchen and told Mrs Deal that I would be out for an hour. Clutching my precious letter, I made my way through the fields to the Mersey banks. I wanted to sit down and think about it, for the letter was precious indeed. Its length, to begin with. I had never before received anything from Louisa but the briefest notes. She had never sent me her love, or called me, except in the formal address, dear Maria. It was full of an intense loneliness that seemed to cry to me from the heart. I forgave the crossness, the grumpy complaints. She was at a halt. She seemed to be surveying her whole life. Everyone came in: Father, Bella, James, Vincent Wheatstone, even Meg Newman. Above all, I rejoiced at a feeling that ran through and through it: a feeling of her devotion to James. It came in sparks and flashes, but it was there.

Even on a spring morning the Mersey water, flowing between high raised banks that control its sudden spites and rages, is grey and unlovely. But the banks are prinked with common little pleasing flowers, and in the fields that day the cows were munching the new grass and over them the clouds were blowing across a blue sky. It seemed to me a lovely and memorable morning, and I walked back to tell Augusta that Aunt Louisa sent her love and welcome.

6

Have you ever come across Meg Newman, Louisa asked. Meg had been that when I last saw her, but she had become Mrs Pickering and Mrs Carpenter. My memory of her was dim; years, and all that the years give and take, would have changed her looks. It seemed unlikely that I would have known her had I come casually upon her in the streets. However, I wanted to be able to tell Louisa something about her when we met, and so, the day before Augusta and I left for London, I rode my bicycle to the Manchester School of Art where, I had been told, Joe Carpenter was a teacher. I had seen the place before: a grim soot-blackened façade that depressed me unbearably, with hideous streets besetting it: a place, to judge from its outside, in which one might expect to hear the clash of iron keys, the echo of doors slamming far away in stony corridors, the tramp of warders' hobnailed boots. I leaned my bicycle against the wall, and from the carrier unstrapped the books that were to be my passport. I couldn't very well walk in, demand to see the principal, and ask for news of Joe Carpenter. So I had decided to sacrifice half-a-dozen of my volumes of reproductions.

I didn't find the inside of the place any more cheering than its outside, but was heartened by the principal's courteous reception, which was all the nicer because my fraudulent gift must have seemed to him almost contemptible. However, he accepted the books for the school library with every appearance of dealing with some such princely donor as Andrew Carnegie. He asked for my name, so that I might go on record as the giver; and when I got as far as Maria Legassick, c/o Dr Frank Cumberledge, he stopped writing, and said: "Dr Cumberledge . . . now where . . . I've had something to do with him, but I can't recall . . ."

There was a youth in the room who was, I suppose, some sort of secretary. He said: "It was that Carpenter affair, sir."

The principal said: "Yes, yes. Of course, that was it," and he said it with so much distaste that I was in a worse position than before, for I could not ask him to elaborate an affair that displeased him. Inadequate as a diplomatist, I thanked him, and he thanked me. I walked out into the corridor, feeling cheated. The secretary came out behind me, and I asked brazenly: "What was this Carpenter affair?"

"Rather unpleasant," he said. "I don't think it would interest you at all."

I decided to be bold. "But it would interest me very much. I came simply to find out what happened to Joe Carpenter and his wife. Those books were a blind."

He looked at me in astonishment, then broke into laughter. "Well," he said, "well! Forgive me, but you don't look the sort of person who would move in Joe Carpenter's orbit."

I don't suppose I did. The sunlight of Italy had long since drained out of my skin. I had recently taken to wearing spectacles; my hair was carelessly pulled into a bun, and my clothes were no dream from the Rue de la Paix. I knew all this, but I resented his making it clear that he knew it, too. I must have looked forlorn; for he said: "Sorry. Perhaps that was rudely put. I'm just going out to lunch. If you really want to know about Joe Carpenter, come and join me."

We went out together, and we might have been walking out of an office in Whitehall. He might, anyway. He was wearing a black felt hat, a grey tie, a black coat, striped trousers, and he twirled a rolled umbrella. He lacked only a despatch-case. It was a bright spring morning. The pigeons and sparrows were taking their midday meal on the cab-rank near the school. Manchester was doing its best, and it wasn't bad at that.

"How do you like our temple of art?" my companion asked; and, giving me no time to answer, went on: "Alas, unconscious of their doom the little victims play with their paints, pencils and pastels, industriously aiming to satisfy His Majesty's Inspectors. Worthy fellows, these inspectors, no doubt. Industrious gents. I wonder what Giotto would have made of them? However, there it is. The time is coming, Miss Legassick – by the way, where – or should it be whence? – did you get that enchanting name? – the time is coming when no one will be able to move one step forward on earth, in any direction, without having first satisfied His Majesty's Inspectors of this, that, and t'other. Armed with certificates, diplomas and degrees, we shall mount on paper steps, fulfilling satisfactorily our task of squashing out every spark of native insight and self-sufficient genius, which never yet in all this wide world gave one-tenth of a tuppenny damn for diplomas, degrees and what have you."

He spiked with the ferrule of his umbrella a rag of newspaper that the gay wind blew by, dropped it into a rubbish bin, and said: "These high thoughts are not my own. I'm quoting Joe Carpenter. He was, as they say, a one, but he misjudged his *milieu*. He should never have come to Manchester. Neither the Irwell nor the Irk has a Left Bank."

He was treating me with the beautiful consideration that a well-brought-up boy would show to his mother, and this annoyed me, so I asked: "Is that high thought yours or his?"

"His, alas. I'm merely Joe's record. Get me running and I play his tune."

We ate in an overcrowded, overheated little restaurant. He ordered for himself a half-pint of lager beer. "I presume," he said, "you take water?"

"Yes," I admitted, "on festive occasions."

He looked at me sharply, as though for the first time wondering whether I took him as seriously as he hoped; then assured me gravely: "The water here's very good: direct from Thirlmere. You shall have some. That reminds me: my name's Waterhouse."

"It's a small world," I said. "Now tell me about Joe Carpenter. Spare me the saga, for I already know a good deal about him. I know about his dog and about his wife. What happened to him? And, especially, what happened to his wife?"

"I saw her off at London Road station."

I sighed. "Tell it your own way."

"Well, Joe was extraordinarily good looking. No one realised quite how good looking till he came to the annual fancy dress ball. I don't know what he reckoned to be – just a god, I suppose. He was wearing nothing but a kind of leather skirt. Maybe he had some sort of pants on under that, but the girls were looking at him with no such proviso. He was gold all over. He'd rubbed gold-dust into his hair and beard and body. He shone. He was a grand sight, leaping about like an amorous buck."

"You were there?"

"Oh, yes, green with envy. I went as David Copperfield."

"Tell me about these girls who were looking at him."

"Well, they were *all* looking at him, but there were two or three in particular. I'd met 'em at Joe's loft. He and Meg lived in a large loft over a stable, not far from the school. Some of the girls used to drift in there to imbibe the true atmosphere as it blows about the heights of Montparnasse. Beer and Lancashire hot-pot and endless jaw about 'trends'. We all used to get a bit tight and sing *Vivent les Etudiants*. You could hear the shackles of convention dropping with a clatter to the floor all round us. Some of the girls arrived home a bit sozzled. There were one or two complaints and Joe had been warned that all this was not within the schedule as understood by His Majesty's Inspectors."

"However," I said, helping myself to a refill of Thirlmere, "it was within the schedule as understood by Joe Carpenter. It tallies with all I know of him."

"Oh, yes, harmless enough if it hadn't been for the girl from Oldham. Do you know Oldham?"

"No."

"You should. It has a railway station called Mumps. That is why we called this girl Mary Mumps. She was a handsome red-headed cotton-spinner, boiling over with red-hot blood. Figuratively speaking."

He ordered sago pudding and prunes, and his mind occupied itself for a moment with Mary Mumps and her red-hot blood. "Yes," he resumed. "Mary Mumps. She would have been all right if some Oldham scout hadn't discovered that she was an artist of genius. It was one of those discoveries never confirmed by competent artistic geographers. Joe used to laugh at her stuff, and once, in his loft, when he had been teasing her more cruelly than usual, she landed him a sock in the jaw that rocked him. She was wearing a green djibbah thing, and that and her red hair and blazing eyes made her look a lovely fury. Joe couldn't resist it. He hit her back, and then they were wrestling all over the floor. Meg went white. I believe she knew from that moment that it was all up. There was a tap in the loft. She drew a bucket of cold water and poured it over them as though they were a pair of fighting cats. At that, they got up, panting, and someone shouted ' Kiss and be friends.' They didn't need to be told twice. And was it a kiss! They clung together till Meg cracked Joe over the head with an umbrella. And so we came to the end of that perfect day and drifted off to our several abodes."

I said : "Shall we blue-pencil a chapter or two and come to the night when David Copperfield went to the ball?"

"Well, Mary Mumps was there, and *negligée* is an approximate description of her attire. She said she was Potiphar's Wife, but even that easy-going old heathen would have tied an extra sack round her. Young Copperfield, standing stone-cold in the wings, had a premonition that this was the night. There was a feeling of something stark about those two, and the trouble broke when Mary's fists came into action. She was always a bit too ready with them. Joe was dancing with what one might call the Second Favourite. She was a Naiad, which could be anything, but was in this case a drip of white clothes decorated with green weed. The Naiad was misguided enough to lay her cheek on Joe's naked golden shoulder. Miss Mumps' almost professional uppercut removed it therefrom; and then, in the language of the classics, all hell broke loose."

Mr Waterhouse was a rather sensational reporter. I doubt whether any considerable part of hell broke loose, but there was a row. A number of young men who wanted nothing more than a bit of dancing, and who realised that anything so undramatic was not likely while Joe was about, got hold of him, ran him out of the place, and threw him into the street. They told Mary Mumps and the Naiad that if they wished to be removed in the same way, they knew how to go about it. Meg was not at the dance: she was in bed with an attack of influenza. Mary Mumps went out after her hero, found him stunned and bloody, for his forehead had hit the kerbstone, and knelt down to lift his head upon her knee.

If this was not all hell, it was a sufficiently interesting sight to come on in a Manchester street: a gilded, leather-skirted, bearded giant who was seen in the light of a street-lamp to be quietly oozing blood upon the lap of a negligibly-dressed young woman. It caused Frank Cumberledge to stop and take a look. He assured Miss Mumps that there was nothing wrong with her friend that a wash, a bandage and a night's sleep wouldn't cure. Joe's loft was not far away, and they tottered off together.

David Copperfield had followed Mary Mumps into the street, and, with no further desire for the joys of the dance, he now started to walk home with Frank, for their ways lay together. That is how he knew the name of the doctor, who was walking back to Didsbury after a night at the theatre, and that is how the name of Frank Cumberledge came to be in the report which Mr Waterhouse was asked by his principal to draw up. For news of the affair got out, and this time it was considered that the school had better get on without the assistance of Mr Carpenter.

"For some days after that," Mr Waterhouse said, "he used to sit on a canvas seat outside the railings of that church near the school. On the pavement, he chalked 'Sacked by bourgeois morality. Starving,' and that damn' great broken-hearted dog of his used to sit by him, slobbering, and with a begging-cup round his neck instead of the usual brandy-barrel. After a time he disappeared, and I went along to see how Meg was getting on. I found her packing. She said that Joe and Mary Mumps had gone away together and that she was going, too. So I went to see her off at London Road station."

"Where did she go to?"

"I haven't an idea."

That evening I asked Frank if he remembered meeting a Mr Waterhouse. It took him some time. I had to supply a clue. "Oh, yes! A chap in fancy dress. He fastened on to me and walked my way. I never heard a man talk such bosh. It was a night when I stopped to have a look at two more-or-less drunks who'd been thrown out of a dance-hall."

That was all it meant to him. For me, I never saw or heard of Meg Newman again.

7

The visit to Louisa in Kensington in the summer of 1909 was altogether happy. Augusta forgot that she had wanted to be a learned woman, and neither Louisa nor I did anything to remind her. I'm afraid we spoiled her: we almost fought for her favours. The promise of her beauty was fulfilling itself before our eyes. We took her out to dine. We took her to theatres and concerts. Louisa provided her with a wardrobe. Suddenly she was no longer a girl. She was a woman.

Louisa gave up her work with the woman's suffrage people. Her lameness was becoming worse, and even when moving about her flat she had to use a stick. She made this her excuse for retiring into a private life; but I think it *was* an excuse, not a reason. If James had not turned renegade, nothing would have prevented her from working at his side. As it was, she accepted the fact. She no longer complained about James. If he wanted to be a farmer, let him be a farmer. She even, now and then, spoke with some enthusiasm of successful experiments on the Tregannock estate. But all the same, I could sense her feeling of loss. She had gambled on making James what it was not in his nature to be, and the gamble hadn't come off. Essentially, James was a peasant – a wealthy one, it is true, but a peasant none the less.

I was surprised that she didn't return to Tregannock, settle down, and have done with it. We had become closer together than I had ever expected we should, and I was bold enough to ask her why she remained in London. She said with a smile: "Because I like living in London and visiting Cornwall. James likes living in Cornwall and visiting London. We get on better that way. It would be another matter if either of us was interested in adultery. We're not, and the thing works."

Nevertheless, I had the sense of her lingering on the field of a lost battle, still ruminating on the little that had been necessary to turn the tide. It was into this void in her life that Augusta stepped: the child she had watched playing at Indians on the lake, with mud on her face and feathers in her hair, now mysteriously a woman, or at any rate quivering like a compass-needle, turned one day to childhood and the next swinging towards a woman's unexplored enticements.

Augusta, I think, loved the aunt she found in Kensington as she had not loved the Louisa of that brief meeting at Tregannock. She took to her from the moment we climbed the stairs, carrying our suitcases, and found Louisa sitting at her tea table , with the spirit-lamp lit under the silver kettle and the muffins under their silver cover; and Louisa got up creakily, leaned on her stick, and, ignoring me, said: "Well, I hoped for something good, but not quite this . . ."

I can see them now, Augusta still holding her suitcase, Louisa dropping her stick so that she could put a hand on each of the child's shoulders; and, holding her away, she looked into her chicory-blue eyes, and her own suddenly became moist. "Well, well," she said. "I hope you're good at putting up with an old woman."

I suppose she was an old woman to Augusta. She was forty-six, and from the time when she was only two years older than Augusta was now she had lived strenuously. Her head and her emotions had been fully engaged. Her beauty was gone, and what had taken its place I find hard to describe unless I call it valour. My own growing love for her was tinged with pity, but I knew her well enough to keep this out of sight.

In any case, I was a fine one to be pitying Louisa! She had known fulfilments. I had known nothing but a drifting of days. My tale was of casual attachments: to Jane Lavernock, to the old woman in Italy, to Frank Cumberledge. Anything deeper or more subtle seemed doomed to die at my touch.

Well, two such women – and Augusta! There was so much that we had to spare and we poured it out, almost competitively, upon her.

Hitherto, my relationship with her, after the few romantic weeks in St Tudno, had been circumscribed by the demands of Frank's home. Now she was all mine, except insofar as she was Louisa's.

We stayed in London for three months. James came up about once a month and joined the courtiers around the young queen. He brought his car with him, and that gave us mobility, especially in view of Louisa's lameness. It was touching to see his devotion both to Louisa and the child. With Louisa, he had what I sensed as a feeling of guilt. She had become reconciled to his defection and never allowed her disappointment to appear. But I am sure he felt that he had failed her. He had let her down with his first luckless marriage; then he had let down her ambition for him; and, though he never spoke of any of this, he treated her with a courtesy and a shy affection that I thought beautiful. It was his way of saying things that his tongue could not speak. When his car was at the door he would say to me and Augusta: "Now, you two, run down. I'll bring Louisa." And very tenderly he would give her his arm. It looked as though for two pins he would take her up and carry her, kissing her on the way. Then he would install her — I feel install is the word: it was so ceremonious — he would install her and Augusta in the car, with cushions behind their backs and footstools under their feet; and when that was done, the two precious packets bestowed, he would turn to me and say: "Hop in, Maria." And I would hop in with no ceremony at all, and off we would go. Motorcars had passed the stage I had known with Lady Jane, and James was an excellent driver. He would grin with pleasure and shout to Augusta: "Better than the drive to Truro in the old Polperro coach — eh?" And, so sensitive had I become to the dear fellow's reactions, I could almost feel, as I sat beside him at the wheel, his body stiffen and his mind go agape as he wondered whether he had said the wrong thing again, whether the old Polperro coach had better lie in the dust with all the wreckage of lives that had followed its appearance at the vicarage on the night of the Tregannock ball.

He took us out to picnic on the Surrey heaths. He took us to race meetings and to Henley. He succeeded in making all his visits memorable; and once I heard Augusta say to him: "Thank you, Uncle James. You are very kind to me and Aunt Louisa."

He looked really surprised. "Kind?" he said in his rather raucous voice. "What d'you mean – kind? I'm not fit to lick the boots of either of you."

I have noticed that – with me at any rate – the news and the weather have a way of chiming. It was on a wet morning that a letter from Miles stirred an uneasiness in my mind. The more so because, on the day before, Augusta had said: "I'm neglecting Daddy shamefully. It's a week since I wrote to him. I'm becoming a mere Hedonist." She was beginning to experiment with words.

I reassured her. Frank knew that she was in good hands, and that he had no reason to worry. He wouldn't want her to spend her time on him. But she wasn't satisfied. "When do we go back?" she asked. "Miles tells me that he's going to spend his summer holidays with a boy who lives in Yorkshire. It's all fixed. The parents have agreed."

Here it was, all over again! I thought of my own sad childish heart when Roger, with Hugo or some other friend, looked in briefly and then disappeared.

"At all events," Augusta said, putting a good face on it, "that'll mean that Daddy and I can go off on a good holiday together. I'll have him to myself."

And now, in the grey drizzle of the next morning, here was a letter from Miles. He mentioned this holiday engagement – "Mellerby's father's an actor. I expect you've heard of him? I must say that attracts me enormously" – and then he went on: "Half-term has come and gone once more, and I found it rather dreary. We licked the old boys as usual at cricket, and I had a decent part in *A Midsummer Night's Dream;* but Daddy didn't come alone, and I thought the woman he brought with him no end of a bore. She's a Mrs Burnsall, dressed all in blue, with a grey parasol. When we went out to lunch at the farm as usual, she came with us, and she came on all our walks. She cheered me like mad during the play. It was most embarrassing, and the chaps chipped me about it. I asked Daddy if we couldn't shake her off for an hour or two, to have some of our good old talks, and he laughed as though the idea was absurd. She was around till the very end, and they travelled back to Manchester together."

Mrs Burnsall swam on my vision, dressed all in blue, with a grey parasol. I felt a disturbance of spirit so deep that I didn't mention the matter even to Louisa. Certainly not to Augusta, who took advantage of the rainy morning to write a long letter to her father.

8

There was nothing much wrong with Fanny Burnsall. It was difficult for me to be impartial, but on the whole I liked her. For the children, it was not difficult: it was impossible. I couldn't blame Frank for wanting to marry again: he was clearly in love with the woman – a childless widow, ten years younger than he was, I should think, and well-to-do. She was a pretty, well-meaning creature, rather clinging, and full of good intentions towards the children.

Whether she and Frank could have handled the affair better I don't know. It's so easy to say how other people ought to be managing their lives at the very moment that we're making a mess of our own. Yes, we're all very, very good at that. What they did was this. As soon as Miles was gone away to Yorkshire with young Mellerby, they were married in a registry office and went off to Scotland for a fortnight. Augusta and I were then still with Louisa. Frank wrote to me from Kingussie and told me of the marriage.

I don't know, (he said) whether Miles had any idea of what was in the wind. I told him nothing before he went away. Augusta is in the dark, too. Fanny and I thought the best thing in the long run would be to face them both with the accomplished fact. Will you be so kind then as to bring Augusta home a week next Saturday? We shall be back then, and I imagine that Miles won't be delaying much longer than that in Yorkshire. Together, I'm sure they'll be able to adjust themselves to the new situation and see how satisfactory it is all round. I've now written to Miles and told him how things are, but please say nothing to Augusta. She might brood, whereas, coming face to face with Fanny, she can hardly fail to realise that she has a friend whom she may come to love.

Of course, dear Maria, you must be considered, too. Fanny and I have talked the matter over a good deal, and I've no doubt that when we meet we shall be able to come to a satisfactory arrangement.

We've been tramping the moors. The country up here is fine and
hard . . .

and so on, with a sort of Viking lyricism. He was on top of the world.
I wasn't.

"You must have some clothes fit to travel in," Louisa had said to
Augusta; and they had gone off in a cab to Bond Street. With Louisa,
only Bond Street was good enough for Augusta. That was something I
couldn't do. I was the poor dependent, the hanger-on, blessed with
five pounds a week out of the charity of a man I scarcely knew. A
loathsome mood of self-pity took hold of me. I was aware of it, and I
hugged it, and I wandered off to Kensington Gardens.

There was the first smell of autumn in the air. A few brown leaves
were on the trees; and, though the sky was blue, I eagerly seized upon
these premonitions of decay and wore them like a garment. I sat there
watching the children sail their boats and the nannies and the
perambulators and the well-dressed little boys and girls, going
through the afternoon routine of their ordered lives and I grieved.

"Fanny and I have talked the matter over a good deal, and I've no
doubt we shall be able to come to a satisfactory arrangement."

That's what I was: something for a happy married pair to discuss –
as they might discuss whether or not to keep a dog that was about the
place they were to inhabit. And that, I said morosely, is how it always
has been. I remembered how I had gone off with Jane Lavernock
when Bella's arrival at the vicarage had made my remaining
unthinkable; and how, when I had returned from Italy, Bella could
hardly disguise her eagerness to see me move on to Manchester. For
two pins, I told myself, I'd put Augusta on the train and let them all
make what they could of the situation when she arrived.

Augusta! The very name pulled me up short. What happened to
Augusta was not a matter in which I could be unconcerned.

9

The weather worsened, and as the train bearing me and Augusta
towards Manchester drew near the city rain began to fall. This had no
effect on the child's spirits which were buoyant at the thought of being
near home.

At Central station we got into the local train that would take us out to Didsbury. About half an hour's journey, I calculated. I was cold with apprehension. Her radiance redoubled my fears.

"What a nuisance this boy Mellerby is!" she cried. "Why should Miles want to hang on there? He knows I'm due back today. It won't be the same without him. But there'll be Daddy."

She was so keyed up now for the meeting that I could have wept with frustration at Frank's command to say nothing to her about Mrs Burnsall. I was sure he was wrong. We stopped at Withington station. I looked through the streaming window, saw the few passengers alight, heard the slam of shutting doors. The train pulled out.

Augusta cried: "Next stop Didsbury!"

What would it be? Three minutes? If that. I could bear it no longer. "Augusta darling," I said. "You won't find your Daddy alone. He's married again. His wife will be waiting to meet you."

I didn't expect what happened. Perhaps, I had thought, she would cry out in anger. Perhaps she would look shocked, unbelieving. She was standing up to reach her suitcase down from the rack, and she swooned. She stood for a moment, her face turned towards me over her shoulder. Then her eyes closed, she swayed, and slumped down across my lap. The train stopped.

To leave the station on the side where I wished to be, you must cross a bridge, and at the bottom of the steps down from the bridge Frank was waiting for us. I noted with relief that he was alone. He saw the porter carrying the suitcases and me carrying Augusta. I am a reed, and I don't know how I did it. Perhaps because I didn't know I *was* doing it.

Frank asked: "What's up?"

"I think she's over-excited," I said. "She fainted."

He took her from my arms. "There's a cab waiting. Fanny'll be terribly upset. She stayed at home to have everything in order for making Augusta welcome."

It is no distance from the station to the house. Only the luggage had made a cab necessary. But there was time for Frank to say: "This is very odd. She's a remarkably strong girl and she's never fainted before."

Through the rain-blurred window of the cab I saw the open door, the lighted passage-way, the vague figure of the new woman. When the cab-door opened, the vagueness solidified into a fair, rather fussy-looking, rather over-dressed, rather ineffective creature.

"Oh, dear!" she cried. "Is anything wrong? Is Augusta unwell? I was waiting to receive her as a daughter."

I said to Frank: "Carry her straight up to her room and leave her to me."

He almost snarled: "I know my business, thank you." But he did as I asked, and I followed them up. Fanny made to come after me, but I said: "I think it would be a good idea if you stayed here."

She looked surprised, for I had said it almost as a command. She stepped into the dining room.

Frank laid Augusta on her bed, and then went down. He returned with a few bits and pieces and did all the orthodox things. He held *sal volatile* under her nose. He lifted her eyelids. He took her temperature, felt her pulse and sounded her with the stethoscope. He laid a hand on her forehead and looked at her earnestly; then pulled an eiderdown over her and went. At the door, his head beckoned me to follow. On the landing he said: "What's the game? She's shamming."

In a way, it should have been a relief to him. But he saw the significance of it, and he looked far more deeply disturbed than if she were indeed in a swoon. I was aware that he guessed I had told her.

I considered it. "Shamming?" I said. "Well, she is and she isn't. She couldn't have controlled a swoon, if it had really been one; and she couldn't control this piece of bluff. It was instinctive and instantaneous, and I should say that means it's far more dangerous than a passing swoon."

He looked at me with a half-mocking smile. "Quite a psychologist," he said. "Knows all about instinctive defence mechanism. And maybe you're right."

His wife had come out of the dining room and stood under the passage light, looking up at us. She made towards the stairs, and Frank signalled to her to remain where she was.

"Will you stay with her tonight?" he asked me.

"You'd have some trouble if you tried to stop me."

"All right, Dr Legassick. The case is in your hands."

He was trying to keep it light, but I could see he was upset.

Fanny called up: "Is there anything I can do, darling?"

"Yes; you can put some soup and toast on a tray and I'll bring it up to Maria. Would you like that?"

"Yes. And send up some coal and kindling. It's a filthy night and I might as well make myself comfortable."

I went back into the bedroom and Augusta looked as though she hadn't stirred. But I saw that she had. When I first came to live here in Manchester, she had had a photograph of her mother standing on her dressing table. After about a year it vanished. I went now to the dressing table to put my hair to rights, and there it was, back in place. I quietly put it face-down, with my hair-brush on top of it. I didn't want Frank to see that when he came in with the soup.

When I had eaten, and the curtains were drawn on the raw autumn night, and the fire was blazing, I sat down to read. Once or twice Augusta stirred on the bed, but I let her be. It was about nine o'clock when I put down my book and said: "I must get to bed now. It's been a tiring day. Shall I see you into bed before I go?"

She sat up. She hadn't shed a tear, but she was deathly pale. "Sleep here," she said. "Sleep with me."

She got off the bed and undressed and put on her night things. "Do you remember the night when Miles filled our tent with bracken and we slept on it together? It was soon after Mother died."

The photograph, and now the name. I chattered about that time in Cornwall – about everything except Mother. That ghost mustn't walk again. She was sitting up in bed, with her knees to her chin, gazing at the wall, and I hoped she was seeing what I was talking about, not slipping back and back. "Miles was with us then," she said.

"Miles will soon be back," I assured her. "And for what it's worth I'm here. Make room on the bracken."

She put her arms round me and cried for a time; than slept with a little bubbling snore that reminded me of Bella's.

When she got up the next morning she seemed well in body and spirit. She was a bit late coming down. I was eating breakfast with Frank and Fanny when she appeared, apologised to Fanny for not having been able to receive her greetings the night before, and then tucked into a hearty breakfast as though this morning were no different from any other.

I was alarmed by all this, and I watched Fanny with apprehension. Leave her alone, for heaven's sake, I prayed, trying to reach the message out into Fanny's mind. It was no good. She fussed. She coo'd. She was determined to fill a mother's place. She got up and put her arms round the child and kissed her. Was this breakfast all right? Was there anything else that Augusta preferred? Augusta said: "Thank you. I am all right."

Fanny burst out: "Now *that's* something we shall have to get settled! 'Thank you.' Thank you what? It would seem a bit odd if you called me Fanny. What do you think, Frank darling? Should she call me Mother?"

Frank had no ready answer. He looked from one to another of them, and I knew he was not deceived by Augusta's calm bearing. She answered for him. "Can't we leave that alone for the moment?" she asked, even managing a smile as she said it. "There are things that settle themselves. Like naming a cat."

She had little more to say, and as soon as breakfast was ended she went back to her room.

Fanny cried enthusiastically: "She's a darling! We shall soon be all in all to one another. And how beautifully she dresses!" Clothes meant a lot to Fanny. She went out, leaving me and Frank alone.

"Another cup, Maria?"

"No, thank you, Frank. Maria is not advising on this. Augusta is right. There are things that settle themselves."

I slept in my own room that night after a trying day in which Augusta politely but coldly endured Fanny's unceasing seductions. I was awakened the next morning by Frank banging on my door. "Get up," he said. "Augusta's vanished."

10

Frank knew from Augusta's letters that she liked her Aunt Louisa and had enjoyed being with her. His first thought was that Augusta had returned to London. He rang up Louisa, who promised to let him know if the child appeared. But there was no news from Louisa that day.

The next day I left the house to take a walk, which I hoped would calm the restlessness of my mind. I wasn't alarmed. I knew Augusta well enough to believe that, whatever she was up to, she would do nothing foolish or irreparable. I ran into Tom Elthorne, coming out of his father's house, and he said: "Hallo Miss Legassick. Any news of Augusta?"

353

I said to him sharply: "Why? What news should there be?"

He blushed all over his ugly pleasing face, pushed a hand through his tangled hair, and said: "Oh, Lord! What a fool I am! I've given it away!"

"Had I better come in and have a talk with you?"

"I suppose you'd better," he conceded. "But the place is in an awful mess. I've been holidaying with my father, but I came home early to do a bit of work in my lab. The woman's on holiday, too. I've been living on buns and tea."

He took me into a shambles of a kitchen. I made coffee and he produced a tin of biscuits. He lit a pipe and tried to be adult. "Now look," he said. "This is dead secret. I promised Augusta to say nothing to anyone, but I *do* think *you* ought to know."

"I'd left something cooking in the lab.," he said, "and then went for a stroll to cool my burning brow. I was pretty well fagged out, and it was cheering to meet Augusta. I didn't know she was back."

They met on one of those paths that thread the Mersey meadows towards Northenden, and she asked him if he could lend her five pounds. "I've never been worth that in my life," he said, "but I knew where the old man kept a bit of spare cash."

She didn't want to tell him why she needed the money, but he said he wouldn't give it to her unless she did. Then she told him about Miles staying with the Mellerbys in Yorkshire and said she wanted to join him.

"Well, that seemed all right to me, so we cooked up a schedule. I gave her the front door key, and before anyone was stirring yesterday morning she nipped in here with a suitcase. We had a grand day in the lab. I think she was a bit impressed with what I was doing. The scheme was that she should travel to York that night and that Miles should meet her. She wrote a telegram giving him the time of the train he was to meet, and I biked into town to put it on in the G.P.O. At the same time I left her suitcase in the station luggage room. That way, you see," he said, looking like a master of cunning devices, "we dodged any snoopers in the local office."

"And you saw her off last night?"

"Oh, yes. Miles will have met her hours ago."

So while we had been torturing our minds as to whether we should inform the police this childish ruse had defeated us all.

"Why she wants to go just because there's a new Mum baffles me," Tom said sagely. "Why, good lord! The old man could fill up this place with a seraglio of Circassian slaves for all I'd care. I can always escape into the lab."

I fumbled in my bag and managed to assemble five pounds. "Talking of the old man," I said severely, "you'd better put this where he keeps his bit of spare cash."

Tom accepted the money coolly. "Thanks," he said. "That brings the experiment to a neat end."

He invited me to visit the lab., and, though what happens in labs is as mysterious to me as Merlin's doings were to Guinevere, I consented. I owed him that much. It was a different lab. from the old shed where he had played at making fireworks. Even I could see that it was a place where serious things could be done, and I pretended to understand more than I did. "I'm having a shot this year for the Boothby medal and scholarship," he said. "Gosh! If that came off it would be something!"

"I hope it will, Tom," I said sincerely.

"This interruption of Augusta's was a bit of a bore," he said. "Still, she seemed pleased. I'd have turfed anyone else out pretty quick. You're not annoyed with me?"

"Well, the resistance had to break somehow. Perhaps you found the right solvent."

He looked at me with his cheeky grin. "We'll make a chemist of you yet," he said.

I didn't want to have Frank, or, worse still, Fanny, rushing to York. When I got back from my walk at lunch time I found them both overwrought. So, it seemed, was Louisa. She had rung up twice during the morning. "She sounds absolutely panicked," Frank said.

We sat down to the meal. Fanny said, sobbing: "I can't eat a mouthful. It would choke me."

Nevertheless, she ate as much as I did. Frank, I could see, was the one who was really suffering.

I said: "I wish you'd both realise that Augusta is no fool. There's nothing for you to worry about. I mean so far as her safety goes. I know where she is."

Fanny cried desperately: "Oh, where? Where?" and Frank, who knew me better, said: "That's all right then. What do we do now?"

"The question is: what does *she* want to do now? I shall join her and find out."

Fanny pressed me to say what I had discovered, but I would not. After lunch I went again to Tom Elthorne's and from there telephoned to Louisa. I gave her the story, and left her tranquil. I knew the Mellerbys' address from Miles' letters. I wrote to him and told him what train I should be on tomorrow. Would he please meet me at York? I hoped he wouldn't get tired of meeting runaway females at York.

I spent the rest of the day packing all my personal things into a couple of suitcases. Nothing was left except my books, and it would be easy enough for Frank to have them sent after me once I had found a new perch. For I had a feeling that I would not see Kingsley Avenue again. I was once more on the march. It seemed my fate.

CHAPTER ELEVEN

I HAD never been further North than Manchester, and when I stepped out of the train at York and sniffed the air of the grave grey city I felt as though I had advanced a month into the year. There was a sharp September smell that alerted the senses and seemed to awaken the wits.

Miles came running down the long platform towards me. Following him, not running but advancing with a lounging grace, was a tall, dark handsome boy whom I guessed to be Hilary Mellerby.

I knew this boy's father – that is, as a member of a theatre audience I knew him. I had seen him act. What I learned later about the family was this. The Mellerbys had lived for centuries on an estate in the plain of York. They had a rip-roaring spendthrift reputation until the time of Mr Mellerby's father. He, uncharacteristically, was a prudent man. But his prudence came too late. Gambling, and then rash speculation in the hope of recouping the gambling losses, had been going on for too long. He sold most of the estate, including the mansion, and settled in the dower house, little more than a "gentleman farmer". His son took to the stage and did well. This was Hilary's father, Haydon Mellerby. When his father died Haydon was well-established and prosperous, married to an actress whose line on the stage reached back almost as far as Haydon's did on the land. It was Haydon who cut with the land altogether, though he could never forget the family's long association with it. He retained the dower house, that was known simply as Mellerbys, and a few acres; and this was his refuge when his life now and then gave him release. His sister Millicent, who had all her father's prudence and circumspection, and who boasted that she had never seen a play in her life, adored him and managed his house. His wife was dead. Haydon was always decrying his folly in having a house so far from London and saying that he must sell up and find something in the Home Counties. But the devil of it was, he said, that if he did he would become a mere actor, and he could think of nothing more humiliating than that. Mellerbys, he said, kept his roots in the dung, and that was worth a lot of money.

2

All this was the aura of the black-curled boy who loped behind Miles, who was presented, and, as he gave me a long hand, smiled from dark-blue eyes. Miles had grown stocky. Side by side, they were like a bulldog and a greyhound. Hilary said: "Father would like you to stay at Mellerbys, if you would care to, Miss Legassick. A train leaves here at half-past two. I think it would be a good idea if we had lunch here, don't you?"

Each of them took up one of my suitcases, which were dumped in the luggage office, and I walked out with them to find myself face-to-face with the ramparts and noble walls of the city. The antique gates through which the centuries had poured, placidly or tumultuously, the minster, the bits and pieces of the past hotch-potched in with modern building: it was all lovely, and the sky was blue, and Augusta was not far away. But so far as she was concerned they were a pair of diplomats, giving nothing, and I did not mention her. We lunched in a dark alley whose shops and houses had upper storeys leaning familiarly together for the exchange of whispers. It was not till we were drinking our coffee that I asked: "How is Augusta?"

Miles said: "In the pink. She would have come to meet you, but she's learning her lines."

Hilary said: "We still have to find an aunt. Are you a quick study? It's little more than a walking-on part."

"What is a quick study?" I wanted to know; and Hilary said: "Someone who can learn a part quickly. The show goes on the night after tomorrow."

I must have looked rather dazed. He smiled and said: "Anybody who comes to Mellerbys needs to be adaptable. There's always some nonsense or other going on. Augusta is fitting in splendidly."

"You'd better wait till you get there," Miles advised me. "You'll see how things are. Now we ought to be moving, or we'll miss the train, and there's a rehearsal at four."

Burton Somers was the name of the fourth station we stopped at. I wondered why Burton Somers had ever bothered to give itself a railway station. It didn't look a place at which anyone would ever want to begin or end a journey. But while it was at it, it had given itself a very nice little station indeed. The railings on either side were painted white and against them rich crimson dahlias were blooming, and michaelmas daisies were beginning to open their flowers. An edging of white-washed stones kept them from intruding on to the platform, which looked as though it wouldn't matter if flowers were growing all over it down to the brink of the line. For the whole place was sound asleep, and the little square full of beast-pens outside the exit-gate was sound asleep, and so was the pub which you could almost hear snoring under the full-bosomed elms that kept the sun out of is eyes. The only thing awake was a youth, wearing an official-looking cap, sitting on a luggage trolley and reading a script. And you only realised that he was awake when he pushed the cap back in order to scratch his head over something that puzzled him. However, he saw with surprise that a train had come in, got up, and began to intone "Burton Somers, Burton Somers" in a voice which suggested that he would be startled indeed if Burton Somers meant anything to anyone. It began to mean something to me when I saw Augusta turning the corner beyond the pub, accompanied by a tall man. Hilary gave our tickets to the youth, who produced his script and asked "Wot's this 'ere word, Mr Hilary?" Hilary said: "Concatenation, Bill. Con-cat-e-na-tion." To me he said: "Bill's a butler. Everybody's someone. Father is ruthless."

This must be father now, with Augusta, within hailing distance. In his country clothes he was disconcerting, because I had seen him only once before, and then he was Hamlet. To find the Archbishop of Canterbury on a bookmaker's stand at Epsom would hardly have called for a swifter adjustment.

However, I adjusted, and thanked him for giving Augusta a roof. He seemed to be thinking of other matters. He strode towards Hilary and said: "She's such a dear little thing. Why did I ever make such a fool of myself?" Hilary replied: "Steady now, steady. You mustn't make too much of it."

Haydon literally beat his brow with his fist. "Oh, my God," he said. "Listen, Hilary. You're *agitated to the marrow* because you've discovered that your father's a cad. You're talking just to gain time. The old man hasn't kissed the girl in a corner. And she's the girl you're in love with. He's seduced her. She's going to have a child, and you know it. You *know it*, you fool. You think me the meanest skunk on earth. Don't you? Tell me frankly – don't you?"

"Yes, I do," Hilary conceded without passion.

"Miles," Mr Mellerby said, "take your aunt and sister home. Leave us here. Heppenstall!" he shouted over the railway fence.

"Sir!" The porter leapt to attention.

"Spare us a minute, Heppenstall. You're in on this."

"There's the three-thirty, sir."

"Damn it! That's in half an hour's time. Come and run through it."

Miles, Augusta and I moved off as Haydon began again: "She's such a dear little thing . . ."

"Well," Augusta said, "you see how it is. By the way: I'm the dear little thing."

It didn't seem to me the moment for discussing such an unimportant topic as her having run away from home. That would have to come later.

3

The dower house was Georgian and charming. "The boys are sleeping in the barn," Millicent Mellerby said. "We had to turf them out when your niece arrived, and now there's you, too. I'm afraid you'll have to share her room."

That suited me. A bedroom makes a good confessional, and I wanted to know what Augusta was up to. One thing clear at a glance was that I had not come upon a broken-hearted prodigal. She was well and happy. "If you'd like to see the barn," she said when my things had been unpacked, "come along now."

It was a splendid barn, much, much older than the house. "Elizabethan," Augusta said. It made me think of a church. The great doors were in the west end, and, on entering, one looked up instinctively to see the glass in the east window. But there was no east window. Slits, that had incongruously been glazed, were high up in the north and south walls, and gave the only light save that which came through the door – a light that was now strong and level, for the sun was well down in the sky. This strong rush of light showed the beaten earth floor, hard as baked clay, and the powerful complexity of the roof-timbers. It was a simple, lovely building that achieved beauty through proportion and purpose. The boys' beds, with odds and ends of belongings scattered round them, made me think of soldiers camping, as indeed they may well have done here, for York was on the road that had known the north-south tramp of legions since Roman times.

"And that's the stage," Augusta said.

The whole of the east wall was partitioned off. The stage was in the middle, and a dressing room was on either side. Backless benches filled what would have been the aisles in a church; "and this," Augusta said, "will be my first appearance on any stage. My last, too. Mr Mellerby says I'm hopeless. But he admits that Miles shows promise. That's as far as he goes with anyone."

The play came and went, as, I gathered, a play always did when Mr Mellerby was at home long enough to give his mind to it. People came in from miles of the sparse countryside: parsons, doctors, squires, labourers. Mr Mellerby and Miles held the tatterdemalion company together somehow, and everybody was as pleased as though they had had a night out at the Haymarket. The play was done on three nights, and until it was over I let the purpose of my visit slide. I had dodged the walking-on part that Hilary had suggested to me, and so was able to chew over the goings-on of this odd family. Although Mr Mellerby talked about having his feet in the dung, it was clear that nothing existed for him outside the theatre. Hilary cared no more for the theatre than I did. He liked to see a play now and then, and he allowed his father's enthusiasm to carry him along in such a moment as this; but in a talk I had with him he called his father "a freak, what the biologists call a sport." All his own love was for the landowning Mellerby tradition. "Of course," he said, "Father's in love with it, too, but only in a histrionic way." I asked him what he wanted to do with himself, and he said he had no idea. "I'm going up to Oxford in the autumn. Perhaps I'll see the light there, but I doubt it."

In contrast to this cool and non-committal attitude, Miles' reaction to Mr Mellerby was worshipful. He had been here now for a month, and he had attached himself to the older man as disciple to master. This was the first actor he had known, and it chanced to be one of rare quality. Haydon Mellerby could do with any amount of hero-worship. I gathered that long before the rehearsals for the play began he and Miles had spent hours in the barn discussing the mysteries. A month is not long, but in so close a relationship it can be decisive. It was so for Miles. Mellerby had no doubt that the boy could find a career in the theatre. There were moments when they seemed to be talking as equals; but for the most part Miles' attitude of what I can only call respectful adoration was moving and rather disturbing to behold. Miss Millicent looked on with veiled amusement. Perhaps she had seen it before.

With all this going on about me, I held my hand with Augusta. I wrote to Frank letting him know that she was well and happy and saying that I hoped soon to be able to discuss her future. The sooner the better, I thought to myself, for the reaction from that shock which had driven her from home was a curious excitement of spirit that I had not known in her before. She was, as she had confessed to me, hopeless as an actress, and Haydon was for ever castigating her about it as unmercifully as he castigated Hilary. "Oh, don't despair," she would say. "Let's try it again. I'll get it in time, you'll see," and off they would go to the barn, and back she would come lit up, almost exalted, beyond necessity.

I said from my bed alongside hers one night: "You're having a good time, darling."

She reached a hand across and squeezed mine, as, I remembered, I used to squeeze Bella's when we were girls bedded down side by side. Augusta said: "Isn't it odd! I rushed away blindly, not knowing what was going to happen. Just to be with Miles – that was all I had in mind."

"Why, darling, what *has* happened?"

She didn't answer, but just squeezed my hand again, sighed happily, and seemed to be at once asleep.

It was Haydon's custom to arrange these affairs when the moon was full, so that the audience would be lighted home. I saw the play on the first of the three nights, but not on the last. I stayed at home talking to Miss Mellerby, who said: "Does it amuse you?"

"Does what amuse me?"

"Watching people walking on clouds. There are three of 'em at it hell for leather."

She was Haydon's twin, but looked much older than he: a tough old thing, given to riding about the country astride a horse as raw-boned as she was herself. She had a face of leather and worked like a man on the bit of land that remained to the Mellerbys.

"A do like this," she said, "always puts Haydon on top of the world; and this time, what with young Miles *and* his sister . . ."

She left it unfinished. The ambiguity of her words disturbed me and I wandered out into the night that smelled of ripeness. It had been a superb month, warming the year up to the moment beyond which it could not go. The moonlight showered upon fields of white wheat and on trees standing tranced, and through the almost tangible milky web of the air the bats were flittering and the owls calling.

I walked slowly towards the barn, where the play must now be ending. It was so warm a night that the west doors were open. From a little way off I looked in: over the heads of the invisible audience to the small, lifted up, compact stage, bright as a picture brought into focus by strip-lighting in a long dark room. And the picture was of this tall handsome man Haydon Mellerby and a girl who was my Augusta. He overtopped her by a head. One of his arms was round her waist and her face was looking up into his. I moved away before the moment dissolved, but never, I thought, could the picture be wiped off the screen of my vision. Miss Mellerby's words came back to me: Walking on air. I saw what she had been trying to tell me, and I wandered disconsolately under the moonlight, stricken again by the unhappy feeling of being always an outsider, a spectator of other people's exaltations and despairs.

Tobacco plants had seeded themselves under the walls of the barn, and the air was heavily sweet with their fragrance. To me they might have been flowers of Proserpine, and I sadly recalled my Milton.

> *that fair field*
> *Of Enna, where Proserpine, gathering flowers*
> *Herself a fairer flower by gloomy Dis*
> *Was gathered.*

Not that there was much of gloomy Dis about Haydon Mellerby, but all the same my heart was full of foreboding.

I was recalled to the moment by the sound of applause marking the end of the play, and watched the people streaming out into the moonwashed night and dispersing on foot, on bicycles, in gigs, and

one or two in motorcars; and then Miss Mellerby came over from the
house and I joined her in what we had to do. For Haydon's delight in
ceremonial had decreed that such occasions as this should always end
with a supper for the players and the back-stage helpers and a few of
the local big-wigs and professional people who were pleased to
bestow their approval on their famous neighbour. Already trestle
tables were being put up end-to-end, and white cloths laid upon
them, and urns of coffee and bottles of wine were carried over from
the house. Candles were placed down the length of the table, and
vases of flowers and bowls of fruit. There were cold meat pies and
cold fruit pies and dishes of sweets. The backless benches were ranged
for seating, and when nothing more was to be done, and all were
standing in their places, Haydon and Augusta, her arm through his,
descended the few steps that led from the stage, walked slowly down
the long room, and stood side by side at the head of the table. A
parson said a few words of grace, we sat, and the meal began.

I had taken a seat at the foot of the table, and looked down its
length through the flattering candleshine, and this long narrow festive
oasis in the old barn, shadowed with all its centuries, seemed more
unreal than anything I had seen on this stage or any other. My mind
was a tatter of wool. I could not believe that less than a week ago I had
left a practical house in Manchester to find a distraught and vagrant
girl, and that this was the girl, sitting at the end of the table, lighted
by the candles in a sumptuous candelabrum of branched silver that
had been carried over from the Dower House. She looked now so
little distraught and vagrant, so far from the child who had swooned
upon me in the rainwashed train approaching a Manchester suburb.
The moment had so exalted her that she had not changed her stage
clothes or removed her make-up, which Haydon himself had applied
with all his art to heighten her beauty. She simply was not the lost girl
I had come to find. She was someone else. She was a woman, fully
conscious of her importance to a man.

But, all the same, she was Augusta, a child. I told myself that Ellen
Terry was a child when she had married C. F. Watts. But it didn't help.
Little good had come of that.

When the meal was ended, the parson who had said grace got to
his feet, thanked Haydon for the play and for the hospitality that had
followed it, and proposed his health. I watched Haydon get to his feet,

handsome, self-possessed, and Millicent turning upon him a mocking smile which showed me that she knew as well as I did what was coming. He was wearing the full-fig evening clothes of the last act and his right hand toyed with a monocle attached to a wide ribbon of watered silk. Augusta, too, knew what was coming. I could almost feel the wild beating of her heart. She did not raise her eyes from her plate. I willed her to look at me, but she would not.

"These occasions," the beautiful voice was saying, "when I am here on the land where my roots belong, and among my own people, are always precious to me. They fill a cup which goes to my lips when the world is too much with me. But precious as they always are, they are this time overflowing with a personal and private joy. I am very glad to see so many dear friends about me, and I want them to share the joy I feel. Well, I mustn't keep you wondering what it is that will make this occasion ever memorable to me beyond all others. In the play which some of you have so ably helped us to perform, and to which the rest of you have given so kind and forgiving a reception, this young lady, sitting here on my right, ends in a moment of deep unhappiness. But you need not waste too much sympathy on her. I am happy to announce – she and I are both happy to announce – that we are to be married."

He waited for the applause. It came – thin, scattered, unbelieving. I couldn't join in. Gooseflesh shivered on my bones. Millicent didn't join in, except with a grin that creased the leather of her face. Miles didn't join in, nor Hilary.

Haydon seemed unperturbed. "Of course," he went on, "we are not thinking of an immediate marriage. We have agreed to wait for at least two years. I drink to Miss Cumberledge and invite you to join me."

We couldn't refuse to do that. We drank, and the gathering broke up. This wasn't Italy. We were all a bit too Nordic to feel at ease. Somehow, I couldn't approach Augusta in that moment. But I saw Millicent put an arm round her roughly. "Bless you, child," she said, blew out the lights on the candelabrum, took it up, and strode off with it to the house.

I followed, and people brushed past me, talking among themselves. "Old enough to be her father." "Old enough to know better."

He was forty-six: thirty years older than Augusta.

365

4

I went straight to bed, so emotionally exhausted that I slept at once and was unaware of Augusta getting into the bed next to mine. When I awoke she was asleep. I left her there and went down to breakfast and found no one at table but Miss Mellerby. While I, as usual, nibbled a bit of toast, she, as usual, marched roughshod over porridge, eggs, bacon and kidneys. "Well, it's in the *Yorkshire Post*," she announced grimly.

I asked where Haydon was. "Oh, didn't you know?" She knew well enough that I didn't. "He went straight into York last night and caught the London train. He's in this new Pinero play and they're starting work on it at once."

"And where are Miles and Hilary?"

"Gone off for a walk. I don't suppose we shall see them today."

"They'll have plenty to talk about, won't they?"

She gave me her grim smile. "We all have, haven't we? I began on Haydon last night. Went to York to see him off and made good use of the opportunity."

"What worries me is what I'm to do about Augusta. Do I take her back to Manchester?"

"You can try. I don't imagine you'll succeed," she said, refilling her large mug of coffee.

I must have looked helpless and confused. She took pity on me. "Augusta was still up when I got back from York last night," she said. "She'd fallen asleep on the sofa in the drawing room. We had a long talk. I think it would not be a good idea for her to go back to Manchester. Do an old hag's ideas interest you?" she grinned. I nodded.

"Very well, then. What with her and Miles, I have the whole story. Losing a mother when you're a child is no joke. I know. I lost mine. It turned all my affection over to my father. I adored him. I wanted no one else. He lived to be an old man. That's why I never married, though, oddly enough, I had plenty of offers. Why don't you eat something?"

I shook my head, and she went on. "I can imagine Augusta going back with you from London, full of what she'd seen and done, anxious to pour it out to him. That's how I used to be. I used to do a lot of fox-hunting, and the best thing about it was being back, with my toes to the fire, giving him an account of every move in the game. That's how Augusta was. And then she found – or thought she'd found – it's the same thing – that now she had no father. She ran – and she ran into a most attractive father's arms. Am I making this all up?"

"I don't know."

"That's how it seems to me, anyway. Haydon can fascinate most women when he sets his mind to it. I've seen plenty of that. And a girl like Augusta, looking for a father, was easy. Mind you," she said robustly, "I don't say there's no sex in it. The girl's as ripe as an August plum."

"What am I to do?"

"Wait till the post comes," she said enigmatically. "It gets here as a rule about ten o'clock. Meanwhile, let the child sleep. I kept her up jawing till three o'clock. Now, I've got some bottling to do in the kitchen."

The letter was from Louisa. "My dear Maria," it began, "before you go on with this letter, read the one which I enclose."

This enclosed letter was from Augusta to Louisa. It was dated two days before this.

My dear Aunt Louisa. – I don't know whether Aunt Maria has told you of the dreadful misfortune that has befallen me. I left London, after the wonderful experience of living for a time with you, more full of happiness than I had ever expected to be. I reached home to find that my father had married in my absence. You have never met my father and cannot know what a wonderful person he is. To find that I had lost him was as though everything solid had slipped from under my feet.

She went on in this banal way, defeated by the attempt to describe the emotional earthquake that had razed all her landmarks; and then she told of her flight and arrival in Haydon's household.

Oh, I love him! she cried. If only I could make you understand how much I love him! He is good and beautiful. He wants to marry me, but not till I am older. What am I to do? Oh, tell me what I am to do. I cannot go home now, and I cannot remain here. I dare not appeal to my father. I spend my time between joy and misery. I am old enough to marry, but I am too

young to deal with the complications that have arisen. What a
fool you must think me; and how easy everything would be if I
had no relatives – no one at all – just me and Haydon and our
two hearts telling us what to do.

At that point I gave it up. I couldn't finish it. I felt like a spy upon
emotion; and what is more I felt a deep unhappiness. I had been at her
side for days: she had told me nothing; she had turned to Louisa! And
I felt something like hatred for Haydon. His fine speech. His nicely-
chosen words. And then away he goes, leaving the child to deal as she
could with all the practical matters. If he had loved her as Augusta
deserved to be loved, he would have said to hell with Pinero and gone
off to Manchester to see Frank.

But if Augusta had confided in me, what could I have done? I
admitted that I had no answer. Like Augusta, I turned to Louisa. I took
up her letter.

This is not a situation that I like at all. Augusta tells me that
Mr Mellerby intends to make a public announcement of the
engagement. Whatever one may think of the rest of the matter,
that at least strikes me as stupidity, utterly indiscreet. It doesn't
help me to think of the man as especially thoughtful for Augusta
or intelligent in his own affairs.

I don't know Dr Cumberledge, though I have talked to him
on the telephone. He rang me up when Augusta disappeared. I
have now written him a long letter, trying to make him
understand that to force Augusta to return to Manchester would
be a great folly. I have offered to have her here indefinitely and
to see that any meetings she may have with Mr Mellerby are
more or less chaperoned. Meet him she must, obviously. To try
to stop that would be another folly. Whether he sincerely
returns her feelings I am in no position to say. If he does, I see
nothing against their marriage when she is a little older. In his
profession he is a very distinguished man, and I have known
several marriages between youth and middle-age that have
turned out well. The one thing I fear is that Augusta's passion
may prove to be no more than a rebound from what she took to
be a disastrous situation at home. I hope you won't join her in

368

thinking Dr Cumberledge any sort of fool or villain. The man has a right to marry again if he wants to, without reference to the probable reactions of over-emotional children. Youth and age have to get on together as best they are able, and if they can't, both sides must make what they can of the consequences.

I have told Dr Cumberledge that you are bringing Augusta here from Yorkshire and that I am awaiting his decision. So do that, will you please, my dear.

Love from Louisa.

This tranquil and thoughtful letter calmed me. Augusta came down and I finished reading it, and in reply to her "Oh, how shall I get through this day!" I was able to say with a smile: "Oh, you will, my dear. It's surprising what we can get through when we have no choice."

Miss Mellerby was forthright. I told her about Louisa's letter and she said: "I thought you'd get one today. The child told me she'd written to her Aunt Louisa. Well, when are you off?"

"We could go on tonight's train."

"Good. I'll be glad to have the place to myself again. Whenever Haydon comes here he leaves some nonsense behind."

We said goodbye to Miles and Hilary. I had telegraphed to Louisa, and in the morning she and James met us at the station. Augusta bloomed into happiness. She was in London, and Haydon was in London. I handed her over to Louisa with a sense of passing to more competent hands a job in which I had failed. James said: "Hop in, Maria."

"No," I told him. " 'You don't think I came to plant myself on you in Kensington, do you?"

It was a suddenly-taken decision. I was as much surprised as they were, and they certainly were surprised. I don't think Augusta even heard what I said. It was a lovely morning, tender and still half-asleep, and she was in London where Haydon Mellerby was.

"What's this all about?" Louisa asked rather sharply.

"Now don't hold things up," I said. "I've taken a job. I'll write or come out and see you as soon as I'm settled. I didn't feel like staying in Manchester. Things aren't the same there now."

James climbed heavily into his seat. "Damn' nonsense," he said. "What d'you want a job for?"

"Because I'm one of the lower middle classes and have to eat."

He had taken to grumbling and muttering to himself, and he did so now as he tucked a rug tenderly round Augusta. Louisa looked both hurt and puzzled, and a pang of joy visited me as I realised that she had wanted me and was disappointed. "Well, it's your affair," she said.

I watched them go, then walked back into the station to get some food.

5

I had picked up a newspaper from a bookstall and turned the pages as I ate. A small item at the foot of a column was headed *Progress of Invalids*, and I didn't expect it would have anything to say to me. But I read: "Lady Lavernock. – A satisfactory night, but condition not substantially improved."

Well, what was that all about, I wondered. I hadn't known that Jane was ill. I hadn't seen her or heard from her since she and Lord Lavernock said goodbye to me years ago in France.

I put my suitcase into the luggage room, and the action seemed to me symbolic. Would I thus for ever be stowing away my few belongings while I sought empty-handed for the next step to take? In the ladies' room I washed and brushed myself into some sort of order and then took a bus to Hyde Park. The calm September morning quietened me in mind and body, and at eleven o'clock I crossed Park Lane and rang at the door of Lord Lavernock's mansion. It was a chance. Jane might be there, but equally she might be at Coverdale or Minstall. Even if she were here she might be in no condition to receive me. My mind went to shreds again as I listened to the bell clanging behind the ornate door. A footman looked at me with contempt. He said he would consult Mr Marmont. He put my card on a vast silver tray where it looked absurd, lost and desolate. I sat there for a moment, listening to the word Marmont – pronounced in a Cockney way – ringing in my mind. It was a puzzle that I couldn't solve.

My reverie was broken by the arrival of Mr Marmont, who to my surprise advanced, dressed in the conventional clothes of a butler, holding out his hand. "My dear Miss Legassick," he said. "It is good to see you again!"

And then my mind clicked. Douze Maisons. The youth who had laid the whip heavily on to Aristide Maillard. All the dreadful consequences that had followed. This was Anatole, who had said boastfully that he would go to England with Madame la Vicomtesse and drive her every day to see the King at Ascot! He looked as though he had learned a little more than that about English ways.

I greeted him warmly, but he insisted on treating me with reserve and respect. The footman came in behind him, bringing coffee and biscuits – a whole silver pot of coffee and a silver ewer of steaming milk. Anatole dismissed him with a wave of the hand and himself poured out my coffee. He stood while I drank.

"How is Lady Lavernock?" I asked. "I didn't know she was ill. I saw a line in a newspaper this morning."

"I told her always," he said, "leave the aeroplanes alone. On the ground you are safe in the motorcar. You are with me. Even for a chauffeur – not me any longer. I must be the butler. It is more dignified. So for a year now another man drive the car – a man with no influence who is afraid to say leave the aeroplanes alone. And so she is always with the aeroplanes. There is a field at Minstall that becomes the aerodrome and a pilot who knows all about the aeroplanes. And so they fly, and so he is dead."

He paused, looking desperately unhappy. "What happened to her ladyship?" I prodded him.

"Broken," he said. "Many of the bones."

There was a ring at the door-bell, and I saw the footman admit Mr Arthur Kopf. He came across to us, and I got up. He looked tired, ordinary, much older. There was grey in his hair. He did not recognise me. Seeing me stand, he said: "Please sit down," and to Anatole: "Is my father at home, Marmont?"

"No, sir. He left for Paris this morning. He will be away for some days."

"Would it be convenient for my mother to receive me now?"

"Oh, yes, sir. I'm sure it would."

"All right. Don't you bother. I know my way up."

He bowed formally to me and went heavily up the great staircase.

Almost to himself Anatole said: "Suddenly all is sad."

"I called," I said, "hoping I might see Lady Lavernock."

"I do not know how long Mr Arthur may stay. I shall speak to her ladyship, and perhaps I shall telephone to you?"

"Yes, please do that."

I thought quickly and decided on a hotel that wouldn't be too expensive for a day or two. I gave him the name.

"Is her ladyship in real danger?"

"Not her life. No. But too many of the bones are broken."

Most of the bones managed to cure themselves, but after the doctors had fussed and fiddled for the next month or two poor Jane's right leg was taken off at the hip.

6

I enjoyed lying doggo in my back-street hotel. It was a long time since I had been alone. I didn't let even Louisa know where I was. It was a time for taking stock, dissociating myself from all the lives in whose affairs I was involved. But looking at the old ladies with overfed snuffling little dogs, the "permanent residents", I hoped the dissociation would not last too long. I was glad when, three or four days later, Anatole rang me up and said that Jane would see me the next morning.

She dismissed a nurse and we sat together in pale September sunshine streaming through the window. She looked very small, lying in an antique four-poster bed, very pale and suffering. A contraption of wooden laths was over her body, to prevent the bedclothes from weighing upon her. She looked like a bit of jetsam on a desolate shore beneath an overturned boat.

She managed a smile. "Don't ask me what happened," she said. "Don't ask me how I am. You shouldn't be here at all, and I shouldn't be talking. It hurts my ribs. That nurse will report me to my doctor and I shall be scolded. You are the only person I've seen except Arthur. He sneaks in every day. Marmont says you were here when he came on Tuesday. How did you think he was looking?"

I hesitated. "Come on," she said. "Tell me what you thought of him."

I said baldly: "I shouldn't have known him if it hadn't been here that I met him."

"Do not ever let my husband know that you met him here," she said. She began to cry.

Off and on I had known Jane now for a long time: in Cornwall, at Coverdale, in France. And, whatever the circumstances, she had seemed to me the image and essence of a free and happy spirit. Her tears moved me to the marrow. I knew that she was not crying for her own woes, for the wreck of her body, for the ending of her passionate curiosity. I leant gently over the cage that enclosed her, fearing to touch her, and kissed her on the forehead. "Dear Jane," I said. "Dear, dear friend." I wiped her eyes. "I shouldn't have come till much later," I said. "But I am glad I did. Now I must go."

She said: "Tell Marmont that I wish him to give you Arthur's address. Then go and see him."

I had no idea what this was about, but I promised to do so. "I shall be seeing Arthur today," she said. "I shall tell him to expect you."

I had been there hardly more than five minutes. The nurse looked anxiously round the door. "All right," I said. "I'm going at once."

Marmont was waiting for me. He was sad and furious all at the same time. He wanted to know what I thought of her, as though that could matter. "Oh," he said, "these damned, damned aeroplanes. When she is well I shall resign as butler. I shall again become a chauffeur and take her about and look after her."

"I expect," I said, "you will do just what she tells you to do."

"Yes," he admitted sadly. "That is how it will be."

He wrote down Arthur Kopf's address in Hyde Park Gate and the telephone number. I rang up Mr Kopf that evening and he asked: "Could you come and take dinner with us tonight?"

I said that I could.

7

Marriage seems the very devil when there's money about. You can do what James Polperro did: turn your girl down and obey your father's orders; or you can do what Arthur Kopf did: tell your father where he gets off and marry the girl you have chosen. It means trouble in any case.

"I don't know," Arthur Kopf said after dinner, "that I should have wanted to tell you anything about this, but my mother wants me to, so that's that."

He must have told Mabel, his wife, what was the purpose of my call. She made her excuses and left us together. I liked her. She was a thin, dark creature, rather too brainy for me, but, I being what I am, that's no disparagement. She was, of all things, the daughter of an East End costermonger whose daring ambition had been to make a school-teacher of her. Once Mabel Duffy found herself among books and the apparatus of learning she was like a hitherto lame bird that finds itself miraculously on the wing. She was at Lady Margaret College on a scholarship when Arthur was at Christ Church, and they met once or twice, though there seems to have been then no more than a tepid friendship between them. I often heard Mabel professing to be without religion and proclaiming her agnosticism, but she had a restless social conscience, and this was why, when a brilliant scholastic career seemed open to her, she chose to become warden of a settlement for girls in the East End of London. She never had any scruples about badgering the rich on behalf of her girls, and a letter she wrote to Lord Lavernock was the beginning of the trouble. He was a generous giver, if the word generous has any meaning when you are talking about a man so rich as that, but he liked to know where his money was going to. He ordered Arthur, who was then learning the ropes in one of his father's companies, to visit this place and report on what it was doing.

I was delighted with Arthur Kopf. A man who can make a great renunciation is always impressive. Not that he said much about that, but bits and pieces that Jane let drop in later years helped to fill in the simple outline he gave me that night. It was one of those "love stories" that can still confound me by their improbability and hearten me by their happening, however improbable. There was renunciation on both sides, and I'm not sure that Mabel's was not the greater. Financially, she gave up nothing: indeed, she gained. But to give up something that satisfied both her brain and her conscience — I didn't know whether it was an act of splendour or of folly.

Well, there they were, not living in squalor: far from it. Squalor does not live in Hyde Park Gate. But the sense of outlawry must have been acute. Lord Lavernock had never so much as seen Mabel. She and Arthur were forbidden to enter any of his houses, and the furtiveness with which Arthur crept to see his mother now and then filled him with shame and Jane with rage. Jane knew that her husband knew, and their always loose fantastic association became embittered.

Jane, who adventured in so many ways, adventured on the stock exchange, and it was she who had arranged Arthur's partnership with her stock-broker. He did the work conscientiously but loathed it. I suppose it was this loathing, hanging about him like a shabby garment, that gave him the look of dull ordinariness which had struck me when I saw him at the Park Lane house. Yet he was, Jane told me, a good and successful stock-broker. There was that much of his father in him, anyway. But there was nothing in him of the child she had awaited as she lay by the stream at Coverdale, hoping for a poet.

"I could put up with being chucked out by my father," he said to me. "It's the feud that keeps me miserable."

The feud was carried to fantastic lengths by a man who had rarely met opposition, and had never, till now, met opposition that he had been unable to overcome. In all his houses and his yacht, and in all the offices that his wide affairs touched, all clerks and servants had received a personal letter telling them, under pain of dismissal, that Mr Arthur Kopf must not be received, and only when Jane was on the premises did anyone dare to disobey. Lord Lavernock had a racehorse that he had named Arthurian. It had had a great career and then been profitably retired for use in his stud. He announced that it was withdrawn from service, and was prepared to say why to anyone who cared to listen. Jane told me that she had infuriated Lord Lavernock by saying that it seemed absurd to deprive the poor horse of his privileges simply because Arthur chose to exercise his. Arthur had left a lot of clothes in various houses. Lord Lavernock ordered that all the name-tapes should be removed and handed to him. He burned them ostentatiously and then had the clothes given away. Any book that had Arthur's name in it was thrown on to a bonfire. Lavernock had been known to cut some of his oldest friends who had taken Arthur out to lunch or supper.

On that night when I first dined in Hyde Park Gate Arthur and I had been talking for a long time when Mabel put her head round the door and asked: "Has Arthur come to the point yet?"

"I'm afraid not, my dear," he said.

Instinctively I had risen as she came into the room. Do you know Augustus John's portrait of Suggia? She was that sort of woman: lithe, bony, angular, lit by flames. The costermonger's daughter. The wind bloweth where it listeth. Her long arms were bare. Her dress was cut low and was of crimson silk. She was a tigress to my mouse.

The silk rustled as she sat down, smoothing it over her knees with an impatient movement of the hands. "The point is," she said, "that I must work or die. But something must be done about Benjamin. You had better see Benjamin. You stay where you are, Arthur."

I followed her upstairs and on the landing she paused to ask: "How did you find Arthur's mother?"

I told her the little I could. "One should kiss that woman's feet," she said.

She switched on a shaded light and led me to the child's bed. "That's Ben." The long hand lay gently on the boy's forehead. He smiled in his sleep. "He's five," she said. "Five yesterday." She looked at me, her face full of wonder that her son should be so remarkable as to have achieved five birthdays. I smiled back at her. I had found her intimidating. At dinner she had talked about things that left me ignorantly floundering. Now I thought: She's all right. We shall get on.

She took me into a small room opposite the boy's bedroom. It was little more than a couple of chairs and a desk in a cave of books. We sat down. "I expect," she said, "that Arthur has told you his father won't receive me. Did he tell you why?"

"No."

"I don't want you to come here under any false impression about me." She told me simply and briefly about her own career, with neither pride nor reserve. "At the end," she said, "I was quite alone. My father died soon after I went up to Oxford, and so far as I know I haven't a relative in the world on that side."

"What do you mean about coming here?" I asked.

"Why, to look after Ben. Has no one told you?"

No one had told me.

"That's so like Arthur's mother," she said. "It was she who put the idea into our heads. You see, Benjamin's arrival was rather difficult. The doctors tell me there can be no more children. I've done what I could for Ben. I suckled him myself," she said proudly. "If there had been other children I suppose I'd have stayed here. As it is, I shall take on this thing they want me to do."

She talked about this thing. A number of settlements and hostels and clubs for girls were to associate under a joint committee of management. "They've asked me to become what they rather grandly call the Director General. It will mean going to an office every day. Well, I see nothing of Arthur all day now. We shall have just as much time together as ever."

"And what do you want me to do?"

"So far as learning goes, just teach Ben to read and write. For the rest, be a good friend to him. In a few years' time he'll be getting sent off to a prep school. You would live here, of course. Don't let Lady Lavernock or me or Arthur or anyone else over-persuade you. Think about it. If you could let us know, say, within a week, that would be helpful. I start on my job in about a fortnight."

I said: "I should like to come."

I wasn't thinking of her, though I liked her, or of Mr Arthur or Ben. I was thinking that now I had a roof over my head again, a den from which I could emerge to keep an eye on Augusta and on what I could not but think this preposterous affair with Mr Mellerby.

CHAPTER TWELVE

MY JOURNAL tells me that it was rather more than a year after this – it was December 1910 – that Mabel Kopf met my brother-in-law James Polperro. Jane was out and about, insofar as she would ever be out and about again. Lord Lavernock had had a handsome Rolls-Royce car specially built for her comfort, and there was a footman whose sole job was to assist her into it and out of it. When out, she could hobble fairly well on a leg and a crutch. Anatole Marmont had been demoted from butler and was in high spirits as the custodian and driver of this splendid mustard-yellow vehicle. Almost always on a Saturday afternoon when Arthur and Mabel were at home Jane would appear and stay to tea. It was at one of these tea times that Jane recalled her meeting with me in Cornwall, when she and her husband had been the guests of James and Louisa at Tregannock. Louisa's remarkable life as Mrs Vincent Wheatstone and as a shop-girl appealed to Mabel, who had read Louisa's book, and she said to me that she would like to meet her. Nearer to Christmas, when she was taking a holiday from her office and she and I were walking in Kensington Gardens, I suggested that we should call at Louisa's flat. James and Augusta were out. It seemed to me that James' visits were a little more frequent now that Augusta was living in Kensington. Frank had wisely agreed to leave her in Louisa's keeping. He had come up from Manchester and had a long conference with Louisa. I was prouder and prouder of this sister of mine. While life blew me about like a straw in the wind, she was rooted. She gave the impression of strength; and it was not surprising that Frank saw the sense of leaving Augusta in her hands. It seemed to me that the situation might have been worse. Now that no one was opposing her association with Mellerby, Augusta became less tense, even tranquil, and, at Louisa's suggestion, Frank occasionally came to town without his wife, and something of the old loving understanding was re-established between him and his daughter. They had recently been to Oxford together to spend a day with Miles who had begun his freshman's year at New College.

I was glad that the situation was out of my hands, but my gladness was not without an anxiety, gnawing ceaselessly. I had asked Louisa whether Frank and Haydon Mellerby had met, and she said: "No. I'm doing my best to prevent it." She looked at me strangely and said: "You know, my dear, I don't think this marriage will ever take place, and I've suggested as much to Frank. The fewer people who get emotionally involved, the better."

"Then what on earth are we all up to?" I asked.

"So far as I'm concerned," she said, "I'm standing by with the lifeboat."

Well, that's how it was. I wanted to cry out a warning to Augusta, but I think she would have smiled forgivingly. She was too, too desperately and dangerously happy, everybody's queen. Louisa loved her. Frank, in his joy at having her back on any terms, couldn't do enough for her. I, she knew, was her humble servant, and she had re-established herself with Miles. As for James, he was her doting old cavalier, there to be commanded, and I suppose that Haydon Mellerby, who was permitted to take her out to lunch, and who had a regular "date" to dine on Sundays at the Kensington flat, was still full of protestations of devotion. Those luncheons with her handsome famous lover, amid the glitter of the best restaurants and under the appraising eyes of Mellerby's stage friends, must have made heady stuff for her, and in my inexperience I could only guess what his kisses did to her.

She was seventeen years old on that afternoon when Mabel Kopf and I called at the Kensington flat. As we were taking tea Louisa said: "James is here for the weekend. I don't suppose he'll be back for a time. He's taken Augusta to the matinée."

I didn't need to ask what matinée. How many times she had seen the Pinero play I don't know. She was not allowed to go alone: Louisa cleverly arranged that she was hardly ever alone: but whenever she could persuade someone to take her out in the afternoon, if it were a matinée afternoon, there they would go, and on to tea at Gunter's afterwards.

"There won't be many more matinées," Louisa said. "The play's coming off."

I suggested: "Mr Mellerby will probably take a rest in Yorkshire."

"No," Louisa said. "A rest seems to be the last thing he has in mind."

I had an idea that she was warning me. She said: "I've heard from Miss Mellerby."

It was characteristic of Louisa that when she had taken responsibility for Augusta she made herself acquainted with everything and everybody concerned. At the beginning, she had written a friendly letter to old Miss Mellerby, and this had developed into a regular correspondence. Miss Mellerby had now written, in the course of her weekly letter: "I was expecting Haydon here when his play ended. All arrangements made. Red carpet, etc. You know. Well, now my lord cancels all that. He'll be embarking at once on a world tour. Away heaven knows how long. How like him. Just his way with women. I've seen a lot of it . . ." and so forth. I could see the leathery old jaws mumbling as she wrote.

James and Augusta came in. It was a cold day. Their faces were glowing. They enormously enjoyed one another's company. "We missed Gunter's for once," James said. "Any muffins?"

I introduced him and Augusta to Mabel Kopf. James had an eye for a lovely woman, and though Mabel's lean looks were not everyone's idea of beauty, I could see that he was attracted. "A good thing," he said, "for us Cornish bumpkins to come up to town now and then. We get mildewed down there."

He sat down. I gave him and Augusta tea and muffins.

"What do you *do* in Cornwall?" Mabel asked. It was a customary opening with her. What do you *do?*" She was deeply interested in people's lives. "Of course," she said, "I know *something* about you. My husband's father, Lord Lavernock, stayed now and then at your place, didn't he?"

"Haven't seen him for years," James said, laying heartily into his food. "Quite out of touch with the upper classes. Just a squire."

Augusta said: "Don't take him seriously, Mrs Kopf. Just a squire, indeed! He's a wonderful man and Tregannock's a wonderful place."

Louisa reminded her: "You've seen it only once, darling, and you were a child. Children grow up, and they go back looking for paradise and find it's a field like any other, with a cow or two in it. Remember, you're not a child now."

"No, indeed," Augusta said gravely. "Does Mrs Kopf know that I'm to marry Haydon Mellerby?"

I trembled for her: it was so heartbreakingly proud and naïve. Mabel answered for herself. "No. Who is he? Should I know him?"

It wasn't a pose or teasing. I had found for myself that Mabel had no interest in the theatre. I explained: "He's an actor. He's in the Pinero play that's running now. He's a good deal older than Augusta, and they won't be marrying yet awhile."

Augusta looked pityingly but with forgiveness at Mabel. To me she said: "My marriage isn't so far off as all that, Aunt Maria. Haydon and I have been engaged for a year now. Another year: that's all I have to wait."

I could see that this was a topic Louisa did not wish to pursue. I had told her of Mabel's interest in East End girls, and she said: "Do you manage to get your girls away for holidays, Mrs Kopf? I used to know a lot more about East End boys and girls than I do now. It was appalling how many of them had never – literally *never* – seen a field or a cow or grazing sheep."

Mabel said: "I hadn't myself when I was fourteen years old. Then some neighbours took me off with them for the annual hop-picking in Kent. All the time I was there I longed for nothing so much as to be home again. I think that was true of most of them."

"There you are!" James said triumphantly. "It wouldn't work. You know, Mrs Kopf, my wife for years has been working on me to have masses of East End children at Tregannock in the summer. Now you confirm my opinion that it wouldn't work."

"Oh, I hope not," Mabel said. "I don't want you to think that that's my opinion at all. There was a lot wrong with me, and with all of us children, and that was one of the things. If children are bored in the country there's something wrong. The cure, surely, is simply more country."

James looked crestfallen, and Mabel smiled at him and said: "You're lucky. If you weren't living in Cornwall I should be worrying the life out of you. In this job of mine, one of the things I have to do is bore landowners beyond endurance to put up with holiday-parties. Cornwall's out of the question – too much money needed for the railway fares. But I promise you the people in the Home Counties shall hear from me."

Louisa didn't press her small moment of triumph. She was watching Augusta, who didn't like the way the conversation had moved so resolutely away from her and Haydon. She was trying to attract attention by making little frustrated noises as she sawed unsuccessfully with a blunt table-knife at the string of a tiny parcel.

"Give Augusta your pen-knife, James," Louisa said.

James, too, was glad to be relieved of the moment. "Let me snip it for you," he said, and took the parcel from Augusta's hand.

Louisa asked: "Is that from Haydon?"

Augusta nodded. We knew that Haydon often had a small present waiting for her, and would send it round during an interval when he saw her at a matinée. It turned out to be a pair of pretty earrings. She held them up proudly, dangling one beneath each ear with her fingers, glad to be in the picture again.

James said: "There's a note, too."

She took it with a smile, and read aloud: "For my dear little one, from her old darling. With apologies that he'll have to miss next Sunday, that dear, dear lunch to which he was so looking forward."

Her voice faltered on the last words, and one of the earrings fell with a small tinkle on to her plate. "But why?" she cried. The poor child had no sense of defending herself or her emotions. "Why? He's never missed before, and he doesn't say *why!*"

Mabel and I had to go. I was happy to feel that she and Louisa liked one another. "Do come again," Louisa said; and Mabel said, with a teasing smile at James: "I should love to. We must talk about putting Tregannock to good use."

As we were walking home she said to me: "I didn't quite get who that beautiful child is."

I gave her my involved explanation: "She's the daughter of a Manchester doctor whose dead wife was the sister of a parson who is married to my sister living down in Cornwall."

Mabel laughed. "No wonder she looks as though she doesn't know who she is or where she is. Her only reality seems to be this actor she's engaged to. Tell me about that affair."

I told her, and she said simply: "Poor child."

2

This was on a Wednesday, and Louisa rang me up the next day and asked if I could come to lunch on the Sunday. "James will be gone back to Cornwall, so now that Mr Mellerby has cried off it'll be just you and me and Augusta. Do come if you can. Things don't look good."

Mabel readily gave permission. She was away from her office till the Christmas holiday was over, and was only too glad to have young Ben to herself.

I arrived at noon, anxious and worried. Augusta had gone for a walk in Kensington Gardens. "My suggestion," Louisa said. "I wanted her out of the way. Read this." It was a letter addressed from Haydon's flat in St James' Place.

My dear Louisa. – Let me give to you personally the apologies I briefly conveyed through Augusta for not being able to join you at luncheon on Sunday. I leave you to imagine how stricken I am. Ever since you have had my little darling under your hospitable roof, this Sunday oasis has been a joy to carry me through the stressful week. How desolate I shall be without its refreshment. But . . .

Ah, the dreadful buts of life! Our play ends with the end of next week, and I have signed a contract to go on a long tour abroad immediately afterwards. What preparation this involves I leave you to imagine. Sunday will be eaten up, and so too will any odds and ends of time during the week after. You hear from time to time, I believe, from my sister Millicent. Perhaps she has told you that I have cancelled a visit I intended to make to Yorkshire. Now I have cancelled the cancellation! The preparations for the tour should be more or less completed by the end of next week, and another week will elapse before we set forth. I *must* spend that week in rest, and nothing refreshes me like a stay in the place that bred me. So to Yorkshire it must be. How can I dare to explain all this to Augusta? She is so young, so sensitive. She will be unable to understand the harsh imperative. So long a separation will seem unbearable to her. And so to you, dear Louisa, I must entrust the task. Explain to her that her loneliness will be no longer than that of a sailor's wife when her husband sets out on a long voyage! Make her see it in some such practical way, my dear, and make her understand that the heartbreak will not be all on her side. Give her lots of love from her dear old Haydon, and believe me ever devotedly yours.

Louisa was taut with anger. "Imagine," she said, "yourself in his place. Imagine you're in love with someone whom you won't see for six months or so – wouldn't you . . ."

She couldn't go on. "All right," I said. "I think I've got his idea. When will Augusta be back?"

"Any minute. She went out at eleven."

By one o'clock we had both begun to fidget. By two o'clock we were torn to pieces with anxiety. At half-past Augusta came slowly in, looked at us both as though she did not recognise us, and crossed over without a word to her bedroom. Taking no notice of us who had followed, she kicked off her shoes and flopped down on the bed. We came out and Louisa prepared a sedative and took it into the bedroom. She was back in about twenty minutes to announce: "She's asleep."

3

I was able later to piece together what had happened. It was Sunday, the day that had always brought Haydon; and Augusta, walking in Kensington Gardens, was desolate. She had no suspicion that the note he had sent with the earrings might be the first touch of a frost that would deepen. It was just that Haydon couldn't come, and the thought was unbearable. And to do Haydon Mellerby justice, none of us ever did know who was right: we in our suspicions, or Augusta in her faith. It *was* a time of intense activity for him. He *may*, being a sensitive if vain creature, have shrunk from the emotional stress of telling Augusta that he would be away for six months, and he may have had no intention of making this the beginning of a break.

In any case, Augusta's faith was absolute, and she was young and impulsive. She suddenly decided to go to Haydon's rooms, tell him that *nothing* must be considered more important than the Sunday engagement, and bring him back triumphantly to lunch. She knew that such an idea would horrify Louisa, but success would cancel all that, and she was sure she would be successful. She had money in her purse, called a cab, and had herself driven to St James' Place. She saw a hansom cab standing outside the house where Haydon had his rooms, and while her own cab was still approaching she saw Haydon come out with a pretty young woman dressed up to the nines. He handed her into the hansom and they drove away.

Again, all this could have been harmless. A long time after this I saw Haydon playing in a London theatre and sent a note round asking if he could receive me. He was friendly and communicative till I mentioned Augusta. Then it became difficult to prise a word out of him. However, he admitted that he had recognised Augusta through the window of her cab, and so had the girl who was with him. She knew who Augusta was, for Haydon had been proud to introduce the child to his friends. The girl said: "She keeps a close watch on you, doesn't she, my dear?"

"I could have smacked her face," Haydon said, "but she was too important to me at that moment. She was the leading actress in the company going abroad with me, and we'd spent a couple of gruelling hours discussing the work ahead. I had ordered the cab to pick us up and take us on to lunch with Harry Chambers, who was also in the company. There was lots and lots to be done that day."

I suggested: "You might have spared one minute to say the right word to Augusta."

"Of course I might," he said. "But do we always recognise a critical moment when it faces us? I don't, anyway. And though I could have slapped that girl's face, what she said gave me a jolt. Perhaps that's what annoyed me. It was the sort of tale that would go round."

"And you minded it all that much?"

"Yes," he said frankly. "You know, Augusta *was* possessive. And so was your sister Louisa. She possessed Augusta. I wasn't allowed much of her, you know."

He began to talk about the play I had seen that night, and then his wife put her head round the door. She was the girl whose face he had wanted to slap. Later, he was knighted and she became a Dame. A most suitable marriage in every way.

4

This was late in 1910, and a year after that I went down to Cornwall. It was a miserable year. To begin with, there was Augusta. Meeting Haydon Mellerby had lifted her out of a pit of sorrow, and now she

was plunged back. As young people will in such a case, she hugged her
misery, she was convinced that life had nothing more to offer, and all
this reacted disastrously on her physical health. She lost her looks, and
all that Louisa could do failed to rouse or interest her. Mabel Kopf
tried, too, and the consequences were unhappy. In Mabel's view, work
was the antidote for most ills, and in the spring after Haydon
disappeared she prevailed upon Augusta to go with her daily to her
office and learn something of what she was trying to do there. Then
in the summer she was shifted from the theory to the practice and
went to live in an East End settlement as assistant to the woman who
ran it. Louisa favoured this experiment. In most of such matters she
and Mabel saw eye to eye. I didn't like the idea myself, and what
would have come of it if things had gone smoothly I don't know. But
they didn't. The girls in the settlement were encouraged to have their
boy friends in in the evenings for dances and games, and one of these
boys took a fancy to Augusta. They were not gentle boys and girls, and
one evening, when this youth was dancing with Augusta, his girl
jealously intervened, thrust them violently apart and smacked the
boy's face. He smacked her in return, and soon the room was in an
uproar. Sides were taken and in a free-for-all Augusta found herself
thrown about like a rugby ball. Her hair was pulled over her shoulders
and her clothes were torn from her back. It was a normal episode to
everybody except Augusta, who was horrified to hear her cavalier
shouting to his girl: "You put yer dirty 'ands on 'er again an' I'll gouge
you! I loves 'er – see? Get 'old of that. I loves 'er."

So she was back with Louisa, and Louisa made a sudden decision.
Her lameness was becoming worse. Her attachment to London was
lessening. She went back to Tregannock for good. It had all been
settled before I heard about it. Augusta had agreed to go. She
remembered Tregannock with affection. Frank Cumberledge had
been to Kensington and given his consent. His wife was expecting a
child, and that, if nothing else, made it unlikely that this was a
moment for Augusta to return to Manchester.

When they were gone, I stayed for the rest of the summer with the
Kopfs. In the autumn young Ben was to go away to a prep school and
my job would be ended. He was a nice child, darkly handsome as
Murillo knew how to make his infant saints. I saw him go off in his
grandmother's yellow Rolls-Royce, she keeping him company and

Anatole Marmont driving. He shook hands with me nicely and said in a grown-up way: "Thank you for teaching me." Well, I hadn't taught him much, except to read and write and to struggle through some fables of La Fontaine in French. But I understand that nowadays that amounts to a miracle-child. I hope he did well. I never saw him again, or Arthur Kopf, who was to be a poet and became a stockbroker, or Jane Lavernock. I saw none of them except Mabel; and I wish I could wipe out of my mind and soul the circumstances in which for the last time I saw her.

5

The day after Ben was gone I breakfasted with Arthur and Mabel and saw them set out: he for the City and she for her office. It was a September morning. I hadn't made up my mind what to do. I walked to Kensington Gardens and sat listening to the first whispers of the dying year. An astonishing year it had been – 1911. Week after week, month after month, the sun had blazed, the rain did not come, and it was only in such an early morning hour as this that there was a little dew, a little freshness, to revive the trees, the flowers, one's own senses. People said it was a good omen for the new reign. Edward was gone. He would disappoint Lord Lavernock no more by failing to keep dinner appointments, and George, the untried king, seemed hardly the sort of man who would want much to do with his father's friends, Lavernock or any other. He was a sailor. Not that that mattered, people said, for the last thing England would want was a navy, or an army, either. Look at this summer! An omen. Settled and perpetual sunshine. Even the new Home Secretary, Mr Winston Churchill, had so little to do that he could take time off to go and fight brigands in Sidney Street. Of course, there were the Germans. But there were always the Germans, and if it should ever be necessary to give them a lesson, well, it would be short and sharp. Meantime, here was this splendid summer, this new auspicious reign, these girls going by me in hobble skirts, tottering as though accompanied by an invisible partner in a two-legged race. Here was the day warming up; the trees were blazing with gold and the ground with crimson, and myself with no occupation, no destination, a rolling-stone once more, without a notion of whither I wished to roll. I called a taxi-cab, went back to the house for my suitcase, drove to the station, and that evening ate my dinner in Manchester.

I did not intend to be in Manchester long, and so I decided to do myself proud and stay at the Midland Hotel. For once in my life I had money to spare. The Kopfs had paid me generously, and I had spent hardly a penny. I slept for an hour or two, took a leisurely bath, put on what I had in the way of a best dress, and went down to dinner. It was rather early – about half-past six – and there weren't yet many people dining, so I could not overlook the two young men. I walked across to them. "Well, Miles. Well, Tom."

We shook hands, and they pressed me to share their table. They were both in evening clothes – not very usual for the casual diner-out in Manchester even at that time when life still retained a good deal of formality. But they were young, aware of themselves, and evidently this was an occasion. I chipped them about their grand appearance.

Miles said: "You have Tom to blame for that. I can't afford this sort of thing, but he's standing treat to celebrate something to do with his stinks."

Tom blushed like a modest hero pretending he didn't really want the medal. He gave me a lame explanation which I didn't understand beyond the pleasing fact that he had made some small discovery which had a commercial use and had been able to sell it.

"So it's my night out," he said, "but, of course, Miles had to decide what we were to do with ourselves. Guess what?"

It didn't take much guessing. "The theatre."

"Right first time," Tom said. "That's why we're eating so early. The show starts at half-past seven. And what about you, Miss Legassick? Shall I ring 'em up and see if they've got another seat?"

I was delighted to be asked, and Tom went off to telephone.

Miles said: "It'll be all right – plenty of seats. It's a rotten play."

"But you can't keep away from it, eh?"

"No, I can't. I think I'd go if there was nothing but a company of performing fleas."

"How is Oxford going?"

"Very well in such time as I can spare from the O.U.D.S."

"And you still want to do it professionally?"

"Rather. It's surprising what that month with Haydon Mellerby did to me. A real pro is a sort of touchstone. You soon find whether you're just playing with a thing or mean it. I've got to thank him at any rate for that, the damned skunk."

His face flushed; we had jumped suddenly on to dangerous ground, and I was glad that Tom Elthorne was coming across the room: much taller since I had seen him last, gangling as though his skeleton were imperfectly articulated, beaming through thick-lensed spectacles. "All right," he announced. "They can do it. Now I shall go into conference with the head waiter."

I remember lobster and Chablis, duck and green peas with champagne, a sweet which was some sort of angelic cloud just condensed to edibility, cheese, coffee and cognac.

"I hope," I said to Tom, "that you've really made a lot of money."

He grinned. "This is what commercial firms call ploughing back the profits," he said. "Now we'd better skedaddle. We mustn't keep Miles from his devotions."

I don't remember what the play was, but it was good to be with the boys. Tom's happiness was really moving. I suppose he was feeling as a writer does on selling his first piece. I remembered how young Dickens on that occasion had rushed to Westminster Hall and loitered there because his tear-stained face was not fit to be seen in the street. Westminster Hall, which has known the trials and obsequies of kings, had known nothing more moving than that dazed boy. Not that Tom Elthorne wanted to cry. He didn't know what he wanted. His mind, which, I imagine, was usually well under control, was gangling like his body. And in this moment he remembered Augusta. I had said that I should soon be going on to Tregannock, and when they had walked with me as far as my hotel, and Miles had got into the taxi-cab that was to take them to Didsbury, Tom turned to me and said in a rush: "Tell Augusta, will you, Miss Legassick? Tell her that I've had this little thing and that I was asking about her." Then he leapt into the cab, the door slammed and they were off.

I went up to bed, but it was a long time before I slept. It's all Augusta, I kept thinking. There was Haydon, and there was Miles all but cursing Haydon. There was that silly Cockney boy at the Settlement, and there was Tom Elthorne. There was Louisa, so possessive of Augusta, Haydon had said; and there was myself. I was aware of a vague jealousy of Louisa, and I knew that I should not be going to Tregannock if Augusta were not there. The thing went round and round in my head as doors banged in the hotel corridor and long good nights were shouted. Who found Augusta, tell me, when like a lost bird she was wandering with Miles towards the vicarage at St Tudno? Who took her in hand and made her sane, and was in love with her so much that she could have killed the odious Miss Vesey, pawing her good night? So it went, till I managed to pull a few tattered rags of sleep about me, to take up again in dreams the theme of waking.

6

While I was sleeping, Mark Cumberledge was getting born. He made an easy job of it, I was told – "Came with what sounded like a cry of joy", his sentimental mother said to me. I looked at him lying in the bend of her arm: his pushed-in nose, his sparse black hair, his pink clutching fist. Miles had told me the night before that he would be sleeping at Tom's house as the child was expected. He continued to sleep there during my short stay in Manchester. It was obvious that he had never become reconciled to the idea of a stepmother, though he had not made a "thing" of it as Augusta had done. There was no reason why he should. Oxford kept him out of the way for much of the year, and he chose, as my brother Roger had done, to spend his vacations, once a duty-call at home had been made, tramping about with his friends. He had something new in mind for the vacation after his next term. "I'm getting a company of Oxford men together – a few girls, too. We're going to revive the old barn-storming idea – go about the country places and play good stuff wherever we can find a hall. Play in the open air if necessary. One of the girls is very good – Celia Duggan. Quite beautiful, too. Well, not exactly beautiful. Not in the usual sense. But extraordinarily vivid. You know the sort of girl I mean? Alive. Every inch."

I thought I knew the sort of girl he meant, but said nothing.

"For an amateur, she was quite incredible as Nora in *A Doll's House*. Her father's in the Army. In India at the moment."

I took note of his brightened face, of his knowledge of Celia Duggan's affairs. "How are you getting on with Tom Elthorne?" I asked.

"Oh, very well. Of course, we're as different as chalk and cheese, not the least bit interested in one another's things; but he's a wide-awake chap is Tom. At the moment he's mad on sound. Can you

390

imagine that? Well, sound is just a noise, isn't it? I don't see what you can do about that."

"No. But I expect Tom does."

We were walking in the golden weather about the Handforth region. (How one walked in those days!) Golden and languorous. The year was dying, like the Dame aux Camellias, with a sort of decorous beauty. We sat in a cottage garden and took tea and watched the swallows draped along the telegraph wires, waiting for their mysterious command to fly south. There were jam-jars full of chrysanthemums by the garden gate. "I'd better buy a bunch for the new mamma," I said.

"Should I?" he asked.

"Well, we don't want to flood the house with them. You do it. It'd please your father."

"Well, of course," he said, "seen in that light . . ."

I couldn't repress a smile, and he asked: "What are you amused about?"

"You sounded so much like a cautious diplomat wondering how far you could commit your country."

"Well, a bob's-worth of chrysanthemums isn't over-doing it, do you think?"

"No. And remember you may want to introduce Celia Duggan to your father some day."

He looked startled, as though the diplomat had been caught napping, but recovered himself and said: "I hope, Aunt Maria, that I haven't given you a wrong impression. After all, Celia is just . . . is just . . ."

He still looked such a boy. I couldn't resist rumpling his hair. "Go on with you," I said. "Buy the chrysanthemums. I'll pay for the tea."

Robins were twittering in a hedge behind us, and the leaves of the blackberry briars were gold and yellow and sepia, against the blue and tranquil sky. Suddenly, as though an unseen bugle had sounded, the swallows took off — lovely, lovely birds. My heart wished them a prosperous journey, and I felt extraordinarily happy.

7

I had come to Manchester to see how Frank was getting on. I was fond of him, though he was no longer capable of giving my heart a twinge. I had ceased to think of him as a hidalgo. I was like that with men. They could flutter me for a time, if they were not quite repulsive, and then I seemed to settle down, even to withdraw a little. Not since Roger and Charles Lester died together had I loved any man, and those two deaths seemed to me to be one.

What with his work and his new son, Frank hadn't much time for me. He spared an hour to take lunch with me at the Midland, and that was about all it came to. He was, reasonably, more concerned about Augusta than about me. That she was with Louisa reassured him. His few visits to Kensington had given him an admiration for Louisa, and I thought the more of him for that. He seemed to be thinking of everybody but me. At half-past one, he looked at his watch and said: "Mark's feeding-time," and that did seem to me the limit when I had gone out of the way to provide him with a really slap-up lunch. "What about your becoming his godmother?" he asked. It sounded almost like a solatium, a booby-prize, and I declined the honour.

"When I get back to Cornwall," I said, "I shall have Augusta, and a whole handful of children at the vicarage. That'll be enough for me."

"Do you hear often from the vicarage?" he asked. "Do you hear from Bella? I remember her so well coming that Christmas-time to Bowdon just before she got engaged to Hugo."

"No," I said. "I rarely hear. I expect she has plenty on her hands without me. She's not much of a letter-writer."

He said: "I hear more often from Hugo. What a good chap he is! I'm afraid he's having a rough moment. Bella had a miscarriage and doesn't seem to have been up to much ever since. A bit of an invalid, I gather."

He looked anxiously at his watch again, and I said: "No! It can't be time for another!"

We parted on that foolish note; and the next day, leaving no address for anyone, I set out on an aimless ramble, anywhere to be alone for once, before keeping my promise to join Louisa at Tregannock for Christmas.

8

Reaching St Tudno on Christmas Eve, I went first, and without warning, to the vicarage. I didn't go at once to the house, but turned into the graveyard that had been my nursery, my playground, my earliest school. It was one of those brilliant winter days that we could count on then with reasonable certainty, but can count on no longer. The sea was calm and blue. The air was full of the scent of winter heliotrope. The stems of the daffodils were pushing up through the grass of the graves, and the brave gold of aconites shone here and there. I knew that in the vicarage garden there would certainly be a camellia or two in flower, but I kept that for later.

There had been a recent burial. The raw wound in the ground was piled with wreaths. Who now? I wondered idly, and walked across to read the inscriptions on the funeral cards.

Bella . . . Bella . . . Bella . . . "Remembering dear Mother with love." And then four signatures, in decreasing legibility. John, firmly. Then Constance. Then Richard. Millicent: a quavering scrawl. Millicent is five, I thought. She was sleeping under the hood of the pram, and Richard was waving his bunch of wilting flowers in her face.

And here was Bella, who had reached a hand from her bed to mine often of a winter's night; and her hands were folded now down there: beneath the flowers, beneath the earth, within the wood, and they would not reach out to anything any more.

My legs went weak, and I collapsed upon the broad grey stone that Mrs Solway and I had so often used as a table, shelling peas on it. And, kneeling by it, I would use it for writing, scrawling large childish letters in a copybook. To the admiration of Thomas May, I had scrawled one morning the whole of Euphemia Emmett's sad story. And on the stone Bella and I would arrange the bits of coloured glass, worn smooth by the sea, and the shells of pink and canary-yellow that we endlessly gathered. "Silly baubles!" Louisa said, her temper sharpened by a morning of scribing for Father. "Why don't you children learn to *do* something?" And Roger, who was at home on holiday, said with his smiling tolerance: "Let them train their colour sense. They're a bit young for the graver preoccupations of life."

I was so shocked that, when I tried to rise, I could not. Hugo reached down his hand, helped me to my feet, and embraced me. We stood silently like that for some time, with the calm winter sunlight falling round us; but, as often happens, there must have been mist stealing up from the Channel and round St Antony's Head, for the lighthouse bell was sounding its sombre measured note. He must be forty, I was thinking. It is five years since I saw him, five years since I saw Bella and the children. I was all wrapped up selfishly in my new-found bliss, my joy in Augusta's beauty and Miles' sad young manliness, and I neglected them all and took my pleasure.

Hugo was shorter than I was, and over his shoulder I looked at the black tent of the yew, weighing down on its crutches, cavernous, like an entrance to the underworld. Its cupped berries had all been stripped away by thrushes and blackbirds – the berries that had looked, as Roger once reminded me, like Shakespeare's jewels hung in an Ethiop's ear. Oh Roger, Charles, Father! All my losses at that moment were one loss; and I, to whom the circumstances of death and burial had been a meaningless, almost a pleasant, preoccupation of childhood, looked about that little grey graveyard by the sea with eyes new-washed by sorrow, so that I became a weight in Hugo's arms, and he eased me to the stone again, saying: "You'd better rest a bit longer, my dear."

After a while I asked: "Where are the children?"

"At Tregannock. Louisa has been splendid. She's taken them off my hands for the holiday . . . A sad holiday . . ."

He looked lost, and I stirred myself out of my sorrow to help him. "John must be a big boy now."

"Yes. Sixteen. He's at Repton. I admire William Temple, the headmaster. That's why I sent him there."

I asked him about them one by one, to keep his mind off that new-turned inexorably sinking earth that was staring us in the face. Constance? She was thirteen. "I'm educating her myself," he said. Richard was eight. He would soon be going off to a prep school. Millicent was five, just learning to read and write.

"I feel ashamed," I said, "that I have to ask you these things. I should have known. I didn't know that Bella was ill till Frank told me. I had no idea that it was serious."

"Don't reproach yourself. None of us knew till near the end. You had your own life to live. You had done plenty in your time for the vicarage. Let's go up to the house now. You'll catch cold sitting there. This winter sunshine is deceptive."

There was a welcome fire in the sitting room, and we sat before it. Through the window I could see that the camellia indeed was out – the camellia that Uncle Reginald had brought from the tangled misty mountains between India and China. I had a feeling that in one way and another Legassicks and their kin would haunt this place through any changes that could ever come. There had been so much bustle in this room just before I went away to live with Lady Lavernock. Bella and Hugo had come down from Hunslet, and it was all a stripping of wall-paper and choosing of curtains and covers, painting and picture hanging; all that agitation of someone settling in with the intention of staying for a long long time. Legassick landmarks were ruthlessly thrown out; but already, when I made my sad return after Gerald Pickering's death in France, things had matured, and now there was such a Legassick feeling about the worn carpets, and the faded wall-papers, and the fabrics clawed by kittens, and the papers and books thrown here and there, that it would not have surprised me to see Father come suddenly through the door with his day's stint of writing in his hand. And this feeling was deepened when I noticed what was part of its cause. "Why, you're sitting in Father's old chair, Hugo!"

"Yes. We bought a new one when we moved in, and this was pushed away into the loft. I was up there one day and sat down in it, and it was so much more comfortable than the new one that I've used it ever since. I don't think you'll find any fundamental change except that we've put in a telephone. I still use a bike to get about the parish."

Tea was brought in, and Hugo said: "I expect, Maria, that you know Mrs Instance?"

"You ought to, Miss Maria," the woman said. "My mother was here long enough."

So even Mrs Solway had succeeded in getting reincarnated to remain among us! There was a family likeness.

"It's nice to see you back," she said. "You'll find things all right. Mr Oldham needn't worry with me about the place, and Miss Constance is beginning to be useful. A proper little woman she be. The spit an' image of what you was at about the same age. I remember you very well – just about the time I got married."

She drew the curtains and lit a lamp. I felt relaxed and at home. Hugo said: "I'd better ring up Tregannock and ask James to bring the car for you."

"No," I said. "Don't do that. Presently I'll ring up Louisa and tell her that I shall be staying here for a day or two. Would you like me to do that?"

"I should indeed," he said. "It would be very kind of you."

9

It wasn't much of a Christmas, but it was a fertile one. At Tregannock were Miles and Augusta Cumberledge and John, Constance, Richard and Millicent Oldham. Miles was nineteen, Millicent five-and-a-half, and the others were neatly spaced between. I said to Louisa: "What on earth are we to do with them all?"

"Nothing," she said. "Leave the doing to them."

What else could we do? Miles was a man, Millicent little more than a babe in arms. Any sort of communal entertainment was out of the question. The way it sorted itself out was that Miles and John Oldham did a lot of walking together, and so did Constance and Richard. As for the young Millicent, she was never happy out of Augusta's company, and Augusta seemed to welcome her as a distraction from her own thoughts.

There was sorrow enough about the house at that time, but none of it touched me very closely except the sorrow of Augusta. She was eighteen, and at eighteen she was to have been married to Haydon Mellerby. She knew now that that was all over. The newspapers had brought the news of Haydon's marriage in Australia to his leading lady. This was between the time of my leaving Manchester and arriving at St Tudno. I had been enjoying myself and had not bothered to look at newspapers. I knew nothing of it till Louisa told me. I asked her what happened.

"Nothing," she said. "Anyway, nothing that Augusta chose to let us see. James and I were going out, and as we went I gave her the paper with the paragraph marked. She hasn't mentioned it from that moment to this."

"Wasn't that rather a hard way to do it?" I asked.

"Do you know of any way that isn't hard?"

No, I didn't.

"Very well, then. I could have smothered her in solicitude, but I couldn't believe she'd want that. No doubt there have been plenty of tears, but she's not a girl who'd want to cry in public."

So there she was, quieter than I had known her, with a deep gravity that made her more beautiful than ever, taking young Millicent off everybody's hands, walking with her, reading to her, helping her with her writing, bathing her and putting her to bed at nights. "What shall we do now, Auntie Gusta?" And Auntie Gusta always found something to do that would cushion the hurt of that small soul.

New Year's Day came, and Hugo bicycled out from St Tudno to wish us sadly a happy new year. James and Louisa pressed him to stay to lunch and he said that he would. He seemed to have an especially warm heart for his youngest child, and Millicent flew to him with an impetuosity that showed she would not want Augusta's company today. Augusta came to me in the great entrance hall where I had long since watched my Uncle Pallace go off into conference with James' father. She came down the stairs, took my arm, then looked back the way she had come. "Do I belong to all this?" she asked. "It looks so grand. I'm quite puzzled sometimes to piece together how I'm here at all."

There was a fire burning, but it was so fine a day that the double doors were open upon the winter sunshine. "I came as a temporary," she said, "and now that Haydon's done with me, I'm a bit lost. I can't stay here for ever, can I?"

I felt insanely flattered that she had opened out to me on this matter that she had not mentioned to Louisa.

"Would you like a walk and a talk?" she asked.

I said: "I should indeed."

"I thought you would. Now that Millicent's got her father, she can do without me for a bit. So I've had a few sandwiches put up. We needn't be back to lunch."

I went to give our excuses to Louisa and James, and James came to the door to see us off. "You watch these Legassicks," he warned Augusta. "They're walking mad, and they've always had parsons in the family. I suppose one of 'em was a monk in the Middle Ages who walked to Jerusalem and back. It's been in the family ever since."

It was an old joke with James, and he laughed at it himself as heartily as he always did, and I answered, as I always did: "You should walk more yourself. You'd be a better man if there were less of you."

Augusta kissed him. She was very fond of him and knew that he treasured her kisses. "Don't take any notice of her," she said. "You're just right."

"Poor Louisa can't walk," he said, "or I'd do a lot more of it."

No, indeed. Poor Louisa's walking days seemed ended, and she hardly moved out of the house except in the car. Indoors, she hobbled on two sticks, and somehow managed to make her progress impressive.

As we walked down through the long field Augusta said: "How they love me! I'm wicked to say I don't belong. Sometimes I think I never belonged to *anything* more than I do to those two. And to you."

We walked down to the village, and then along the creek to St Tudno vicarage, and on from there along the path that fringed the sea. It was a walk I had taken long ago with Roger, on that day when I told him how it was between me and Charles Lester – or, rather, there was no "between" about it: it was all my own out-going, with nothing responding to it, and I discovered that as long as Roger lived nothing could respond.

A bit of gorse was blooming, and the pale sunlight fell upon it and upon the water placidly slapping the rocks tumbled about in the gulch at our feet.

"Let's sit here and eat our sandwiches," Augusta said; and when we had eaten them she poured herself out to me, as I had poured myself out to Roger.

I let her go on. That, I felt, was what she wanted: to say it and have done with it. Her pride in him: that was the key-note. Nothing much about herself. She couldn't see, she said, how a man so handsome, so famous, so personally fascinating, had ever taken the slightest notice of her. When they were working on the play he was so exacting, so sharp with her at times. When she found that all the sharpness was directed against a phantom, given a name for the purpose of an hour's entertainment, and that she, Augusta, was something else, she was dumbfounded. When everyone else was packing up one night and moving out of the barn, he said: "You stay, Miss Cumberledge. We'd better go over our bit again. You must try and get some animation into it." It was a bit designed to show up the nature of a philanderer, stealing a hug and a kiss. That night she knew that he was not kissing the phantom, the name on the programme. I can imagine how she pulled away from him, startled, her breast heaving. She said to me: "It was shattering. No one had ever kissed me before – not like that. I was trembling from head to foot, and I wouldn't have been, would I, if I hadn't liked it, if I hadn't wanted it?"

He kissed her again, and she found herself responding, surprising herself with the discovery that she, too, knew how to kiss – like that.

When they came in, old Miss Mellerby said: "You look a little feverish, my dear. You'd better go straight to bed."

"I did," Augusta said, "but I didn't sleep. I lay there, living it all over again and again, and thinking how that old lady was going to be surprised. Well, I don't suppose she was. I was the one to be surprised. Were you? Or did you believe in it as I did?"

"It's more important to ask whether he did. I think he did. He's not the first man I've known break off an engagement, and a man isn't necessarily a worse man because of that."

"Thank you, Aunt Maria," she said. "I'd rather hear that than some soft nonsense. It's what I've been trying to tell myself. But perhaps it's a bit harder for me than it is for you."

"Much harder, my dear."

She began to gather up the sandwich-papers and orange-peel and put them into our basket. "Nineteen hundred and twelve," she said. "This year I shall be nineteen. If things had gone as we planned, I should have been married for about a year."

She stood up tall and slender, looking over the quiet sea to the white tower of St Antony's light, the pale winter sun shining on her pale hair. "Do you remember," she asked, "when we first met? You rowed me and Miles out beyond the lighthouse, and the sun was going down and someone said it would soon be rising in America. I asked if it would take with it all the things that had happened to us that day in Cornwall."

I remembered – as I remembered all that had happened that day – and said so.

"It used to be quite a thought of mine when I was a child," she said. "The sun picking up news in the East and then scooping up more over Europe and carrying on with it to America, and on across the Pacific to the East again. Adding and adding, till it was crammed with men's goings-on."

She turned to me, smiling at her own fancy. "Perhaps it's the same with us," she said, "as we go through our days. We remember and remember, and there's always something else for remembering! I remember my mother. I was weeping for her when we first met, but now I'm reconciled. Perhaps one becomes reconciled to everything."

It was half a question, and I had learned the bitter answer, but I didn't give it. She seemed on the way to finding it for herself.

We walked back the way we had come, and I asked her whether she remembered Tom Elthorne. "I ought to," she said. "I don't suppose I shall ever forget him. It was he who arranged my journey to York."

"He meant well."

"Oh, yes. He's a well-meaning boy."

I told her of my dinner with him and gave her his message. She didn't seem much interested.

"I wonder whether I shall be here in the summer?" she asked.

"I expect Miles has told you about his barn-storming scheme? He says that St Tudno is on his schedule. I should like to meet this Celia Duggan."

"Oh, he's talked to you about her, has he?"

"If I'd let him, he'd talk to me about nothing else. She seems to be Mrs Siddons, Rachel and Ellen Terry happily united in one little undergraduate. She can't be much older than I am. Perhaps if I'd been that sort of a girl . . ."

"Now! Augusta!"

"All right, darling," she said. "No bitterness."

The bitterness was bound to fester for a time, but she kept it to herself. So far as the rest of us were concerned, she had spoken the last word.

CHAPTER THIRTEEN

MILES CALLED his company The Oxford Strollers, and a fortnight before they arrived in St Tudno, his Publicity Department, as he called it, was busy. The Publicity Department was a nice boy named Michael Miskin, known as Mickey. He couldn't act, and had the sense to know it. He was one of those people who in more spacious days became patrons of the arts. To him, the theatre was a temple, and he its humblest servitor. He was always there ready to give a hand with the hard work and the dirty work, and he spent his money freely. He had plenty to spend. He was twenty-one, a Somerset boy whose family had been settled there longer than the Polperros had been settled in Cornwall, and his coming-of-age had given him a handsome income, bequeathed by his dead mother.

We knew nothing of this when he arrived. Miles had written from St Austell to say that the company would be with us in a fortnight's time, and that Mr Michael Miskin, the publicity agent, would be coming along at once. Would we put him up?

Augusta and I were walking from the house towards the high road when we saw this young man bicycling towards us through the long field. He jumped off and said: "Hallo! Are you any of the Tregannock people?"

We admitted it, and he said: "Good. I believe you're expecting me. I'm Mickey, the bill-sticker."

We hadn't heard that he was Mickey, but assumed that bill-sticking was a part of publicity, and that therefore this must be Mr Miskin. On the handle-bars of the bicycle was a basket, and there was another on the carrier at the back. They were encased in waterproof material, and when he removed this at the house we discovered a fine confusion: hand-bills, stick-up bills, tooth-brush, pyjamas and paste-brush all most comradely together. "I suppose," he said, "you can find me a bucket and a bag of flour?"

I promised that we could, but must have looked rather surprised, for he explained: "I'll have to make some paste and get busy slapping things up. Would you two care to come with me after lunch?"

James and Louisa were out, and would not be back till evening. Augusta showed Mr Miskin his room, and then we three sat down to lunch. He said, belatedly, how glad he was to meet Augusta, and from Augusta passed to her brother. "I'd do anything for Miles," he said. "Wonderful chap. Can't act myself. Never wanted to. Said to him: 'Look, Miles, shows like yours are ruined for want of publicity. Arrive in a village, find six people yawning on a bench in a stable and a horse looking over the door. Leave all that to me.' He did, and here I am – fortnight before they come. Time to work up enthusiasm. Always a fortnight ahead of 'em wherever they go. Sowing the seed. Finding a hall. Finding digs. Well, let's make that paste."

We made the paste, and he gave Augusta a dozen large bills announcing the show's coming. "Everything there except the dates. Fill that in. Make a nice clear job of it."

We must have been an odd-looking trio: Mickey carrying the bucket of paste, myself burdened with those little hand-bills that he called throw-aways, Augusta with a roll of posters. We got to the large gate leading to the road, and there Mickey paused, contemplating the granite pillars from which the gate hung. "Just the job," he said. "Two posters, please."

He slapped paste on to their backs, and with a fine professional touch fixed them to the pillars, which, I imagine, had never before in their hoary lives known such defilement. He walked to the other side of the road and regarded them with pleasure, like a painter looking at his picture hung on the line. Two women and a child from the village, passing by, stopped to read. Mickey cleared his throat meaningfully to call my attention, nodded even more meaningfully towards them. I tumbled to it and humbly, blushing, gave them a hand-bill each. They passed on, and Mickey said: "Good. You're getting the idea."

We combed the village. We called at the Polperro Arms, which received us with surprise, but Mickey was an ingratiating person. He downed a pint of ale, and Augusta and I toyed with shandy-gaff. Mickey extolled the virtues of the theatre and left a poster exhibited over the bar. A little pile of throw-aways was left for distribution. Mickey had a fine touch with villagers. After all, his family more or less owned a village. At the smithy, where young Mr Rowe had long succeeded old Mr Rowe, he joined in the discussions of the parliament. They were talking about the chances of war with Germany, and the feeling of the house was against. But Mickey disagreed. "You wait," he said. "Couple of years at most. My father's a Territorial colonel. I'm a lieutenant. We talk about these things. You wait."

However, sombre thoughts didn't weigh heavily on him. We scattered our throw-aways, left a poster on the smithy door and one in each of the three village shops, and then Mickey said we could call it a day. He had already, he said, before calling on us, seen the parson about the use of the church hall. The parson reminded me that it was time I was back with Hugo, so there I said goodbye, and he and Augusta strolled back together towards Tregannock. "Tomorrow," he said to Augusta, "perhaps you'll come with me to Falmouth. Must see local newspaper people. All helps."

Mr Michael Miskin, I pondered, wandering homeward along the creek, was no leaver of unturned stones.

2

Back then to the children. They had stayed at Tregannock for a month or so after their mother's death. Then John had gone back to Repton and Richard to his first term at prep school. Constance, at thirteen, was her father's pupil, and the five-year-old Millicent was mine. There was no need for me to be there at all so far as the children were concerned. Things were not as they were in Father's day. His fruitless writing had left him with little time for us, and had eaten into our own time. Hugo was not a writer, nor had he any ambition except to be a good parish priest. He had had leisure to be schoolmaster to John and Richard while they were at home, and he had leisure for Constance now. He would take Millicent off my hands when Constance was ready for the university. It was the sudden vacuum in his own life that I was there to fill. He asked me with his usual diffidence if I would stay. "It's asking a lot, my dear − perhaps too much. But if you could just be about . . . come and go as you please . . . but just be about."

So Augusta stayed with Louisa and James, and here I was, back where I had started, with the loft new white-washed, my books on their old shelves, my bed in its old corner – Aunt Maria, aged thirty-six, the odd-job woman, spectacled, gruff, who sometimes felt as though she had lived through a hundred harsh and disappointing years, and sometimes felt a child who could do with a Euphemia Emmett to kiss and fondle. That afternoon, when I came back from my expedition with Mickey and Augusta, it seemed to me that all through my life I had been the Mickey – not one of the players, but the bill-sticker, the stander-by, the indispensable one who, as I remembered Father saying in a sermon on John the Baptist, was happy to pave the way and do without the glory. But was I happy?

3

A fortnight later I had come in from a massive struggle with flowers and fruits and vegetables that had been dumped in the church for the garnishing of our harvest festival. I loved the way our people treated the church with the same sort of happy familiarity that they gave to their kitchens. One stout woman threw a pile of enormous leeks before the altar and said: "Well, there they be, Miss Legassick, with my regrets. A fine lickey pie they'd have made, but if the Lord God wants 'em I suppose I'd better pretend He's welcome to 'em." She looked regretfully at the leeks, and then took out a few of the best. "He won't miss these," she said, and carried them off; and I thought of Samuel reproving Saul who had kept the best of the Amalekites' cattle when God had commanded him to destroy them all. I remembered it because of Samuel's stern words: "Stubbornness is as idolatry and teraphim," and I used to wonder when a child what teraphim was. I thought it was something to do with turtles, and was disappointed when Father explained that it was a sort of family idol that the Hebrews were forbidden to have.

Happy at being plunged back into this old atmosphere of my childhood, I made my way to the loft, and had hardly settled down when I heard Miles' voice on the outside stairway, shouting: "Are you in, Aunt Maria? May we come up?"

We! I knew at once who was with him. Celia Duggan, daughter of the colonel in India, came in.

She was an actress, if only an amateur, and the little I had heard about her had told me she was exceptional. I was still romantic enough to think of any actress as a flashing, glamorous creature, and was taken aback by a girl who was as quiet as a pool in a wood. There was nothing about Celia to catch the imagination except this quiet. She was of middle size and brownish: brown skin, brown eyes. Her brown hair was coiled into two Chelsea buns that hung above her ears. A seemly young person, who was quietly dressed, carried herself beautifully, and spoke in a quiet voice. Just about as old as Augusta, I guessed. But not an Augusta. I made this reflection almost with satisfaction. Nobody must be like Augusta.

She shook hands with me and said: "So this is you. I wondered if you really existed."

Those were the first words she spoke to me, and as she spoke a faint smile spread over her face, like light falling through the trees of the wood upon the pool.

There has been some correspondence in the newspapers lately about gabbling and muttering on the stage, and an old-timer – one of my generation, I guess – asked: "Where are voices like Celia Duggan's? Her voice was an oboe played by a master."

That was it. She had a woodwind voice, clear and cool and sweet, like a dove's. I lived to see her famous, and, splendid actress though she was, half her art was always in her voice. Even then, when she was little more than a child playing Juliet in our St Tudno church hall, my heart was choked when I heard her say such things as:

> Come, gentle night, come, loving black-brow'd night,
> Give me my Romeo; and, when he shall die,
> Take him and cut him out in little stars,
> And he will make the face of heaven so fine
> That all the world will be in love with night.

The slight, trembling hesitation on those words "when he shall die" (spoken in a kind of incredulous whispered parenthesis) was an artist's signature.

Well, there she was, and when she said: "I wondered if you really existed," I answered gruffly: "Oh, I'm real enough, like an old teak bollard."

She said: "Miles loves you so much. He'll talk for hours about St Tudno and how you healed his wounds and his sister's."

"Have you met his sister? Have you met Augusta?"

"Yes. Miles and I slept at Tregannock last night. She came to my bedroom and we had a long, long talk. What a beauty she is! If I could be envious, I'd envy her."

"Can't you be envious?"

"No. Only thankful. I've been given so much."

She said it simply and without pride – humbly, almost. But at the same time with complete assurance. She never doubted herself.

Miles seemed restless and ill at ease. Suddenly he said: "I've asked Celia to marry me."

The little room clouded. It was so abrupt, so impetuous, that one felt he had not intended to say it. It had torn itself out of him. He looked troubled, and Celia sad. For me, what could I do or say?

We had all been standing. All I could say, feeling ineffectual, was: "Do sit down."

I sat, and Celia perched herself on the arm of my chair. Miles remained upright and began to pace the room. "Not now, of course," he said. "We'd have to wait a bit. We're more or less beggars, the pair of us. But it would be a stimulus, wouldn't it? An incentive."

Celia said: "Miss Legassick, I'm so sorry about this. We shouldn't drag you into it."

"Don't say we," Miles put in, contrite. "It's my doing."

Celia said: "I've known for some time how Miles feels about me. But I did hope he'd leave it alone at least till the tour was ended."

"The tour," Miles said, and this time he couldn't keep some bitterness out of his voice. "The tour comes first. The tour is everything."

"But it is, isn't it?" she asked reasonably. "We're both professionals, or hope to be. We can't play fast and loose with our work. If I'd been able to say Yes, that would have been a different matter. It could even have helped things on. I see that."

Again the cloud. To me, the room seemed filmed with disaster, like Louisa's bedroom when Bella and I left the oil lamp smoking.

It was Celia who at last broke the silence. "I don't know, Miles. That's all I told you, isn't it? I don't know. I'm very fond of you, but that's not enough, is it? Not for me, anyway. I can't say Yes if I don't know. You wouldn't want me to, honestly, would you now, if there was a chance that I'd have to go back on my word?"

She had got up and faced him, pleading. They were no longer a young man and a young woman who hoped to be professionals. They were children, hurt, bewildered. Miles was biting his lip, and I saw with horror that he was trying to prevent himself from crying. He made a strange gesture of renunciation, as though putting aside all joy, all hope. "All right," he said unsteadily. "I see I'm in the wrong. Let's leave it and go on as we were. Forgive all this, Aunt Maria."

I was too stricken to speak. I kissed them both.

Miles said with a wintry smile: "Well, we're due at Tregannock for lunch. We have to walk it, so we'd better get going."

I stood at the window and watched them walking down the road. It was the window through which I had pushed the tent and sleeping-bag on that wonderful day when the ebbing tide shut us into the Ruan River and all life seemed to lie happily before Miles and Augusta. Well, I reflected sadly, they are both getting a taste of what life is about.

4

The next day the sea was like silk, and in the morning I rowed myself across the creek to have a swim from the little jetty. I had persuaded Hugo to buy a dinghy. It was a shame to have these children growing up in such a place with no knowledge of the sea. Hugo was well-to-do, and I promised myself that, if I were still with him next summer, there would be a sailing boat, too. The fact is, I was rather desperately clutching at my own childhood, trying to recreate the ingredients of a long-lost peace and serenity.

I had my swim, and dressed, and was lying in the sunlight, when I heard voices and footsteps coming along the path which, on that side, leads down to the water. I recognised the voices at once: Augusta's and Michael Miskin's. They burst through the bushes and saw me lying there, my bathing-suit hanging out to dry on the thorny sloes. They seemed a little taken aback.

"Oh, Aunt Maria," Augusta said. "We were taking a walk."

Since coming to live at Tregannock she had got back all the lovely colour that she had lost in London, and the colour was heightened by the walk and by her obvious excitement. Taking a walk . . . A pretty long one, too, I reflected, to bring them from Tregannock to that side of the creek.

"I'm unemployed," Mickey said. "There's not a man, woman or child in St Tudno who doesn't know that the players will burst upon them tomorrow. I've practically sold out the house for the first night."

"It's meant too much beer-drinking in the Polperro Arms," Augusta chided him.

"You're a one to talk," he said. "What about the gallons of shandy-gaff?"

They were already on surprisingly easy terms. They could talk nonsense together.

"Tomorrow," Mickey said, "I move on to St Ives. So Augusta thought I'd better see something of your country. Pretty marvellous, too. Somerset's better, of course, but my part of it isn't on the sea."

We sat there idly watching the idle water. It was some special day or other, and Hugo had run up a flag on the staff above our small grey tower. It hung motionless. Bees were at their work in the bushes behind us. Their buzzing had an urgency. Not much time was left for honey-gathering. The gulls were too lazy to do a thing. They just sat on the water, rocking gently.

"St Ives will be my last port of call," Mickey said. "Then I must rush straight back to camp. My father's very strict about it."

He talked to us about his father and his home. "It's a bit more crumbly than Tregannock," he said. "Tregannock's built of granite, and that lasts. We're Ham stone. I expect you know it, Miss Legassick? Honey-yellow – like Augusta's hair."

He turned and smiled at her, and she seemed to like the comparison better than she had liked Tom Elthorne's remark that her hair was like Lyle's golden syrup.

"Still," Mickey said, "Ham stone takes more watching than granite, and so, as I say, we're a bit crumbly. Elizabethan to begin with. There's a miniature of a Lady Miskin that Nicholas Hillyard painted. That's the oldest thing we've got. Hillyard painted Elizabeth, you know. Miskins have been there ever since. I wonder how much longer that sort of thing can go on?"

On such a day the question seemed incongruous. On the hills the ricks looked like houses of solid gold. The harvest was in, as it always had been, as it always would be. Next Sunday Hugo would be thanking God for it all, and we would sing the harvest hymns without a doubt that we would be doing it again in a year's time. It was a day to believe in continuity.

"Why shouldn't it go on?" I asked.

"Oh, I don't know." He pulled a stalk of grass and began nibbling it like a child. He looked very young. "As a family," he said, "we're wearing a bit thin. We've got a bad habit of being killed off in wars. The long gallery's full of pictures of Miskins in uniform, and every other one of 'em died in some schemozzle or other. They began in the Civil War and have kept it up ever since. The Boer War was the last to do for one of 'em."

He pulled out a pipe and lit it, and said: "It was all right so long as the family was fruitful. If one was knocked off, there was another to carry on. But there were only two in my father's generation, and, as I've told you, the Boers took one. Then there was just my father left, with two sons. Always sons. Odd, isn't it? In all the Miskin history there's never been a daughter."

"So you have a brother?" I said.

"I *had,* but I killed him."

Augusta and I looked at him in consternation.

"I was at Eton then," he said. "In the summer holidays we always got up a cricket match for the village boys. It was quite a thing, with tea-tents for the village people and all the rest of it. That year it was a pretty bad bit of weather, raining day after day, and I was keen to practise batting, but couldn't get out. So my brother and I – he was just a year older – did what we often did. We went up to the long gallery to practise there on a strip of matting, with stumps socketted in a block of wood. It wasn't a picture gallery then. It was more or less of a shambles. All the same, we were forbidden to play cricket there. The windows are pretty ancient and interesting, and I suppose Father thought we'd smash 'em. Well, that's where I killed him. I just swiped wildly at a ball and it hit him in the temple. It was as simple as that."

He knocked out his pipe on his heel, as though knocking out an intolerable memory. He brusquely went into a new subject. "What d'you think of this new king?"

"I'm afraid," I said, "kings have never meant much to me."

"Better than Edward, anyway," Mickey said. "Father detested Edward. Father's rather a stern soldierly type. He didn't like all that gutsing and musical comedy stuff. He says that when war comes it'll be better to have someone like George who's done a bit of practical work in one of the Services."

"What d'you mean – when?" Augusta asked. "Don't you even say 'If'?"

"Father doesn't anyway. He says it's as certain as tomorrow's breakfast. We'd better get back."

They were both very quiet. I noticed that on the rocky path she took his arm.

5

The Oxford Strollers were gone. They were a gay, amusing lot, not very talented, except Celia and Miles; and all the boys adored Celia and all the girls adored Miles. But those two were unhappy. I find in modern novels that boys and girls are ready to fall into bed together at the drop of a hat, as they say, all in fun; and perhaps two wars have had something to do with that. Celia was fastidious, almost strait-laced. I doubt if she had ever given Miles as much as a kiss. She loved him – I was sure of that – but she was cool, keeping herself in check, as I have seen her do on the stage, level and contained, so that when the moment to let go came the effect was doubled. For whatever reason, her moment with Miles had not come.

They had taken lunch one day with me and Hugo, and I mentioned Michael Miskin's view, and his father's, that war was not far off. Miles laughed. "We all know Mickey," he said. "I hope he made clear to you that his father is his god. I don't take very seriously his passings-on of wisdom from the oracle."

Celia said: "Don't be too sure of that, Miles."

"Good lord!" Miles said. "Men are civilised now, aren't they?"

"Then why do they go on building dreadnoughts if there's nothing to dread?"

"Oh, you know what the Services are. They have to keep something stirring to justify their existence."

Celia said: "My father is in one of the Services. I've always considered his existence justified."

"I beg your pardon. I didn't intend a personality. But, good God! D'you mean to tell me that all we've learned, all we've done, leaves us still like hordes of barbarians, glaring at one another over fences, panting to throw rocks?"

Celia said quietly: "That is exactly what I mean to tell you. I know a lot of my father's friends in England. I hear them talk, and I don't find their talk comforting."

Miles appealed to Hugo. "What do you think, Uncle?"

"My religion," Hugo said, "teaches me that man is born to sin and iniquity. My experience teaches me that my religion isn't so far out."

Miles turned desperately to me. "Auntie. Let's have your view. Then I'm sure we shall be fifty-fifty."

I longed to comfort him, but I could not. I remembered a talk with Mabel Kopf. In her energetic way she had dashed off to Germany to find out what was being done there for the sort of luckless young people she herself had to deal with. "I don't like that place," she said to me. "I found most of the people smooth enough on the surface, but deep down I felt a loathing for this country. The father of one of the women I was dealing with was a Prussian officer. I met him at a dinner. He'd drunk rather a lot and his tongue began to wag. He said to me: 'Why are you bothering about trifles, Mrs Kopf? You will soon have something serious to occupy your minds over there.' It was the sort of hint that came my way pretty often, but never quite so rudely. I had a feeling that there was something brewing up."

I said to Miles: "I'm in no position to speak with authority. But a witness whose intelligence I trust was in Germany not long ago, and I'm afraid her vote would be against you."

Miles wouldn't have it. "The Germans are civilised people," he burst out. "Their science – their music –"

Hugo said: "My dear boy, we may have to leave out the music and face the science. As for their being a civilised people, I doubt if they've ever been as civilised as the Greeks, and they were pretty warlike. Every great civilisation has been warlike, including our own. How on earth do you think we got hold of India, Canada, South Africa?"

There was a long, uneasy silence. Nobody was eating. At last Miles said: "Well, if you're all right and I'm wrong, I propose to remain wrong. Nothing would induce me to take a hand in war."

"Why should you?" Celia asked. "We have our army and our Territorial Army."

That sounded sensible to me, and I am sure to Hugo. But, whatever his views on fighting may have been, Miles had already seen farther than any of us.

"You all have very odd ideas," he said. "If war comes, it will be immense. Your army and your Territorials will be a flea-bite. The government will use every emotional appeal to stampede men into the Territorials, and the time could easily come when they'd stop appealing and use compulsion."

He spoke with such conviction that we were awed, and convinced. He pushed away his unfinished food and stood up. "That's what I think," he said. "You can't talk about this matter as if we wouldn't be involved. We would be – up to the neck. It wouldn't be the poor bloody redcoats fighting for us in the Crimea this time, or Wellington's scum of the earth being mown down at Waterloo."

I had never heard Miles swear before, never seen him so passionately excited.

Celia said: "Supposing you're right. Supposing it came to that and all your friends were involved. Would you still stand out?"

"I would."

She looked at him with sad speculation. "I think that would be a pity," she said.

6

Now they were gone, and I walked over to Tregannock. James was himself working the home farm, and he came in to lunch from the fields, looking robust and agricultural. But Louisa was not robust. She walked into the dining room heavily on her two sticks and complained that she was having difficulty in holding them. Some rheumatic affection – I suppose we should call it arthritis today – tended to tie her fingers in knots. The Strollers' visit had tired her, though she did not mention it. There had been Mickey and Augusta, Miles and Celia in the house. Her increasing disability made James cross, though not with her. It was, I suppose, that blind, undirected crossness that comes if we haven't the philosophy to understand and accept the inevitable. It was monstrous to him that his Louisa should be afflicted in any way; and when, just as she was about to sit at the table, one of the sticks fell from her hand, he burst out: "If you'd kept away from that damned horse and all those harridans, this wouldn't have happened." He helped her down into her chair.

There was a time when she would have flown out at that. She smiled and said: "Nonsense, my dear. It's the Cornish climate. It puts mildew into everybody's bones if they stay here long enough. Anyway, this is just one of my bad days. It comes and goes."

"Yes, I know," he said. "That's true so far as your hands go. But what about your legs? That's nothing to do with climate."

"Well, such as they are, they'll have to do. Be a dear and cut my meat. I can't manage a knife and fork today."

I watched his great red hands cutting up the meat, and the beautiful solicitude of his face. He muttered: "Thank God you didn't have your way and keep me in Parliament. There'd have been no one to look after you."

She laughed at him mischievously. "Yes," she said, "I averted a national peril. You might have become Prime Minister."

He had his father's liking for wine, and filled his glass with Pommard. He took a deep draught and said: "The country might do worse. For one thing, I'd find an excuse for getting in before the Germans made a move."

"You've been talking to Michael Miskin," I said.

"Yes, I have. That's a sensible boy."

I asked where Augusta was, and he said: "I motored her over to St Ives first thing this morning, and I'll bring her back this evening."

My mind said: "For St Ives read Mickey."

Louisa said to James: "I had a letter from Mabel Kopf this morning. She proposes herself for a visit. Could we put her up for a few days next week?"

"Of course we could put her up," James said. "This damn great barrack could put up a regiment. But *should* we? That's another matter. Haven't you had enough?"

Louisa said: "I've never had enough. I want all that's going."

Unwittingly, she summarised in those few words all that, through the long years, she had more and more seemed to me. Now that she was sitting, her face was tranquil, almost with an autumn tranquillity, ripe and experienced. All that she lacked of autumn was tenderness. She never had that.

"I can guess what la Kopf wants."

"Well, of course," she conceded. "It doesn't take much guessing. She's a one-idea'd woman. But it happens to be a good idea. The snag about Cornwall has always been the cost of bringing the children here. I've promised to find the money, and now she'd like to take a look round to see if the place is suitable. If it is, we'll have a party down next summer."

James looked sulky. "It's very kind of her ladyship to come and look at our place," he said. "I hope it meets with her approval. If she'd like another dozen bathrooms she must let me know. Why don't you drink some of this Pommard? It'd put a bit of blood and bone into you."

"Thank you, James," she said. "Give me a little, and fill up with water."

"Don't be blasphemous," he reproved her. "I know only one verse of poetry – by a chap named Chesterton.

And Noah he often said to his wife when he sat down to dine,
'I don't care where the water goes if it doesn't get into the wine.'

"That shows that even a poet has moments of common sense. You better take his advice."

"I never met Noah," she said, "so I don't know what wine did to his blood and bones. The Bible tells us that his drunkenness shocked his sons. I did once meet Mr Chesterton. He looked like a jelly that hadn't set. So, please, a little wine and a lot of water."

"Well, I must hop it," he said. "We're threshing."

When he was gone Louisa said: "Come up to my room."

James had had an electric plant installed, not primarily for the lighting of the house, though there was that, too, but in order that a lift might be there for Louisa's use, now that she found stairs tiresome. I was afraid of it, as I am of almost anything new. I gave Louisa an arm as far as the lift door, which was in the back of the hall, and said: "I'll run up the stairs and meet you at the top."

"Nonsense," she said. "Get in."

I got in, and when the lift started to go up I said: "Are you sure you can stop it?" I pictured us shooting out through the tiles of Tregannock.

"The question is," Louisa said, "will it stop itself? It's temperamental. Last week it stopped halfway to my room, and there

I had to sit till James had motored over to Truro for an electrician. He was a very airy electrician who explained that these things are still experimental but will be reliable some day."

Louisa's room used to be on the first floor, but, now that the lift was there, she had gone up to the second whence she had a wider view. She hobbled along to her door, and, indicating the one before it, said: "That's Augusta's. It's handy for me to have her near me. She's a dear child. James gave her a rather extravagant cheque for her birthday, and she bought a typewriter. Now that there are days when I can hardly hold a pen it's a great comfort to have a secretary."

She sat in a chair placed to give her the famous Tregannock view.

"Then I suppose," I said, "I shall see less and less of Augusta. She doesn't disturb the vicarage much nowadays."

A pang of jealousy showed me a picture: Louisa sitting here in this charming room, looking through the window as the colours of the falling woods changed with the passing year, and the hawks hung against the blue sky or the rolling cloud-billows, and Augusta served her and adored her. We couldn't give her this at the vicarage.

"There are some letters, of course," Louisa said, "that I *have* to struggle through. There was one to Frank about this young Michael Miskin. Augusta seems fond of him, but I don't know whether it's more than that. As for him, I'm afraid he's head over heels. He asked me for a 'private interview' — poor boy! fancy putting it like that! — and poured out his soul. He's finished at Oxford, with a Third in whatever he was studying, and is going back to live with his father in Somerset. He wanted to know whether I would approve of his asking his father to write to me, proposing a visit by Augusta to Somerset. He said: 'Of course, she'd have to be accompanied, and as it might be a strain for you, it would have to be her other aunt.' "

She looked at me with a faint smile, which may have been of sympathetic amusement with the ways of the young, or of ironic enjoyment of all that was wrapped up in those three words — the other aunt. The other aunt, who had been the other sister when Bella went long ago to meet Hugo's people at Bowdon.

Ah, well, I thought; it would have been very nice to be asked for my own sweet sake, but God save us from self-pity.

"What did Frank say?" I asked.

"He sees nothing against her going if she wants to. Naturally, he would like to see her settled. It's not likely that she'll ever go back to him, especially as there's this other child on the way."

"I didn't know about that. I seem to live like the fire-brigade — never called in unless there's trouble."

"Well, for once let's discuss something ahead. There seems no doubt that Mabel Kopf will be bringing some of her boys and girls down here next summer. I sha'n't be able to give them much beyond my blessing, but we'll want some sturdy hands. Miles has promised to come and bring a couple of boys from Oxford. It would help if you could come, too."

"All right — if I'm still here. But you know how it is. By then, someone may have put me in charge of a failing grandmother in Korea."

I left her, and, fearing that the lift might stick halfway, walked downstairs.

7

Augusta and I travelled to Sherston in the following April. It had been for me a dull winter. With John Oldham away at Repton, and Richard at his prep school and Constance in her father's competent hands, I had to make do with the small Millicent, a sluggish and lethargic child heavily endowed with the qualities of her mother, Bella. However, Hugo congratulated me on her progress in reading and writing, and there was the Christmas break when Miles, after a short visit to his father in Manchester, came to stay at Tregannock and took me out now and then on the rousing walks that we both loved. He brought me some news of Tom Elthorne, who, I knew, had opened a tentative correspondence with Augusta and, unencouraged, had dropped it. On a winter's day of calm sea and sunshine Miles had said: "Aunt Maria, we've never been on the Ruan River since that time when Augusta and I first knew you. Let's go there now."

And so we did, rowing up the Ruan River among the winter-struck oaks, which even yet had a tatter or two of gold and amber flapping on their bones. "What a philoprogenitive man my father is!" Miles said. "There are children all over the place."

"Oh, come, Miles! Only two."

416

"Well, believe me, two can seem to be all over the place. I spent most of my time with Tom."

"You mean Tom spent most of his time in the theatres with you."

"We got some walks in, too. He's properly cut up because Augusta gives him the cold shoulder."

"That's your fault. You shouldn't have brought Michael Miskin along. What's Tom doing?"

"At the moment he's just pottering about in his own laboratory. But he's on the look-out for a job with some big chemical firm — something like Brunner-Mond's. He's not in a hurry. He says it's got to be a job where he can experiment. And, of all things, he's joined the Territorial Army. Can you believe it! And he's nearly as blind as a bat. I don't know what's coming over people."

I didn't answer, and after a moment he asked: "Is your silence a reproof?"

"No, Miles. It's a question you must answer for yourself. Let's hope no answer will be needed."

In the Ruan River the winter quiet was profound. No birdsong, no rustle of leaves, not so much as a sigh from the flood tide. We grounded the boat and sat on the shingle, eating our sandwiches. All the jolly stir of our former visit was absent. No tent to put up, no firewood to gather, no meal to cook. We sat there shrouded in a moment that was immense and inapprehensible. Even to speak seemed out of place. But presently Miles said: "The devil of it is that I'm coming to think you people are right. We've got a few German under-graduates, you know, at Oxford, and one of them asked me up to his rooms not long ago. We talked of this and that, and I suppose it would have been just another call on a man if a couple of his fellow Germans hadn't drifted in. And d'you know what they began to talk about?"

I didn't.

"How they were going to get out of England in case of a call-up!"

Again the silence, and then he said: "Still, it doesn't alter my opinion about what *I* ought to do."

We started back early, for the days were short. I asked him: "How is Celia?"

"Oh, very well. We're rehearsing a Strindberg thing. She's going to be great in it. She amazes me the way she gets the hang of a character – the very guts of it."

I looked at him sadly, and he said: "We never discuss this German thing. Don't think that *that* could ever come between us. We're great friends. Of course, her work is tremendously important to her."

We drew into our own creek with the dusk deepening and the sky towards Tregannock all a crimson smoulder with a drift of homing rooks across it. He helped me ashore and said hopefully: "Thank you, Aunt Maria. Another good day to remember."

8

The house called Sherston is about five miles from Yeovil. Michael Miskin met us at the Yeovil railway station, and I had to pinch myself hard to assure myself that I existed, that I was there with the other two. I was, in that moment of reunion, so overlooked and forgotten that I would not have been surprised if they had walked out and left me standing there. I suppose charm is the inescapable word for Michael – not a word I like, but there is no other. Michael had only to smile at you with the light blue eyes in his rather irregular face for you to be captive. And Augusta was beautiful. They were both young. She was twenty, he twenty-three. Beauty, charm and youth, meeting and kissing. Is it any wonder that I was not there? Indeed, they were walking away when Augusta exclaimed: "Oh, the luggage!" and they turned back, and there was I, feeling inseparably a part of the luggage. "Miss Legassick!" Michael said. "How beautiful you're looking!" And of course I was looking beautiful, just as, to him at that moment, the engine driver was, and the engine, and a consignment of bananas being tipped out of the guard's van, and the litter-basket, spilling over with empty cartons and crumpled newspapers. "Thank you for bringing her," he said, as though I had brought the King of China's silken daughter, jingling with bells. Oh, Celia! I thought. You could be all this to Miles!

We got into Michael's motorcar, a red sporty-looking affair, all open to the blue and white of the May day. They sat together in front, and I at the back among the luggage. "Father wanted to send the Rolls and the chauffeur." Michael said. "Thought this a bit disrespectful. I'm afraid you'll find him a formal type, but he's fundamentally sound."

It was comforting to feel that he was at all events sound enough to take a liking to me. He was waiting under the *porte cochère*, a tall man, thin-faced and lean of build, with a brushed-up white moustache. He was wearing blue tweeds and a tweed hat stuck with fishing-flies. He waved back a man-servant, took off his hat, and himself opened the car doors. He greeted me first, but naturally it was on Augusta that his attention was fixed. He took her young warm hand in his, on whose mottled skin the bones and blue veins stood out, and he held it for a moment, looking at her intently. Then he smiled at her, and there it was again. The Miskin charm. That's how Michael will look, I thought, if ever he becomes an old man. I thought of Haydon Mellerby's smile, about which there had always been too much of the Sweet Nell of Old Drury for my liking, and of Tom Elthorne's grin, and they both seemed a long way from this present moment. "Now come in, please," the old man said. He gave me his arm up the steps as though I were a dowager approaching dissolution, and we went into the house.

9

It was an immensely old house. Tregannock had been built in one piece and done with, and not so long ago at that. Sherston, shining golden in the spring light, looked cohesive and proportional and beautiful. But inside you had to learn your way about; you found stairs that didn't lead you where you expected to go, corridors to unsuspected rooms that some Miskin had added heaven knows when or why. Low walls surrounding a hidden garden would call from Michael or his father some such remark as: "Oh, there were rooms here. These are just the stumps of the walls. I think it was Repton who decided to sweep this lot away." But now there would be no more of it. Such as Sherston was, it was likely to remain, hoary with the past, but with no future save the furtive nibble of dissolution.

My bedroom window gave upon a view that was pleasing and extensive but had none of the beauty that Louisa looked at through her window, for the land was flat and there were no great woods. It was an odd little room altogether, painted in ox-blood red and boasting no luxury. I pulled open the door of a cupboard and found a bath inside. It was of enamelled tin, boxed in, and provided only with cold water. Every evening, before dinner time, a footman poured in a few buckets of hot water. Once I had shut the cupboard door behind me there was no way out for the steam. After the bath, I let it drift through my bedroom and out of the window as well as it could. I had a feeling that this was a spartan household and that, normally, cold baths caused the steam problem not to rise. Everything in the house was like that. Cold water, lamps and candles. I was sure that if Colonel Miskin were in the last extremity of rheumatism's tortures he would not want a lift. He would crawl upstairs on his hands and knees, hurl himself into an icy bath, and hope the shock would do him good.

Augusta loved it all; Michael loved Augusta; and Colonel Miskin seemed in his reserved way to approve of the pair of them. There is not much more than that to be said about our visit to Sherston. But I must tell of a talk I had with the old man just before we returned to Tregannock. We had stayed on into June, and one evening after dinner when Michael and Augusta had gone, as usual, to take a walk in the twilight Colonel Miskin invited me to join him in the garden. He had coffee and brandy carried out to that enclosed spot whose walls had once been the walls of rooms. Now these walls were grown with roses, and stone pots of lilies filled the air with honey-scent. For the rest, the place was a lawn. "My father laid it out as a bowling green," the colonel said. "Before that, in *his* father's time, it was a kitchen garden." It was all like that: every Miskin tinkering and changing, each change absorbing change and inviting change, time without end.

We sat on a stone seat with a stone table before us. Colonel Miskin carried a cushion and a rug. He put the cushion for me to sit on and draped the wrap over my knees. "You mustn't catch cold," he said.

"What about you?"

"I never catch cold."

He poured the coffee, gave me a tot of brandy and lit a cigar.

We sat there companionably in silence for a time, then he said: "I may change this place myself. It'd make a useful miniature rifle-range. But perhaps it's a bit late for that now."

Well, there it was again. I had no doubt what he meant. I felt as I sometimes did at St Tudno when the day was still and sunny, and, apparently without sense or reason, the warning bell would sound from the lighthouse on St Antony's head. The fog would be creeping up the English Channel and would soon be over us.

He sensed the uneasiness in my silence, and put his hand on mine. "Sorry," he said. "Not a good theme for a night like this, I'm afraid. But there are so many heads in such an awful lot of sand that I sometimes feel inclined to jump up and blow a trumpet. Not that I could," he added. "We've always been soldiers of a sort. We wait till we're told what to do."

Bats were flittering above the secret garden. To the west, over the wall, you could see part of the house. A balustrade ran right round the top of Sherston, and high up there, leaning upon it, and looking into the sunset were Michael and Augusta, small and lonely-looking against the embered sky. His arm was round her.

Colonel Miskin became aware of them at the same moment as I.

"It's a long time since Michael's been up there," he said. "He and his brother used to go up, playing at being on the look-out for Parliamentary troops. You know Cromwell's people knocked this place about a bit. I had to stop that game. Some of the stone's none too safe. I don't remember seeing him up there from that day to this."

He drew on his cigar, refilled my coffee-cup and gave me more brandy. "I expect he's taken her up there to tell her the news," he said. "I let him know this morning, and I've written to Augusta's father and to your sister."

Now I needed the rug. His words made me feel cold. I knew what it was that he had told Michael, and my heart wept for Augusta.

He said: "Augusta is lovely, and what's more she's lovable. I imagine that by now Michael has asked her to marry him. And I'm happy about that. Did Michael ever tell you that Miskins never have sisters? Perhaps that's what turns their thoughts to lovely women. They *always* marry lovely women. My wife," he said simply, "was very beautiful. When the time comes – let's be fair," he amended, "and say *if* the time comes – I shall be most happy to have her for a daughter. Michael wants to marry her out of hand. That is what I can't consent to. But I have gladly consented to the engagement."

The two figures, wrapped together as one, moved across the fading light of the sky and disappeared.

I asked him: "How long do you expect them to remain engaged?"

"They're young," he said. "I've told Michael that if what I fear hasn't blown up in two years, then they can marry."

"Two years," I said, "is a long time when you love as they do."

"I know very well how they love," he said. "I, too, have loved, and because of that I cannot expose the child to the risk of so great a sorrow."

"If they married tomorrow," I said, "and war came next year, and Michael was killed, how could her sorrow be greater because they had had that year together? When you love," I argued, "you'll strike any sort of bargain. And the chance of sorrow is always in the bargain, war or no war."

He would not be moved. We stayed for one day after that and then went home. For a long part of the journey we had a railway compartment to ourselves, as we had had that night when I broke to Augusta the news that she would find her father remarried. I watched her twisting on her finger the ring that Mickey had given her. She looked up from it to me and said: "I'm so happy and so miserable. Two years! Do I always have to wait two years? It was two years I had to wait for Haydon. Well, I'm glad about that now. But this is another matter."

"Mickey is not Haydon Mellerby," I said in a desperate effort to reassure her.

"I should think not," she said. "But two years! I don't like the sound of two years."

10

It was the easier for Augusta to comfort herself because she would soon be seeing Mickey again. This was June. In August Mrs Kopf's gang, as James called them, would be arriving, and Mickey was one of those who had volunteered to look after them. Miles was another. There was to be no Oxford Strollers tour this year. On those two, and on me and Augusta and a Miss Levy who would bring the party from London, the job would rest. There were to be ten boys and ten girls, all about fourteen years old. The boys were to sleep in tents in the field that lay before the house, and the girls in rooms on the top floor. James, grumbling all the time about the damned nuisance the children were sure to be, was for ever turning up with some new idea for their pleasure. It was he who hired dinghies and sailing boats and men to be in charge of them, and a day or two before the gang was due a fine marquee came over from Truro and went up in the field near the tents, with flags gaily fluttering over it here and there. This, he explained, was the common room, where the gang could get together to talk or read or write their letters home, and where perhaps we could stage an entertainment or two in the evenings. Chairs and trestle tables were put in. "Anything," he grumbled, "to keep 'em out of the house."

A week before this Mickey and Miles had arrived. They, with me and Augusta, spent some time drawing up a schedule, covering every day of the visit. We didn't want loose ends, a "what shall we do next?" state of affairs. We submitted it to James, who said: "Sounds fine, but you'd better add 'wind and weather permitting'. Shouldn't be surprised if it pours every day and you've got the whole gang on your hands shouting their heads off. Anyway, it's a bad idea to show the poor how the rich live. Puts wrong ideas into their heads."

He was only half serious, but it was mighty like the philosophy of old Mr Polperro, who insisted on all the hat-raising and other ways of keeping the poor in their places.

"Anyway," James said, "don't bother me. I've got to go and see about the cricket-pitch." He was having part of the field mown and the pitch rolled. "I've bought a couple of footballs, too," he said. "You know what these gangs are like. Even if it's eighty in the shade, the little hooligans will want to run and kick."

Louisa said: "I think if we leave the whole thing to James and this Miss Levy we sha'n't go far wrong."

She looked at his red glowing face with affection, knowing well the small value of his grousing. "He'll have to do my part, anyway," she said. "I'm afraid I'm not going to be of much use."

She was looking frail. She was fifty, and she seemed more. She didn't get about now more than she had to, and when she did she walked with obvious pain. James looked at her sadly. "There's one thing you'd better make up your mind about, my girl," he said. "When this lot's over you must have an electric chair to get around in."

"If we were Americans," she said, "an electric chair wouldn't sound too good. Off you go now and roll the bumps out of your cricket-pitch. You'll never roll mine out of me, I'm afraid."

Hugo had given me a dispensation to stay away from the vicarage until this affair was over, and I spent much time with Louisa in what she called her eyrie, looking out over the countryside. I went up there with her after this discussion with James, and when we had sat silent for some time she said: "I'm afraid this Colonel Miskin is a bit of a fool."

I had liked him and I defended him, but added: "I agree that he's mistaken in not allowing Mickey to marry Augusta right away."

She gave me a long considering look, faintly smiling. "They're so hopelessly in love," she said, "that when I say he's a fool I mean he's a fool if he thinks he can allow them to be together without marrying."

It took a moment for this to sink into my mind. When it did, I must have looked stricken with consternation. In reply to my feeble "How do you know?" she said: "By looking at them together. Don't forget that James and I were married in that way long before the Church took a hand. I know what I'm talking about."

I was sure she was right, but I could not take it as calmly as she did. "What on earth can we do?" I asked.

"I don't know what you're going to do," she said. "For me, I've given her some sensible advice, and I'm rejoicing."

I left her and went downstairs and found Miles in the hall. "Augusta's pushed off with Mickey as usual," he said. "Let's have a walk."

It was very hot. We walked no farther than the rose garden and sat on the granite coping of the pond, listening to the drip of water over the edge of the alabaster basin. He was a year older than Augusta but seemed, now, younger, though when we first met he was the one in command. He could not conceal his feelings. "Isn't this lovely?" he asked, watching the fishes appearing and disappearing among the lily leaves, flat like green plates mottled with burgundy red. "I wish Celia could be here. She loved this pond."

"I'm sure," I said, "that James and Louisa would have liked to have her. Did you ask her?"

"No. It would have seemed a bit pushing, don't you think? After all, apart from the acting, we don't see much of one another."

"But, my dear boy, you saw enough to ask her to marry you last year."

He dabbled his fingers in the water. "True enough, but you know she said she didn't want to."

"No, no," I protested. "She said she couldn't make up her mind."

"Same thing," he said. "Anyway, near enough to the same thing to make me rather nervous about asking her."

Again the hot afternoon silence, in which we could hear the metallic whirr of a dragonfly's wings above the lilies. "It seems so much worse," he said, "seeing Mickey and Augusta so happy."

11

The day before the children arrived Mabel Kopf paid us a visit, as a field-marshal might make a visit to the front line when the troops are about to go into action. She went down to the creek and examined the dinghies and sailing-boats and impressed on the men in charge the importance of their task. She inspected the marquee and the boys' tents with their folding canvas beds, and instructed me to have the blankets laid out in the sun every day. She went up to the girls' attics, and I almost expected her to command James to give her a few trial balls on the cricket-pitch and a kick or two at the footballs. Our cooking arrangements were approved, but our schedule was amended in several particulars. "The boys seem to be dominant in everything," she said. "You must share all responsibility equally. The girls mustn't have a sense of being underlings."

She had travelled on the night train, spent the day with us, and taken the night train back to London. James drove her to Truro, and returned calling for a whisky and soda as soon as he was in the house. "If, as you once foolishly hoped," he said to Louisa, "women were given a share in government, that woman would be a Cabinet minister. You see what we have fortunately missed. Well, now that she's gone, we can forget that she's been and go ahead as we intended. How wise of Mickey and Augusta to have kept out of sight all day. What have they been up to?"

"Oh," she said, "probably getting about among the highways and hedges as we used to do."

"Good," he said, unable to take even so clear a hint.

He had arranged for a wagonette to meet the children at Truro the next day, and Miles and I went in to welcome them. They were all tired from the day-long journey in a train grilling under the August heat, a pale and apathetic crew. Miss Levy, a dark young Jewess, was as pale as any of them, though she miraculously had still some resilience. She said briefly: "I'm glad we're here. They've been a handful."

She turned to the children. "Now, Jack," she said. "Up you go."

Jack looked at the wagonette. "What? More flickin' ridin'? I fort we was there."

"You soon will be," Miles assured him. "And you'll be riding in the open air. You'll feel a bit fresher."

"Oo are you?" the boy demanded.

"You can call me Miles, and this is Miss Legassick. We'll be about all through your holiday, and I hope we'll be able to give you a good time."

"You better," Jack said briefly. "I didn't want to come. I was pushed into it because my Ma's sick of me. Got a match?"

He produced a half-smoked cigarette from his pocket. Miles looked a question at Miss Levy, who nodded. Miles lit the fag-end, and Jack climbed into the wagonette. The others, as though they had been waiting for a lead, followed. When they were all aboard Miss Levy whispered to me and Miles: "That's the one you'll have to watch – Jack Edwards. The others adore him."

Most of the children, clutching their sad-looking little bundles, began to doze as soon as the wagonette was on the move. We had climbed Carnon Downs and had descended to the Norway Inn when James met us, driving his car. He turned and waited till we drew near. "Well, children," he shouted, "I've come to meet you and lead the convoy home. Not far now. Up there among the trees." He waved towards the wooded hills on the left.

Jack Edwards leaned over the side of the wagonette. "Oo are you, Fatty?" he asked.

"You can call me Mr Polperro."

"That's a funny name. Can I come in your car?"

"Certainly. Hop down," James said.

Jack hopped down and climbed, in alongside James. "I likes goin' fast," he said. "Drive like 'ell, Mr Poll Parrot!"

The name was a howling success. The stop had wakened the dozing children, and they began to intone: "Mr Poll Parrot! Mr Poll Parrot! Drive like 'ell, Mr Poll Parrot!"

Miles, who was sitting with the driver, turned round with an angry look on his face that I had never seen there before. "Stop it!" he said. "D'you hear? Stop that senseless noise, all of you."

The effect was miraculous. Silence. Miss Levy looked at Miles with admiration and whispered to me: "I'd never have dared to do that. Mrs

Kopf says I must use nothing but kindness. But really it doesn't always work."

James and Jack Edwards had disappeared. In a Trappist silence we jogged slowly after them, up through the leafy quiet of the autumn woods, out on to the highroad, and at last through our tented field, where the flags hung down disconsolately above the marquee, and where Jack Edwards, standing alone, was taking pot-shots with a catapult at nothing in particular.

12

Well, here was Louisa's old dream come true at last: Tregannock no longer wasting itself but dedicated to social service. It wasn't a howling success. The weather was too hot for football. Cricket tended to be Jack Edwards at the stumps, someone bowling to him, and everyone else chasing the ball that he slogged about the field. They got tired of it, deserted one by one, and left the field to him. The boats were shunned after the first day when a party of four was taken sailing. It was a breezy day, and as soon as we were out of the creek, Barty Spargo and myself in charge, the boat, which had been sedately upright till now, heeled over in a gust. Consternation seized our passengers. One, who had been assuring us with pleasure as we doddered down the creek that she was going to be sick, promptly was, and could not be persuaded to perform the operation over the side. The others, as the boat scudded along leaning heavily to port, were sure that she was going down, and this conviction deepened when the wind caught a handful of sea-crest and threw it in their faces. There were shouts of "Let's go back," "Take us 'ome, mister," but Barty, who bore with them good-heartedly, assured them that the St Just shore was now nearer than home and that we would soon be there. In the sunshine on the beach they took off their shoes and stockings and paddled timorously on the edge of the tide. This looked like being a happier outcome, but the girl who had been sick now ventured far out in an effort to regain prestige, stumbled on a submerged rock, and fell down. She had only to stand up again and walk out, but this she refused to do. She called out that she was drowning, and the others took up her theme, shouting mad confused instructions to me and Barty. He waded in, took her by the scruff of the neck, and dropped her on the beach, looking as disgusted as if he had been handling a half-drowned cat.

"You'd better take off your clothes," I said. "They'll dry in no time in this sun if we spread them out."

She was horrified at so indecent a suggestion. I had noticed that, for all their rough speech and manners, they were excessively prudish. A little cove, gold-paved with sand and warm as an oven in the afternoon blaze, opened off the beach. "Take her in there," Barty said. "I'll keep the others away."

He herded them down the beach and set them to gathering drift-wood for boiling the kettle. I took young Nan into the cove and at last persuaded her to undress. She did so with her back to me. When I had spread her thin bits of clothing one by one on the sand I turned and found her lying full length on her back, with her hands decorously placed where hands are placed in old pictures of Eve being expelled from Eden. The little body, with half-formed breasts, was very thin and white. A great wave of compassion surged over me. I think I had been more inclined than any of us at Tregannock to be cross and impatient with the children, with their bad manners, their rude speech, their loud wrangling ways. I saw now how self-defensive this was in a world that must be as strange to them as the Indies to the first explorers. No wonder they tended to keep together in gangs, as it were rejecting us. I looked at the flat stomach that must be feeling drained and wrenched after her sickness, at the little thighs hardly thicker than her calves, the stubbed and broken finger-nails, so modestly disposed. I was sitting by her side and leaned over and kissed her forehead. She opened her eyes and looked at me without smiling. Her eyes, which I had not bothered to notice before, were beautiful: a disturbing sea-green. Lying there naked in the sun on the sand, she looked like a small sea-creature washed up on the tide. She had yellow hair, like Augusta's, spread out on the yellow sand. The sun made her pale flesh pearly. And madly a thought rushed upon my mind: From what Eden is this little Eve locked out? For what sin, for whose sin, is she, so young, denied so much? And, thinking this, I was ashamed, and I kissed her feet. She opened her sea-green eyes upon me again and looked at me with what I took to be a depth of comprehension beyond her years. At last the shadow of a smile lightened her small sad face. She said: "It's all right. Don't worry about me."

I thought it a beautiful thing for her to have said, but deep in my heart I could not accept that absolution.

Her name was Nan Lovel. When she had dressed and we had joined the others by the roaring fire on which the kettle was boiling, I found myself disposed to fuss over her, to be sure that she had plenty to eat and drink; and when occasion offered later that day I asked Miss Levy to tell me something about her. She was from Stepney and her father was dead. She had no brothers or sisters. Her mother, not yet thirty, had been sixteen when she bore the child. She worked in a pickle factory. Nan attended a board school and took a bit of bread-and-scrape to school with her, to eat in the streets when at liberty between noon and two o'clock. She was out of school at four, and her mother came home at six. "So at any rate," I said, "she does have someone to look after her in the evenings."

Miss Levy sighed. Sighing was her greatest accomplishment. "Well," she said, "it's not quite so simple as that. There's a pub on the corner of their street. Mrs Lovel goes there most nights. Sometimes she takes a jug and brings the beer home, and sometimes she wants company and drinks on the premises. Then Nan just stays in the streets till her mother comes out. She doesn't seem to like playing with other children."

"She doesn't look as though she gets enough to eat."

Miss Levy sighed again. "I'm afraid not," she said. "Mrs Lovel never cooks anything. Even if she did, it couldn't come to much on what she earns. There's a Wesleyan parson near Nan's school. Sometimes he takes her in at midday and she shares a meal with him and his wife, but she dodges him whenever she can. She's got that she doesn't like company, and she's rather terrified of what she thinks the grandeur of that poor parson's home."

We were talking in the great hall. Miss Levy looked about her at a grandeur that surpassed what the Wesleyan parson could offer. As though two disparate thoughts had run together in her head, she said: "Miss Legassick, I don't know why we do any of this. What's the good of these bombastic palliatives?"

She looked a little startled and said: "I beg your pardon. I'm not criticising anything."

"Then it's about time you began," I said, and went out angrily: angry with I hardly knew what, but in no mood to reprove even Jack

Edwards whom I found sitting in the old punt in the middle of the lake, slinging stones from his catapult at our fat sluggish carp.

13

Our beautiful schedule had more or less broken down. Miles' angry outburst in the wagonette made the children distrustful of him; and Mickey and Augusta didn't want to be disturbed. They would have pulled their weight had things run smoothly, but they were not sorry to have an excuse for deserting. It was James who saw the solution of the problem. The lift in his car had made him *persona gratissima* with Jack Edwards, who had given up calling him Mr Poll Parrot. Indeed, Jack was now so much in James' camp that a boy who used the derisive name Jack had invented found himself knocked flat with a few swingers that bloodied his nose and loosened his teeth. The routine now became this. James would say each morning: "What do you think we should do today, Jack?" and Jack would have it all cut and dried. He himself, of course, would go riding in the car with James, and he would choose two others to share the honour. Those who were left would be apportioned between me and Miss Levy. Sometimes these two sides would be commanded to play cricket together. Sometimes they would be given separate assignments. In the evening, Jack had his own means of obtaining a report on the day's conduct, and anyone who fell short could count on not being chosen to go in the car the next day. The car was the trump in Jack's strategy. All the children adored it, and James bowled them through the county and fed them like fighting-cocks.

So a kind of peace, a routine of a sort, settled on us, thanks to Jack's ability to impose his will and to James' perception of the boy's quality. "Jack's one of those fellers," James said to me, "who'd be promoted from the ranks in the field," a farsighted remark, because so he was in March of 1918. The war had then only a summer to go, but Captain Jack Edwards didn't live to march in a victory parade.

Perhaps it is not surprising that in the early part of the war, Jack was a despatch-rider. Like young Marmont when Jane Lavernock met him in France, he was fascinated by motors. He didn't want merely to ride. He wanted to know how the thing worked, and James, who was himself as much interested in the mechanics as in the driving, spent hours with the boy in the garage where he had an inspection-pit. They would crawl about in it, oily and ineffably happy.

Jack was a thief. In the higher walks of life he would have been called a kleptomaniac. He didn't steal for gain, but he couldn't resist picking up anything that came his way. When the epidemic of thieving came to light, no one suspected him. I was not surprised when first one child and then another began to complain that their things were being "nicked", for small things of my own had disappeared unaccountably: a fountain-pen, a sketch-book, a pair of gardening-gloves. I reported the matter to James, but what could we do except keep our eyes open? And, unhappily our eyes were not sharp enough.

14

There was a half-basement under Tregannock. I had never been in it, but had often looked down through the windows that were for half their height below ground level. I suppose that somewhere down there, when Tregannock was an establishment, the laundry work had been done, and no doubt coal and wood were still stacked there. Also, though everyone had forgotten it, there was a good deal of paraffin oil, left over from the time before James had the place electrified.

The petty thieving went on, and at last James decided that something must be done about it. He and Jack Edwards were coming up from the garage one evening after putting away the car, and I walked down to meet them. Jack's proudest possession was a watch – a very cheap one that never told the right time, but it was a thing of prestige all the same, for no one else had a watch. James said: "We really must do something about this stealing, Maria. It's too bad. Jack's had his watch pinched."

Jack was moving off when James said: "Just a minute, Jack, I've got an idea. You know more about the children than we do, and you have a better chance of finding out what goes on. I'm sure you can get to the bottom of this; and when you do I don't want to know anything about it. Keep it among yourselves. Better still, keep it between you and whoever is the thief. Don't let's make a row about it."

Jack seemed pleased to be given a detective's job. "You trust me," he said confidently. "I'll see it stops."

And it did stop. What is more, delighted children found their small bits and pieces reappearing as mysteriously as they had gone. Even my few things met my eye one day, placed where I couldn't fail to find them. James congratulated Jack, who said airily: "Oh, it was nuffink. It was easy."

What wasn't easy was James' fur coat. This was an ancient moth-eaten garment that hung in a closet under the stairs. It was utterly disreputable, and James had no doubt forgotten that he owned it. There was almost always someone in the hall or passing through it, especially during that crowded fortnight of the children's visit; but, by chance, there was a moment when Jack found it unoccupied, and in one of his lightning forays for loot he came upon the coat, whipped it hastily to the front of the house, and dropped it down to lie outside a basement window. That night he slipped out of his tent, opened the window as he had often done before, and put the coat with the rest of his pickings.

The tragedy that followed developed through a thicket of ifs. If Jack had not learned to like and respect James. If James had not asked him to find the thief. If this had not touched Jack to the quick of honour. If honour had made him say frankly "I am the thief." But that was the rub. No one had trusted Jack before, and he did not want to lose James' esteem. If he had left the coat where it was. No one would have missed it. If, having decided to dispose of it, he had hauled it out and thrown it behind a thorn bush or done any one of a hundred things with it.

We know exactly what happened because, though he need have said nothing, he told the police. When he had returned all the trifles, the bulky coat tormented him. It was James', and so, beyond all the other stolen things, it had to go back. But he never again found the hall unoccupied. At last he decided to destroy the coat by burning. The garage was never locked, and at one o'clock of a morning he went there and unstrapped a can of petrol from the running-board of the car. He took it to the basement room, poured some over the coat, and stuffed the coat into the fireplace. He stood back and threw a lighted match towards the coat, and was appalled. He had not realised the dreadful combustibility of petrol. The instantaneous savage *Pouff* made him leap back towards the window. "I kicked something over," he said. "It must have been the petrol can." Leaving the floor awash with doom, he climbed out of the window and ran. If he had come hammering and banging at the locked front door, the house in all probability would still have been lost, but lives could have been saved. However, he ran, terrified.

15

At midnight I had stood at my open window looking out on the countryside, still and silent under the rain of moonlight. The serenity comforted me, for it had been a bad day. Louisa had seen little of the children, and it had for so long been her dream to have them here, to see Tregannock giving help where it was needed, that she had decided to spend the whole day downstairs, a thing she hadn't done for a long time. The children took their meals in the marquee, and she joined them there at lunch. They had become more or less accustomed to the rest of us, but she was a stranger, an odd stranger, too, hobbling about with a stick in either hand, and, when she sat, lowering herself slowly with James' help. They looked at her, open-mouthed and mute, and, try as she would at her most gracious, nothing could she get out of those with whom she talked save a muttered Yes or No. At last she fell silent, and I could feel her deep distress. So could James, who looked unhappy; and this mood communicated itself to the children. Even the noisiest of them stopped chattering; and in the silence Louisa turned to me and said: "Do you remember a night long ago, my dear, when we all ate a meal in the garden at St Tudno? It was night, and there were candles burning on the table, and old Thomas May came wandering up from the graveyard and joined us. Roger was there, and he twitted old May about being the skeleton at the feast."

"Yes," I said, "I remember."

The children were listening, gaping.

"Well," Louisa said, "I feel a bit of a skeleton today."

The confined air in the marquee was burning hot, and she looked distressed. "I remember," she said, "that you wanted me to go in and say good night to Father, who was writing as usual. I didn't. A silly little point, but I've thought of it again and again. I wish I had gone. I come round to thinking so much when it's too late to do anything about it. I wish I'd had these children here years ago."

It was enough to petrify the hungriest jaws, and the feast slowed down in a chill.

"I'd better leave you all to yourselves," Louisa said.

433

She got up, and James tried to take one stick from her and give her an arm as usual. But she said: "I'm all right, James. Stay and entertain the children."

She hobbled slowly out, and the blaze of sunshine hit her suddenly, causing her not to see a tent-peg. Her foot caught in it, and she went down with a crash.

James and I ran and lifted her up. She was wincing with pain, and now indeed she had to take an arm – two arms, mine and James'. We almost carried her to the house, into the lift, and to her room.

"Get her into bed," James said. "I'll motor in to Penryn for a doctor."

"What's the point?" she asked wearily. "What can he tell me that I don't know already? – that now I've put the tin hat on it."

She tried to smile, and James didn't stay to argue. I got her into bed, and stayed there till the doctor came. She hadn't broken anything, he said but her old troubles had been terribly shaken up and revived by the jolt. He was an old man whom we had known all our lives. He said: "Now you do as I tell you, my girl. I feel responsible for you, you know. I brought you into the world."

She asked: "Is that something to thank you for?"

He looked at her sadly. He was about to answer when James burst in: "It's something I have to thank him for, anyway." He bent down and kissed her and ran out of the room.

There was not much the doctor could do save advise her to stay where she was. When he was gone I asked if I should sit with her awhile, and she said: "Go and help with the children."

And that thrust me at once from Louisa's sorrows to Miss Levy's. When I got down into the field the children were coming out of the marquee. A small girl saw Louisa's two sticks lying on the grass, picked them up, and began to give an imitation of Louisa hobbling. Miss Levy, who was always a tense young creature, was more than ever in a worked-up mood. Louisa's damping effect on the children during the meal had disturbed her; and she could not make allowance. She could not see that this little girl's grotesque aping, and the laughter that it caused, were an escape from the tension they had all felt. She went up to the child and slapped her sharply on both cheeks. Then – the worst thing she could do in the circumstances – she herself began to cry penitently. The children, seeing so to speak, the government fallen, began to mill around and shout, some for and some against Miss Levy. I said to Jack Edwards: "Do something with them, Jack, for heaven's sake."

Jack Edwards shouted: "Come on now, you kids. Fall in, all of you. We're going for a route march. I'm Sergeant Edwards. You and you – you're corporals. You march at the end of the file and see nobody strays."

Soon they were marching – I didn't know and didn't care where. Then I comforted Miss Levy, and found her deeply and volubly unhappy. I listened to her life-story, gave her a sedative, and told her to stay in bed till it was time for her to see the girls into theirs.

It *would* be this afternoon that Miles, irked by the children's distrust of him, had pushed off altogether. He had gone over to St Tudno to take Hugo's children sailing. At all events, I thought, as I sat in the hall with a cup of tea, not much more can happen today, and at the weekend the children will go. But there was still to be a sharp unhappy incident.

As I sat drinking my tea Augusta and Mickey came bustling in. They brought with them that air of radiant excitement that Louisa's insight had taught me to interpret. I was pretty well tattered, and the flood of their happiness disturbed me, offended me, perhaps made me jealous. Poor Louisa. Poor James. Poor Miss Levy, sleeping, I hoped, and for a moment forgetting the sad tangle of her life that she had wept out to me. Poor Miles, trying to forget with Hugo's children that Celia had not written to him since he arrived at Tregannock. For that matter, poor me! Maria, universal aunt, receiver of confidences, looker-on at other people's loves, from the moment under the yew in the dawn so long ago up to now when these two occasionally spared me a side-kick from among the glowing glances they were directing upon one another.

Mickey rang, and tea was brought to them, and Mickey said: "We're back a bit early today. How are the children getting on? We rushed home because we felt rather self-reproachful. I'm afraid we haven't exactly been pulling our weight."

"No," I said, "I'm afraid you haven't."

Words regretted as soon as spoken. Oh, damn you, you old moralist, I thought. You're not talking to John Stuart Mill back from discussing *On Liberty* with Mrs Taylor. You're talking to two people blazing with love, and you love them yourself.

"I'm sorry," I said, for the glow had faded from their faces and brightness seemed fallen from the air. My words must have sounded to them a condemnation of all the joy they had had of one another.

Augusta said: "We've been walking all day. I think I'll go and rest." She went, leaving her tea untouched.

Mickey's anxious eyes followed her, as though I had delivered a mortal wound. When she had disappeared round the bend of the stair he said: "You're right in a way, Aunt Maria, but . . ."

I said: "My dear, I know all about the buts, and I should have taken them into consideration. However, this has been rather a special day."

I told him of all the specialities, and of course his first thought was for Augusta. "Augusta will be appalled," he said. "She loves her Aunt Louisa so."

"I'm afraid I've hurt her," I said. "Make my peace with her, there's a good boy."

"I certainly will," he said, and kissed me. "You're an old dear."

The kissing pleased me. I was not so sure about the old dear.

16

The top floor was a warren of small rooms, once the servants' quarters. Three of them had been knocked into one to make Louisa's bed-sitting room, into which the lift opened. My cubicle was next door to this rather fine room; then came three more where Miss Levy and the ten girls shook down on camp beds. Each cubicle had a window on one side. On the other it opened upon a narrow corridor. James' quarters were on the floor beneath this, where Miles, Mickey and Augusta also slept.

I stayed up for a long time talking to Louisa that night. When she was asleep I got into bed with a book, hoping to tire myself. But it had been too exciting a day: sleep would not come: I put on a dressing-gown and sat at the window, looking out into the cool of the moonlight. Restless still, I opened my door and began to prowl. I had never explored this part of the house, and now made my way through its tortuous geography, thinking of the bustling days of Polperro entertaining, when every one of these dog-kennels would house a valet or a lady's maid, and even in the corridors, I had been told, you would find servants sprawled out on mattresses. I opened some of the doors, and looked at the dust on shelves, and the grey swags of cobwebs hanging in corners and the blue quiet crosses drawn upon the floors by the midnight moon leaning on the window-panes.

I'm not a nervous person; I had been brought up too familiarly with graves ever to expect them to gape at midnight or at any other hour, and certainly the dusty attics of an old house – and not so old as all that – had no skill to twang my nerves just because the time was getting on for one in the morning. But I am often led to ask all the same why I was moved that night of all nights to hover about like a leathery old bat in a dirty belfry. Because, if I hadn't done it we should perhaps never have found the ladder.

There it was, an iron-runged affair, fixed to the wall at the end of a corridor and leading to a trap door which obviously opened upon the roof. I climbed up and tried to lift the trap with my hands, but the hinges resisted, tightened by years that had never seen them used. But I was determined to get on to the roof and look upon the wide moon-washed world that I knew would open before me there. So I tried again, this time going up the ladder with my back to it, and so I was able to get my shoulders under the hatch. I had to heave like Atlas trying to throw off the world. I groaned, and the hinges groaned, and my groans won. At last, dry unoiled creakings told me that the job was done, and then I went down again, came up right side forward, and pushed the door open.

I looked about me at the flat lead roof, with tall chimney-stacks rising out of it here and there, and at the great range of country now revealed to me. It was an enchanting spectacle: the earth was a vast grey-blue placid sea, dotted with islands large and small, which were woods and little copses; and tangles of milky mist were drifting over this sea, and small ships lay unmoving here and there. They were cottages and barns, but my fancy rejected the prosaic fact and took alarm for one of them which was clearly in distress and sending out a fiery signal. I knew it was only a bonfire that had caved in and rushed a constellation into the night; but it was a night so enchanted that I should not have been surprised to see the other ships pull up their anchors and sail in mercy across the phantasmal ocean.

The clock over the stables struck one. I moved to the parapet to look down on the stables – a parapet that was not an august balustrade such as I had seen Augusta and Michael lean upon, but merely a coping hardly more than a foot high. Then I saw what I might have expected had I given the matter a thought. The ladder I had climbed from the attics was a fire escape, leading to this other iron ladder that now caught my eye. Fastened to the wall, it ran down the house to the ground. It looked as though it had been long forgotten. Kneeling and peering over, I saw that it was so overgrown with rampant climbers that only luck had shown me its existence.

I stood for another moment watching the cottage bonfire die down again, and then climbed back into the attic maze. "Don't drop that hatch behind you." I stopped at the bottom of the ladder. Why had that thought rushed upon me? Why had I left the hatch open? Association of ideas, I told myself reasonably. You saw the bonfire blaze and thought it was a ship alight, with lives in danger. However, feeling a perfect fool, I nevertheless went into one of the attic rooms where I had seen old newspapers lying. I took an armful of them, tore them up, and laid an unmistakable trail through the tortuous passages. Then I got into bed, wondering if I had been struck moon-crazy, and tried to sleep.

I could not. Sitting up in bed, I was obsessed by the day: Louisa's fall, Miss Levy's hysteria, Augusta's coldness. And then my mind played with that far-off moment that Louisa had recalled when we ate at night in the garden with candleshine unwavering on the table, and, when Louisa was gone, we sailed out in *Norah* and Charles Lester ran her on the sand-bar. All save Louisa and myself had guttered out like the candles on that table: Father and Roger and Bella, Charles, Thomas May, Mrs Solway and Gerald Pickering. I shivered and watched the fiery flakes dancing up past the window into the moon-blue night. The bonfire was still at it.

But the bonfire is on the other side of the house.

I leapt to the window and craned my head out, looking down. I was appalled by what I saw. Billows of smoke, dusky-red with the fire shining upon them from inside the house, writhed upward, and the fiery flakes that had called me to my senses were shooting swiftly through this turgid slower-moving stream. Now and then from a window down there a belch of flame shot as if from a cannon's mouth, and I could hear two sounds which filled me with dread: a fierce crackle which spoke of the hold the fire had upon the food that fed it, and a deep-throated roaring which you never have, even in the milder example of a bonfire, unless the fire has won and is ravening, consuming all that goes upon it.

I rushed into Louisa's room and found her sitting up in bed, with her bedside light switched on. She said almost calmly: "Do you smell the smoke?"

"Yes," I cried. "The house is on fire."

"Have you warned Miss Levy?"

"Not yet."

"Then do it at once."

"You," I said. "You first."

She looked at me in a blaze of anger. "Get the children out," she said. "Don't stand there wasting time, you fool."

Still I hesitated. I knew that if anything was to be done for her I must do it. After her fall that day she would have difficulty in getting out of bed, much less walking. I took her under the armpits and began to heave her up. She cursed me in words I had never heard from her lips before, telling me still to get the children out, and at that moment the electric light went dead. In the sudden darkness the window brightened. The look of it frightened me. There were flames now – not sparks, flames – writhing up amid the smoke. "Go!" she shouted. "Go, you crazy idiot. Come back to me when every one of those children is out."

Then I rushed from the room and opened the door of Miss Levy's. She was out of bed and was standing there gazing at the lurid window whose light showed her face aghast. I forced myself to some sort of tranquillity.

"Miss Levy," I said, "there's nothing to worry about."

She looked at me, wringing her hands, and I could feel the poor wretch calling up all her resources, striving to meet the moment. She tried to speak, but could not.

"Get all the children *at once* into the corridor," I said. "Never mind their clothes or anything else. Get them into the corridor."

They occupied three of the small cubicles. I got them out of the room we were in, and she routed them out of the others. I counted them – twelve. They could see the flames, hear the roaring. The dusky light fell on the sad white-clad file, sobbing, shouting, ready to panic. "Girls," I said as quietly as I could, "there's a ladder, and I'm going to lead you to it. You'll all be safe in the garden in a few minutes. Now follow me; and, Miss Levy, you be the last please, to see that no one misses the way."

I was glad I had laid the paper trail, for, strive as I might to seem self-possessed, terror was tearing me: terror for my own sake, terror for Louisa's, lying there helpless in this house which with every passing second was, I could feel, nearer to a doom which nothing could now turn aside.

I shot up the ladder and counted the children as they followed – twelve. I knelt and looked over the parapet. It was a long way to the ground, and some of the children were very small. One look over, and they would be terrified. We were on the eastern edge of the house, and at that moment, looking back down the long lead-sheeted roof, I heard a slow grinding sound, and then a crash. The western end of the roof had fallen in. The fire was through from ground floor to attics, and triumphal banners of flame roared up, waving in a coruscation of glowing embers.

At that the children began to scream, and now, I thought, the panic is on. Then I heard a voice calling me from below, and, peering over the edge, I saw a little group of people standing there and gazing upwards, reddened by firelight. It was Miles who had seen me looking over and had now shouted.

"There's a ladder leading up here," I yelled. "It's hidden by the climbers. Find it, and come up at once."

The weight of the children rolled off my mind. "There's a fireman coming up," I assured them confidently. They would know what a fireman was. I was able to take stock, and saw Mickey down there and Augusta and a few people drawn as people always are to a scene of disaster. There was the estate fire-engine, a hopeless antiquated thing as useful for this task as a squirt from a fountain-pen filler. And there was a row of men hurrying buckets of water from the lake: a forlorn, impossible endeavour.

Then Miles' head appeared over the parapet. I whispered: "They'll be terrified of the climb down. You must help them one by one. For God's sake be quick."

"Where's Aunt Louisa?" he asked.

He was grimed, with blood-shot eyes. "Never mind Louisa," I said. "Here's the first." I handed a child over.

It went better than I had feared, for some of the bigger girls made the descent alone, two or three close behind one another.

"Twelve," I counted, with a groan of relief; and then Miss Levy went and Miles came back and stood with me on the roof. Poor begrimed dishevelled boy; he looked like something from the pit, and in my heart he shone like an archangel. He asked again: "Where's Aunt Louisa?"

It was an awful scene now. The hole in the western end of the roof was a volcano-vent through which flame and smoke and sparks poured with a triumph of roaring.

Miles said to me quietly: "Look at that."

It wasn't at that terrifying inferno that he was looking: it was at the lead floor under our feet. A part of the lead slowly rose, swelled like a bubble, then collapsed.

"No time to lose," he said.

I went down the ladder into the corridor and he followed me. Now it was fearfully hot there and swirls of smoke made us cough and stung our eyes. I ran. The smoke thickened as we drew nearer to Louisa's room and as we came to the door it rushed out at us in dense entangling coils. It was coming up through the opened door of the lift-shaft. There was no lift. Louisa was lying there, her head over the shaft, suffocated and dead. She must have rolled herself out of bed, and dragged herself to the lift-door, and somehow opened it. And the lift wasn't there. Later on, when the blaze was ebbing and the autumn dawn was making the east rosy, I learned where the lift was. "The whole of our floor was blazing," Miles said, "and we had to run for it. He wouldn't come with us. He said he had to get to Louisa."

So while the others ran out of the blazing house James entered the lift. I remembered how the light suddenly went off in Louisa's room while I was talking to her. It was an electric lift, and the electricity failed at that moment. I could only hope that James, immobilised in the shaft that offered a fearful suction to the flames, died quickly.

Miles and I carried Louisa's body up the ladder to the roof, but we never got it to the ground. By now the whole floor was bubbling and the air was a tremor of fearful heat. Miles was exhausted, and Louisa was heavy. He got on to the ladder ready to receive her, and said quietly: "Sorry. This ladder is almost red-hot. Save yourself before it's too late."

He climbed back and helped me on to the ladder, and I reached the ground with blistered burning hands. He came after, and we stood with the little crowd watching, mesmerised, the last agony of the great house. All save this part where we stood was now a hollow white-hot shell, and the end came quickly. The rain of melted lead poured down amid a falling chaos of flaming beams and rafters. And even then we stood there, stupefied like cattle whose byre has been destroyed and who don't know where to turn. Birds were beginning to sing as though nothing had happened; and I suppose one house and two lives are not much to pass out of the world.

CHAPTER FOURTEEN

Y OU CAN look over the hedge of the house called Little in Sight
and see the small inlet where Barty Spargo gave Miles his first
lesson in handling a dinghy. That was eight years ago. Now it was
August 5th, 1914. Things don't change much at St Tudno, and so I was
not surprised to see Barty there fiddling with his dinghy as he had been
doing on that far-off morning. I wished him good-day, and he looked
up and returned my greeting, and said: "Well, Miss Legassick, seems
they ole Germans 'ave to be given a lesson." It was nine o'clock. The
war was ten hours old. Barty put his fishing-tackle into the boat and
took up his oars. "Well," he said, "I'm goin' to see if I can find an ole
bass."

I watched him out of sight, and the small incident reminded me, as
things so often did, of Father. In a sermon, he was speaking of St Peter,
and told how, after the crucifixion, Peter was lounging on the shore of
the Sea of Tiberias, and said casually to his fellows: "I go a-fishing."
There are times, Father said, when in face of great disaster, there's
nothing left but to get on with the common jobs of life. What else,
indeed, is there for any of us to do?

Now, with the world's crucifixion not ended but begun, Barty said:
"I go a-fishing," and rowed away whistling into the splendid morning.

2

Nan came across the dewy grass and said that breakfast was ready. After
the disaster at Tregannock, when I stood in the dawn watching the fire
die down behind the gaunt walls and staring empty window-sockets, I
felt a cold hand slipped into mine, and looked down to see Nan
standing there with chattering teeth. Her feet were bare in the dew,
and she was wearing nothing but a nightdress filthy with smoke. Miss

443

Levy had recovered her senses enough to take the girls into the marquee, commandeer the blankets from the beds in the boys' tents (for the boys were up and dressed to see the sights) and wrap the girls up warm. Nan had escaped, and there she was, and it touched me deeply that in this moment when the world seemed sunk she had come to me, for I felt that she had come not to seek comfort but to convey it. She was pitifully thin and white, and I hurried her to the marquee to join the others.

Some of the village people took the children to their homes and fed them and put them to bed, and during the next few days found clothes for them to travel in, and Mabel Kopf, who had come from London on hearing of the fire, took them away on the third day. A wagonette was hired to carry them to Truro, and I could not hold back my tears as I watched them go and thought of what had happened between one ride in a wagonette and another. Before going, Mabel Kopf said to me in her abrupt way. "Would you like to adopt that girl named Nan Lovel?" I looked so surprised that she didn't pursue the matter then, but said: "I'll write to you," jumped into the wagonette, and called to the driver: "Off now. We're ready."

She did not write for a few months. Mickey had gone back to Somerset and Miles to Manchester to see his father. Augusta and I were with Hugo in the vicarage. Mrs Kopf's letter said that the conduct of Nan's mother had become impossible, and it had now been necessary to take action against her for both cruelty and neglect. "I have talked to the magistrates," she said, "and I have no doubt that if you wanted to adopt the child it could be arranged with all necessary legal safeguards. Nan herself talks of you as a sort of angel beneath whose wing she would gladly shelter."

I didn't see it like that, but I did know that after our day on the beach the shy creature had had some feeling for me; and, without going into the boring and troublesome details, I need only say that here she was, and that she went by the name of Nan Legassick. I had not till now discovered, and never did discover, any longing in her for her mother or her home. She had been with me for six months and we were happy together when the war broke out. Nan was then twelve years old.

3

You must think of me henceforth as a well-to-do woman. I suppose if some lawyer had wanted for any reason to see me a year ago he would have summoned me to his office. Now the lawyer who was the agent for the Polperro properties called upon me day after day to clear up this and explain that. James was the last of the Polperros. His sister, whom I used to watch, when I was a child, stepping out of the great coach on a Sunday morning, had long been dead, and her husband, too. There were no children. In my loft, where my Uncle Pallace had fried our fish breakfast on a memorable far-off morning, I found myself most unexpectedly entertaining to sherry and biscuits (borrowed from Hugo) this stout purring old gentleman who talked to me for hours about things I didn't understand and didn't want to understand. What it came to was that James had made large benefactions to Cornish charities and had left the remainder to Louisa. He added: "Should she predecease me, or for any other reason fail to inherit, then this residue will pass to her sister Maria, my dear friend of many years."

I was touched by this, for I had done little enough to earn James' affection; but the lawyer was more concerned to point out the beauty of the words "or for any other reason fail to inherit". He said: "It's lucky I insisted on that going in. If it had simply read 'should she predecease me', we should have been in a pretty mess, for who could have proved which of them died first? The lawyers would have had some nice pickings arguing over that."

I begged him not to argue over it now: it was not a subject I wished to contemplate. He apologised, and said, sipping his sherry: "Of course, the advowson of St Tudno will be in your hands."

Melancholy though the whole business was, I could not help laughing at that. "You mean it will be my job to choose the parson?"

He meant just that; and added: "And to pay him."

It all seemed crazily upside down to me. I pictured myself going in every Saturday morning and handing Hugo his pay-packet. "I can leave all that to you?" I asked.

"Oh, yes," he said easily. "You can leave everything to us."

I said: "Thank you. I'd like to do that. And to begin with, will you buy me the house called Little in Sight? I see it's in the market again."

4

There was no reason why I should remain any longer at the vicarage. John Oldham was twenty and at Oxford. Constance, at seventeen, was a girl with something of Louisa's independent spirit. She was acting as Hugo's housekeeper, but I didn't see her content to remain long in St Tudno. She was studious, and wanted to go up to Oxford. When I moved into Little in Sight she took over the loft. Richard at twelve was still at a prep school, and Millicent, heading for ten years old, was being tutored by Hugo. But she was a dull child, not likely, I thought, to come to much.

No, there was no reason for me to stay, and I was glad to have for the first time in my life a place of my own. I could afford to live in rather a grand way, with a few servants, but that was the last thing I wanted. A hermit-crab like me could do with a close shell, and Little in Sight was just the thing. It was full of memories: of Father taking me to call on old Mrs Mitchell and her parrot and cat and candles innumerable; and of Gerald Pickering in the happy hey-day of his promise. He, especially, was in my mind as I watched the workmen scraping dingy papers from the walls and bringing the place back to the all-white light-filled cottage that he had made it. There were three small bedrooms, and one of them was made into a bathroom, a rare feature of a St Tudno house. There was a dining room, a kitchen into which I introduced all that was then known of labour-saving devices (which wasn't much), and the sizeable room with windows looking on the creek, where we had been entertained by Mrs Mitchell.

It was on a March night of 1914 that for the first time I drew my curtains, lit my hanging lamp, set a match to the fire, and lay back relaxed in a chair, looking at the few pictures, the many books, the sparse furniture that I had bought. I felt like a wanderer home at last, and when, later, I got into my bed I listened for what to me were the sounds of home. They came through the open window: the voices of the owls and the curlew, and the sighing of the tide flowing in from the Carrick Roads: incomparable trilogy. Now and then, I thought, drowsing off, I should hear too the wings of swans flying over. But that was something else, not of the earth, an added grace of wild strength and freedom that belonged to heaven.

5

Quiet, which I prize beyond most things, can be terrifying to some people, and it was so to Nan. The voices of the night, which for me only deepened its peace, frightened her. Being at Tregannock with a gang had been one thing; being alone in a bedroom in a rather solitary cottage was another. She didn't sleep well and she was alarmingly thin. She was not a beautiful child. Only her eyes were startling: those sea-green eyes which had moved me when I first observed them as she lay on the sand after her ducking. She had a little snub nose and a big mouth. But I thought she was good value for the moments when the big mouth and the green eyes conspired in a startling smile. Her brow was broad and calm. She would do.

The summer of 1914 was very warm, and I took to sleeping on the bit of grass that lay between the back of the house and the creek-water. She slept alongside me. This proximity comforted her and gradually made familiar the things that at first had frightened her. Then they began to enchant her. She would wake in the dawn to find wagtails running in the dew, almost within reach of her hand, or to see a hedgehog waddling about on his spiny affairs, or rabbits nibbling the grass. Once, an owl was still calling in the daylight, and, seeing the thing there before her eyes making its fussy querulous noise, she recognised it for what it was and began to lose her fear of night sounds.

When the spring tides were up, there was plenty of water to permit a dive from the stony ramp that shut our garden off from the beach, and she was staggered by the heroism with which I did this. I was able to use her desire to emulate, and soon had her unafraid of the water and shoving along on a tentative breast-stroke. After a rub down, we would each take a big jug, and walk to where Gerald's hippocrene gushed from the rock. This, too, was something she didn't like at first. Water wasn't "safe" unless it came from a tap. This ice-cold elemental spring, leaping from among the ferns and moss into the morning light, lacked the virtue of having oozed sluggishly through miles of convoluted leaden intestines. "Our Mother says . . ." she would begin, in explanation of this or that fear or fancy; for the woman who had starved and thrashed her was not yet obliterated as Authority. But gradually "our Mother" faded out and Nan began to adjust herself to her new world. The dead white of her face became

447

warm ivory, and she looked less starved. But she did not put on flesh. Soon she was eating like a horse, but never looked more than a whippet.

It was in June that I received a letter from Tom Elthorne.

Dear Miss Legassick. — Dr Cumberledge has given me your address and I'm taking the liberty of writing. I don't know whether you've been keeping in touch with my distinguished career. In case not, here is the score to date. I managed to get my Doctorate of Science and then wangled a reasonably good research job with a firm of industrial chemists in Lancashire. Now I've applied for, and got, a similar job with a more important firm in London. Put thus briefly, this doesn't do justice to the brilliance of my achievements, but it must serve for the moment. I begin with my new bosses in about a month's time, and am filling in the interval with a tour on a fearsome motorbike. I'm now in Plymouth, headed your way. I shall take it kindly if you prove not too horrified to see me soon pulling up at your garden gate. Can't say when, but, till soon (I hope)
yours affectionately,
Tom Elthorne.

For "heading your way" I read "heading Augusta's way," but he was unlucky. Augusta had done the sort of thing Louisa would have done when young, the sort of thing I had done myself because necessity forced me to it. She had taken a job. It isn't startling now. Two wars have changed all that, but even so recently as in 1914 few young women worked unless driven to it. Augusta was driven in a way, but not by economic necessity. She could have stayed with me as long as she liked. She was driven by her need to be near to Michael Miskin. She persuaded Hugo to write to a parson-friend of his in Yeovil, asking him to look out for some suitably ladylike work for his niece, and there she now was doing I hardly knew what in a lawyer's office and boarding with the parson and his wife. She didn't write to me often, but from her few letters I gathered that she disliked both her job and the parson; but she was able to see a good deal of Mickey. I didn't like the arrangement because I was told that Colonel Miskin knew nothing of it. He was, Augusta said, the sort of man who would disapprove of the women of his family – even potentially of his family – earning a living. And so there was this clandestine and rather furtive association that troubled me; but I could do nothing about it.

Tom didn't come after all. On the last day of June I received a second letter from him.

Dear Miss Legassick. – I expect you saw the papers yesterday. Or don't you see the papers in St Tudno? Anyway, this assassination of the heir to the Austrian throne has made me change my plans. I'm in the Territorial Army, you know. I'm making for London to explain the situation to my new bosses. I do hope I can screw a promise out of them to hold some sort of job for me when the war's over. For I'm sure this does mean war, though I haven't met a soul today who agrees with me. We shall see. Forgive this breaking of my engagement, and if Augusta's about, give her my greetings.

Ever,

Tom Elthorne.

6

About a month later war was declared and Barty Spargo went fishing. A few weeks after that Miles came down to St Tudno and stayed at Little in Sight. He was finished with Oxford. We rowed out in the dinghy one day and just drifted on the tide. I had been disturbed and hurt by his querulous attitude to me and Nan and everyone else since he arrived; and I thought to lull him into a better mood. We had left Nan behind. She remembered him as the young man who had shouted at her and the rest of them when they arrived in Cornwall last summer. She avoided him as much as possible. We were now at war, but it was the old scene of peace. It didn't heal him. He looked both wretched and rebellious.

"What are you going to do, Miles?" I asked him.

"Do?" he said sharply. "Why, what I've always said I'd do – keep out of it."

I chided him gently, with my hand on his. "No, no, my dear boy. I'm not talking about that. I mean what are you going to do now that you're down from Oxford?"

449

He looked contrite, but still spoke with this new unlikable asperity. "I don't know why I ever went to the place. Three years wasted. What can Oxford teach an actor?"

"So it's still the stage?"

"Of course. What else could it be? But I suppose this damned war will knock the theatre endways."

"It may give you a chance," I said. "Probably lots of young actors will join the army."

That made him furious though I had not said it to hurt him. He went red with vexation. "That's a pretty mean remark. D'you think I'm looking out for some dead man's job? But that's how it will be. That's what everyone will think."

I took up the oars and pulled lazily over to the St Just side. We went ashore and lay in the sun. I thought he had dozed off in the hot silence, but suddenly he sat up and said: "Aunt Maria, what do you *really* think of me?"

He looked defenceless, torn by something I did not fully understand, and I could not strike him. Not that I wished to. He was stuffing tobacco into his pipe with trembling fingers. "Really," he said, trying to smile. "No punches barred."

I thought of him and Augusta, forlorn and piteous children, making their way down to the vicarage after their mother had died. I had done what I could to heal their wounds, and now he was a man, asking for healing still, and there was nothing I could do for him, nothing whatever. The world suddenly seemed monstrous, shameful, and all this bounty of nature, this corn on the hills, this smiling sea, this fulfilling sun, a mask of infamy.

I began to cry, thinking of him and of Augusta, who both must suffer, and of all the sorrows of which their suffering would be no more than a tear-drop in this sea. And having begun to cry, I found all that I had to cry for welling up in me, harrowing me, and at the same time giving me ease: Louisa and James, Father, Bella, Roger, Charles Lester and Gerald Pickering. Here, on this small bit of land and sea, I had found and lost more than I could bear. So I went on weeping.

I looked at him through my tears, and he said: "You needn't cry for *me.*"

I wasn't crying for him or for myself. I was crying for incurable and eternal woes.

"I'm going," he said. "I'm joining up."

He tried to light his pipe, then threw the match down from his shaking fingers. "When I said I wasn't, it was the last clutch at an attitude I can't keep up."

I dried my eyes and said: "You must do as you please. I love you. I shall always love you. A uniform on your back will make no difference to that."

"It's the men," he said.

And, of course, there was that. The men he had known at school and at Oxford, the men he had talked about to me and the men whose very names I had never heard.

"They're joining up in scores," he said.

The herd instinct. Well, if you like. After all, we are of one herd or another, say what we will. It didn't, and doesn't, seem to me ignoble. I could imagine the bond that was already forged, and its challenge to a sterner and bloodier test.

"I'm loathing the very thought of it," he said. "In a way, I'm despising myself. Well, there it is."

He left it at that. I asked, "Have you told Celia?"

"I only made my mind up this morning."

"You'll write to her?"

"Not on your life. That would make me despise myself still more."

We went to a shack in a cottage garden and ate our tea and tried to make it one of those days we had often known: the wasps in the jam-pot, the butterflies, the birds waiting for crumbs, life safe and happy. But we had no words. Whatever we were, we were not happy, though we were at peace with one another as we had not been since his arrival, and for the three days he stayed after that he was very loving and gentle.

7

It came and it went. I shall say no more about it than that. Plenty has been written about it – so much glory, so much shame. Outside the two gates – the lych-gate leading into the graveyard and the gate leading to the vicarage – there is the granite monument that we put up; and on it there was room for more writing, as though we had foreknown our unteachability. For we needed the extra space, and now we have used it. The names belonging to the second war were added long long before time had mellowed the granite on which those of the first were inscribed. Now that I am very old, I sometimes totter out of the vicarage on a November day and look at the red poppies, scattered before the granite roll-call, ready for the service in which we shall remember the men of two wars, as though shame forbade us to hold a separate service for the men of each. Get the sin and folly over in one do, and then forget it. There the poppies are; and I think of McCrae's lines:

> *If ye break faith with us who died*
> *We shall not sleep, though poppies grow*
> *In Flanders fields.*

There must be sleepless ghosts hereabouts.

Apart from this monument, nothing seems changed since I was a child. The same sycamores stand on the grass along the vicarage wall. The same letter-box is let into the side of the byre with the V.R. monogram entwined upon it. Victoria Regina. I look at it, and I think of some St Tudno mother dropping her letter into it. "Dear Jack, thanks for yours. We was interested in what you said about this woman Miss Nightingale. Mind you watch this frostbite." How many letters had Hugo dropped through that slot addressed to Lieutenant John Oldham? And there the name is in the first list – John Oldham, whom I had seen tagging up the hill on a May day with Constance and Richard and, in the pram, young Millicent, still feeding on Bella's milk.

Somewhere in Somerset there is a monument with Michael Miskin's name on it, and somewhere in Manchester one with the name of Miles Cumberledge.

CHAPTER FIFTEEN

YOUNG RICHARD OLDHAM finished at his prep school just at the time when Hugo received news of John's death. Constance had joined the WAAC, which is to say the Women's Army Auxiliary Corps. Hugo was lonely without her, and was looking forward to John's coming home on an overdue leave. Well, the telegram came instead. Hugo said little. He was quite traditional about it all, and carried on with his work. Few realised as I did that something was dead in him. He said to me: "I think I'll postpone Richard's going on to Repton." He didn't say why, but I knew he couldn't bear the emptiness – John never to come on leave again, Constance away in France. That was in 1916. So Richard stayed, and he didn't go to school again.

I saw a lot of him. He was constantly running along the creek to see me and Nan, who was of his own age. I saw no reason why the war should gloom their lives, insofar as I could prevent it. I did what I had long wanted to do – bought a Falmouth quay punt, and took them out whenever I could. They were quick pupils and could soon sail her themselves. Richard was a good swimmer, and I let them do as they pleased. They swam and sailed and walked together through all that misery, and I did what I could for Hugo by making a luncheon arrangement. He came to me one day and I went to him the next so long as the war went on after John's death. I cleaned the church brass for him and saw to the flowers and gave him all the companionship I could.

After lunch one day he said to me: "Can you spare a minute, Maria? I've found something that may interest you."

He walked me up to the loft. On a long trestle table was an array of leaves: sycamore, oak, beech, and many others. Alongside them were their images drawn in pencil. They were not very good drawings, but they were better than I could have done. They had a fluent grace. Hugo picked up one of the sheets. It showed a spray of hawthorn leaves and berries. "See the signature?"

It was signed: N. L.

"I suppose that's Nan Legassick," he said.

I said, flabbergasted: "Well, I'm darned!"

"Maria, you're getting too fond of that expression," he reproved me.

I apologised; and he said: "Here's something else."

It was a sheet of paper on which was written: "Flowers and Leaves, by Richard Oldham and Nan Legassick."

"A book!" I cried.

"Looks like it. Here you are."

This time it was a page of Richard's writing – a careful and accurate account of a beech leaf from bud to autumn withering.

"I knew Richard was a bit of a botanist," Hugo said. "But I didn't know it had come to this."

"I hadn't the faintest notion that Nan drew," I confessed.

"I suppose she does draw – in a way," he conceded.

"Well, something can be done about it," I said rather crossly, disliking the belittling tone. "I'll have a talk with Mr Mompsen."

2

Cornwall has the good fortune of being continually refreshed by "foreigners", especially artists. Some come there to live, and some to die. Old Mr Mompsen told me more than once that he had come to die, but he was taking a long time about it. It was in 1916 that he appeared amongst us. The grandson he had been bringing up, both the boy's parents being dead, had been killed on the Somme. He had no one left, and he fled from a place too full of memories. Higher up the creek on the opposite side from mine, where the water dried out into mudflats at low tide, there was a quay with a grassy plateau behind it, and on the grass was a cottage. There he set up: a thin gentle old creature who didn't find it easy to make contact with his fellows. He bought a dinghy, but never rowed out of the creek and never even ventured upon it unless the day was perfect. He was unable to grasp even so elementary an idea as that tides came and went, and the consequence was that I saw him one day sitting in his dinghy, looking up-creek towards his cottage which was unaccountably cut off by a long stretch of mud. I rowed out to him and introduced myself and said: "You live over there in Quay Cottage, don't you?"

"I'm afraid so," he said. "What shall I do?"

"Well," I said, "it would be a good idea to invent a pair of mud-shoes. You know, something like snow-shoes. Then when you get caught out like this, you drop anchor and walk home."

He looked at me gravely and said: "I'm afraid I haven't an inventive mind. I'm a stupid sort of person."

"Well, come and land on my lawn and drink a cup of tea. You can row home when the tide turns."

I left him sitting on the lawn in a deck-chair and went in to make the tea. When I came back, he was drawing in a sketch-book. He tore out the sheet and handed it to me. "Something like that?" he asked.

And there he was, floundering along on his mud-shoes, with a few contorted trees on the bank, inquisitive birds over his head, and in the distance Quay Cottage, by some magic transformed into a place from which a tribe of gnomes and elves might at any moment troop out.

"Oh," I said, "I knew you were Mr Mompsen, but I didn't know you were *that* Mompsen."

He looked pleased. "It's only a blob," he said. "How did you know?"

"True, it's only a blob, but it's a Mompsen blob. I have your edition of *A Midsummer Night's Dream*."

We began like that. He stayed till the tide came in; and thereafter he often dropped in to tea. Sometimes I rowed across to Quay Cottage and took tea with him. He had a competent village woman looking after him, and the little place was as neat as a captain's cabin. Behind the cottage was a large shed, and that was his studio.

I had known his work for years. In his own line he was a master, and no Christmas came round without a "gift-book" appearing with his illustrations. The fairy plays of Shakespeare, *Gulliver's Travels*, Hans Andersen's tales: those were the sort of thing he enlivened with his own imaginative touch, which not merely depicted but illuminated, pushing the story across into his own vividly created world. He was a curious little creature to have drifted into our homespun village: dressed always immaculately in a navy-blue lounge suit, with spotless linen, neat triangle of crimson silk handkerchief, and white spats.

Even when he was in his dinghy he was thus attired, with an umbrella lying on the thwart beside him. We became very friendly. Sometimes he joined me and Hugo at lunch, either in my cottage or at the vicarage. We were all sunk in grief. It was a bond. Though never mentioned, it held us together. We had our immortals.

3

It was very charming to me to see Mr Mompsen rowing Nan on the creek. Now, in 1917, she was fifteen. I never had any Pygmalion trouble with her voice. I never had to emphasize that the rain in Spain falls mainly in the plain. That mother of hers, whatever her faults, had taught her to speak well. She was not a native Londoner, but had drifted there from some part of the country that had conventional speech. Nan was a great reader, and I bothered very little with her education. I saw that she always had books, that they were worth reading, and that a dictionary was at hand. I had had little more education than that myself, apart from the languages I had picked up on my travels. I noticed that Nan was best pleased when a book was illustrated. I had a lot of bound volumes of the old *Strand* magazine, and she would pore for hours over the drawings by Sid Paget, Gordon Browne, H. R. Millar and the rest of them; and there was, too, my one book illustrated by the celebrated monogram M M, which was Matthew Mompsen. I had seen her copying the pictures through tracing paper, but, as that is a common game with children, had taken no notice. I didn't know, till Hugo showed me her work, that she was doing her own things. Indeed, walking home that day, it occurred to me that what I had seen in the loft was probably traced from some book she had come upon. But then they were signed N. L., and that would have been cheating if they had been traced, and Nan didn't cheat. She was startlingly honest.

I saw little of Augusta now. When Michael Miskin went overseas, she remained at her job in Yeovil. She wrote to me: "I shall stay here till I know the worst. I don't suppose that will be long," and indeed it wasn't. Whatever angels may have been at Mons were unable to help him. All his bright light was blown out in the first puff. I wrote at once to Augusta and invited her to come and stay with me. No answer came, and it was from Frank Cumberledge that I heard she had turned up in Manchester. "She's pretty well shattered," Frank wrote, "and I don't know what to do about her. She's all nerves and sense of sin. She is dedicating herself to Fanny." (That was her step-mother.) "She is convinced – God help her, poor child! – that she is being afflicted for her conduct those years ago when she walked out of the house because Fanny was in it. Everything, she says, has gone wrong with her since that day. She castigates herself for having chosen what she calls an utterly selfish way of life. Even something that happened at Tregannock, when you had those children down there, is in the indictment she brings against herself. I haven't got the hang of it, but she was selfish even there, she says, neglecting her obvious duty and causing Michael Miskin to do the same. Forgive me, dear Maria, for putting all this on your shoulders, but I'm trying to write myself out of a confused state of mind about her. We try to surround her with peace and quiet – not easy nowadays – and I hope she'll pull out of this phase before long. I don't suppose you hear anything of young Tom Elthorne? His father tells me that he never got out of England. He went down with appendicitis just when his battalion was going overseas; and in hospital they discovered that he'd been putting up a big bluff about his eyesight which, it seems, is worse than any of us suspected. What with that and a lot of people leaving the chemical firm he was about to join, he's been discharged as medically unfit, and ordered to report to these chemical people. I suppose in these days chemicals are seen in a new light. Anyway, that's where Tom is, and his father, being an honest man, says thank God for it."

There was more, but that was all that concerned Augusta. I wrote several letters to her in Manchester, and when they were unanswered concluded that I was associated in her mind with her sinful days, and so decided to abide my time. Frank kept me in touch. Towards the end of 1915 she took up Red Cross work in a Manchester hospital and went on well enough till Miles was killed. Then she had a relapse. Miles, I suppose, apart from the strong bond between them, deepened by their mother's death, would ever be associated with the flight from Fanny and the "sinful" days with Haydon Mellerby. She was very ill indeed, and Fanny, whom I had always liked, though she was a bit of a fool, had to endure a new outpouring of penitential affection. Augusta was desperately trying to get back to the point where she conceived herself to have gone wrong. She even called upon Miss Vesey, who had loved her too much and taught her Latin too little, for Miss Vesey was associated with that moment. "It being school holiday time," Frank wrote, "I've packed the three of them off to Redcar on the north-east coast, where the air is vigorous." At the end of a month they came back with Augusta apparently recovered. "Tom Elthorne writes to her regularly," Frank told me, "but she never answers his letters." I could guess why. It was Tom who had organised her escape from Fanny.

She took up her Red Cross work again. In the summer of 1918 she at last came to see me. It was four years since we had parted – four such years for all of us! I had parted with a girl, and here was a woman. She was tall, much thinner, grave and collected. I hadn't known when she would come, and there she suddenly was. She walked round the house, carrying a suitcase, and found me lying on a mattress on my patch of lawn, asleep in the afternoon light. She sat down on the grass and waited for me to wake, which I soon did, sensing a presence alongside me. We both got up and embraced, and I said: "Oh, my darling!" There was nothing else I could say. I felt like a beggar who had once been rich and finds himself enriched again. She overtopped me, and I had to look up a little at her blue eyes. There was a faint perfume about her, and I breathed it hungrily, still holding her. At last she put me gently aside, as though she were the adult, I a child. I hadn't known what to expect. Frank's letters had so distressed me that a trembling bag of bones and nerves would have given me no surprise. But I knew that whatever hell she had had to go through was behind her, and that she was out on the other side.

I must have looked so much a fussed old hen that she said: "Dear Aunt Maria!" and patted my cheek with her gloved hand. I was very happy. There had been no need for more than these few words and we were beautifully at one.

I picked up her suitcase and said: "Now come in and have some tea and let me show you my little cottage."

We drank our tea and I looked at her with frank and foolish admiration: the long slender legs, the ripe breasts, the beautiful face that was the lovelier for its gravity. Now that she had taken off her hat, her hair shone with its remembered sheen of sunny wheat.

"Poor Nan!" I said, but even as I said it I knew that I loved my little duckling as much as I did this proud young swan. She was all mine. And that was something that I saw Augusta could never be again.

"Tell me about Nan," she said. "Father has said something about her, but not much. I ought to know her because she was with the others at Tregannock. But I'm afraid she made no impression on me."

"She wouldn't," I said. "Nan's not an impressive person. But she grows on you. And she's only sixteen."

She gave me a long cool look, and I knew she was looking not only at me but back at her own life. Her look said to me: "Yes, but one can be *something* at sixteen." She was sixteen when she met Haydon Mellerby. She said: "You know, Aunt Maria, you love people too easily." She filled my cup and added: "It's not a good habit." And again I knew that she was thinking more of her own life than of mine.

"I'm too old to grow out of it," I said. "And I wouldn't want to if I could. It's no good trying to stop up the vent of a volcano. It keeps bursting out."

"Oh, your love isn't *that* sort," she said, "It's more of a habit, like a shepherd's care for silly sheep."

"Well, it's a good habit, and I intend to cultivate it."

We got up and walked to the window, and there was the quay punt that we had christened *Curlew*. Richard was pulling the mooring-buoy aboard and Nan was lashing the tiller. They looked a pair of happy ragamuffins. Nan was bare-legged and wearing little but a short grey skirt and a red pullover. Richard wore nothing but a pair of khaki shorts. His body shone like autumn leaves in sunlight.

Augusta looked at them, a smile on her face. "So that's Aunt Bella's boy," she said. "How young he looks. And that's Nan. They make a beautifully unsophisticated picture."

We walked out into the garden. Nan was rowing them ashore, putting her back into it heartily, and I thought of a day when Miles and I and Augusta were rowing to Falmouth and I let her have a go at the oars. She, too, was unsophisticated then. The word worried me. It seemed to suggest a distance that she had travelled. It put a small cold space between us. I noticed for the first time that her unobtrusive clothes were sophisticated.

Seeing us standing there, Richard shouted over Nan's tousled head: "How's it for tea, Aunt Maria?"

He held up with pride for my inspection a few fish threaded on a string through their gills. They added to a rather primitive picture.

459

Nan tied up the dinghy and came ashore, a shake of the head tossing the tangled hair from her eyes. She had then the sort of beauty that I liked best. Her sea-green eyes were shining. She embraced me and said: "It's been a lovely day, Aunt Maria. Thank you for *Curlew*."

It was a pleasant little habit of hers, whenever she came ashore, to say "Thank you for *Curlew*." She loved the boat as though it were a living thing – as indeed a boat becomes to those who love it.

She stood there, her legs sturdily apart, rubbing her wet hands on her skirt. *Curlew* was knitted in white letters on to her red pullover. She was taking an eyeful of Augusta. She held out her hand. "I remember you," she said. "You were at Tregannock."

Augusta took her hand, and Nan added: "I was glad when Aunt Maria said you were coming. She's been longing to see you."

Richard, too, shook hands. "Nan's not going to worry you, Aunt Augusta," he said. "We thought you might be here when we got back, and so we talked the thing over. You and Aunt Maria will have a lot to say to one another."

Augusta laughed. "My dear Richard," she said, "I'm not your aunt. Your father and my mother were brother and sister. I'm your cousin."

He looked at her gravely, swinging the fish in his hand. "It's terribly complicated," he said. "Really, I could never have the cheek to call you just Augusta. You look so old."

At that, I had to intervene. "Now come and have tea," I said "and tell me what's all this nonsense about Nan not making a nuisance of herself."

Nan answered for him. "We thought it would be best while Miss Cumberledge is here if I stayed at the vicarage. Richard's father says it'll be all right."

Augusta said: "My dear, that's not at all necessary. I wouldn't dream of driving you out of your own home."

"Oh, I shan't mind," Nan assured her. "I like being at the vicarage. So that's all settled."

"But is it?" I asked.

"Oh, yes, please," Nan pleaded. "I'm sure you and Miss Cumberledge will get on better without me."

4

Augusta stayed for a week. She looked more my Augusta when she got into her country clothes, though even these were country clothes as conceived by *haute couture*. You know those girls you see in the advertisements, sitting on a shooting-stick, or standing on the edge of a moor with a gun that looks as well-bred and unused as their brogues, or stroking a retriever when you can see at a glance that they're more at home with poodles. She took a long time over her toilet, and while I was in the garden fuming to be off, wearing the things that a man in Falmouth knocked up for me, she would be dilly-dallying in front of a mirror. She was no longer interested in sailing, and as Nan and Richard wanted to do nothing else, we saw little of them. Even when we went one night to take dinner with Hugo at the vicarage, those two bolted their food, asked us to pardon them, and rushed away to do something or other aboard *Curlew*.

Hugo had asked Mr Mompsen to join us at our meal, and the courtly old creature was at his best with Augusta. I suppose that before fleeing from London he had known a lot of women of that sort. He was attentive, even deferential. A beautiful perfectly dressed woman was something he didn't see much of in St Tudno. He had been for some time now supervising Nan's drawing, and I asked him how she was getting on. "She will do well enough," he said, "but not excellently. At the moment her work is abominable."

I expressed my sorrow at this, and he said: "Oh, it's nothing – just a necessary phase. Before I began with her she had a natural fluency, and I had to destroy that. I had to reduce it to bedrock, so as to have something to build on. That's where we are now. From this point we shall slowly go forward. She will be able to walk very nicely, but she will never fly."

Augusta said: "I don't think she likes me, Uncle Hugo. She fled to your arms at the first sight of me."

Hugo, looked at his sister's child. His face was round and his body fat. Peering through his thick lenses, he was like a wise old owl gone to seed. "She doesn't dislike you," he said. "She's afraid of you. Remember, my dear, she's only just out of a London slum, and you're just out of a Parisian bandbox."

Augusta flushed. "She seems quite at home with Aunt Maria."

Hugo chuckled and patted my hand, and when he chuckled his body heaved about in his chair, as I imagine Dr Johnson's did. "Maria," he said, "is another kettle of fish. Indeed, did you ever see a woman who looked so much like a kettle of fish?"

Mr Mompsen said: "Miss Legassick is the World's Mother *manquée*. Even I feel that she has adopted me as her baby."

"Please stop," I begged them. "These well-turned compliments will swell my head."

Augusta said: "Still, Uncle Hugo and Mr Mompsen are both quite right. I see what they mean."

We went on to the terrace to drink our coffee, and Hugo alone also drank brandy. He had become a *bon viveur*, as indulgent to himself as he was to everybody else. It was a beautiful night, with a violet western sky and a great quietness. We could hear the subdued voices of the children out there on *Curlew*. I said to Hugo: "Don't you ever feel like writing books as Father did?"

"Ah, my dear," he said, "now you're trying to take *me* in hand. Well, there was a time, you know, when I dreamed of writing books, but not as Father did. D'you remember when I first came down here with Roger?"

I did indeed, and we were lost in silence for a while, thinking of that old time.

"Of course," Hugo said, "we were going to move the world, the pair of us. I think if Roger had lived I might have been different. But there; perhaps every hog thinks he'd have been a better pig in a different sty. Dreams are so easy."

No one spoke for a long time. We were all thinking of dreams that had foundered – with friends, with sons, with brothers, with lovers. It was a terrible moment, made the more poignant by the voices of the young dreamers coming to us across the quiet water.

Augusta said: "I feel a hundred years old," and got up. We walked home in silence along the creek, and she was not my child, not my girl. She was a woman who shared my own agonies. She spoke only once. "Such a lot is dead in me," she said, "and I'm not sure about what's waking up."

The night had turned a bit cold, and when we got in I lit the fire. We stayed up late, talking, and our peaceful solitude loosened her tongue. At last she spoke of the things that had been hinted in Frank's letters, and I made a pot of tea and let her run on. For the first time, I was glad that Nan had chosen to be absent while Augusta was with me, and was pleased with the instinctive wisdom that had shown the child what to do.

Augusta told me of the day, more than three years ago now, when Colonel Miskin had called at the office in Yeovil where she worked and had asked permission to take her out to lunch. Halfway through the meal, he took the telegram from his pocket and handed it to her without a word. She read it and watched him going on eating as though it were a matter of no moment at all. Augusta tried to be as brave as he seemed to be. "I didn't cry," she told me. "I felt too dead to do even that. Presently he wiped his lips with his napkin and said: 'Well, I'm afraid that's that. Let's not bother about coffee.' He walked me back to my office, shook hands, and said goodbye as though we had been spending a pleasant hour together. I was thinking with contempt of the stiff-upper-lip tradition. All that day somehow I couldn't think of Mickey at all. I was thinking of his father, almost hating him. That night he shot himself."

"Oh, my dear!" I cried. "I didn't know that. Your father never told me."

"I didn't tell him," Augusta said. "What would have been the point? I've told nobody but you."

We sat by my little old-fashioned grate, listening to the logs purring. Augusta said: "Doesn't it feel *safe* here? But I shall never feel safe again. I'm terrified when I think of the life I've led, the way I've *clung* to people: Mother and Miles, Haydon and Mickey. And, for that matter, you. I feel as if I shall never dare to make a friend again, much less take a lover. I *have* given, haven't I?" she asked rather wildly.

"Darling," I said. "You've been a very loving girl. Don't reproach yourself."

"I don't reproach myself. I reproach whatever it is that throws everything back in my teeth."

"Well," I said, trying to lighten the moment. "I haven't been thrown back yet."

She kissed my hand and said: "No. But I wish I was this girl Nan, so that I could start with you all over again."

My clock struck one, and she got up. "I'm a bit jealous of her," she said, meaning it. "They say sorrow fortifies the character."

"I should think that depends on the character."

"Well, it hasn't done *me* any good. I'm a cautious, watchful creature, all too aware that I'm tired of giving."

"Don't think of it like that," I warned her. "You've given a lot, but you have also received a lot – even from Haydon Mellerby."

"Perhaps that will occur to me some day. It doesn't now."

She kissed me good night, and I sat there till the embers were grey. Then I went to my bed, feeling unhappy. I didn't sleep at all. I knew that she had revealed herself to me as she had never done to Frank, insofar as I could judge from his letters. It looked as though the war was wearing to an end, and what would she do when that came? She could do as she pleased, for she was reasonably well off. When Mr Oldham, her mother's father, died, he had left a lot of money to his daughter. She had tied it up for the benefit of her two children, wisely allowing them not capital, but only interest, with reversion of the whole to whichever should survive the other. So now, with Miles' death, it was all Augusta's. Hence, I thought, her clothes, her shoes, her lovely bags and gloves. Shoes, bags, gloves! I laughed at the trivia that were whirring in my addled sleepless brain, and saw that the dawn had come. I got out of bed and walked to the window, huddled in a dressing-gown, and there, amid the pearly mists on the water, was Mr Mompsen with a shawl wrapped round his head and another round his shoulders, stroking his dinghy slowly and aimlessly to and fro. His housekeeper had told me he hardly ever slept. He looked like some poor old soul adrift on the Styx, too feeble to get across to those who had gone before and whom he wished to join. It was a picture of such utter loneliness, such sorrow unobtrusive and unobserved, that I crept away from the window, hating the thought that he might see me.

5

On her last day with me I asked Augusta if she had decided what she would do when the war was over. She said: "I shall go to London and wait and see."

I said impetuously, not having thought a thing about it till that moment: "I shall go to London, too. I shall find a flat for me and Nan, and we can use this place for holidays."

"That will be a blow for Richard. I notice that he hardly ever gives a moment to young Millicent. It's Nan all the time. He seems to grudge even the hours she spends with Mr Mompsen."

"He'll have to put up with that. It's too valuable both to Nan and the old boy. I wish I could think of something to do for him."

"For Richard?"

"No. For Mr Mompsen. He breaks my heart."

She smiled. "There you go again. When are you going to learn that broken hearts are in the fashion and that there's nothing you can do about it? You can't adopt the old boy and bring him up. How is my cousin Constance?"

"I haven't seen much of her. She's twenty-one, and in the WAACs. She was home on leave about a year ago. A very responsible sort of young woman. Rather as my sister Louisa used to be."

"It will be a good thing for Uncle Hugo when she's back. What a dear he is."

"I'm afraid he'll have to do without her. She didn't strike me as the sort of girl who'd stay at home. She'd been hoping for Oxford, but you know the war stopped that. I asked her if she'd try to get up there when she was demobilised, and she said No. It would be time to be getting on with something, but she didn't have any clear ideas. Still, I'm sure Hugo won't see much of her."

We were drinking our morning coffee in the garden, and Nan and Richard came rowing down from Mr Mompsen's cottage. Richard always hung about there when Nan was with the old man, and then they walked or rowed home as the tide dictated. I asked them if they would like coffee. Richard said: "We had it with old Mompers," and Nan said: "We're going to take *Curlew* out. We just looked in to say goodbye to – to –"

She had never decided what to call Augusta.

"Just call me Augusta."

Nan held out her hand and said formally: "Well, goodbye, Augusta. It's been nice having you."

Augusta burst out laughing. "You haven't been having much of me, have you?" and Richard said gravely: "I'm afraid that's been my fault. I hope we haven't been dreadfully rude."

"Never mind me," Augusta said. "Look after Nan. Off you go now, the pair of you."

They gladly went, Nan calling back over her shoulder: "Mr Mompsen was pleased for once."

Hugo, making calls on parishioners along the creek, looked in to wish her goodbye, and then the pony and trap arrived that I had hired to drive her to Truro, where she would catch the Manchester train. I didn't go with her. We both disliked formal farewells.

6

Those last months of the war dribbled along, and November came, and we read in the papers about the riotous scenes in London. I hadn't felt like rioting. I walked along the creek with Nan and left her at the vicarage, and went down to the church. The air in the graveyard was scented with winter heliotrope and the trees were as still as though that pause in history had petrified them. I went through the little rounded doorway beneath which Norman heads had bowed, and I sat enclosed by the cold stone walls that had been the setting for so much of my life. I read for the thousandth time the thanks of King Charles the First to his people of Cornwall for having been so kind to him in his day of tribulation, though that had saved neither his throne nor his head. I read the memorials of men of our parish who had died in wars by land and sea; and I looked at the grandiose memorials of Polperros, whose corpses were housed between walls, and I thought of the humble souls who had to make do with a slit in the cold earth outside. James Polperro and Louisa were neither in nor out. Not a bone of them had been recovered for burial; and, thinking this, I thought of the May morning when they were young and I surprised one of them riding away and the other wild and desolate. Father, and the mother I couldn't remember, and Bella were outside, and a line on a stone spoke of Roger.

Thinking of the life and the death that these stones and that bit of turf on the edge of the sea had known for nine hundred years, I felt older and sadder than any of it, a survivor, still afloat on the spindrift of time that would soon be extinguished in the ever-rolling stream. I knelt on the hassock I had used since I was a baby, and I prayed for us all, living and dead. Then I went out and stood under the tent of the yew tree, to draw what courage I could from those old limbs that had seen it all, withstood it all, and, knowing neither hope nor despair, still lived on.

7

On May the 21st 1919 I was forty-three years old, and I didn't tell anyone that it was my birthday. However, I decided to have a loafing day, and as the children, who had been fitting out *Curlew*, were taking her off for her first sail, I went with them. For one thing, they had told me that Constance would be going, and it seemed to me a good chance of getting to know something of that young woman. She was twenty-one and had just been demobilised. She was a tall girl, calm and quiet, with no looks to speak of, but with what I could only call an air. When you met her, she did not slide off your consciousness: you were aware of her. She was a person. She was brown: hair and eyes and complexion: and her broad brow and quiet manner suggested a mental stability. She and Nan got on well together.

It was a good day. We started early and sailed down to the Helford river and ate our lunch aboard. Richard had been fussing about the boat ever since we started and said he was not satisfied with her performance, so he and Nan stayed aboard to see to this and that, while I rowed Constance ashore. We found a sandy nook embraced in arms of rock and lay down there in the sunshine. She had a warm rich voice. She said: "Father tells me you've taken a place in London."

I had. It had seemed to me that London would soon be flooding with demobilised people and that I had better act quickly. So I had spent a week looking about me, and was lucky. Rider's Yard, which opens off the Marble Arch end of Oxford Street, had been a mews. A number of flats had been built on two sides of it, and a small house filled the third side. It was minute: a living room and a kitchen on the ground floor, two bedrooms and a bathroom up above. It was a perfect perching-place for me and Nan when we were not at Little in Sight, and I had managed to get a long lease. From time to time since then I had gone up on a spending spree, and now the place was ready. The brass knocker shone on the olive-green door. A ray of sun, which visited the yard at noon, lit up the white paint of my four windows and of the pretty fanlight. I told Constance all about it.

"I hope we shall see something of one another," she said. "I shall be in London as soon as my man's ready for me."

Her man, it seemed, was a Lieutenant-Colonel Guy Halliday. "I was a chauffeur. I used to drive him about."

"A chauffeuse, surely?" I said pedantically.

"I used the word once," Constance said, "and he told me it sounded suspect."

I asked her why he hadn't driven himself, and she said: "Oh, colonels didn't do that sort of thing. Besides, it would have been awkward. He had only one arm."

She picked up handfuls of the warm sand and watched it dribble through her fingers.

"He knew my cousin Miles," she said. "That's when he lost his arm — when Miles was killed."

She wasn't a fluent talker, but bit by bit I learned of Guy Halliday, a Territorial officer, who might well have got out of the army on the strength of his lost arm, but insisted on staying in it and became attached to G.H.Q. "He's forty-five now," she said.

His father was a builder. "Not like old Rees at St Tudno," Constance explained, meaning our carpenter-builder-undertaker. "He's the sort whose board you see flaming over about a mile of activity when some enormous work is going on. I suppose he'd call himself a constructional engineer."

Guy had been engaged in this very profitable family business; but the war had changed his thought. "His father's still alive and active and there are two other brothers, so Colonel Halliday thinks they can get on very well without him. He wants to go into Parliament, and so of course he will."

Of course. The words told me all I needed to know about her opinion of him. "There'll be a good deal to do," she said, "before that, and so I'm learning shorthand and knocking father's old typewriter about, and I read a lot of stuff he sends me."

I gathered that their commerce had not all been as officer and chauffeur. There had been long talks about the world and what to do with it, and this man of more than twice her age had found an eager convert. "What party will he stand for?" I asked.

"Oh, Labour, of course."

"Your father won't like his typewriter being used in such a cause."

"Oh, well," she said. "I don't tell Father much, and I gather that old Mr Halliday won't like his son being used in such a cause."

The ghost of Louisa rose before my eyes. But the living energetic figures of Richard and Nan laid it. They had put on bathing things and dived overboard and were swimming towards us. "Good heavens!" I cried. "It's too cold for that sort of nonsense."

Constance said: "I'll bet there was a time when you wouldn't have thought so," and of course she was right. I said: "I'm afraid I'm becoming a proper fussy old hen where Nan is concerned."

"Oh, well," she said. "I suppose Richard will take her off your hands one of these days. Thank God there are those who will see that they live in a safer world than ours."

What was making her tick, I wondered: Guy Halliday or the dreams he had put into her head?

8

When I first met Augusta wandering with Miles towards the vicarage she was thirteen and Constance was eight. They saw little of one another then, and they did not meet again till, in this summer of 1919, they met as strangers. They took to one another. Augusta had come down to spend a day or two with me before going on to London. She had bought a small open motorcar – the sort of sporting thing that, I remembered, Michael Miskin had driven when he met us at Yeovil. I wondered whether that had influenced her choice. She was in high spirits – rather too high: a bit feverish – and she drove me and Constance to Truro to take lunch with her at the Red Lion. She told us about the flat she had found – on the Bayswater Road, overlooking the park – "and that," she said, "is what they call an amenity, and I find you have to pay for amenities. The place is going to cost me the earth, and it's absurdly big."

Constance said: "I wish I could afford to share it." She told Augusta about Colonel Guy Halliday – out of the army now, and henceforth called Mister – who was clamouring for her to come to London. "He's got an office," she said. "His father's been more accommodating than he expected, and is allowing him to use a room in the firm's premises. So my job's ready, but my pay isn't going to be much to begin with, and flats are very dear nowadays."

I didn't like the idea of either of them being solitary in a flat, and especially I didn't like it for Augusta. There had been too much disaster in her life. I dreaded the thought of her being alone, with time to brood. Always, till now, there had been Louisa or James, or myself, or Frank. Constance would be good for Augusta.

The thing was turning over in my mind as we walked about the town after lunch. We found ourselves in a small park and sat down there, and I said: "I could help, Constance, if you'd allow me."

"How do you mean – help?"

"I'm rather a rich woman through no fault of my own," I said apologetically. "If Augusta would permit you to share her flat, paying half the rent would be nothing to me. Indeed, it would take some of the guilt off my mind."

Augusta said gaily: "Do you feel guilty because you're rich, darling? It makes me feel fine."

"It's not being rich," I said. "It's having riches that I've done nothing to earn."

"Oh, well," she said, "when Mr Halliday's Chancellor of the Exchequer I expect he'll relieve you of worry on that head. Don't you think so, Constance?"

Constance was not inclined to find it an amusing topic. "Forgive me," she said. "I'm only beginning to think about such things, and so far I'm not terribly good at thinking. But thank you, Aunt Maria. I'll gladly accept your offer if Augusta can put up with me."

Augusta said she could. "If you can manage it, we could drive up together. I go the day after tomorrow."

And go they did, though I had some trouble in persuading Hugo. We finished a day-long argument in the graveyard, and I told him what was clearly true – that she'd go anyway, and it would be better if she went with his blessing.

"There were so many of us," he said forlornly, thinking of Bella's prolific days. "Now there'll be no one but Millicent and Richard, and half his time Richard's running about with Nan."

"Well, you've got me," I comforted him.

He said ungallantly: "Oh, you! Everyone's got you."

CHAPTER SIXTEEN

BATCHLEY WAS one of those places into which octopus-London was sticking a tentacle. You could still call it rural. There were cows in the fields, market gardens and orchards that sent stuff into London, and old-fashioned shops in the High Street. There were also multiple stores, a cinema, a taxi-rank outside the station of the Metropolitan railway. A few fields had hoardings in them announcing that they were "ripe for development"; others had already ripened and borne a small harvest of factories: nice factories that didn't make much smoke and had playing-fields outside and welfare officers inside. Batchley, in short, was doomed as an agricultural area, and each year's burst of apple and cherry blossom could well be the last. It had never quite made up its mind whether it wanted a Liberal or a Conservative to look after its interests in the House of Commons, and could indeed have gone on comfortably without either; but now a few people from the factories had got together and a notice in a window over a High Street shop announced it to be the headquarters of the Batchley Labour Party. Guy Halliday went down there and had an interview with the committee. More and more, they decided between them, Batchley would fill up with people who wanted a world fit for heroes to live in, and all who assembled at the meeting were full of starry-eyed conviction that to provide such a world would not be too difficult, given a Labour government. Guy Halliday's address did nothing to shake their conviction. It was delivered to only ten men, but it was his first public speech and he put into it all he had. He was elected as Batchley's prospective Labour candidate, and agreed to face a public meeting a fortnight later.

This was in the autumn of 1920. Nan and I had come up from Cornwall to spend our second winter in Rider's Yard. She was happy enough in Cornwall, but she loved London. She hated the parting from Richard and Mr Mompsen, and the old man was desolate to see her go. She didn't any longer need his tuition: he had given her all she could possibly take from him: but the lessons went on just the same for his comfort. I think she absorbed some wisdom from him, too. The poor little skeleton I had cried over as she lay naked and shivering on the beach had become a most loving and intelligent young friend, established as a person in her own right. Mr Mompsen came to take tea with us the day before we left, and I had a feeling that we were seeing him for the last time. When I shook hands with him it was like taking a bird's foot, so thin and brittle. Richard rowed him home, and then came back to spend the evening with us. He was a sensitive boy, and I could see from his face that something unusual had happened. He put a small portfolio on the table and opened it to show three drawings. "One for each of us from Mr Mompsen," he said. "Farewell presents, he says."

And so they were. With so much else that I loved, he is buried in our graveyard.

Nan was young enough to shake off the sorrow of leaving him and Richard and we settled down to our winter routine. She would go off self-confidently day after day to make her beautiful meticulous copies of drawings and tapestries in the Victoria and Albert Museum and to visit the art galleries. She needed no guidance. She had learned to live on her own and to pursue her own phantoms. She would bring home leaves and twigs and berries from the parks, and look at them for hours, and her sketch books were full of the ducks from the park ponds and the deer from Richmond.

Our little yard had a cloistral quiet, and we would sit there happily by the fire, the murmur of Oxford Street falling upon us with no more disturbance than the murmur of the sea falling on ears at St Tudno. I looked up as a sheet was torn, crumpled, and thrown on the fire. "Rotten," she said. "I can't get it."

It appeared to be the entrancing curl of a twig of corkscrew hazel. She left it, and came and sat at my feet.

"What is it all going to add up to?" I asked.

"Books," she said. "Richard will write them and I'll do the pictures."

"You've had that idea for a long time now, haven't you?"

"How did you know?"

I told her of the drawings and writings that Hugo and I had found.

"Oh, heavens, auntie," she said. "Did you see that stuff? What a nerve we had! I couldn't draw and Richard couldn't write! Did you weep for us?"

"No. But happily heaven sent us Mr Mompsen."

She said gravely: "How lucky I am! I'm always having something sent to me – you, and Mr Mompsen, and Richard."

The letters flowed between them every day. She sent him drawings; he sent her little pieces of writing. I felt content: it looked as though something I had set my hand to might have a happy issue at last.

We were in this relaxed affectionate mood when the bell rang. It was Constance, and Constance as usual meant news of Mr Halliday. It was eight o'clock, and I asked her if she had dined.

"Good lord!" she said. "I rarely do anything so impressive as that. I take my midday meal at a Lyons' place in the City, near the office. Apart from that, I live on nibbles."

"You look very well on it, my dear," I told her; and she did. She looked tranquil, as though her work satisfied her. She spoke of this. "I'm one of the lucky ones," she said. "I met one of my fellow WAACs today. She can't find a job for love or money, and that's not surprising with so many demobilised men clamouring for work. And here am I – dropped right into the one job I would have chosen above all others."

I wondered, as I had often done, whether the job would have seemed so desirable had her boss not been Guy Halliday. There was no doubt whatever that her feelings were engaged pretty deeply, but whether through admiration or love, or on that difficult ground where both meet, I did not know and could not ask. Nor did I know anything of his feeling for her.

"You're pretty late getting away from the office, aren't you?"

"Oh, this is nothing," she said gaily. "I'm often later than this. Tonight I've been staying to type Mr Halliday's speech for the Batchley meeting."

I said I knew nothing about the Batchley meeting, and that she mustn't assume that all the world was aware of Mr Halliday's engagements and intentions. She looked a little confused at that, but carried it off by saying, half seriously: "Perhaps they will be before long."

Nan had disappeared into the kitchen, and now came in with a tray on which were a pot of tea, two boiled eggs, a rack of toast, butter, marmalade, and two apples. "I've brought you a nibble," she said with her endearing smile. "Now you needn't run away. I know that Aunt Maria likes to have you around for a talk. She doesn't see much of you, or of Augusta."

Constance thanked her and turned gratefully to the little meal. "I don't see all that much of Augusta myself," she said. "I'm often in bed before she gets home at night and away in the morning before she's awake. I wade out through a litter of glamorous clothes and an atmosphere of exhaustion. Sometimes it's one o'clock or later when I hear a car door bang outside and a hearty male voice shouting 'Well, cheerio, old thing.'"

"I hope at least," I said, "that it's always the same voice."

"Oh, I'm too muzzy to tell at that hour of the night. But I wouldn't bet on it."

I made a note of all this, but didn't want to question Constance or anyone else about Augusta's doings. She finished her meal and got up. "You're not off already?" I chided her.

"I'm afraid so," she said. She picked up an attaché-case from the floor. "Still a few things here that I must take a look at." Hesitantly she added: "You've never met Mr Halliday. Why don't you come out to Batchley and hear him the night after next? It's only half an hour's run from Baker Street metro."

"My dear, I've never been to a political meeting in my life."

"Then you should be ashamed of yourself," she joked, and added seriously: "This won't be the usual run of things, you know."

2

But it was, or I supposed it was, having no measure. Nan didn't come with me. "I *must* get some drawings done to send to Richard," she said, and that, I knew, was imperative with her. Nothing would avail against it. They were a determined young pair: the goal, and the unremitting push towards it. It made me happy. Our little house was handy for Hyde Park, and Nan had spent the day there, taking a few sandwiches to eat. She came back with a sketch-book full of scribbled notations, as she called them, mostly of stripped November trees, having the gnomish look she had caught from Mr Mompsen's work.

The day was dusking when I got into a train called Sherlock Holmes at Baker Street, and that gave me a feeling of being bound on some mysterious quest. A client from Amersham had looked in at No. 221B, and unfolded a story not without a point or two of interest, and here we were, off to sniff around it like bloodhounds. But the uninspiring suburban litter of factories and streets, the mournful November crepuscule, the banal ordinariness of the jarring journey in all-but-dark, left me in little hope of a romantic conclusion. Constance's exalted view of the occasion seemed even less admissible when I alighted at Batchley. Only one other passenger got off the train, and it was now quite dark save for a platform lamp or two whose shine fell upon reiterated advice on how to care for my liver. It didn't feel like a political, or any other, resurrection day; and in the little town there was no surge of people or thud of drums. Indeed, asking my way to the meeting, I found a distressing lack of knowledge concerning its whereabouts, even its existence. But I ran into Constance, and at once it was clear that my conclusions were wrong, and that we were on the doorsteps of heavenly mansions.

We went to a little hall that could never have been lovely and through wartime's neglect had become hideous. It could hold only a couple of hundred people seated on hard wooden chairs, and although it was almost time for the meeting to begin it looked lonely. Behind the platform was a door with a tatter of red plushy stuff half drawn across it and, over it, the assurance "Righteousness Exalteth a Nation". This was in bilious green, and, like the family mottoes that have lost touch with the descendants of those who coined them, had a shame-faced look and was peeling away from the wall like a backslider edging off furtively from true doctrine. Fifty or so people failed to abolish the atmosphere of cold stuffiness, but their pipes emitted a fog that swirled about the three or four naked electric bulbs.

I hoped, for Constance's sake, that it was going to be all right. We were sitting near the front, and now and then she would look over her shoulder to see if the place was filling up, quite unable to credit the senselessness that failed to crowd the hall and demand an overflow meeting. "I'm afraid the local tennis club is having its annual dinner," I comforted her, and she looked annoyed at this inadequate pleasantry.

The plushy dusty rag in front of the platform door rattled back – brass rings on a wooden pole – and a few people came out of the room behind there. I knew Mr Halliday at once by his empty sleeve. He had a hale clean-shaven face, grey hair, and an honest look. He was well-dressed in the conventional fashion of the men you see coming by scores out of Baker Street station in the morning, bound for their offices. Indeed, he looked that sort of man not only in dress: what some people call, with a small sneer in the voice, an ordinary decent Englishman, though I don't see much wrong in being that.

I joined Constance in starting a hand-clapping welcome, but we didn't raise a storm: just a patter of rain on the window. The platform gentlemen bowed and smiled as though the Albert Hall were rising towards them in delirious praise, and sat down behind a water-bottle that looked oddly forlorn on a green cloth fringed with bobbles.

The chairman, who could have been a bookkeeper from the synthetic cheese factory near the station, said he would not speak for long in introducing Labour's prospective candidate, but all the same he spoke on and on in the midst of a grey dingy silence. Then Guy Halliday spoke – more good-mannered restrained applause when he rose – and I don't remember much of what he said, but I do remember thinking with a heavy heart that this was not the stuff to give the troops. Constance assured me afterwards that Guy's facts and figures were unchallengeable and added up to a masterly presentation of Labour's case. I am prepared to believe that it did, just as I am prepared to believe that raw cod liver oil is good for me. But nothing would induce me to drink it.

However, the people seemed to like Guy more than they had liked the chairman, who had been bombastic. Guy gave an impression of humility, of not being there to serve any private end, of sincerely, for everybody's good, desiring what he rather drably called a "good clean-up of this mess we're in." I imagined that he would be an excellent committee-man, which in fact is what he became when he entered Parliament, but for public occasions any party would want a bit more glitter, if it was only on brass.

Constance, Guy Halliday and I all went back to Baker Street in the same compartment. I noticed that she called him Mr Halliday, and sometimes sir, and that he called her Miss Oldham. He asked me how I thought things had gone, and, struggling for truth, I said that they couldn't have gone better, adding the mental rider "in the circumstances".

At Baker Street he called a taxi and asked if he could drop us anywhere. He said to Constance: "Do you live near here, Miss Oldham?" That was another thing to note: he didn't even know where she lived. I told him we'd find our own way, and when he was gone we walked through a deserted Baker Street to Oxford Street and so into Rider's Yard. It was nearly eleven o'clock, and Nan was waiting up for us. To my surprise, Augusta was there, too, looking extremely sophisticated, as though she had "come on", as they say, from some distinguished social occasion.

I hadn't seen Augusta for some time. I kissed her and, looking at her clothes which belonged to a dance floor rather than to my little room, I said: "This is a bit late for me to be out, but a bit early for you, I imagine. Are you off somewhere?"

"No," she said. "I've been left rather flat. I had a dinner-date, and naturally one expects to dance after dinner, but my cavalier decided otherwise."

She said it lightly, almost flippantly, but I could see that something had hurt her. She was in rustling golden silk, with golden shoes, and she was carefully made up. Sitting there with Nan and Constance, she was almost exotic. "I should have felt dreadful," she said, "if I'd gone home at that time of night, so I asked him to call me a cab, and came on to have a talk with you."

"Well, here I am."

She looked at Nan and Constance, and seemed uneasy. "What about lunch tomorrow?" I asked. "I can always give Nan a bit of bread and cheese and send her off bird-watching."

"I'd love that," she said, and got up. Constance said she'd call a taxi, and they went out together. "I'll be here at a quarter to one," Augusta called back.

I suddenly felt weary and in the presence of something difficult. Nan made me a pot of tea and cleared away her work from the table. "What time did Augusta come?" I asked.

"Soon after ten. I think she'd been crying. She went upstairs and made up and then seemed more calm. Isn't she beautiful? Do you think I shall ever be beautiful?"

"No. But you'll be happy, I hope."

"I'm happy now," she said. "But I wish I was beautiful as well."

"What did you and Augusta talk about? Or shouldn't I ask?"

"Oh, it was innocent enough. She did all the talking – about when she and her brother first met you, and how happy you all were together, and how lucky I am to be living with you."

"Well, if she thinks that lucky," I said, sipping my tea and warming my toes, "there's nothing to prevent her coming and living with us."

"Oh, yes there is."

"Why – what?"

"Well, everything. Not giving in, for one thing. Even if you're unhappy, you may want to fight it out on your own."

"Do you ever feel like that, Nan?"

"A little, sometimes," she said with delightful candour. "But I'm not restless like Augusta. I know exactly what I want to do. And so I plod along. And spending all our summers with Richard makes such a difference. He keeps me steadfast."

I loved the word. It said what I myself felt about Richard.

3

Since coming to Rider's Yard I had seen Tom Elthorne once or twice. The first meeting was by chance. I was walking through Berkeley Square in the dusk of a late autumn day when he turned in from a side street, and there we were, face to face.

"Well – Miss Legassick!"

I was taken aback, because this was not Tom Elthorne. It was, at the very least, Thomas Elthorne, Esquire. I hadn't seen him since before the war began, and the memory of a gangling youth was difficult to reconcile with the man before me. My mind made a rapid calculation. Augusta is twenty-six. He must be nearing thirty. He was still thin and rakish, and wearing thick spectacles, but he was well-dressed and had an air of confidence and success. Whatever he was now doing, he clearly was no longer making fireworks that didn't go off.

He raised his black Homburg hat and we exchanged civilities. Then he said: "Come and have a drink."

"Mr Elthorne!" I protested. "I am not accustomed to entering public houses."

He laughed. "Dear Miss Legassick! I wouldn't disturb the respectability and serenity of a pub by taking you into it. No, no. I live near here. Let's go to my place."

One of the Berkeley Square houses had gone over to offices on the ground floor. Above that were a couple of flats, and he took me to one of them. The sitting room looked on to the square, and I stood there gazing out as the darkness deepened, thinking that Tom Elthorne had done very well for himself. He switched on the lights and an electric fire, and pulled the curtains, and put me into a comfortable chair. It was a lovely room, but rather bleakly furnished. No pictures. No frills. "This is just my doss-house," he said. "I eat out."

He put sherry before me, and lit his pipe. "I always understood," I said, "that one didn't profane good wine with a pipe."

"That's just a classy notion," he said. "I'm a rude provincial."

He didn't look it. He had an aura of authority.

We drank to one another's health. "I hope the world's treating you well, Tom," I said.

"I can't complain."

He didn't tell it all then, but we had other meetings, and gradually I pieced it together. The war gave importance to the firm he had joined, and he prospered with the firm. He was able to contribute things of his own. I never understood what, but "one or two small discoveries," as he called them, attracted attention in the Ministry of Munitions, and by the time the war was over he was a person of some importance. What surprised him was that he revealed a talent for administration. "All very well being a chap producing the goods," he said. "The executives are the ones who get the money." An executive who knew also the scientific principles involved was a rarity; and that is what Tom was. "Our plant became rather notable," he said, "and of course B.A.C. began to cast an eye on it."

I asked him to explain B.A.C., and he said: "British Associated Chemicals. They absorb everything in the long run, and they absorbed us soon after the war ended. I'm a B.A.C. man now."

I only slowly discovered that he was quite an important B.A.C. man. He remained what he called an executive, with the job of travelling about the country, keeping an eye on the associated factories, preventing duplication and waste. "Of course, we've got factories abroad, too, but I don't touch those. That's another job. Then there are the over-all executives who keep an eye on the lot of us."

"Well," I said, "let's leave it at that now. You must tell me about the inter-stellar executives some other time."

He laughed. "Oh, I expect it'll come."

He had taken me out to dinner. We were in the dance-mad phase after the war. We watched the swirling couples on the dance floor, the remnant, the salvage, from the incredible holocaust. "Do you dance, Tom?" I asked.

"No call to," he said briefly. "No girl to dance with. It doesn't interest me much, anyway."

"Do you ever hear from Augusta now?"

"Good lord, no. Why should I?"

"I just wondered."

"It will probably surprise you to know," he said, "that I had quite a crush on her at one time."

He sipped his coffee, thinking of that time, and presently added: "She rather cold-shouldered me. Of course, I know there was that actor, and I heard from Miles that that had busted up. Then when Miles was killed I tried again. I wrote three or four times, but she never answered. It's years since I saw her."

"I don't think she would have answered an archangel," I said. "It wasn't only Miles, you know."

I told him about Mickey, and he said, like an adult commiserating with a child: "Poor girl. The war was too hard altogether on some of them."

We looked at the dancers, flushed, excited, body to body in a way that would have horrified me when young, heads on shoulders, lips down on hair. They had endured too much for too long. They seemed intoxicated, orgiastic, in the mere joy of being alive. I remembered all this when Augusta and Constance had left us on that night of Guy Halliday's dreary meeting, and I fell asleep understanding pretty well the sort of thing Augusta would have to tell me in the morning.

4

The next day, when Nan had gone off with her wrapped food and drawing things, I rang up B.A.C. and asked if I might speak to Mr Elthorne. I found that Mr, Elthorne was not easy to speak to. The switchboard girl put me through to another girl who sounded tremendously Girton and dubious about intrusive women who wouldn't say plainly what they wanted.

"Well," she said at last, "I'm not at all certain that I can contact Mr Elthorne. But I'll see. Hold the line, please."

I said: "Tell him it's his Aunt Maria from Manchester, to speak to him about a personal matter."

"Very well, I'll try. He may be in conference."

I guessed that being in conference was Mr Elthorne's customary get-out; but soon he was on the line.

"Tom," I said, "could you accidentally be taking a drink in the foyer of the Café Royal at two o'clock?"

"I could," he said, "but why?"

"I shall be lunching there with a girl – a girl with hair the colour of Lyle's golden syrup."

"Oh, get on with you, you interfering old hen," he said rudely.

"Call me what you like. But will you be there?"

"Possibly."

"Good."

"I'm making no promise."

"Good. Two o'clock sharp."

Augusta turned up looking delicious. I was proud to be going out with her, both for her beauty and her style. We set off for the Café Royal in a taxi, and as soon as we were away she startled me by asking: "Do I look a bitch?"

"Darling!" I said. "Please don't say things like that."

"I'm asking you," she persisted, flushing. "Do I look a bitch?"

"No. Of course you don't."

"I ask because I was taken for one last night."

I took her hand and said: "I knew something unpleasant had happened. But please don't think of me as a chaperon."

She laughed at that, and I was glad she could laugh. "Surely," she said, "a chaperon is someone one dodges, not confides in."

"Well, if you want to confide, I'm here."

481

She confided during our meal. "I don't think," she said, "you ever met a man called Sacker?"

"No."

"It was when I was working in Yeovil to be near Mickey. But I'll have to go further back than that – to that time when Mickey and I were at Tregannock. We didn't give you much of a hand with the children, did we?"

"I'm afraid not, my dear. You were otherwise engaged."

A little uneasy with herself, she managed to ask: "Did you guess how we were engaged? Was it obvious?"

"I'm afraid I'm not good at noticing things like that. Louisa told me."

She said simply: "We couldn't help it, you know. We weren't cold people, either of us. It went on at Yeovil."

Amid the rattle of crockery, and the running of waiters, and the balancing of trays, and the smoke and chatter, it seemed strange to be listening to this primitive story of two passionate young people who couldn't help it. I accepted it: they couldn't help it, as Louisa, all those years before, had not been able to help it.

"This man Sacker," Augusta said, "was a friend of Mickey. He knew Miles, too. They'd all been up at Oxford together. He was with Mickey on a long visit just before the war started. I didn't see him again until a few weeks ago. Then I met him at a dance. I was there with another man, and Sacker came across and introduced himself."

Sacker had had a hard war. He was a rich young man, and he was making up for it now by having a gay peace. They talked about what she had done in the war, and about what he had done, and a little about Mickey.

"He's one of those handsome, hungry-looking men," she said. "The man I was with said 'I don't like his type.' "

However, the memory of Mickey made him attractive to Augusta. They dined and danced together several times. "It began to be pretty obvious," she said, "that he was trying to make me."

"Make you?"

"Oh, darling, that's just an expression. He was trying to get me to bed. It's almost expected nowadays."

They had had dinner, and Sacker said: "Don't let's dance here. There's a place out towards Maidenhead. Rather fun."

She agreed to go, and in the taxi Sacker put his arm round her. She didn't mind that: dancing nowadays meant arms intimate enough: but when he tried to pull her on to his knees she said: "Please don't."

He seemed to think that a little resistance was part of her technique, and began to kiss her. She pulled herself away from him, sat in her own corner, and said: "If you want to dance, let's go on to this place of yours. But it will be the last time I shall dance with you, there or anywhere else."

He still didn't take her very seriously. "Really! "he said. "Dancing will be fun with that threat hanging over me."

"It's not a threat," she told him. "It's a simple statement. I have no intention of meeting you again – to dine, to dance, or for any other purpose."

"I was hoping that the other purpose would turn up before long."

"You are mistaken."

"Oh, come. Don't talk like a child. Everybody's doing it nowadays. And it would be nothing new for you, would it? It was obvious that you were having it with Mickey, and I expect there've been a good many since then."

She had taken off her gloves, and with her bare hand she gave him a stinging smack to the face. Then she slid back the screen and asked the driver to stop. The driver did so, switched on the light in the car, and came round to the door.

Sacker was no longer the cavalier, the dining-and-dancing man about town. He had seized her wrist and was twisting it, looking furious.

The taxi-man said: "A bit of trouble, miss?"

"He was an oldish man with a big moustache," Augusta said. "We seemed to be miles from anywhere, and he looked comforting."

Sacker said: "This is nothing to do with you. Get back to the wheel and take us where you were told to."

Augusta said: "One of us is going to walk home, Mr Sacker. Is it to be you or me?"

The taxi-man said: "No argument about that, miss. Now, you, get out."

Sacker asked haughtily: "Are you addressing me?"

"Too true I am, mate. Get out or I'll bloody well chuck you out."

Sacker said: "Have a go at it."

483

The man reached in a large hand, took him by the collar and pulled him on to the road. Unfortunately for himself, Sacker then aimed a blow. It went wide, and that large fist hit him like a hammer in the solar plexus.

They left him lying there and drove back towards London. Augusta gave my address as her destination, and when she was landed at the door she fumbled in her bag for the fare. He said: "No charge, miss. The show was worth the money. But don't be such a silly little bitch in future. Got daughters of my own."

"Well, there it is," Augusta said. "Not the sort of story one would tell a chaperon, is it?"

I said: "It's not the sort of story I expected you'd ever be telling anyone, darling. I should be talking nonsense if I pretended to like any part of it. It rather disgusts me."

"Then you *do* think I'm a bitch?"

"I think you're a fool, or at any rate that you're acting like one. You ought to find something better to do with your life – the life that Mickey loved, and that Miles loved, and that I love."

She sat for a time silent, twisting on her finger the engagement ring that Mickey had given her and that she could not bring herself to part with. At last she said: "Thank you. I hate you for saying that, but I'd have hated a bit of soft nonsense even more."

5

It was a stupid and commonplace incident – too stupid, too commonplace, for Augusta. She didn't, as they say in Cornwall, "belong" to be putting herself in the way of such humiliation: this mauling without love, without even friendship. I knew well enough that, because of the repressions of the war, this sort of thing, and worse things than this, were happening everywhere. But not for Augusta, please, I prayed.

I thought of Tom Elthorne, and now I was sorry that I had asked him to be hovering about at two o'clock. It had not been easy for Augusta to tell her cheap little story, and it had not been easy for her to accept my reproof. She was very quiet, and I had been hoping that Tom would meet a sparkling girl. But it was a minute before two, so I called the waiter, paid for our lunch, and walked out with this silent Augusta to the foyer, aware of men's eyes watching her, aware that she was aware of them.

Tom wasn't there.

I could do nothing about it. I had no excuse for lingering, so we walked out into Regent Street, and there she said: "Thanks for the lovely lunch, darling. I think I'll go straight home. I didn't sleep much last night for thinking about things, and I'll catch up." She got into a taxi and went. I made my own way home on foot, dawdling and shop-gazing, and when I got there Nan, who had returned before me, said: "Oh, auntie, you're just too late for a man with a most exciting voice. He said would you ring him up – a Mr Elthorne."

It hadn't occurred to me that Tom's voice was exciting, but now that I came to think about it I remembered that it was one of the nicest things about him. I had contrasted it in my mind with Mr Guy Halliday's earnest sombre tones.

I rang up B.A.C., and was pleased to be able to tell the Girton girl that Mr Elthorne urgently wished to speak to me.

"So sorry I didn't meet you," Tom said. "I'd like to explain, but I have to go into conference any minute."

I asked: "Do you always keep a tame conference on the premises?"

He laughed and said: "Don't be too hard on me. But, look. Could you take dinner with me tonight? Then I'll tell you all about it."

"I'd love to."

"Good. Rules' do you? At eight?"

"Yes. Now go and confer. I can hear the delegates champing for you."

He was waiting for me in Maiden Lane, and we went to the upstairs room. He ordered oysters and hock to be going on with, and said: "D'you remember meeting me and Miles in the Midland in Manchester years ago and joining us at dinner? I'd just had my first little invention, and that was my first dinner. I was terrified of the waiter."

I remembered, and assured him that he had carried it off very well. "But don't temporise," I said. "Come to the point. Why did you let me down?"

He ground red pepper on to his oysters, took a drink of the wine, and said: "I was there all the time. I watched you and Augusta go into the downstairs room and then I took a table in the gallery so that I could keep an eye on you."

"That was rather cold-blooded."

"Yes. You know, it's a long, long time since I've seen Augusta or had a word from her. I wanted to see how it would hit me. Rather like an experiment. You introduce one chemical to another, and sometimes there's a satisfactory reaction. Well, I was able to take a good look at Augusta and there was no reaction whatever. She left me stone-cold. So I vamoosed."

"But, my dear Tom, she's incredibly lovely."

"So am I, but girls don't fall in love with me for that."

"Do girls fall in love with you at all?"

"Oh, rather. My path is strewn with woman-wreckage."

I looked at him, and somehow I could believe it. He was no Romeo who would bleat under a moonlit balcony. You could look at his features, as I now did, and dismiss them one by one as nothing much. But they added up, all the same, to an attractive face; and the thick spectacles could not disguise the ironic humour that played upon it.

"Well," he said, when I had completed my survey, "what's your verdict?"

"Sorry, I didn't know I was staring."

"They're all like that," he said. "In my magnetic presence they can never quite understand what makes their hearts flutter."

"Do you get out much in this odd world?"

"What's odd about it?"

"Nothing, I suppose. I used the wrong word. The inevitable can hardly be called odd. All this dancing and kicking over the traces was bound to come after what we've been through."

"Yes, indeed," he said gravely. "Especially as they think it's now all over and done with and that the world is back where it was before the war started."

"Isn't it?"

He took a drink, then shook his head slowly. "Oh, no. Oh, no, indeed. But let's not go into that now. Let's go back to your question. The answer is that I don't go out much, except with safe old ladies."

He smiled, and I loved his smile. "I hope," I said, "that you'll include me in the number." I wavered, wondering whether to say it; then I said: "I've lost so many people, Tom: my sister and her husband; Miles; a young Oldham nephew; that boy Augusta was engaged to. Do I sound as though I'm cadging for company?"

He said: "You're the dearest of all my old ladies – indeed, the only one. The trouble is, I'm beginning to suspect you of ulterior motives."

"I'm sorry," I said. "I shouldn't have worried you about Augusta. But she'd got into rather an unhappy spot."

"Then let her get out of it," he said, "as I had to do."

I wondered what that meant, and he said after a moment: "I did love her, you know. I never told her so, because for a long time I didn't realise it, and then I hadn't the right. However, as you know, I did keep in touch with her, in a temperate sort of way. I didn't let myself go, though it was hard not to, and I would have done it if she'd as much as lifted a little finger. But it was perfectly clear that she didn't give a fig for me. I accepted that, and now, for me, she doesn't exist – not in that way. So, my dear, don't try blowing on dead embers. There's nothing so dead as a broken friendship or a love that misfired. I've known both. I'm not talking through my hat."

I was reproved, and again apologised.

"I know how you feel about Augusta," he said, "and so there's no need for you to apologise. But I'm not a fire-brigade. As I told you, I turned up to have a look at her, and she was worth coming to see. She's more beautiful even than I remembered. I had you both in view for the best part of an hour, and not for a moment did I feel that I wanted to go down and say how d'you do. Is that clear?"

"It couldn't be clearer."

"Good. That's why I asked you to dine tonight. I didn't want you to have illusions. So now we may as well finish dinner."

We did so, and then he took me on to the second house of a music hall. "My low tastes," he said, "but any day I'd rather see Little Tich than Henry Irving."

He was most attentive, and found a taxi-cab and put me into it.

"By the way," he said, "my secretary is most annoyed with you."

"I'm sorry. I seem to be sorry about everything tonight. What have I done wrong now?"

"For one thing, you ring me up, and she doesn't like people to ring me up. For another, you ask for Mr Elthorne. It should be Dr Elthorne."

"I'll remember."

"Good. And ring me up any time you like."

487

6

That winter passed into the spring of 1921. In January a letter came
from Hugo.

Dear Maria. — I don't often *use* people, but I've been rather
shameless with Henderson, whom you may know — the parson
at St Augustine's in Falmouth. He has a brother who is a
publisher. The firm isn't important, but it has a sound
reputation. I expect you've heard of Henderson and Gooch?
Well, Henderson was down here visiting his brother, and they
took that walk from Flushing round the headland which passes
my door. They looked in, and I gave them tea. Richard was out
botanising, so I invaded the loft and showed them what Nan and
Richard were up to. Henderson — the publisher one — was
interested. He read a bit of Richard's stuff, and was kind enough
to say that it had a lovely freshness. Nan's drawings pleased him,
too. Heaven knows she turns out enough to give a basis for
judgment! What an industrious child she is! I told Henderson
that they had the idea of a writer-illustrator collaboration on a
book, and he said: 'Tell 'em to call it *Native Woodnotes*.' Well, it
didn't go much further than that. I *did* sound him about the
chances of his publishing the book, but all he would say was:
'There's no reason why they shouldn't send it along. A
publisher's ready to look at anything.' When I told Richard about
this he wondered whether you could spare Nan at once? I
suppose you'll be coming down in May in any case, but he
would love to go ahead and says that there's a lot to do in
bringing his side of the book and Nan's together. She would stay
here at the vicarage, of course; but would you find her absence
intolerable?

How is Constance? We hear from her regularly, but in a
rather dry way. All her letters contain the lethal phrase 'Shall be
writing more fully soon,' and end 'yours with love in haste.' If
you are not so deeply up to the neck as she appears to be, give
me some account of her.

I didn't often entertain in that little house, but it happened that I had
asked Tom Elthorne and Augusta to take dinner with me and Nan that

night. Tom and Augusta would have to meet soon, and they might as well get it over. I didn't try surprises and deceptions this time. I told them both who would be there. Tom laughed and said: "I shall be like a Philistine in the National Gallery. I won't even buy a postcard at the door"; and Augusta said: "What an odd creature he was! I didn't know he was in London. What's he doing with himself?" When I told her, she said: "Rather surprising. I never thought he'd come to anything."

I was seeing more of Augusta. As they say nowadays, she had seen the red light. The episode with Mr Sacker, trivial in itself, had shown her the *tendency* of the life she was living; and it chanced that at this moment the Dolly Andrews scandal blew up. The papers were full of it. I hadn't known that Augusta had drifted into the set of young people who surrounded Dolly Andrews, a rich girl little more than a child, whose frantic doings found an almost daily place in the gossip columns. It came to its disastrous end soon after the taxi ride with Mr Sacker, who was himself involved. He turned up at a party in Dolly's flat – Augusta was not present – so late that everybody was more or less drunk. It was quite normal to kiss one's hostess, and Sacker did so, but the kiss was more prolonged than seemed good to Dolly's drunken lover of the moment. He shot at Sacker with a revolver, missed him, and killed Dolly.

That is the bleak outline round which the newspapers blared and embroidered. The shock to Augusta was so severe that I sent Nan off to share the flat with Constance, and nursed Augusta for a week in my own place. She got over it, and now she was back with Constance again, and Nan with me. Anxious though I was about her in many ways, I felt pretty sure that her disorderly life was over. I was almost impious enough to thank God that Dolly Andrews had been killed in time.

My little dinner was quietly successful. Tom need not have feared the wiles of a *femme fatale*. Augusta was altogether charming, but met him on the ground of an old acquaintance and nothing more. He spoke of Miles and she deftly turned him off. I had noticed a quirk in her: she would not speak of the men who were dead to those who had not served. No fault attached to Tom so far as not serving went, but there it was. She rarely would speak even to me of Miles or Mickey. It was the fact that riotous young men like Sacker had suffered a hard war that drew her to them.

So it was a quiet domestic evening, and over our coffee I produced Hugo's letter and gave Nan the good news that there was at any rate a chance of her book being published. She made no bones about wanting to be off at once to join Richard. She didn't even ask if I would like her to stay. She was a frank little creature who knew nothing of deception.

Augusta drove us to Paddington the next morning in her sporty car, and when the Riviera Express had pulled out she turned to me and said: "I'm glad she's gone. She has Richard, and I have only you."

"You have Constance," I reminded her.

"Oh, Constance! Constance and her one-armed hero. I'm rather tired of that warrior. Let's go somewhere."

We did. We drove about the Home Counties and had lunch and dinner in pubs, and we didn't get back till quite late. Such a happy day, re-established with one another. I went up to the flat. Constance was not there. "Another meeting, I suppose," Augusta said. "Well, sit down and let's go on talking."

We talked until eleven o'clock, and then Constance came in, and Guy Halliday with her.

Augusta had not till then met what she called the one-armed hero. Constance introduced them, and Guy said: "Do you mind if I sit down for a moment? I feel very tired."

Augusta asked: "Could you do with a drink? Whisky?"

He said yes, and she produced the drink from a cabinet which I noticed was pretty well stocked. Our day of blowing about in the open car had brought colour to her cheeks, which had been pallid since her breakdown. She hadn't touched her hair, and had a wild wind-blown look. Constance, who was turning over papers at a small desk, looked every inch the faithful secretary: her hair severely parted in the middle of her head, her clothes neat, trim, unobtrusive.

Guy said to her: "Don't bother, Miss Oldham, if you can't lay your hands on it. Bring it along in the morning."

She looked a bit flustered, as though caught out in dereliction.

"It's here," she assured him. "I copied it from *The Statist*. I shan't be a moment."

Guy explained: "We've been over to a meeting in Hackney, and ran into a pretty smart heckler. He had me beat with some of his

490

questions, but Miss Oldham says she has the answers. I thought I'd take them home and study them tonight."

"Why?" Augusta asked.

She was sitting back in a chair, with one attractive leg thrown over the other. Her question seemed to surprise him. "Why? Well, one likes to have a point like that settled, and the sooner the better. Anyway, I'm usually up till one or two in the morning over something or other, and it may as well be this."

"Forgive me," Augusta said, "but you look as though you do too much sitting up. You look very tired. You ought to go home and straight to bed."

Constance, who had found what she was looking for, turned with the papers in her hand, surprise on her face at Augusta's impertinence. I am sure that is the word she was using in her mind. Guy looked surprised, too. But Augusta went on, smiling: "Besides, this is my flat. I'm not sure I approve of politicians turning up as though it were a House of Commons committee room."

It was lightly spoken, but Constance said, outraged: "Really, Augusta!" She looked as shocked as if a guttersnipe had thrown a well-deserved egg at the Prime Minister.

It was a touchy moment, and to my relief a smile came upon Guy's rather stern tired face. "You and my father would get on well together. He's always telling me that I overdo things."

He finished his whisky with an appreciative smack of the lips, and said: "I really think I'll take your advice. I feel pretty well all in tonight. Bring these figures along in the morning, Miss Oldham. Now I'd better find a taxi."

"You needn't bother," Augusta said. "If you don't mind an open car, I can drive you. I haven't put my car away yet. We'll drop my aunt at her place and then I'll take you on."

However, I didn't intend to leave Constance quite so abruptly as that. "It's no distance for me to walk," I said. "I've been sitting in a car all day and a walk won't hurt me."

We watched them go. Constance put the papers into the attaché-case that she would take to the office in the morning, and then carried the solitary symptomatic glass to the kitchenette, washed it and put it where it belonged. It is almost, I was thinking to myself, as though she is trying to wash a terrible scene from her memory. Then there was nothing else for her to do, and she sat down. "I didn't realise," she said, "that he would want a drink. I'd have offered it to him myself."

"You didn't realise either," I said, "that he was very tired, and at that moment probably sick of public meetings, *The Statist*, and the whole boiling. You didn't realise that you were very tired yourself. No one offered *you* a drink. What shall I bring you?"

"Oh, nothing," she said.

I made Ovaltine for herself and me, and when we were sipping it I said what I felt in my bones to be true. "You know, my dear, that man doesn't love you, and never will. Go on working for him if you want to, and be devoted to the work if you want to be, but don't be devoted to him."

She looked at me, stony-eyed, and said: "I don't know what you're talking about."

I took her hand and said: "Another thing. You're building him up into too much of an idol. You're seeing him as something he can never be. You think you're assisting at the making of a great career, but there's no greatness in him. I think he's good and honest, but he's only medium-sized."

"I don't know what you're talking about," she repeated dully.

"Oh, my dear, don't go on saying that nonsense."

"All right," she said. "I admit it. It is nonsense. But what can you *do* about nonsense of that sort? What can you *do*?"

She looked desperate, and I said: "Once you face the facts, you need do nothing. I've lived long enough to know that time will do it for you. Perhaps it doesn't always make a very satisfactory job, but it allows us to go on. And that's something."

She said. "Stay till Augusta comes back. I shall be all right tomorrow, but tonight I couldn't face her alone. I'm afraid we should quarrel."

"Why?"

"Well—"

She couldn't go on for a time, then regained control of herself and said: "Because I'm all on edge. I knew tonight, before coming here, that he wanted nothing from me except my work."

It seems that after the Hackney meeting she had been a bit too officious. In a committee room behind the platform she told him that she knew the answers to the questions that had bothered him, and he seemed annoyed that she should drag up his inefficiency in the presence of other people. He agreed to go to her flat and pick up the papers, but in the taxi on the way there he said: "You know, Miss Oldham, there's no reason at all why you should attend these meetings of mine. You work hard enough all day. Give yourself a rest now and then."

Constance said to me: "I thought he *liked* my being there, but all of a sudden I realised that I was boring him. The way he said it! It was plainly telling me that he'd prefer my *not* being about so much. So I was pretty desolate, and then Augusta . . ."

"Don't blame Augusta," I said. "She's been about – far more than I like – with people whose first impulse with a guest is to say 'Have a drink'. And it happened that your Mr Halliday wanted a drink, and there it was. He certainly looked very tired, and her offer to drive him home was natural enough. She was in an expansive mood after a happy day with me."

"I've been thinking of leaving this flat," Constance said. "I don't like the company she keeps."

"That's not your business, and I don't think she'll keep that company any longer. Please don't quarrel with her. When will she be back?"

"She shouldn't be long. Mr Halliday lives at Hampstead with his father."

Augusta came in soon after, and I said: "Darling, I'm going to be terribly lonely with Nan away. Would you like to come and stay with me for a bit?"

She said: "But what about Constance? *She'll* be lonely if I go."

It was spoken so sincerely, and she so obviously had no sense of having scored in snatching Mr Halliday away, that Constance said, with an easing of the tension in her face: "You go if you'd like to."

"Yes," I said, "put a brush and comb and nightdress into a bag and come now."

She laughed. "Oh, darling! Even to stay with *you* I shall need more than that."

In a quarter of an hour we were on our way, walking through the cold midnight streets.

"How did you like Mr Halliday?" I asked.

"Oh, not such a bore as I feared he might be. I discovered an extraordinary thing about him. He was there when Miles was killed. That's when he lost his arm."

Constance had told me that, but I had forgotten it. Oh dear, I thought. Poor Constance!

7

Nan wrote to announce her arrival at St Tudno. "Richard met me at Truro. He has a motorbike, and we had a wonderful journey to the vicarage, with my suitcase strapped to the pillion-seat, and me sitting on the suitcase, holding Richard round the waist."

Yes, I could understand that that would be very wonderful, and that I need not expect to see much of Nan ever again. Augusta was eating breakfast with me, wearing a dressing-gown of peacock-blue silk. "Darling," she said, "you've got a barometer-face. There's a depression approaching from the west."

"I'm afraid I've lost Nan," I said.

"Well, you've still got me," she said, buttering the toast which was all she ate at breakfast. And after a moment: "What a shameless lot of people you've known! How we all *use* you!"

"Yes," I said, trying to be gay. "I'm the port from which you all go sailing off on your voyages."

"And I alone come sailing back. Isn't it odd. Here's little Nan. Eighteen, isn't she? And obviously she's going to be off your hands in no time. And here am I. Twenty-eight. I've had voyages enough, God knows, and I'm back in port. You're too good to all of us."

It had taken Nan a week to find time to write to me, and during that week there had been a shuffle. Tom Elthorne looked in on me one night and declined my offer to go out to a meal. "Just scrape up something," he said, "and let's eat here. You know what the gossip-writers are now. We've been out together quite a lot lately. They'll be writing darkly about a promising young scientist and an unknown lady from the provinces."

So we ate what there was in the house, and sat by the fire and talked, and I was glad to see that Tom and Augusta were easy with one another. We were three old cronies with shared memories and with the tact to keep away from those that had better be left to die. There was every chance for a bad mistake. Tom might have said: "D'you

494

remember the day, Augusta, when I packed you off to York?" but I soon gave up worrying. They knew where they were, and that was on a footing of merely pleasant reminiscence. I was glad that Tom didn't once refer to Miles. He sat there smoking his pipe and telling us something of his own doings, and I felt as happy as an old hen with two rather nice chicks.

"By the way," Tom said, "the secretary who resents your existence so deeply will trouble you no more. She's just left me to get married. What odd things women do! I don't suppose you could suggest a suitable substitute – preferably one guaranteed man-proof?"

"Well," I said, "I have a niece . . ."

Augusta laughed. "Aunt Maria is like Queen Victoria. If there's a good job going, she can always fish up a nephew or a niece. She suffers from the curse of the Coburgs."

"I don't care if the candidate is a Coburg or a commoner, so long as she can type, write shorthand, keep a few files in order, and swear off men for the rest of an unnatural life. Do I know her, Maria?"

"Well, you know Dr Cumberledge?"

"I do indeed."

"His wife's brother was a parson who married my sister, and this girl is one of their daughters. She's here in London – secretary to a man who for some reason or other wants to be an M.P."

"Will he give her up?"

"Well, I suppose she can leave him if she wants to. Secretaries aren't nationalised yet."

"Is she any good?"

"I should think she's just what you're looking for. Shall I speak to her?"

"Yes, do, and if she's interested, bring her round to see me."

It was a long and difficult talk that I had with Constance. She didn't say it, but she left me in no doubt that she thought me an interfering old busybody. But it seemed clear to me that Guy Halliday did not think of her, and had never thought of her, as more than a useful secretary. She would be hurting herself and embarrassing him if she continued to hang about like a dog determined to be faithful despite kicks. She was white and miserable when I left her, and her last word concerned her loathing for people who tried to run other folk's lives. It was the worst hour I had ever spent with one of my young people, and, heaven knows, between them they had given me experience enough; but the next day Constance rang me up and said in what sounded a normal voice that she would like to go and see Dr Elthorne.

I don't know what poor Constance was expecting, but she was very nervous. I didn't stay for the interview – only long enough for Tom to shake her hand, put her in a chair, and say: "We're old friends, Miss Oldham. I know your Aunt's husband, Dr Cumberledge. He took some glass splinters out of my face when I blew up a retort I was fooling with. So if I ever find fault with you, which I undoubtedly shall do, I give you permission to say 'You weren't always perfect yourself.' "

I crept out of the room, cheered by the smile that dawned on Constance's face, glad that I had been brave enough to be a busybody.

A few days later Constance called to say that Guy Halliday was allowing her to go without notice and that she had found a flat more conveniently near to the B.A.C. offices than the one she had shared with Augusta. "I never did like that place – too luxurious for a parson's penniless daughter."

I went along and saw the small box she had found right up under the tiles of a place in Chancery Lane, and I bought her a few odds and ends to make it look less bleak.

"I hope the B.A.C. people are paying you well," I said. "They're rolling in money."

"I can't complain, and I like Dr Elthorne."

I was glad she had said it. I hadn't dared to ask her.

"You'll find him all right. I've known him since he was a schoolboy and I can give him a good testimonial."

I looked round the rather dim little place, and it wouldn't be much, I thought, even when my few home comforts were in place. And I looked at the rather plain brown girl standing there grave and undemonstrative in this first room of her own. I kissed her and said: "Be happy, child."

"I think I shall be happier than I was," she said simply. "I shall start without illusions."

8

Augusta was living with me now. As soon as she heard that Constance was leaving the Bayswater flat she got rid of the rather long lease she had taken on it. She was more deeply shaken than she cared to admit by her narrow squeak of being involved in a scandal, but happily she was able to laugh at herself. "Darling," she said, "I'm a shockingly bad sower of wild oats. One little fistful has put me off for ever. I want to creep under a protective wing. Could you spare one?"

I was only too glad to do so, especially since the letter had come from Hugo, telling me that I would not need to shelter Nan any more.

My dear Maria. — I don't quite know whether I'm telling you of an accomplished fact or asking your advice. Richard let drop the other day that he and Nan would like to get married in the coming spring. They are the same age — nineteen — and that seems to be absurdly young, but I'm not sure that thinking so is any more than a convention. Of course, I did the heavy father business: took him into my study for 'a serious talk', but really I was surprised how little there was to talk about. I asked him if he thought that he could keep a wife, and he said: 'Oh, yes, well enough. We don't want much,' and went on to explain that they have ideas for lots of books that they want to work on together. 'Of course,' he said, 'they're not the sort of books that bring in a fortune, but I'm sure they'll be saleable, and if we can keep body and soul together by doing what we love doing — well, that's all we ask.' I said they wouldn't find living in London very cheap, and he laughed. 'London! Good lord, we wouldn't live there if the king offered us free quarters in Buckingham Palace. Oh, no. We shall stay here where our stuff is — trees and birds and beasts and fishes. We'll find a cottage with a bit of garden, and what we grow there and the fish we catch will more or less keep us.' Really, my dear, he made me feel quite envious. Fancy living like that, and writing no more sermons, attending no more mothers' meetings, and organising no more outings for the children. However, I must be careful what I'm saying. I forget that I'm writing to the patron of my living!

But, seriously, my dear, when I see how hard those two work, how devoted they are to one another, I can *not* see why I should ask them to wait. But I'm a selfish brute, and I think of my own loneliness if they go. John dead, Constance away — it would leave only Millicent. So if you think the whole idea is not quite crazy, I should ask them to stay here — with my patron's permission! The barn would make an excellent studio, and goodness knows there's room enough in the house.

I suppose we shall see you in May? I wish it could be sooner. For the first time in my life this question of loneliness is becoming a bit obsessive. It's that that makes me selfishly wish to have these two about the place. When Bella married me, she was only a year older than Nan is now.

Ever lovingly

Hugo.

I showed the letter to Augusta, who said: "Of course they should marry," and I wrote to Hugo and said: "Of course they should marry, but tell them to wait till I'm down there in May."

CHAPTER SEVENTEEN

BEFORE GOING back to Little in Sight for that summer of 1921 I bought a nice hat in Bond Street. I kept it a secret till the wedding-day, and when Hugo had married the young people I walked out into the graveyard, wearing it. Augusta and Constance joined me, and Augusta said: "You know, darling, you look like a hanging judge come into court in a floral wreath instead of a wig."

Well, perhaps I did. The years had not given my features much enchantment, but I reproved her all the same. She appealed to Constance. "Doesn't she?"

Constance kissed me, and said: "Take no notice of her. Dr Elthorne, at any rate, would approve of you, whatever you wore. He has a surprisingly high opinion of you."

"What is surprising about that? You're as bad as Augusta."

I took off the hat. In the light of cold reason, it certainly looked over-gay for a hag. It was like one of the floral circles that Mrs Solway sometimes wove for me as we sat on a tombstone. I would gather the flowers for her; and I once stole a few that I thought would make the thing especially chic. They were shining irresistibly in a wreath on a grave, and Thomas May caught me at it. "Put 'em back, Miss Maria," he commanded sternly. "Don't 'ee know that when a poor ole spectre appears at the Mercy Seat 'e do wear the spectre flowers from off 'is grave? For Tom Rowe to come forrard without they there would be like an ole 'orse appearin' in a May Day show without ribbons in 'is tail."

"The Judgment Day," I assured him with inherited ecclesiastical certitude, "is not a May Day show."

"That it bain't," he agreed, "which is why a soul like Tom Rowe can't afford to neglect precautions."

Constance put her arm through mine. "What are you dreaming about, darling?" she asked.

There was Euphemia Emmett's tombstone, and Thomas May's grave, and the memorials to Father and Roger, and the great yew, and the May sun shining on the sea that had given us so much joy and so much sorrow.

"If I don't dream here," I said, "where should I dream? We'd better get up to the house. They'll be drinking the bride's health."

It had been a wedding without fuss. Nan and Richard had worn the clothes they would be going away in, and when we had drunk their health Richard said casually: "Well, we'll be on our way."

They were to spend their honeymoon on the road. They slung on their rucksacks, gave us a wave, and were off with as little ceremony as though we did not exist. They would walk to Truro, spend the night there, and then go wherever they felt like going.

It was all so casual; they were so obviously without problems, without doubts of one another, that the remembered anguish of her own affairs must have bitten into Augusta deeply. She and I were to join Hugo and Constance at dinner in the vicarage that night. I said to her: "You'd better come home and have a sleep now."

I walked along the creek, wearing my absurd hat and holding her arm, and suddenly she said: "I hope my new affair goes better than the others."

2

I had not seen or heard anything of a new affair, and her remark so astonished me that I said nothing. In the days to come I was able to piece it together. That night when she drove Guy Halliday home to Hampstead he said: "You're Miss Oldham's cousin, I take it? She told me she was sharing a flat with a cousin."

Augusta said yes – her mother was the sister of Constance's father.

"Then Miles Cumberledge must have been your brother?"

That was how it began. The fact that the one-armed hero had lost his arm in the same shell-burst that killed Miles was bound to affect a girl whose devotion to her brother had been almost as great as mine to Roger. However, the surprise of the thing was too great for a quick reaction. It merely made her mute, and they had little more to say to one another at that time.

Augusta herself took the next step. The stirring up of Miles' memory caused her to write to Guy Halliday, suggesting a meeting. She said modestly that she expected to be rebuffed, knowing well from Constance that Guy was a busy man. However, he answered, asking her to meet him at a restaurant in the City, near his father's office, where he had a room.

They talked about Miles while they were having a drink, and afterwards while they were eating their soup. "We had a small table," Augusta said, "and we were facing one another. We both ordered roast beef, and when it came he pushed his plate across to me and said: 'Would you mind cutting up my meat? Very small, please?' "

She did so. "I can't explain it," she said, "but it seemed to put us at once on to an extraordinarily intimate footing. It was obviously nothing to him. Someone must have been doing it every day; but now *I* was doing it. It was something a mother did for a child, and it made me feel tender towards him."

When she pushed the plate back she couldn't look at him. She feared that a sense of dependence might embarrass him. However, he was not embarrassed. After all, he had been without an arm for six years. He said: "One feels such a fool having to ask a stranger to do a thing like that. When you get to know people they just do it without being asked. Still, it's a new experience for me to feel like Nelson."

She looked at him enquiringly. "Nelson?"

"I suppose Lady Hamilton did it for him. Romney was always painting her. Well, almost always. This is the first time my meat has been cut by someone fit to be painted by Romney."

She was surprised. He was not the sort of man she had expected to edge in with a compliment. She had formed her opinion of him from Constance's talk, and that had suggested a very one-idea'd man, a dedicated missionary with no frivolity. Now that he had himself mentioned his disability she dared to refer to it. "I suppose," she said, "being without an arm has given you plenty of opportunity to say things like that to helpful women. You may even have said them to Constance."

"Constance? Oh, Miss Oldham. No, I assure you. I'd as soon have said it to the nun who was my nurse in France."

"We'd better get on with our lunch," she said.

She had always been attractive to men, and knew it. She was used to the compliment that was the first probe towards an opening. Never before had a compliment made an occasion go flat. She couldn't understand it, but to me it seemed clear enough. She had gone there to talk about Miles, who was dead, and dead Miles was never far in her thought from dead Mickey. She had tried to bury them both. Her excursion into the post-war nonsense had been nothing but that. It had turned to ashes, and she was ready to face the thought of Miles and Mickey again, but now with a calmer, almost accepting, mind, that kept all of its love and none of its frenzy. When she was asked, however tentatively, to forget them and to think a little of herself, it seemed a betrayal of her new and better mood.

"I felt ghastly," she said. "I didn't know what had come over me."

She tried to talk again of Miles, and even of Mickey, but she didn't feel that this was a man with whom she wished to talk of either. She watched him fumbling with his overcoat and didn't help him. She left that to a waiter, and when he was gone she wandered into one of Wren's churches and sat there, feeling desolate and abandoned. Presently Guy Halliday came in and stood looking down at her. She was sitting at the end of a pew, and instinctively she moved on a little to make room for him. Neither spoke for a long time. They sat there in a silence broken only by an occasional shuffle of feet, with the wintry light lying dead and flat on what could have been the glory of the windows. Guy said very quietly: "Miss Cumberledge, I feel that I made you very unhappy. Honestly, I don't know why. I watched you when you left me, and saw you come in here. So I followed, because I should be unhappy, too, if I felt I had hurt you."

"You know, darling," she said to me, "the place had something to do with it. I'd been so used to stuffy flats reeking of alcohol and cigarette smoke and to night clubs blaring with dance tunes. And here was this place. Well, it was another world, where people didn't shout and rush about, but folded their hands and listened."

Guy said: "May I go on speaking to you?"

She nodded, but it was a long time before he could find his words. Then he said: "I think this is a good place to talk about love. May I?"

"If you want to."

"When you drove me home the other night you told me that Miles was your brother. I lay awake thinking about him. I loved that boy, you know. I was old enough to be his father, and he confided in me as he would have done in a father. I expect you know that he hated being a soldier. He made no bones about it to me. He said once: 'I hope to God I'm killed before I have to kill someone else.' Well, he was. He would have had to be killed anyway. You could feel the fate on him. So I was glad it came like that."

A few wanderers in the church stopped at the pew end, gazing up at the pearly windows. When they had moved on, Guy said: "He sometimes talked to me about you, and so in a way I've known you for a long time. There was a moment when I was very close to you. Miles told me of you and Michael Miskin and how happy he was about that. He said 'Mickey's a grand chap and they'll have a grand life – if they're lucky!' Well, you weren't lucky, were you? I read Michael's name in the casualty lists, and that day I couldn't get you out of my head – or for days afterwards. You'll think it crazy, but I tried to send out thoughts that would reach you and comfort you for Miles' sake."

She said quietly: "Thank you, but they never reached me."

"How could they? They'd only do that in a fairy-tale. I don't want to pretend that you meant anything to me at all, except insofar as you were a reflection of Miles."

"And what did Miles mean to you?"

"It's difficult to say. He made the beginning of the war tolerable for me. Then, as a person, he faded, but he remained as a symbol of all the beautiful lives that were being wasted."

"And I'm the shadow of a symbol."

They were silent then until at last she said: "Thank you for what you've told me. But please don't ever talk to me again about Miles or Mickey."

"Very well. But let's meet sometimes, shall we?"

She gave him no answer, and they walked out of the church together. Each of them seems to have felt a reluctance to part. They stood there in the grey winter city street and he said: "I'm sorry I dragged in Lady Hamilton. Romney would have dropped her like a shot if he'd once set eyes on you."

With that he smiled mischievously. "It was quite enchanting," Augusta said. "It was a new man. I could understand how Miles took to him."

On this lighter, happier note they parted, with nothing arranged about meeting again.

By that May day when Richard married Nan they had met often. I think this rather sober-sided man, whose smile was rare but delightful, this inward-looking man with a purpose and a hard will to pursue it, was inevitably the sort of man to whom she would turn in revulsion from the company she had discarded. He was twenty-one years older that she, and was not, I should imagine, an impetuous lover. Indeed, at this time when she first mentioned the matter to me there had been, so far as I knew, no talk of love between them. But she spoke of "this new affair of mine", and I don't think she would have done that if it hadn't reached a stage of serious intention. But the wedding of those two young, unspoiled, inexperienced creatures had touched her, filled her with memories of her romantic and ill-considered absorption into Haydon Mellerby's life and her passionate all-giving love for Michael Miskin. Watching those two stride off with rucksacks on their backs like children going for a holiday, Augusta must have felt as old as the hills, as experienced as Cleopatra, and filled with a sense of loss as she considered the staid companionable man to whom she was half-committed. She took my advice and went to bed, and I carried a deck-chair out to my patch of lawn and sat in the spring sunshine, thinking how little time ago it seemed since she and Miles, lost children, had here wandered into my life, and how I had done what I could to reassure them and make them feel that all was not finished. Well, there was nothing I could do for her now. What was left, she had to do for herself.

3

Soon after I had gone back to London in the autumn of that year the first book of Nan and Richard was published. I was pleased with it, and pleased with the inscription in the copy Nan sent me: "For my dear saviour." I think Mr Mompsen, too, would have been pleased with it had he lived. The drawings had great charm if little strength; and, as for Richard's part in it, the simple clarity of his writing, his obvious love of the things he so minutely observed, touched just the note needed in a book of that sort. It did well enough, and I may as well say here, and have done with it, that they went on to do better — well enough to give them that modest sufficiency that was all they asked for. Richard had no invention, but Nan had; and soon after this she began to write simple tales for children, doing her own pictures for them, and this helped to put a bit of jam on their bread and butter. They were unambitious, devoted to one another, and wonderfully happy. I had given them my quay punt for a wedding present, and was amused to see as the years went by how often it was the basis of Nan's children's books; though they were grimmer when, from time to time, she remembered her London childhood and built tales around it.

I went back to town that year rather earlier than usual because Augusta, who had returned soon after the wedding, wrote to say that she and Guy Halliday were about to be married. She had been in a quiet mood when she left me to visit her father in Manchester before going on to London. I guessed that, for the first time since she had fled to York so long ago, she intended to take counsel with him, and that at any rate was something to be glad about. Her only reference to Guy as we parted was: "Think of me, won't you, darling? I've got an idea that this is it."

She looked sad and lovely, and there were tears in my eyes as I said: "If you marry that man, he'd better watch his step. He'll have me to deal with."

She called up a smile and patted my cheek as she leaned out of the carriage window. "Now don't be more of a battle-axe than you can help," she said, and then the train pulled out.

When I went up in the autumn she met me at Paddington. I prided myself on being a connoisseur of Augusta's moods, and a new mood was clear from her face and voice as she embraced me, enveloping me in a faint delicious perfume. It was a mood of serenity, altogether different from the effervescent, almost feverish, mood that Haydon Mellerby had induced and the rapturous exaltation of her fulfilment with Michael Miskin. I said to myself: "She has found someone who makes her feel safe, and God knows that's what she has needed."

She looked at me and laughed. "D'you know what you're trying to do, darling? Trying to 'read me like a book'. Aren't you?"

I said: "I'm so happy."

"Good," she said. "So am I."

The next day I went with them to a registrar's office and saw them married. The only other person there was Guy's father, a crusty white-haired old gentleman who stood on the pavement with me and watched them drive away, Augusta at the wheel. They were going to tour in Scotland. "Not my idea of a wedding," the old man said. "But there it is. It'll have to do. Like to come and have lunch with me?"

I excused myself, and he said: "Good. I've got plenty to do in the office."

He held up his rolled umbrella, stopped a taxi, and drove away. "No frills," I thought. "The Halliday touch."

4

On a Saturday morning about a week later this old gentleman rang me up and said: "I promised to give that boy of mine a house for a wedding present. I've been told of something that sounds as if it might do. Like to come and have a look at it?"

I said that I'd be delighted, and he called for me the next morning in a chauffeur-driven Daimler. He was very stout, very cross, and as the chauffeur tucked an enormous bear-skin rug around us he grumbled: "No need to do that. I'm capable of handling a rug. I've told you before not to treat me like a child."

The chauffeur gave the rug an extra tuck, gave me a confidential wink, as if to tell me to take no notice of tantrums, and off we went, tending north-west. "He'll be bringing my titty-bottle next," the old man said.

It was a charming day, a hang-over of summer, but Mr John Halliday wasn't having that. "It ought to be winter," he said. "Weather like this is all humbug. You look out. You'll be up to your knees in snow before you know where you are."

It was interesting to be here with John Halliday in person. I had thought of him as nothing but a notice-board: that immense white notice-board, with nothing on it but the name John Halliday in red, which announced to the public that another vast skeleton of steel would arise to be clad in stone or concrete and to shine with a thousand windows and to house an army corps of office workers. I learned later that he had begun his life as a hod-man, carrying the bricks up a ladder to platforms whereon the brick-layers were raising their buildings in the slow laborious fashion of that time.

"Tell me something about this girl Guy's married," ' he commanded. "You're a relative of hers, aren't you?"

"Well, I've been more or less *in loco parentis* for a good many years."

"Look – I went to a board school, so you can leave out the Latin, if that's what it is. I've never found anything yet that I couldn't say in English."

I thought of Charles Lester's father, met but once, and that long ago. "I'll bet Guy was taught Latin," I said.

"Of course he was. Guy's another matter. He learned it and I hope by now he's forgotten it. But we're not talking about Guy. I'm asking about this girl."

His white moustache bristled at me, but I refused to be intimidated. "Oh, fair do's," I said. "If you want me to talk about Augusta, we must have a proper swap."

So he talked about Guy: Eton and Christ Church: and I soon gathered that Guy could do no wrong. I became emboldened and asked why Guy had taken up Labour politics. "Somehow, I shouldn't have thought you'd approve of that."

"No more I don't," he admitted. "But what's approving got to do with it? The world's full of things we don't approve of, isn't it? But we've got to put up with 'em all the same. What Guy wants is going to come one of these days. I hope I'm dead before it does, that's all. I believe in bosses, and there'll always be bosses, and I think I make a better boss than some chap sitting on his backside in Whitehall. That's all the difference there'll be in the long run; but if that's how Guy wants it, let him have it."

He had gone rather red in the face. We were visible in the chauffeur's mirror, and he slowed the car, looked over his shoulder, and said: "Your heart, sir."

"Damn my heart."

"Very well, sir. You told me to remind you."

"Damn it, drive on and mind your own business."

"Now, come on," he said, "and tell me about this girl."

I gave him an expurgated edition of Augusta's biography, omitting Haydon Mellerby and making the association with Mickey respectable. I diplomatically praised Guy and spoke with pleasure of his value to Augusta in a shattered moment of her life.

"Well, she'll keep him out of politics. That's one good thing," he said.

"I doubt it, Mr Halliday. I haven't seen much of Guy, but I should say politics is the one thing he wants."

"At all events, it gives him something *besides* politics, and that's all to the good. I don't know what's come over him. He wasn't like this when the war started."

"The odd thing to me," I said, "is that so many men *are* the same as when the war started."

"It's all this stuff in Russia," he said hotly.

"Well, of course, there is that, too. It wasn't a very nice country, was it?"

He sighed unhappily, suddenly looking much smaller. "You know, Miss Legassick, I don't know where I am in this world. I really don't. And that's a fact. Well, it'll all have to work itself out without me."

"Yes, one way or another, it will," I assured him.

Near Maidenhead we left the main road, made a tricky turn or two, and came to a white gate. A path led through a bit of paddock to the front door of a small Georgian house. The usual thing: a porch on pillars, a nice fan-light, the whole flat-fronted and, I noted with satisfaction, having still the small panes in the windows. The chauffeur helped Mr Halliday to alight, and then Mr Halliday helped me, and, to my surprise, someone opened the door from inside. I had thought the place unoccupied.

"Lunch ready?" Mr Halliday asked the woman who stood there.

"Yes, sir."

"Good. Come on, then," he said to me. "Let's eat first and look afterwards. Tinker," he said to the chauffeur, "you'll find something in the kitchen."

He led me into the dining room where a fire was burning in a basket grate enclosed by an Adam fireplace. Every piece of furniture, I saw, was contemporary with the house. Whoever had owned this place had loved it. The walls were empty – not a picture. Mr Halliday, standing straddled before the fire, said: "Nearly all the pictures were portraits. The Colbys had a mania for having their mugs reproduced. They built the house, and small though the place is as these things go, they had Sheraton to see to making the furniture on the spot. Then they set about getting themselves painted, and they've been at it ever since. So far as I can make out, it's all they've ever done. Old Miss Colby, who died six months ago, was painted by a chap called John. She was the last of 'em except for a nephew who doesn't want the place. He's farming in Rhodesia. All the pictures have been packed off to him, and I bought the rest as it stands, lock, stock and barrel. It's not a difficult place to keep up, and there's only a few acres of land, mostly grass. Think it'll do?"

I looked through the window across the misty landscape to the Lombardy poplars standing up out of a huddle of willows. "That's the Thames," Mr Halliday said. "It's the boundary on that side. They could have a punt." Beneath his phlegm, he was clearly anxious that I should be pleased, that I should say he had done Guy and Augusta proud. I said it. "You've done them proud, Mr Halliday. They should be very grateful to you. The taste of the whole thing is perfect."

"Taste?" he said. "Well, that's what I want your opinion on. I don't know much about taste. I'm a builder. That's my side of the thing, and I know this house is *built*." He kicked the skirting-board heartily, like Dr Johnson refuting Berkeley. "You won't kick this place down in a hurry," he assured me.

The woman who had opened the door was, I gathered, his own cook, whom he had sent here overnight. She brought in our meal, and we ate it off Crown Derby china. We drank Pommard from lovely glass, and Mr Halliday became mellow and confidential. We moved over to the fireplace for our coffee, and he lit a cigar. "One of old Miss Colby's," he said. "There's boxes and boxes of 'em. She smoked like a Bradford mill chimney, I'm told."

Presently he said: "Well, go and toddle round. I've seen it all more than once, and the fewer stairs I climb the better."

It was all right. Wherever I went I found the loving care that had impressed me in the dining room. It was no bigger than the St Tudno vicarage, but it had a better shape, better fittings, more delicacy. It was a perfect little house. I said so when I came down.

"Did you go right up?" he asked. "Did you find that big attic?"

I said that I had.

"A grand playroom," he said. "The sooner they get a few children in it the better I'll be pleased. I'm getting on, and so is Guy. It's about time I had some grandchildren. I've managed to help myself to most things, but that's something I must have a bit of help with."

He went on about it: a pony in the paddock, a boat on the river. He could come down at weekends and see how they were all getting on. He was thinking of his childhood, building a compensating dream. "I never had a pony, or a boat, or tuppence to rub together, come to that."

We walked as far as the river, watched it sliding by, green and cressy. "Now what are them chaps with the red blobs?" he asked.

"Moorhens."

"And them with the white blobs?"

"Coots."

"I've got to learn these things," he said. "You've got to learn all sorts of things if you're to keep up with the youngsters."

Against a sky that was now become smoky with mist, a muffled sombre purple, the tall pencils of the poplars stood solemnly up and the river smell had density.

"I've missed a lot in my time," he said. "I've got to catch up and keep up."

He held out his hand and, rather surprised, I gave him mine. He said: "Well, thank you for that girl."

A strange, awkward compliment, but I wondered whether Augusta would ever have a finer one.

5

Mr Halliday never saw his grandchildren swimming in the river, or poling a punt, or riding a pony in the paddock, for he didn't live much longer. Guy entered the House of Commons in 1922, winning a by-election, and the next year Ramsay MacDonald formed the first Labour ministry. It lasted for only nine months. The old man was pleased and annoyed. He had no use for the Labour Party, but Guy was a member of it, and therefore, he concluded, there must be more to it than his age and make-up permitted him to understand. Either he or Guy must be mistaken, and he was humble enough to think that perhaps he was. Though he damned the government when it was formed, he damned still harder when Baldwin came back as Prime Minister. As he had once said to me, he didn't know where he was. He smelt change in the air, realised his own inability to change, and, perhaps for the first time in his hard-hitting, go-getting life, suffered the agonies of indecision. He had taken to coming down for weekends to the small white house near Maidenhead, and one weekend when Guy was away in his constituency, I was there, too. It was in June of 1924, and the paddock in front of the house was alight with dog-daisies and buttercups and the tall red spires of sorrel, and here and there, if you knew where to look, you could find clumps of snaky-spotted fritillaries. Guy had wanted to have the paddock turned into a formal garden, but Augusta had fought him on it, and won. The old man had backed her. This was no place for paths and flower-beds and horticultural fiddle-de-dee. It was where his grandchildren were to run. With them in mind, he had been playing about, too, at the riverside. He had had a landing-stage built, and behind it was a strip of lawn, and, looking out on lawn and river, a little open-fronted building where you could sit with the afternoon sun pouring in to bless you. It was a charming cunningly-chosen spot, with the old willows hunching their green shoulders at the edge of the lawn on either side.

This was where Mr Halliday liked to take his tea when the weather was fine, and during that visit I walked down there with him, carrying the tea-basket. Augusta asked to be excused as she had letters to write. It was the time of year when, lovely as this was, I thought St Tudno lovelier, and I should have been there; but Augusta had sent me the news that she was expecting a child. I at once came anxiously down, because a year ago she had had a miscarriage. And now she had had another. What the old man did not know was that the doctor had warned her against trying again.

So there he sat in his biscuit-coloured tussore suit and panama hat, panting a little from the short walk and feeling the heat. The punt that he had ordered a year ago when the child was expected was tied up to the landing-stage. I gave him his tea, and he asked, as though I were responsible: "What's the matter with Augusta? She's a fine healthy-looking girl."

She was. Despite her misfortunes, she had never looked better. She was at the ripe peak of her beauty, tall but full-bodied, calm and majestic. A week ago she had sat here with me, and suddenly, out of a quiet moment, she had said: "I can't bear the thought of having children. They die. Miles and Mickey . . ."

I looked at her, startled, and she was trembling. "If there was another war," she said. "Imagine it . . ."

I couldn't. I still believed in the war to end war. The situation was beyond me, and I could not speak. I could only take her shaking hand and hold it tight.

"And if they don't die," she said, "their mothers may. Look at me. I've been more or less tangled up ever since my mother died. One nonsense after another. I can't bear the thought of dying and leaving children to fight it out."

I tried to lighten the moment.

"My dear," I said, "I never saw anyone who looked less like dying. You'll live to be an imperious old lady with an ebony cane, the terror of your grandchildren. And even if a bus knocked you over, the children would still have Guy."

"Fathers marry again," she said; and the whole thing rushed back at me, and I was in the train for Didsbury, telling her that in a few moments she would be meeting a new "mother".

"You can't understand," she said, "– how could you? – the terror that shakes me when I'm carrying a baby. It kills them before they're born."

"It's hard on Guy."

"It's hard on everybody. On me, not least."

She spread out on the lawn the gay cushions that were in the little tea-house, got down on them, and fell asleep. I sat there watching her for an hour, and then she woke and said: "I feel better. I tell you everything, don't I, darling? I worry you with everything. But that's enough of that. I'm glad I got it off my mind. You must forgive me."

And so what could I say to that disappointed old man? Only some nonsense. "Oh, don't take this too much to heart, Mr Halliday. These things happen, but there's plenty of time."

"Not for me, there isn't," he said truthfully. He died suddenly before the summer was out.

6

And then, despite the doctor's warning – "Just to show him, and just to teach myself not to be a fool," Augusta said – there she was, and it was again June, three years later, and she sat on the lawn behind the landing-stage, suckling her son. He was named Philip, after the grandfather who had never seen him, and he was three months old. She had had a bad time, but she was over it, and she was radiant. When she had fed the child she put him into a large washing-basket in which we carried him about, a pink blanket under him, a pale blue blanket over him. "Now he'll sleep," she said. "I never knew such a boy for sleep."

She stood for a moment looking down at him with a pride which suggested that Philip's ability to sleep was quite out of the ordinary, as, of course, was everything else about him. "Look at the way he sucks!" she would say. "Did you ever see anything like it?" And if he howled: "He's like a young bull of Bashan. Did you ever know a child with such lungs?"

Having to be contented for the moment with observing this negative excellence of his doing superbly nothing whatever, she sat beside me and said: "Look at his finger-nails. Aren't they perfect?"

"They're not bad as finger-nails go," I conceded. "Where are Nan and Richard?"

"They went off in a punt after lunch. Drawing coots and watercress and things, I expect."

She didn't care where they were or what they were doing, so long as they were about. She had wanted everybody to be about in her moment of triumph. She was like a playwright who had pulled it off at last and wanted all the family there on the first night. Frank Cumberledge, a widower now for the second time, had come down from Manchester, and I had brought the rather reluctant Nan and Richard with me from St Tudno. Nan did a lovely water-colour drawing of Augusta nursing Philip, and that seemed to exhaust her interest. They were something to draw; and now she was off in the punt with Richard to find something else. These two were still incredibly dependent on one another, sharing happily their small celebrity. They could do without anything and anybody so long as they had their work and one another. They had gone into London once, to take lunch with Richard's sister Constance, but I gathered they didn't establish a close touch. However, it was a duty, and it was done, and now they could get on with what interested them. At the moment it was feathers. They brought back new ones every time they went on the river or into the fields. Nan had taken to wood-carving, and from a block she could print a feather that looked so light you could almost blow it off the page.

Frank was gone back now to Manchester. I felt rather ashamed of the way we had drifted apart. After all, in my moment of deep stress, he had given me a home and something to bind my life around. But

513

he had become almost a stranger, and an old sad one. His second wife had died that spring, and he looked defeated. We took a long walk together, and he said: "Well, Maria, how cleverly you've avoided involving yourself with anyone. You're the born, spectator, aren't you? – always on the side-lines watching the poor devils tumbling in the mud, even though they score an occasional goal."

"Oh, I wouldn't say that," I chaffed him. "I know that I've kept out of the battle, but I've been quite a useful Red Cross van."

"Well," he admitted, "you've never been far from Augusta when she's needed you." He added, almost with a little malice: "It looks as though she won't need you much longer. She seems settled at last."

It rather nettled me, and it rather alarmed me. "Oh, you wait," I said. "You'll see me taking on her grandchildren."

It wasn't a very heartening walk under the lazy white clouds of that June day; but if I gave him any reason to think me a little offended or aloof I had reason to regret it. For when, the day after this, I saw him off, he said, looking through the window of his car: "Well, goodbye, Maria."

"Au revoir, I hope."

He put the engine into gear, looked at me for a moment, and said: "No. Goodbye. I'm a doctor. I know what I'm talking about. But keep it to yourself."

Giving me no time to answer, he waved a thin hand and was off.

Well, then, sitting there in the warm sunshine, with Philip sleeping in the clothes-basket, and Augusta's head nid-nodding by my side, and Nan and Richard away round the silver bend of the water, I thought of all these lives I was involved in – for I felt involved, whatever Frank might say – and of the lives whose knots had been cut – Charles Lester and Roger, Gerald and Meg, Miles and Mickey, and James and Louisa – and I floated bemused on this sea of living and dying till the bee-humming day drugged me to insensibility, and I didn't stir till Augusta nudged me, saying: "He's waking up. Look at the way he's rubbing his fists into his eyes! Aren't they beautiful?" Then I staggered back to consciousness, and said: "Fists? Fists? What on earth is it this time? D'you think he's going to be a prizefighter?"

7

The one person who hadn't obeyed the royal command to come and glorify Philip was Augusta's cousin Constance. She was at St Tudno, spending the summer holiday with her father. The day after Frank had left us, I went too, taking Nan and Richard with me. Nan was shrewdly aware of the moment. I treated them to a journey in a first-class compartment, which we had to ourselves, and as we passed over the bridge at Maidenhead, she waved her hand roughly in the direction of the Hallidays' house and said: "Goodbye. We've paid homage at court and may now return to our provinces."

"Where we shall find Constance," Richard said.

"Oh, well, we've got plenty to do," Nan assured him. "It'll keep us out of her way. Have you seen Constance lately, Aunt Maria?"

"No. I've been at St Tudno all the summer, except for this visit to Augusta. I'm looking forward to seeing her when we get back."

"When we called on her in London the other day," Richard said, "she was packing for the journey. We thought her a bit of a drip. We didn't see why she shouldn't nip out to see Augusta's kid, but she was quite cross when we mentioned it. She gave us tea in that foul little flat of hers. God – what a place to live in!"

"One lives where one's work is," I told him. "You should think yourself lucky that you can live and work where everything is to your taste."

"I should have thought," he said, "that she could work in Falmouth. There must be jobs of a sort there. Then she could live at home. Father'd be glad to have her. Now he has no one but Millicent, and she's not a joy."

They disturbed me. For the first time since their marriage, their complete dependence on one another, their willingness to see the rest of us as outsiders unprivileged to share their happiness, struck me as dangerous. Life wasn't like that. I had seen too much founder. There was no harm in a life-line or two.

"I liked Augusta's husband," Richard said. "But we didn't see much of him, did we?"

"Maidenhead's rather a long way out," I told him, "for a man whose work is in the House of Commons. Even if he managed to catch the Maidenhead train, there'd be two miles to walk. It might be possible if he drove a car, but that can't be done with one arm. He uses a small flat in town most nights, and of course he's at home for weekends and when the House is up."

"I'd find it a bit fragmentary," Nan said.

I rather lost my temper. "Don't carp, child," I told her. "People have to put up with life as it is. Be thankful that you find yours satisfactory, and leave the rest of them to make do as they can. I daresay they find more than you are aware of."

She could always win me with a contrite look, and she gave me one now and followed it with a smile. I tried to look sternly at her. Then I smiled, too. "Here's the man coming to announce the first lunch," she said. "Let's go along. Isn't it lovely, Richard, to be travelling with a wealthy benefactor?"

"Yes," Richard agreed, as we shoved along the swaying corridor. "We usually have to make do with a sandwich in a bag and a bottle of pop."

8

I didn't see Constance on the night of our arrival. I took a taxi from Truro and was dropped at Little in Sight, glad to be back, for long journeys were beginning to tire me. The next morning I had got up and eaten my breakfast and had gone out on to the road when the postwoman came along. "Only one for you, Miss Legassick," she said, "but if you're on your way to the vicarage, would you save me a journey?"

I took the letters and went back into the cottage to read mine, and was struck by the handwriting on one of the others. "Miss Constance Oldham." I knew that hand. It was Guy's.

My own letter was from Tom Elthorne. "My dear Maria." He had taken to using the Christian name, and I liked it.

> I intended to talk to you about Constance before you returned to your rustic cot, which I must visit some day – will you have me? – but, being a coward, I kept on dodging it, for who cares to face the sibyl? So I write, to greet you on your arrival, and also to talk about this affair of Constance (Miss Oldham to me in the office). Now and then work piles up and I have to ask her to stay late. Until a month or two ago she didn't mind this, but then she began to make difficulties, and at last it came to her

refusing to stay. Well, that's reasonable, and I can always find someone else, but I prefer Constance who is used to my works and ways and excellent at her job. I said: 'I suppose you've found a boy-friend, and I shall soon have to look out for someone else?' She reacted with a blush and informed Dr Elthorne (though in well-chosen words) that he could mind his own damned business.

We have a rule here in the office that telephones must not be used for private conversations, which is why my former secretary (now married to a lecturer of the London School of Economics, God help her) thought you a pestilential old butter-in. Well, one day when Constance was out the girl at the switchboard rang through to say that a gentleman wanted to speak to Miss Oldham and, on being told she was not there, asked if he might speak to me. It was Guy Halliday, and he asked me to tell Constance that he would be late at the House and would not be able to call at her flat. If she had anything else on hand, she was not to hang about for him. I passed on this message, and she seemed a bit embarrassed, but not unduly disturbed. 'I'll be glad to have an evening to myself,' she said.

Now they were both so almost childishly open about it that there's no reason to fear anything fishy. Most nights, he doesn't go to Maidenhead, and obviously she's doing secretarial work for him in the old way. How she came across him after their break I don't know, and how he could be such a fool as to take her on again I don't know either. But they *did* have a long association in France and elsewhere, and he has an innocence that I admire and distrust. Explosive possibilities belong to my trade, and I don't want a blow-up here. I've known Augusta since we were children, and I don't think she'd react quietly to this situation. When she married I gave her a silver *entrée* dish, and I feel that a marriage thus personally blessed must not be allowed to drift into even the chance of danger. Handle this, my dear Maria, with the exquisite tact with which you tried to plant Augusta on me. Or perhaps even with a little more.

With love,

Tom.

I walked slowly along the creek towards the vicarage, pausing to cup my hands and drink ritually of Gerald's hippocrene.

"Thank you for yesterday's luxurious travel, Auntie. Now, you see, we're back to our own bare trotters."

I turned, and there were Nan and Richard, not exactly with bare trotters, for they wore sandals, but with bare legs. Richard wore nothing but khaki shorts, Nan a lime-green djibbah. "Where are you off to?" I asked.

"Oh, anywhere," Nan said. "Maybe to Tregannock. Have you been there lately?"

"No. I can't bear to."

"It's fascinating," she said. "All sorts of strange things growing up out of the ruins. Yes. Let's go there, Richard. I can go on drawing there day after day."

They waved in their happy way and were off, leaving on my mind, as always, their sense of being for ever *en passant*.

I watched them for a moment with an oddly-mixed feeling of envy and compassion, and turned to see Constance coming towards me. She gave me a kiss and said: "I was just coming along to your place. How are you, did you have a good night?"

All dutiful. The right kiss, the right questions. We walked back together to Little in Sight and sat on the lawn.

"Augusta sends her love," I said.

"Thank you."

She was twenty-nine. She looked thin and had a London pallor and a lassitude I did not like. "Let's go sailing today," I said. "Not that there's much wind, but we could dodder about. It'll do you good. You've had too much Chancery Lane."

"I've not had too much anything," she said. "Always too little."

She alarmed me. "Darling," I began, but she put a hand on mine and stopped me. "Don't commiserate," she said. "I couldn't bear it. And don't explain that life is life, full of wonder, if we only know how to see it lavishly scattered about us. It hasn't been like that for me. I've had nothing. I wanted to go to Oxford. The war stopped that, and all the dreams I had of what could follow it. Perhaps poppycock, anyway, but I never had a chance to find out. And then I met Guy, and I thanked God I'd missed Oxford. And then Guy met Augusta and . . . Oh, I've had nothing, I tell you – nothing at all."

We sat on deck-chairs, watching the tide flow in over the mud-flats, and I delayed giving her the letter that was in my handbag. I had a premonition that it was not a happy letter, and I hoped that sitting here in this native place, with the stress of London far away, and with so perfect a morning embracing us, would soothe her, fortify her to receive, perhaps, a blow. Her fingers were fiddling with everything: with her handkerchief, with the stuff of her dress, with her bobbed hair.

"Nan and Richard are just gone along," I said. "They're going to spend the day mooching and drawing at Tregannock."

"I'm glad they condescended to speak to you," she said bitterly. "They don't seem aware of my existence. They rather nauseate me — all wrapped up in one another — almost physically."

I was deeply distressed. Constance had always been a difficult girl, though full, it had seemed to me, of fine possibilities. Without Louisa's beauty, she had all Louisa's ambition, but she couldn't meet a reverse, as Louisa had done again and again, and come out the stronger for it. As she had reminded me, she had missed Oxford and she had missed Guy, and seeing her sitting there with every nerve exposed I wondered whether the best thing now would not be for her to stay where she was and make what she could of life as she found it.

I took the letter out of my bag and gave it to her, fearfully. "Here are some letters for your father, and one for you. The postgirl left them, and I was on the way to hand them over when I met you."

She looked at her letter, and her face flamed. "The postgirl has no right," she said, "to give letters to anyone save the persons to whom they are addressed."

I couldn't help saying: "Oh, come child. Don't make a bitterness of every small thing. We're rather easy-going in St Tudno. More than once I've found my letters dropped in the road."

"It's not a small thing," she said, very angry. "A letter is a most private matter — almost sacred."

"Oh, God, Constance," I groaned. "Whatever has come over you?"

She got up, trembling, and tore the unopened letter to shreds.

"I don't need to read that," she said. "I can guess what's in it. I suppose you know whose writing it is?"

"Yes."

She stood gazing at the glint of sun on the water, her face lit with a shine of angry despair. I reached for her hand and pulled her back into her chair. "Nothing," I said, "is the worse for telling. It may even make it better. Here I am." I continued to hold her hand.

"What's this – a confessional?"

"It's anything you like to call it. But don't let things fester, child."

"You'll be ashamed of me," she said, calmer.

I didn't answer that, and after a moment she said: "If he hadn't been Augusta's husband I shouldn't feel so bad about it. Not that I feel all that tender towards Augusta. She took him away."

"While we're at it," I said, "let's get it as straight and honest as we can. There were the two of you. Guy chose Augusta. Isn't that right?"

"I suppose so."

"You *know* so – don't you?"

"Yes. But she can't have loved him as I did."

"I can't say whether that is so or not. But, alas, it has nothing to do with the question. Guy had made his choice. I can imagine many a man walking out of church watched by half a dozen girls who love him more than the bride on his arm. But that's the girl he wanted to marry, all the same."

She didn't see Guy for two years after he was married. Then she went to one of his public meetings. When it was over, she lingered till he couldn't help seeing her and speaking to her. He said: "Hallo, Miss Oldham! Quite like old times. How was I tonight?"

After marrying Augusta, Guy had used his father's house in Hampstead when detained in town. Now the old man was dead and he had rooms in Lincoln's Inn. This was no distance from Chancery Lane, where Constance's flat was, and as the meeting had been in a hall in Farringdon Street, it was natural that they should walk the short distance to their homes together. They strolled along Fleet Street, and Constance, I can well imagine, was in a seventh heaven at this recreation of an occasion that had been dear and familiar. They discussed the matters that had occupied him at the meeting, and Guy laughed. "I thought all your allegiance was to big business nowadays," he said. "Don't tell me you still keep up with my stuff!"

She assured him happily that she indeed did – that this was all that really interested her. She ventured even to take him up on things that he had said, and, engrossed in their conversation, they walked two or three times round Lincoln's Inn Fields before he said good night and went to his rooms.

If, instead of discussing such matters as the export-import gap they had been singing love ballads to one another, Constance could not have been more uplifted. She didn't go home to bed but walked down a side street to the river, watched the moon on the water and the towers of Westminster against the starry sky, and felt anew the wonder of knowing Guy and talking with him about matters that were, she was sure, beyond Augusta's range.

That was how it began all over again, and it went on as Tom had told me in his letter, by her becoming his unofficial secretary. Guy must have been extraordinarily insensitive not to be aware of Constance's feeling for him. Or was he aware of it, and yet willing to take advantage of it? It seemed strange to me that he never mentioned it to Augusta, but, so far as I know, he never did.

Constance's bitter happiness was bound to end, sooner or later, in disaster for her. There came a night when he was to call at her flat for some material she had been preparing for him, and then they were to go together to a meeting at Hatch End. When he arrived, she was not in her sitting room, and he heard her calling from the bedroom. He didn't want to go in there, but she continued to call, and it at last penetrated his rather dense mind that it was the voice of a sick woman. She was in bed, burning with influenza. She began to apologise for letting him down, but he cut her short, put his hand on her forehead, and asked: "Is a doctor looking after you?"

She said no, and he told her impatiently that that was stupid of her. She could see that he was as much alarmed for himself as concerned for her, and remembered that during the influenza epidemic that killed millions after the war he had been near to death. She had no telephone, but he said he would find one and call a doctor, and then began to hurry off, saying that he mustn't be late for his meeting. She called him back to tell him proudly that his notes were ready. She had worked on them while shivering and burning, and there they were, lying on the table near the bed. He said: "Thank you, Miss Oldham, but I think I've managed to cover all that"; and off he went. She knew that he was afraid the notes were infected.

She lay there, in the small room I knew well, a room with only a skylight for letting in the day, and she was tossed on a storm of emotion. She could feel his hand on her forehead and she could sense his repulsion which shrank as if from a leper. The doctor called, gave her a sedative, and said he would be back in the morning.

This was three months ago, towards the end of March. Her convalescence was slow, and what shocked me as she told me the story was that I had still then been in London and she had not let me know that she needed me. I chided her for this, and she said rather sullenly: "How was I to know that you would want to bother with me? I'm not accustomed to being bothered about. Even if Guy had married me, I should never have wanted him to *bother* about me."

It was this almost savage spirit of isolation that made her so difficult.

Ten days after he had called for the notes which he didn't use, Guy wrote to say that he had learned from the doctor that she was getting out again, and suggested a meeting in Lincoln's Inn Fields. "In the open air I should be tolerably sanitary, I suppose," she said. However, she met him, and they quarrelled. She told him that she thought he had behaved cruelly in not once looking in to see her when she was ill, and he said with equal frankness: "I couldn't risk taking influenza to Maidenhead. My wife was expecting a child. She's had it now – a boy."

"You wouldn't have cared if I'd died," she said.

"Oh, you're wrong," he assured her. "I should have cared a good deal."

"I should have been difficult to replace, I suppose. That's how much you cared."

"I managed very well for two years before you turned up at my Farringdon Street meeting. I could see then that you were longing to work with me again. I don't deny that that was useful to me, but I was thinking of you more than of myself. I know that the theatre and things of that sort don't interest you and that you lead – well, a quite unnaturally solitary life. I hoped this would help to pull you out of it."

That started the quarrel. He pitied her! That was what his words meant. All her work was not service from her to him but a dole from him to her. Looked at in that light, it was more than she could bear, and she flamed at him.

Thank God, she said one funny thing. "You know how you are when you get like that," she said. "I wanted to taunt him, and I said 'You didn't send me so much as a bunch of grapes!' As soon as I said it I saw what a lunatic thing it was, and I started to laugh – rather hysterically, I'm afraid. But at least it allowed us to part with a smile, for he saw the joke, too. 'If I'd known you were pining for that,' he said, 'I'd have raided the vine-house at Hampton Court.' "

That was how they parted, and just before coming down to Cornwall she had recovered enough to write and ask him whether, on her return, he wished her to continue with the work. This letter which the postwoman had handed to me was no doubt his answer. "And what," Constance asked me, "can he say but no? Yes or no, I'm sorry I wrote and asked him. No more of that."

I said: "You have avoided mentioning the important thing, and it's not for me to put it into words. But I assure you that there's something to be said for being an old maid, as they call it. Look at me!"

She called up another faint smile. "Well," she said, "I suppose you have your points."

CHAPTER EIGHTEEN

AUGUSTA HAD motored up from Maidenhead to do some shopping, and I took her out to lunch. I rang up Sir Thomas Elthorne and asked him if he would join us. He agreed to do so, and was waiting for us in the foyer. He gave us drinks and grinned at us. "Remember the last time?" he asked. "I sat upstairs and watched you and this *femme fatale* lunching below."

"That was a long time ago, Tom. You've been knighted for three years, and it was well before that."

His hair was grey. He looked distinguished, like one of those people we see today in the advertisements, carrying an impeccable overcoat over one arm, an impeccable suitcase in the other hand, and getting into an impeccable aeroplane that one presumes never has engine-trouble but arrives at its destination with impeccable punctuality.

Augusta, I thought, was looking wonderful, all things considered. And there was a good deal to consider. I was never sure how her marriage had turned out, and it was not something I could ask her about. But I often wondered. The men who had attracted her had all been romantic. Miles, Haydon Mellerby, Michael Miskin. I know that her feeling for Miles had had a more than sisterly intensity, like mine for Roger. Whether she had loved Haydon I could never be sure, but hers was a nature that would inevitably be dazed and subjugated by his *panache*. As for Mickey, even to my older and experienced eyes the boy dazzled. And then – Guy Halliday. I could never quite see it or believe in it. Perhaps she had been dazzled too much and wanted to get out of the sun. Those unhappy abortive pregnancies may have meant more than appeared. Then Philip came, and she began to bloom again. He was six now, and in the true line of succession – a glorious child. On this day when we lunched with Tom, Augusta had been a widow for two years.

I don't think she had ever dreamed, as Louisa had done, of turning her husband into a man of note. If she had, Guy would soon have cured her. I saw a good deal of him and found him a bit gritty. His left-wing convictions were sincere but purely intellectual. He had never known poverty: his reaction to injustice had none of the passionate and romantic fire of men who had endured it, seen their families suffering because of it. He was a legislator, not a crusader. His calm confidence that the cure of this sorry world was almost a mathematical problem galled me. Men were not wholly right or wholly wrong, as he seemed to think. I had seen too many of them to believe that. Even that greedy shark Lord Lavernock had shown me a spot of gold.

Guy wasn't doing much public speaking towards the end. I suppose his party realised that he was more useful in other ways, and he didn't mind that. He was not ambitious: he was content to do as he was told. Hard work in committees doesn't get into the headlines.

His death was dreadful. He had been at home that day and was to go to London in the afternoon. Augusta drove him to the station, but did not stay to see him off. He stood there waiting for his train, and a small boy was bouncing a ball on the platform. Guy was aware that an express was due, and warned the boy not to play in so dangerous a place. The boy persisted and the ball rolled towards the edge of the platform as the train was roaring into the western end of the station. He ran after it, and Guy leapt to grab his collar. The boy, at last seeing his danger, turned in panic, pushed Guy away, and in doing so toppled him over on to the line. Not much appeared in the papers. The main point made was that the train, which pulled up, was half an hour late in reaching Paddington.

2

Constance was living with me at that time. When she came down to St Tudno in 1927 and at last faced the fact that she was not, and never would be, more than one of Guy's friends – hardly that: a useful acquaintance was more like it – it seemed to me that, if she was not to be entirely wasted, her life must take a new direction. I disliked everything she was doing: her job with Tom was something that could be done by any girl who could write shorthand, type a letter and use average commonsense. It wasn't good enough for her, her wretched little flat wasn't good enough, and I went along to the vicarage in a crusading spirit and said as much to Hugo. I thought that Hugo himself needed a bit of rousing. Millicent, who was housekeeping for him, said: "Father's in his study. I don't know whether he can be disturbed."

"Well, I'll go and see," I said, marching towards the stairs.

I didn't like Millicent. She was a slothful and sluggish girl who had never been out of Cornwall and had been unable to find there, as her brother Richard had done, enough to fill a lifetime with work and wonder. I had, more or less unprofitably, interfered in all sorts of lives, but I felt no desire to interfere in Millicent's.

I knocked on the door which we Legassick girls had approached with awe in Father's time, and Hugo shouted: "Come in." He was sitting in an easy-chair, smoking a pipe and reading a third-rate novel. He rose and yawned. "Hot today," he said.

We talked of this and that, and somehow he got on to the subject of curates. "I sometimes wonder whether I could do with one here," he said, (and that startled me when I thought of our little church and handful of people) "but", he went on, "I don't know. There's a lot of poor stuff about today. It was the war, of course. Curates ran short and they pushed half-educated men through a half-educated theological course and turned 'em loose regardless of consequences."

I listened to him amazed. "My dear Hugo," I said "the war ended in 1918. It's now 1927. Nine years. Those curates are either bishops or dead of old age. And in any case, why should you talk so contemptuously? Those boys did what they could. The war caused them to miss the university, and they had to take what was going. You were one of the lucky ones. Besides, there are other ways of getting educated than going to a university. They could use their spare time to good purpose."

I looked fiercely at the book he had put down, and he had the grace to seem embarrassed. "You don't think, do you," he said, "that life has been the same for me since John was killed?"

If the rest of his speech had surprised me, this shocked me. "Oh, Hugo," I said, "don't put it on to poor John. That's cowardly. People we love and depend on die every day, whether in peace or war. Why, good heavens, if we used that as a screen for laziness the world would stop. And though John is dead, you have other children. I don't think you need bother about Richard. He's self-sufficing. But what about Constance?"

"She rather baffles me," he said. "She doesn't confide in me. I don't understand her."

"You don't take any trouble with her, my dear. She'd confide in you if you did. She confides in me."

"I did take trouble with her, you know," he said. "Before she went off to the war I was preparing her for Oxford. Her Latin is excellent."

I didn't tell him that she was worried by something more than the state of her Latin. I said: "This job she's doing in London doesn't use her. It's just pottering. I'm going to advise her to throw it up."

"Will that mean my having her back here?"

"You needn't be alarmed. I think I shall be able to persuade her to do something more intelligent. But it'll cost money. You're a well-to-do man."

"You're a well-to-do woman."

"I know I am. But I want to involve you in this. I want Constance to share my little place in London and to study law. It may have drifted down to St Tudno that women can become barristers. I want you to pay for her keep with me and find the money for her training. If you put your hand in your pocket, she'll feel that you're interested in her. At the moment, she feels utterly deserted. Well, goodbye. Think it over."

I was halfway through the door, wondering whether I had made an enemy for life, when he said: "Maria, one moment."

I went back, and he said: "Would you mind very much if *I* put this to Constance? Let it seem like *my* scheme? If she likes it, I could say that I'll consult you about putting her up and keeping an eye on her."

My fears turned to a glow of joy. "Oh, Hugo," I said, "that's by far the best way to do it. Thank God you're not so deep in sin and iniquity as I supposed."

He took my hand and said: "You know, Maria, you and I could have made a do of things."

I was pleased, but pretended to be shocked, and hurried out of the room, thinking: "Poor Bella!" I had always guessed, but would never face it clearly, that she hadn't come up to scratch.

3

That was six years ago, and now in 1933 when I was lunching with Augusta and Tom Elthorne, Constance was beginning to make a meagre living as a barrister. It had been a time of great changes. Hugo was dead, and I could weep my eyes out about Hugo. I'm too ready to judge. I began with my doll Euphemia Emmett whom I would catch out in some fault, if it was only the sad fault of being young and beautiful no more, and I would throw her over the gun'le of the dinghy and leave her callously to dry on a tombstone. One way and another I had found fault with everyone except Roger, and I sometimes wondered whether even he would have escaped if death had not enshrined him, beautifully living, in the amber of memory. I have often damned myself when recalling the way I confronted and affronted Hugo, charging him with laziness and indifference when the seeds of his dying must already have been painfully springing up within him. He let me go on. He said nothing. He did as I wished. It took him three years to die, and the last of those years was horrible. I spent that year at the vicarage, doing what I could, and that came to no more than giving him my company. He had a curate at last, a hearty youth named Nethersole, who was an Oxford rugby blue and exploded through the parish on a red motor-bicycle. He organised a football team and an amateur dramatic society and gave boys boxing lessons, and for aught I know may even have talked about the things of God, but I didn't see how he could find time for that. He was not so much a muscular Christian as a Christian muscle-man. But there goes Maria Legassick again, with the judge's wig on her head. However, he didn't worry me much, for he didn't live in the vicarage. He had rooms with a widow in a house on the creek.

Until the end of his last painful year Hugo was able to get about. Indeed, he insisted on doing so, for he had a horror of lying in bed. "There are circumstances," he said, "in which a bed is altogether too much like a coffin. One lies there with a feeling that there's nothing more to be done except the screwing-down." He had to spend time enough there, goodness knows, and little of it was spent in sleep. I read to him. "Before I die," he said, "I want to hear all the novels of Jane Austen once more."

"I think," I said, "that Father would have prescribed Jeremy Taylor's *Holy Living and Holy Dying*."

528

He managed a smile, and said: "I'm afraid I was never of the old man's metal. He was a great man after his fashion. I was never a great man after any fashion. D'you remember how Bella and I fell upon the vicarage when we first came here and uprooted every trace of him?"

And "do you remember?" became a theme song, whether we were sitting in the summer sunshine looking across the graveyard to the sea, or interrupting for a moment in the bedroom the tale of Elizabeth or Emma. "D'you remember that first time I came down here from Oxford with Roger? We two, and you and Bella, and your father, and that queer bird Thomas May. You and I are the last of them, and you'll outlive me by half a century, I expect. You have the leathery look of a survivor."

Another time, he fell asleep as I was reading, and awoke to interrupt my voice by saying: "Thank you for looking after Constance. She'll be all right now. It's been nice having her down for all her holidays." He dozed off again, and I sat looking at him in the light of a fading day, and somehow all I could see was the boy who met us with a brougham at London Road station in Manchester, and drove with us to Bowdon. Bella slept on his shoulder, making her characteristic bubbling noise, almost like the sound of a baby sucking. In his sleep his face occasionally twitched with pain and I could feel his hand, which I held, close upon mine convulsively. Then he woke up again and said faintly: "Give my job to young Nethersole, there's a dear. Not a bad boy."

So far as I remember, those were the last words he spoke to me. He died with *Emma* half-finished – such a pity. I gave his job to Henry Nethersole, who didn't want to live in the vicarage. Life was becoming more difficult for the clergy as for other people, and the vicarage was too big to be run on the stipend. I was glad. Someone had shocked me by speaking of my "declining years". Well, I thought, I'll end them where they began. So I paid Mr Nethersole a rent for the vicarage, and that, with his stipend, allowed him to take a small house on the creek and employ a housekeeper. I turned over Little in Sight rent free to Richard and Nan, who had been living there during Hugo's long illness, and as they couldn't afford much furniture I let them keep what was in it, except my books and pictures, and I gave myself a high old time furnishing the vicarage to my fancy. I sold the lease of my place in London, and now my role and Constance's were reversed. When I was in town I stayed with her, not she with me. As well as her chambers in Fountain Court, she had a flat high up in King's Bench Walk. Well, it was hers fictionally. I paid the rent.

4

For one born as I was into a family richly studded with parsons on both sides, I knew remarkably little about curates. Jane and the Brontë girls could give me points on that. However, during Hugo's last year I got to know one who has my gratitude. He took Millicent off my hands. Not that she was on them strictly speaking. She was no concern of mine, but I am unable to see a boy or girl lying about without girding up such loins as I have and looking round for a job or a mate. Mr Nethersole's brother spared me that. He was older than Mr Nethersole and so different as to be beyond belief: tall, thin and grim, with an inquisitorial look that lightened only when it fell upon Millicent. Then it was like the look of an experienced wolf regarding a lamb about which something ought to be done. He was engaged in the mission field – in some such place as Accra, I think, and had come to spend a holiday with his brother. He told us that he was able to speak to the children of his parish in their native tongue, and gave us an example of how this sounded. It was remarkably like the noise a boy makes when he draws a stick sharply along iron railings, but Mr Nethersole assured us it meant "Suffer the little children to come unto Me." I could see the way the wind was blowing, and when Millicent told me that they were engaged I begged her and him to say nothing of it to her father. To their credit, they did not. I felt I had done something to make up to Hugo for my rudeness about Constance. Mr Nethersole had gone back to Africa by the time Hugo died; and soon thereafter Millicent packed up and went off to join him. So there were those four children whom I had first set eyes on long ago dawdling up the hill with a nurse pushing the pram. One was in Africa, one was a bit of English dust in Picardy, one was happy with his Nan at Little in Sight, and Constance, on that day when I lunched with Augusta and Tom, was defending a man who had tried to strangle a girl with a silk stocking under a bush in Hyde Park.

5

It was perhaps not the most savoury topic to go with lobster mayonnaise and Chablis, but I told them about it, because I was very proud, as I said to Tom, of having rescued Constance from the routine of his vast impersonal office. "I hope she gets him off," he said. "It would be a wonderful reward for all your solicitude to have a sadistic monster turned loose among us, ready to have another go."

Augusta said: "I admire Constance. All those false starts: the war, then fiddling around with Guy's political work, then that dreadful time in your office, Tom. I can imagine nothing viler. After that, to settle down to the slog of reading for the bar. It takes some doing – the sort of thing I'm quite incapable of."

"It's your hair," Tom teased her. "I told you years ago when I was a cheeky little boy that it's the colour of Lyle's golden syrup. Women with hair that colour never make good secretaries or accountants or lawyers or what have you. They make satisfactory wives and reasonably good mothers. That's about all you can say for them. And talking mothers, how's that boy of yours? Don't forget that I'm his godfather."

"I think he's settling down fairly well," she said. "He and a friend named Ginger Cranbrook will be with me next weekend. It's half-term, and I've vamped the headmaster into allowing them to come to me instead of my going to the school. I'm dying to meet Ginger Cranbrook, of whom I hear in every letter Philip writes. The last one ended 'Ginger Cranbrook and I send our fondest love.' "

"You see," Tom said to me, "as I said, it's the colour of the hair. Even men who've never met her send their fondest love. Augusta, may I come down next weekend to chaperon you? This Cranbrook sounds dangerous."

"Come by all means," she said. "You'll be able to keep Ginger Cranbrook engaged and leave me some time for Philip. But I warn you, you'll have to work hard. Mr Cranbrook is a demanding character. Listen to this."

She fumbled in her handbag and produced a letter. "Yes, so and so and so and so. Ah, here it is: 'Ginger Cranbrook says he hopes as he's coming there'll be something to do, not just messing about. I told him we have a paddock, and he says better get a cricket pitch cut in it and practice nets. He prefers a medium slow bowler if you can find such

531

a thing. He knows about the punt, and says he hates anything shabby on the river. I hope there's time for a new coat of varnish. He'd like to sleep out in a tent, but not if it's a bell tent. Something like a small marquee is what he has in mind. He's a good swimmer, and thinks if there's no spring-board at the bathing-place, which there isn't, it would be a good idea to have one.'"

She looked at us and laughed. "That's how it goes," she said, "but of course you haven't seen the spelling."

"I'm dying to meet the man Cranbrook," Tom said.

Augusta said: "You can have him all to yourself. Just find if he'd like a race-course laid down for his next visit, with a stable of thoroughbreds."

"I think," I said, "that I'd better be there, too. May I come?"

"Well, yes," Augusta said, "if Ginger Cranbrook agrees. I'll write and ask him."

6

There was no cricket pitch, no new coat of varnish on the punt, no spring-board, and no marquee. Ginger Cranbrook had to put up with the indignity of sleeping under a roof. He didn't seem to mind any of these things and was, in his aggressive and demanding attributes, altogether a creature of Philip's imagination. Philip was new at school, and I suppose a boy a year older than he could easily become endowed with mythical qualities. Ginger just mooched about rather gloomily, ate a lot and slept like a dormouse. I ventured to ask him if he was enjoying himself and he conceded: "Well, it's better than school."

"You know," Tom said to Augusta one evening when we were at dinner, "what Philip has been doing is telling you in his own fashion what he wants here for himself. You'd better see to it before the summer holidays."

I asked: "Should he be given everything he wants?"

Augusta said, almost sharply: "Of course he should."

I began: "When I was a child, the only toy I had apart from home-made ones was a doll that became horribly battered . . ." but Tom interrupted me.

"My dear Maria, that was a very long time ago."

"Yes," Augusta said. "And you belonged to a very poor family. I expect your father had his work cut out finding money to send his son

532

to school. Nothing left to buy toys for daughters. It's not like that with Philip."

"Don't spoil him," I said.

"In reason," Augusta said, "I shall give him everything I can. This world's not likely to give him much."

"What do you mean?"

"It's quite clear what Augusta means," Tom said. "We've had one war. We've done next to nothing about all those things it could have taught us. And when I say we, I mean the whole damn' human race. The consequence is that ten to one we shall have another. Look at this maniac beginning to rear up now in Germany. We haven't heard the last of him."

"Yes," Augusta said, "that is what I mean. What I can do for Philip I shall do."

"If the world is going to be as grim as you suppose," I said, "wouldn't it be better to train him in fortitude?"

"Philosophically," she said, "that's a splendid idea, but mothers are not much given to philosophy."

A gloom fell upon us, even though it was a lovely summer evening, full of the late songs of birds.

"D'you remember Armistice night in London?" Tom asked. "No, of course not. Neither of you was there. I was. People kept on giving me drinks and I got a bit tight. I dived into one of the fountains in Trafalgar Square. It sobered me, and I lay on my back, looking up at the sky, with the buses full of roaring people hooting and honking all round me, and mouth-organs were being played, and there was a policeman wearing a coloured paper hat sitting on the edge of the fountain, kissing a girl who was wearing his helmet. Suddenly everything seemed fantastic and I began to shiver and to think of all the men who had been killed . . ."

Augusta broke in: "Shut up."

"Sorry," Tom said. She got up and left the room and he went after her, and I sat there for a long time with the darkness deepening and the birds one by one falling to silence. When at last I went out into the hall Tom was standing there, looking abashed. "I think she's gone up to see if Philip's all right," he said; and she came slowly down, pulling a light cloak round her shoulders, looking infinitely sad. She had had sorrows enough, and at that moment she looked as though, like rooks coming home to a tree, they had all thickened at once upon her. She put an arm through Tom's and said: "Let's go on the river and be quiet for half an hour."

It was about nine o'clock, and ten is my bedtime. I stayed up till half-past, and still they had not returned. I went up to my room then, and a moon was rising, and in the moonlight I saw them trailing up from the river arm-in-arm.

Soon after that I went back to St Tudno to spend the rest of the summer in my vicarage. Early in September I received a postcard from Philip. "Dear Gran" – that was what he called me – "had a grand holiday in a place in France with Mother and Uncle Tom. Now I'm back in stinking school. Philip."

A little later an almost casual note from Augusta said: "Could you put me and Tom up for a fortnight or so? We are to be married, and I have a fancy for getting the job done down there where once I was happy."

Mr Nethersole did the job, and I lodged for a fortnight with Richard and Nan at Little in Sight, leaving the vicarage to Tom and Augusta.

7

I enjoyed my time with those two young people, and I think I was good for them. She was the only girl in the world and he was the only boy. Far too much so, I thought. They gave a sense that even St Tudno was metropolitan and that they would like to live in a shack in Lamorran Woods. Occasionally, they went up to London on the business of their books, and they returned with the joy of prisoners who had finished working out a sentence. They were happiest of all when sailing the quay punt. They would be out in her for days, dropping their anchor at night in some quiet creek, sleeping on the sand of deserted coves, cooking on beaches, and Nan for ever drawing: the curl of a wave, a tree isolated on a rocky point, the dance of wind-blown corn, the heavy lolling clouds or the clouds that raced with racing weather. They knew the coast and all its juttings into headlands, and recessions into bays and creeks, from Newlyn to Falmouth and thence up the roads to Truro.

They gave me coffee on the lawn at Little in Sight, and Richard, his brown-baked body stretched on the grass at my feet looked up and said: "I suppose nothing has changed here since you were born, Aunt Maria?"

Well, that was a pretty good stretch. I was fifty-seven. "Oh, there's been change enough," I said. "My father used to drive a pony trap about the parish, and now Mr Nethersole has a motor-bike. And that means a very big change indeed in the roads. They were all white dust when I was a girl. We used candles and oil-lamps in the vicarage, and the old witch who lived here hadn't even oil-lamps. It was all candles. She didn't have a well, either, as you have. She had to walk halfway to the vicarage to get water from a spring. All you have to do is touch the button of your electric pump."

"Tell me about the old woman who used to live here," Nan said. So I told her about old Mrs Mitchell who had been a lady-in-waiting and became a village crone, and I knew that her vivid mind was already seeing another of her books for children. "You can call it *Cordelia in Candleshine*," I said with a laugh.

"How did you know I was going to call anything anything?" she asked, surprised.

"Oh," I said, "I'm not such a fool as I look."

She got up and kissed me – the woman who had been my little starved and bony waif lying naked and ashamed on the sand. She still had the strange sea-green eyes that had moved me then. And her kiss moved me now to a mood of sentimentality, so that I asked Richard if he remembered the first time I had seen him – that time when I came back to the vicarage after old Mrs Kopf had died, and he was dangling a bunch of wayside flowers in the face of Millicent lying in the pram. But he didn't remember a thing about it, or about my short stay then at the vicarage, and that was my fault, for all my heart and time were given to Augusta and Miles. But I was sorry he didn't remember: I found myself more and more looking backward for consolations.

He said: "I do remember Augusta from that time. She was so beautiful. She still is. I hope she'll be happy with this chemicals man."

I laughed at this description of Tom. He had indeed been a chemicals man since I had first known him, but somehow it seemed an odd phrase to apply to Sir Thomas Elthorne, D.Sc.

"I sometimes wonder," Richard said, "what those chaps have got up their sleeves. They go on and on finding things out, just for the fun of it, or, I suppose, because they can't help it. And then the rest of us are faced with the consequences of it. Look at that chap, for example."

That chap was the tame gull named the Ripper, because he had a cold, inhuman and murderous look in his eye.

"You see," Richard said, "these chemical chaps discover how to drive ships by oil. Then the engineers shoot the waste into the sea and chaps like the old Ripper cop it."

They had found him starving, oil-clogged, and unable to fly, and had brought him home and cleaned him up. Here he was now, disinclined to leave a cushy billet with all found.

"And poor old Ripper's just a small example," Richard said. "Sometimes it's not just a gull, it's men, thousands of 'em copped out in a war. Flame guns, gas – all that sort of nonsense."

"Well," Nan said, "there'll be no more of that sort of nonsense, I hope."

She took the coffee-cups in to wash them; and I said to Richard: "Why did you say that? You've scared her."

"Well, you can't dodge everything, even with the sort of life we lead. Sometimes when we're getting about the country we go into a pub for a drink. You meet all sorts of types there, you know. Cornwall's full of 'em – old naval officers squatting down on the edge of the sea, old soldiers, and so forth. The world's never settled down, has it, since the last lot? Well, you hear these chaps talking, and they say surprising things sometimes. 'Have to knock the – 's for six next time, and have done with it once for all.' That sort of thing. Makes you think."

The Ripper was on his knee and he was feeding it with a biscuit and scratching the top of its head. "Well," he said, "thank God I know something about the sea. I think I could be quite comfortable in the Navy."

Nan came back, and he said casually: "Look at this chap, Nan. That's what these chemical men do. They land you with a responsibility, and once you take it on it's round your neck for life."

8

I had no doubt that the chemicals man would make Augusta happy. The highflown romantic side of her had twice been cruelly deflated. She now could, and did, laugh at Haydon Mellerby. "Once," she confided to me, "when Guy had been unspeakably dreary, I went all on my own to see how he affected me. He was playing a youngish man – he always does, have you noticed? – and really he revolted me. Like an old satyr pretending to be a faun. What a young fool I was!" She laughed – whether at the past young fool or the present old satyr I don't know. But she never laughed at Mickey. She never even mentioned him. The flesh had healed over the gash of that wound, but there would always be the scar. It seemed to me that her marriage to Guy had been a grab at something safe and solid, but with the safety there had been, I fear, an intolerable dullness. If safety is what you want, better have it, as she had it now, with someone who shared your memories. With Tom, she began at any rate with a solid basis of friendly affection, and she might well go on to something better. I said to her, during the honeymoon at the vicarage: "Why don't you take Tom to see that lovely Ruan river? D'you remember the day we spent there with Miles, when the tide ebbed and locked the door on us, and no one but ourselves could get in?"

She said: "That was one thing. This is another." And musingly she repeated my own words: "No one but ourselves could get in." She said: "There are experiences like that. I want to keep them locked up. Tom and I must make our own things. I think we shall."

I moved back into the vicarage after they had returned to London and made ready to receive Constance who was coming to join me when the Courts rose for the long recess. I heard from her occasionally, but she hadn't much time or inclination for letter-writing. I was finding my association with her deeply satisfying on an unemotional level. I had loved Augusta perhaps too much, if only because of the solace her beautiful young presence brought to me when my life, like hers, was in bits; but I could never love Constance. Her gratitude for the way I had taken her in hand and almost compelled her into her profession was deep and sincere; and on my side was a great respect for the way she had taken and used that opportunity. Gratitude on one side and respect on the other made a sufficient basis for our relationship. It was without passion and anguish, and I was beginning to feel that a bit more of that sort of tranquil life would do me no harm. In our quiet rooms in King's Bench Walk we might have been during the winter evenings a couple of Trappist hermits, so little we spoke to one another, she, as often as not, working on the documents of some case she was concerned in, I reading or entering up the journal on which this all too wandering and diffuse record is founded. But then I am no novelist; I seek simply to tell something of the people in my life.

I was surprised then, about a week before Constance was due at the vicarage, to receive a rather long letter from her. It was to ask whether she might bring with her a Mr Hans Mohl. He was a student at a German university.

> You and I, (Constance wrote) haven't talked much about Germany, but I expect you know as well as I do that things are boiling up there rather badly. Those who know the country better than I do, especially Henry Rogers, whom I believe you've met, and who is often there on business, are horrified at what is happening. Henry has seen bands of thugs, belonging to the party led by this man Hitler, parading the streets and sometimes bashing people almost to pulp. Only last week, he returned from a quick visit and said he is convinced that we are at the beginning of something horrible. Jews, in particular, are the subjects of increasing violence, and a good many of those who have the money and the luck are leaving the country. Henry brought with him a young man named Hans Mohl. Hans' father is a textile man with whom Henry has had business for years, and he has watched Hans grow up and has a great affection for him. The Mohls are not Jews, but Hans was engaged to a young Jewess. She was denounced to one of these gangs of ruffians, and they lay in wait one night and attacked her as she and Hans were walking away from his father's house. They killed her. Perhaps unintentionally, but they killed her. Hans, trying to protect her, was battered with knuckle-dusters. There were passers-by, and he shouted to them to help, but they hurried away. There – that is what Germany is coming to. They hurried away. Physically, Hans was not much the worse, but psychologically he is shattered. His father prevailed on Henry Rogers to take the boy to England for a rest. That is how I met him. Henry thinks a long holiday in a quiet place might help to pull him round, and that's why I'm writing to you.

And so on.

538

9

Hans Mohl wasn't much fun. He was nothing to look at — young, fair and slight, and incurably anguished. When he and Constance arrived, he dumped a large suitcase on the floor in the hall. I tried to put it on one side, and couldn't budge it. "My books. Please, I shall carry it," he said, and somehow he did. I later saw "my books" ranged on a chest of drawers in his bedroom. They were in four or five languages, and were about many things: history and chemistry, astronomy and physics, painting and sculpture, biography, poetry, theology and philology. My little maid reported to me that when she went into his room one morning he was shaving, with a piece of paper stuck into the frame of the mirror. I tried to chaff him about beginning his studies at so untimely an hour, but he was not chaffable. He said: "Always I do. It was Greek. Sometimes it is Persian. Now, especially, I must do so. Thus I forget."

I tried again to make the moment a bit easier. "Are you aiming at being a Renaissance man?" I asked. "*Uomo universale?*"

"So I try," he said, "but not successfully."

I fear he was right. Those Renaissance men had a good deal of the swashbuckling ruffian mixed in with their learning. "Poor Mr Mohl," as Richard said, "is just a poor little mole."

"And that," I said, "is a poor little pun." But it was near enough. No joy fused Mr Mohl's erudition into a sparkling reaction to the business of living. Goodness knows, the shocking experience he had been through was enough to damp a tougher squib than he appeared to be; but, leaving that aside, I had a feeling that he was the sort of man who would bore like a wood-beetle into a hundred matters and produce from each nothing but a little pile of scholarly dust.

He was at once an easy and a difficult guest. He was easy because he kept out of the way. Every morning he dutifully made up his bed and dusted his room. Then, after breakfast, he would take the books he was working on to the loft and stay there till lunch time. From two to four he would walk, not because he liked walking but because walking was necessary to keep him fit. That poor ass the body had a job to do in housing the mind, and so it must be in working order. Usually Constance went with him on these walks and appeared to enjoy doing so. After tea he went to the loft again and stayed there till bedtime, save for the evening meal break. "Thus," he said to me, "I am not a nuisance."

But the very fact of his being so damnably unobtrusive made me acutely aware of him, and I found him hard on the nerves. Nan and Richard did their best in the beginning, inviting him to their cottage, to a day out in the boat, to share their working rambles, but he was determined not to be a nuisance. "In England," he said erroneously, "all are so good. I must not intrude." So they gave him up, and I heard them singing in unison as they marched along the creek arm-in-arm:

> Old King Mohl was a merry old soul,
> A merry old soul was he.
> He called for his ink and he called for his scroll,
> And he called for his dictionaries three.

Constance was with me. She flushed with displeasure. "To jeer at a man in a moment like this!" she said. "It's indecent."

I had to explain that they would not have done it had they known all the facts. I had decided, I told her, that there was no point in dragging other people's sorrows into lives that were not concerned.

"I disagree, Aunt Maria," she said. "They *are* concerned. We are all concerned. To me, the horror of Hans' story is those people hurrying by when he called for help. They thought they were not concerned. They will find out."

Nan and Richard, reaching a bend of the creek, turned and waved. "I wonder," Constance said, "whether it ever occurs to those two that they are themselves very much like Mr Mohl? More than any I know, they are unthinkable apart. They make up one being, and that being shuns company like the plague."

It was true in its way, but I protested. I couldn't bear to hear criticism either of Augusta or of my little changeling Nan. "They are certainly one being," I said, "insofar as that is possible to two human creatures. It isn't wholly possible, you know. But say they are, they make a sociable being enough. Think how they invited Mr Mohl to make any use of them he liked."

"That's just conventional manners," she objected. "They were glad enough, I'm sure, when *his* sort of manners made him feel that he mustn't intrude."

This seemed to me a rather bad return to a side of Constance that I didn't like. I let the matter drop. On her side, she ended it by saying: "Heaven help the survivor if anything happens to one of them as it has happened to Hans' girl."

It was a remark that darkened the sky for me.

I did what I could for Hans Mohl while he was with me, but I was not sorry when he and Constance returned to London. I didn't at the time understand his real significance, though when I think of him now it is the significance of the man, rather than the man himself, that floods my mind. He was, so far as I was concerned, the first pebble to fall from what still looked like the fairly solid face of western civilisation. Soon they would fall, these pebbles, in increasing ones and twos, then in an avalanche that made a breach, unrepaired up to this moment in which I write. Some would spread over Europe and America, some would die where they fell or die a death whose fortunate arrival was miserably postponed. They would add up to a gate through which terror would stream; and science, stirred from its peacetime jog-trot, as it always is in time of war, would take its leap forward and stun us with horror at Hiroshima. The horror would shamefully lull itself to a sleepy acceptance, and we would at last wake up to find ourselves in the Frankenstein grip of poverty, hopelessness and despair in which the world today waits, dull-eyed and dull-hearted, for God knows what.

That is what, to me, Mr Mohl means when I bring him back to mind. The man himself lingered for a time in England and then went to America. None of us heard of him after that.

CHAPTER NINETEEN

I WAS glad that in her way, which was not an exuberant way, Constance was happy. She was never notable in her profession, but it gave her work that she enjoyed doing and a meagre living. She would not have been able to afford the rooms in King's Bench Walk if my purse had not taken most of the weight. Lord Lavernock died in the middle thirties, and I was touched to find that that hard unscrupulous man, in whom I had detected here and there (when his vital interests were not concerned) a quality of tenderness and affection, had remembered me in his will. Through all the years since I had left Italy on the death of his mother, I had neither seen him nor heard from him; but I think the old woman must have reported to him a fondness for me whose depths I had not suspected. The five pounds a week that he had told me I was to have for life had been punctually paid – £250 out of the blue appearing each New Year's day to my credit at the bank. I had thought it might end with his death, but here in his will was a charming tribute to "the love and service the said Maria Legassick gave my dear mother," and an instruction that the £250 a year should be compounded into a lump sum which, if invested, would produce the same amount. Also, as a personal "thank you" from him, I was to be given a little picture by Tiepolo.

Lord Lavernock disposed of millions to universities, art galleries, libraries, and all those other institutions which permit rich men to hope that they have made their peace with God. My bequest was only a dewdrop out of the ocean, but I found it a cool and refreshing little dewdrop, a crystal into which I could gaze and see so much of my youth: dear Gerald Pickering, and crazy, generous Jane Lavernock, and Uncle Pallace creating the garden at Dorking, and Louisa turning up there with James in pursuit. All this I could see as I looked at the

Tiepolo picture, which I remembered admiring in old Mrs Kopf's Italian villa. As for the lump sum of money, I didn't want it. I arranged with a lawyer to leave it invested as it was, but to pay the interest to Constance. She was not a girl apt at speaking words of thanks, but I think she was developing a little affection for me, and she was not quite so angular as she had been.

She had even softened towards Augusta. It was rather a moving moment when I became aware of that. I was, for the first time, really enjoying living in London. When living in Kensington and in my little house near the Marble Arch, always I had been glad to fly home to St Tudno. But these rooms I shared with Constance in King's Bench Walk took hold of me at a deep level, and sometimes I would linger there when the spring was far advanced. In the Temple I could feel antiquity more deeply than among the crumbling stones of our churchyard. To be shut into that quiet place, with the roar of Fleet Street to the North and the timeless tides rising and falling to the South, was to be shut into history itself. The great plane trees and the lawns, the sparkling fountains, the worn and echoing pavements, the coming and going by day and the deep silence of the night, the chapels and the monuments, the crooling and fluttering of pigeons, the thoughts that besieged me of what here had come and gone through the centuries – the Great Fire sweeping so much away that now was there again and already soaked into by the ages: all this made me hear the voice of history more clearly than in our village where ever since the time when our Norman church was built, and before that, no tale had been told save that of men who ploughed and reaped and fished the seas, and died.

One night in December, after Constance and I had eaten our evening meal I went out, as I often did, and wandered through the courts and narrow lanes, listening for such whispers as these. I returned half an hour later with my mind tranquillised, as my nocturnal rambles never failed to make it. I had become a believer in the virtue of silence and doing nothing for some long stretch of the day. So I sat there in the quiet firelit room, my hands folded in my lap, half of me watching Constance, and half of me surrendering to the inflow of peace. I had given her a Sheraton secretaire. She was sitting with her back to me, rummaging in its drawers and pigeon-holes. Some papers were put on one side; some were torn up and dropped into the waste-paper basket. Presently she took up a slender packet tied in red tape, and sat quite still, looking at it. Then she half turned in her chair, looking towards me, and said, with one of her rare smiles: "I suppose I passed judgment on these by tying them with red tape."

"What do you mean, my dear?"

She came and squatted on the rug at my feet, holding the small packet in her hand, and said: "My love-letters, as I used to think."

She pulled the two ends of tape and the letters fluttered down to her knees. "I kept every scrap he ever wrote to me," she said. "As you see, he didn't write often."

I knew that she was talking about Guy. Had she been Augusta or Nan, I should have placed a hand on her head, but one didn't do that to Constance. I sat very still.

"D'you know something about yourself?" she asked. "You've become different."

"So I should. I shall be sixty in May."

"You used to be rather fussy. You used to make me writhe with the thought that you were watching me, looking after me, keeping me in the straight and narrow way. You were the same with Augusta and Nan."

"Ah," I said. "Augusta!"

"Yes. She was always first, wasn't she? I remember when you came to St Tudno — well, the first time I was *aware* of your coming. I was eight years old. You hardly looked at me. You were out all day, and once all night, with Miles and Augusta."

"You remember that?" I asked, surprised.

"Yes."

In the quiet room, with no light save that from the small shaded lamp on her desk and the firelight falling upon her somehow utilitarian-looking slight figure, there was silence for a moment, and then she said: "She was so beautiful. I was madly jealous. A child can be, you know."

I defended myself. "She was unhappy and helpless. Her mother had just died, and Augusta had worshipped her."

"I didn't worship mine," she said. "I disliked her. All the time you were there I used to cry at night and wish I had someone to love me as you loved Augusta, and that I was beautiful like her."

I was shocked. It was dreadful to be looking into these unsuspected depths; but it was good for her. It was a pity, I thought, that she had sealed it all down till now. I kept quiet.

"When you came to live in London," she said, "after the war, you kept an eye on me, but I didn't want it then. I had Guy. Everything was different after I met him. I joined the WAACs simply because I wanted to get away from home. But I loathed it. It may have been just bad luck, but I was with a coarse lot. I used to read Latin, with Oxford in view, and that amused them. One day, one of them thrust a book into my hand and said: 'This is the stuff you want to read. Teach you something.' It was illustrated – a translation into English of a dirty French book called *The Lady Who Gave Herself to the Embraces of a Bear*. The bookshops were full of that sort of thing. I looked at one of the pictures and was violently sick in front of them all. And of course that amused them enormously."

Your King and Country need you. Poor child!

"Oh," I said, "that sort of tale's as old as the hills. The Greeks were very fond of it – Europa and the Bull, Leda and the Swan, and endless nymphs and satyrs."

"Somehow," she said, "it was different." I could believe it.

It was no wonder that things seemed different after she had met her earnest one-armed hero. She must have felt like Andromeda rescued from the sea-monster.

She said simply: "I always wanted to be loved," and added after a moment: "But of course Guy never loved me, and never gave me even the shadow of a reason for thinking that he did. I just mesmerised myself into believing that I was all in all to him. They talk nowadays about inhibitions. I suppose I was completely knotted up with inhibitions. I used to try to devise ways of showing him how I loved him, but the very thought of making an advance froze me."

I said: "My dear, if he had loved you, he would have devised the ways."

"I see that now."

The little enamelled clock on the mantelpiece gave eleven quick silvery strokes, and the slow majestic boom of Big Ben confirmed the verdict.

"Bedtime," she said, and began to tear up the letters one by one and drop them into the dying fire. "Nothing but memoranda," she said, "formal and dead. But I kept every line."

She got up, and brushed her hands together as though brushing those barren moments out of her life. The gesture poignantly reminded me of old Thomas May brushing his hands when he had dropped earth into a grave.

At the door she paused and said: "I'm glad Augusta gave him some years of happiness. We ought to go and see her some day."

She shut the door quietly, and I sat there for a long time, feeling that the moment was incomplete, that I should have embraced her, kissed her; but, such as it was, the moment was done with. It was as complete as Constance could make it.

2

This was in December of 1936. Philip was nine-and-a-half – a year older than Constance had been in that time she had reminded me of – the time when she had cried at night because I loved Augusta too much and too obviously. The prep school he was attending was in Hertfordshire, and I had gone down there once with Augusta to see him at half-term. When she introduced me to the headmaster, he said: "Legassick? That's not a usual name, is it? I knew a man at Oxford – Miles Cumberledge – who had Legassick relations down in Cornwall. I was there not long before the war with a little gang touring the country with plays."

All that old unhappy moment came back – unhappy for poor Miles, who was sighing for Celia Duggan, but madly exciting for Augusta in the first dazzle of her meeting with Mickey.

"Lady Elthorne is Miles' sister," I said. "You must have met her at that time, and me, too."

"Good lord!" he said. "The names put me off, of course. Lady Elthorne – Miss Cumberledge. They didn't click."

So Mr Worrall asked us to take tea with him and his sister, who looked after the domestic side of the school, he being a bachelor. "I don't suppose Philip will mind seeing the backs of the pair of you. He's anxious to be off with Si Custis, who's teaching him something about the way Americans play rounders. They call it baseball, I believe."

The school was in a house not much bigger than my vicarage. It had no more than thirty boys, I think. To one side of the lawn in front of the house there was a group of lime trees in flower. We took our tea there in the shade, with the scent of the limes drenching the air. Augusta, ever anxious to know whom her precious Philip was associating with, asked: "Who is this Si Custis?"

"A nice boy," Mr Worrall said, "apart from the savagery he imports into the honourable game of rounders. His father's at the American Embassy in London."

Si being thus briefly disposed of, Herbert Worrall became reminiscent, and we had to hear, unhappily, of his achievements in various roles from Shylock to Mr Darling in *Peter Pan*. Miss Worrall spoke no more than once. That was to say: "When Herbert was only six, our mother called him into the dining room after dinner, stood him on a chair, and he recited to her guests the whole of the *Wreck of the Hesperus*, without one fault. That was his introduction to the art of acting."

Mr Worrall blushed. I guessed he had told that story once too often, that we ourselves had been in danger of hearing it, and that his sister was warning him not to be a bore. "Well," he said, "I expect you'll want to see a bit of Philip."

So we went to see a bit of Philip, reluctantly surrendered to us by Si Custis.

"Si thinks cricket's a sissy game," he said; and as we carried him off to the village to pretend to eat another tea in his company, we found that Si, and Si's opinions, and Si's deeds, occupied his mind almost as desperately as Mr Worrall's was occupied by the loss to the English stage that his school-mastering had brought about.

3

By the summer of 1937 Augusta and Constance were seeing a great deal of one another. Augusta was forty-five – five years older than Constance. They both seemed young to me, and Augusta seemed younger than Constance. That may have been because she didn't seem very young to herself. This caused her to pay a lot of attention to her clothes and to her personal appearance. It had become almost a habit for us all to be together at Maidenhead during the weekends, and often enough in those relaxed moments Constance would come down to breakfast wearing a rather dim dressing-gown, a cold-water looking face, and hair that a comb had tugged back over her forehead with a hit-or-miss gesture. But Augusta didn't appear at breakfast. A tray with orange-juice, coffee, and a few dry biscuits was taken to her bedroom, and it might be eleven o'clock before she joined us, her clothes, her fingernails, her face having what Tom called a Cadillac look. Certainly she gleamed like some high-class unused car on the show-line at Olympia. The hair which had fascinated me when first I saw it was as glorious as ever, and she was as slim as a reed. She boasted that she hadn't put on an ounce since she was twenty. It often happened that Constance brought work with her and that, not having bothered to change out of her dressing-gown, she would be wearing heavy horn-rimmed spectacles and reading papers when Augusta came down. I remember a June morning when Augusta appeared wearing a suit of white linen with a dark blue belt and dark blue shoes. The morning sun streamed upon her, making a startling apparition of mature beauty. She looked at Constance who had chosen – she would! – the darkest corner of the room and was tying up the papers she had been reading. "Well, darling," Augusta said, "how are torts and malfeasances this morning?"

Constance didn't mind. That was the happiest thing one could say about the new relationship between them. They accepted one another with a simplicity that bridged the enormous gulf between them. Constance slipped the papers into her brief-case and got up. "Happily for me," she said, "they're still about. Well, I must go up and wash. Mr Custis is going to take me on the river."

"Go up and wash," Augusta said. "What an extraordinary expression!"

But Constance wasn't biting. She smiled and went.

Aaron Burr Custis, who claimed to be descended from the controversial American Aaron Burr, was the father of Silas Custis – Philip's "Si". He was a widower of about forty. His work at the American Embassy was concerned with trade, and Sir Thomas Elthorne was a representative of British trade with a big T. They had met at Mr Worrall's rather foolish little prep school, and had taken to one another. Mr Custis came often to Maidenhead to join the weekend parties. He was a slim dark man with blue eyes and fine white teeth. The eyes and the teeth joined often in an irresistible smile. I was glad to be beyond all that sort of thing. I should have found Mr Custis disturbing. He disliked his Christian names, and insisted that we all call him A.B. For myself, brought up in an age of formality, I could never call him anything but Mr Custis.

Mr Custis knew England well. He had been a Rhodes scholar at Oxford, and his education there had included the handling of a punt. While Constance was upstairs, fulfilling her threat to have a wash, he appeared wearing flannels and a New College blazer and carrying a picnic basket. Augusta said: "It's going to be marvellous on the water today. I wish you'd asked me to come." She looked at his slender athletic figure with admiration, and as he returned her look it was obvious that, on his part, he thought she was worth inspection.

"My dear Lady Elthorne," he said, "it's your punt. But I didn't know that being on the river interested you much."

"It doesn't," she said.

This ambiguous and provocative reply startled me, but seemed only to amuse him. "Well," he said, "we'll need more provisions than we have in this basket."

"Oh, I eat nothing," Augusta said, "and anyway there are tea-gardens all over the place. I'll come."

Tom had gone up to town and would be travelling back after lunch. Augusta went up to get a parasol. Parasols were out of date, but they suited her. While she was away Constance came down. "All ready," she said, aglow with scrubbing. "Let's be off."

I said: "We're waiting for Augusta. She's decided to join the party."

I could see that she was surprised and displeased. But she kept it under. "In that case," she said, "we'd better settle down for an hour with a good book."

"She's only gone for a parasol," Mr Custis said.

"Don't you believe it," Constance assured him. "She's one of those artists who never know when a picture's finished. She'll start again, and one extra stroke will lead to another."

The picture looked all right when Augusta appeared in a quarter of an hour. The parasol was of dark blue silk, with wheel-spokes of white.

I walked with them through the sunny morning down to the landing-stage, and watched them move off: Mr Custis standing up with the pole, his shirtsleeves rolled over sun-tanned arms; Constance sitting with her back to him; Augusta, in the shade of the parasol, facing him, reclined on cushions. Antony and Cleopatra, I thought with a smile.

> The barge she sat in, like a burnished throne
> Burn'd on the water . . .
> > For her own person,
> It beggar'd all description. She did lie
> In her pavilion.

There was no pavilion, but the parasol helped.

4

I still find it incredible, but I had learned to drive a motorcar. I never dared to use it in London traffic, but kept it at Maidenhead for ambling about the country roads. I took it out of the garage after lunch and drove into Maidenhead to meet Tom. As I purred along at twenty-five miles an hour I was thinking of Augusta, and I was thinking how incredible it was that I was only fifteen years older than she. When I first met her she was thirteen, and those fifteen years made me an adult looking at a child. But now, in what I was beginning to think of as tattered old age, the gap seemed to have widened, not diminished. Impossible, seeing her reclining in the punt, to think of her as a woman who was moving on to the wrong side of her middle years. She was as beautiful as ever, even though her beauty now was sophisticated and called for care. If I had been a forward little girl, I could have been her mother. I felt like her grandmother.

I was puzzled and a little disturbed, and I realised that my cogitations had made me overlook the clock on the dashboard and that I was going to be late for Tom's train. I always thought that I was going faster than I was. I pushed the car up to a perilous thirty miles as I was approaching the station and never quite realised how I had got into the collision. But I had, and Tom, coming out of the station and crossing the road to see what had caused the small crowd to collect, was hard-hearted enough to grin and say: "I knew you'd do it sooner or later, Maria."

He was a business-like person. He put me into a taxi, called at a garage and arranged for my car to be picked up, and then took me on to his doctor's. It wasn't much of a collision, but it had banged my knee hard against the dashboard, and my knee-cap was cracked. I was strapped up, and the taxi took us home. Tom brought out a nice Madame Récamier sort of seat, but made of wicker, for me to recline in. He put it on the terrace looking upon the paddock, and went in and ordered tea, which he carried out himself. "It must be most gratifying to you," I said, "to have so charming an injured damsel to wait on."

"I was rather hoping," he said, "that a charming uninjured damsel would be here to wait on me. Where's Augusta?"

"The last time I saw her, she was reclining on cushions beneath a parasol in the punt, looking like youth on the prow with pleasure at the helm, pleasure being Mr Custis and the helm a pole. In between them was Constance, looking like a bar of carbolic soap. I do wish that girl would realise that virtue is not necessarily allied with sackcloth and flat heels."

"She's a queer creature," Tom said. "How old is she?"

"Five years younger than Augusta. And she remembers that I neglected her when she was a child."

"Well, now she's a woman, and she hasn't learned that men neglect those who neglect themselves."

"Oh wise young judge! But not so wise as all that. She doesn't neglect her mind. Augusta's not a bad linguist and she's fairly well read, but intellectually Constance could eat her in a mouthful."

"Well then, she ought to look out for someone like the Lord Chancellor to bite on. She came to me this morning and said that Custis had asked her to go punting. 'I do want to,' she said, 'but should I?' What can one do with a woman like that? I said: 'My dear Constance, obey the dictates of your womanly heart.' She blushed, and looked as if I'd booked a double bed for them at Brighton."

"She overcame her scruples and arranged to go. And at the last moment Augusta, dressed to kill, said she'd go with them. It was unkind of her, or at any rate most thoughtless."

"I agree," he said, "but don't ask me to tell her so. I married her for better, for worse."

"I hope the better predominates."

"Yes," he said, "by ninety-nine and nine-tenths per cent. But she can't resist trying to fascinate a man if she likes him. And she likes Custis as much as I do myself."

"She must have plenty of opportunity when Constance isn't about. I'm sorry it happened today."

"So am I. Not that it matters fundamentally. Custis would never want a woman like Constance. He would be thinking of nothing but making a day pleasant for her. He wouldn't bother to ask Augusta because he knows that, more or less, all her days are pleasant. And another thing, he knows what she and I mean to one another. I'd trust him and her together in a thirty-foot boat crossing the Atlantic."

"Well," I conceded, "small boats being what they are, and the Atlantic being what it is, that would certainly not be so dangerous as walking together through a barn full of hay."

"I'd let 'em do that together, you horrid old woman. I hope your knee is giving you hell."

I loved his defence of Augusta, and I knew it was well-founded. "Tom," I said, "do you realise you've never kissed me?"

"Well, I'm not going to start now. We're overlooked from the windows and these tales get round. They should be back soon, so we'd better get down to the landing-stage. In my wife's company, I shall feel safe from Delilahs like you."

My Récamier couch was a useful contraption that could be pushed like a wheel-barrow, and there would be no jolting, for Tom had had a smooth path laid down to the water. It was pleasant, the heat going out of the day and the river idling by, green and tranquil. Tom lit his pipe and held my hand, and for a long time we said nothing. Then he said: "Maria, do forgive me for saying that I felt a little hurt. I felt that – perhaps by ever so little a bit – you had some doubts about Augusta. Don't have any more. Sitting here like this, waiting for Augusta, I feel that I'm waiting for something I couldn't possibly get on without, and something I can count on, absolutely. All right?"

"All right, Tom."

"I suppose there are plenty who think she's just a beautiful woman, and that that's a matter of luck. She's beautiful all right, but there's more to it than that. She comforts me. Do you know what comfort means?"

"Well, my father would have told me to watch that syllable *fort,* which means strong."

"And he'd be right. *Comfort ye your hearts* doesn't mean coddle them, but make them strong. That's what Augusta means to me. And that's enough of that. I thought I'd better tell you, because I know that Augusta has always meant a lot to you."

He knocked out his pipe. "Well, here they are – coming round the bend."

5

I enormously enjoyed being an invalid. I was absurdly healthy and could not remember being laid up for a single day before this, except with the things children do get laid up for – measles and what not. It was quite charming, as soon as they were out of the punt, to have three people fussing over me. Mr Custis insisted on wheeling me back to the house; Tom walked alongside, looking sympathetic; and Augusta kept urging Mr Custis to watch the bumps in the path and yearning towards me as though I were on a hospital trolley, being wheeled in for an operation that had a chance in a hundred of succeeding. As for Constance, she carried the luncheon-basket and said: "There aren't any bumps. The path's as smooth as a main road."

"Your judicial exactitude, darling," Augusta said, "would no doubt draw ringing cheers from bench and bar at the Old Bailey; but if my sympathetic heart demands bumps I shall have them – hundreds of them."

"I've warned you often enough," Constance said to me, "that you should not drive a car. Half your time, as you sit at the wheel, you're wool-gathering."

"Miss Cumberledge, you must not disturb the patient," Mr Custis said with a dead-pan face. "She'll have a relapse."

I gave a deep artificial groan. "There," Tom said. "She's relapsing."

"She's told us herself," Constance persisted, "that the doctor has diagnosed a cracked knee-cap. A few days with her leg up should put that right."

I said: "I refuse to put my leg up. What d'you take me for – a can-can dancer?"

"I must say," Tom said, "that for a country parson's daughter you have an unsuspected range of licentious allusion."

Oh, you self-torturing little fool, I was thinking, why don't you join in the fun – such as it is?

I had expected Augusta's intervention in the punting-party to bring Constance home rather gloomy, but I hadn't thought we should be treated to such an open display of raw resentment. Everybody, I think, was aware of what was eating her, as they say. We were damped, and finished the journey in silence.

This was a Saturday. It had been arranged that Constance should stay over till Monday. But she said she must take a train early on Sunday. She explained that she had to appear in court on Monday morning and that she wanted to go over her notes on the case. After breakfast Tom had wheeled me to the terrace, and as I sat alone there Constance came out. "You know," I said, "that this case on Monday no more exists than Augusta's bumps on the path."

"That's true," she answered. I waited for her to go on, but she didn't, and I hadn't the heart to pursue the matter. She was standing, embarrassed and silent, by my couch when Mr Custis appeared, driving his car out of the garage. He left it standing and came towards us, wearing his town clothes. "I've come to say *au revoir*, Miss Legassick. Miss Cumberledge has set me a good example and I've decided to get back to town." He turned to Constance. "Can I give you a lift, Miss Cumberledge? It'll be a bit cheerier than travelling in a dismal Sunday train. I've explained to Tom and Augusta, and I'm off at once."

She thanked him and went in to say her goodbyes. I said to him: "Good for you, Sir Galahad."

He didn't smile, but said: "She was miserable all yesterday. Augusta shouldn't have done that, you know. And I really do have work to do."

"I'm sure you have," I lied.

"Anyway, I couldn't bear the thought of her sneaking off like something unwanted."

Tom and Augusta came out to wave them goodbye, and as I watched the car move off – a great gleaming pike to my little buckled-up gudgeon – I understood more than ever why Tom had so great an affection and admiration for Mr Custis. I sat there wondering whether it wouldn't have been better for Constance to get over it on her own; but, all the same, it was a lovely thought.

Augusta brought a deck-chair and sat by my side. "Now, dear Aunt Maria," she said, "this is the moment when you tell me what a bitch I've been."

"I wouldn't say that, my dear; but you are at times capable of very bitchy conduct."

"Yes," she said. "I'm ashamed of myself." She clearly meant it, but I didn't think the matter should rest there. I told her, with no holds barred, what I thought of yesterday's episode. I reminded her that, though there had never been a dog's chance of Constance marrying Guy Halliday, it was she who had, in fact, married him, and that this thought was always at the back of Constance's mind, however much she might repress it. "And that," I said, "is one of many reasons why you seemed to me to be behaving like a half-wit, and a cruel one at that." I told her of what Constance had said to me not long ago – that, even as a child, she wanted to be loved. "You've never wanted, have you? Your parents, and Miles, and that dreadful Mellerby man, and Mickey and Guy and Tom – and even myself. You've been surfeited, and still you snatch at other people's crumbs."

She began to cry; and while she was crying Tom came out and looked at us, half-amused, half-anxious. "You giving her cold steel, Maria?" he asked.

"No," I said, "boiling lead. She deserves it."

He raised her up from the chair and put an arm round her slender waist. "Come on in," he said, and they went indoors where she could have her cry out on a cosy sofa.

6

During the remainder of my semi-invalidish stay at Maidenhead Augusta fussed around me like a dog who has been given a flick of the whip and knows he has earned it and is trying to make up. Back in London, Constance was morose. I didn't want any of it, sweets or sulks. Let 'em both stew in their own juice, I thought. They're middle-aged women. If they can't sort out their own affairs now, they never will. London was becoming stuffy; the Thames wasn't the Carrick Roads; I packed up and went down to Cornwall. I was in a sour temper, because I wanted people to want me, to depend on me, and neither Augusta nor Constance did, I told myself. And why should they? Weren't feelings like mine, if they were given rope, just the same as those that animated the "saviours" who destructively popped up now and then in history, like this frothy little maniac strutting in a dirty mackintosh all over Germany? It was a wild comparison, showing how disturbed my feelings were, and anyway it didn't calm me. I still wanted to be wanted, as ardently as Constance had wanted to be loved.

And so my heart leapt up as the train slowed into Truro station and I saw Nan and Richard on the platform. They spotted me through the window and ran with the moving train, and Richard was inside, almost before we came to a standstill, lifting down my suitcases and carrying them to the platform. There Nan embraced me, a brown, gypsy-looking creature – a sort of maritime gypsy with the sea in her eyes. She was wearing her favourite green, with sensational sandals made of black-and-white goat-skin. Her bare legs were as slender as a girl's.

"We've got a taxi waiting," Richard said.

"How are you?" Nan asked anxiously.

"How should I be?" I snorted. "As tough as an old boot. Surely you know by now that age cannot wither nor custom stale my infinite capacity for being a battered wreck making for God knows what port."

They laughed, and Nan said: "From what Constance told us, we wondered whether to have an ambulance ready."

We went out to the taxi. "And what has Constance been telling you? I trust I sha'n't find that you've taken the precaution of having a grave dug outside my own drawing room window."

Nan put an arm through mine. "Constance rang up this morning. She seemed properly fussed and said we mustn't fail to meet you. Something about an accident you'd had."

"Nonsense. The girl herself told me I'd be well if I kept my leg up for a week."

"She may have told *you* that, but she told us to take great care of you because you're very precious. And so you are."

"Do I look at death's door?" I demanded. "Don't chatter. Let me close my eyes."

I put my head back and closed my eyes to keep in the tears. The dear children! All the dear children: Augusta and Tom, Constance, Nan and Richard. So this is what it has come to, I thought. I'm not to look after them any more. They're to look after me. I'm to be precious!

I didn't open my eyes till we were past Devoran and a high tide was seeping into all those narrow cracks and crannies scribbled on the face of the low land that the water-birds love. And rising beyond that was the fine hill fleeced with the little twisted Rackham oak trees over which on a long ago summer night the flames of Tregannock rose up beautiful and terrible, consuming the house and James and Louisa, and so much of my life as it had been till then.

"You were there," I murmured to Nan.

"What, darling?"

"Oh, nothing. My mind was rambling."

You'd better let it ramble *forward*, I told myself; and I thought of young Philip, Augusta's son and Guy Halliday's. He, at any rate, was not too old for my clutches. And so, a few days later, I wrote to Augusta and said it was time he got to know something about St Tudno and boats and swimming. But he didn't come that year. Augusta wrote to say that Tom was off to America on B.A.C. business. He would be away for at least six months, and she and Philip were going with him. "Mr Custis and Si are going at the same time, so we'll be quite a family party."

7

When Nan and Richard brought me in from Truro, Mrs Flesch met me, looking oddly ill-named. She should have been called Mrs Bones, and her bones seemed as brittle as a heron's. Indeed, she looked altogether like a heron: tall and grey and melancholy, speaking not often and then harshly. She was another of them, a successor to that poor boy Mohl that Constance had found. Constance had found Mrs Flesch, too. She was involved in good works of one sort and another. She strove to make life easier for everybody but herself. She said to me: "Who's looking after the vicarage while you're away?" and I told her that Nan and Richard went in now and then and that a woman from the village gave the place a go over every week. She said: "You ought to have a housekeeper. I've got the very thing for you." And she produced Mrs Flesch. Like Mr Mohl she wasn't Jewish, and she wasn't much older than he. I suppose, for all her gaunt and worn-out look, she was not more than thirty. Her husband had been a barber, a calling that affords outstanding opportunities for talking too much. He hadn't liked this new Parsifal in the comic moustache and dingy mackintosh, and had often said so in just those words, I gathered. And now, if he knew anything at all, which, being dead, I suppose he didn't, he knew that upstart paranoics above all things dislike being laughed at. She had a few stumbling words of English, and I didn't dare put her on the train alone. Richard and Nan had gallantly come up to town and taken her to St Tudno. Richard's German wasn't bad. They had stayed in the vicarage with her for the first week, and then she said she thought she would be all right alone. And alone it was. The woman who had been coming in once a week couldn't stand this stranger who was dumb so far as English goes and whose haggard face was rather frightening. So she had ceased to come. However, Richard and Nan kept Mrs Flesch company when they could, and now and then took her for a walk or a sail or to a meal with them at Little in Sight. They were dear and understanding young people, and Mrs Flesch adored them.

When I was a child and a young girl, one of my jobs was helping to clean the brass in church. I hated it and took an especial dislike to a smug-looking eagle. I used to stick a dollop of brass-polish in his eye and hope it hurt. Perhaps for this reason, I have never been much of a polisher. I found the vicarage shining. Brass, wood and silver were gleaming like a usually dingy rustic town hall when a passing prince is to look in and swig a cocktail and shake a bunch of municipal paws. Mrs Flesch took me round and asked in her flat voice: "Will it do nicely?" and, calling up the little German I knew, I said enthusiastically that it would do very nicely indeed. All our communications for a long time were like that: she speaking in fragmentary and atrocious English and I replying in German to match. Old Mother Kopf had talked a lot of German and a few words had stuck with me.

8

It was good to be home. Now, more than ever, the vicarage was home to me, everything round about seeming so changeless that it comforted my heart in a world that was already beginning to mutter threats of disastrous change. Mrs Flesch was the reminder of things breaking adrift, of love lost. She gave me an ear through which, even to our placid stream, there came a far-off sound of cataracts. But indeed, it seemed very far off, and St Tudno drowsed; and even Tregannock, to which I went one day with Richard and Nan, had so settled down in ruin that it had the tranquillity of tales told long ago – such tranquillity as one feels when looking upon the Colosseum in Rome, or, nearer, upon our own grey and beautiful Restormel. The place soothed rather than disturbed me. Lady Mary Lacey and Louisa and James and the bloated winy face of old Mr Polperro looking out through the window of his lumbering silk-lined coach — all was absorbed into eternity. *Chickenanam sandwiches.* The little child, sitting on a chair in the great hall, watching Uncle Pallace's hodden-grey figure moving over the chequer-board floor, seemed not me. She, too, was buried beneath this avalanche of years, and the springing willow-herb, the briars and the ragwort, beautiful under the sun, were rooted in her half-remembered dust.

"You seem a bit tired," Richard said.

"Well, yes," I admitted reluctantly; and Nan said anxiously: "What has tired you, darling? We tried to arrange everything to save you trouble."

I said: "I'm tired because I've made an enormous journey — right through all that has happened since a May morning long ago when my Uncle Pallace brought me to Tregannock. It was the first time I entered the house."

And as they rowed me up the creek towards the vicarage, it was in that May morning rather than in this late summer afternoon that I was dwelling: May, and the dawn bursting about me in bird-song, and poor Euphemia Emmett going to her last resting-place, and Louisa's white furious face coming out from Roger's dark tent of yew, and her words accusing me. I'd better start from that point, I thought suddenly. I surprised myself, because till that flash of thought I hadn't intended to write anything, but now I fell victim to the curse of the Legassicks. As soon as I got in I looked up my old journal, and that evening I switched on the lamp at my desk and began to write. And that was a change, when you came to think of it. Father had written by candlelight. Now at the head of the creek there were all those small new houses, and people coming to and from them in motorcars, and motor buses taking them to Truro and Falmouth. Yes; even upon St Tudno change was creeping as imperceptibly as the first spoonful of salt water spills west upon the mud-flats when the slack is ended and the tide is coming in.

CHAPTER TWENTY

MR BUSHELL lived at the head of the creek where the water petered out into mud. But he sailed, nevertheless, coming out as soon as his little ship would float, and hurrying home before the outgoing tide stranded him. He had a large boathouse where his garden met the creek, and we had gathered there – he, Mr Nethersole and I – to go through the books. There were hundreds and hundreds of them on trestle tables.

Everything was being scraped together. In Falmouth the iron railings were being cut off people's front garden walls, and in St Tudno the very graves were ravished – those, that is, whose occupants had been so high and mighty that their resting-places were fenced with iron. I sat on the tomb where I had often shelled peas with Mrs Solway and watched the fierce oxyacetylene lamp flames searing through the metal, and I wondered what old Thomas May would have said to all this. "Well, Miss Maria, 'twill save a bit of bother come resurrection day. The poor souls'd have trouble clambering over they ole iron fences. Now they can step straight out, bound for glory." Something like that, I supposed.

But there was no Thomas May, no Mrs Solway. It was a quiet house of three women: myself and Nan and Mrs Flesch. Just beyond the lych-gate, through which the dead used to be carried when they arrived on a handcart, and to which they were now borne in a shiny motor-hearse, there was a memorial cross bearing many names for so small a place, including that of Richard's brother John, Hugo's son. There was room for more, and more were being provided. Richard, rather elderly for that job, but refusing to take advantage of this, was an R.N.V.R. lieutenant.

Everything was wanted. After the iron, paper. Mr Bushell had organised our collection. Every cottage combed through its

Keepsakes and Sunday school prizes, and I had ransacked the library accumulated by Father and Hugo and myself. And there we were, with all that stuff lying on the trestle table s in the boathouse – Mr Bushell, Mr Nethersole and I. We had to sort it out – some for hospitals, some for the troops, and the sorriest rubbish of all for pulping. Books in the first categories were laid on tables: the others were remorselessly hurled into a pile on the earth floor.

I found it an agonising job as I turned back covers and read inscriptions. *Jessica's First Prayer*. "To dear Mary, with love from Jim. Remembering May 21st." What had happened on May 21st? *Christie's Old Organ*. "For Jill from Dad, on her 9th birthday." Would the troops want to read *Christie's Old Organ*? Better chance it on someone in hospital. *The Book of Common Prayer*. "For Margaret from Mother. 'Be good, sweet maid, and let who will be clever.'" I wondered about Margaret. Had she been good? Or clever? Or neither? Dean Farrar's *Life of St Paul*. Oh, pulp, surely?

I plodded on, but Mr Nethersole brought a fine abandon to his job, puffing at a briar pipe and shouting his decisions like an umpire as he doomed the books to one destiny or another. "Meredith? Who reads him now. Pulp!" And smack goes poor Meredith to the mud.

"Gosh!" he shouted, "I'd save these for the bindings alone. But" - ruffling the pages – "what stuff! Oh, how boring! Pulp!"

He was about to hurl the book down when he noticed the author's name and almost blushed. "I beg your pardon, Miss Legassick."

"It's all right," I said. "Pulp!" and I took the volume from his hand and threw it to the floor, and after it I threw the other eighteen morocco-bound books of the set. "Pulp!" I cried, the tears stinging me. "Pulp! Pulp!"

It had been a hard decision. No one had wanted them. Louisa had not wanted them, or Hugo, or Bella. They had been stored in the loft; they had gone with me to Frank's house in Manchester, they had after many years come back with me to Little in Sight and then to the vicarage, where their birth had been accompanied by so many pangs for all of us – Louisa and Bella and me. I had never opened one, but love and forbearance had kept them by me. And then came this – what Mr Bushell called the Emergency; and all must bow to the Emergency. So, feeling dreadful, I had rowed that heavy load up the creek and put them with so much else, resolved not to pass sentence

myself, hoping that one or the other would speak a word of reprieve.
But now the sentence on a life's labour was passed and with pain I kept
back my tears as the Emergency opened its ugly mouth and swallowed
up so much of my youth.

2

When Richard went Nan was lonely at Little in Sight. The quay punt
was laid up on the beach, with the mast and boom and bowsprit taken
out of her, everything stripped down to a bare hull covered with
canvas. Now and then Nan would slip under the canvas and spend an
hour or two aboard, saying that she must keep the boat to rights against
Richard's return, but little enough there was to do, and I could well
imagine the sad sessions that went on there in the twilight between
herself and the absent lover. Sometimes I would see her rowing alone
in the dinghy – out past the vicarage, out into the roads, over to the St
Just shore, or perhaps north to the mouth of the Truro river, into
which, with field glasses, I could see her disappear, seeking the
consolation of being where she had been with him. Or she would go
off on the walks they had done together: into the woods, along the
beaches, out on to the headlands where now was the living flame of
gorse and now the dying fire of ling and bracken. She would take her
canvas stool and her sketching-block and pencils, but she didn't do
much, and sometimes when I was writing behind my black-out
curtains, I would pause, and think of the black-out curtains at Little in
Sight, and Nan there, solitary as Mrs Mitchell was among her candles
on those winter evenings when Father and I would pay the old witch a
call.

These nights were terrible for me, for through the memory of my
years the faces and the voices went streaming like a marching host,
and now I was at the saluting-point as they all passed by, and now I was
one of them, and everything was one thing; and the thing was the vast
haphazard business of getting from one end of life to the other. I
would put down my pen, and give up all pretence of writing, and
listen to the owls and the curlews and the herons – sounds that had
charmed my childhood but seemed now filled with menace,
reminders of what had existed before men came and might well,
when he was gone, go on with their forlorn and desolate crying. And
sometimes the wind was high, thrashing through the eucalyptus trees

and slamming the waves down on to the shore, and Mrs Flesch would look in with her thin scared face and ask: "We are safe?" for she always feared that trees would fall and was hardly to be persuaded that seas could rise so high and no higher.

So I talked to Nan about it, and Little in Sight was let, and she came to live at the vicarage. We spent our evenings together and invited the scared Mrs Flesch to spend hers with us, too. There we would sit, Mrs Flesch reading, Nan turning over portfolios of work that she and Richard had done together, and I writing away. The company was no distraction to me. Being together comforted us all. And in the daytime fears thinned out.

3

Occasionally a letter came from Augusta or Tom. Mr Custis had been recalled to Washington, and Tom, just before the war began, wrote to him, asking if he could fix up quarters for Augusta and Philip who, he thought, would be better out of the way when the storm broke. Mr Custis had a mother, a widow, living in a small town in Maine, and that is where they now were. Before sailing, they came down to St Tudno to say goodbye. Richard was still with us, and he and Nan took Philip off in the quay punt so that Augusta and I could be together. I didn't ask them to do it, but they thought with one mind and knew what I would want. Our visitors were with us for three days, and I think Augusta knew that these were the last three days we should ever spend together. As they were. On the afternoon of the third day we walked up the hill away from the vicarage until we came to a lane running to the right, and there was a field gate over which you could look back upon the roads, blue and tranquil that afternoon. We both paused and leaned on the gate and there were the white sails of yachts and the russet land rising beyond. Augusta laid an arm over my shoulder and said: "It was here."

"Yes."

And the moment was back with me. I was leaning on this gate, returned from my long time abroad, Gerald's tragedy behind me, and I was wondering what welcome there would be at the vicarage. A young voice asked me if this was the right road to St Tudno, and there they were. It was Miles' voice that had spoken, and Miles was to die in the arms of Guy Halliday who was to marry Augusta. And now there was Philip. The unpredictability of life swept over me in a wave, and I could only say foolishly: "Yes – it was here. I hope you're not sorry you ever set eyes on me."

There were small wrinkles in her skin, and the wonderful hair looked dry, like a flower that has lain pressed in a book for too long. But all the same, it was the flower I saw: the violet that had charmed my eyes here, by this hedge-side. And that is all I ever see, even now.

She hadn't answered my silly words, but the pressure of her arm round my shoulder became warmer, and I knew that she did not speak because she could not.

She drove Philip back to London the next day. On our little gravel sweep she kissed us, then got into the car with a brightness that deceived not even herself: "What nonsense it is. Rushing off to the States like this! Ten to one, there'll be no war after all."

She waved, and was gone; and I knew that she was as finally out of my life as if she had been carried in her coffin over the granite slats beneath the lych-gate.

Richard said: "She's wrong, and I expect she knows it. Of course there'll be war." And she was hardly in America before we were making the black-out curtains, to hang in mourning across the windows of our houses and the windows of our souls.

Richard was the next to go. He was forty-seven, but he didn't look it, and I am sure he didn't say it. He was as lithe and fit as a young panther. The life he had lived for so long on land and sea, and the abstemiousness of his days, had kept his appearance almost boyish. "I expect they'll make me a cabin-boy," he said, "till I start to grow a beard. Then it'll be too late to throw me out."

Nan did not try to dissuade him. It was what he wanted. He served as an ordinary seaman in a battleship, and then went to the King Alfred training-school for officers. The day he wrote to say that he had "passed out" with a commission a letter came from Tom. I read it sorrowfully. My world was emptying.

My dear Maria. – Here's another one off to America. I shall be flying out in a day or two, and between now and then I shall be up to the ears, so forgive me – I can't come to say *au revoir*. Nor can I say much about the reasons for my going. Of course, in war time supplies are important, and now that we haven't one ally left either to bless or badger us, all the thinking about supplies has to be done by ourselves. And all sorts of chemicals are involved in supplies. A trade commission is going out, and B.A.C. has been asked to submit a name to the government. Mine has been submitted and approved; and that's all I can say about it, except that in Washington my opposite number will be Custis. So that takes a pain out of my neck. I shall go with a good heart. I hope I shall occasionally have a chance to see Augusta and Philip, but that's as may be. They have settled down happily in Maine with Custis' mother, and they'd better stay there. I don't suppose you want to buy the house at Maidenhead? No, I guessed not. Anyway, Augusta has asked me to put it into the market. All my love, my dear, and all my thanks for more things than I can remember, much less say.

Ever,

Tom.

From time to time, food parcels reached us both from Maine and Washington, and we were glad to have them, but for us three women life was very, very empty; and Nan's hair began to grow grey. She kept herself busy, writing and drawing, but I could have wept as I saw her from time to time put down her pen or pencil and sit staring before her. She heard regularly from Richard, 2nd Lieutenant, R.N.V.R., who was in a motor-launch. The M.L.s, as they were called, were pretty little things, camouflaged in blue and white, looking for all the world like a rich man's idea of a nice weekend toy. There were a good many of them up and down our own waters, based in the Penryn river, and we had been aboard one, invited by her captain who seemed no more than a boy and was a friend of Richard's, a fellow-student at King Alfred. Young Dancey explained their speed and showed us how powerful for their size the armament was, so that we ceased to think of them as things to lounge on of a summer's weekend. We went ashore and climbed the hill, walking towards St Tudno, and Nan said, breaking a long silence: "Yes, you can see they could give a good account of themselves so long as they're not hit."

And that, I suppose, is one of the things she thought about when she stopped working and stared ahead. For the hulls of the brave little ships were plywood. They belonged to what was called with irony and

565

affection the Plywood Navy; and when sometimes our night silence was broken by the sound of shooting out there on the open sea beyond Falmouth harbour it was not comfortable within the same flash of thought to include those shots and plywood. Nor was it comfortable to think of Constance, doggedly sticking to the rooms in King's Bench Walk, so near the river, so near the City, so near the Docks that were being bombed night after night.

4

Early in December of 1941 Richard wrote giving us the dates of a leave that was overdue. As soon as Nan had left the house that day I rang up Constance and asked her to put a letter into the post at once, giving some imaginary but urgent reason for my travelling to town the day after Richard was due. I had no intention of being about for longer than it takes to say How d'you do? when Nan and Richard were together. I forget what Constance trumped up, but it worked well enough, and I packed Mrs Flesch off to Flushing where a friend of mine was ill and needed someone to look after her small children.

Richard arrived at about three o'clock on the afternoon before I left, so I had with him just the fag-end of one day. I had wondered how he got away with the lie about his age, for I had noticed the youth of all the men in the M.L.s on our local water. The beard was the answer. It hadn't a grey hair, and in a service wherein beards flourished no one would know whether the face behind the beard belonged to a man of fifty or a boy of twenty.

I recall it as a placid evening. There was no howl in the weather to suggest what the sea could do to men in small boats, and anyway it was a topic no one wanted to raise. The war was not mentioned. We stood in the garden and watched the sun go down in purple dusk over the end of the creek, and then we went in and opened an American parcel from Tom and talked of him and Augusta as we made a meal of the good things they had sent us. After that we sat by the fireside and played rather silly games with cards. But it sped the hours along, and we all knew that that was what we were trying to do. Those two had never wanted company other than their own. They would be glad when I was gone. I knew it, and didn't resent it.

A taxi came the next morning to take me to the station. Nan kissed me and told me to look after myself, but Richard didn't kiss me.

When the taxi drew away he stood there at the salute, the morning light falling upon the one wavy ring round his cuff. As the taxi turned out of the gate under the bare sycamores I looked back, and already he and Nan were clinging together, their arms wrapped round one another's shoulders, his face bent down upon hers.

5

There was no need for Nan to tell me to look after myself in London, for those nights of bombing that had worried me so when I thought of Constance living through them were ended, at any rate for the moment. It was dusk when I arrived on that December day, and black-out time, so that I felt rather than saw the ruin that had fallen on part of King's Bench Walk. Constance was not there to meet me. She had written to say that she might be late in getting home that night, but I had my key and let myself in to the loved familiar room. I didn't switch on a light. (What a world, I thought, where one doesn't dare to show a little light!) With a small torch I groped around till I found some squares of cardboard that seemed to have been made to fit the windows, and as I fixed these up I noticed that most of the window-glass was gone and that paper was stuck across the gaps. I put the cardboard into place, drew the curtains, and pressed a switch. At that moment Constance came in. She kissed me in the way-without-warmth that was characteristic, and said: "I thought I'd be later, but I managed to cancel a meeting."

She put me into a chair. "I'll make some tea," she said, "and when you've rested we'll go out and see if we can find dinner somewhere."

She went into the kitchen, and I sat looking about me, taking in the room for the first time. There were pock-marks in the walls, and near my feet a hole in the carpet had singed edges. My little picture by Tiepolo was gone; so was my cabinet containing a collection of Copenhagen figures in porcelain and stoneware.

Constance came in with a tray. She poured out the tea and put a couple of biscuits in my saucer. The tea made me feel a bit better. I dared not ask what had happened to my things. Clearly Constance had had a bad time, but she had told me nothing of it. She said: "It looks a bit bleak, don't you think? But I hated the idea of being driven out. It wouldn't have been easy to find a place, anyway. Well, let's hope they've got something else to think of for the moment. We haven't seen them since May. Off and on for nine months was enough."

There was no fire in the grate. She poured me another cup of tea and switched on a feeble bar in an electric gadget near my feet. "Your stuff's all right," she said. "I have a friend living out at Harpenden. He's got it all there."

I thanked her, and said: "What *did* happen? You kept me pretty well in the dark."

"You must have read in the papers what was going on."

"Reading is one thing. Seeing this hole in the carpet is another."

"Oh, that! Well, it was the worst night – the worst for me, that is. When you see the place in daylight you'll realise that I've been lucky. It's amusing to reflect that that night I was worrying my brains about how to put up some sort of defence for a man charged with arson! I didn't feel at all sympathetic to him when the night was over."

She said she had thought she would be safer under the bed than anywhere, so she had gone into the bedroom and squirmed into position. "This house wasn't hit, but there was a mass of flying stuff. The windows went and the walls were filled with mementoes. I smelt burning, and crawled out from under the bed to have a look. A bit of flaming wood from some less lucky house had been thrown through the window. So you see, if I had bunked the chances are the room would have been burned out. It was quite a sizeable bit of timber. However, I had a couple of sand-buckets handy and put it out. This was towards the end of the show, so I stayed where I was and gave myself one of my rare tots of whisky. The worst bore was cleaning away the glass the next day. I put up a poor case for my arson man, and he went to gaol."

"Well," I said, "now that I've seen with my own eyes what you're going through, I sha'n't have a moment's peace thinking about you. You should have gone to America, like Augusta."

She stiffened at once, so that I hastened to add: "After all, it's her business to be where her husband is."

She said: "She didn't wait for him, did she? She was in America before the war began. For all she knew, he would be here through it all."

I had lost the point, and I was sorry I had raised it. I hoped that was the end of it; but she said as she walked to the kitchen with the tea-tray: "I don't want to be like anybody who chooses this moment to go to America, and especially I don't want to be like Augusta."

Well, that put me in my place. I said: "It's very kind of you, my dear, to take me out tonight. What time do we go?"

"We'd better move off in about an hour."

"May I snatch a sleep till then? The journey's tired me."

"Of course you may. You'll find everything ready in your bedroom."

But I didn't sleep a wink. She had drawn the curtains, and turned down my bed, and lit one of those poor little electric things, but I lay on the bed thinking: Why can't I love her? She was resolute, brave, hard-working, filling her life with purpose in a way Augusta had never done. She had looked after my pictures and knick-knacks, and that is something Augusta would not have thought about, but all the time there was a hardness on which I bumped and from which I recoiled with dismay again and again. I know, I told myself, that there was the matter of Guy Halliday, but even he, I felt, was on my side. Augusta had given him a few years of happiness. Could Constance have done that? I doubted it, and I felt disloyal to Constance and altogether miserable.

We walked through the dark streets to a restaurant I had used in happier days, and sat for nearly an hour on a bench in the foyer till a table was vacant. The place had been famous for its food, but it gave us poor stuff, dressed up and sauced, and I thought it repellent. However, I was able to get a decent bottle of wine. The head waiter was a naturalised Italian with whom I had once or twice talked in his own tongue. He came from the town where I had lived with Mrs Kopf, and because of this, I suppose, he remembered me. And so I was able to wash down my food with something palatable.

"You said," I reminded her, "that you had cancelled a meeting. I'm sorry if I've upset anything for you."

"Oh, it was nothing much. Just a few of us who get together now and then to discuss what we shall do after the war. Mr Derwent, my friend who lives out at Harpenden, is one of us, and he wanted to get home early tonight anyway."

Well, I thought, this certainly looks like a matter of form with Constance. I remembered how, while the last war was still raging, she and Guy Halliday had discussed what to do with the world when it was over.

"Is it rude to ask what sort of things you discuss?"

"Well, naturally, we're a left-wing group."

"Why naturally?"

She said, with a smile of self-understanding that was rare with her: "I being what I am, it seems natural enough. I suppose you think a pattern is repeating itself?"

"That had occurred to me."

"Well, it's a pattern with a difference. I'm not in love with Henry Derwent. And I must say that makes life a lot simpler. I think your sister Louisa would have approved of me – though perhaps not of my political party."

"What has it to do with Louisa?"

"She was politically minded, wasn't she? You wouldn't know that she was one of the heroines of my youth. Father used to talk to me about her. He believed that she was using her poor husband as a way of compensating for not being able to stand for Parliament herself."

"He was right."

"Well, our little group want me to stand, after the war. But not, thank God, as a Liberal."

"Do you like the idea?"

"Immensely. Talking in the Courts has been a help. I'm not afraid of a public meeting. In fact, I've discovered that I'm rather good at handling one."

"You would carry on," I said, "where Guy left off."

The remark went home. She looked confused for a moment, then said, almost defiantly: "There is that, too."

How admirable she was, in so many ways! I left my food almost untasted and sipped my wine, and thought: If only you could love the living in memory of the dead! I put my hand on hers and said: "Why do you want to help people? Do you love them all that much?"

She didn't withdraw her hand, but it didn't respond to my touch. "I love justice," she said. "I find that enough to be going on with."

6

I went back to St Tudno in time to say goodbye to Richard, and my journey was ruined because of what had happened on the day before I left London. A food parcel from Augusta had reached the vicarage and been re-addressed to me by Nan. Constance had said she would spend the whole of this last evening with me, and I had been wondering what I could do to make it cheerful. The parcel came in the afternoon, and when I had opened it I thought here was the answer. A fine piece of ham, tinned vegetables, tinned peaches and apricots, biscuits, coffee, tinned milk, sugar, and, so carefully packed that it had come through safely, a small bottle of cognac. Spread out on the kitchen table, it looked sumptuous. I gave myself a high old time. I boiled the ham, had the vegetables ready for the time of Constance's arrival, put the peaches and apricots in dishes for "afters", and prepared the coffee in which I, at any rate, would enjoy a dash of the cognac. I laid the table in the sitting room with great care. We would eat and drink, and then settle down to a good game of chess, which was a relaxation we both enjoyed. I even rummaged out a scuttle of coal from Constance's hidden meagre ration, and lit the fire just as she was due.

The night was cold and wet, with a wind moaning through the courts and alleys of the Temple – just the setting for a gay fiesta. Constance came in, wearing a mackintosh that dripped with rain. Wet streaks of hair were plastered to her forehead. She stood there for a moment, sniffing the good scents and smiling. "What have you been up to?" she asked. "Bribery and corruption?"

I told her where the dinner had come from, and her face became the hideous blank I knew only too well. She hung up her mackintosh where it would drip into a tin pan, and came back pushing the wet hair out of her eyes. "I'm afraid," she said, "you'll have to eat that on your own. Don't bother about me. There's plenty in the larder."

"There's half a loaf, a scrape of butter, and a bit of mouse-trap cheese."

"What's wrong with that? It's all that thousands are having nowadays. There's a war on," she said without humour. "We're on soldiers' rations."

"I can't imagine a soldier who wouldn't add to his rations if he had the chance."

"Let me put it quite straight," she said. "If some American had sent this, I'd have eaten it with pleasure and posted a note of thanks. But I won't take it from any English runaway – least of all from Augusta."

She brought out her bread and cheese, and made herself a cup of tea. I ate from Augusta's largesse, but not much. Still, I did enjoy the coffee and brandy. I said: "Looking at this on the transcendental plane, I admit that you are right. But that is good ham. Don't waste it."

She wouldn't be jollied out of her mood. She said: "Please, Aunt Maria, don't go on about this. There are such things as right and wrong."

"I agree," I said, refilling my coffee-cup and tipping in more of the excellent cognac. "But for myself, the older I become the less I am dogmatically certain that I could tell one from the other at a glance. And there is such a thing as doing wrong out of love, and doing right out of a most unpleasant moral self-satisfaction."

And – would you believe it? – instead of having our game of chess, we spent the evening in this sort of exalted discussion – ethics, social responsibility, the importance of Right Choice. We might have been John Stuart Mill and Herbert Spencer having a cosy heart-to-heart; and when I yawned and got up Constance said: "Thank you, Aunt Maria. That's the first time you've done me the honour of talking to me as though I were a responsible being."

I groaned, took a night-cap of cognac, and went to bed hoping I would have happy dreams of Augusta chasing peach-fed hogs across the prairies.

7

When I left in the morning, Constance said: "Give my greetings to Mrs Flesch," as though to remind me, I thought, that she was not all words and wind. She had played her part in rescuing Mrs Flesch, and a good many other unfortunates, from the hell that life had become for them in their own country. But Mrs Flesch was not there to receive Constance's greeting.

She had never been more than an unhappy ghost among us. To our village worthies, anyone from the other side of the creek was a foreigner. How much more she! Speaking badly a few English words and never shedding her frightened and fugitive air, she was not well received; and, when the war began, dislike hardened into distrust. However, in the village at the head of the creek she was welcomed in one home. She rarely went out except as a shadow into the dusk; and during one of these bat-light flittings she heard the crying of a child. She found the child, with disordered clothes, being held to the ground behind a hedge by a village lout whose intention was obvious. Mrs

Flesch was the last person I would have expected to react violently in any situation, but she reacted violently now. Taking up a stone from the ground, she smashed the youth on the head. She left him there, dazed and bleeding, and took the child home. Naturally enough, alas! when the young violator was sent to prison she was regarded with less favour than ever. In St Tudno, we didn't want foreigners interfering in our most private affairs.

Only the parents of the child warmed towards her, and now and then the father would call for her, take her to spend the evening in his house, and escort her back to the vicarage later. He had done this while I was visiting Constance, but that evening he did not escort her back. It was the evening the bomb fell.

We were not much troubled by bombs in St Tudno, but there were a few, and this one solved all the problems of that hospitable little family and of Mrs Flesch, too. So, if you care to look into St Tudno churchyard, you will find her memorial and that of the few who died in our village. Some of the more philosophical villagers, able to discern cause and effect, said it was a judgment on her. Be that as it may, that is why, when Richard went, life at the vicarage was reduced to me and Nan.

8

Nan's rather precarious financial life with Richard had taught her to scrounge in all sorts of ways. Just as we Legassick girls, when young, had learned to harvest the fruit and nuts, mushrooms and berries of the fields and hedges, so it was with Nan, and now it was more necessary than ever. We spent hours on bottling and jam-making, and I could usually find a fish or two if I bothered to take out the dinghy. We grew vegetables and we kept hens, both for eggs and for the pot. Not that we were up to the gruesome business of slaughter. We would leave that to Barty Spargo, and go for a walk during the execution.

It was the hens that took us down to the beach on a March evening in 1942. There is a point called Penarrow. Some say it should rightly be called Pencarrow, which means the point of the corpses, for there bodies were washed up from the wreck of the *Queen* transport, returning from the Peninsular War – that old tragedy of which I had told Miles and Augusta so long ago. On the point were deposits of

573

oyster shell that the tides had pounded to grit, and we carried baskets to bring this grit for the hens to peck at and scratch in.

It had been an exceptionally heart-lifting day for March, clear and warm. There had been a pleasant scent all day, compounded of the bonfire smoke from a burning that Barty was carrying on in the graveyard and the flowers of the winter heliotrope. The sea was of glass.

I had been out earlier in the day and brought back a useful bass; and I had noticed then that a few M.L.s that had been lying fairly close under the land on the St Just side had been joined by more. Now, as we went along with our baskets, we saw that still more had come. A small fleet of the pretty blue-and-white things lay there, just off the spot where, on a spit of sand, I had looked with sorrow on the white, naked, skinny body of the child from London who was here with me now, and who stopped, and looked across the quiet darkening water, and said gravely: "I don't like the look of that. Do you?"

We stood still, looking at the little ships, listening to voices that came clearly across the water, though we could distinguish no words. They were talking to one another through loud-hailers. "No," I said. "I don't like the look of it."

We were used to seeing them slipping in and out in twos and threes; but this slow build-up of what was obviously a Force – a build-up that seemed now to have reached its culmination – disturbed me deeply.

Nan said: "I wonder if Richard is there?"

She had uttered my own disquietude. Whatever that collection of ships was for, it was clearly something formidable. The growing dusk was wiping away their colours. They were shadows that were still talking to one another through what had become for me and Nan a deep expectant hush.

We had forgotten what we had come for. We stood arm-in-arm, our baskets on the shingle, gazing across the water. Suddenly the hush broke. A sharp *rat-tat-tat-a-tat* came from the direction of the ships and we heard the *zing* and *zip* as stones on the beach about us were struck. It came again, and I couldn't make out what was happening. Nan said: "Well – of all the things! They're firing at us. Get down!"

We threw ourselves to the shingle, and for a time the machine-gun bullets whined and struck about us. Then they stopped and we sat up.

Nan's face was white in the dusk. "I like it even less," she said. "Someone must be very jumpy to do a thing like that. And you don't get all that jumpy unless something desperate is in hand."

We carried our baskets home thoughtfully, and spent a miserable night. At the first crack of day Nan came to my bedroom. "They're gone," she said. "All of them. Not a trace left."

It was some time before we knew that they were gone to storm their way by night up the miles of fortified river to St Nazaire. Richard was with them. A few days later we saw the pitifully small remnant return, and Richard was not with them.

9

It was about a year after this that I handed Nan what I had written — right up to those words "Richard was not with them." Three nights later, as we were sitting together after supper she put down the last page and looked for a while into the blue and green flicker of the salty fire-logs. She said: "It's a pity it's not a novel. Novelists are like God, aren't they?"

"Well, they can pretend to be, but I suspect they arrange other people's lives rather more skilfully than their own."

"You could have done a wonderful picture of Richard turning up after an heroic escape through France."

"I've tried not to be heroic about anything. Life's rather ragged, and I've just put it all down as it came about. But yes, I do wish, my dear, that I had been able to do that heroic bit, and that it was true."

"It never will be," she said. "Never for one moment did I hope. I knew it was finished."

We were silent for a time, and then she said: "There's no point in my staying here now, and I don't want to, anyway. I don't want to look at this sea and these lanes and fields and woods. It all belonged too much to us, and now there's no us any longer — only me. So I shall go as soon as you can do without me."

"I seem to have spent my whole life doing without. They go, one after another, all the people I love."

She asked: "Have you loved me?"

"Yes. Leaving men out of it, you have been my third — Augusta and Louisa and you. But I'm not sure of Louisa. I'm not sure that I ever loved her. I admired her enormously, but love? No, I'm not sure. Perhaps you're my second-best."

"Why do you love Augusta so much? She's not even related to you. And now that I've read what you've written, I see that she's caused you plenty of trouble."

"When you love someone, you don't much remember the trouble, only the joy. And Augusta has given me more pure joy than anyone else on earth. That's all I can say."

Nan was not very demonstrative, but she came and knelt in front of me and pulled my head down and kissed me. "Thank you," she said, "for making me your second-best love. I feel like Shakespeare's wife who inherited the second-best bed. But that's something, isn't it, if your husband is Shakespeare."

She smiled, and I was glad that even in the midst of her sorrow she could see a point of humour. I have not found life to be now all fun and now all grief – more like a circus where one is not sure whether to weep at the pathos of the clowns or laugh at their antics, and so, somehow, does both.

"Well," she said, "I don't suppose I shall run away tomorrow. If you'll have me, I shall stay till the war's over. Then I have a fancy for finding a little cottage – something like Mr Mompsen's, where there are mud-flats and birds running about at low tide. A place on the Thames estuary would suit me fine. And it would be handier for London. Don't forget I'm a Cockney."

10

That is what she did when the war was over. First of all we had Victory in Europe – the second victory in Europe in my time, following with sad speed upon victory in the war to end war and to create a land fit for heroes to live in. Then we had Victory in Japan, and the manner of it caused the world to hold its breath. For the first time in history, victory bells were a dirge and a disaster.

But there it was. It was victory, and Nan and I made a celebration of burning all our black-out curtains on the beach. Then we walked round to Penarrow Point and came to a stand there. It was the first time we had walked that way since we saw the small blue-and-white ships, the plywood armada, assembled in the dusk for their dash into the watery valley of death. The gallant six hundred, or however many they may have been. But no poet had thought them worth a song.

We didn't speak, but stood there looking at the ghosts of men and ships, and beyond them was the sand where Miles and I had sat and he had wrestled with his demon and decided to go off to the brief encounter that ended in Guy Halliday's arms. I wondered whether Nan, who had read my book, was thinking of that, too. There was, indeed, much for both of us to think about.

We walked back, and she said: "I feel rather badly about leaving you, but you realise, don't you, how impossible this place is for me? I shall come to see you now and then, and you'll have Constance for a companion."

Coming back in the taxi from Truro the next day, after seeing her off, I thought that yes, I should have Constance. I couldn't make any pretences to myself. It was a duty to be done rather than a joy to be looked for. Poor Constance. Millicent had offered her a home in Darkest Africa, but, rather than Millicent and Mr Nethersole's missionary brother, she had chosen me. It was a compliment of a sort, if not a high one. It was in the time of those abominations called doodle-bugs that she had been walking in a London street when one of them exploded. She was far enough away to escape death, but she was carried to a hospital suffering profoundly from the shock of the blast. She recovered – up to a point. She was almost dumb. She could speak but little, and to understand what that little meant was difficult. And that was the end of her not unsuccessful career as a barrister and of all her hopes of a public life. She had been for a long time in a place where what they called speech therapy was practised on her; but now her case was considered hopeless, and she was returning to St Tudno.

The morning mail had arrived by the time I was back at the vicarage. One letter, addressed in Tom Elthorne's handwriting. I didn't open it at once. It was time I had some good news and I hoped this was it. I hoped this was to give some hint of a not too distant return now that the war was over. So I dallied. I made some coffee and carried it out on to the lawn where the sun was shining. I sipped my drink, twiddled the letter about, hoping, and, being experienced, doubting.

My dear Maria – Augusta and Philip join me in sending our love. What a ghastly thing to have happened to poor Constance! I remember her so well from the time when she was my secretary at B.A.C. I never had a more conscientious girl or a more ambitious one. I don't think she was ever ambitious for herself. She never dreamed of a 'career' as something that would bring her glory. But she did so deeply feel the needs of people, and so much wanted to do something to smooth the path a little. How dreadfully like an epitaph this sounds!

I'm afraid I haven't anything very helpful or hopeful to say to you so far as our small family is concerned. We were looking forward to coming back to England soon – at any rate I was, but I can't speak for Augusta, and so far as Philip is concerned he's dead against it. He's settled wonderfully well in America, and wants to go on to Harvard when Si Custis goes there. Moreover, he wants to take American citizenship, and what that boy wants he gets! His mind is now playing with the idea of atoms as mine used to play with a few elementary chemicals in those old Didsbury days when you were with Augusta's father.

Well, the thing has been settled for me, and I stay here. I'm clearing up the side concerned with the English Government's job that I was doing, and now B.A.C. has stepped in. They want their whole set-up out here to be immensely bigger than it was before the war. We're to have quite a place, almost as imposing as the London show. Lord Lavernock has been out to brief me. I'm to supervise the setting up and then to remain in charge. So there it is. I don't suppose you knew that *your* Lord Lavernock, who had a finger in every profitable pudding and pie, was a financial power behind B.A.C. I gather that *my* Lord Lavernock, his son, had an awful bust-up with the old man at one time, and pushed off to work as a stockbroker. He remembers you – I may say very favourably – as a person who for a time looked after his son. He and his father came together again when the old man was trotting towards death's door, and with the title the new Lavernock – newish – inherited the B.A.C. interests. He gives more *personal* attention to it all than his father ever did, and now he's chairman of the Board, so I'm lucky to have him on my side, which I think he is – and I don't know for how much of it I must thank you. Anyway, he has rather a mother-fixation, and it seems that his mother thought you quite something.

So you must, my old dear, thank yourself to some extent that we're all fixed here, though I humbly beg to claim a crumb or two of credit. Of course, we'll fly over now and then. In the meantime, Augusta, at my elbow, says I'm to send you lots of love. No, she says, make that L. a capital. So lots of Love from us all.

Ever,

Tom.

11

You can call this: "Epilogue".

Constance and I were back where we had both begun, in St Tudno vicarage. There was no one else. We hadn't even a maid. None of us Legassick children was ever religious in any formal way, with a stylographed set of rules and beliefs. I rarely go to church, and Mr Nethersole, who has become old and staid, often chaffs me with being the village atheist. I reply by pulling his leg about his importance as a bishop's brother. For Millicent's husband is now the bishop of some dusky diocese, and Millicent, in her rare letters, has all the airs of a female prelate. I'm surprised she doesn't sign herself, with a cross, "Your Mother in God."

When Constance joined me she had no airs, unless an extreme and almost ostentatious humility could be so called. We had no maid because she insisted on being my servant. She got on to her knees and scrubbed. She cooked the food and did the washing. She lived as though in a convent, and took to wearing a rosary. She never missed a service in church, and with gladness polished the brass that, when a child, I had reluctantly given a spit and rub. She saw to the altar flowers and stitched at every rent that appeared in Mr Nethersole's surplice.

She was convinced that, for reasons obscure to me, God had punished her for pride and ambition, and the only good thing I could see in this attitude was that it was rare in female politicians. And I guessed that, unknown to herself, the poor girl was taking refuge not so much from the wrath of God as from the notice of men. She came back to me dreadfully self-conscious about her affliction. I worked

579

hard not to allow myself to seem aware of the strange sounds that were all the speech she could manage, and as the years went by I literally was not aware of them. They began to make sense to me and, when we were shut down of a winter's night, we could and did talk to one another. It had been like learning a foreign language, and I learned it. But she had a terror of humiliation if anyone else talked to her, and that is why she shut herself up in the house as in a convent and worked like a humble lay-sister. She would never go into the church until she was aware that all the congregation was assembled. Then she would slip into a back pew, and, as soon as the service was ended, bolt out and through the gap into the vicarage garden like a startled hare.

The only person she would tolerate except me was Nan. She knew what Nan had meant to her brother Richard, and every summer, when Nan would come down for a few weeks, Constance would be seen beyond the confines of vicarage and church. It was an odd communion that those two had. A look, a nod, a smile, a grasp of the hand, made up their currency, and they would go away in the dinghy to places where they would be unlikely to meet anybody and achieve a strange mute happiness together.

Nan had become a beautiful grave woman, thin and white-haired, with still the sea-green in her eyes. We never talked about Richard, but sometimes, when she would absently smile, I could almost see him at her side. Never did I feel more certain that there was communion with the dead than when Nan was with me. Her visits were all too few – each as brief and dazzling as an April smile.

I don't need much sleep now, and on May 21st, 1950, I got up early. It was my birthday, though I didn't imagine that anyone would remember that, and I didn't want anyone to. The less said about birthdays the better when you're seventy-four. I dressed warmly and went downstairs and through the french window on to the lawn and looked north and east at the sight unchanged since I had crept down on a birthday morning long ago, carrying Euphemia Emmett in a boot-box. As then, the air was full of writhing mist and the day's eye was in the east, and I thought of how Father had once said what a wonderful sweep of imagination it had been when poets first called the humblest of flowers the daisy, which is the day's eye, thus shedding the perennial light of the world upon the small and passing joys of life. And thinking of Father, I stepped through grey dew upon which the feet of birds had left their small patterns that a touch of the sun would wipe away as though the tracks of these little lives were of no moment. But now the little lives were bursting with joy, as on that other morning, and like an idiot I began to quaver:

> *New every morning is the love*
> *Our waking and uprising prove,*

and my very soul meant it, and the love of all the people I had known was about me, blessing me. Whether, before, I had loved them much or little or not at all, I loved them then and found it hard to split life up into hate and love. All my years became one thing – my ending sojourn – and I felt it as something full of worship and wonder.

The sun came up over St Just, and the milky mist eddied and swayed like a congregation of ghosts caught out at cock-crow; and, as though that morning everything was out to meet an old fool's mood, a cock did crow at that moment. Over at St Just he was, and the call came across the water, brave as trumpets sounding on the other side.

The rays of light poured like loosed arrows into the heart of the great yew, and within its cavern I could see many things: a little girl standing in the dawn not only of a day but of a life; Roger, sunny as a god's child eager for his kingdom; Louisa, aching with unharnessed energy, mortal and divine; and, oh dear, I thought, this is a wonderful birthday; it is giving me yesterday in the only way I want it. I shall spend today thinking of them all and loving them in a special way.

I looked at Father's grave, and Bella's, and Hugo's; and the alien shared grave of poor Mrs Flesch; and in the strengthening warmth of the sun I went in and prepared breakfast for myself and Constance.

While I was laying the table she came in, grey and quiet, seeming surprised to see me up but saying nothing about it. I was beginning to find her all-but-silent presence comforting. After breakfast she said: "I shall row into Falmouth today. We're short of all sorts of things."

If the weather made it at all possible she would row the long way round to Falmouth and back rather than walk to Flushing and cross in the ferry. That way she met fewer people, and she enjoyed the loneliness of the water. I walked down to the beach with her, and thought how once I would cut through the graveyard and jump over the wall. No jumping now. I pushed out the dinghy and strolled back

581

to the house and was washing up the breakfast things when I heard a sound that was rare in our parts: the long melodious gurgling of a horn on an expensive motorcar. I took no notice of it: such worldly and successful sounds were not for me. A moment later I was listening, thunderstruck. Outside the front door voices were singing:

> Happy birthday to you, happy birthday to you.
> Happy birthday, Maria Legassick, happy birthday to you.

I walked to the front door, the dishcloth in my hand, and on the gravel where the light of the oil-lamp once shone on the Polperro coach that night when Louisa, in mother's altered dress, brushed past me and Bella, and was driven away to the Tregannock ball, there stood an immense blue and grey Cadillac car, shining with material well-being. There was a speck of dust on the mudguard, and I instinctively stepped forward and gave it a wipe with the dishcloth.

"Hey, steady!" one of the two young men said. "We use nothing but doeskin on that."

I said: "You're Philip."

"Yeh. This is Si Custis."

They were tall, spare and handsome, carefully dressed. They shook hands, but did not kiss me.

"Come in," I said.

Philip said: "Just for a minute. We stayed at the Green Bank in Falmouth overnight, and we're due to see Land's End by lunchtime."

They came in. I was glad Constance was gone. She would not have been happy with Guy Halliday's son and Augusta's. They seemed anxious to be off, a duty done, but they stretched their long limbs in chairs, and Philip said: "We thought we'd do England before settling down. Si and I are both in physics."

Si said: "Nuclear."

"Mother said to arrange it so's to be at St Tudno for the 21st. She remembered it was your birthday. So this is St Tudno. Sort of quaint. I just remember visiting with you here before the war."

"It doesn't change much," I said. I led them to the window. "You see that little quay over there? The first day I met your mother we dived off there."

"A cute place for a dive. I've brought a present. From Mother. Fetch it, Si."

When Si was out of the way, he kissed me timidly. "From Mother," he said. "She said not to forget the kiss. And to say that she remembers everything. And that some day she's going to fly over and see you again."

"Give her my love," I said.

Si came in with a parcel, and we unpacked it on the table. "Go easy," Philip said. "Something delicate, Mother says."

She had remembered my love for bits of Royal Copenhagen porcelain. It was a lovely little piece: a weeping faun, his face hidden in his hands, his back bowed in sorrow. I looked at it with tears in my eyes. "Give her my thanks," I said, "and say I love her."

"Sure," Philip said. "And she'll come when things are not too pressing. Now, Si . . ."

They got up. We shook hands rather formally and I walked with them to the door. They manoeuvred the splendid monster carefully, and drove out, turned left, and stopped for a moment to wave and to shout again "Happy birthday!" Then they were gone, the horn dripping expensive honey behind them.

I went in and looked at the little weeping faun, desolate amid the debris of packing-paper. All the sorrow of the world was in his attitude. But there was no sorrow in my heart. She had remembered me and she had said she would come again. I knew she wouldn't, but I was glad she had said she would. I decided to say nothing to Constance. She would see the faun amid the other bits in my collection and think it was one she had overlooked. I kissed the crown of his weeping head and put him in place. Then I cleared away the rubbish, took up my dishcloth, and went back to the kitchen. I was sorry that the dishcloth had hurt the feelings of the beautiful motorcar. You must buy a bit of doeskin, I said to myself. Not that you're ever likely to need it. But just in case.

Howard Spring

Fame Is the Spur

Born into poverty, Hamer Shawcross is arrogant and ambitious. Entering politics he becomes a cabinet minister, then Viscount Shawcross. Ann, his wife, loves her husband but will allow nothing to diminish her commitment to the Suffragette Movement. This passionate novel is set against social and political changes of the early 20th Century – the rise of the Labour Party, Suffragettes, the challenge to the power of the landed gentry and the aftermath of the 1914-18 war.

Hard Facts

In 1885 the young curate, Theodore Chrystal is struggling to come to terms with life in a working-class district of Manchester – a shock after having lived amongst the dons and landed gentry of Cambridge. Dan Dunkerley is the ambitious young printer who establishes the penny journal, *Hard Facts*, to help create a new future for himself, his family and those around him. Here, amongst poverty, violence and prostitution Theodore must learn some 'hard facts' of his own.

HOWARD SPRING

THE HOUSES IN BETWEEN

Born in 1848, Sarah Undridge was three when she witnessed Queen Victoria opening Crystal Palace. Throughout her life Crystal Palace remained for Sarah a shining symbol of hope. However its glory was always obscured by 'the houses in between'. This powerful tale chronicles an eventful life that lasted almost one hundred years. Set mainly in London and Cornwall, it is crowded with Cornish fisherman, politicians, saints and sinners – the many people who knew and influenced the indomitable Sarah Undridge:

I MET A LADY

In 1916 the impressionable fifteen-year-old George Ledra is sent from Manchester to Cornwall because of his ill-health. Here he meets Hector Chown, a professor of Greek. Hector is living in a derelict house with his actress niece, Sylvia Bascombe and her young daughter, Janet. The story of how their lives become entwined spans the years of uncertainty between the two world wars and ever present in the tale, the house becomes a symbol of the fragility of their world.

Howard Spring

There Is No Armour

Edward and Blanche Pentecost have grown up in a modest but artistic home. Their security is suddenly shattered by the conversion of their father to harsh religious beliefs. Only gradually can they break away from his control. Edward becomes an artist while Blanche marries an unscrupulous financier whose schemes bring many to ruin. While Edward looks back on the previous fifty years, his son and Blanche's daughter must face the impending devastation of the Second World War.

Time and the Hour
(Third in the *Hard Facts* trilogy)

Time and the Hour opens in Bradford in 1912 with a group of young people who later move to London. In the mid 1930s they are confronted by the influx of persecuted Jews and the looming tragedy of the Second World War. This is a compelling saga of personal challenges, a tale where a child discovers the true identity of his mother and where romance is tempered by the terrifying reality of the growth of fascism in Europe.

OTHER TITLES BY HOWARD SPRING AVAILABLE DIRECT
FROM HOUSE OF STRATUS

Quantity		£	$(US)	$(CAN)	€
	Dunkerley's	6.99	11.50	15.99	11.50
	Fame Is the Spur	8.99	14.99	22.50	15.00
	Hard Facts	6.99	11.50	15.99	11.50
	The Houses In Between	7.99	12.99	19.95	13.00
	I Met a Lady	7.99	12.99	19.95	13.00
	A Sunset Touch	6.99	11.50	15.99	11.50
	There Is No Armour	7.99	12.99	19.95	13.00
	Time and the Hour	7.99	12.99	19.95	13.00
	Winds of the Day	6.99	11.50	15.99	11.50

ALL HOUSE OF STRATUS BOOKS ARE AVAILABLE FROM GOOD BOOKSHOPS
OR DIRECT FROM THE PUBLISHER:

Internet: www.houseofstratus.com including author interviews, reviews, features.

Email: sales@houseofstratus.com please quote author, title, and credit card details.

Hotline: UK ONLY: 0800 169 1780, please quote author, title and credit card details.
INTERNATIONAL: +44 (0) 20 7494 6400, please quote author, title, and credit card details.

Send to: House of Stratus Sales Department
24c Old Burlington Street
London
W1X 1RL
UK

Please allow following carriage costs per ORDER
(For goods up to free carriage limits shown)

	£(Sterling)	$(US)	$(CAN)	€(Euros)
UK	1.95	3.20	4.29	3.00
Europe	2.95	4.99	6.49	5.00
North America	2.95	4.99	6.49	5.00
Rest of World	2.95	5.99	7.75	6.00
Free carriage for goods value over:	50	75	100	75

PLEASE SEND CHEQUE, POSTAL ORDER (STERLING ONLY), EUROCHEQUE, OR INTERNATIONAL MONEY ORDER (PLEASE CIRCLE METHOD OF PAYMENT YOU WISH TO USE) MAKE PAYABLE TO: STRATUS HOLDINGS plc

Order total including postage:_____Please tick currency you wish to use and add total amount of order:

☐ £ (Sterling)   ☐ $ (US)   ☐ $ (CAN)   ☐ € (EUROS)

VISA, MASTERCARD, SWITCH, AMEX, SOLO, JCB:

☐☐☐☐☐☐☐☐☐☐☐☐☐☐☐☐☐☐☐☐☐☐☐☐

Issue number (Switch only):

☐☐☐

Start Date: Expiry Date:

☐☐/☐☐   ☐☐/☐☐

Signature: _____

NAME: _____

ADDRESS: _____

_____

POSTCODE: _____

Please allow 28 days for delivery.

Prices subject to change without notice.
Please tick box if you do not wish to receive any additional information. ☐

House of Stratus publishes many other titles in this genre; please check our website (**www.houseofstratus.com**) for more details